BROKEN
HEART

By Michael John Matsler

Library of Congress Control Number: 2018909265

Matsler, Michael John, author
Broken Heart, title

ISBN 978-1-7326532-0-7
1. Fiction, Historical. 2. 18th Century. 3. Canada – French and
Indian War; United States – New York – Revolutionary War;
France – French Revolution.

Published by Jonnycat Publishing Company
37 Felter Hill Road
Monroe, New York
mmatsler@riderweiner.com

Cover design and maps by Michael John Matsler, with
appreciation to the New York Metropolitan Museum of Art,
Creative Commons, and the Public Domain Project.

Printed in the United States of America

To James, Jonathan, and Li – and to all those who yearn to be free

"When the righteous cry for help, the Lord hears; and delivers them out of their troubles. The Lord is near to the broken-hearted, and saves the crushed in spirit. "

- *Psalm 34:18*

Author's Note

Broken Heart is set against the background of the tumultuous 18th century in Canada and New York, and revolutionary France. The story follows the adventurous, tragic and miraculous life of a French gentleman soldier turned farmer in the Colony of New York whose life with his American wife and children is brutally upended by the War of Independence before he undergoes an uncanny metamorphosis.

The romantic life of Michael Hector St. John de Crèvecoeur is nothing less than an epic saga spanning the Battle of Quebec in 1759 to the American Revolutionary War to the French Reign of Terror. Although war is never far away, this is not a story about war in the conventional sense. It is the tale of a man searching to escape tyranny and hoping to find the true meaning of freedom.

Readers not at ease with the French language should not feel discouraged by occasional words or phrases in that language; the meaning will be clear from the context. I use British spelling for the same reason, to evoke the feel of the place and time. British orthography ends with the American Declaration of Independence for symbolic purposes, except when British subjects are speaking. Symbolic clues and allegorical allusions are seeded throughout the story to undersore both the secular as well as the spiritual themes.

Maps of Canada, New York, French Normandy and Paris are found at the end of the story to help the reader navigate.

The cover of the book is no less symbolic: *Aeneas Fleeing Troy with his Family* by the Italian artist Agostino Carracci. The medallion is composed of the French and American flags excerpted from John Trumbell's painting *Surrender of Lord Cornwallis.* The back cover is a sampler from 1778. I tip my hat to the New York Metropolitan Museum of Art for its support of Creative Commons and the Public Domain project.

Table of Contents

PART ONE: GUILTY IN DEFENCE

Chapter One: *False Like a Canadian Diamond*

Michel-Guillaume turned his gaze heavenwards. A flock of doves sailed across the light blue sky, unfurled wings the colour of canvas. Their bellies bounced forward through the air like so many ships surging against the sea. But where was the ocean? Only waves of young wheat whispering in the sunny breeze of a gentle May day. Voices were floating from over yonder, beyond the horizon of grain. Muffled laughter and the scratching of a fiddle wafted through the air.

Panic seized him. Enough of hide and seek. The desire to find his family squeezed his young heart until he thought it would burst. With frantic fingers he clawed at the forest of wheat surrounding him, tall stalks like the bars of a prison. His feet rebelled, refused to take him where he wanted to go. But after an eternity the veil of wheat parted, revealing the apple orchard, small twisted trees sadly in need of pruning. Looming beyond sat his father's château, worn brick walls sagging. An utter silence stole in.

Heart pounding he raced through the apple grove and into the herb garden, its forlorn bounty as neglected as the lugubrious manor house. But there was no one about. Vanished the voices, the violin, the laughter, the joy. Only the cold, dark château empty of life.

He stumbled to the stables, struggled with the plank of oak barring the enormous doors too heavy for his small hands. There was no one inside. Even Pegasus was gone. Not so much as a trace of his saddle or bridle or his favourite blanket, mother's last loving gift of Easter before she died.

He wandered, forlorn, among the dark empty stalls, confused eyes searching. A sudden rustling from the rafters above made him jump. A pair of turtledoves nestled together, watching him.

Fingers of daylight beckoned him back outside. The sudden brightness made him blink. He squatted in the dirt, sat down in the primordial dust of his ancestors. Angrily he clenched his little fists and gritted his teeth, refusing to give in. *I will not cry. I will not surrender.*

Small pebbles emerged from the ground about his feet, miniature mountains of Zion rising from the desert. They glittered enticingly in the sunlight. He thought of his slingshot; thought of Father François. "And how many stones did little David pick up? Not just one; he picked up all five."

He scooped up the pebbles. Anger forgotten, he admired the sparkling treasures in his hand. He picked out the largest and held it up to his eye.

Soft light radiated from the depths of the diamond, reigning on the throne set into the ring by a master jeweler from eons ago. Without needing to look he knew what was inscribed on the back of the silver band: *Semper Fidelis*.

"From my father to my mother, and so from me to you," he murmured to his beloved, slipping the precious heirloom onto her slender finger.

They stepped out of her mother's parlour into the sunny garden, early lilacs and primrose petals a palette of yellow and orange and purple against the white picket fence laced with ivy velvet-green. As they embraced, a distant church bell began to toll. Michel-Guillaume felt the warm kiss of sun on the nape of his neck grow suddenly cool. The light of the garden dimmed as shadows rolled across the neatly trimmed English lawn. He looked upwards.

Doves. Droves of doves so thick they eclipsed the sun. But these were not the soft buck white *tourterelles* of Normandy and England. Boldly coloured with reddish bellies, these were *tourtes voyageuses*, the passenger pigeons of the western lands. Even as he watched, the advance guard of these new world birds grew larger, breasts swelling like a tidal surge, powerful, overwhelming, invincible. There was a difference in their eyes, in their beaks now longer, heavier, rapacious.

"*Des goélands...des goélands....*" As Michel-Guillaume Jean de Crèvecoeur mumbled in his troubled sleep, he now saw the gulls – *les goélands* - come cascading across the steel-grey ocean of the vast sky, row upon row. Huge outspread wings filling the sky, beaks like dark, protruding bowsprits slicing through the air.

"*Des frégates....*" The frigate-birds followed, rolling up the estuary with the morning sun rising behind them, majestic, indomitable, terrifying. As they soared past, prow-like beaks grimacing horribly in a silent scream, gun-ports, dozens of them in a double-row, opened up in their clapboard bellies bulging like the hulls of ships and mutely belched forth a volley of round iron eggs from blue-wreathed nests of smoke and fire, all the more terrifying in their complete soundlessness.

Crèvecoeur woke up in a cold sweat. He stared upwards and saw Sagittarius suspended in a smoky spiral. Sitting up, he smelled as much as saw the last dying embers smoldering in the camp-fire. The glowing dark-red coals pulsated like a living heart. A sudden flame flared up, mocking him.

He fumbled for his stockings, laid out on his haversack to dry out before the fire. As always he struggled with the gaiters, then the minor agony of his stiff shoes which never seemed to fit right.

He glanced at the dark figures strewn about the camp-site. Not a few were snoring loudly. He got to his feet, irritated by the pinching of his shoes. He felt a surge of envy for the Canadian militiamen and their native companions, excused from the sartorial pretentions of the elite army regulars. They wore moccasins.

The young French officer didn't bother to bring his pistol; the spyglass would do for the moment. His compass and surveyor's kit he also ignored. He donned his hat and quietly slipped out of the camp onto the crude trail they had hacked out the day before leading to the bluff. He could barely discern the way in the dim gloaming of the dawn.

As he rounded a bend in the path he felt a light tap on his shoulder. He whirled and instinctively cocked his fist. Megeso's eyes were level with his. They glittered sardonically. Wordlessly he motioned with his head to the clearing ahead where the first light of the eastern sky was glowing. Crèvecoeur let Megeso take the lead, but only by the span of a sparrow's wing. It would not do for either to follow the other.

Crèvecoeur took in the crisp morning air, grateful to exhale the bitterness of the night. The breeze was gentle, the love-songs of the thrushes joyous. Dark brooding hemlocks competed for territory with majestic maples, outstretched limbs lifted upwards to form the archway of a sylvan cathedral. Their light-green leaves, reborn only a few days earlier, were the visible proof of the promise of the resurrection to come written in the winter. The crown of the trees formed the vault of the cathedral, leaving an opening like an oculus through which the still greater vault of the universe could be seen. The stubborn moon would not let go and the stars still proclaimed the glory of the heavens.

The two young men emerged from the forest, one garbed in grey woolen breeches and puffy white blouse, the other wearing only a deerskin skirt. The sun lingered below the mountains to the east but the proof of its presence was plain to see in the rapturous canvas of the clouds painted red, pink, orange.

Megeso suddenly whirled around, a grin flashing across his coppery face. He gave Crèvecoeur a hard push to the chest throwing him backwards before breaking into a run into the open clearing. Crèvecoeur, swearing, jumped back to his feet and chased after his companion. Panting, half-cursing half-laughing, they raced across the rocky clutter of the cliff-top towards the edge, shoving and hitting each other as they ran. Megeso pretended to stumble and as Crèvecoeur gleefully strode forward he fell to the ground over the outstretched foot of his friend, who surged ahead.

"Damn cheating snake!" Crèvecoeur yelled out, cursing for not having thought of the trick himself. He scrambled back to his feet but it was too late. The contest was over.

They threw themselves onto the ground, crawling the last few feet to the edge, and peered over the abrupt lip of the cliff-top. Ninety vertical yards below the greyish green of the Saint-Lawrence River roiled past the base of the cliff, a rocky foot jutting out into the water. Looking to his right Crèvecoeur discerned, two miles away to the southwest, a forested island. The humped ridge rose up out of the river like a breaching whale.

The woody eastern tip of Orléans Island split the water like the prow of a ship, dividing the river into two channels. The northerly channel was sandy and shallow, impassable even at high tide for any vessel larger than a sloop. The southern channel held deeper water, but was treacherous with submerged rocks and hidden shoals.

Crèvecoeur crawled back a few feet and sat down. Taking out his spyglass, he trained his left eye on a point in the southerly channel just east of the island. He focused, found what he was looking for: the wooden buoy bobbing in the brisk current, its twin a few hundred yards further away. He was skeptical the trick would work, but orders were orders and, after all, there could be no harm in trying to lure the enemy into false waters.

He backed a few more prudent feet away from the cliff-edge and squatted, Indian style like his friend. He glanced at him out of the corners of his eyes. Even after three years Megeso was a mystery, he mused. Behind the stoic dark eyes simmered a reservoir of fire which could suddenly erupt into an outburst of passion only to subside and disappear just as quickly, like the fabled volcanoes of Iceland. Harsh as the winter, generous as the summer. His sharp brow and aquiline nose made him look every bit the eagle whose name he bore in the Abenaki parlance. A white ring of bone from a bear he had killed graced an earlobe and a scalping knife dangled on a lanyard over his brightly painted torso, keeping company with a small pewter cross.

A sparkling in the dirt at his feet caught Crèvecoeur's eye. Absently he picked up the object, a small stone glittering with streaks of iron pyrite. He turned it over in his hand. He stared at it, sea-blue eyes suddenly aflame, russet-red eyebrows tensed in a frown.

"I had that same dream again, last night," Crèvecoeur brooded out loud.

Megeso looked at his friend. He saw the sparkling stone and understood.

Wordlessly he got up and went over to a clump of birch trees. He bent down a moment, straightened up and came back, holding a length of vine, some birch bark and pinecones, and a handful of moss.

Sitting down cross-legged, in a flash he had fashioned a hoop out of the vine and bark, lacing it together with the moss. Pinecones and a hawk's tail feather from his own belt completed the ornamentation. He rose and approached Crèvecoeur solemnly, holding his handiwork in front of him. He motioned for the lieutenant to stand up.

"Take off your hat."

Crèvecoeur obliged.

"Incline your head."

Crèvecoeur bowed his head.

"Repeat what I say."

Megeso chanted a prayer in the Algonquin tongue, pausing after each short verse to allow his friend to mimic him. Satisfied, Megeso lifted the ring heavenward as though for a blessing from above, then passed it over Crèvecoeur's head and onto his shoulders.

"*Capteur des rêves*. It will capture the demons that bring you the bad dreams. My gift to you. Wear it every night when you sleep." Megeso's chiseled brown face broke into a grin.

The young French officer forced a smile.

"I will make it a point of honour to do so."

He gave a mock bow, sweeping his cocked hat in a grand flourish before plopping it back on his head.

"And I have a gift for you." He extended his hand and opened it up to reveal the gleaming stone.

"A Canadian diamond."

The two friends shared a laugh. Megeso put the reminder of Samuel de Champlain's folly into his leather pouch. *Faux comme un diamant du Canada*.

The wind was picking up now. It came from the northeast, a rare occurrence for that time of year. Crèvecoeur put the *longue-vue* up to his eye again and looked downriver. The small island called Île aux Coudres came into view. It was uninhabited except for a few ponies, living peacefully among the hazelnut trees for which the island had been named, utterly indifferent to the vanity of humanity.

Crèvecoeur put the spyglass back into his pouch, glancing around him. The spot they were standing on would be a good place for cannon. From there they could be trained upon any point up or down river. Every enemy vessel coming from Hazelnut Island to Orléans Island to the southwest would have to sail under a steady barrage of fire.

But the cannon were in Québec, far away to the southwest. It was a good twenty miles as the crow flies to the spot where he was standing on Cape Torment, but since cannon don't have wings the guns would either have to go by boat to the fishing village of Saint-Joachim at the foot of the Cape, or by land along the cart-path from the Lower Town, across the Saint-Charles River, then northeasterly past Beauport; and even then the Montmorency River and the tremendous waterfalls where it entered the Saint-Lawrence blocked the way. Regardless of the route the cannon would still have to be hauled up the mountain.

Ever since the fall of Louisburg in 1745, fourteen long years ago, there had been talk of putting artillery on Cape Torment, or on Orléans Island, or fortifying Pointe-Lévy on the south bank to protect Québec. But nothing had ever been done. The king and his councilors had other priorities.

Even the governor, himself a native-born Canadian, gave little heed to placing guns along the Saint-Lawrence. There was no need. The river was too treacherous for ships of the line; the winds almost always blew from the west and the narrow channels made it impossible for large, square-rigged warships to tack. One need only recall, he was fond of saying, the fiasco of Admiral Walker in 1711 when the British Navy had last attempted to challenge the river. No, any serious attack was bound to come up from the south, from New-England and New-York, as the events of 1757-1758 had proven. " 'Tis Amherst moving up from Lake Champlain we should worry about," the governor scoffed.

It was General Montcalm who issued the order to scout out Cape Torment. He had ridden up post-haste from his command post in Montréal last week. By then everyone in Québec knew the advance squadron of the British Navy had been espied snooping around the mouth of the Saint-Lawrence. The militia's signal fires along the river had been blazing all night.

Crèvecoeur's crew was digging out the puny moat along the walls of the Upper Town, facing the Plains of Abraham, when they saw the general's entourage, banners waving, thundering towards them from the west along the Sillery Road. They passed a scant few yards away, tossing up clouds of dirt in their wake. They disappeared through the gates of Saint-Louis below the king's coat-of-arms and on into town, to the granite elegance of the governor's château, oblivious to the angry cursing from the grimy men showered with their dust.

An hour later a captain reemerged from the gates and rode up to Crèvecoeur, not bothering to dismount. "You are to report to His Excellency the Marquis," he said stiffly, then whirled his horse around and vanished back into town.

After a long wait Crèvecoeur was allowed into the great hall of Château Saint-Louis. Lieutenant-Général Joseph-Louis, Marquis de Montcalm stood over a huge oak table strewn with maps, oblivious to the beauty of the river below framed by mullioned windows. Pontleroy, his chief engineer, was pointing to a chart, a map drawn by Crèvecoeur the prior month. Crèvecoeur's own immediate superior was also there: Captain Dumas, in command of the Colonial Regulars who reported not to Montcalm, but to Governor Vaudreuil. The governor evidently was still lingering upriver in Montréal.

Crèvecoeur removed his *tricorne* and bowed deeply. He tried not to fidget, waiting for the general to address him first. The marquis was absorbed in his thoughts, frowning down at the map. Pontleroy cast gun-grey eyes at the young lieutenant.

"His Excellency recalls the fine work you did at Fort Carillon last year."

"Sire. You are too gracious," Crèvecoeur murmured, head still bowed.

The general looked up from his charts. Pontleroy regarded Crèvecoeur coldly. The nostrils in his long thin nose dilated.

"You will speak when asked." His voice was ice. "Captain Dumas will allow you to accompany a detachment of men to Beauport. There you are to trace out a main line of defence on the higher ground above the beach, from Beauport to the Saint-Charles." The engineer ran a finger along the lines on the map marking the north bank of the Saint-Lawrence just east of the Lower Town. "Your trench-works will accommodate 14,000 men."

Crèvecoeur's face twitched. Fourteen thousand. So the decision had been made. It was on the beaches of Beauport the main attack was expected and where the defences were to be concentrated. He glanced at Capt. Dumas, who acknowledged the question in his subordinate's eyes with a quick nod of the head.

"I will design the redoubts," Pontelroy continued. "As for you, after you lay out the trench-lines get up to Cape Torment. Find the best spot you can for at least one battery. I need not tell you time is a luxury we no longer have. Although," he smiled sarcastically, "there are some, it would appear, who do not comprehend the urgency of our situation." He deigned a contemptuous look at the governor's empty throne-like chair.

"How many days did he have you waste trying to turn that silly ditch along the west wall into a proper moat? It's solid rock underground. It has to be blasted. Too bad they built the walls first," Pontleroy mocked. "Many are those who do not want to hear the truth."

While the engineer spoke Crèvecoeur saw the trenches bristling with almost the entire combined French and Canadian forces and their Indian allies. Montcalm must be pulling all eight of his French Royal Army regiments out of Montréal, leaving that town totally open to any attack from the south. Only Brigadier Bourrassa at Fort Carillon on Lake Champlain stood in the way of General Amherst coming up from New-York.

Montcalm saw the young officer's furrowed brow and pensive look.

"Lieutenant. We received word yesterday that General Wolfe set sail from England February 16 with 8,000 troops bound for Halifax."

The marquis' large, warm hazel eyes were tense under the gentle arch of his black eyebrows, face lined and tired. Abruptly he strode over to the huge windows looking southeasterly over the river.

"If ever we had an Achilles' heel, it is over there," he fumed to no one in particular. He was referring to Pointe-Lévy on the opposite bank of the Saint- Lawrence directly across from the town.

"But," continued the marquis, turning around, smiling sardonically, "it is true, is it not, that our great governor, with his vast military experience and profound knowledge of the arts of war, knows better than we. After all, has he not just been awarded the Great Cross of the Order of Saint-Louis? Why waste time, money and effort fortifying Pointe-Lévy to prevent the enemy from seizing the high ground when all one needs do is show them that magnificent medal and watch them flee in terror? We defer to his superior wisdom."

Pontleroy exhaled nervously, his own Great Cross a-glitter. "If his Excellency would allow me," he murmured, using his staff baton to point to the map, to the lip of the Lower Town jutting into the river. "By my calculations, the English guns, even their 24-pounders, should not be able to reach the Upper Town from Pointe-Lévy and ought to fall short of the Lower Town, except perhaps the outer fringes of our batteries...."

Standing now on the cliff-top of Cape Torment, taking in the cool morning breeze like the breath of truth, Crèvecoeur brushed away the memory of the tense council of war in the governor's château. There was work to do. He regretted leaving his compass and transit behind at their bivouac.

"Let's go back," he told Megeso. "I need my equipment. We'll bring up the men. They can start digging and cutting down trees after I lay it out for them. Then we'll ride back to town and report to my captain."

If Megeso did not respond it was not due to a lack of understanding of the French language, which he spoke quite well thanks to the missionary school. Megeso stood calmly still, looking pensively at Crèvecoeur. His piercing eyes glittered.

"Come on, let's go." Crèvecoeur gestured with impatience.

Megeso's face betrayed no expression. Then, silently, he turned his head towards the rising sun of the east. He raised his left arm and pointed.

Crèvecoeur saw nothing. He fumbled for his spyglass, found it, raised it up to his better left eye and focused.

There, far to the northeast beyond the forested green of Hazelnut Island, he saw what his friend could see with his naked eye alone: squares of tiny white dancing on the shimmering blue crest of the horizon. As he watched, transfixed, the white objects seemed to grow, like Indian corn pushing upwards towards the sky as top-gallants were followed by royals and then the billowing snow-white mainsails of a dozen ships rolling over the water, jibs in full bloom over bowsprits pointing forward like eager foxhounds. Flags fluttered happily from the tops of the masts.

Warships. British warships.

Chapter Two: *The Blasphemy of Truth*

The sharp pinging of picks and shouting of men vibrated in the air. Galloping over the crest of the hill, Crèvecoeur and Megeso saw below in the distance an infinitely long line of dark objects bobbing and weaving all the way west to the town along the bluffs parallel to the river, looking like an elongated millipede writhing its legs in some kind of death throe.

Thousands of soldiers and militiamen, *en petite tenue* stripped down to their linen shirts, were furiously digging along the line Crèvecoeur had laid down only a few days before. At least one of the redoubts, on the rocky beach above the high water mark, was almost complete, with a gang of men infilling the palisaded walls of wood with dirt from the trenches above. To the right, north of the trenches in the meadows, thousands of buff-coloured canvas tents marked the army's encampment.

The tiny hamlet of Beauport boasted only a few houses flanking a plain board and batten-sided chapel. Flags fluttering outside the largest house announced the quarters of General Montcalm. In the yard next the house a large campaign tent had been pitched. The flaps of the entrance were tied back, guarded by the royal colours and Colonel Bougainville's standard.

Crèvecoeur saw his commander's tent planted in the meadow behind the houses. He let his horse drink at a trough then picked his way through a small apple orchard towards the tent. Megeso wordlessly parted company and disappeared.

Crèvecoeur spotted the short, sinewy figure of Captain Dumas talking to Bernier, the army's chief quartermaster. Dumas, usually calm despite his Gascon temper, was agitated, gesticulating with his arms, shouting at the quartermaster.

Bernier wore a pained expression on his round face beneath white wig and black hat. He winced with each verbal exclamation point Dumas punctuated digitally in the man's face.

"How do you expect me to feed my thousand infantry on only three hundred pounds of salt pork and five hundred loaves of bread a day?" the captain fumed. "Do you think I am Jesus Christ himself? That I can miraculously feed the multitudes on five loaves and a couple of fish?"

The captain thrust his lean, square jaw in the quartermaster's face. "I find it impossible to believe Governor Vaudreuil would ever issue such an order. Only two days ago we were told to expect full rations through September, long enough to force the enemy to give up any siege and go back to the devil's den they came from. Do you think I'm going to order my men to scrounge through the forest for nuts and berries like we had to do at Fort Chambly, as if they were Indian squaws?"

Bernier, himself a plump, well-fed man, shrank back. He shrugged his shoulders, holding up soft, pink hands in feeble supplication.

"It's not the governor's orders. In fact, he opposed it. He believes as strongly as ever the town cannot be taken. The English Navy will never be able to manoeuver past Île d'Orléans and even if they did succeed they can't sail any further west. Cape Diamond protects the Upper Town. No army could possibly scale that cliff, and from there our cannons protect the Lower Town below."

"So it was General Montcalm, then."

"At the urging of Commissary Bigot."

"Bigot!" Dumas spat in disgust, as though expelling the bile he felt for the king's chief civilian administrator, in charge of all financial affairs and supplies from Québec to Nouvelle Orléans and in the process becoming the richest man in New-France.

"It is they who have made the decision. I myself can take no position," Bernier hastened to add. "I am only a subaltern. It is not for me to decide."

Glimpsing the momentary look of resignation on the captain's face, the quartermaster saw the opening he had been watching for. With a quick, short bow he hastily took his leave and scampered away on silk-stocking'd legs.

Only then did Dumas notice Crèvecoeur on his steaming mount. "What are you doing here, lieutenant?" he asked, irritation replaced by surprise.

Crèvecoeur quickly dismounted and, removing his hat, bowed stiffly.

"Yes, yes," Dumas gestured impatiently, never one for formalities. "Out with it."

"The English armada has arrived." Crèvecoeur felt a sense of relief to impart the weighty news, as if a ship's master dumping ballast. "By now just east of Île aux Coudres with a strong northeasterly wind in their sails. I counted a dozen ships."

"*Crisse de tabernacle.*" A pious man, Dumas allowed himself a mild oath. His dark eyes blazed what his mouth would not utter. With effort he regained his composure, casting his gaze off to the east as though trying to verify with his own eyes the British warships.

"So, twelve ships, you say. That must be only their vanguard. Would you agree, lieutenant, the wind is bound to shift? Let's hope soon. That will stop them for a while. I suppose you've told Captain Le Mercier. At least he'll be spared another battery for down here."

"You're the first one I've seen. I rode all morning from Saint-Joachim."

Dumas nodded. He looked pensively at the blue sky above. A flock of passenger pigeons was flying westward, as if leaving behind the antagonists to their fate.

"Well, my son. General Wolfe comes a-knocking on our door to the east; General Amherst knocks on our door to the south while Johnson would like to sneak in through the back door in the west," he mused. "There'll be a lot more ships behind the dozen you saw, of that we can be certain."

Dumas searched his memory, found what he was seeking.

" 'Though an army besiege me, my heart will not fear; though war break out against me, even then will I be confident'," he murmured.

His ebony eyes suddenly flashed lightning. "You can bet your soul that while my men are reduced to half rations Bernier and Bigot will still find a way to dine in the high style they so richly deserve. Bigot with his *foie gras* on silver plate and fine wine in crystal, and his beautiful mistress Madame Péan keeping his bed snug and warm."

He allowed himself a grim smile.

"Truth is, our heads are between the hammer and the anvil. We all thought the king would be sending us another 4,000 troops and 400 guns; he gave us one- tenth those numbers. Bigot promised beef and bread aplenty; he delivered mostly rum. And now they've decided to send most of our paltry rations and half our ammunition fifty miles upriver, for 'safekeeping'."

Spleen purged, Dumas' eyes softened. " 'Obey the King's command, I say, because you took an oath before God…Since no man knows the future, who can tell what is to come?' "

His face brightened. He smiled at himself as though reflecting on his own foolishness. He slapped Crèvecoeur on the back affectionately.

"Come along, lieutenant. Let's find the masters of our fate and report to them what you saw."

They mounted their horses and picked their way past the chapel towards the bluffs overlooking the river. The trench-works before them cut a mud-brown gash through the green of the meadows all the way west to the mouth of the Saint-Charles River, on the north end of the Lower Town, where it fed into the Saint-Lawrence. Although nearly five miles distant, they could see the makings of a new wooden bridge spanning the Saint-Charles.

The Lower Town was dominated by the spire of Notre-Dame-des-Victoires, overshadowed in turn by the château atop the cliff and the cathedral with its seminary. New ramparts had been built along the waterfront. Cannon barrels poked out of the gun-ports. The docks were devoid of masts except those belonging to five or six small barks. What few ships the colony possessed, along with a brace of French Royal Navy frigates, had already been moved upriver.

Sweeping his eyes from the Lower Town to the tip of Orléans Island lying south of him, Crèvecoeur saw the mile-wide expanse of mud flats and rocks exposed by the low tide of the river all along the beach. The jagged rocks protruded from the viscous muck like demons' teeth sown in the gums of hell.

In the trenches work had stopped for the midday meal. Exhausted men had flopped down on the ground, dripping wet with sweat, guzzling the contents of their canteens, whether water, applejack or rum depending on individual tastes. The militiamen sat apart from the soldiers. The heat didn't seem to bother them as much; they sat cross-legged, puffing contentedly on pipes or native *calumets*. Several card games were underway and someone broke out a fiddle.

Crèvecoeur shifted self-consciously high up in his saddle. He felt the sting of resentful looks, sensed a murmur of disapproval, and imagined the snickers he heard were at his expense. What great exploits had he accomplished in his young life to merit his exalted status? Nothing compared to his captain, the victor over Braddock and the hero of Fort Duquesne four years ago. Unlike the governor who, Montcalm liked to remind everyone, had never so much as commanded target practice, Dumas did not flaunt his medals and did not flinch under fire. That Dumas had taken a liking to him, Crèvecoeur thought, was only due to his knowledge of geometry and triangulation. It was Dumas who had received the general's permission to pull Crèvecoeur out of the LaSarre Regiment and it was through his grace he had the right to a horse, even though he felt as though he always had one foot in the stirrup and one foot still on the ground.

"Hey, lieutenant there! By the Blessed Virgin, get off your high horse a moment and have a drink on the house," came a raucous voice from below.

It belonged to a beefy, burly man in white linen homespun like his *compères* but with a beet-red knit cap atop curly dark-brown hair. He was relaxing on the grass, clay pipe in one hand and goat's bladder canteen in the other. His companions guffawed. The man in the red *tuque* gestured invitingly with his canteen, leering at the young lieutenant with large brown eyes.

Crèvecoeur was tempted, not for the drink but for the companionship. The ways of the people here intrigued him. No peasant in France would dare speak to a superior that way. But then, the farmers and merchants, fishermen and backwoodsmen of Canada did not view themselves as peasants. They were free men beholden to no one but God; and even then not as much as their parish priests liked to hope.

Crèvecoeur glanced at his captain a few paces away; thought of the white sails and lance-like bowsprits cutting downriver at that very moment. He tried to look impassive and dignified and in so doing looked ridiculous. More guffaws from below. He felt his face flush, angry at letting himself be perturbed.

On the beach two redoubts were under construction a hundred yards apart. Soldiers were planting long wooden poles with sharpened tips into the ground in front of the walls, made of logs stacked horizontally, while others were putting a field gun into place on a rampart. Their corporal looked out over the open terrain towards the river, as though seeing the defenders sweeping the beach with musket and artillery fire while the invaders were forced to slog their precarious way through the muddy shallows. Even if the enemy were able to overcome the redoubts, they would still have to contend with an uphill climb over exposed ground to assault the trenches above.

At the closest redoubt they came upon Le Mercier the artillery chief conferring with Pontleroy and Colonel Bougainville. Dumas and Crèvecoeur dismounted and approached the trio. They lifted their three-cornered hats and bowed, deeply. The superior officers lifted their own three-cornered hats and bowed, less deeply.

"*Messieurs*, Lieutenant Crèvecoeur has an urgent report to convey."

As Dumas spoke he noticed his junior officer open his mouth. Dumas caught the lieutenant's attention with a frown. Crèvecoeur checked himself and clamped his lips. They waited on the colonel, heads bowed in deference to his military rank and social status.

Louis-Antoine, Count de Bougainville was not Montcalm's aide-de-camp for nothing and was already a renowned philosopher of natural history and member of the Royal Society of London to-boot. He had just returned from France, pleading with the king for more assistance and, as all the troops knew thanks to the rumour mill, to subordinate the governor to Gen. Montcalm. It was Bougainville who suggested the king placate the governor with the Order of the Great Cross of Saint-Louis, and in the process the count did not object to receiving the medal for himself as well. The brilliant medallion enameled ermine and white, bristling with golden *fleurs-de-lys*, glittered on the count's breast, a testimony to his diplomatic finesse.

Bougainville pursed his Cupid-like lips in a slight smile.

"I was pleased to present to his Royal Majesty your map of New-France. The king and his ministers were impressed."

"Your Excellency is too kind," Crèvecoeur murmured, avoiding Pontleroy's smoldering stare. Without waiting for the requisite invitation to speak, he blurted out, "Captain Pontleroy sent me to lay out a battery on Cape Torment. But at dawn this morning I saw at least a dozen enemy warships on the horizon just beyond Île aux Coudres. I don't think there is time to set up cannons on the Cape."

Bougainville remained impassive. He glanced at the engineer, who ejected an oath, fuming.

"Lieutenant, it is not for you to think. You are to execute the orders given to you." Pontelroy looked away in angry disdain, towards Orléans Island a mile away as though seeking a solution on its rocky shore.

"Damn it all. One more week. Just one more." He exhaled sharply before turning sardonic eyes to Dumas.

"So be it then," he allowed, in a voice that would freeze fire. "Your lieutenant's wish to be excused from the assignment is granted." He abruptly turned his back to them.

Crèvecoeur felt his face flush at the insult but held his tongue. After more bowing and lifting of the hats directed towards Bougainville, Dumas and Crèvecoeur took their leave. The captain looked towards the third redoubt a half mile away to the east, where the mounted figures of Montcalm and his senior officers were contemplating the works. Dumas ordered his lieutenant back to camp to rest up and rode on himself to inform General Montcalm of the turn of events.

The men were all working in the trenches and the camp was deserted except for their company quartermaster and his cooks, already two sheets before the wind and barely able to stand up to stir the simmering pots. Crèvecoeur went to the quartermaster's waggon and helped himself to a tent. He pitched it as far away from the latrines as possible, then borrowed some hot water from the fire for a badly needed shave.

Crèvecoeur felt listless. He wasn't in the mood for a nap and the quiet of the camp vexed him. He went into his tent and rummaged in his pack for his sketch-book. He made himself comfortable on the grassy ground and opened it to the drawings he had made, charcoal studies of native plants and birds he had observed here and there he had found intriguing. Finding no inspiration in his sketches, he took out a small leather-bound book, a quill and ink powder. He mixed the powder with a bit of water in a tiny cup the size of a thimble, made from an acorn. He began writing in his journal, using his knees as his desk.

It had been several weeks since the last entry. He started; stopped; began anew. "Surveyed the bluffs around Beauport...laid down trench-lines...."

This was not satisfying. For whom was he writing? For a brief instant he saw her oval face. The nub of his quill caught on the rough paper. Angrily he fumbled for his blotting-cloth. Despite himself he remembered the company's last mardi gras celebration and that night of drinking and debauchery in the Lower Town, and his disgust with himself the morning after. "Forgive me, Amelia..."

That occasion and numerous others did not find their way into his journal. Nor did the horrific scenes he had witnessed after the battle of Fort William Henry, or his own feelings of bloodlust and hatred which overwhelmed him, transforming him into another creature altogether, one he did not recognise nor care to remember....

He opened the journal to a new page. He yearned to see his father, to talk to him, even as the image of his angry face appeared on the blank page. He dipped his quill into the acorn of ink.

"30 May 1759. My dear father," he began. "Since our only means of communication with France is now via the Ohio to Louisiana, and is limited to official correspondence, I cannot send you a letter. But were I able, I would tell you about some of the practices of the farmers hereabouts I know would interest you.

"In late winter they harvest maple sugar, which the native people taught them long ago. It requires nothing more than placing a sharp tap through the bark of the tree to divert the watery sap into a pail. They boil the sap and so distill it into a thick sweet syrup. Cane sugar is far too dear, so maple sugar is a fine substitute and serves as a local currency for bartering. The Abenaki say it has great medicinal powers as well.

"They also rely on honey. They have an ingenious method for finding wild beehives. They mix up a batch of hot bees' wax and honey with vermillion dye which turns the mixture bright red. They place it out in a tray in the early afternoon when the bees are most active. The bees are attracted to the concoction, diving into it and so dyeing themselves bright red. After that the farmer can follow them back to their hive in the forest and mark the tree, which he chops down before making a fire to produce smoke, chasing away the bees and allowing him to seize the hive..."

Crèvecoeur thought of the beehives on his uncle's estate just east of Caen, how his mother had delighted in concocting new recipes for the honey. He saw again her *sauterelles à miel* she would have Cook bake for him for Lent, little pastry grasshoppers glazed with honey he would place in a small pouch she had fashioned for him. How she would laugh when he would march around the garden and stables, haranguing the hired hands against their wicked ways, advising them to repent before it was too late, a budding John the Baptist munching on locusts and wild honey.

But then the night his brother was born, the cold rain borne on a heartless wind, Father François trudging wearily down the stairs where he, Michel-Guillaume, waited with his uncle in the flickering candlelight. He saw the look in the priest's eyes, the slow nod of the head, and he instantly hated him, hated everything he stood for, hated everybody and everything in that one horrible moment.

He tried to run past the priest up the stairs but was held back by the men. He snatched the open Bible out of the feeble priest's hands, slammed it shut and threw it on the tiled floor, then broke free and ran out into the storm of the night sobbing blindly....

"...And you! You! You're so ugly not even your own mother could love you," came a loud voice from outside Crèvecoeur's tent. Another voice, low and angry, hissed out a profane curse. A third voice, and a fourth and a fifth chimed in, a regular chorus of cussing and swearing.

Inside his tent Crèvecoeur hurriedly put down his quill and journal. More cursing; and now laughter.

"That's not true. Of course his mother loves him," came a mocking voice. ""One monkey always loves another."

A muffled retort; then the sounds of scuffling and jeering. A heavy thud, hoots of laughter. Crèvecoeur felt his pulse quicken. He got to his feet and stepped outside.

Near the wood-pile two bodies were writhing on the ground in a cloud of dust before a semi-circle of soldiers snarling like a pack of hungry lions, shouting encouragement to one and curses on the other. The monkey was pinned to the ground by a burly youth with a shock of chestnut hair whose left arm and balled fist rose up and down onto the head of his victim as though chopping firewood. The soldiers paid no attention to the lieutenant.

Crèvecoeur felt his own blood boiling, anger doubled by frustration at the lack of effect his rank produced on the men. He strode to the combatants and gave a hard kick to the ribs of the chestnut-haired private who rolled over, howling in pain.

The spectators fell into a sudden, sullen silence broken only by the whimpering of the soldier and the gasping of his victim.

"What are you all doing here back at camp? Where is your corporal?" Crèvecoeur barked, trying to sound martial but annoyed at the lack of gravitas in his voice.

After a moment one of the younger soldiers finally spoke up.

"It's our platoon's turn for firewood detail. We were told to take care of it now before nightfall." Unlike his older companions who refused to look directly at the lieutenant, the freckled youth stared boldly into Crèvecoeur's eyes even though his Adam's apple was bobbing up and down. He was clutching a long-handled axe.

"And so instead of cutting up wood you cut up each other? Have you forgotten who the enemy is?"

"Stéphane deserved to be beaten," the freckled private muttered defiantly, gesturing with the axe-head towards the object of their hatred whose swollen face and bleeding nose attested to the condemnation by his peers. "He was speaking treason."

"It's not treason to tell the truth." Stéphane winced in pain. His boyish face was bruised and bleeding. His remark was met with low grumblings from the assembled. "All I said was, our trenches might hold off an English attack this summer but then they'll just keep coming back year after year until Québec falls. The English have their king behind them. We don't. So multitudes of men are going to die for no good reason."

"There he goes again. It's nothing short of blasphemy. What more proof do we need?" The freckled private pointed an accusing finger. "Liar! Traitor!" several soldiers snarled their agreement, lunging towards the author of the despised words.

"Enough!" Crèvecoeur exclaimed, stepping between them, his own fists balled. "You!" he ordered Stéphane. "Get over there and wait for me. You others, I could have you all court-martialed. I should not have to repeat the captain's orders. No fighting in camp, no cursing, no blasphemy. I asked you before, where is your corporal?"

"With the others down at the western trenches," was the surly reply.

"Go back to your company," Crèvecoeur commanded. "You, Stéphane, come with me."

Seeing the soldiers hesitate, Crèvecoeur raised a balled fist. "I told you to move!"

"We were ordered to gather firewood."

"Who ordered you?"

"It was Duflot. Like you, one of Captain Dumas' aides. You don't outrank Duflot."

"I'll deal with Duflot. Get back to the beach or I'll have you court-martialed. Move it!"

Their freckled-face leader shrugged and, still glaring, led his companions down the path back towards the beaches.

Their departure only increased Crèvecoeur's anger. Why couldn't this self-appointed apostle just keep his damn mouth shut? Crèvecoeur whirled around and grabbed the private by the shoulders. Seeing the boy's bruised and swollen face yet gentle eyes only increased Crèvecoeur's rage at this young man who was the cause of so much trouble.

"Heed what I am telling you," Crèvecoeur almost hissed through clenched teeth. "I could have you shot for treason. Do you want that? Do you?"

The private reflexively moved his head from side to side although retaining a calm irony in his eyes that exasperated Crèvecoeur even more. Finally the soldier opened his mouth.

"As God is my witness, I only –"

"Don't talk to me about God!" Crèvecoeur raged. "I don't want to hear about God!"

He shook the boy violently. His angry blue eyes made the fiery red of his hair seem even more aflame. "Now listen! For your own sake I am going to ask you be assigned to another company. But they will be watching you. You will keep your mouth shut. Do you hear me? One more slip up and you will be shot. Keep your 'truth' to yourself. Do you understand? Do you?"

Stéphane nodded his head gently, soft brown eyes serene as ever.

Crèvecoeur felt his grip relaxing. There now, he told himself, the boy's fate would be in the hands of others. Let the private's captain and Dumas deal with the trouble-maker. He would wash his hands of it.

He gestured to Stéphane to follow. Brooding, he heard the boy's meek footfalls behind him. Was the youth not simply a coward, trying to justify his weakness by this pretense of virtue?

Angrily Crèvecoeur picked up a stone and, glaring at Stéphane, hurled it as hard as he could at an innocent tree.

Chapter Three: *Hold Up the Sceptre and the Crown*

"We believe there is a large English fleet in the mouth of the Saint-Lawrence. How large we don't know. We also don't know what the enemy's plan of attack might be; but understand there will be an attack. And the most likely target is right here, at Beauport."

Dumas looked at his company officers one by one, bringing each one into his fold. The light of the dying camp-fire flickered on the mostly young faces. Behind Dumas stood his aides-de-camp in the shadows.

"We don't have the forces or the resources to go on the offensive. Rest assured that our valiant governor the Marquis de Vaudreuil would like nothing more than to attack the enemy. But prudence dictates otherwise. We will let the English exhaust themselves in futile offensive maneuvers and wait them out until autumn forces them to abandon the fight.

"But it is of paramount importance for an army under siege to keep up its morale. There was an incident today involving a private who was too outspoken in his personal views. You must be careful to nip such talk in the bud. Outright treason and cowardice will be dealt with harshly; but make sure you don't overreact. Be gentle as doves but clever as serpents."

Dumas bowed his head. "With God on our side we cannot fail. Let us pray."

The officers in the light of the fire followed the example of their captain. Crèvecoeur, in the shadows with the other aides, did not. He fidgeted impatiently, casting his glance at the play of the light of the dying fire. Someone had sacrificed an old crosspiece from a fence with the iron nails still embedded. The nails glowed brightly red from the intense heat. The lieutenant turned his eyes away, irritated.

After dismissing his officers Dumas pulled Crèvecoeur aside. "Kicking a soldier in the ribs is perhaps not the most effective way for a young officer to garner respect. Yes, I heard about it. Never mind how. Watch that temper of yours. I don't want to have to tell you again. Do you understand me?

"Now listen. This evening Governor Vaudreuil issued a proclamation. All civilians residing east of Montmorency whether in villages or on farms are to take to the woods as far as possible away from the river. You will ride with a few cavalry Captain de la Roche-Beaucourt will provide, and a dozen mounted militiamen under Captain DuChêne. You will proceed eastward to Île aux Coudres. On your way you will announce the governor's proclamation."

Dumas reached into his tunic. "Here. Take this. It's the proclamation in writing with the governor's seal. Leave a man at each village to act as relay. At Baie-Saint-Paul set up a post to keep an eye on the English Navy if they moor at Île aux Coudres. Report back to me through your relays if you find out anything useful. General Montcalm agrees with the governor's decision, but adds that under no circumstances are we to go on the offensive. You are not to engage the enemy. May God be with you."

With these instructions Dumas left his lieutenant to his own devices.

Crèvecoeur was impatient to get underway, wishing for daylight. He glanced beyond the encampment of Dumas' Colonial Regulars towards the distant fires of the militia, still blazing strong. A faint snatch of a song and the scratch of a fiddle were carried by the light breeze of the night. He went over to the cavalry's camp to introduce himself to Roche-Beaucourt. But the officer's aide-de-camp curtly turned him away. "The captain has already retired. Report tomorrow morning at dawn."

Sleep was obviously not uppermost in the minds of the militia rank and file. The civilian soldiers had wisely set up camp as far away as they could from the colonial and royal armies. Not so far as to muffle completely the sounds of serenading and fiddling which only seemed to intensify as the evening wore on. Clearly the festivities were just beginning.

No one in the militia camp paid any attention to the uniformed lieutenant of the Colonial Regulars wandering among them in his buff-and-grey and three-cornered hat. Crèvecoeur was looking for an officer, any officer, to direct him to Captain DuChêne. Although no two men were dressed identically they were all dressed alike, that is, in accordance with their own fancy. Officers and soldiers were indistinguishable. Every camp-fire seemed to have its card game and dice. Those not in the mood for gambling were singing or drinking or, in many cases, doing both, with equal verve.

"Hey there. Lieutenant!" came a raucous voice from the flickering shadows. "Did you lose your horse? Or did you decide to see what it's like to walk among the mortals?"

The burly man in the red knit cap was relaxing on a log, feet comfortably propped up on a stump. He was grinning at Crèvecoeur.

"My offer still stands. Pull up a log and take a load off your legs." He made a flourish in the air with his canteen before finishing the gesture with a swig.

"I am looking for Captain DuChêne."

"Yes, yes. Of course you are. But first, sit down and have a drink."

"I need to speak to Captain DuChêne. It is important."

"No doubt. Here. Take it. Make yourself at home."

"First I must see Captain DuChêne."

"Absolutely. Now, I'm sure you'll agree: this here's the finest applejack in all Christiandom. No, go on, take it. By the Blessed Virgin, tell me the truth: isn't that the best you've ever had?"

Resigning himself, Crèvecoeur grasped the goat's bladder and took a sip.

"You drink like the Virgin herself. Don't be shy. Do me the honour."

Crèvecoeur threw back his head and drained the canteen.

"Ah, that's my boy!" red cap chortled, taking back the canteen with enormous hands, fondling it fondly. As if by magic another goat's bladder appeared in his paws. He hefted it with satisfaction.

Crèvecoeur wiped his lips with the back of his hand, suppressing a wince from the burning in his throat.

"Now, about Captain DuChêne. I must see him."

"I understand that."

Crèvecoeur blew up.

"Man, will you not tell me what I need to know? I need to see Captain DuChêne!"

"You are."

"I am what?"

"You are. You *are* seeing Captain DuChêne. In the flesh. And he is pleased to make your acquaintance. Now, as I said before, pull up a log and let's talk."

Half a canteen and an hour later Crèvecoeur pulled out a copy of the governor's proclamation from his pocket and unfolded it. "Here, you can read it for yourself," he said, passing it along to DuChêne.

The militia captain swept it away with a flourish of his big brown hand. "I don't know me letters. But I know what it says. My colonel has informed me. It won't work."

DuChêne shifted on his log and sighed contentedly.

"Like I said, it won't work. The folks around here won't go for it, don't you see."

As he spoke he swept his muscular arm out as though unveiling a portrait. "These are our farms, these are our houses, our villages, our churches. This is our land."

He paused. A thought had occurred to him. It was time for a smoke. Philosophizing called for tobacco. He pulled out a greasy clay pipe, the original white stained a muddy brown. From a fold of his homespun he produced a pouch from which he pinched a bowlful of tobacco. He took a stick from the fire and lit his pipe, puffing blissfully. For an uncomfortable instant Crèvecoeur was fearful the Canadian would insist on sharing his pipe. His fears were, for the moment at least, unfounded. DuChêne appeared lost in thought.

Finally he stirred from his reverie. "There is nothing in the good God's world better than good aged Virginia tobacco!" he mused. "Far better than the local weed the Indians around here peddle. Vile stuff, that Indian tobacco! Although," he reflected, "our native friends say it has magical powers."

The Canadian took another grateful puff and grinned. " 'Tis a pity Virginia is an English colony. If it weren't, I would have no need to feel guilty for smoking smuggled contraband. Or for aiding and abetting the prosperity of our heretic enemy."

DuChêne gave the lieutenant the benefit of a beatific smile. "What a blessed God he is, He who gives us forgiveness through confession! And I have a jolly big need for confession, don't you see? The more I sin the more I confess; and the more I confess, the closer I feel to Him our Lord Almighty. Besides," DuChêne winked at the young officer, "with Father René on the other side of the confessional, forgiveness and absolution from sin take less time than you can say hail Mary, since the good father is all the more anxious to get it over with and have a smoke for himself."

DuChêne frowned. "But I must pray you forgive me! I must have left my manners at home! Here..." With a pinch of grimy thumb and forefinger he broke off the tip of the long pipe stem and passed the instrument on to the lieutenant. Crèvecoeur, seeing he had no choice, took it, feigning a nonchalance he did not feel.

"Yes," DuChêne continued to ruminate as he rummaged in his pocket for another pipe, "not only did the good Lord give us tobacco to enjoy for its own sake, but the Indians are mighty adept at using it to concoct all manner of medicines and poultices and...and the like. Also keeps away the black flies."

As the Canadian smoked another pipe he twiddled a small cloth pendant worn over his heart with sausage-like fingers. Crèvecoeur recognised the home-made *scapulaire*. Most of the militia wore one kind or another. Here a feminine hand had lovingly embroidered the image of the Virgin Mary holding her blessed infant.

Crèvecoeur puffed as shallowly as he could, willing himself to relax and not gag. Fortunately the giant Canadian was paying no attention. Someone had begun strumming a homemade lute. A fiddle joined in and voices were rising.

DuChêne freed his lips from his pipe and, unfolding himself up to his full height, gleefully chimed in with an oily baritone:

> *"Take heart, brother Canadians!*
> *Face our fate like Christians*
> *Hold up the sceptre and the crown*

25

Brave soldiers and militiamen
Fight on to the end of time,
Never let them down.

Let us call upon the angels and the saints
That He may tender to us His Hand
Let us call upon the Holy Virgin
That Her Blessings protect our land
That Her Blessings protect our freedom
And save us from the enemy brigand."

DuChêne finished the ballad with an emphatic "Amen", and took a final swig. He belched contentedly.

"Well, my boy, the English heretics may have their navy, but we Canadians have our God. At least we know what we are fighting for."

DuChêne looked Crèvecoeur in the eyes.

"Do you know what you are fighting for?"

Chapter Four: *Father René's Gift*

The tolling of the church bell reverberated in the Sunday morning air as they galloped into the tiny parish of Sainte-Anne-de-Beaupré, boundary proclaimed by a large wooden cross next to the road. Blue smoke and the smell of burning maple issued from the houses in the village. With the call to mass there was certain to be no one at home except the lame or sick.

They slowed to a trot as they approached the cross. DuChêne raised his hand, signaling a halt. He and the militiamen got off their horses and knelt in the dust, heads bowed. Crèvecoeur, regarding them impatiently, fidgeted. His horse felt his irritation and snorted, jerking and pulling against the reins, confused by the signals he sensed from his master, not knowing whether to stop or to go.

They continued into the village, past the small stone church nestled into the graveyard. Crèvecoeur pulled up his mount, glancing at DuChêne. This was the Canadian's parish; this was his priest; this was his country. It was understood the militia captain would take the lead.

DuChêne had the men dismount and enter the church through the plain wooden doors, removing their headware and scraping their boots on the iron blade set in the stone step. Crèvecoeur came in last. Like the others he knelt and crossed himself obligingly, but emptily, mechanically. In the pews women, all in black skirts, white shawl and cap, were also kneeling, children wriggling next to them. The few men present were elderly. Their priest, a diminutive, beaming bald man with a booming voice, was performing the Eucharist in mangled Latin, waving the incense burners and jingling the Sanctus bells with enthusiasm. He held up the panten, then the chalice and kissed it. After giving thanks and a blessing, he brought the body and blood of Christ to his lips with gusto.

Father René flashed a smile to the newcomers, bald pate a-gleam in a beam of morning sunlight streaming from the window. DuChêne and another man, seeing their wives, went to kneel with them. Then, rising to their feet, they partook in Holy Communion before returning to their places.

The priest raised his hands. "People, have faith! Forget not the trials and tribulations of your forefathers who, despite every adversity, courageously persevered through the Grace of God to carve out from this wilderness a piece of His Kindgom for you and your children, forever and forever, may it please the Lord Almighty. Let us take inspiration from mighty King David and his Psalm 140, so appropriate in these troubled times." The priest closed his eyes, reciting from memory.

" 'Rescue me, O Lord, from evil men. Protect me from men of violence, who devise evil plans in their hearts and stir up war every day....' "

As the priest recited the psalm in his thunderous voice, so much at odds with his short stature, Crèvecoeur absently cast his eyes about the church. Seeing nothing interesting about the backs of the kneeling devout, he glanced again at the clergyman in his robes, then let his eyes wander up above, to the crucified figure on the cross.

Crèvecoeur's jaw tightened and he looked quickly away. Through a side window he saw a plain wooden cross painted white serving as a tombstone; then another and another....Listlessly he heard the priest invoke the prophet Elisha, under attack by the furious King of Aram and his legions of howling warriors, calmly praying for his trembling servant to see God's chariots of fire driven by angels surrounding them in a protective ring.

"Open your eyes, beloved! And you will see that those who are with us are more than those who are with them." With a hymn and a final benediction the priest concluded the mass.

René strode over to greet DuChêne, who towered above him. DuChêne whispered in his wife's ear, tousled the hair of his children, and, grabbing the priest by the elbow, motioned with his meaty hand for his men to follow them out the side door into the graveyard before donning anew his red knit cap.

As Crèvecoeur stepped outside he saw the priest's arms gesturing in agitation. Father René's face had turned beet red, matching the colour of the militia captain's knit *tuque*, and his eyes blazed.

DuChêne looked down at him in sympathy from his great height, nodding his head and sighing. With relief he espied Crèvecoeur approaching. "Ah! Here's our lieutenant! René, I present to you Michel-Guillaume Jean de Crèvecoeur, lieutenant in the Colonial Regulars. Lieutenant Crèvecoeur, Father Philippe-René Robineau de Portneuf, pastor of the parish of Sainte-Anne-de-Beaupré."

Crèvecoeur doffed his tri-corn and inclined his head obligingly. Father René's face went from thunderclouds to sun in an instant. He clasped the young man's hands in both of his and ratcheted them vigorously, beaming.

"Blessings be upon you!" he exclaimed. "So you are the messenger who has come to prepare our way. Or are you Hector, come to defend our Troy?"

Not knowing what to say, Crèvecoeur said nothing. He forced a smile in return, more to stop himself from wincing from the iron grip of the priest, who seemed oblivious to his own strength.

"Jean DuChêne has enlightened me as to the purpose of your visit." Father René's light blue eyes glowed. "Bowl of coffee?"

Crèvecoeur nodded his head, hoping the coffee was as strong as the priest's handshake. With relief he got his hands back and let himself be guided by the priest who strolled next to him, one hand clasped to the young man's shoulder, one hand onto his elbow, the better to steer him along the right path. DuChêne gestured for the other men to remain behind and followed along.

"Let us go into the presbytery. Anne-Marie will have returned from mass by now and should still have the pot on the fire. Although coffee is under rationing, the priesthood is not without its privileges."

The priest's timber-framed dwelling looked ancient. Like the other houses in the hamlet it had several outbuildings including a barn, all built in the style of Normandy with a pigsty and sheep corral attached. An orchard in back and a large vegetable garden completed the bucolic scene. Geese and chickens, chased by a scolding rooster, scurried across the yard, protesting angrily. An image of the cock, in brass, adorned the roof of the house, serving as weather-vane. Only government officials and clergymen had the right to *porter girouette*.

Inside the great-room a stooped, grey woman in grey dress and grey shawl turned from her bustling by the fire. She tied a pure white apron around her waist, then crossed herself and came over silently to attend to the priest as he shed his robes, revealing the plain, homespun attire of the man.

Anne-Marie looked even more ancient than the house and was even shorter than the priest. She gave a quick curtsy to his guests then hung the vestments in an armoury from which she pulled out a tray of dishware. She quietly set a small table- the only table - for coffee and retreated back to the fire.

"Come! Pull up a log and make yourselves comfortable," Father René invited them, indicating several chairs arranged against the wall.

DuChêne, befitting his gigantic stature, chose the largest chair, a huge oaken baroque throne blackened by the ages, with a well-worn seat. Crèvecoeur selected an English chair with a Windsor back, several of whose spindles had the look of recent repair. Father René pulled up a tall homemade stool crafted out of maple he had made himself, allowing him to sit at eye level with his guests, more or less.

Anne-Marie poured out coffee into three brown earthenware bowls and Crèvecoeur produced the proclamation. Storm clouds returned to the priest's face and as he grasped the parchment his eyes flashed lightning. He had to hold the document at arms'-length in order to focus and as he did so the loose sleeves of his linen blouse fell back, revealing muscular arms and, all around his right forearm, the unmistakable livid scars of sabre wounds.

Father René read the proclamation silently to himself and handed it back. He folded his arms across his broad chest and contemplated the young officer a moment, pensively. "You know, in all honesty, I almost tore up your precious document. But I know you are only doing your duty. And, God preserve me from insulting my dear friend the governor, who is also doing what he feels is his duty to his people. But, by the Blessed Virgin! We are going to stand our ground and defend our homes."

He closed his eyes a moment, reflecting. " 'Have I not commanded you? Be strong and courageous', " he recited. " 'Do not be terrified, do not be discouraged, for the Lord your God will be with you wherever you go.' "

The priest opened his eyes and smiled anew, blue eyes radiant.

"Have some more coffee."

As Anne-Marie once again officiated over the bowls DuChêne saw an opportune moment to take out his pipe and pouch. Father René gleefully produced his own pipe, a native *calumet* with soapstone bowl; and a clay guest pipe for his young visitor, politely breaking off the tip of the stem first before proffering it. Crèvecoeur, realizing with dread he was trapped, took it, smiling as best he could.

Soon the room was filled with sharp blue smoke and the soft sounds of contented puffing broken only by a few muffled coughs. Anne-Marie gave a disapproving look then silently slipped outside.

"How are your yellow beans doing?" DuChêne inquired between puffs.

"Not bad, not bad. How fares the sick calf?"

"She has died, I'm afraid."

"I'm sorry to hear that."

"My brother's well has been dug."

"So I have heard. Let's pray it brings forth pure water."

"Amen."

"I would like to drop by and give it a blessing."

"He would be pleased. Did your grape vines survive?"

"Well, yes and no. The native vines of course are sturdy. The best ones come from Île d'Orléans. But their fruit is not as sweet as our good French vines produce. So, the question is finding the right grafts. Most have withered on the primary vine. Very few take hold and flourish. But, you can't know in advance just by looking at them. Looks can be deceiving."

"Amen."

"The only way you can know is through the test of time. Have those apple seeds I gave you last year sprouted?"

"Yes."

"Good, good. There too we'll just have to wait and see. You can always tell a good tree by its fruit but don't be deceived by the bad ones. They may survive to produce robust apples but the taste might turn out to be bitter."

"Then at least my pigs will be happy! Lieutenant, where are you going?"

Crèvecoeur had stood up, trying to look nonchalant. "Have to visit the backhouse," he croaked.

He groped his way through the thick blue fog to the side door, undid the latch and stepped outside into the precious clean air. He exhaled with relief and gratefully gulped in a few deep breaths. Rounding the corner of the house he heard the sound of sobbing. Anne-Marie was seated on a stump, plucking the evening's dinner, weeping as she worked, her wrinkled face half-hidden by the worn white bonnet and long strands of iron-gray hair. She looked up at the lieutenant, eyes red and wet.

"I know why you are here. You have to convince him. You have to make him understand…" the woman implored. She looked beseechingly into the young man's eyes. Crèvecoeur averted her gaze, looked down at her rough hands. The ancient woman's fingers worried the feathered carcass as though it were a set of rosary beads.

"He is so stubborn. He won't listen to the truth. Oh, why must men hate and kill each other so? Why can they not learn?" She brought to her nose a scrap of linen rag.

Crèvecoeur stood there awkwardly, eyes avoiding the woman's.

Anne-Marie understood. "Please excuse me," she murmured and, head down, went back to her plucking.

Crèvecoeur found the latrine and was making his way back to the priest's dwelling when Anne-Marie stopped him. She pulled at his sleeve with one hand and pressed with the other a small cloth patch into the young man's own hands.

"Please. Please take this. He will protect you."

Crèvecoeur glanced at the object in his palm. It was a scapular. He hesitated; then thanked her. "I will treasure this always, my dear lady." He politely put the patch into his breast pocket and instantly forgot about it as he stepped back inside the house.

DuChêne was seated by the fire sharpening a hunting knife. Father René had taken down an old musket from above the fireplace mantel and was oiling it.

"He who is forewarned is forearmed," he intoned cheerfully. He was using a chair as a makeshift worktable on which sat a small iron mold and several pewter bullets. An iron pot was suspended over the fire and several pewter plates were teetering precariously at the edge of the work-chair, awaiting their trial by fire.

"Our poor Anne-Marie," the priest mused absently. "She will surely regret the sacrifice of our best dishware! But, the Lord giveth and the Lord taketh away; blessed be the name of the Lord." He took a poker to the embers, checked the contents of the pot.

"Yes, poor Anne-Marie," he repeated. "She has had so many trials and pain in her life. You see, she is Acadian, from the Melanson clan near Port-Royal. When the English rounded up all those poor French farmers in 1755 and deported them – imagine, deported them from their own land they had worked so hard to fructify for a hundred years! – her ship was the one where the prisoners overpowered the crew and sailed to Québec.

"But her last brother died during the mutiny. She had lost another brother and nephew at Fort Beauséjour and yet another brother long before, when the Massachusetts Rangers captured Louisbourg in '45. She hardly knew her father; he was killed defending Port-Royal from the English in 1710. Now her only living relation here is nephew Joseph. He has hooked up with the militia at Baie-Saint-Paul. He's a bold man, that Joseph! His men have elected him their captain. But that only adds to his loving aunt's agony.

"Yes, poor Anne-Marie. May the Lord watch over her."

Father René finished reassembling his weapon and put it back up over the mantelpiece. He turned, wiped his hands on his breeches, came over to Crèvecoeur and embraced him.

"You must go now. Thank you young man for doing your duty. I, too, must now do my duty."

Father René smiled at the lieutenant. "As King Solomon teaches us, 'Fear God and keep his commandments, for this is the whole duty of man...' Let it be said of me that I have fulfilled my duty to God in all good conscience."

Father René slipped his priestly vestments back on and walked DuChêne and Crèvecoeur outside. He embraced Crèvecoeur one more time, then reached into a pocket and produced a ring made of pewter. He handed it to the young man, pressing it into his palm.

"Please accept this gift in remembrance of the truth."

Crèvecoeur looked at the ring. It held a circular form made of wax the size of a small coin on which could be read, in raised letters, "*Agneau de Dieu*".

Father René smiled.

"Peace be with you, my children."

Chapter Five: *The Chains of the Captors*

They had arrived at the tiny fishing village of Baie-Saint-Paul long after nightfall. DuChêne woke up a villager he knew, to the vociferous displeasure of the man's wife, and the harried husband let them sleep in his barn. The miniature cavalry had shrunk to a handful of militia, all the regulars having been posted at each village they had passed along the way.

"In the morning you will see the English ships," the man whispered to them, as if afraid the English – or his wife – were eavesdropping. "They are at anchor on the lee side of Île aux Coudres. They arrived two days ago."

Now at first light Crèvecoeur found himself flat on his stomach, spyglass clamped to his left eye, on a hill overlooking the river and island nearby. He counted thirteen vessels, anchored in the deeper water of the channel between the island and the shore. The closest was a small frigate, the *Squirrel*, then a large warship, *HMS Devonshire* which bristled with too many big guns to count. There was the smaller *Centurion*, and *Pembroke*; then another frigate. The largest vessel was furthest away in the deepest water, bow turned upriver.

That would be the admiral's flagship, the lieutenant thought. Despite the early hour several rowboats sat on the island's rocky beach and there were a number of sailors wandering aimlessly around, looking like bored children in search of something to play with. Several island ponies eyed the mariners warily from a safe distance.

Crèvecoeur retreated a few yards then found a new location further to the south, the better to train his glass on the admiral's flagship. "*Princess Amelia*" was the vessel's name, boldly embossed on the gunwale near the bowsprit. Crèvecoeur cursed softly under his breath.

"Why do you torment me like this?" he muttered to several dark clouds floating on the southerly horizon. At that moment he felt a soft, soothing breeze caressing his right cheek. He closed his eyes a moment, then looked again at the sky, this time more to the west. Black clouds were gathering over the mountains. A storm was approaching.

Abruptly he got to his feet, recklessly challenging any English sniper to shoot, wishing the enemy would attack, launch a raid, anything, that he might feed his fury, vent his frustration, kill, anyone, everything. He wished for a tomahawk, wished to drive it deep into the heart of the nearest innocent maple, settled for a handful of stones glittering on the ground under the morning light. He scooped one up. Opening his hand, he saw the diamond ring. With a cry of impotent rage he flung the rock away, as far as he could into the trees. *"Why don't you just curse God and die?"* Job's wife screamed.

Returning to the village, his anger melted into surprise. The tiny hamlet had been invaded by a homespun squad of militia and a few Abenaki scouts, instantly doubling its population. Their horses were tethered in a meadow next to the blacksmith's shop where the smithy was banging out a new horseshoe or two. The Abenaki were off by themselves, laughing in a semi-circle around several contestants caught up in a tug-of-war, the rope pulling them first one way, then the other.

DuChêne filled in the lieutenant. "Seems like our governor has had another slight difference of opinion with our general as to how to conduct this war."

He chuckled, oblivious to the look of smoldering irritation on the young man's face. "You recall meeting Auntie Anne-Marie, from yesterday? At the chapel? Well, that's her nephew Joseph over there. Joseph Saulnier. Governor Vaudreuil told him to high-tail it back to his village here with a few men and braves and see if they can lure the enemy into an ambush, or at least find a way to take a few prisoners, preferably officers. The governor would like to know what the English plan of attack might be."

Crèvecoeur looked with dismay at the Canadian. "But I'm under orders from General Montcalm to not engage the enemy."

"Don't worry. You won't have to. But, lest you forget, you are an officer in the Colonial Regulars. And the Colonial Regulars are under the orders of Governor Vaudreuil. As is the militia."

"That may be; yet it was Captain Dumas who conveyed the general's wishes to me, and I owe obedience to my captain."

"You speak true. Well, he's not *my* captain, and the general's not my commander."

But you are under my orders on this assignment, Crèvecoeur almost blurted out. The absurdity of the idea then hit home and the lieutenant burst out laughing in spite of himself.

The Canadian's look of defiance melted into suspicion, then he too chuckled, although inspired by a different vision.

"There's only one true commander, and it's not them!" DuChêne's eyes sparkled. "Even though they flatter themselves otherwise."

"Well, no, it has to be one or the other. It can't be both."

"You are correct on that last point, I'll grant you that."

"The king is above us all."

"Correct again."

"But the king is not here."

"Not the earthly one. Can't argue with you there."

"So we must obey those to whom he has delegated his authority."

"Yes."

"Therefore –"

"Therefore," the Canadian concluded, "you shall obey your master, and I shall obey mine."

Crèvecoeur frowned, opened his mouth then shut it finding nothing meaningful to say. He looked away, irritated.

In the field next to the blacksmith's the Abenaki had all joined in the tug-of-war, split into two screaming teams, Megeso caught in the middle, being pulled this way and that. Seeing his friend, Crèvecoeur strode over and was soon pulling on the rope as hard as he could. In an instant rough hands shoved him up to the middle in front of Megeso and the howling took on a derisive tone as the two were flung violently like puppets back and forth, powerless to control the combat or the outcome despite all their will and effort, until finally the other team won, drawing them over the middle line marked by a spear thrust into the ground and sending them sprawling head over heels.

The victors let out a raucous whoop and pounced on the losers. Crèvecoeur felt himself being grabbed by the hair and in an instant the horrible scenes of massacre at Fort William Henry flashed through his brain. The mocking, leering face above him, muscular arm raising the tomahawk high in the air, then a relaxing of the grip, the taunting laugh of the victor and then only blue sky.

A new face from above entered into Crèvecoeur's line of vision. Megeso's eyes were as sardonic as ever. His grip, however, was affectionate as he pulled the lieutenant up to a sitting position next to him on the grass.

"He who kills the bear gets to eat," Megeso remarked.

Crèvecoeur couldn't help but be disturbed, as always, by the several dried, hideous scalps dangling from his friend's belt, a testimony to his prowess as a warrior. Megeso had explained to him once before the significance and the story behind each gruesome talisman: this one came from an Iroquois, this one from a Maine settler. The western Abenaki hated – and feared – the Iroquois, just as their Huron cousins did; the eastern Abenaki tribes resented the New England English for having stolen their lands and pushed them into Gaspé. The New Englanders hated – and feared – the Abenaki for their bloody raids into the Penobscot and down the Connecticut River, and in revenge for which numerous American Rangers themselves boasted bloody trophies hanging from their leather belts as souvenirs of their own cruel retribution.

Crèvecoeur, sitting cross-legged, picked absently at a blade of grass, hunched over, eyes downwards. Megeso, sitting cross-legged, leaned back on his elbows, head thrown back so that his eyes were skyward.

"Look above," he exclaimed softly.

He pointed up to the blue vault of the sky. The yellow orb of the early morning sun was hanging low over the mountain peaks to the east while the pale ghost of the full moon was still suspended over the river valley to the west, just ahead of the advancing clouds, fading imperceptibly into the oblivion of the light of the day.

"That is Glascoop driving away the devil Malsumis. Glascoop always fulfills his promise to return. His light is good."

Megeso fingered a triangular ornament dangling on a necklace of beads around his neck, one of two items of jewelry he proudly displayed on his chest, in counterbalance to the scalping knife and gruesome trophies around his waist. The other item was his pewter cross.

"The world of the dark belongs to Malsumis. His realm is where evil is born. But he will always run away from the light."

"Well," Crèvecoeur replied, still hunched over, eyes turned back towards the ground, "if that is so, why doesn't the light just simply stay all the time so that Malsumis can never return?"

"Tabaldak wants it that way. He created Glascoop; he created Malsumis. But one day Glascoop will finally kill Malsumis and then there will be nothing but light."

Megeso again pointed upwards, to the west, where the false light of the moon had almost completely disappeared.

"See. Already Malsumis has run away. He is afraid of Glascoop."

There was a stirring among the militiamen. "Fall in!" a voice yelled. None too hurriedly, bodies in twos and threes ambled over towards the voice. Some of the faces were covered with grey beards, some belonged to mere boys. Most of the young men were clean-shaven although stubbly. The greybeards wore a quiet, somber look; the boys swaggered to cover up their fear. The older men all bore the stoic expression of fishermen and farmers the world over who accepted that there was a greater master of their fate above themselves.

The voice belonged to their leader, a middlin'-sized man of perhaps forty. His band gathered around him in a circle, the militia's interpretation of falling in. Crèvecoeur could not hear what Captain Saulnier was saying but even from where he stood he could see the fire in the man's eyes, blazing with a desire to wreak vengeance on the lion which had destroyed the lives of his loved ones. DuChêne and the few of his own remaining militiamen joined in.

Crèvecoeur, uncertain of his role, wordlessly walked with Megeso over to the Abenaki scouts standing proudly apart from the white men, silently watching, like so many red-tailed hawks perched quietly in the treetops surveying the meadow below, waiting for their moment to pounce.

The doors of several houses were open. Women-folk with young children in their arms, at their feet, watched with the same stoic expression as their men-folk. In the doorway of the church stood a man in priestly robes. He, too, was observing the events unfolding before them all, but with a look of fearful resignation in his eyes.

At a word from their captain, the militia, Abenaki at their side, moved off and onto the road, hardly more than a wide trail, leading away from the hamlet towards the south. Their march took them after a few minutes to the same smaller path Crèvecoeur had trodden an hour or so before, running to the bluffs overlooking the river and the English ships in the channel below.

Reaching the cliff-edge the militia spread themselves out along a long line parallel to the river.

"That's it, my boys! Make yourselves look like a long snake, ready to strike!" their captain shouted. "Go ahead! Make noise! Let the English bastards hear us!" Saulnier swaggered up and down the line of men now lying prone on their stomachs, indifferent to any danger from the ships below.

Standing among a clump of pines with Megeso, Crèvecoeur tried to estimate the distance from the militia's crude line and the nearest frigate rocking peacefully in the morning current. Surely they were too far away for their muskets to reach or do any harm; but not so distant as to protect themselves from the ship's own guns. The English sailors and soldiers lounging on the decks were clearly visible, and several could now be seen pointing up towards them, shouting.

An officer appeared on the poop-deck, by his bearing and uniform the commander of the ship. He spread his legs slightly apart to thwart the yawing of the vessel and, hands clasped casually behind his back, looked languidly in the direction of the militiamen on the cliff-top. He let loose an enormous yawn, an old scruffy lion regally contemptuous of the intruders disturbing the peace of his morning ruminations. The officer now came about, turning his backside to the enemy. He rocked jauntily on his heels, glancing from right to left, admiring the view of the spars and rigging presented by the other vessels in the channel. His men below cheered and, after a hearty Huzzah! went back to their business on deck, totally ignoring the pests on the cliff as if they were so many gnats, in emulation of their commander.

Saulnier was beside himself with rage. He stormed back and forth along his line. "*Ossie de crisse de ciboire de tabernak!*" he swore. "Damn those pigs! Fire away! Fire, I say!"

His men obliged with enthusiasm, if not with precision. The musket fire in the open space of the cliff-tops sounded like so many Chinese firecrackers popping off sporadically and at random. Their musket balls all fell far short of the target, throwing up tiny bouquets of water as they plopped harmlessly into the river. The British soldiers and sailors paid them not the slightest attention. DuChêne and the older militiamen instantly rested their arms, but a few of the younger men and boys eagerly reloaded, aimed, and fired again as if by squeezing the trigger harder the balls would go farther.

Saulnier reluctantly ordered a cease-fire and the last of the muskets fell silent. Wisps of acrid smoke dissipated in the breeze, now blowing stronger from the southwest where dark grey clouds, growing blacker by the minute, covered almost a third of the sky.

They waited, watching the indifferent men on the ships below. The vessels were turning a bit more on their anchors now as the wind starting playing with the current of the river. The gun-ports in the ships' sides were all closed and no effort was being made to open them. On deck, preparations were underway to counter the coming storm.

Saulnier, resigned, saw that the enemy was not going to let themselves be provoked. He had his militia form up and they returned to the village, their steps lighter by the few less ounces they carried equal to the ammunition they had wasted.

The majority of the men took leave of their captain, farmers who lived outside the village anxious to tend to their fields recently planted with oats, fishermen who were anxious to secure their boats. The British warships anchored a few rods away might just as well have been in the estuary of the River Thames. The Canadians had work to do, and they did not care to listen to proclamations. Saulnier agreed with his men they could go under pledge to come back within the week. The Abenaki had already melted away back into the forest, Megeso excepted.

By mid-afternoon the storm came crashing down all around. DuChêne led them back to the barn where they had spent the night, taking refuge from the tempest outside, along with the barn's owner, taking refuge from his tempestuous wife. Desrivières, for that was the beleaguered man's name, managed to smuggle some smoked cod and bread from the larder for his guests while a few men from the village ate from their own provisions. Hunger satiated, they convened their council of war. From the open barn door they could see through arrows of pelting rain the bay down below, brown muck exposed by low tide with the island beyond.

Saulnier was still smarting from the insult of the morning. "If the bastards won't attack us, why, then we'll attack them!" he proclaimed. He looked eagerly around at the assembled, sprawled haphazardly amidst the hay. To his amazement they did not jump up to their feet in excitement at his idea. Several were picking at their teeth with a straw. Several without teeth, older men, looked at their captain blankly.

DuChêne was puffing contentedly on his pipe, relaxing on a stump in the open doorway. Silence hung over them like the blue smoke from the tobacco broken only by the patter of rain. He took his pipe out of his mouth long enough to murmur: "*Un ange passe...*" then went back to his cogitating, looking up at the threatening sky as though seeing the angels themselves flying by.

"I suppose," he mused, "there could be no harm in taking a few skiffs over to the island and scouting around. As long as we don't get too carried away."

"We can muffle the oars," Saulnier's corporal agreed, speaking with a Swiss accent.

Saulnier, grateful for the opening, nodded his head. "Who can say? We might be able to get our hands on an officer or two."

They convened the next morning long before dawn as agreed. The storm was over and the tide was up. Desrivières had three skiffs at the ready on the rocky beach. After twenty minutes' rowing the tiny armada made landfall on the eastern point of the island. Upriver towards the west they could barely discern the shapes of the anchored ships emerging from the gloom of the night.

The war party followed Desrivières along a path towards the ships, running parallel to the shore yet hidden by the trees along the forest fringe. By dawn's glow they saw a long, wide meadow sloping down to the gravel at water's edge and beyond, the ships at anchor. A herd of wild ponies was grazing peacefully. Even from their vantage point in the woods perhaps a quarter-mile away the warships were imposing.

There was activity on the decks. A small boat was lowered over the gunwales and onto the water. Oars propelled the craft onto the rocky beach, spooking the ponies who, with angry snorting, dashed to the opposite side of the meadow, glaring at the intruders. A band of sailors disembarked carrying small buckets, commanded by a young lieutenant who directed his men to the meadow in front of the woods where the spies were in hiding. As they advanced they began to fan out, stooping down now and then.

"A foraging detail," DuChêne murmured. "Gathering mustard greens and dandelions to garnish the admiral's dinner."

The ponies did not seem to appreciate having competition for their food. Their leader took a step forward and pawed at the ground, glowering at the humans. A pair of sailors put down their buckets and glared back, mockingly. One of them, a stocky tow-headed youth, moved his leg up and down in imitation of the pony chieftain. The pony snorted and shook his head. The sailor snorted and shook his head; then started advancing toward the herd, which began to fidget in agitation. The leader reared up and let loose a loud whinny whereupon the two sailors rushed the herd. The ponies bolted away, to the uproarious laughter of the sailors' peers.

"Spencer! Burris!" Their lieutenant was furious. "Leave the damn ponies alone!"

The detail went back to foraging, gloomily, finding mustard greens and dandelions less exciting than ponies. As Saulnier and DuChêne weighed their strategy in whispers the English officer took the next move out of their hands. He signaled his men back to the boat.

By noon the wind had picked up again, blowing strongly from the west. The channel was choppy, making it hard going for the skiffs shuttling between the admiral's flagship *Princess Amelia* and other vessels of the vanguard. Through his glass Crèvecoeur could see the admiral and officers conferring on the bridge. Clearly they were impatient. The winds showed no signs of turning.

Late in the afternoon another skiff was rowed ashore. The three sailors pulled up the boat to high ground, as though planning on spending some time on the island. They made their way up the slope towards the forest.

Saulnier had his men retreat further into the woods, away from the path. They watched as the three sailors, one of them the stocky blond from the morning, hiked past them heading towards the eastern end of the island, armed only with leather shoulder bags. Saulnier's band followed at a discrete distance.

The sailors were easy to track as they stuck to the trail and made no effort to be silent. On the contrary, they sang as they walked. After a mile they veered to the south and emerged from the woods into a grassy field leading down to the water. From there the view was open all the way downriver to the northeast. The sailors evidently had been sent to see if the rest of the fleet was nigh. There were no vessels in evidence. The contrary wind was too strong all up and down the Saint-Lawrence.

To the right on the western fringe of the grassland were the ponies, grazing with one eye turned towards the disturbers of their peace. The tallest sailor motioned to his companions. They huddled together, whispering as though fearful the animals understood English, then one of them broke away and sauntered casually back up the slope towards the forest.

Saulnier's band shrank back. The tow-haired sailor entered the woods and turned back down the path toward the ships. The other two away in the meadow produced a length of rope from a shoulder sack. The tall mariner fashioned a loop at the end and began twirling the rope in grand circles.

After a few minutes came loud yelling from the forest beyond the ponies. The stocky sailor emerged from the woods waving and screaming at the animals, which turned and bolted towards the other men. The sailors closed the circle on the frightened ponies, bumping into each other in confusion and terror. The rope sailed out and the noose found its target, like a bowline around a bit, on the neck of an unfortunate beast while the others broke loose and galloped away.

The three sailors converged gleefully around their captive. The pony strained at the rope, eyes wide with fright, ignoring the handful of grass proffered by one of its tormentors, caught in a snare over which it had no control and desiring only to be free.

The men now began disputing their prize. The stocky blond fellow grabbed the mane of the animal and hoisted himself onto its back only to tumble to the ground. The tall sailor took his place on the pony, kicking up its hind legs to rid itself of its unbidden master. The stocky blond swung himself up behind the other so that now there were two on the back of the beast, looking for all the world like Don Quixote and Sancho Panza.

At Saulnier's wave of the arm his war party, pistols drawn, dashed out of the forest and surrounded the mounted knight errant and his servants. Saulnier looked back towards the woods at Crèvecoeur who had lagged behind, unwilling to disobey Captain Dumas' orders. Saulnier, excited, signaled for him to join them. Crèvecoeur, realizing he was the only one in their party able to speak English, went forward reluctantly.

The ensnared sailors, two of them still mounted on their steed, had been regarding their ragtag captors with a look of haughty disdain which melted into a more respectful aspect as they saw the uniformed officer approaching them. Crèvecoeur understood the role expected of him and acted his part accordingly. Sweeping his gaze over the three sailors, he asked in English: "Are you all of the same rank?"

"I'm an able seaman" the tall one responded, surly. He jerked his head behind him. "Burris there is ordinary, as well as Tomkins."

"Very well. Mr. Tomkins, you will please step forward. Thank you. Slowly remove your shoulder bag. Now extend your arms. I am sorry but we must take certain precautions."

After Tomkins' wrists were bound tow-headed Burris was made to dismount and be bound in turn; then their leader, whose name was Fitch.

"You are prisoners of war and therefore entitled to all which such status implies."

Crèvecoeur's formality only served to increase the captives' apprehension.

"What are you going to do with us?" the blond sailor blurted out. He had undoubtedly heard of the horrors of the surrender of Fort William Henry.

"Be easy," Crèvecoeur replied, repressing a surge of sympathy he felt for the scared youth. "We won't feed you to the cannibals."

"But our mates will think we've deserted. That we're turncoats, traitors."

Crèvecoeur reflected a moment. He reached into his side pouch and pulled out a stub of artist's charcoal and a scrap of sketch paper. Using his pouch as a writing table, he printed as best as he could a message to the intention of the captured sailors' superiors.

"My compliments to the gallant officers of His Majesty's Royal Navy: Greetings. We have this day taken into custody three sailors by the names of Fitch, Burris and Tompkins, respectively. Your men are to be commended for their vigourous and courageous resistance. They are unharmed. Rest assured they will be treated honourably in accordance with our custom. Respectfully, etc etc."

Crèvecoeur read the missive out loud, then placed the note in Burris' pouch.

"I'll leave it on the path in the forest in plain view."

The rope was removed from around the pony's neck. It stood there a moment, then, suddenly understanding it was free, bolted away. The English sailors, hands bound by rope, and the Canadian militia, hands holding the rope, shadowed by a French lieutenant and his Indian companion, watched the creature as it flew effortlessly away, unshackled by the invisible chains binding its fellow creatures.

Chapter Six: *That Special Spot in Sussex*

The whitewashed walls of the Dauphine Redoubt were dazzling in the morning sunlight. Inside, the barracks were gloomy despite the light from outside filtering in through open windows and doors. Through the openings Crèvecoeur could see the courtyard where soldiers were drilling and beyond them to the north the blue curve of the Saint-Charles River far below where it met the Saint-Lawrence. Beyond the new bridge over the Saint-Charles the road, flanked by brown trenches and earthworks, cut northeasterly along the beaches to Beauport.

Crèvecoeur resumed pacing the cool flagstone floor of the room. DuChêne sat on the edge of his bunk puffing on his pipe, unperturbed. Saulnier was as impatient as Crèvecoeur, anxious to present his prize, proof of a mission fulfilled.

A young orderly dressed in the pale grey of the Colonial Regulars appeared in the doorway of the corridor. To Saulnier's disappointment the orderly addressed Crèvecoeur, also in grey, and ignored the two militiamen.

"His Excellency will see you now."

They all went down the dark corridor then up a flight of stairs and through an open doorway into a vast room spanning the width of the building. Unlike the gloom below, here everything was bright, serenely cheerful thanks to windows on both exterior walls. The atmosphere itself was lighter, refreshed by the cross-breeze from the open windows. In the middle of the bright, cheerful room sat a bright, cheerful man. His portly figure was stuffed into a brilliant scarlet waistcoat with old-fashioned silver lace collar and sleeves covering a camisole of emerald green. The ermine and gold Cross of Saint-Louis glittered over his heart.

He was seated at a regal carved oak table with an Italian globe of the world at one end, pouring over a document held in one hand with the aid of a round magnifying glass grasped by plump fingers. As he read, his large head bobbed up and down and with it the white, curled bob-wig on top, like a boat riding up and down on the swell of the tide.

Hearing the boots on the creaking pineboard floor, Pierre de Rigaud, Marquis de Vaudreuil et de Cavagnial , Gouverneur de la Nouvelle-France et de la Louisiane et Lieutenant-Général du Roi, looked up.

"Well, gentlemen, what is it?" The governor's large, calf-like eyes fell upon them, puzzled.

The orderly coughed. "Your Excellency may recall...the three English prisoners?"

The governor's bovine eyes beamed. "I do, indeed!" he chortled, slapping a plump thigh in delight. "Excellent work. Excellent! No, do stay, my child," he said to the orderly who had bowed to take his leave.

"Now, how shall we put to good use the fruits of your endeavours? Why, we shall interrogate them, of course!"

The governor paused, frowning. "Unfortunately, we are not proficient in the English tongue. A barbaric abomination of our own shared linguistic heritage from the times of the Norman Conquest, this English language! Too many German words mixed in. They know it, themselves! Just look at their officers. See how they all strive to speak French even amongst themselves, in acknowledgement of the one true, pure language! The language of Corneille, Racine, Molière! This sublime verbal unity of music, art and philosophy! What more proof does one need of the truth of our superior culture?"

He frowned again. "However, as I said, we do not speak that barbaric tongue. But," he beamed, turning his round face to Crèvecoeur, "I...we... have learned that you do."

Understanding his cue, Crèvecoeur stepped forward and made a reverence, grandly sweeping his *tricorne* in a graceful arc to the floor and back up, narrowly missing the apoplectic face of Saulnier.

"Yes," his Excellency continued, "we have learned from your Captain Dumas that you have spent many years in England and are thus conversant in that language.

"Now, see here what we have done." The governor chuckled. He tapped a plump finger against his temple for emphasis. "We have kept the three sailors separated from one another. Thus separated, they are in complete ignorance of the fate of their companions or what they say to us or not say. Voilà!" With a dramatic flourish he had seen at the theatre in Paris the governor brought both hands together with a loud clap in front of his chin and beamed at Crèvecoeur.

"What say you? You have spoken to the three. Which of the three shall we question first?"

The lieutenant cleared his throat. "Your Excellency has acted wisely. Their leader – the tall one named Fitch – should be questioned last; the first one should be the short blond sailor called Burris. He is fearful and not very astute."

"Yes, yes, I – we – follow your reasoning. Splendid!" the governor again clapped his hands together in exuberance. His eyes gleamed. "Perhaps we shall succeed in providing a bit of surprising intelligence to our dear Montcalm. Orderly!"

"Sire."

"Go fetch Fitch."

"Sire?"

"Fetch Fitch forthwith."

"Fetch Fitch first?"

"Bring Fitch forth, I say."

Nonplussed, the orderly looked at Crèvecoeur for help. Crèvecoeur again cleared his throat and took another step forward, doffing his hat and inclining his head.

"If it please your Excellency…may I be so bold as to praise the shrewdness of his Excellency's thinking, so much in advance of his humble servants. I see that, by bringing the leader Fitch first out of his cell, we shall deceive his companions into thinking their leader is the first to be questioned; and thereby prepare the soil of their brains for the seeds your Exellency will be planting. If I may be allowed, Sire, bravo! *Bravissimo!*"

Vaudreuil beamed anew. "Perhaps, my child," this to the lieutenant, "you would be so good as to accompany my orderly and execute our plan, as you have so cogently described. We will occupy ourselves with other business for, shall we say, three-quarters of an hour, so that our stratagem may have its effect."

Crèvecoeur bowed and departed with the orderly, leaving behind a steaming Saulnier and a chuckling DuChêne. They descended the stairs onto the barracks level and proceeded down another flight of narrower stairs into the even darker, danker basement below where their captives were locked up, each in his own make-shift cell. They brought Fitch back up to the ground floor and pushed the sailor into a small side room. A staff sergeant looked up in surprise. The orderly quickly explained. The sergeant nodded his head, then went to a door and opened it, revealing a pantry of sorts. Fitch was shoved into the closet and the door was banged shut, then locked with a heavy key produced by the sergeant.

Crèvecoeur and the orderly stepped outside into the courtyard to kill time.

"You're from Bordeaux?" Crèvecoeur guessed, judging from the orderly's accent.

"Close. Arcachon."

"How is it you became the governor's orderly?"

The private, barely old enough to shave, smiled. "Divine intervention. I would like to believe it is due to diligence and aptitude, but the truth is, Captain Dumas is my mother's cousin. He arranged it."

Crèvecoeur offered his hand, English style. "Michel-Guillaume."

"Jean-Luc. Jean-Luc Lespérance."

The orderly shook his new friend's hand. "You have lived in England? What's it like?"

Crèvecoeur looked at the younger soldier, then cast his eyes away.

"The weather's cold. The food's terrible," he replied, curtly. "But," he finally added, "the girls...are beautiful..."

"I can imagine. I don't believe I have ever laid eyes, or any other part of my body, on an English girl. I saw a lot of English merchants, though, around the warehouses in Bordeaux." Jean-Luc grinned. "My grandmamà used to tell us she was descended from Henry the Second and Eleanor of Aquitaine and if so, that would mean I ought to have a claim to the English throne!"

"I suppose the Georges of Hanover might have something to say about that."

"They needn't worry. I wouldn't want to be a king. Seems to me a king is like a prisoner of sorts, only that his shackles are invisible and he lives in a very large, fancy prison whose bars are just as invisible."

"I suppose..." Crèvecoeur paused a second. "I suppose we are all...prisoners in one way or another."

Jean-Luc looked at the lieutenant quizzically. "Well, I don't know about that. We all have duties, we are all under the orders of someone, true enough. We all must obey a higher authority. But it's not the same as being in a real prison cell. And then, when we're off-duty, well, then we're perfectly free to do what we want."

"And what do you want?"

The orderly paused, opened his mouth to reply, shut it and frowned.

"Well. I suppose I don't really know. It's easier to describe what I *don't* want. I don't want to be poor. I don't want to be wretched. Leprosy doesn't appeal to me. Neither would the priesthood. I can't imagine being a priest, going through life celibate."

"I have news for you: priests don't."

Jean-Luc laughed. "Well, I know. I was talking about the ideal. But see, that's the problem, isn't it? On the one hand you have the ideal, and on the other hand, the reality. What we ought to do compared to what we want to do. I don't like feeling guilty, so I wouldn't want to be a priest."

"A priest is just a man. If priests are guilty then so are all men. If men are not guilty then priests aren't either. I suppose," Crèvecoeur continued, speaking to himself as much as to the other, "I suppose the best way – actually, the *only* way, is to have your wants align with the ideal. Like those passenger pigeons up there."

He pointed upward, where a majestic flock of the native doves rode the waves of the air as though lifted up by an invisible hand. "They don't think about flying, I'm sure. They don't *need* to think about flying, or about anything they do. They just *do*. That, I guess, is real freedom."

Lespérance was puzzled. "If not thinking is freedom, then that means thinking is the opposite of freedom. To think is to be in prison. But we can't help but to think! Therefore..."

"We're doomed!" the lieutenant concluded.

The orderly laughed again. "I'm not ready to stand condemned, at least, not just yet. I've got me whole life ahead of me. And," he almost whispered, suddenly self-conscious, "I've found myself a beautiful girl. She told me last night she wants to be my wife. I haven't asked her father yet, of course. This wouldn't be the right time, would it? To tell you the truth, I'm a little scared to ask him."

"What's her name?" Crèvecoeur put in politely.

"Angélique. And she is, too!"

Lespérance gestured down towards the Lower Town. "Family's in the fur trade. Own a warehouse on the quay. They have a trading-post at Saint-Charles; a couple of mills, too. They have a sloop but it's on 'loan' to the Colony. The vessel's name is Angélique, after my fiancée."

The private grimaced. "That's one debt never likely to be repaid. You see, Captain Le Mercier wants to destroy the English fleet with fireboats. On the other hand, though, if his plan works, why then, maybe my father-in-law will go down in history as the man who saved Québec! And whose son-in-law is heir to the English throne, to-boot."

After a moment the orderly asked: "You ever think of getting married?"

The lieutenant started with a jerk. He glared with smoldering eyes at Jean-Luc, startling the private. The younger man blinked, a shadow of confusion crossing over his face.

Crèvecoeur struggled to compose himself. He cast his gaze towards the Saint-Charles valley far below in the distance. He was silent a very long moment.

"I'm sorry," he finally managed, abruptly.

He took off his hat, looking at it as if seeing it for the first time. His fingers worried the felt of the brim. A few strands of reddish hair freed themselves from his queue, liberated at least for a moment by a soft breeze wafting up from the west.

With the back of his hand he brushed away the errant wisps of hair. In the parade-ground nearby a company of town militia was assembling, shepherded by an impatient Colonial Regular officer. He began instructing the civilian soldiers in close-order drill. His angry commands were met with irreverent laughter.

Crèvecoeur, irritated, retreated. The governor's orderly followed him. They went up the small incline in the shadow of the building to the chaplain's cozy white-washed house next to his vegetable garden. The summer squash was flowering and the grape vines were flourishing, heedless of the human activity around them.

Crèvecoeur broke off a grape leaf.

"I was in boarding school, south of London..." he murmured.

He caressed the leaf absently in his hand.

"It was in a small village in Sussex, not far from Lewes, the market-town."

His fingers stroked the surface of the grape leaf. Its fibres though soft were resilient and therein lay its strength.

"After my mother died, my father sent me to her cousins in England. His health wasn't good and neither were his finances. My relatives didn't quite know what to do with me, so they packed me off to school."

Crèvecoeur opened his hand and watched the grape leaf float to the ground.

"I was in my fourth year. My last year. The school mistress had a daughter, several daughters, actually. Amelia was the youngest. "

He smiled at the memory.

"I remember the day I first saw her.... We were at the May-Day festival, students, families from the town. I saw her, in her beautiful white dress. She came to me, like in a dream...I asked her to dance. I pinned a rose to her garland she was wearing like a crown of flowers, I looked into her eyes, light brown, soft and radiant like amber and she smiled at me, so sweet, so gentle. When she twirled around the May-pole her long chestnut hair came undone and the rose slipped from her hair, I stooped down, picked it up for her, fastened it back on her garland. A thorn pricked my thumb. She was saddened, but then laughed, a sweet lamb's bell and she took my hand in hers. She wetted her finger and put it to the wound, to stop it from bleeding.

"There was a small stone chapel near the school, and a beautiful, shady cemetery. An old, narrow path wound through the trees, leading to a gazebo. Someone had planted rose bushes against one side where the sun filtered through, and there were grape vines climbing as high as the roof. It became our favourite place. Our special spot. Our own special spot...."

Crèvecoeur reached out for another grape leaf, touching it but this time leaving it secure on its vine.

"No one ever comes here, it's so quiet, so wonderfully peaceful. No one ever bothers us here, no one even knows we are here. Our special place....Only the doves in the trees know.

"It's our special world...I teach her French, she corrects my English. She tells me about her family, her childhood, her whole life; and then I repeat what she says, in French so that she can practise by telling me again what she has just said, in French this time. And then I tell her my story in French, and she repeats it in English so that I can learn to say it just as though I were English. We tell each other everything, as long as our memories can stretch....

"My mother's cousins introduce me to a cartographer and surveyor in London. He publishes maps, performs surveys of towns, counties, estates. It doesn't pay much but it's a respectable position, being a surveyor and map-maker. I travel a lot around Kent, Surrey, Sussex, surveying, sketching.

"Amelia writes to me in her charming French. I love the soft curves of her script, the sweet shape of her letters, her mistakes in grammar.... It's so...so easy, so...pleasing...to write to her. I want her to see everything I am seeing, learn everything I am learning. I want her to feel everything I am feeling....

"A year goes by, a wonderful year....now it's near Michaelmas and the weather is wet, cold. The season for working in the field is over for now, so I go back to the drafting-table in London. I take leave for a week, a precious week to be with her.

"Our special place is there as always and we don't care if it's drizzling and cold. She's so warm, so soft, so lovely in the rain!

"Her father is dead, you see; so I go to her uncle and he agrees to our engagement. I have my mother's diamond ring I sent over for, from my father's vault. The diamonds sparkle, just like her eyes. Her fingers are so slender and graceful, so white, so cool. The ring glides on so easily as if created just for her. The church bell is ringing....

"But now...now... she's...fallen ill...she's lying, she's lying there, sick in bed. So pale, so weak. Her eyes are closed. I kiss her eyelids. Over and over again I kiss her eyelids....Open your eyes, please open your eyes. Please open them....She's... she's dying? You can't die Amelia. You can't die. You can't die. You can't die...Please don't die Amelia! Please God don't let her die...."

The orderly found himself crying, standing next to the lieutenant of the Colonial Regulars, two young men crying together in the courtyard of the Dauphine Redoubt, three thousand miles and a universe away from that special spot in Sussex.

Chapter Seven: *The Governor's Prophecy*

Governor Vaudreuil was still seated as they had left him an hour earlier, as though he and the chair were one piece of furniture. He had been joined in the room by Le Mercier, the captain of artillery. In fact, the room served as the captain's quarters. Le Mercier appeared irritated by the usurpation of his chair by the ample seat of government so royally represented by the ample governor.

Next to the large desk cluttered with maps and compasses another young officer sat, on a folding campstool. On his knees balanced a portable writing chest, whose top was open to allow the smooth writing surface, on which was affixed a rectangle of parchment, to glide forward beneath the waiting quill of the scribe.

Crèvecoeur and the orderly marched the blond Burris into the chamber and had him sit on a camp-stool in the middle of the room. The governor clapped his hands together in delight, rubbing them and looking at the terrified sailor as though contemplating a holiday banquet. He motioned for Crèvecoeur to come near.

"Ask him how old he is." He whispered, unnecessarily.

"How old are you, Mr. Burris?"

"Seventeen...sir."

As the governor whispered Crèvecoeur questioned the captive then relayed the responses back in French. The scribe's quill scratched the parchment noisily.

"What is the name of your ship?"

"The *Pembroke*, sir."

"Who is the commanding officer?"

"That would be Captain James Cook."

"How many guns?"

"I...I don't really know for sure...maybe 50? I'm not a gunner, sir."

"You understand, don't you, that we have already questioned Fitch. He has told us everything."

"Sir?"

"We know all about your plans."

"My plans, sir? I don't have any plans. Except to get back home as soon as possible."

"Who is your admiral?"

Burris looked confused. "You mean our rear admiral? There's Admiral Saunders, sir. But he's not with our group. Then there's Holmes but he's also behind us. We have Rear Admiral Durrell with us, in the *Princess Amelia*. But he don't confide in the likes of me."

"How many vessels are you at Île aux Coudres?"

"Well, I don't know...there's my ship, then the admiral's. There's the *Devonshire*–"

"How many cannon?"

"I guess maybe 60? 70?"

"Go on."

"Then there's the *Squirrel*, the *Centurion*...maybe five gunships and seven or eight transports."

"How many soldiers on board?"

"Oh, a lot! A thousand, I'd guess. I don't know exactly. I don't pay them much attention."

Vaudreuil hoisted himself up. Lace-sleeved hands clasped behind his back, he strolled over to a point just in front of the sailor and looked down at him. Burris shrank back.

"Do you know who I am?" he asked, Crèvecoeur translating.

"No, sir. General Montcalm, sir?"

The sailor's response bought him a glare followed by a look of disgust.

"So, you know who General Montcalm is, do you?"

"Of course, sir. We all know that much. And a very great general you are, too. We know all about your military genius."

The governor was miffed. "Anyone else amongst the leaders in New-France come to mind?"

"No sir."

"No one else?"

"I am sorry but no, I can't think of anyone else. No one of significance, anyway."

Crèvecoeur, seeing the governor's face grow red, hastened to intervene. "May I suggest sire asking the prisoner about General Wolfe and his intentions?"

Vaudreuil reasserted his authority. "Tell him we know all about Wolfe's plans, that we intercepted correspondence addressed to Amherst in New-York, that...we believe Wolfe wants to skirt around Québec, join forces with Amherst and then attack Montréal...."

Crèvecoeur did as directed. But it was clear the sailor knew nothing about anything beyond the gunwales of his own ship.

"Alls I know is that Captain Cook is anxious to get underway. Every morning it's the same routine. At dawn there's no wind so we're all hoping...we go to stations and wait...but then when the wind comes up, why, it's always a-blowing from the west agin' us. So, we're stuck on that damn island."

"Where is your captain's destination?"

Burris looked surprised. "How am I supposed to know? Something about sounding the channel west of us upriver...they call it the 'Traverse' or something like that. Supposedly it's treacherous but our captain thinks that talk is all bilge water. He's dying to show we can make it through all right. Should be easy as cake, says he."

Hearing Crèvecoeur's translation, Vaudreuil snorted in derision.

"Easy as cake! Well, my children, what say we about that? Easy as cake! The Traverse! We know what our own pilots would say about that! Rocks and shoals and rapid currents with the spring winds in their faces and no room to manoeuver big square-rigged ships! Without perfect winds and the buoys we took away they will never make it. Easy as cake, indeed," the governor sniffed. "Well, we'll make them eat crow."

Before having the last sailor, Fitch, brought up the governor conferred with his officers. "I have a plan," he announced. He brought a forefinger to his generous nose then tapped his temple, smiling broadly. "If this fellow Fitch is as taciturn as I am led to believe, and if he knows as little as his fellow sailors, why then we will do most of the talking. Then," the governor gave a wink and a nod, "we will allow them to return to their ship, as though so much small fry being tossed back into the river."

A defiant Fitch was brought into the room and placed on the camp-stool, Crèvecoeur again translating for the governor. "Mr. Fitch. We have intercepted correspondence from your commanding officers that they intend to take the town of Québec from the east, from the coast of Beauport. Is that still the plan?"

Fitch stared at the lieutenant; then looked away, feigning indifference.

"They must know through your spies that we have over twenty thousands of trained troops from all over New-France and the Louisiana territory plus even more militia and Indian allies waiting for you behind impenetrable lines defended by hundreds of guns and mortars. Therefore, Mr. Fitch, we believe the letters we have intercepted are decoys, mere tricks to try to deceive us into thinking the English attack will be at Beauport. So tell us, Mr. Fitch, where is the real attack to take place? Québec itself? That would be foolish, indeed. The cliffs of Cape Diamond cannot be scaled and the town is surrounded by fortified walls impervious against any assault from the west.

"The only thing your officers will accomplish is the useless waste of thousands of your troops' lives. Is that what they want? Is that what you want? To lose an arm or a leg or your head or drown in the river only to have what's left of your fleet go back to Halifax or New-York come October?"

Fitch stared at his captors defiantly and said nothing.

"Very well, Mr. Fitch. But Québec cannot be taken."

Fitch gone, Vaudreuil rubbed his hands. "If, by luck and the Blessed Virgin, that young man's superior officers should hear of what we have this day said; and if what we have said should not dissuade them from attack; why, then, may they think that we are attempting to deceive them into believing that Beauport is our strongest point! Thus deceived, may they conclude that Beauport is our weakest, and attack there!

"But, of course, an English attack against the coast of Beauport presumes that their warships will find their way safely through the Traverse. And that, gentlemen, we know will not happen." The governor sat down with a contented sigh in Le Mercier's chair, oblivious to the frown of the captain of artillery.

"Truth is, the English fleet, General Wolfe's Grand Armada, will never succeed in navigating that channel."

Chapter Eight: *Beware of False Prophets*

A large crowd was gathering along the waterfront in the Lower Town under the warm sun of late June. "Look!" exclaimed a young lad, clad in the leather apron and leggings of a blacksmith's apprentice. He was pointing excitedly to a spot downriver, to the east. "There's another one. And another!"

A collective groan rose up from the civilians on the quay who then succumbed to a somber silence as the white billowing sails of three English warships emerged into view two miles away, pushed westward by a favourable wind. Their fellow citizens and militia on the Saint-Charles could see from their more northerly vantage point what the townsfolk at Place Royale could not: not just three but one dozen, two dozen, three dozen vessels and still they kept on coming, slowly, relentlessly, out of the Traverse and into the broad expanse of the river basin separating Orléans Island from the cliffs of Pointe-Lévy.

The cordwainers and chandlers, weavers, coopers, bakers and tavern-keepers, and even the brothel owners, all closed up shop as though for some morbid holiday. All along the waterfront, from the Lower Town to Beauport, and on the heights of the Upper Town, people quietly stood, looking with dread and awe across the Saint-Lawrence. By the end of the afternoon English warships, frigates, sloops, transports and tenders lined the opposite shore of the bay, rocking peacefully at anchor, molested by neither wind nor current nor cannon fire from the unfortified heights of Pointe-Lévy. It was a vision rendered even more terrifying by its cold, silent majesty.

Most of the lower townspeople, spirits subdued, filed sooner or later through the open doors of the church in the centre of the Place Royale, taking the place of others who were leaving, resembling a progression of pilgrims. Despite the twilight the interior of Notre-Dame-des-Victoires was unlit by any candles, there being none to spare, and the people prayed in the dark, among the crowded pews, the narrow aisles, around the altar. Twice before God had answered the Town's prayers and turned away the English ships. Would that He intervene again, they prayed.

After leaving the church merchants and gentry gathered at the Lamoureux warehouse a scant fifty yards away, where an impromptu meeting was taking place. From that vantage point it was impossible to forget the peril they were facing. Although they could not see all the enemy vessels, they could discern enough to imagine the immense forest of masts and spars rising up from the darkening line of the river formed up like the crescent blade of a scimitar lying on its side. The silhouette of Pointe-Lévy on the opposite shore loomed harmlessly above the vessels, like an impotent giant. It was a sight as maddening as it was sickening to the townsfolk.

"It does us as much good as Sampson without hair." Jacques Lamoureux was bitter. "Why do we have no guns up there?" he asked for the hundredth time, gesturing with his one good arm. He and his family had as much to lose as anyone. Their depot, their merchandize, and their fine stone house all stood exposed. The batteries lined up on the quays to their immediate right and left only made matters worse. They were living next to one of the enemy's primary targets.

Lamoureux' daughter Angélique tried to console him. "Our men are brave. God knows we are in the right. He'll protect us from this evil, papà."

Lamoureux brushed his daughter's light brown hair and forced a smile. "God helps those who help themselves."

The men at Lamoureux' warehouse agreed to petition the governor to send militia across the river in the hopes of securing Pointe-Lévy. Crèvecoeur and Jean-Luc listened in silence, then ambled away in the direction of the Royal Battery, crew watching anxiously at their posts.

Jean-Luc spoke up first. "You know, a few days ago after we learned Wolfe and his fleet had reached Île aux Coudres the general and the governor had another row. I thought the Château was going to explode."

Crèvecoeur recalled General Montcalm's bitter sarcasm while looking out the mullioned windows of Château Saint-Louis on that fine May day. "Don't tell me. Let me guess. The general wanted to put artillery at Pointe-Lévy and the governor didn't."

"Your guess is correct. The governor did not accept that English boats could ever anchor in the bay, and he didn't want to take away any armament from Beauport, or the Town, or Montréal."

"Well, perhaps Lamoureux' petition will change his mind."

"We'll see. The governor can be awfully stubborn. But, he loves his people. If it comes from the townsfolk, well, maybe then he'll listen."

Night had fallen and the dark of the celestial dome glittered with the sparkle of stars too many to count. The waxing moon hung low and its reflected light was further reflected by the stones of the houses huddled at the foot of the cliffs. Crèvecoeur could only imagine the terror of the people behind the stone walls. He gazed over the river at the ships. The same false light bathing the town was illuminating the enemy's vessels. Anxiety was lurking there, too, behind the wooden gunwales, but it was the tension of the hunter rather than the terror of the hunted; and these hunters did not have the added fear for wives and children.

Despite the gloom and thanks to the moon Lespérance espied a becloaked and hooded figure hurrying along the street from the Lamoureux warehouse. "'Til later," he threw over his shoulder as he started after the figure disappearing in the dark. Crèvecoeur watched his new friend join up with his beloved and felt a pang as he saw them, together now, halt in their steps by an unspoken accord, as if by suspending their movement they could also stop time.

Deep in thought, the lieutenant almost bumped into a shadowy figure emerging from an alleyway. The spectre held up a tallow lantern in front of him, sputtering and smoking. He was dressed in rags and his hair, unkempt and wild, hung down, framing his gaunt face. In the flickering light Crèvecoeur could discern the man's eyes searching his own, as though seeking something important. Their eyes locked a moment, then the apparition slipped past, muttering below his breath. The figure made his eccentric way up the unpaved street, pausing at each group of amused soldiers he encountered, holding up his lantern, searching, only to resume his path before vanishing around a corner into Saint-Pierre Street.

Crèvecoeur moodily climbed the switchback path to the Upper Town. His captain had granted him twenty-four hours' leave, his first break in two weeks, but the lieutenant had nothing to celebrate, no family to see; and so he had passed his time wandering around the Lower Town, brooding, lost in thought.

With the coming of the English ships that afternoon his reflections had deepened. The same sun shining on the cross atop Notre-Dame-des-Victoires, rising above the people of the Lower Town, shone also on the cross of the masts of the English ships rising above the men and boys on deck below; and the wind and the rain assailing them every third day swept down on the land-locked defenders as well.

Without realizing it the lieutenant had escaped the afternoon heat by slipping into the shade of the church and, still deep in his thoughts, had mechanically walked in the footsteps of those in front of him, up worn stone steps and through a rounded portal into the cool of the sanctuary. He found himself on his knees on the cold stone floor. He bowed his head, for the first time since he could remember.

He did not know what to pray or what to pray for. And so he finally asked simply to be given the wisdom to let the prayer come of its own accord. He thought of the English sailors and soldiers, perhaps praying as well at that same moment, in the immemorial custom of all warriors since the dawn of time about to come face to face with the truth. Lost is the luxury of postponement, the fiction of another day, for that other day has arrived.

Rising from the floor he did not know if he discerned any difference, or felt any different. They cannot both be right, he found himself thinking, but they can both be wrong….The face of DeChêne flashed into his mind, and he saw again Father René, scarred hands polishing his musket, blue eyes glowing in utter serenity. "Who is *your* master?" DuChêne smiled.

Now, climbing up the switch-path in the cool night air, he saw that the moon had ascended higher overhead leading a multitude of stars too numerous to count. At least, he thought, for the few hours of the night, it will be Malsumis' turn. But Glascoop will return triumphant.

At the top of the road, silhouetted against the starry sky, crowds of civilians and soldiers had gathered, pointing to a spot to the east behind Crèvecoeur. He turned around and looked.

In the distance downriver bright flares of orange and red were blazing on the water. A cheer rose up from the crowd. The fireboats….The flaming objects drifted lazily towards the shadowy, irregular chain of English ships curved like a scythe in the distance. Now several of the dark shapes swung around as though trying to fix a broadside against the approaching fireboats. But rather than firing they retreated away from the flaming craft, shifting themselves northeastward. Only after maneuvering themselves away from the floating danger did they fire several cannon, not at the fireboats, for that would be pointless, but instead as a warning signal to their companion ships farther away downriver.

For several anxious moments Crèvecoeur and the hushed crowds on the ridges of the Upper Town watched the luminous, ponderous dance of the fireboats and the shadowy forest of masts and hulls, until a sudden thundering reverberated from across the water as the fireboats exploded. Some of the civilians cheered, but quickly fell silent as they all realised the boats had exploded too soon, too far away from any of the English ships to do them any harm.

"One hundred thousand pounds," a man muttered near Crèvecoeur. His voice sounded hoarse, choked. "One hundred thousand pounds from the royal treasury, up in smoke, just like that."

The voice belonged to a portly gentleman in an elegant suit. He took a pinch of snuff, sneezed, and thus expelling his disgust at the waste of good silver as he cleared his nose of phlegm, Commissary Bigot, the chief financial officer of New-France, turned his ample rump to the sorry sight and grimly waddled his way back to his waiting coach on the street above. With a crack of a whip over the heads of the horses a liveried coachman drove his master away, far away from the people of the town and the sight of the smoldering ruins.

Chapter Nine: *The Battle of the Acorns*

There was a muffled thudding sound followed immediately by soft cursing.

"Quiet!" Captain Dumas hissed. "Lieutenant!"

Crèvecoeur went over to the figures huddling in the dark. He whispered to them crossly and then stood by as other dark shapes descended the slope, slipping and stumbling on the rocky trail leading down to the beach from the road above. He did his best to organize the clumsy shopkeepers and schoolboys who made up most of the impromptu raiding party, lining them up on the beach. Dumas' handful of Regulars and town militiamen were already boarding the small vessels of all shapes and sizes manned by royal mariners charged with ferrying the assault force across the river. At a whispered signal, one by one the civilians took to the boats. A large party of Abenaki followed in their long war canoes and swiftly overtook the Europeans in their awkward craft.

After an arduous climb they reached the top of the ridge just as dawn broke. The Abenaki, familiar with the deer-trails, took the lead, the civilians lagging far behind. By mid-morning they were directly opposite the Plains of Abraham on the north side of the river, unfurling like an undulating flag held horizontally to the sky, lapping at the walls of the Upper Town and the redoubt on the cliffs of Cape Diamond. Inside the walls, the huge convent complex of Sainte-Urséline, the imposing cathedral, and the grand Château Saint-Louis dominated the houses. To Dumas's dismay clusters of townspeople crowded the cliff-tops of Cape Diamond, scanning with excitement the ridges on the opposite shore where they guessed their heroes to be readying their valiant attack on the enemy's guns.

Crèvecoeur trotted with Megeso and the Abenaki war-party, scouting far ahead of their companions held back by the stumbling townsfolk unaccustomed to carrying heavy muskets and canteens up steep slopes, or enduring the merciless black flies swarming around kerchief'd heads and necks seeking out the least patch of exposed flesh sticky with sweat. The Abenaki warriors, skin glistening with bear fat to thwart the biting pests, threaded their stealthy way to a granite outcropping screened by hemlock. Megeso tugged softly at Crèvecoeur's arm. Below was a rolling meadow ending in a flat shelf of rock overlooking the river, directly opposite the town on the far shore, perfect terrain for the batteries the English artillerymen had just erected. A fresh-cut road descended to a clearing away in the distance where red-coated troops stood in drill formation awaiting the next command.

They backtracked along the deer-path. Crèvecoeur was annoyed to find the main corps of militia and civilian warriors so far behind. He was impatient to report to his captain and launch the attack before the English realised their oversight and supplemented their forces around the new batteries; and before his own fears got the better of him.

They heard a sudden firing of muskets. They broke into a run, dropping to a cautious pace as they approached the point where the gunfire had flared. The Abenaki fanned out far to the left and to the right of the deer-path, to outflank any hostile force but also to protect themselves from any mistake by their own allies. Crèvecoeur stuck close to Megeso, following his friend's lead in deference to his greater skill in forest fighting.

After several minutes they heard muffled shouting from close by. They were all speaking in French. The lieutenant yelled out his identity. He continued to cry out his name as he and Megeso advanced carefully through the underbrush, crouching low to the ground, pausing to listen. Finally they heard a reply, from Captain Dumas signaling them to approach. They emerged into a clearing at the same time as their native companions from all the points of the compass.

In the middle of the meadow were standing Captain Dumas and his aides. Near the captain militiamen were milling around, hovering over a trio of figures on the ground, obscured by the grass. One of the figures, a youth, was sitting with head down, sobbing, a length of bloody linen around his right arm. Nearby lay an older man on his back, face to the sky, as though sleeping peacefully in the grass. Next to him was another prone figure, equally immobile. None of the other civilians were to be seen.

With tremendous effort Captain Dumas kept his voice level, almost nonchalant, although he could not suppress the Gascon flame in his eyes.

"Well, lieutenant, it would seem our citizen brigade has difficulty distinguishing friend from foe." He glanced sideways at the Abenaki. They were looking at the scene with an undisguised look of contempt and disgust. Dumas dropped the pretense of calm and swore out loud, albeit under his breath.

"Damn them all. Not only do they shoot at their own kin, they bolt like scared rabbits at the sound of their own musket fire." He spat on the ground.

"The English have set up their batteries but they've taken hardly any precautions to guard them," Crèvecoeur submitted hurriedly. "We saw a battalion but they're camped far away. The guns are vulnerable. At least we can take out the guards and spike the guns with one bold attack -"

With another curse and abrupt gesture his captain cut him off. "We've already lost our native brethren. Look at them. No self-respecting brave will have anything more to do with this mission. They believe it is doomed now. The spirits have cursed it."

Dumas bent down and picked up a Brown Bess an unknown school-boy had flung to the ground in fleeing. Dozens of its companions along with an assortment of canteens, belts, cartridges and even shoes lay scattered in a long, wide swath tracing the flight of their owners back to the river. "We don't have a strong enough force left. There is nothing we can do but turn back."

It was almost twilight by the time the remnants of the raiding party carrying the dead, the wounded, and the discarded made it back to the boats. Their native allies had long since departed. The civilians huddled miserably near the boats, too ashamed so much as to even glance at their companions in arms. Dumas said not a word to them. In near silence they embarked and began the gloomy crossing of the river, now in darkness.

Just as they reached the opposite shore they heard the crash of thunder. Looking up at the sky, they saw nothing but glittering stars and a few wispy clouds. Again, the boom of thunder, from back across the river, followed by a crashing sound. Again and again they heard the thunder and crash, thunder and crash, but now they all knew what it was. The bombardment of the town had begun.

After an hour of forced marching in the dark they crested a hill and saw before them flames flickering towards the sky within the stone walls of the Upper Town. They encountered groups of townsfolk on foot, many with carts pulled by hand or donkey or horse. Whatever their direction or destination they all held in their ears the relentless roaring of the enemy's thundering guns and the less frequent retort from their own cannon.

Dumas ordered Crèvecoeur to lead the militiamen and civilians back into town, and gather whatever information he could before reporting back to camp. The lieutenant and his party pushed their way through the Saint-Jean Gates and the mass of panicked citizens clogging the narrow streets until they finally regained the Dauphine Redoubt. Just as they arrived within the walls of the fort a tremendous explosion went off behind them, barely five hundred feet away. Crèvecoeur took a deep breath as he recalled the engineer Pontleroy's estimate of the range of the English guns.

Confusion reigned inside the barracks. Hands were busy not with muskets but with buckets. Every portable container from piggins to hogsheads was pressed into service by men scurrying into the streets to the fire brigades forming up around the town wells in a desperate attempt to quash the flames licking at the roofs of houses.

Colonel Bazin, in command of the militia, was not at the redoubt. "Try down below, in the Lower Town."

The lieutenant and Megeso felt a relief of sorts as they made their way along the steep road carved into the north side of the butte, the Côte du Palais, winding down into the village below. Here the eerie whistling and crashing of cannonfire were muffled by the rocky walls of the cliffs rising above them as they descended.

They found the Lower Town in turmoil. Militia had encamped in every possible field and opening between the houses and depots to the west and north, towards the Saint-Charles, as far away as possible from the reach of the enemy guns. On the waterfront, looking towards Orléans and Pointe-Lévy, sailors manned the town's batteries along the ramparts, but their guns remained silent. For the moment, at least, the enemy cannon were trained only on the Upper Town. The few civilians remaining below the Cape could be seen milling around Notre-Dame-des-Victoires where, inside the darkness of the church, a constant prayer vigil was taking place. The rest of the townsfolk had placed their faith in their feet.

Colonel Bazin already knew about the débâcle at Pointe-Lévy. The colonel, eyes bleary from lack of sleep, fearful of an English raid against the waterfront, had no time to waste on the junior officer and dismissed him with a wave of the hand.

Crèvecoeur suddenly felt his own weariness overtake him like a tidal wave. He had gone two days without sleep. His legs ached, his feet were blistering from the army's regulation shoes which never seemed to fit right. An overwhelming numbness took hold of his senses.

"I don't think I can make it back to camp," he mumbled to Megeso, barely looking at his friend.

The Abenaki brave, impassive as always, nodded. "Sleep, then."

He said it simply, hiding his disdain at the Europeans' compulsive need to be always doing something and to dominate everything they did. They were like acorns believing they created the forest which gave birth to them and which they no longer needed. It was that restless drive that had brought the first French here; it was what now compelled the English to come and take away what the French had. It was what had driven the Englishmen from Massachusetts to plunge further and further into the Abenaki domain. This incessant urge to take. To subdue. To possess, consume, and take again; and never feel satisfied.

The young officer had stumbled his way over to a low crate sitting on the quay and plopped down on it. Megeso joined him. If he was tired it didn't show.

The enemy guns abruptly fell silent. The eerie calmness settling over the river was as unsettling as the cannon fire itself. The pre-dawn glowed in the sky to the east and across the river on Orléans emerged the blurry white of thousands of tents and smoke from enemy camp-fires, rekindled anew for another day of siege. Moored in the sound were warships, frigates, transports and, on one of the vessels, General Wolfe. What was he planning, Crèvecoeur wondered drowsily. Where was he going to attack? Here at the Lower Town? The beaches of Beauport?

Behind him, visible through an alleyway, were the Place Royale and the front façade of the church Notre-Dame-des-Victoires. The portals were open, as though beckoning. Sleepily, the young man thought of the cool, dark interior, recalled the penitents kneeling on the stone floor, the smooth cherry pews, the crucifix above the altar.

Crèvecoeur was too exhausted to move, too drained to be afraid, too tired to care whether he lived or died. He slumped into a deep sleep.

Chapter Ten: *Chasing After the Wind*

The booming of cannon roused him. He tried to open his eyes, felt a surge of panic as it seemed his lids were cemented shut. He felt a tight grip on his heart and his lungs were squeezed as though in a vise. He fought to breathe. It was dreadfully cold. He was lost in a dark world that made no sense and where he was a total stranger. He felt imprisoned by a certainty of utter, complete horror.

He tried to move his legs, his arms but could not. They refused to obey as if no longer a part of him. And yet he was conscious of moving, of being pulled downwards by a tremendous weight, then catapulted at great speed through total darkness.

Gradually, almost imperceptibly, a floating sensation overcame him. He felt bathed in a soft light which he could perceive if not see. His breath came easily now, effortlessly, peacefully.

He opened his eyes. The crucified figure of Jesus was before him. Looking down on him from the niche above the altar, upon all the people gathered among the pews, on the steps of the church outside, spilling out into the Place Royale into the morning sun.

Crèvecoeur started with a jerk. He moved to get up but felt a restraining hand on his arm. It was the elderly Lamoureux.

"Easy there, young man," he said, looking intently into Crèvecoeur's face. "I want to make sure you are all right."

"I'm sure...I mean...how did I get here?"

"Deacon Thomas and I saw you slumped on the quay. We were afraid you had hit your head. So we carried you into the church."

"Thank you," Crèvecoeur mumbled, mouth dry as cotton. "I suppose I was very tired." He looked at the older man, who returned the gaze with a sorrowful look.

"It is I who thank you, for having tried to answer our petition. My daughter Angélique has told us all about it." Lamoureux managed a smile. His hair and neatly trimmed beard had turned even whiter over the past few days. "Even in the midst of death and destruction life goes on. I have given my consent to your friend Jean-Luc's own petition."

He glanced up at the figure of Jesus on the cross; then returned his eyes to the young man next to him. "Yes, I verily believe that love conquers all, even if we blind ourselves to it. How can I stand in the way of my beloved daughter and her own happiness? I am an old man and I don't have much time left in this vale of tears. Thank God for that! But she, her...fiancé, and you, you have your whole lives ahead of you, God willing. Wasn't it King Solomon who said, 'Be happy, young man, while you are young, and let your heart give you joy in your youth'?"

Both men jumped to their feet as an enormous explosion went off nearby. It seemed to shake even the stone walls of the church. Crèvecoeur pushed his way through the crowd and ran down to the waterfront.

To his right was the *batterie de la Reine*, the Queen's Battery. It was a scene of utter devastation. The remains of a caisson lay on its back, broken wheels turning languidly in the air, cannon pieces and body parts strewn on the ground in a bloody heap, sailors writhing in pain, others tearing off linen shirts to make bandages and others bringing buckets of water. One of their own cannon had exploded.

The site sickened Crèvecoeur. He turned away, forcing himself not to retch. He tried to summon up within himself the furies of anger, to chase away the sirens of fear. This time there was no answer to his summons. He was perplexed to discover that the gods of wrath chose to remain silent. And yet neither did he feel fear. The knot in his stomach and the pounding in his head he had come to expect when confronted with violence were absent. He was aware only of a strange sensation of detachment, as though he were merely floating among spectators viewing a theatre-piece.

Before him stood the king arrayed in armour, the Lancastrian coat of arms emblazoned on his royal banner, Henry V and his knights before the walls of Harfleur, the French seaport town, challenging the besieged governor and his terrified citizens to surrender or suffer the terrible consequences. Crèvecoeur closed his eyes, saw Amelia's mother in front of her classroom, portfolio opened on the lectern before her, heard her declaim as her students read with her –

> "...if not, why in a moment look to see,
> The blind and bloody soldier with foul hand,
> Defile the locks of your shrill-shrieking daughters;
> Your fathers taken by their silver beards,
> And their most reverend heads dashed to the walls;
> Your naked infants spitted upon pikes,
> Whiles the mad mothers with their howls confused
> Do break the clouds as the wives of Jewry at Herod's
> bloody-hunting slaughter-men
> What say you? Will you yield, and this avoid?
> Or guilty in defence, be thus destroyed?"

Brooding, lost in thought, the lieutenant found himself crossing over the Saint-Charles onto the road to Beauport. Behind him the enemy guns on Pointe-Lévy awakened. With a pang Crèvecoeur thought of Lamoureux, his family, the terror of the townsfolk, or at least, the stubborn or fatalistic few who remained.

All day and all night the bombardment thundered on, then the next day, and the next until it seemed as though the entire month of July 1759 had dissolved into one never-ending day of incessant pounding. Tension, terror, monotony: the defenders in the trenches and in the camps to the man wished now for the enemy to attack, to put an end to the interminable torment of waiting.

"28 July, 1759," Crèvecoeur wrote in his diary. "Father: I do not know if I shall survive this ordeal nor if I shall ever behold you again. But should I be required to die here, may it be said that I died honourably, doing my duty, however that duty may be defined or to whom it may be owed. I confess that the certainty of the nature of that duty is no longer clear; even as I affirm the existence of the duty itself.

"General Montcalm and Governor Vaudreuil, I fear, will never see eye to eye about anything, to our great disconsolation. If ever there were a need for unity in thinking and spirit, now is the time.

"A fortnight ago, even while Gen. Wolfe was putting in batteries on Montmorency and massing his elite grenadiers on the island across from us as though preparing to attack Beauport, English warships slipped by Cape Diamond under cover of the bombardment and Wolfe himself was seen scouting out the terrain as though planning an attack on Québec from the west, notwithstanding all his preparations here downriver to the east. What Wolfe's plans are no one can figure out. Capt. Dumas swears that either the English general is a master tactician and the slyest fox in the world, or is hopelessly befuddled and indecisive.

"The entire Upper Town is aflame. The cathedral has suffered greatly. It is as if the enemy were attempting to destroy not only the body of our people, but our souls as well.

"Two days ago we were cheered by a bit of good news. Capt. Saulnier's Acadians and Abenaki ambushed a company of grenadiers fording the Montmorency above the falls. We drove the enemy away with heavy losses. The Governor was positively beaming. He rode around our encampments, himself announcing the good tidings to encourage us.

"But, I fear, the enemy's incessant back-and-forth and our dwindling rations are a daily reminder of the desperate situation we are in. Saulnier's skirmish was like a handful of wood chips tossed upon the fire which flare up for an instant but which are quickly consumed.

"Our soldiers complain openly about their reduced portions. No more beef, no more wine; but native tobacco aplenty. 'Tis a poor substitute for the nourishment we need. Worse, the local folk no longer accept *la monnaie de carte* in payment for food, as if they had any food to spare themselves. ' *C'est faux comme les diamants du Canada'* they've taken to saying. They don't want false money; our soldiers don't want false food. We all yearn for that which is true but don't know where to find it.

"We have learned the enemy raided the village at Pointe-aux-Trembles and captured a dozen of the Colony's most beautiful belles. The English also found flopping in the net several of the

Upper Town's leading gentlemen engaged in a secret mission of their own, it seems. This is not the time to be caught with one's *culottes* down. Let us pray that the breeches of our soldiers are firmly fastened when the attack comes.

"Last week the Governor ordered our militiamen to stop shooting the native doves gracing our skies. I don't think he is so much concerned with the doves as he is with the waste of ammunition. Needless to say, the effect of the prohibition has been to encourage even more restless souls to take up the sport.

"Yesterday the Governor refused to pardon two soldiers and a sailor caught stealing wine from a doctor's house in the Upper Town. They were hung at sunset and their bodies are still dangling from the scaffold. I doubt this will have any effect on the thievery which seems rampant.

"Now that this horrible month of July is almost over I must still do battle with myself. Would that the enemy attack! Cannon fire, musket balls, bayonets, all that I would prefer to the affliction of waiting. It becomes harder to endure with each passing day. I find myself praying that Wolfe attack us, now, and put an end to the torture of uncertainty."

Crèvecoeur cleaned his quill and put away his ink. He stepped outside his tent. Instantly he regretted it, as swarms of mosquitos attacked.

The early evening air was heavy and humid. The defenders were somber. Even the militiamen camped over yonder were quiet, fiddles silent. No one was shooting at doves in the air. Everyone was waiting. Yet no one quite knew what they were waiting for, which only served to deepen the pervading sense of dread.

Across the Beauport Road Crèvecoeur saw Jean-Luc emerge from the rambling house serving as Governor Vaudreuil's field quarters. Crèvecoeur hailed him. They wandered over to a clump of birches overlooking the trenches and the river beyond, swatting mosquitos as they strolled. The enemy's camp-fires on the island were small specks of red in the gloaming.

"Wolfe dispatched a letter to Montcalm and the Governor. Wolfe demanded our surrender. I've never seen the old man's face get so red. He sputtered, 'it's as if a servant came to the lord of the manor to demand the keys to the Château.' I need not say that the old man refused to yield."

Jean-Luc's own face darkened. "Wolfe also demanded an end to all sniper attacks by civilians hiding in ambush downriver. Threatened to burn every house and barn on both sides of the Saint-Lawrence unless the attacks stop. Said he cannot guarantee the safety of any civilian they encounter."

Crèvecoeur felt the familiar flush of anger welling up from within.

"Damn their arrogance. How does he expect simple folk to react when their land is invaded? Their way of life threatened, their language, their beliefs? Does he think the Canadians are ignorant of the fate of the Acadians? Look what the English governors did to them. You know," he continued, anger flowing into disgust, "it's all vanity. Nothing but vanity. Ordinary folk are just pawns to them."

"Well," Jean-Luc rejoined, eyes flashing, "let the English see how pawns can fight!"

He laughed in spite of himself. "The governor wrote back he would rather die than be guilty of dishonouring his people. He had Bigot surrender three good bottles of fine Bordeaux to send to Wolfe. You should have seen Bigot's face."

"What's Montcalm's plan?"

"Well, as always, of course, he and the governor don't see the world through the same glass. The old man wants to attack. The general doesn't. He thinks that's exactly what Wolfe wants us to do."

"And so we wait."

"And so we wait," Jean-Luc echoed.

The next day, Sunday, opened with a barrage of rain and hail, a hard, pelting punishment even for men used to the violence of nature. But then, in an instant, the squall passed and a breeze from the north kicked up, bringing a refreshing respite from the oppressive heat of the previous day. Even the cannon seemed to observe a respectful silence. Birds could be heard twittering in the meadows and in the surrounding forests, joyous praise to the giver of life to those who would hear it.

The church bell in the village of Beauport sounded in the clear air, a defiant call to the faithful and faithless alike. It was echoed by the peeling of the bells reflected over the water from the Lower Town. The governor had ordered the silencing of all church bells by day but by common accord the edict was ignored.

By and by the parish priest came by. If the troops in the trenches and encampments could not come to mass, then mass would come to them. He walked, barefoot and bare-headed, among the anxious, tired, somber soldiers of the Royal Army, stopping every now and then to pray and hear confession. By late afternoon he had made it as far as Dumas' Colonial Regulars in the camp awaiting their watch in the trenches.

"Remember what the Lord commanded Moses to tell the Israelites when He promised them deliverance from the chains of Pharaoh:

> *'I am the Lord, and I will bring you out from under the yoke of the Egyptians. I will free you from being slaves to them, and I will redeem you with an outstretched arm and with mighty acts of judgement. I will take you as my own people, and I will be your God....'*

Crèvecoeur was not among the penitent saints, forming a long quiet queue to await their turn at absolution. He turned his back to the impromptu confessional and wandered over to the militia camps. He found DuChêne seated on a log sharing a pipe with Father René.

The priest saw the young officer's surprise. "I couldn't sit still on such a beautiful Sabbath day."

"But how did you get past Wolfe and his camp on Montmorency?"

Father René winked. "You're safe if you follow the right path. Smoke?" He extended his scarred arm towards Crèvecoeur, pipe bowl cradled lovingly in the palm of his hand.

"No, thanks anyway."

"That was a powerful good sermon you missed," DeChêne remarked to Crèvecoeur between puffs. He turned his head towards the priest. "Powerful good. Isaiah, did you say it was? I liked the part about the music. Say it again."

Father René obliged. " 'And you will sing as on the night you celebrate a holy festival; your hearts will rejoice as when people go up with flutes to the mountain of the Lord, to the Rock of Israel...the voice of the Lord will shatter Assyria; with his scepter he will strike them down. Every stroke the Lord lays on them with his punishing rod will be to the music of tambourines and harps....'"

"You see," DuChêne filled his young friend in, "Father René's idea is that, since music is divinely inspired, those who make music are pleasing to God. But, I ask, are those who make music badly pleasing to God? I hope so, for then He must be mighty happy with me."

A few tents away someone began strumming a guitar. Soon another joined in, then a fiddle, tentative at first before taking the plunge and launching full force into a jig and reel. Voices chimed in, louder and louder accompanied by the banging of clubs and the clanging of pots. As if swept by a tidal wave the whole Canadian encampment joined in the *tintamarre* with every conceivable device with which to make, or approximate, musical sounds.

DuChêne jumped to his feet, bellowing at the top of his lungs. The militia on duty in the trenches below let loose a wild cheer, then joined in. Their colonel strode around the camp like a captain on his ship, grinning widely, arms waving encouragement to his comrades.

"Play on, fiddles! Sing out, my boys! We'll show them what Canadians are made of."

The rough-hewn symphony of six thousand men thundered in the evening air, rolling over the neighbouring French troops watching their backwoods cousins with open mouths, roiling across the waters to the English soldiers and sailors before echoing into eternity.

"Well," Father René mused, "it may not be flutes, tambourines and harps, but nothing is more divine than music from the heart."

From across the channel the enemy camp-fires winked.

* * * * *

It was at the crack of dawn that the enemy's own concert of cannon-fire began, seemingly from all around the entrenched defenders, from the channel in front of them, from the east off the heights of Montmorency, from the English frigate *Centurion* which had slipped during the night into a position just to the east of the trench-works half a league away from the beaches. The tide was out and the dragons' teeth of jagged rocks jutted from the miles of mud flats. The defenders' drums tattoo'd the general alarm and call to arms as all troops rushed to the bluffs to reinforce their comrades in the trenches.

From his position on the bluffs at the midpoint of the defensive line, Crèvecoeur watched and waited near Dumas and his other aides. The enemy ships' cannon were too far away to reach the entrenched defenders, although dozens of missiles fell around and about the redoubts on the beaches in front of them. The trenches with their solitary redoubt away to the east were taking a pounding from Wolfe's guns on the Montmorency heights. The defenders' guns fired back, but to what effect, Crèvecoeur could not know.

The morning air was hot and heavy despite a dank breeze from the west. The leaden sun beat down on the defenders waiting, waiting, forever waiting in the trenches. The tension was becoming as unbearable as the sun.

Across the channel the defenders could see thousands of red-coated grenadiers standing stock still in formation on the shore of the island opposite, before marching onto scores of flat-bottomed barges, slender glittering bayonets pointing upwards to the heavens like the cynical spires of some perverse church. Hours went by as the troops embarked in the distance, while from the enemy's anchorage across the river at Pointe-Lévy ships could be seen under sail, taking advantage of the favourable wind from the west, the harbinger of another July storm a-brewing.

The ships, a couple of frigates and dozens of smaller transports, groped their way across the channel towards the defenders, bearing towards a point to the west of the beaches, while from the island in front of the defenders barges full of scarlet soldiers rowed their ponderous, clumsy way directly towards the centre of the shore where the two redoubts, defenders and guns at the ready, were waiting.

A rider galloped in with a message to Dumas, in charge of the defenders' centre.

"Wolfe's troops forded the base of the falls at Montmorency. They're attacking the redoubt and Colonel Lévis' flank."

"Grenadiers?"

"Some. Also regular infantry. The advance is led by Highlanders. Looks like General Townshend is in charge."

"Lévis is holding out?"

"We've lost a lot of men. But so has the enemy. They seem to have given up any assault on our defenses. The colonel says he's confident he can hold his position. But he thinks the enemy intends on bypassing him altogether to join up with the others about to attack you. "

Dumas thanked the messenger and dismissed him. The man galloped off full speed to notify the governor encamped on the western end of the trenches. Dumas turned to Crèvecoeur.

"I want you to pass the word to General Montcalm -"

But at that moment the general himself accompanied by his staff, banners flying in the breeze, came charging up. They dismounted. The captain quickly filled in his commander.

"So Wolfe has finally played his hand. He has deployed Townshend and Murray to our left and General Monckton to our right; but it seems his main thrust is to be right here, at our centre." Montcalm gave his officers a tired, tense smile. They looked at the barges bouncing towards the beaches, the defenders' cannon balls plopping in the water around them. A missile made a direct hit and the red-coated grenadiers in the unlucky craft were thrown into the murky water like toy soldiers swept from the play theatre by an upset child. Yet still they came on.

"This is madness," the general mused. "See how the tide is rising now. They waited too long. They will be up to their belts in water. And they have precious little artillery cover. What is Wolfe thinking?"

He turned to his aides. "Pass the word up and down the line: under no circumstances are we to advance to meet the enemy. Hold our ground. Let the enemy come to us. Hold our cannon fire as well until they regroup on the beach. We don't have ammunition to waste. Let every shot count."

The sun was now past its apogee. Thick, black storm clouds reared up like enormous demons from the southwest and overspread the sky, swallowing up the orb and throwing the earth into a grey half-light. The wind started whipping up. Slowly, ineluctably the floating crescent of reddish barges crawled closer to them, fighting currents and wind, while to the east the thumping of cannon continued.

In the trenches and redoubts the defenders readied their muskets as they saw the first wave of the attacking barges come to a lurching halt a hundred yards out in the surf, spilling out their contents of red-coats into the wash. One by one the landing craft jerked to a stop on the half-submerged shelf of mud and rock and their grenadiers jumped out clumsily, arms raised high above their heads holding their muskets over water reaching above their thighs. More than one slipped and plunged body and all into the water, ruining once and for all powder, musket, uniform and dignity, suddenly realizing he was nothing but a wet man.

Seen from the trenches it appeared as though hundreds of grotesque, giant lobsters had risen from the waters, steel antennae quivering in the air above their heads, lurching towards the strip of the shore. They might have looked silly if they were not so terrifying. These are not men, their intimidating uniforms proclaimed. They are machines, killing machines, indifferent to death and thus unstoppable and they are going to overwhelm you. And yet, Crèvecoeur saw, turning a human being into an unfeeling machine also made it easier, much easier, to wish to destroy him.

The lobster-backs slogged their way through the water, aiming at a point far to the left of the redoubts, until the first few wavy lines in the lead made it to firmer ground, trying to form up but in so doing creating a barrier to their comrades struggling ashore behind them who, exhausted, began spilling around the flanks of the first ashore like a stream encountering a tree falling suddenly in its midst. Behind them, gasping for breath, came officers, swords held high for attention, shouting out commands upon deaf ears.

Out of the chaos and confusion lines, somehow, began to form on the beach. Drummers beat out a rhythmic tattoo. The *Centurion* out in the channel to the west had crept closer to shore on the tide and redoubled its bombardment of the redoubts. The defenders now fired back at the English vessel so that a thick blanket of acrid smoke hung over the beach and bluffs above in the heavy, hot air of the late afternoon.

From the easternmost redoubt artillery was firing upon the grenadiers pinned on the beaches far to the left. Two field guns in the middle redoubt, muzzles pointing at the beach in front of them, opened up. The English troops in the centre squirmed under the fire, looking like one enormous, quivering jellyfish, expanding and contracting along the sides. Suddenly an otherworldly scream of rage emanated from the organism and it began to move with a jerk towards them. The jellyfish disintegrated into hundreds of individual grenadiers, yelling out in unison and launching themselves into a furious charge, breaking all ranks, while their frustrated officers, sabres waving helplessly in the air, tried to maintain a semblance of control; and failed.

The defenders in the redoubts panicked. They abandoned their cannon and mortars and scrambled back up the slopes to their entrenched comrades.

"Fire! Fire, now my boys! Fire!" The commands screamed out from all around in the trenches. Against the charging grenadiers fifty yards down the slope, a thousand muskets went off from the first row of defenders atop the bluffs along a thousand-yard line. As they fell back to reload the second line advanced, fired, fell back to be replaced by the third row, in a regular, mechanical rhythm devoid of thought. With each volley dozens of grenadiers fell to the rocky ground where the beach began its long upward slope to the bluffs above. Here the rocks gave way to grass, thick tufts of slippery green. The grenadiers soon discovered it was impossible to climb up the slope without using their hands, encumbered by their weapons.

They began to fall back, under a barrage of musket balls, flinging themselves down onto the ground behind anything they could improvise as a shield, rocks, driftwood, fallen comrades. Some dove into the redoubt freshly abandoned by the defenders from where they attempted to return fire back up the bluffs.

And then the clouds opened up. The earthly artillery was replaced by a celestial one. Cannon fire and musket shot were supplanted by lightning and thunder. A drenching downpour ensued. Defenders and attackers alike ceased firing, hunching over where they squatted, sat or lay, covering their muskets and powder horns as best they could with tunics, coats or shirts. The land fell silent while the heavens proclaimed their rage.

Crèvecoeur felt his heart still pounding. He peered through curtains of rain at the blurry scarlet figures below on the beach and about the redoubts. He sensed more than saw the grim determination on grimy exhausted faces, the whispered exchanges, the hands and fingers fumbling along the barrels of their muskets, groping the slippery shanks of the bayonets to confirm their readiness; and he imagined more than heard the muffled commands of their officers as the grenadiers hurriedly regrouped themselves into a semblance of order, bayonets once again pointing heavenward.

Crèvecoeur looked at the defenders huddled three and four deep in the trenches. Perhaps one in three had bayonets; virtually none of the militia had them and they comprised the majority of the troops. If the grenadiers breached the dirt walls, the defenders' muskets would be useless.

The rain slowed to a drizzle. But the grenadiers did not charge. One by one the defenders raised their heads and roved widening eyes over the tops of the trenches. They saw the attackers form up, not to attack, but to withdraw. Their drummers set the cadence as best they could, drum-tops soggy from the rain; and then fifers piped in with an audacious Scottish air. The grenadiers marched away, heads held high, away from the bluffs and back down to the water. Those that could walk, that is. As the invaders receded from the beach, like the tide they exposed behind them the bodies of hundreds of their comrades, some writhing and groaning, most not moving.

From the trenches came a loud thundering cheer; then another, and another, all up and down the lines along the Beauport bluffs. Behind Crèvecoeur, on a small knoll, sat Montcalm on his mount. The soldiers and militia in the trenches within eyesight of the general turned to him and cheered again.

Montcalm, whose worried look seemed etched into his face, permitted himself a smile and he doffed his hat, bowing to his men despite the light rain. Dumas and the other commanding officers in the vicinity congregated around the general along with his aides. Riders were dispatched out in all directions, meeting along the way messengers hurrying in.

"Lieutenant, I've sent Duplessis' company to secure the beach," Dumas said calmly, as though discussing plans for a parade drill. "Pick a burial detail for tomorrow morning. From the looks of things it will have to be a big detail. In the meantime go with the surgeon's corps down to the beach. Save whatever poor souls you can save. The parish priest will follow you, no doubt. Pull aside any English officers still alive fit enough to talk and we'll chat with them tomorrow."

Dumas' dark eyes focused on the scarlet backs of the proud grenadiers, once again waddling through the surf, waist deep, hoisting themselves up into the boats, exhausted arms failing them, falling back into the water, hoisting themselves up again.

" 'Vanity, vanity. All is vanity....Our purpose is to fear God, and die,' "he murmured.

He shook his head in pity.

"Poor bastards. Chasing after the wind."
He looked at his young lieutenant and smiled.
"Just like us."

Chapter Eleven: *The Governor, the General, and the Truth*

"Splendid, gentlemen, splendid!" Vaudreuil exclaimed. Casting aside protocol, he had not waited for the general and his entourage to enter the manse but instead had rushed out himself to greet them. Now, standing on the veranda, he watched impatiently as the officers dismounted, fidgeting uncomfortably in his battle-gear.

He was wearing his old-fashioned brass helmet which was too large for his head and a matching brass breastplate which was too tight for his torso, making it difficult for him to breathe. His excited state made the act of respiring only more labourious. His discomfort did not dissuade the governor from waving his elaborate sabre, dull and rusty which, like the armour, he had inherited from his father, the first governor of Canada.

Having dismounted and handed over their horses to the governor's grooms, Montcalm and his officers stepped up onto the porch. The general bowed, doffing his *tricorne,* as did the other officers.

"Yes, yes! Salutations to you, too. Salutations all around!" The governor's helmet and breastplate rendered any return bowing impractical if not impossible. "Pray follow me inside," he gestured, calling out to his servants to attend to his guests and serve them with the celebratory libations he had arranged in anticipation of this moment.

As the servants fussed over the officers, taking away their dripping cloaks and hats, the governor seemed to realise he was overdressed for the occasion. "Pray excuse me an instant," he muttered, exiting into the adjacent bedchamber with his valet, whence the sounds of grunting, groaning and panting emanated, intermingled with a few choice soft oaths. A final exhalation and exclamation of triumph and the governor reemerged, the Order of the Cross of Saint-Louis glittering over his heart, only slightly askew.

He beamed at the general, standing wearily across the salon; and, grasping a proffered goblet of amber inspiration, raised his hand high in the air, signaling a toast.

"On behalf of His Royal Majesty, our divine king and kin, Louis the Fifteenth, King of France and Navarre, Louis the Well-Beloved, His Most Catholic King and Protector of Canada and Louisiana; on behalf of all his loyal and devoted subjects, his glorious officers and gallant men; and, oh yes, on behalf of the Blessed Virgin, the saints and Lord Jesus himself, we dedicate this day to you, this splendid victory over a formidable adversary, this historic moment of triumph which will be recorded in the annals of history and all time as perhaps the supreme battle, the ultimate victory, the crowning achievement of good over evil, the proof of the pudding that God has blessed this people and has, once again, destroyed the enemy at our doorsteps as He twice before has done; and so on behalf of...on behalf of all the aforesaid above, I – we – offer this toast in commemoration and rememoration and celebration of you. To your everlasting salvation and well-being. Gentlemen!"

Montcalm took a step forward and, glass in hand, inclined his head slightly.

"Thank you."

He threw back his head and tossed down the brandy. The officers and even the household servants joined in a rousing cheer. The clinking of raised glasses was followed by a contented moment of silence.

"Well!" exclaimed Vaudreuil. "Well! I hereby convene the Governor's Council of War on this date in the year of our Lord, 1759, the thirty-first day of July. Gentlemen, pray be seated."

All duly sat. The governor, however, could not contain himself. He immediately sprang back up.

"What a glorious day this is. Let us dispense with formalities." He beamed at Montcalm. "Please do tell me all the wondrous details of your tremendous victory over the enemy. You understand," the governor hastened to add," you understand that I was myself totally engaged in directing the defenses here at Saint-Charles against what appeared to be an imminent assault by Monckton. And so what I have learnt of your heroic exploits has come to me only by hearsay. Therefore, pray be so kind as to indulge the desires of your devoted servant."

"Wolfe chose a frontal assault on our centre. The mudflats and rocks and tides worked against him. His grenadiers went amok and charged without waiting for Townshend and Monckton to reinforce them. Then the storm hit."

Montcalm was gazing somberly at the governor with tired eyes, then allowed himself a wry smile. "Perhaps indeed we owe this moment of respite to God's benevolence and pity."

"Respite?" Vaudreuil exclaimed, puzzled. "Pity?"

The governor looked around him at the faces of his officers seated in the salon. "Gentlemen! I – we - perceive today's battle as a monumental victory! Most assuredly the decisive, definitive engagement of the enemy's entire campaign!" he proclaimed. "Tis through the Grace of God we have vanquished the heretic enemy and through His Grace we shall persevere 'til autumn's first frost drive Beelzebul away."

Vaudreuil began waddling to and fro in the centre of the salon, his version of pacing, the better to focus his thoughts. He came to an abrupt halt and, smiling, gestured over their heads, pointing heavenwards.

"Do you not see that God has spoken? He has spoken through the lightning, thunder, wind and rain that have doused the enemy's powder and drenched the wicked ardour in their evil hearts. Have we Canadians not witnessed twice before His merciful response to our supplications and prayers?"

The governor pivoted, spinning his outstretched arm to the southwest. "Let us never forget why we Canadians rechristened our glorious church over there in Place Royale "Our Lady of Victories" upon the news in 1711 that God's mighty hand had swept the entire fleet of Sir Hovenden Walker onto the rocks in a sudden tempest not unlike the one we have just seen; and how a scant 21 years earlier Sir William Phipps and his troops, on the beaches of Beauport not far from this very spot, ran away as though pursued by an invisible horde of avenging angels, never to return.

"Gentlemen! Once again, the Lord has answered the prayers of His faithful servants. Let us be grateful! Let us be humble! Scribe! Write this down. I declare in the name of our Most Gracious King and Holy Protector of the Faith, Louis the Fifteenth, that the morrow, the first day of August in the year of our Lord 1759, shall be a day of prayer and offerings and that there shall be celebrated a special mass in Notre-Dame-des-Victoires in humble thanksgiving to our Saviour.

"Now. My friends. My children. Let us turn our attention back to the things of the world. What else can our dear General Wolfe now do except retire to Orléans and lick his wounds? And what more need we do except wait 'til September and his inevitable retreat lest the cold of winter come to ensnare and annihilate him?"

The governor looked expectantly at the general. Montcalm, pensive, said nothing in reply. Colonel Bougainville and Colonel Lévis exchanged glances, but remained silent. Finally Le Mercier spoke up.

"I think Wolfe's done with attacking Beauport. He won't want to try that again. That means he will either assault the Lower Town; or try his luck by attacking the Upper Town from the west, on the Plains of Abraham. But Cape Diamond protects the Lower Town and his men would face a hellish climb up to the top. That's why I say we move half our guns away from Beauport and put 'em up along the western walls of the Upper Town. "

Vaudreuil snorted in derision. "The Upper Town? The Plains of Abraham? We need not concern ourselves there. The enemy's fleet will never be able to land enough forces upriver and even if they did, the cliffs are too steep for them to scale. No, I view such an attack as impossible."

Captain Dumas spoke up. "If it please your Excellency...I have reconnoitered the lands around Sillery and Saint-Michel and I tend to agree with his Excellency that an attack *at this moment* is improbable. I feel compelled nonetheless to point out that there are in fact several trails running from the shore to the cliff tops which determined troops, under the right conditions, might climb...and once on the Plains, would be able to assemble in regular formation. If they succeed in reaching such a point, then an assault from the west would be practical. There are several small hills upon which the enemy can place artillery. The walls of the town would provide but little defense.

"Lt. Crèvecoeur here questioned some English officers captured on the beach today. One of them boasted that Wolfe's secondary plan was, in fact, to disembark at Cape Rouge, or perhaps Saint-Michel, and attack from the west against the Upper Town. Truth is, – "

Vaudreuil cut him off with an impatient wave of the hand. "What's the truth?" he almost sneered. "Pray, tell me, what is the truth?"

The governor swept his arm around the room before supplying his own response to his question. "Is it not true we have just turned away the redoubtable English Army? That we have almost twice the number of men as they, firmly entrenched behind solid defensive lines? That we are only a scant few weeks away from the onset of the cold season against a foe with no supply lines for a winter campaign? That we are willing to fight to the death to defend our hearts, hearths and homes; and, not least of all, that we have God on our side?"

Commissary Bigot took a pinch of snuff and gave a dainty sneeze into a silken handkerchief. "Well, my dear governor, it is certainly true our own food stocks are running dangerously low. Perhaps it would be wise to summon back some of the stores we sent down to Batiscan for safekeeping. Especially if the enemy were to position itself between our supplies and the town."

The governor nodded at the suggestion, putting plump finger against fleshy nose, his sign for discussion. The Council decided to have Bougainville's cavalry shadow the enemy's movements, moving in parallel to any English ships which might attempt to sail upriver past Cape Diamond, and to move the colony's supplies back to Québec once the enemy's intentions became clear.

The Council of War adjourned for the night just as the last of the thunder rolled away in the distance and the drizzle faded to a muggy haze. But as they shrugged on their cloaks they heard a clatter of hooves followed by a knocking on the door. A servant opened it, letting in the out-of-breath rider.

"Missive for General Montcalm," he wheezed. "Boat came ashore under a flag of truce. It is from General Wolfe."

Montcalm undid the wax seal and unfolded the document. He held it at arms'-length, the better to focus. His expression grew grimmer, then relaxed into a sardonic smile. He handed the letter to an aide.

"Here, convey this to his Excellency the Governor."

The aide obliged, walking the ten feet separating the two leaders, and handed the missive to Vaudreuil, with a bow. Vaudreuil's puzzled expression turned to one of derision, then contempt as he read the letter.

"The nerve of that man. What unspeakable cheek! Such temerity! This is an effrontery. Such arrogance!" The governor was almost choking. "He has just lost the battle and six hundred of his most elite troops, and he demands once again our surrender! That should we fail to heed his most generous offer, the guilt of the ages will be upon our shoulders, in retribution for the calamity that will fall upon our women and children!"

The governor tore the document to shreds and let the pieces waft to the floor-boards before crushing them with the heel of his boot. "I declare, General Wolfe must be the devil himself."

Crèvecoeur and the governor's orderly stepped outside onto the veranda. From across the water came a rhythmic, clanging sound.

"I'll confess," Jean-Luc murmured. "I prefer church bells to cannon fire."

"Or to Herod's bloody-hunting slaughter-men...." Crèvecoeur muttered in English.

The bells fell silent, yielding to the croaking of the bullfrogs in the marshes.

"I suppose I'd better learn English if I want to ever press my claim to the British crown," Jean-Luc replied. "Was that from the Bible?"

"Shakespeare."

The church bells resumed, at a slower cadence this time, as though the unseen hands pulling at the ropes were growing weary.

"Maybe Wolfe will give it up after all." Jean-Luc smiled hopefully. "Perhaps the Governor is right. Listen. After all, the bells are still chiming."

Crèvecoeur, still brooding, looked at his friend with a sudden surge of sympathy.

"Or tolling."

Chapter Twelve: *The Nerve to Forgive*

The waggon was finally loaded when the first of the missiles struck. The cannon balls whistled before crashing into the widow Barbel's house nearby. The oxen lowed and grunted in terror, straining at their harness, shaking the waggon and its contents of furniture, pots and pans, and the miscellany of household life. Then the redoubling of their terror from the shock waves of the explosions from the three remaining guns in the Royal Battery as they replied to the enemy fire.

Crèvecoeur grabbed the reins of the beasts and tried to calm them. Jean-Luc grabbed the sleeves of Lamoureux' indentured servant and tried to calm *him*. The servant, a Basque farm lad brought down from the tranquility of the family mills inland, was beside himself with panic. Jean-Luc shook him hard and slapped him.

"Pull yourself together! We're almost done."

Another cannon ball hit with a sharp crack sending an avalanche of stone down into the street below. The air swirled with dust and debris. Smoke rose from a house where the enemy's heated missiles had found timber, igniting it. The servant broke free and ran as fast as his terror-stricken legs and the rubble-strewn street would allow.

Jean-Luc cursed. He yelled after the servant but more to vent frustration than to change the coward's mind. He suddenly whirled.

"Where's Lamoureux?" he exclaimed. Frantic, he looked back at the house, the last of six attached dwellings on the street lining the waterfront. "He must have gone back inside. Damn! We've got to get out of here. I'll go fetch him."

Jean-Luc ran into the house. A moment later a red-hot cannonball sizzled through the air and crashed through the roof with a grinding smash. The oxen bolted and bucked, throwing Crèvecoeur to the muddy road. He felt the ground shake, the air vibrate, heard the heavy rolling sound of masonry tumbling to the earth. He scrambled to his feet and rushed through the white cloud of plaster dust billowing out the door.

The interior would have been dark were it not for the gaping holes in the walls and the roof above where the missile had smashed its way from the top of the house to the bottom. Crèvecoeur stumbled over the debris in the central hall. The formal salon to the left seemed to be empty as was the dining hall to the right. He advanced towards the back, passing the staircase leading to the upper floors.

Crèvecoeur heard before he saw Jean-Luc. The orderly was on his knees in the rubble, talking in an urgent tone of voice.

"Lamoureux?"

"Yes, it's him. He's not responding."

Crèvecoeur saw the bloodied head and shock of grey hair cradled in Jean-Luc's hands. Lamoureux' eyes were closed but he was breathing. A thick oak beam lay across his legs. With great effort they heaved it away then, with the orderly grasping the man's shattered legs and the lieutenant lifting him up from under his torso they began the arduous task of evacuating him, and themselves, from the death trap. Each movement provoked a low, sickening groan from the elderly man.

Crèvecoeur, inching his way backwards, cursed as he stumbled and almost lost his grip. Painfully they managed to move into the centre hall. Crèvecoeur glanced over his shoulder at the open doorway looking out into the daylight where the rear of the ox-cart was visible. Crèvecoeur swore again.

"Stop. We have to clear out the cart first. Put him down."

Even as he spoke the terrifying crack of cannonballs hitting stone thundered from over them and the floor-boards shuddered underfoot. From outside came a roaring sound like the Montmorency Falls as a cascade of stone collapsed from the upper wall of the house onto the ox-cart. The two young men looked at each other and then, as though of one mind, eyed the door under the stairs. Jean-Luc managed to open the door and they worked their way down the narrow steps into the basement.

The cellar was typical of all the houses in the town. The open *soupirail*, small window high up in the foundation wall, let in enough daylight to illuminate the solid stone pillars supporting, cathedral-like, massive stone arches which in turn supported the vaulted ceiling. Here, unlike the floors above, there was no dust or debris and the dank, stale air was as refreshing to them as a cool stream in summer. They made their way over to a camp-bed under an archway evidently serving as Lamoureux' sleeping quarters while waiting out the siege.

As they placed him on the cot the older man uttered another groan of pain and his eyelids fluttered.

"Can you hear me? Are you thirsty? Can you drink?" Jean-Luc was frantic.

Lamoureux' eyes seemed to move but his lips did not. As Jean-Luc stared helplessly, canteen in hand, Crèvecoeur examined the man's legs. His baggy wool breaches, originally a dusky brown, were coated with a powder of greenish-white lime dust. Crèvecoeur slowly moved his fingers down the man's thigh towards an ominous dark stain. As he encountered a large swollen protuberance an electric hiss of agony welled up from the man's very being.

Crèvecoeur looked at his friend. "He needs a surgeon."

Without more he scrambled up the rickety stairs and left the house. He skirted the pile of stone crushing the cart and oxen and hurried his way northward along rue Saint-Pierre, then turned onto Saint-Paul, hugging the base of the cliffs forming the northern ramparts of the Upper Town. Here townspeople and militia were in evidence, venturing out more boldly, feeling secure from the enemy's cannon under the lee of the cliffs.

Crèvecoeur marveled at their fortitude, wondered how they managed to feed themselves, how they kept their sanity in an insane world. Ahead he saw the Palais de l'Intendant, Bigot's mansion, peeking above high palisaded walls forming a false façade of security. All around in every garden and field were the tents of soldiers and militia.

He entered a large building converted to a hospital. Every square foot of floor was occupied by the injured and the dying. Most were townspeople, a few were soldiers or militiamen. Some were groaning; most suffered in silence. Some were sitting, heads thrown back against the cold stone of the wall, eyes staring blankly, forlornly, into space; more than a few were stretched out on the floor, the lucky ones on coarse wool blankets stained with blood. Nuns in once-white aprons attended to them in hushed whispers. Crèvecoeur stopped one of the good sisters.

"We have no surgeons here to spare, sir. Try the Hôtel-Dieu in the Upper Town."

Crèvecoeur went up the Côte du Palais, the steep road wending its way to the Upper Town. He followed the ramparts to the high stone walls encircling the complex of buildings housing the Augustinian order of monks and sisters. Their hospital's gothic wooden portals were wide open, above which "Hôtel-Dieu" stood out in relief.

Crèvecoeur ducked inside the cool recesses of the fortress-like structure. As with the hospital below, every room, every inch of corridor was devoted to the sick and injured. Despite the thick walls, the muffled sounds of cannon and the thumping of their missiles hitting somewhere in the town could be felt.

After several inquiries Crèvecoeur found himself in a smallish chamber on the main floor, illuminated by an arched window whose panes had long ago been shattered. A man lay on the bed, looking up at the ceiling upon whose plastered surface a mural had been painted eons before depicting, in faded blue and gold, angels hovering around the fount of their love and the source of their life, the mocking crown of thorns transformed into a halo of triumph.

Sagging on a hook next to the bed was the bloodied dark green coat of an officer in the American Rangers. A good sister was hovering around the upturned face of the patient, wearing his own crown in the form of a bandage stained dark with his blood.

She gently soothed his sweating brow with a damp cloth, then let the man sip from a cup she held to his lips. He winced in pain as he raised his head, supported from underneath by the nun's hand, but eagerly let the source of life flow into his parched mouth. Satiated, he lay his head back down on the pillow and gazed into the good sister's eyes. He reached out with his arm and took her hand in his and pressed it.

"Thank you," the man murmured in English.

Still holding the man's hand, the nun looked at Crèvecoeur questioningly.

"I have a civilian in the Lower Town, with a badly broken leg. I need a surgeon."

The nun's eyebrows rose. She permitted herself a wry smile, large green eyes gentle.

"We have scores all around us in need of healing," she said softly. She looked back down at the injured man, eyes now closed but tensed with the pain of his suffering.

"Doctor Soupirant will be back in a moment. You can talk to him."

The man opened his eyes at the sound of the conversing in the foreign tongue and directed them to the French lieutenant. As Crèvecoeur gazed into his eyes with his own there was a flash of recognition as both men realised they had seen each other before. Now in an instant the injured enemy stretched out helpless on the bed was transformed from an indifferent foreign thing into a familiar, sentient human being.

Seeing the French officer searching his memory, the sick man spoke up first.

"Fort William Henry," he said simply.

In an epiphany it flashed back into Crèvecoeur's memory. The brutal scenes of massacre. The bloodlust, the anger, the hatred, the fear. The dark wilderness where dozens of unarmed British and American soldiers under Montcalm's pledge of safe passage were slaughtered by France's native allies run amok. The general, beside himself, cursing in impotent rage at the native chieftains, powerless themselves to control the fever of evil coursing through the veins of their warriors. The cries, the pleas for mercy from the captives, the anguished screams, the demonic yells. The English grenadier who, tomahawk in hand, Crèvecoeur killed with a thrust of his bayonet only to realise the man was not attacking him but defending his own self from a Huron he had wrestled to the ground….

"You were there, near General Montcalm, after he put himself between the savages and my company…and you helped me and my men get to safety. You conveyed to us the general's apologies…."

Crèvecoeur forced himself to look into the injured man's eyes, and gave a brief nod. That seemed to satisfy the American, for he turned his gaze back to his nurse.

"I am not a Catholic, as you may have surmised…."

The good sister put a finger to her lips, hushing him.

"You need rest."

The man lay back, closed his eyes. In a moment he drifted off to a troubled sleep.

"How did he get here?" Crèvecoeur whispered.

The nun gently eased her hand out of the American's and took Crèvecoeur aside.

"They brought him here yesterday. They said he was with a detachment of Gorham's Rangers. Our militia ambushed them. This man was their captain. His name is David…I cannot say his family name, I think it is Scots. He was shot in the leg. While he was lying on the ground an Indian began to club him with a *casse-tête.* One of our Royal officers intervened and saved the poor man. The doctor does not believe the head injury is too serious but he couldn't remove all the lead from his leg…."

She looked with pity at the sleeping man. "He seems to have something on his heart which is bothering him."

At that moment a short man in a bloody frock came bustling into the room. He was unshaven and his eyes were bleary. He glared at the lieutenant, then spoke to the sister.

"Still alive? If not, let's get him out of here and make room for someone else."

Doctor Soupirant went up to the bed to see for himself. As he felt the man's pulse the patient woke up and opened his eyes.

"Thank you, doctor." The injured man looked intently at his caregiver.

Soupirant brushed aside the gratitude and, dropping the man's wrist felt the back of his neck, then the man's forehead. "Fever," he muttered. "More wet cloth."

The nun obligingly placed a damp rag on the man's forehead. He raised a weak hand towards her. She held it in her own as he looked into her eyes, searchingly.

"What is it like, heaven?"

The good sister raised her brows, smiled, and shook her head gently.

"I wonder if I shall be allowed to enter...." He squeezed her hand, looked at her imploringly. "I have done so many bad things...evil, horrible things....I have murdered...." He sunk his head back down onto the pillow. "That day...when we were attacked...we were...were killing women and children in the village, burning their houses...destroying their lives...."

He looked up at the ceiling as though searching for something.

"And yet after all that I was saved....Can you forgive me? Please...forgive me...."

Exhausted, he closed his eyes once again and fell silent.

Doctor Soupirant turned to leave but Crèvecouer tugged at his sleeve.

"What do you want? I have other patients to attend to."

"I need you to come with me to the Lower Town. I have a civilian with a fractured leg. It's bad."

Soupirant was annoyed. "Find someone else. I have too many things here requiring my attention. Your friend will have to pull through on his own."

Crèvecoeur lost his temper. He grabbed the doctor violently by both arms and forced the man to look into his eyes.

"My 'friend', Jacques Lamoureux, can't make it on his own. He'll surely die without help."

"Lamoureux?" Crèvecoeur felt the doctor relax. "Jacques Lamoureux? All right," Soupirant sighed. "Let me grab my bag."

As they stepped off the ramparts onto the Côte du Palais leading down to the Lower Town they could see below Bigot's palisaded palace and the militia's encampments. Near the bottom of the hill they passed by the scaffold where the blindfolded, decaying bodies of the two wayward soldiers and their sailor sidekick dangled on the hangman's rope. Soupirant snorted.

"See those scoundrels? Hanging's too good for them. Teach them to break into a man's home and steal his wine. To think they had the nerve to ask for forgiveness."

Rounding the corner onto Saint-Pierre Street the doctor stopped and surveyed the broken houses and rubble-strewn road with dismay. The distant booming of the enemy's cannon from across the river did not bother him as much as the sound of crashing further up the street as the missiles landed. The air was heavy with the acrid smell of smoke. Flames licked at house-tops while frantic residents clung to the ladders built into the roofs and tried to douse the fire with small leather buckets. The doctor balked.

"We can't go into there!" He made to turn back. Crèvecoeur grabbed him and pushed him forward.

"You've come this far. There's no turning back."

Half-pushing, half-dragging the man of medicine and doctor of philosophy, the lieutenant picked out a path through the debris. They reached the short street called Notre-Dame leading to the Place Royale and the church, tall steeple rising heavenward, crowned by the forged iron cross on whose three points were the *fleurs-de-lys* of the King of France. At that moment came a netherworldly whistling in the air and the deafening crash of iron into stone as the base of the church steeple and half the roof were demolished, as if by a giant invisible hammer from the sky. Although the steeple was no longer recognizable as such the iron cross was still there, resting on the rock of the rubble, pointing to the sky, albeit at a slant.

The lieutenant threw the doctor through the doorway into Lamoureux' broken dwelling and dragged him down to the basement sanctuary. Jean-Luc was kneeling next to the cot, holding the old man's hand. His head was bowed.

Jean-Luc was weeping. He lifted his head, slowly, wearily. He glanced at the doctor, then turned wet eyes upon his friend.

"You should have brought the priest."

Chapter Thirteen: *Timeless Love*

Thick brown smoke hung low and heavy, like an evil fog, seeming to smother the entire Saint-Lawrence valley to the east. Day by day it grew darker and heavier as Gorham's Rangers began executing General Wolfe's orders with a vengeance. DuChêne was beside himself with worry mingled with fury.

"I'm going to go back to my village," he told Crèvecoeur. "My colonel got approval from the governor to send my company yonder. Said we have free reign to do what we must to stop Gorham.

"You recall our friend Desrivières? At Baie St.-Paul? He's in hiding now, in the woods, with the rest of his village. Joseph Saulnier is with him. He sent word through Father René that his Swiss corporal turned his coat and went over to the enemy. The traitor be damned! The Swiss led Gorham to our cache of powder and munitions and then set fire to the houses in the village with his own guilty hand. May the Lord have mercy on my soul for what I will do to him if I get my hands on his hateful neck."

"Is your family safe?"

DuChêne paused. "So far, yes, as much as I know. My wife and children were to go with my brother into the backcountry, to our Huron friends towards Montréal. I can only pray they did what I told them...."

"Look, let me go with you. I'll ask Captain Dumas for permission."

They set out at dawn the next day, DuChêne with his company of twenty militiamen on borrowed horses and a small party of Abenaki. Crèvecoeur was glad to find himself riding with Megeso again. They forded the Montmorency upriver and then stopped at the first small hamlet on their path, Ange-Guardien, village cross depicting a wooden carving of the eponymous guardian angel. DuChêne's village, Sainte-Anne-de-Beaupré, was seven miles' ride to the east.

The people of Ange-Guardien had not left their village. On the outskirts of the hamlet farmers were finishing up with the wheat harvest as though the war did not exist. In the village mill grain was being ground, tended by the miller and his family who glared coldly at the militia company passing through their sight.

The village smithy, asked by DuChêne for leave to water their horses at his trough, stopped his pounding long enough to jerk his head to the adjacent yard then resumed his work without a word.

After giving their horses water DuChêne approached the blacksmith.

"We would like some hay for our horses."

"We would like some coin for our hay."

"We have no coin to give you."

"Then we have no hay to give you."

"My friend. Do you think the English are going to give you money for your hay? Or for everything else they will take? Your livestock. Your lumber. Your tools. Your larder."

"We have sent word to them we want no part in this war. General Wolfe wrote he will let us keep our houses and farms, our customs, our church. He promised he will not molest us."

"In every war you have to decide which side you are on. By not deciding you are, whether you know it or not, taking a side. Here."

DuChêne had reached into his pouch and counted out several cardboard cards. He extended his open hand to the man, palm up, displaying a king of diamonds and several lesser cards underneath, all with the neat, prim signature of the Commissary of New-France.

"Keep your damn *monnaie de carte* for yourself!" the smithy cried. "I don't want play money. I want the real thing! Precious lot of good Bigot's playing card I-owe- you's will do me after the English take over Québec – "

DuChêne slapped the smithy so hard in his face the man almost fell backward. The smithy was a strong man but DuChêne was stronger. He also had a good four inches on the other. As the blacksmith raised his hammer DuChêne laid him out with a blow to the jaw, sending the man reeling backwards into the leather folds of the bellows. DuChêne tossed the playing cards on the floor and he and Crèvecoeur rejoined their men outside before leading their horses to the smithy's barn with its store of hay.

Unlike Ange-Guardien, DuChêne's village was almost deserted. The only chimney smoke in evidence came from the presbytery, whose bucolic barnyard was marred only by ducks, geese and chickens eternally disputing for their territory in a cacophony of cackling and scratching, chasing and honking. DuChêne had his company dismount and take their midday meal.

Inside the timber-framed dwelling they found Father René seated at the rickety table, reading the Bible. He flashed them a cheery smile, snapped the Scriptures shut, and carefully placed the Bible in his bulging saddle bags sagging on the table top, next to his *cartouchière*, the box without doubt loaded with the musket balls and cartridges of powder he had fashioned with his own hands.

"I knew I could count on you," the priest said affectionately, hugging his giant friend. "You are a pillar of strength." He smiled at Crèvecoeur. "My Hector as well."

He embraced Crèvecoeur; then turned slowly towards Anne-Marie, on the hearth tending the fire.

Stooped over was she, her back turned towards them. Carefully she rearranged the small burning pieces of wood with a poker; then replaced the poker in her hand with a ladle, and brought it up to the kettle suspended above the fire.

Slowly over the kettle hovered her arm, stirring the contents with the ladle. Below the kettle embers glowed. Their deep red oscillated, waxing and waning, pulsating like a living heart, pumping waves of heated, shimmering air rippling upwards, carrying wisps of spiraling smoke.

An ember popped. Bright orange sparks flew heavenwards. They were glowing, dancing like fireflies, before fading into a black nothingness.

A hissing sound came from a hidden spot within the fire. The embers spit and crackled, the fire breathed and exhaled. In feeding itself on the fibres of wood, it was destroying the source of its own sustenance; but in the process sustaining something else. As Anne-Marie slowly stirred, the sweet smell of simmering stew infused the air.

The small wall clock ticked. There was only a single hand. If the weight and counterweight hanging on the brass chain below moved, if the solitary hand on the face of the clock budged, it was imperceptible. Yet still the clock ticked.

A shaft of sunlight slanted its hazy way through the lone window in the west-facing wall and fell upon the back of the woman. In its soft, silky milky buttery light could be seen motes of dust suspended lazily in the air. A few wisps of sprite-like smoke stole into the light and laced ghostly white arms around the motes like suitors stealing onto the dance-floor to waltz away with their belles in an eternal pas-de-deux.

The alabaster skin of Anne-Marie's frail, wrinkled hand looked more than ever like dainty porcelain when cupped in the large, strong hands of Father René tanned chestnut-brown. Her eyes themselves were of the same reddish brown and their glowing seemed to wax and wane like the embers of her fire as she looked softly into the eyes of the priest, gazing into her with his own orbs, blazing gently bright blue.

The clock ticked but the hand did not move.

Chapter Fourteen: *Where Satan Cannot Go*

They met up with Captain Saulnier at the Abenaki village in a clearing in the forest. Without wasting a moment the two militia captains convened a council of war.

"Gorham laid waste to Baie-Saint-Paul. He burned Les Éboulements to the ground. Saint-Joachim will be next," Saulnier informed the newcomers bitterly. "I bet they come by way of the river. If so, then that's where we can set a trap for him."

"How many men does he have?" DuChêne asked softly.

"A company of American Rangers is usually around a hundred. It seems that's about what he has."

"And we're only fifty."

Saulnier looked at Father René. "The men of Saint-Joachim will be willing to join us once they know they have their fighting priest at their side."

"Joseph." Father René had placed a hand on the man's arm. "Whatever happens you must stay out of harm's way. For the sake of your aunt. You are the only one she has left."

Saulnier brushed off the priest's hand. "I know how to take care of myself. Nothing's going to happen to me."

"Joseph." This time the priest's voice was sharp. "We are all mortal. My time is coming. Your time will come. But let it be not now, may it please the Lord. Anne-Marie has already lost everyone else near and dear to her on earth. She will have no one to comfort her in her last days but for you."

Saulnier's eyes betrayed a momentary look of indecision. DuChêne intervened.

"I have a plan to propose. Me and René know the village and the marshes and the path leading up from the water. You know the woods along the backside of Cape Torment. I'll take my militia south down to the village. We'll join up with the local men there. You and your men will skirt the edge of the forest to the east of us before turning south, so that you can protect our flank in case the enemy sends a detachment by land from Baie-Saint-Paul. You'll approach the village from the east and meet up with us there."

"But I have only a dozen men."

DuChêne looked at Crèvecoeur. "Our lieutenant here will go with you along with our Abenaki friends."

Crèvecoeur flushed. About to protest, he saw in his Canadian friend's eyes a look that forestalled discussion. Father René too was watching him intently, blazing blue eyes speaking their own unspoken words. Crèvecoeur took a deep breath before nodding his head reluctantly. He glanced at Megeso, observing the diplomatic exchange with a keen eye. He too seemed to understand.

They broke camp quickly. Horses were left tethered in the Indian settlement; they would go on foot, more practical in the woods. In silent acquiescence there was no last embrace, no parting words. By an unspoken common accord neither party looked back as they went their separate ways.

Saulnier forged ahead on the narrow forest path as quickly as he could, as if to reach the village ahead of their friends. The trail, on the flank of the mountain, twisted and turned, following the contours of the slope. Sunlight filtering in through the canopy of late summer leaves showed them they were now heading southwest and that an hour had elapsed since their departure.

"Past that rock the trail goes down to a grassy clove then meets up with the path from the eastern villages. From there we'll be less than an hour to Saint-Joachim."

At the summit of the next hill the hemlocks of the forest thinned out and were replaced by groves of canoe birch as the slope led them downwards into a meadow. Some Abenaki ran ahead and disappeared into the woods on the other side of the field.

"We're coming up to that junction," Saulnier informed them. "From there it won't be long. Come on, let's push it."

But the party came to an abrupt halt. An Abenaki warrior came trotting back, motioning for them to stop. Gesturing with his arms and hands he made them understand the danger ahead, a large body of enemy troops. Megeso stepped forward and the two conversed in hurried whispers.

"Ninety men," he reported. "American Rangers. Come from the east. Heading now southwest on the trail to the village."

Saulnier swore under his breath. "Damn them. They came overland after all. They've cut us off." He glared. "We'll attack them from behind."

Alarmed, Crèvecoeur shook his head. "That would be futile. We can't do it from the trail. We'd have to somehow get ahead of them while they're still in the woods and flank them for a broadside attack. All we can do is tail behind until we see a way to outmaneuver them."

They set off, single file, looking out for any rear guard the Rangers might have posted. Crows cawed in the distance from up ahead, a sign both of the transition of woods to meadows and the presence of men. Saulnier's band were treated to the same avian welcome when they reached the forest edge. He raised his hand and they halted. They could see far ahead green-coated Rangers on a fast-march through the grass, and houses poking above the tree-line marking the outskirts of Saint-Joachim; and farther away, towards the greenish-grey of the Saint-Lawrence River sparkling in the afternoon sun, the white spire and cross of the church. If DuChêne and Father René had arrived, they were hidden by the trees flanking the village.

"Come on!" Saulnier commanded, bolting onto a nearly invisible trail to his left. Deer would have had a hard time on this path but Saulnier raced on, Crèvecoeur right behind him, cursing at himself for not having gone with DuChêne, forgetting that a leaf must go where the current will take it. They were on the path ordained for them and they would make the best of it.

They were closer to the village though still a half mile away, on its eastern flank, some thirty yards higher in elevation. They could see clearly now the several small jetties poking out from the marshy beach and what they saw alarmed them.

Two frigates swayed at anchor with dozens of landing craft close by. A line of red-coated grenadiers, bayonets glittering in the sunlight, tall buff-coloured hats like bishops' mitres, stood watch over the landing. The barges were empty save for sailors waiting by shipped oars.

Saulnier and his men turned their eyes back to the direction of the church spire visible above the trees where a dog was barking furiously. There was a retort of musket fire. The barking stopped. They heard now the gruff, muffled sounds of human barking. From the church came the crack of muskets followed by a louder volley of gunfire. Then the infernal wailing of a legion of men screaming as though from one gigantic throat swelled through the air, unleashing in one stupendous exhalation all the primordial furies tormenting the human soul since time immemorial.

Through the foliage Crèvecoeur could glimpse flashes of red streaking from the left and flickers of green rushing in from the right to converge upon the middle where the church was. The primordial scream merged with a primordial, collective moan from the centre. More musket fire, but sporadic, half-hearted.

Crèvecoeur saw there was no way to reach the village except by continuing along the path leading down to the grenadiers near the jetties; or by backtracking to the forest trail. The steep slope in front of them was impossible. He turned and ran as fast as he could back to the trail, heedless whether his companions followed or not.

They were, in fact, right on his heels, Saulnier foremost. Finally regaining the forest and the main trail to the village, Crèvecoeur paused long enough to take a hurried gulp from his canteen, feeling a surge of gratitude that Megeso was right behind him. The rest of the Abenaki had vanished into the forest.

He felt a hand gripping his arm. He looked into Saulnier's eyes locked into his own. His eyes were blazing with a strange light.

"They are a company of grenadiers and a company of Rangers. We are a dozen." The Acadian was glaring fiercely at Crèvecoeur. "I outrank you. I order you to bring my men back to camp safely."

He suddenly shoved Crèvecoeur to the forest floor, bowling over the militia behind him like so many pins, and bolted out of the woods into the open meadow descending into the village. As he ran he was screaming at the top of his lungs every profanity, every curse he knew – and he had a vast vocabulary to draw upon.

Unconsciously Crèvecoeur and company counted down the seconds they reckoned remained before Saulnier could reach the semblance of shelter offered by a screen of apple trees behind the first of the village houses at the far end of the field. The Acadian was within touching distance of the trees when a dozen puffs of blue smoke appeared from within the orchard, then a pattering of popping and Saulnier fell over backwards into the tall grass.

Crèvecoeur could only stare at the spot where Saulnier had vanished. Nobody said a word. Even the crows were muted. From the village as well no sounds could be heard. But as quickly as a sabre can be drawn from a scabbard, there came a heavy thudding then a whooshing sensation, sounding like a thick rug being lifted up and dropped back onto the floor-boards, pushing outwards waves of air. In an instant the rooftops of the village were ablaze orange-red. The wooden white spire of the church topped by its iron cross soon disappeared in clouds of black smoke.

Crèvecoeur motioned for Megeso to come with him, back onto the narrow side trail on the ridge above the village. From there they could discern the last of the grenadiers queued up along the path to the river, waiting their turn to embark, the frigates' decks already teeming with their red-coated fellows. Off to the west a body of green-coats was moving along the twilit road, away from the burning village and down towards the hamlet of Saint-Anne-de-Beaupré. As the now invisible Glascoop cast its last rays over the distant mountains upriver, Malsumis peeked behind them above the eastern horizon. The village was a blazing inferno.

They spent a miserable hungry night in the forest. Crèvecoeur tried, but failed, to not think about the dreadful task awaiting them in the morning. Megeso, too, was troubled behind his mask-like stoicism. Quietly he padded off into the woods and, in the fading light of the dying day, found what he was seeking. With a knife he peeled away small strips of white birch bark, then gathered several small boughs of green hemlock. To the recipe he added one large acorn. Carefully he arranged the objects in a small, neat pile on the ground on top of a layer of dry leaves and pine needles. A few expert strokes of his striker against flint together with a few short blows of his own breath and the sparks took hold.

Megeso sat down on the forest floor, cross-legged, before the tiny burning pyre. From a pouch he sprinkled a dark substance onto the flickering flame. The faint smell of the burning tobacco did not travel much farther than the circle of light from the fire. The flames quickly consumed themselves into a small pile of ashes, sparse tendrils of smoke twisting upwards. Megeso's eyes were closed. He appeared oblivious to the world. He was seeking to enter that place where Malsumis could not penetrate.

In dawn's dim light they carried Saulnier's corpse past the smoldering remains of the village along the one and only road. They paused long enough by a blackened barn to rummage around, searching for what they knew they would be needing. They repeated the process at each dwelling they encountered until every other man was armed with a pick and a spade, or at least a hoe or an adze while others scrounged up scraps of clapboard spared by the fire.

The smoky shell of the church loomed ahead. The blackened posts stood like tall silent sentinels over the ruins. All around the foundation, in front and on into the cemetery in the side yard, lay dark, grotesque shapes on the ground. Their living comrades came to a halt and as of one mind stood in respectful silence for a moment. They fanned out among the corpses.

Each one had been scalped. All except Father René, that is. The American Ranger who had run him through with a bayonet vented his frustration at having no trophy of hair to take away by crushing the priest's bald head with a tomahawk. Crèvecoeur removed his waistcoat and gently placed it over Father René's head and torso.

DuChêne lay close by. As he bent down over his friend he saw the round scapular, its leather neckstrap slack alongside, resting on the man's chest. Crèvecoeur fingered the scapular with its leather tether, hesitated, then let it slip back through his fingers.

The scattered packs and pouches had been ransacked of everything resembling, in the enemy's eyes, ammunition; and thus they overlooked the priest's Bible. Father René had marked a page by placing inside a folded piece of paper. Crèvecoeur carefully pulled the paper out, noting where the priest had placed it.

He unfolded the paper. On it was writing. It said: "My Brother, when you lay my mortal remains in my final resting place, know that I am going to where the enemy can never go. Satan can have my body, but Jesus has my soul. When you give your final blessing to me, kindly recite Psalm Three. May God bless you."

All day long they dug into the earth. Crèvecoeur, shovel in hand, let himself drift into a reverie. The shovelfuls of dirt he saw his arms tossing out of the trench could have been the soils of his youthful Normandy and the grave the resting place of his mother.

"The Lord giveth, the Lord taketh away: blessed be the name of the Lord." Father François made the final sign of the cross over the gentle mound of earth and Michel-Guillaume fell to his knees. Someone was screaming and crying in his ears, hands were clawing at the dirt before his eyes, and he felt rough fingers clutching his shoulders, pulling him away but he

refused to be taken and kicking and shouting he threw himself back onto the dirt....

By and by the women-folk of Saint-Joachim began to appear. When they had fled, whither they had flied to, did not matter now. They filtered onto the grounds of their church and fell to their knees crying when they had identified a husband, a father, a son.

After all the graves were dug they placed each body into the womb of the earth, one by one. A piece of wood was driven into the ground in front of each grave and on it Crèvecoeur drew the initials of the man, or boy, in charcoal. When it came Father René's turn, Crèvecoeur slowly wrote out the name in full.

He opened the priest's Bible. The people gathered around. Crèvecoeur read out loud the note René had written, then his Psalm.

> " 'O Lord, how many are my foes! How many rise up against me!
> Many are saying of me, 'God will not deliver him.'
> But you are a shield around, O Lord; you bestow glory on me and lift up my head.
>
> To the Lord I cry aloud, and he answers me from His holy hill.
> I lie down and sleep; I wake again, because the Lord sustains me.
> I will not fear the tens of thousands drawn up against me on every side.
>
> Arise, O Lord! Deliver me, O my God! Strike all my enemies on the jaw;
> break the teeth of the wicked. From the Lord comes deliverance.
> May Your blessing be on your people.' "

Crèvecoeur snapped the Bible shut and placed it in René's bag. He felt a smoldering sensation welling up from within the deepest part of his being. *Requiem eternam dona ei Domine, requiescat in pace* he heard from somewhere behind him.

He stepped back and nodded his head.

In unison, all around the cemetery, spadefuls of soil floated down upon the just as well as upon the unjust, and the last rays of the late August sunlight fell upon the sinners as well as upon the saints.

Chapter Fifteen: *An Unappealing Messenger*

"12 September 1759. We have only a few weeks before the first frost. Yet still Wolfe has not left us. Now it seems he is bent on attacking us once again at Beauport. All day long his transports and sloops have been maneuvering back and forth in the bay before us. We are on a constant state of alert. Everybody is on edge. The Governor is convinced the assault will take place right here, on the east side of the Saint-Charles; and maybe upon the Lower Town as well.

"He has pulled back towards our camp the Guyenne Regiment from where the general had positioned them a few days ago up on the heights near the Plains of Abraham. The General was not pleased, but did nothing to countermand the Governor's decision. I think he, too, believes Wolfe will strike us here.

"All the sky east and south is filled with black smoke such that the morning sun can no longer be seen from where we are. The enemy has put to the torch every house, every barn, every field. Even Ange-Guardien has not been pardoned. And yet, the enemy is not totally heartless. They sent to us a boatload of our women and children who had been spared. I was pleased to find among them Aunty Anne-Marie. She is now with the good sisters in the Ursulines' convent.

"The General has ordered every other militiaman to be integrated into our regular troops rather than forming a corps apart. My captain is not happy. He wants to use the militia where they fight best: on the flanks, quick sorties Indian style, or in ambush. They have not been trained to fight in formation or to hold a line. But, he is, as always, loyal to his duty and said we'll have to learn to make it work. He has always told me that no matter how bleak our circumstances may seem to us one day, there is a purpose to it all which transcends our own individual situation, and the good which arises therefrom is there to see if we only know where to look and how to see it. If that is true, then I confess I must be blind.

"I am weary of thinking in circles. I am weary of thinking. I am tired of eating the moldy bread in camp and drinking the

101

brackish water our cisterns offer. How I long for fresh bread and pure water!

"I must put down my pen now. I wonder if I will ever write another word in this journal. Or if I will ever see my father. And yet, although I cannot see him, I feel he is with me even now as I write and that he has always been with me even in my darkest moments. But enough. I hear the drummers beating out the call to evening Orders."

Crèvecoeur emerged from the isolation of his tent into the society of his fellow creatures. The enemy guns still boomed from Pointe-Lévy but found little left to destroy in the smoldering ruins of the town.

The watchword for the night: general alert. The attack was bound to come right here where Dumas and his men were encamped, near la Canardière, the mudflats where the Saint-Charles River merged into the Saint-Lawrence. Near the Lower Town, on the other side of the Saint-Charles, were the royal troops of the Guyenne Regiment, banner hanging limply in the still evening air. The other regiments, Béarn, Languedoc, Royal-Roussillon, LaSarre, stretched out to the east towards Beauport.

Montcalm's field command lay close by, not far from the governor's borrowed manse. Dumas instructed his aides to keep their horses saddled, at the ready to relay messages. To them he entrusted communications with the water-borne watchmen plying the shallows in their birchbark canoes.

Crèvecoeur and his fellow aides Duflot and Sanssouci drew straws to see who would get to sleep first while the other two stood the first watch. Crèvecoeur drew the long straw. He returned to his tent in the fading light, glad the enemy's guns had fallen silent. Inside he sat on his cot and pulled off his shoes, savouring the relief from removing that constant source of discomfort in his life. He lay back on the cot, stretched out still clothed although minus the tunic, waistcoat and belt, clasped his hands behind his head as a pillow, and stared straight up at the peak of the tent. He let his eyelids drop.

He knew he needed rest but sleep would not come. He tried to will himself to slumber and gave it up as futile. He tried to conjure up a happy memory but could summon only sad ones. He was like a passenger pigeon with crippled wings trying to regain the gift of flight through his own doomed effort. He gave up the effort.

His eyes opened and he gazed again into the grey blankness. In the half-light he dimly discerned the round hoop of Megeso's *capteur des rêves* hanging on a strap. He raised himself up, took it off the strap, placed it over his head and onto his shoulders, then lay back again. He closed his eyes.

He again saw Megeso, squatting on the cliff-top in the morning sun fashioning the hoop, his solemn ceremony invoking the heavens. Glascoop chasing Malsumis. Tabaldak wants it that way. The hoop of wood with a pinecone talisman of feathers hanging around Crèvecoeur's neck, the sailors' rope hanging around the pony's neck. The pony flying free. Peasants ploughing in the fields, the yoke of the Egyptians around their necks. The tall burly man in the red knit cap. Sheep trailing behind them, a lamb leading their way. Please accept this gift, in remembrance of the truth, blazing blue eyes shining, the lamb in the pocket of his tunic.

"Wake up. Crèvecoeur, wake up, damn it." The voice was harsh, unforgiving. It was Duflot.

Crèvecoeur sat up with a start.

"Come on. Get your shoes on. Lazy bastard. It's my turn."

"To be lazy or to be a bastard?"

"Go to hell. Come on, move it."

"All right. Shut up, damn you. Give me a second."

He fumbled in the dark for his satanic shoes, felt instead the pair of Indian moccasins Megeso's mother had given him. He didn't hesitate for long. He slipped them on and stepped outside into the world, buckling his too-loose belt and slipping on his tunic.

"What were you doing with yourself in there?" Duflot leered. "Catch you at a bad time?"

"Go to hell."

Crèvecoeur squinted groggily around the dark camp. All was quiet.

"What's the matter?" Duflot grumbled. "You think I'm trying to trick you? It's your watch, all right."

"Sanssouci's down by the canoes?"

"I hope so. I don't know where else he would be." Duflot yawned. "Have fun. I'm hitting the sack."

"Sweet dreams."

Crèvecoeur picked his obscure way down to the marshy beach and the jetty. The soldiers on picket duty in the trenches hardly looked up as he passed. Half asleep, he thought. The enemy's cannon were sleeping, too. As he approached the jetty an excited Sanssouci came running up. He almost bumped into Crèvecoeur coming down the path in the darkness.

"There's a lot of noise from across the water. Sounds like the enemy's embarking. I thought I best tell the captain...." Sanssouci's voice trailed off as he hesitated, suddenly uncertain, as though he did not want to be the one accused of sounding a false alarm.

Crèvecoeur said nothing; he was intent on listening. "I don't hear anything," he finally said.

"What should we do?"

"Go down to the jetty, I guess."

Although invisible in the darkness they knew the ebb tide was nigh. The marsh reeked with the putrescence of rotting vegetation and the wooden planks they were walking on were already decaying though only a few months old.

"I suppose," Crèvecoeur thought out loud, "if the enemy plans on attacking here they will want to come in on the tide. That means four o'clock or so. If that's what they're up to, then we ought to hear them getting ready about now."

They reached the jetty, scanning the peppery-greyness before them. Above, through shrouds of clouds, a few stars glowed in indifferent passivity, a reminder of the meaninglessness of the projects of men. Across the water the low hills of Orléans Island were only a vague silhouette. Along its western tip, pointing like the bowsprit of a warship at the guts of the Lower Town, a few dots of orange light glowed. The only sounds were the serenading of frogs and the occasional splash of a turtle, oblivious to the human drama in their midst.

They kept their voices to a whisper. "I'm glad I didn't wake up Captain Dumas for nothing," Sanssouci admitted ruefully.

"I doubt if he's asleep."

"I don't want to give a false alert."

"You mean, you don't want to be the boy who cried 'Wolfe'."

Sanssouci nodded his head in the dark, taking the other's remark seriously.

Crèvecoeur remembered that Sanssouci did not speak English and so explained the play on words.

"Oh. 'Wolfe' means *loup,* like the animal? I suppose then he feels obliged to live up to his name. I hope that doesn't mean we're nothing but sheep."

"If we're sheep, let's hope we have a good shepherd...."

A loud thud reverberated across the tops of the water, followed by several more. Crèvecoeur peered vainly into the darkness, frustrated that although his eyes were open wide he could not see. Now came a clattering sound, then scraping noises and muffled voices from the island, and an indefinable feeling against their faces as though a great mass was moving, displacing the air as it lumbered. There was no mistaking it now: the enemy's transports were being boarded.

"Where are the canoe-men? If we can hear that, they can too."

"I don't know."

"All right. Stay here. I'm going up to see the captain."

As Crèvecoeur expected the captain was not asleep. Rather, he was gazing up at the celestial dome above them, calmly absorbed in a quiet contemplation.

"Captain, sir. We can hear the English embarking."

"All right. Let's take a stroll over to the general."

They picked their way among the tents to the general's own, grander version. They found him with his aides and chief of staff around their fire. He waited patiently as the captain and his lieutenant doffed their tri-corn hats and bowed.

"Any news, gentlemen?" Montcalm's tired smile only accentuated the sadness in his eyes.

"It appears the enemy is either embarking or preparing to do so as we speak."

"I see. Well, this is not unexpected. If they must attack, an attack just before dawn makes the most sense for them." The general's voice was soft, almost casual. He thought a moment. "I want our men to have as much sleep as possible. God knows they are worn out. Let us suppose the enemy has begun to embark as you report...and let us assume the process will consume three hours or so. They will be able to row across the channel in a few heartbeats since the tide will be with them."

The general pulled out a large watch from his deep pocket. He smiled. "Yes, gentlemen. This is, indeed, an English timepiece. A Graham pocket clock, they call it. Not very accurate, though. I have had to learn how to compensate for its false readings. If this instrument is to be believed, it is now one hour past midnight. Let us therefore allow our men to escape the worries of this world another hour before snatching them back to our hell. Do you agree, gentlemen?"

The general dictated two short letters, one for Col. Bougainville at Cape Rouge ten miles upriver, the second addressed to Governor Vaudreuil in his house ten rods away. The general handed the second letter to Dumas.

"If you would be so kind...."

Dumas passed the letter to Crèvecoeur who conveyed it to a sleepy Jean-Luc. He took it upon himself to wake up each of the company commanders before the call to assemble. First he went to rouse Duflot from his slumbers.

Duflot resisted.

"Come on, let's go," Crèvecoeur insisted.

"Go to hell. It's just another false alarm."

"It's the general's orders."

A muddy shoe came flying through the dark and hit Crèvecoeur in the chest. He felt his face flush. He strode all the way into the tent. He grabbed the frame of the cot and turned it over, spilling its living load onto the ground. For good measure he heaved the cot onto the object now lying on the floor. He gave the object a sharp kick then stepped out of the tent. He pulled out all the stakes, removed the two poles, then threw the canvas down onto the enraged bundle below. He was about to give the struggling beshrouded thing another good kick when a voice stopped him.

"What the hell is going on here?"

Crèvecoeur whirled around. Captain Dumas was standing stock-still. The lieutenant felt even if he could not see the blazing anger in his commander's eyes. In an instant he found his brain racing to fabricate an explanation, an excuse, a *lie*.

As though reading his thoughts Dumas cut him off at the pass. "Don't compound the sin. You will report to me later today at noon. Carry on." The captain turned his back and walked away.

At two o'clock the drummers beat out the energetic rhythm of reveille, *la Diane,* with its initial long beat followed by five quick ones; then a few moments later the rapid irregular fire of *l'Assemblée,* summoning the soldiers to fall into line. Within minutes they were in their places in the trenches.

Crèvecoeur joined Sanssouci down by the river. Sounds of activity continued from across the channel. A canoe bumped its nose into the jetty. "The enemy's on the move, that's for sure," the watchman reported. "I saw a dozen barges. Packed with grenadiers."

"All right. Go back out and keep an eye open," Sanssouci replied, yawning. He smiled, weakly, as if to hide his fear. "Why do the bastards always choose the nighttime to do this? I'm dead tired. I don't know which is worse: no sleep, or hardly any food."

At that moment musket fire echoed over the river from the west, from beyond Cape Diamond. The firing stopped almost as soon as it had begun.

"What was that all about?" Sanssouci wondered out loud.

"Don't know."

They stood still, ears now straining as well as eyes. The frogs had fallen silent and the turtles splashed no more. Quiet reigned all around them broken only by the eternal flowing of the river, making a soft whispering sound as the current meandered by and the tide crept in.

"I hope that wasn't our food boat being captured by the English," Sanssouci fretted.

Crèvecoeur could only shrug in the darkness.

A half hour later the other canoe-man came by. "The enemy barges are still just off the island. They haven't moved."

Crèvecoeur left Sanssouci with his thoughts of food and climbed back up the bluffs through the trenches where the stench of fear and weariness mingled with the odor of sweating men who had not bathed or changed their clothing for weeks. Senior officers were gathered around Montcalm, who by all outward appearances was living up to his name, only his eyes betraying the turmoil within. Crèvecoeur bowed, made his report. It was received with a nod of the head.

A cannon boomed once from the north side of the Upper Town. Unconsciously they all counted to ten silently to themselves. There was no further firing.

A look of puzzlement broke the calm equanimity of the general's countenance. He ordered a junior officer to go into the town post-haste to inquire of Chevalier de Bernetz, now in charge of the defenses of both the Upper and Lower Towns.

By and by the sky to the east began to awaken. Duflot came up from the beach.

"The enemy grenadiers have returned to their camps. The barges are empty."

Crèvecoeur received the news with an odd mixture of relief and frustration. He found himself again cursing the waiting yet dreading the fighting. And now they would have to endure that peculiar kind of hell all over again: the battle with one's own fear.

The general ordered his troops to retire. Six thousand weary souls on either side of the Saint-Charles retreated to their rest. Exhaustion and fatigue recognise no distinction of rank. Officers and privates alike threw themselves willingly into the arms of Morpheus and into the peace of oblivion.

Their peace was short-lived. Just as Glascoop was peeking over the horizon, the officer sent into town returned, accompanied by a militiaman whose ranting could be heard even before he came into view. Dumas turned out from his tent as did the general's aide Capt. Montbeillard. Crèvecoeur, too, came out, having found sleep impossible.

Seeing the officers, the Canadian rushed forward. He was alternately wringing his hands then throwing them up into the air. Whether he was sobbing or gasping for breath it was hard to tell. His long, loose hair fell all over his face, conspiring with his toothless gums and his terror-stricken eyes to give him all the appearance of a lunatic gone beyond the bounds of madness. It was though he had seen the very devil himself.

"He's here! He's here! He's here!" the man wailed. He threw himself onto Montbeillard.

The officer seized him with both arms and shook him.

"Get hold of yourself. What are you saying? Who's here?"

But the militiaman was too distraught to speak. He sagged to the ground, sobbing, Montbeillard's hands slipping up to the man's armpits before the officer threw him off in disgust.

"The man's lost his senses."

Dumas spoke up, addressing the junior officer.

"Where did you find him?"

"He found me, sir. I was going to see Chevalier de Bernetz like the general told me to do; but when I was about to go up to the Upper Town I see this crazy man here come running pell-mell at me down from the hill leading up to the Plains of Abraham. He says it was life or death, I had to take him to General Montcalm, says he. He says Wolfe has landed...."

Dumas stooped down and picked up the wailing bundle of skin and bones from the dust. He gave the man a slap. The man's crying turned into a weird chuckling.

"Tell us what you know. Tell us!" Dumas slapped him again.

The man's chuckling was now a bizarre laughing. He stared at Dumas, eyes shining with tears.

"I'm the only one! I'm the only one!" he cackled.

Dumas shook him again. "The only one what?"

"The only one left! The only one to survive!" The man gave a violent tremble as though something had departed from his body. He stopped laughing. His voice dropped to a whisper.

"It is Vergor. Captain Vergor. At Anse au Foulon. Wolfe's soldiers!" He was shrieking now. "Wolfe's men! They climbed the cliffs! They've taken the Heights! It's too late! It's too late!" He gave another cry and fell again to the ground, sobbing.

Montbeillard prodded the man's tattered backside with the disdainful toe of an elegant boot.

"He's stark raving mad. Anse au Foulon! Impossible."

"No! It's true!" the man moaned. He beat his fists into the dirt.

"What do I do with him, sir?" the young officer asked.

"I don't care. Just get rid of him." Montbeillard was thoroughly irritated. He glanced at Dumas, as the young officer led the sobbing Canadian over into the militiamen's camp and out of sight.

"I'm going back to sleep. Go up to the governor's and see what he has to say about this. If you find him awake, that is. You can wake me up if you learn anything important." With that Montbeillard returned to his tent.

But Dumas did not go up to the governor's. He was staring at the smoldering embers in the fire-ring as if looking for answers in the ashes.

They were all startled by the sound of popping from beyond the Upper Town. Dumas made up his mind. Quickly he made for General Montcalm's tent.

"Rouse the troops," he ordered over his shoulder to Crèvecoeur. He hurried past the general's startled *garde du corps* and strode directly into Montcalm's tent.

The general soon emerged in an agitated state. He frantically dictated a letter to a scribe while struggling into his *jusqu' au corps*. An orderly brought over his horse. Montcalm grabbed the reins to hoist himself into the saddle but then remembered he had forgotten to don his sabre.

From the Colonial Regulars' camp came the beating of the call to arms. Like a wildfire in dry brush the call was picked up within seconds by each battalion and in the militia. Montcalm hurriedly dispatched commands to his aides right and left, who passed them along in turn to subordinates before mounting their horses and rushing off with their commander in a gallop towards the bridge over the Saint-Charles, his senior officers and chief of staff not far behind, battle flags streaming.

Dumas and his Colonial Regulars reached the bridge in haste but then in frustration had to mark time. The flimsy structure was jammed with the Royal Roussillon ahead of them. Marching in unison was not allowed for fear the structure would collapse from the vibrations and so the soldiers shuffled forward awkwardly.

They could see ahead of them the Guyenne Regiment swarming up to the Heights just to the west of the Upper Town's walls and the figure of Montcalm on horseback in the lead. Far off to their right up the Saint-Charles they saw a group of militia and Indians negotiating the much more narrow old bridge.

An eternity passed before they emerged from the bottleneck of the bridge. As each successive wave popped free it fanned out and overspilled onto the road and surrounding terrain, rippling forward like a tidal surge onto a beach. They passed at a run the General Hospital, then the Commissary's palace, through the hamlet of Saint-Roch then the mad scramble up the slopes, each man and boy among them overcome with a frantic urge to see what awaited them at the top.

The Plains of Abraham was a misnomer. The topography was rough, uneven, irregular, more brushland than grassland. From the Saint-Jean Gate and Dauphine Redoubt, anchoring the northwest angle of the town wall, the ground swept sharply upwards towards the heights of Cape Diamond to the southeast overlooking the Saint-Lawrence River, like a tilt-top table set at a slant. Running along the southern ridge came the road from Sillery off to the west; the road from Saint-Foy formed the northern boundary of the Plains with its smattering of houses and farms. Between the two roads lay, closest to the town walls, a thin grove of trees which petered out into an expanse of grassy meadowland and brush sloping upwards to the west where, five hundred yards distant, a long scarlet line now stretched three-deep from south to north.

The scarlet line did not move. It resembled a picket fence, a very long red one. The uniformity of colour was marred only by a splash of dark green along its northern flank. The uniformity of height was broken only by two small clusters of figures on horseback at either end of the fence. But for the scarlet, the fence seemed to be just another feature of the landscape, so calm, so serene, so patient was it standing there, as stoic and inevitable as the rocks in the field.

There was nothing calm or serene among the white-coated defenders gasping and panting for air as they milled around in front of the town walls and the Saint-Foy Road, Montcalm on his horse in their midst, shouting out commands, gesturing with his sabre now right, now left.

"Stay put," Dumas said. He galloped over to the general and other senior officers buzzing around him. The captain rushed quickly back and shouted out orders directly to his troops.

Crèvecoeur found himself, on foot like everyone else, running as fast as he could westward along the road, past the houses of the hamlet, and then off to the right where the ground rose up to form a low forested ridge. Dumas, directing his companies, ordered Duflot to post the town militia which had joined them and Crèvecoeur to handle the Abenaki. Crèvecoeur spotted Megeso. They silently clasped hands and went to his chief. Crèvecoeur with the help of his friend explained the captain's orders and the Abenakis' role.

From their vantage point they had a clear view of the Plains. To their left the French Royal regiments clad in white were struggling to form up in front of the trees. To their right, almost at a perpendicular to the road, stood the three-deep lines of Monckton's scarlet-red grenadiers.

Monckton's flank was exposed. Dumas' regulars were at that moment maneuvering behind the Abenaki and militia crouched along the ridge, hoping to fall upon Monckton's rear at the right moment. But as if reading their thoughts, Townshend could be seen galloping up in the distance from the rear leading a regiment to seal the exposed flank; and to the English general's left were marching at double-time Colonel Howe's light infantry up the road followed by a regiment of American Rangers. Where on earth was Bougainville's cavalry, Crèvecoeur wondered.

A field cannon boomed from the English lines. A French artillery piece replied. The enemy's troops stood stock-still like statues. But not the French. Far off to the left, the middle of the French lines, the Guyenne and Béarn Regiments, began to advance to the shouting of officers and beating of drums while to their right the Languedoc and LaSarre, closest to the Saint-Foy Road, also stepped out.

Crèvecoeur saw with alarm that the LaSarre and Languedoc troops were advancing far too quickly. They were in a three-deep formation proceeding over more or less even ground whereas the Guyenne and Béarn were encumbered by a series of shallow ravines and thorn bushes and their own narrow, deep-column formation.

But oh what a glorious sight, Crèvecoeur thought. The luxurious soft royal white of the coats fringed with blue, capped by the elegant black of the three-cornered hats sporting a dashing array of coloured cockades: red, white, green and blue. In the lead, huge regimental flags, white cross against red and black squares, and their drummers in rich blue and red brocade. Just as bright white clouds carry within them a rainbow of colours, the royal regiments displayed among them homespun shades of black, brown and red, the militia's uniforms which were everything but. The whole resplendent multi-hued cloud of men and boys went surging through the golden grassy brushland and as they rushed forward now a terrible wail of fury and hope escaped from their collective throats.

The scarlet fence stood still.

The white-clad regulars and homespun militia in the leading edge of the cloud – to call it a line would do a disservice to geometry – was now less than a hundred yards from the enemy when one of the French soldiers, unbidden, abruptly stopped in his tracks, raised his musket and fired. His companions immediately followed suit. The troops directly behind them ploughed into their backs just as they were firing and so too the soldiers rushing forward in the third line like an accordion being squeezed. The regiment's officers swore furiously and hastened about, trying to restore order.

The scarlet line did not move.

The Royal Roussillon and Béarn Regiments in the middle by now had caught up to the troops on their right and, spurred on by the musket fire, precipitated themselves forward so that they now were in advance of both their right and their left. Eighty yards, seventy yards, sixty yards from the enemy.

The scarlet line did not flinch.

A loud bang boomed out from a knoll to the English right and a cluster of white coats went down, like sheaves of wheat mowed down by an invisible scythe. From somewhere behind the defenders' lines a cannon retorted in reply without seeming to make any impression upon the enemy.

A French officer's sabre flashed in the morning sun and another volley of musket fire resounded, this time from the entire French line. Gaps suddenly appeared in the scarlet fence. Then, from up and down the enemy's line could be heard commands to fire. A shudder rippled along the fence, barrels were raised, and muskets went off, company by company with the measured cadence of a drumbeat.

The English muskets had longer barrels and greater range than the French models from 1728 as proven by the dozens of white-coated soldiers who now fell to the ground. The Canadians stepped forward and fired in their turn, then they too dropped to the earth, not because they were hit but to reload which, to their way of thinking, made more sense to do lying down rather than standing up like the regulars were trained to do. The regulars, seeing scores of their militiamen falling to the ground, assumed they had been hit by devastating fire and were seized by panic.

At that moment, at the shout of an English command, the entire scarlet line, no longer a fence but now a wall, moved forth as one magnificent perfect body. The front row of grenadiers stepped forward in a perfectly timed cadence, knelt on one knee with perfect precision and they and the second row together raised muskets to cheeks, aimed and fired one thunderous volley in perfect unison.

The French troops, in imperfect unison, turned and ran. As their comrades fell right and left like ripe apples from a tree regulars and militia alike took to their heels as fast as the thorn bushes and men ahead of them would permit.

From Crèvecoeur's right came the popping of muskets. It was Dumas' Colonial Regulars who were now firing upon the English flank anchored by Townshend and the American Rangers.

Crèvecoeur understood. Fighting down his own fear, heart beating against his chest like a drum, he called out his Abenaki warriors. He heard Duflot do the same with the militia. They ran as fast as they could down the slope of their small ridge and onto the roadway to take up positions behind any object they could use for cover: trees, fence posts, boulders. Instinctively they knew what had to be done.

As Monckton's troops in the centre began to chase the French in headlong flight from the field, Townshend and the Rangers were trying to move up the road when Dumas began to fire upon them from the side. Now, as the English came running forward to avoid Dumas, they were met with a barrage of fire from the Abenaki and militia.

As the English dove for cover, the defenders retreated a few paces down the road toward the hamlet, stopped, reloaded, and fired again, repeating the maneuver until reaching the first of the several houses. During this time Dumas had been swinging his men along the woody ridge parallel to the road where Crèvecoeur had been, shadowing the English, preventing them performing any flanking tactic, harassing their lines, diverting them as long as possible to allow the main body of the French to escape down the slopes to the Saint-Charles.

Crèvecoeur's mind was racing as fast as his heart was pounding. He did not know what to do. He struggled to think clearly. He could see off to his left Moncton's forces cutting at an angle across the field heading to a point on the road behind him. The militia and Abenaki were scattered among the houses and barns but it was an impossible position.

A couple of militiamen ducked into a house and began firing out of a window up the road. Crèvecoeur yelled at them to get out of the deathtrap but had to give it up as futile. English field artillery began to bombard the houses and the road beyond.

The Abenaki decided it was time to take their leave. Duflot from behind a stone well was trying to shout out orders to the militia but they were too spread out to hear. Seeing the Indians padding away, the Canadians too commenced to flee from behind whatever cover they had been hiding as Moncton's men began to shoot at them from the field.

The Abenaki chief had waited, stoic and dignified, for his warriors to retreat. He turned his regard to Megeso, crouched behind a fence with Crèvecoeur. As despicable was the thought of running, the notion of capture was intolerable.

The three began their escape, crouching low, avoiding the road, running through a patch of Indian corn which soon gave way to a field of barley, hoping the grass might give them some cover. Crèvecoeur sensed behind him Duflot and a few of his militiamen.

Up ahead the road ended at the Saint-Jean Gates, flung wide open to allow gaggles of militia and irregular groups of regulars to flow through into the town while above, on the ramparts of the walls, sharpshooters were firing at the grenadiers who had begun to emerge from behind the grove of trees where the French troops had assembled only an hour before.

English field guns were now firing from the houses the Canadians had just abandoned, four-pound balls smashing against the stone walls of the town. From behind Crèvecoeur came the whistling of musket balls. One more minute, he heard himself praying. One more minute and we'll be at the gates.

The Abenaki chief went down. Megeso stopped and whirled. He stepped towards his fallen brother. At that moment Crèvecoeur felt a searing pain in his thigh and the back of his head as he stumbled to the grass. He looked up helplessly, cursing through clenched teeth, his head spinning, saw the walls so close by, saw his friend now hesitate, looking at his chief, then at Crèvecoeur and as their eyes met Megeso was hit square in the chest with the sickening sound of a musket ball.

Crèvecoeur felt himself falling into that peculiar, terrifying bottomless hole of utter blackness only unbearable pain can produce. He had fainted.

Chapter Sixteen: *Welcome to Paradise*

The anvil on which he was lying was hard and cold. The back of his head was pounded by the blacksmith's unmerciful hammer while the sadistic mechanic gleefully poked a red-hot iron into the back of his thigh. But Crèvecoeur was in a realm where the pain had been so continual that it became unremarkable, then dull; and now nothing more than a sensation of numbness.

Voices floated through him, coming from far away. The iron left his leg, the blacksmith went away. Birds busied themselves around his leg. He felt their wings brushing against his skin, now poking him with their beaks. His leg was elevated and dropped by invisible forces then something tight was wrapped around it. The forces grabbed his shoulders and turned his body over, raised his head from underneath and eased it down onto something soft.

"There. That's over with. Who's next?"

Crèvecoeur knew the voice from somewhere else, somewhere far, far away and a long time ago. He felt himself slipping back into the free-fall, into the black hole and was seized by a feeling of terror as he fought to pull himself back out. Something gripped him tightly and he came to rest. He opened his eyes.

The good sister was regarding him attentively with her deep green eyes as if seeing into his soul.

"There now. Don't try to move. Rest."

She took her hands away from his shoulders and folded them across her middle, watching her patient to make sure he followed orders. He was only too glad to oblige. Doctor Soupirant's face hove into view. His eyes were bloodshot as always and his brow creased with fatigue. A low grunt escaped from his lips.

"Good. You're conscious. I guess that means you're alive. I've been losing too many patients lately. Not good for one's reputation." The surgeon's gruff visage disappeared.

"Water," Crèvecoeur heard himself groan. He closed his eyes as he felt the nurse's hand cradle his bandaged head from underneath and the cold lip of the tin cup against his own and then the trickle of cool water. He drifted back into a deep sleep which even the dull throbbing pain in his leg and head could not penetrate.

When he awoke he experienced a moment of panic as he was sure his eyelids were open yet he could see nothing but blackness. He then realised it was merely the absence of daylight but whether it was dusk or dawn or somewhere in between he could not know. But then he was overcome by a sensation of peacefulness and was content to surrender himself to the flow of the water, letting himself drift in the current lead where it might.

By and by the filtered light of the dawn stole softly into the room and glowed all around. The worst of the pain was gone and Crèvecoeur was in that in-between place where the memory of the pain was still alive and the complacency of forgetting had not yet set in. It is that place where gratitude is most keenly felt.

He saw the angels, blue and white, above him in the air and the halo around the head seemed to glow, not from any reflected light but from a source within. He heard soft footfalls approaching and turned his head towards the door to the small room.

The good sister had entered, carrying a wooden tray on which half a loaf of bread sat next to a bowl. Steam came out of the bowl. Crèvecoeur suddenly realised he was famished. He devoured the bread despite the admonishments of his nurse and did not stop to wonder how it came to be that there should be fresh baked bread about.

He was forced to sip the broth it was so hot but even so he went at it without pausing. He was able to eat from a sitting position, the sister having propped a folded blanket behind his back, and she gently wiped remnants of soup from the whiskers which had sprouted on his jaw and around his mouth.

Still hungry, but satisfied for the moment, he lay back on the pillow and gazed at the nun.

"Thank you."

She nodded, smiled, fussed around the bandage on his left leg.

"You are the same angel that cared for that injured American Ranger…David…."

"The same servant," she murmured in reply. "It was in this same room as well. You're in the same bed as he."

"How fared he?"

"I pray for him every day. I pray he is where he begged to be right up to the moment he left us for a better place."

Crèvecoeur thought a moment. "How is it you are able to bring fresh bread?"

As if in answer a presence made itself felt in the doorway. Crèvecoeur turned his head. A foot soldier in the uniform of a Royal American infantryman was regarding him with bored blue eyes. He looked hardly older than a boy.

Crèvecoeur, startled, returned his gaze to the sister and their eyes met. She nodded her head, slowly.

Crèvecoeur slumped back into the pillow. "So it's all over then."

He felt a bitter taste in the back of his mouth. Unbidden, the image of DuChêne, of Megeso, of Father René flashed past his eyes. *Requiescat in pace.*

He turned again towards the sentry. "I suppose congratulations are in order," Crèvecoeur addressed the youth in English.

The young soldier stared blankly back.

Crèvecoeur repeated his words. The puzzled expression on the young man's face made him look more and more like the backwoods farm boy he most certainly was.

Finally the youth muttered, "*Entschuldigung.* I speak English only a little."

Crèvecoeur, curious, asked, speaking slowly: "Where do you come from?"

"Bremerhaven. North Sea. Mine family...we are now in Pennsylvania." The young German lad stepped all the way into the small room and stood at the foot of the bed. "Mine family, there is mine father and mine mother. And I have brothers and sisters."

"Where in Pennsylvania?"

"It is a small village near-by Philadelphia. The name is Germantown. Our farm is five miles away. We are not all in Pennsylvania. First, mine uncle said, he come with us. Then he said, no, he go better to Nova Scotia. He is gone to Lunenberg near-by Halifax. Many people from Hamburg and Bremen go there. There is free land for farms. The Indians there are friendly. They are not friendly in Pennsylvania. Maybe I go to Lunenberg after this. He is a good uncle. Mine uncle has the same name as I."

"And what is your name then?"

"My name is Johann. Johann Metzler. What is your name?"

Crèvecoeur reflected a moment.

"Michael. Michael Hector St. John."

Another day passed. Or perhaps it was two or three. Crèvecoeur lost track of time and found he did not care. He was propped up in bed, engrossed in a game of backgammon with Johann, when a familiar voice hailed him from the doorway. It was Duflot.

"Thought I might find you here. You look ghastly. Don't let the girls see you for a while. You need a shave, too."

Crèvecoeur was regarding his *confrère* intensely. "Aw, go to hell," he said. He smiled. "It was you who saved my skin, wasn't it?"

"It was distasteful work, but someone had to do it. Besides, I didn't want the lobster-backs to get to you before I had my chance to get even."

"I owe you my life. "

"Maybe someday I'll collect that debt."

Poor Johann was looking at the two French officers exchanging these strange words with a puzzled expression on his broad country face. Crèvecoeur sought to enlighten him.

"This man is my friend. He saved my life. He brought me into the town. He brought me here."

Now it was Duflot's turn to look puzzled, not understanding English. "What did you say?"

"I told Johann here what a son of a bitch you are."

Duflot nodded. "I thought so."

Johann folded up the wooden backgammon board, understanding the two others wanted to talk. He posted himself just outside the open doorway, leaving them alone in the room.

"You can sit down here on the bed. I won't kick you, I promise." Crèvecoeur was impatient now. "What day is it? What exactly happened? Is it really finished?"

"Today is Thursday. The twentieth day of September. In the year of our Lord 1759. A day which shall be recorded for all time as the day a French lieutenant – "

"Stop with the bilge, will you? Tell me what happened! Have we lost the war? Has Montcalm surrendered?"

Duflot regarded the other calmly. "General Montcalm has, indeed, surrendered. He surrendered his soul to the Lord about, let's see, the day after the battle…which would have been on the 14th, I think. He died of his wounds, my friend."

Duflot let the news sink in before continuing. "General Wolfe was killed, too. On the battlefield."

"And the governor? Captain Dumas?"

"Our valiant leader, the Marquis de Vaudreuil, lives on to fight another day. He's taken what's left of our troops upriver towards Montréal. Bougainville and Lévis are with him. I don't know about our captain. I suppose he escaped all right. They were all heading down the hill towards the Saint-Charles the last time I saw them. None of our Colonial Regulars are still here in the town, as far as I know, 'cept for you and me and a few other injured men. We're the lucky ones, I guess."

"And so the English captured the town?"

"Well, no, not exactly that. Colonel Ramezay…capitulated, two days ago. Said there was only enough food to last another week. Vaudreuil wrote him a letter allowing him to give up if he thought it necessary. All the militiamen had deserted anyway. General Monckton and General Murray are in charge now. Monckton's put his soldiers to work rebuilding all the houses they destroyed so his officers can have comfortable winter quarters in the style they so richly deserve."

"What's going to happen to us?"

"Well, I suppose that's a good question. I can answer part of it, though. Yesterday the general read out a proclamation. Said all Canadians who take a pledge of allegiance to the Crown of England and foreswear taking up arms forevermore will be allowed to return to their homes, farms, shops as if nothing had ever happened…promised they can keep the French language, the Catholic rites, even I suppose their dreadful tobacco, and the English will not bother them, as long as they never forget who their new masters are. The Canadian families are swearing allegiance already by the droves here in the town."

"Yes, but what about us?"

Duflot hesitated. He looked away, out the solitary broken window a moment, then turned his gaze back to Crèvecoeur, a smile in his eyes.

"Most of 'us' are going to go back home. You see, there are about a thousand royal French troops taken prisoner. Monckton, says he, has arranged for them to be shipped back home, to France. I'm going with them. We're supposed to be departing any day now."

Crèvecoeur reached out with his right arm to grab Duflot, as if by clinging to his mate he could hitch a ride with their ship. The effort made Crèvecoeur wince in pain and he dropped his arm to the bedside.

"I'm going with you," he gasped. "I'd like to see my father…."

Duflot, who had stood up, looked down with pity.

"If it were up to me, I'd say, sure, come along. But our new masters have decreed that all injured officers, and all invalids – I am sure you recognise yourself – in hospital must remain here in town. Monckton is trying to negotiate some kind of prisoner exchange with Vaudreuil. He plans on using you like *monnaie de carte*. I'm sorry, old boy."

Duflot gave Crèvecoeur a jaunty salute and turned to go to the door.

"Duflot. Do me a favour."

"Sure. What is it?"

"When you get to France look up my father, will you? The château is up on a little hill near a village called Pierrepont, about a dozen miles west of Caen. Let him know…I'm safe and sound…."

"The ship is supposed to be taking us to Le Havre. I'm going to my family in Poitiers so I guess I can go through Caen just as easily as Paris." Duflot gave a cheery wave of the hand and left.

Crèvecoeur felt suddenly empty, and very alone. He heard no more of a prisoner exchange, and admitted to himself he felt relieved.

By October he was able to walk again. He still had headaches and dizziness but they were now infrequent. Boredom and a lack of exercise were his new tormentors. Therefore when the English major came to fetch him and lead him to the Dauphine Redoubt he would have jumped with joy had his leg permitted it. As it was he almost outpaced the English gentleman and would have beaten him to the general's quarters had his leg not pained him so much on the stairs.

It was strange to see seated in the large, bright cheerful room a different figure in a different uniform.

"The French lieutenant from the hospital. Sir." The major was crisp.

Brigadier General James Murray was surprisingly young. But then, so had been General Wolfe.

Crèvecoeur bowed his bare head stiffly, errant strands of long reddish hair escaping from his queue just above the raw spot in the back of his skull, still sore, where he had received the blow. He felt awkward in the borrowed English ensign's uniform. The only articles of his former life he had managed to save were the scapular from Anne-Marie and ring from Father René, safely tucked away in his breast pocket.

"*Veuillez vous asseoir,*" General Murray said to Crèvecoeur in impeccable French, indicating an armchair nearby. "*Je sais que vous avez été blessé en défendant l'honneur de votre pays.*"

Crèvecoeur sat down and smiled in appreciation. "Thank you, General. That is most kind of you." He replied in English.

Murray's look took on a heightened interest. "*Mais c'est vrai que vous parlez admirablement l'anglais.*"

"If I could speak English as well as your Excellency expresses himself in French, then I should consider myself accomplished indeed."

Murray chuckled in spite of himself. "You show a lot of spirit, lieutenant."

The general was looking at Crèvecoeur intently. "'Tis pity fate would have it that you should be born a Frenchman."

"But were it not so, I would not have had the honour of meeting your Excellency."

Murray's smile was genuine. "I see that you are a follower of Leibnitz."

The general stepped over to the large carved oak table – the same one at which Governor Vaudreuil had been prone to preside only weeks before – and put his finger on the large

Italian globe adorning the corner of the tabletop, the true spherical shape of the earth dominating the flat surface of the imagination. The general turned the globe on its axis until his phalanx rested on the prime meridian, smothering London under his manicured digit.

"Therefore it should be apparent to you that we are witnessing the proof of Leibnitz' Law of Continuity and the unfolding before our eyes of God's predetermined harmony of order." The general's demeanor was relaxed, almost nonchalant.

He turned his gaze back onto his captive. "It is the destiny of the British Empire to fulfill the role God has assigned to us."

"I must admit to your Excellency that Leibnitz is too profound a thinker for my modest intellect."

"Perhaps then Hobbes would be more suited to your temperament."

"Or Montesquieu. *Si vous voudriez m'en accorder cette petite indulgence pour l'amour-propre de mon pays.*"

Murray's smile broadened. "*Exaucé.*" He reflected a moment, then continued: "I understand you were an aide-de-camp to Captain Dumas."

Crèvecoeur tried to stifle his surprise. How could Murray have known? From Duflot? Some deserter from Beauport? Sailor Fitch? He thought of his new German friend Johann. Perhaps his linguistic abilities were not as limited as he let on.

"Captain Dumas is an heroic fighter and a shrewd leader of men," Murray continued, seeing the look in his captive's eyes. "He does not choose his aides casually."

"If I may be so bold sire to ask whether Captain Dumas is still alive?"

"I have every reason to believe he is. He has been observed at Pointe-aux-Trembles in the company of Colonel Bougainville."

Murray continued observing Crèvecoeur intently. "You would not be harbouring, by any chance, a desire to rejoin him? Such a decision would not be a wise one. *La Nouvelle-France est finie.* The end of this theatre-piece has been written. It is only a matter of time."

"I do not want to rejoin them."

"I see." The general pursed his lips. He continued: "The British Army can be an El Dorado of opportunity for an intelligent, talented young man. Particularly one skilled in mathematics and literate in the two languages. Yes, I am aware of your abilities as a surveyor and cartographer. Then too, you are of noble descent."

"Your Excellency's confidence in me is most kind and I am honoured to be made a party to such trust. But I cannot raise my hand against my captain, or my former companions in arms."

Murray's eyes softened and he allowed himself a slight nod. He turned his attention back to the globe and absently gave the sphere a twirl. "I must confess my admiration for your loyalty and devotion to principle. They only add to my regret to not be able to welcome you into our brotherhood of arms. 'Tis a pity."

The general looked again at his captive. "There is a troop ship sailing for Halifax next week with our walking wounded. You will be on it, provided you pledge to not take up arms ever again against his Royal Majesty."

"Is there an alternative? My most ardent wish is to return to France."

"The alternative, lieutenant, is to remain here in Québec as a prisoner of war. As to sending you to France, I am afraid that is outside my purview. However, you might be able to procure a berth from Halifax to England and from there on to France, if you are able to afford the passage."

Crèvecoeur could not help but smile as he imagined the reaction of the ship's master to an offer of *monnaie de carte* in payment for the voyage across the Atlantic. Taking the young man's smile to mean acquiescence, General Murray nodded his head to the major still standing formally at attention.

"Please make the necessary arrangements for Lieutenant Crèvecoeur here."

With that Crèvecoeur was led out of the Dauphine Redoubt.

The maple trees were radiant with the red, orange and yellow of leaf-fall as Crèvecoeur was rowed out from the Lower Town to the waiting English ship. He saw with a pang in his heart the ruins of the Lamoureux house. The streets at least had been cleared of rubble. Stone and wood were stacked in neat piles next to houses waiting to be rebuilt. Scaffolding encircled the steeple of Notre-Dame-des-Victoires, townsfolk busy repairing the damage, the cross once again pointing heavenwards. The British flag with its own crosses of Saint George and Saint Andrew fluttered everywhere along the waterfront and above the ramparts of the Upper Town crowning the tops of the cliff, glittering with the false diamonds of Canada in the morning sun.

The sail down the Saint-Lawrence was as brisk and pleasant as the shipboard rations were repugnant and scarce. As they passed below Cape Torment Crèvecoeur searched with his eyes the spot where he and Megeso so long ago it seemed had fought to be the first to reach the cliff-edge. They skirted Île aux Coudres; at anchor on the western tip stood an English sloop, and in the meadows ponies grazed peacefully.

The next day's weather turned nasty and violent as the ship sailed past the Gaspé Peninsula through the Gulf of Saint-Lawrence into the Atlantic Ocean. English soldiers and captives alike were to a man violently ill in the rank, dark holds below the main deck. Crèvecoeur had never felt so sick in his life. He longed for his bed in the hospital, the hot soup and fresh bread, the soothing smile and gentle green eyes of the good sister. To fight off nausea, and fear of shipwreck, he forced himself to review in his mind every book he had ever had to study in English, from the Book of Common Prayer to Shakespeare and Milton.

By the third day the storm had gone from tempest to hurricane. It was impossible to stand up even if one had the strength for the ship was rolling and yawing as though on the back of a giant, wild bull whale bucking and plunging this way and that. It was all they could do to grasp onto the ropes criss-crossing the hold, designed for that very purpose, sitting in misery on the planked deck, awash in human effluent too disgusting to describe. With each lifting up and crashing down it seemed as though the entire vessel were being beaten by an enormous hammer and with each impact the ship should surely break apart and let the raging waters of the ocean pour in.

Through the fog of his misery the image of Jonah flashed through his mind, fleeing from the face of God into the stormy seas of His wrath. More than one wretched soul writhing on the wet planks of the hold could be heard muttering the Lord's Prayer throughout that terrible day and the next.

But then, as quickly as it had begun, the gale disappeared. The ship now seemed to only drift, bobbing in the swells. By and by a dim light filtered in through salty portholes. A soldier groped his way painfully to his feet and peered out. He sat back down in disgust. "We're in the doldrums," he muttered. "Out in the middle of the bloody ocean."

There was a loud banging on the decks above. A shaft of dusty yellow streamed down into their midst. A hatchway had been pried open. An officer appeared and ordered everyone topside. They were only too glad to oblige. One by one they climbed the ladder and emerged into the brisk air and bright light of day, stepping over the mess of broken spars and rigging cluttering the deck. The mizzen's broken top-gallant mast hung by a splinter aloft. Sailors were everywhere replacing shredded sails.

The midday sun was hard aft to larboard. Crèvecoeur approached an ensign. "Why is the sun not off our quarter bow?" he asked, puzzled.

The ensign looked at him with a wry look on his face. "I don't know about you, mate, but I'm glad just to be anywhere alive."

"Yes, but shouldn't we be bearing southwest if our destination is Halifax?"

"The storm blew us way off course. We went in a big circle. I guess we have to pick up the easterlies now to get back to where we want to go."

Crèvecoeur digested the news. "I've never been to Halifax," he mused. "What's it like? I heard it's a grim place."

"Oh, it's much, much worse than that," the ensign replied cheerfully. "It's a bloody, wicked place. Filthy barracks, filthy slums, mud and crud all over the streets. Prostitutes and taverns everywhere. It's a regular Sodom and Gomorrah, it is. I can't wait to get there!" he enthused.

The afternoon winds picked up, filling the sails. They surged westward through the night and the next day. Crèvecoeur tried to estimate their speed but had no point of reference. It was irrelevant anyway as the knowledge would do him no good.

The next morning an excited buzz ran through the holds. "Land. I see land!" Soldiers jostled around the portholes to get a peek.

Crèvecoeur ignored the hubbub. He was thinking how he could survive the winter in the wilds of Nova Scotia let alone afford passage back to Europe. But then, what, exactly, did he propose to do in France, other than visit with his cold father and, in passing, fight with his brother over the eventual inheritance? Norman Calvados unlike most of France did not recognise any right of primogeniture. And even if he inherited, was he prepared to oversee the estate, such that it was? The income from the tenant farmers was not enough to keep the château and outbuildings in good repair. Perhaps he would have to become his own tenant, a farmer himself. If so, he would have the grandest farmhouse to live in of any farmer in Normandy though with a roof which leaked worse than the most humble peasant *chaumière.*

His reverie was interrupted by excited shouting and a stampeding towards the ladder leading up to the hatchway, now wide-open. He too felt a surge of joy in spite of himself, but he held back, seeing no point queuing up for an hour for the ladder then three hours on deck waiting to disembark. He leaned back against the cold gunwale. What was the hurry? Where was he going to rush off to? His mind drifted. He amused himself with absurd thoughts. *Maybe after landfall I should migrate to Lunenberg, learn German, hire myself out to Johann's uncle.* Phrases popped into his head from long ago. Faces, images…a voice from somewhere reciting Milton. *"Nor love thy life, nor hate; but what thou livest, live well. How long or short permit to Heaven. And now prepare thee for another sight…."*

He sensed the vessel come to a standstill. Waves slapped against the stationary hull. He heard, and felt, the releasing of the anchor chains, sending a subtle vibration along the hull. He saw in his mind's eye the heavy black irons splashing into the water, the crews around the capstan now, tender boats rowing up to the ship from the shore….

One of the English laggards sprawled not far from Crèvecoeur hoisted himself up.

"Don't know which is worse, this bloody ship or that cursed hell-hole Halifax," he groused.

"Aw shut your trap. You know damn well inside two hours you'll have gills of good island rum pouring down your greedy gullet," his companion rasped. "Hurry up. Get your arse up the ladder."

Crèvecoeur too got to his feet, bringing up the rear. He stepped onto the deck and admitted he was glad to feel the breeze and the sun on his skin. He found himself in a sea of soldiers and sailors, officers shouting out orders, trying to organize the men to disembark. He could not see anything except the heads of those around him and the blue sky above criss-crossed with darting gulls crying out their shrill calls.

Crèvecoeur's line shuffled forward inch by inch. Finally his group neared the gunwale. They heard men ahead grunting and cursing their way down the rope ladder to a boat waiting for them below. Now Crèvecoeur's line reached the railing and the horizon opened up before their eyes.

The laggard from below decks let out a whoop of joy at the sight. "Well I'll be damned! Lord, Hallelujah!"

The town lay some two hundred yards away, docks crammed with vessels of all sorts and sizes. Above them rose a magnificent brick edifice capped by a cupola, with stepped gables in the Dutch style; and all around similar buildings stretching back away from the docks. To their left was a large fort and behind that the blades of a windmill churned lazily in the breeze. In the distance the tall, elegant gothic spire of a church pointed heavenward. On the open parade ground in front of the fort a company of red-coats was drilling. To Crèvecoeur's eyes the town appeared cheerful, tidy, busy, prosperous.

"Halifax is a lot bigger and grander than I've been led to believe," he remarked to his companion in misery.

The English soldier gave him a look of disdain. Then he broke out in a guffaw, nudging his buddy. "This frog-eater here thinks we're in Halifax!" he snickered.

"Halifax?" The buddy too gave a derisive snort.

"My friend," the laggard said, turning a mocking gaze upon Crèvecoeur, "this ain't Halifax."

"Then where are we?"

The boatswain who had been directing the soldiers onto the rope ladder looked at them with a broad grin on his face.

"Welcome, gents. Welcome to paradise," he proclaimed.

"Welcome to New-York."

PART TWO: KNOW THY ENEMY

Chapter One: *A Curse on Tyranny*

"Steady, boys, steady. Pike-men, at the ready! Rope-men, stand by! On the count of three: one, two, heave!"

With a heavy huzzah! the team of pike-men pushed upwards on their long poles, slowly raising the giant wooden H from inside the barn-to-be, the rope-men on the outside taking up the slack on the safety line looped around the beam and running down to the bull-wheel on the ground, an old ship's capstan around which ran the rope. The slack end of the line was fastened to the ox-cart, oxen coaxed into motion by the blacksmith's young boy John, proud to be at the head of the rope-team.

A loud cheer rose up from the frolickers as the first of the barn's massive oak frames came to an upright position. Men rushed over to hammer in the tree-nails through the temporary bracing. They repeated the procedure until, one by one, all five H-frames had been raised and the horizontal plates made fast along the top, creating a rectangular box.

The mid-June sun reigned directly overhead. An aroma of roasting pork and goose wafted through the sultry air. "Dinner time, lads!" Thomas Bull bellowed. The stout house-wright was already munching on a goose thigh. Hearing the cue, a knot of children skirmished to bang on the tocsin serving as signal bell next to the well. Bull's Negro slave Rodney broke out a fiddle.

A group of older boys and girls gravitated towards the music, girls on one side of the fiddler sitting on a stump, boys on the other, shyly stealing glances at each other while younger siblings ran amok on the grass in a game of tag. If the children weren't interested in food, the grown-ups were, and cider and beer, the better to wash it down.

"A toast!" proclaimed the grateful owner of the farm on whose land the new barn was being raised by neighbours come from miles around. "I offer a toast, to my esteemed friends; and to our good house-wright Mr. Bull. Thank you, Thomas." As St. John raised his cup with the left hand his right reached out to Bull, who hastily transferred the goose thigh to his left hand before extending a greasy right paw.

Bull exchanged his neighbour's hand for a tin cup of cider. He cleared his throat.

"Ahem. An' *I* propose a toast - to our noble friend here and his lovely bride. An' to our, to our, ah...." Thomas hesitated only a moment, looking around him with eyes royal-blue like the sky. He raised his cup higher in the air. "An' to our sacred rights as free Englishmen...under a good king. Here's to King George! Here's to his birthday tomorrow!" He brought tin cup to lips and drained it in one gulp.

"Hear hear! Long live the king," a raucous voice yelled out. "Of Prussia." Laughter greeted the joke.

"Here's another for you." A man of middlin' age stepped forward. Like all his neighbours Nathaniel Roe was dressed in a pale homespun blouse which failed to hide his strong, wiry frame. The man lifted up his black felt hat and smiled around, then raised his cup. "A toast to our *friends* in Parliament. Long live Isaac Barré."

Cheers competed with catcalls.

"And a drink to our friends Parliament refuses to seat. Long life to John Wilkes!"

Here the jeers were louder than the cheers.

Thomas' eldest brother John, called the Captain in deference to his old militia rank from the time of the French wars, took his turn. "*I* say Edmund Burke's the greatest friend America has. To Burke and the Whigs!" Capt. Bull proclaimed. Taller than his brother and just as stocky, he shared the family's prominent nose and ruddy cheeks.

A tall, austere man came forth. He was hatless despite the bright sun. His thick hair, prematurely grey, was combed back into a pony-tail, held neatly in place by an ornate gold and enamel clasp, lending an air of elegance to the rustic setting. Judge Henry Wisner, for all his prestige, held aloft a simple tin cup grasped by the strong hand of a farmer and mechanic.

"My toast is closer to home. Why look to England for protectors to thank? To our philosopher king Benjamin Franklin. And to our kindred spirit in Boston, John Hancock."

"Hear hear," voices chorused roundly.

"But", another chimed in hoarsely, "let's not forget the Sons of Liberty and Captain Isaac Sears in New-York City."

A woman slipped her arm through the judge's. She pushed back her white bonnet, letting out wisps of iron-grey hair the same colour as her husband's. She snatched the cup out of his hand and held it out in front of her at arms'-length.

"Why should only men be allowed to celebrate liberty? I, yes I, a woman, offer to toast." Mrs. Wisner raised her cup in the air. "*I* wish to praise a lady. Oh, I am so tired of hearing of *men*. Let us hear for once of the fairer sex. But whose womanly song calls out to our ears? Is there no one but ancient relics like good queen Elizabeth or distant foreign females like Catherine the Great? Is there no woman on our shores alive today, known to farmer, tradesman, or judge –" here a nudge to the side of her husband – "worthy of our praise?"

Sarah Wisner looked around her at the blank male faces, not expecting any serious response to her question. "Well, of course there is! They may not know her in London, Paris or Petersburg; or for that matter, in Boston, Philadelphia or Charleston; but *we* know who she is, don't we? To us she is great."

"Mercy, Sarah! Hush now. She'll hear you." Mary Carr Bull, Thomas's wife, admonished. "You know how modest she is. You will mortify her."

Sarah tossed off the contents of the judge's cup and wiped her mouth with a dainty sleeve.

"Judge Wisner!" Mary Bull protested.

The judge assumed his most dignified air. "There are certain matters outside of my jurisdiction. And best left that way," he added, with a wink to Thomas.

Sarah Wisner put a hand on Mary's sleeve. "Now, Mary, say no more. You must learn to be more tolerant." She smiled to remove any offence from her remark. "Just look over yonder. Our dear Sarah Bull needs no public adulation. Her progeny speaks for her."

Sarah Wells Bull's progeny, in fact, was everywhere in evidence and all around her. If not all twelve then at least six of her adult offspring were there at their neighbour St. John's barn-raising frolic; and no less than two dozen grandchildren and great-grandchildren. There were times, visitors would remark, when half of Ulster County and most of neighbouring Orange seemed to be descended from Sarah and William Bull.

The matriarch herself was standing in the middle of an imaginary circle in the grass of the yard behind the new house, built the autumn before by her son Thomas, under contract with their distant neighbour in consideration of seventy-five pounds. She was holding her left arm aloft and clutching in her hand the end of a dozen slender white ribbons made of old flax linen-cloth while a gaggle of giggling children raced around their human May pole. Someone – maybe herself – had crowned her head with a garland of wildflowers.

"A remarkable lady," remarked the constable, freshly elected, of nearby Goshen Township and proprietor of the Yelverton Inn two miles down the road. His drawl simmered with the Welsh overtones of his ancestors. "Even more remarkable is seein' how kindly the dear marm treats a sinner like me."

"Owning an inn is a respectable occupation," Judge Wisner observed. "One cannot be granted a licence without proof of good character and moral behaviour. And to be elected constable! Such an office would be incompatible with a dissolute character."

"But," Yelverton pointed out, "the election to such office *is* compatible with being the owner of an ordinary and serving up on election Tuesday plenty of good, free rum and lots of it." He flashed a grin of yellow teeth before raising his cup to his lips.

"'Tis good for you I'm going hard of hearing in my advancing age. If I had heard what you just said I would be duty-bound to enforce the law against bribery and have you arrested."

"But I'm the constable! I can't arrest myself."

"That would be odd, I'll grant you that." Judge Wisner held out his cup for another round of cider, brought around by a demur dark-haired young woman. "I suppose I could call upon our county sheriff, Jesse Woodhull over yonder, to clap you in irons."

The judge smiled at his hostess. "Thank you, Mrs. St. John. And congratulations, my dear," he added, gesturing with his cup towards her rounded midsection.

"Aya, I thank thee, Judge," came her reply, a suggestion of Boston in her voice. As she filled his cup she gave the judge a shy smile. "There's a-plenty more a-coming, I pray." Green eyes sparkling, she moved on with her pitcher to the inn-keeper, then to the house-wright.

"On the other hand," Wisner continued his ruminations, "I could declare the election a fraud and then you would no longer be constable."

"Ah, but then, if I were stripped of that office, it would fall on the runner-up. You wouldn't want that, now, would you?"

"Claudius Smith? No, I suppose you might be right. Being constable calls for a level head, and a sober one, and not a hot head. On the other hand, he is a bold, courageous fellow, that Smith, and they say he has a generous heart as well. Which he wears on his sleeve, perhaps to a fault."

"Is it wrong then to be honest in what you say?" Sarah Wisner asked. "Should we rather be dishonest in saying only what others want to hear?"

"My dear," Judge Wisner replied, "if a man has a wart on his nose would it be a virtuous thing to call his attention to it, and thus hurt his feelings, notwithstanding the truth of the statement?"

"Ah, but there, my dear husband, you place your finger on the true issue. 'Tis not so much what one says, but what one's purpose is in saying it. What is important is what motivates the heart of the speaker. If his motives are pure, if his intentions are honest, then what matter the words?"

"But, Mrs. Wisner," Nathaniel Roe injected, having listened to the debate with interest, "God knows how hard it is for me to read a news-paper, let alone the hearts of men. I can only judge by what a man says and does."

"Or how good he is at holdin' his likker," Yelverton threw in. "That's the real measure of a man, by me! You can keep y'r beer and y'r cider. Show me the man who can take his gill of rum and then ask for more without flinchin', and I'll show you a worthy fellow."

"But Abe, is that not cider there I see in your cup?" Thomas Bull asked politely.

Yelverton took a hasty swig. He turned the cup upside down to show nothing dripping out. "You see naught of the kind. As you will notice, it is empty."

Their host, Michael St. John, had circled back, even as his wife was orbiting away. He was carrying a hefty jug. "I thought I heard a call for grog."

"A welcome statement! I like what this man says." Yelverton was the first to hold out his tin. "An' I like even better what he does."

"You ought to like it," Wisner observed, "since it undoubtedly comes from your own store."

"The rum, yes, the water, no. But both the rum and the water are the product of a free people."

Judge Wisner winced as the Negro fiddler, scratching out a popular Scottish air, hit a sour note.

"Then I accuse you, Abijah Yelverton, of base hypocrisy. You charge for your spirits. You ought to distribute your rum free every day, not just Election Tuesday."

"No tavern-keeper hereabouts, not John Brewster, not Zach DuBois, pours out rum as freely as I so long as a man has coin or good credit! See here. I have principles, after all. An' the rights of a free man. So, I am free to make money!"

Yelverton downed half his cup before raising it high.

"Another toast!" he yelled out. "Here's to Lord North and the repeal of the Revenue Act!" A loud Huzzah! rose up from the frolickers.

Thomas Moffat, owner of the nearby grist mill on Crommelin Creek, raised a mug.

"I offer a toast to the Quartering Act."

Jeers and boos met his offering. "A pox on forcing Parliament's soldiers on a free people," a voice yelled out.

"But the City's misery is our gain," Moffat pointed out. "A garrison needs lots of flour and beef. We all profit from the presence of the troops and, since they are some seventy miles distant, we endure none of the hardships. An' even better, Gen'r'l Gage pays us in good English sterling. God knows we need coin. We get the money, without the inconveniences."

"That's not true. We do endure hardships we ought not. We all pay taxes that they may eat and drink and be clothed in their fine fancy uniforms," a feisty sunburned man with straw-blond hair interjected, a hint of anger in his voice.

Elihu Marvin had joined the group. Like most of the circle he was just north of forty summers, give or take a decade, among the first or second generation of European immigrants to the wilderness just west of Hudson's River and south of the old Dutch village of Wyltwyck now called Kingston. Albany was a three days' walk to the north and the City of New-York a ferry boat ride from the village of Newburgh plus a two days' march to the south.

"But at least the taxes we pay are imposed by our own elected Assemblymen of our own Colony," Moffat rejoined. "Among whose members we find you yourself, Judge Wisner! As well as our neighbour George Clinton."

"But," Nathaniel Roe pointed out, "the Assembly voted the money under duress. Lord Hollingsworth ordered the Assembly dissolved if they continued to refuse."

"That smells awfully like tyranny if you ask me," Marvin shot back, looking with blazing blue eyes at Moffat. "It's the Stamp Act of '65 all over again. Parliament treating us like slaves. Maybe it's true they dropped the tax on paper and paint, but they kept it on the tea! And they still force us to buy all our necessities from England. We're not even allowed to make our own door hinges."

"You do it anyway, Eli!" Judge Wisner chuckled. "As well as ploughshares, anvils, hammers, nails, horseshoes."

"A man's got to make a living, don't he? Besides, you forgot to mention cooking-ware. Your women-folk are my best customers."

"How dare you accuse us of complicity in crime, Mr. Marvin," Sarah Wisner laughed. "Especially in view of the fact it is the royal governor who appointed my good husband judge."

"Our acting governor, dear," Wisner corrected his wife. "Cad Colden is still just a humble farmer at heart. And lieutenant-governor of New-York in his spare hours."

Yelverton, not hearing the edge of irony in Wisner's words, spoke out, a burr to own his voice. "Beg to differ with you Judge, but Cadwallader Colden is neither humble nor a farmer. The richest family in Ulster County! 'Tis not enough they own the monopoly on the ferry boats in Newburgh; he gets a salary of two thousand pounds a year for being lieutenant-governor and God knows how much in rent from his tenants."

"I can tell you what I owe him," a young man, Jonathan Tuthill, spoke up. "Twenty bushels of wheat and ten cords of firewood a year for the right to farm a hunnerd acres of his land. An' he credits me two shillings six pence a load to take wood down to his depot on the river, although what he does with it I don't know."

"He ships it down to the City, to His Majesty's troops, that's what he does with it," Thomas Moffat informed him. "For the ripe sum of four hundred pounds a year he supplies Fort George with firewood and candles. By duly approved Act of our Assembly."

"For which we pay the taxes," Yelverton groused.

"But Abe, you as constable are paid by our taxes and licencing fees," Thomas Bull needled him.

"Hardly a-tall. I'm mostly paid out of the fines I collect. It's the county sheriff who gets paid a salary. Like our good judge here. An' it's my misfortune to live among such a group of law-abiding and pious citizens. Nary a Sabbath-breaker nor disturber of the peace in sight. A little less rectitude and a wee more frivolity would be healthier for my purse."

"What, am I hearing Abijah Yelverton pleading poverty?" Thomas Bull feigned incredulity. "With the prices you charge for victuals and drink!"

"All scrupulously within the limits imposed by law," the tavern-keeper replied solemnly.

"And not a penny less!" Moffat rejoined. "There's the mark of the shrewd businessman."

"I have no choice but to charge as much as the law allows. Since Parliament closed off our foreign ports we're forced to buy our molasses and sugar from English traders only, who can't meet our demand. So they jack up their prices. As their prices go up, so must mine."

"There you go again, blaming Parliament." Richard Bull, Thomas' younger brother, offered a smile which fell short of his eyes. "Is it Parliament's fault it cost so much money to defend our frontiers against the French and the Indians? Was it Parliament that provoked Pontiac to go on the warpath? Or was it our own people who insisted on pushing into the Ohio valley?"

Elihu Marvin's eyes flashed. "It was us in the Colony of New-York what paid for Gen'r'l Amherst's army to go up to Quebec in '59, warn't it? It was our own blood what was spilt fighting Pontiac, warn't it? Go ask your brother Cap'n John what he thinks about that. He was there."

Marvin spat on the ground, narrowly missing Richard Bull's boots. He looked at Nathaniel Roe, watching the discussion intently.

"Go ask your dad, Nat. Go ask Cap'n Roe. He was there with Cap'n John. Ask 'em whose blood was spilt. We all had family and friends what lost lives there."

Marvin was staring hard at Roe, whose older brother David's bones had never been recovered. In response Roe raised his cup high in the air.

"A toast!" he proclaimed. "A toast to peace and prosperity and good will to men."

"I second that!" Thomas Bull, standing more or less in the middle between Marvin and Richard, waved his felt hat in the air. "Here's to good neighbours and friends."

The evening sun was slipping behind the chalky ridge of the Shawangunk Mountains to the west when Bull stopped work for the day. Most of the folk had already left. Home for many was a five-mile walk or cart-ride away.

"We're after bein' done with the rafters. Let the boys have a bite to eat and let 'em git home before dark. We'll put on the shingles tomorrow."

The shingles in question, freshly riven and shaved that afternoon by teams of older boys, were stacked in neat piles on the ground, guarded by Bull's son George, proud his team had won the contest for producing the most.

"The last thing you'll do," Marvin said, gesturing at a wooden box-like structure sitting in the grass, "is to put the cupola on top. I'll send my slave boy Cato back tomorrow to help you."

St. John shook their hands. "Thanks to you two friends my new house will stand forever, and my new barn will outlast the house. Come on. Supper's a-calling. Let us eat, drink and be merry."

They went over to the make-shift table, tomorrow's wall-boards placed on barrels, where Mrs. St. John was spreading out leftovers from dinner. St. John gave her a hug, then brought over a large brassy object and set it on the boards, a shiny tin-plate weather-vane in the form of a rooster.

"Thank you, Elihu, for making this for me. Perhaps tomorrow Cato will do me the honour of placing it on my new cupola."

"My pleasure. I'm obliged to my nephew Yelverton for smuggling the tin-plate for me."

St. John poured out another round of cider. He smiled at his neighbours.

"I offer a toast to a land where every farmer is free to put up his own weather-vane and to keep it there despite which way the wind blows."

He raised his cup high.

"A curse on tyranny."

His two friends solemnly raised their own cups and clanked them together with his.

"A curse on tyranny."

The breeze from Canada had chased away the humidity of late June and the dirt of the roads was dry. The morning sun illuminated the full glory of the yellow mustard in the meadows; and the bright orange of the day-lilies, standing at attention and saluting their waggon-cart as they trotted by, was glorious. Even Purgatory Swamp just to the south smelled sweet that morning. The wild roses guarding the limestone manse of the old William Bull homestead were still in bloom, white and pinkish petals looking like pearls of snowflakes after a spring snowfall.

With a gentle tug of the reins St. John bade the horse to stop and the animal obliged, then of its own accord advanced just enough to align the side of the waggon with the landing next to the white picket fence garnished by hollyhocks and red-orange trumpet vines. Mehetable offered her cheek; St. John took her lips. He sprang out of the cart and dashed up the three steps to the landing to take his wife's hand and guide her down to the grass. From out of the waggon he retrieved her sewing basket and small bundle of fabric. Hand in hand they strolled across the yard and onto the low stoop, broad Dutch doors wide open to let in the cooling breeze.

Over in the barn, from across the way, field hands could be heard on the threshing floor bundling hay, and from the pen outside the bleating of sheep and the mournful lowing of cows. A couple of older boys was busy with knives under an oak tree, where they had raised up a slaughtered steer with block and tackle, and which had likely provoked the distress of the bovine nearby. The pigs in the neighbouring pen, however, were grunting in delighted anticipation, sniffing the scent of the steer's offal in the air, soon to be offered to them as a mid-morning treat.

"And here we part company for the day, my dearest," St. John gave Mehetable another kiss.

He saw a flicker of anxiety flash across her eyes.

"No need to feel shy, my dear. You are amongst friends and neighbours."

" 'Tis not me for whom I worry."

"Then it must be your father in Boston. He is an able man. And a careful man. And, most importantly, a good man."

"I worry about him, that is true enough." She looked intently at her husband, hesitated, then smiled. "I suppose it's all just the flux and fuss of a woman with child."

"Even more reason you must not fret. For our child's sake."

Mehetable glanced away, looking across the sunlit grassy yard, the prosperous pens full of the fat of a generous land, the bountiful orchards, and yonder to the south, to the low hills where their own farm lay, near the hamlet called Blooming Grove just across the invisible border between Orange and Ulster Counties, as though she were seeing something even further beyond.

"What a paradise God has given to us...." she murmured.

"Mehetable! Is that you I hear? Don't be shy, girl, step on in," came an alto invitation from inside the house.

St. John gave his wife a hug and a squeeze. "Don't you worry now. Everything will be fine. Here, your basket and cloth. We shall have the finest quilt in all the Colony."

The women-folk gathered together at Sarah Wells Bull's quilting bee were in a merry humour. They finally had a chance to escape the demands of their homes if only for an afternoon. The baking was done for the week and the washing would be done on the morrow. Today was their day.

Their escape was not total, however. Crawling around their feet on the reed mats covering the wide pine floor-boards of the Bull's long-room were several young children, watched by a couple of older girls not quite of the age to partake in quilting but old enough to lead the children in reciting their ABC's.

"Phebe! Let Mrs. St. John have her place." Hannah Holly Bull, Capt. John's wife, sounded severe but her face was serene. It was the serenity born of a stubborn will to survive, to persevere through countless childbirths and premature mournings, whispered rumours of wars and massacres, and a thousand and one daily chores needed to overcome another day which left no room in her heart for petty annoyances.

Phebe, thick reddish-brown hair neatly braided under her butter yellow bonnet, obediently vacated the chair and called out to the fledglings to gather 'round her by the spinning wheel in a corner of the room. Her blonde cousin Patience sat next to her, a slim volume in her hand. "Daniel, Esther, Chrisse! Come take your place." Phebe tried to sound severe like her mother, but her register was too high and the young children giggled.

Hannah, auburn hair under her cap still as thick and luxuriant as her daughter's, had risen to give Mehetable a hug and lead her to the seat of honour at the quilting table, in ordinary life the guest bed, relocated for the occasion and placed on wooden risers. The other women ensconced around the rectangle greeted the newcomer in turn, hands busily rummaging in their sewing kits. Squares of fabric of various colours were strewn here and there on the linen backing-cloth.

"I am sorry for the tight space," Hannah smiled.

"There's plenty of room, Mrs. Bull," Mehetable demurred. "Although perhaps not so in a few months' time, God willing."

"When do you suppose the blessed event will occur?" asked her neighbour on her left. Esther, Capt. John's sister, bit her lower lip slightly. None of her four children had survived infancy.

"Methinks early December, ma'am."

Margaret Bull Horton, another sister, patted Mehetable's hand gently. She and husband Silas lived not far from the St. Johns', near Otterkill Creek, in a fine house erected by Thomas upon his sister's marriage. Over the following thirteen years the footfalls of little feet were frequently heard on its floorboards. Only two of their five children thus far had been the occasion to don mourning clothes.

"We will be sure you and baby have all the best of care, my dear."

"I thank thee, Mrs. Horton."

"Oh, please, do call me Margaret. After all, we're neighbours now."

"Mehetable." This from the matriarch Sarah Wells Bull at the opposite end of the table. "I don't know you've ever been introduced to our good friend here Mrs. Colden. Elisabeth, Mehetable St. John."

"Pleased I'm sure to make your acquaintance." Elisabeth Colden's smile, though warm, had a regal air about it. Although she, like the others, wore a cap and shawl, hers were of silk, with elegant borders of gold and silver threads.

"Likewise, I am sure, ma'am," Mehetable murmured shyly.

"My husband's father, Cadwallader Senior, speaks very highly of *your* husband, Hector. Although," she added, "we are all a little bit confused over his name. In his correspondence with my father-in-law your husband signs his letters as 'Hector St. John'. Therefore my father-in-law refers to him by that name.

But my husband Cadwallader Junior knows him by the name of 'Michael'. And so, when my two Cadwalladers talk about your Hector and your Michael we have oft-times quite a tangled skein of wool to unwind before we know quite whom we are talking about."

"My dear Bess," Hannah Bull placed a calloused yet gentle hand on her friend's arm, "we have much the same muddle when we discuss your husband and your father-in-law! It will not do to merely say 'Cadwallader' for then the other knows not a-tall whether one means Cadwallader the lieutenant-governor, or Cadwallader the attorney.

"I think, my dear, you should ask your father-in-law to have our Colonial Assembly prohibit parents from naming their offspring after themselves! Each child, after all, is its own individual and should have its own identity; and this would make things less confusing."

"But what then, good sister-in-law, shall we do with all of us named 'Mary'?" asked Mary Carr Bull, Thomas' wife, smiling at her young niece and namesake sitting across the table. "Or with our dear Elisabeth, whose husband's sister is also Elisabeth! Perhaps the Parliament should place a tax on repetitive Christian names."

"At least," Elisabeth Colden observed, "our dear new neighbour Mehetable carries a name few here in Ulster County have. If you don't mind my asking, are you from Massachusetts-Bay?"

Mrs. St. John nodded her head, blushing. "I was raised near Boston, where my mother was from; although I was born near New Rochelle, in Westchester County, where my father's father had settled after coming over from France."

A moment of silence ensued as the women finished threading their needles and searched in their kits for pins to fasten their squares of fabric in place on the linen backing of the quilt-to-be. The tall, majestic floor clock ticked from the hall with a reassuring regularity.

The long-room was exactly that, spanning the length of the tall stone house completed forty years previously. When Captain John inherited the place – his father William having died and his mother Sarah remarried - he repaneled the rooms in the latest Georgian style. The elegant moulding gracing the fireplace and windows, painted buttermilk blue, testified to the family's prosperity, as did the eighteen panes in each of the sash windows, arranged nine-over-nine.

"I'm sorry, Mary – Mary Carr Bull! - but I must borrow a few of your pins. I'm afraid I've run out." Hannah sighed. "My husband refuses to let me buy more. He says he'll be...struck by lightning first rather than buy any more merchandize from England. Says we'll just have to make do with substitutes."

"That's easy for a man to say!" Mary, Thomas' wife, spoke out, indignant. "Our men need only wrought iron and wood to fashion the tools *they* need. Try to make fine sewing pins and needles out of wood or iron."

"Well, when I was a young lass we did one better," Sarah Wells Bull remarked. "When my man and me was just married and was livin' in our log lean-to, just over yonder where our smoke-house is now, an' I needed to darn his britches and me my skirts, I used bone needles our Indian friends gave me. Times were hard back then. We were prett' near the only white folk this far in from the river."

Mrs. Colden reached for her friend's and placed a soft object in her upturned palm. "Here, Hannah, have this pin cushion. Isn't it lovely? I adore the pink satin on top and the white silk below, and those little gold tassels."

"Oh! Elisabeth. I couldn't...." Hannah protested. But her eyes said otherwise, entranced by the perfect, shiny steel slivers standing at attention in the pin cushion.

"Of course you can, dear. You must. For the comfort and happiness of Mehetable's baby. Is this your first time?" Mrs. Colden, looking at the young woman, hazarded a guess.

Mehetable nodded. "Aya. I pray all will be well."

Mrs. Colden nodded her head shrewdly. "You are the only girl in your family."

Mrs. St. John smiled. A faint flush in her cheeks brought out the small freckles in her face, in pleasing contrast to her hair so black under the bonnet it almost bespoke of blue. "I have a brother, Samuel. An' distant cousins, in Westchester."

"Where will you baptise baby?"

"There, Bess, time enough for that I'm sure," Hannah interjected.

"Oh, no ma'am, I don't mind. We would be thinking of our meeting-house in Blooming Grove but for there is no regular preacher right now. My husband has mentioned Pastor Tétard who is with the French Church in New-York City."

Elisabeth Colden's eyebrows arched slightly. "Catholic, then, I suppose? I was not aware Catholics were allowed in New-York."

"No ma'am. Protestant. It is a Calvinist church, of the Company of Geneva. Reverend Tétard sometimes preaches up in Westchester as well. He married us there."

Mrs. Colden nodded, understanding. "Your father is descended, then, from the French Huguenots. That explains New Rochelle. What is your family name? We have many friends amongst the Huguenot settlers in New Paltz and Newburgh."

"Well, my father's name is Tippet. My mother was a Merrill an' her family was of the Congregation Way. I reckon for that reason my father fit right in, what with him being from the Protestant Calvins."

"Tippet...interesting name. I don't believe I have ever met a Tippet before."

Mehetable gave a shy laugh. "My father's father pronounced it *tippé.* But my father gave up long ago and so we're now just plain *tippett,* like what one does with a pitcher of tea when pouring out."

"Or like the robe the Presbyterian pastors wear around their shoulders," Mrs. Colden observed, smiling in return. "Is your father still in New Rochelle?"

"He is a merchant, like his father before him, an' so he has a house and depot in New Rochelle, but he lives mostly in Boston now since my mother's death." A cloud passed over Mehetable's eyes. "Times are not good for him. He deals mostly in Medeira wine but now he's forced to go through English middlemen and the prices and the taxes are too high for his customers. An' anyway his customers won't buy wine anymore."

"You must tell your dear father that he has a new customer," Mrs. Colden smiled. "I shall write to him myself."

There was a hub-bub of excited voices outside. One of the older boys who had been butchering the steer came running in. "Ma! Ma! The cat-whipper's come by! He's just outside the door. Wants to know if you have shoes in need of mending."

Hannah looked up from her stitching. "Don't get blood on the floor, William, or you'll be licking it up! Tell 'im to go 'round back, to the summer kitchen. I'll be there in a moment. And don't call him a cat-whipper. He'll be offended." She resumed her needlework, finished her row.

"Yes, I declare this will be a fine quilt! Excuse me a moment while I do my business with the cobbler. I have shoes to mend, all right, but don't know if I have enough coin. Perhaps he'll take some hides in exchange." She went out into the centre hall. The clink of a door latch rising and dropping was heard.

Sarah Wells Bull gave a little dry chuckle. "How spoilt we have become! Tradesmen comin' to our home to wait on us hand 'n foot. Young lady," she addressed Mrs. St. John, "count your blessings you can raise your children in civilised society, where vendors an' weavers an' cobblers come right to your front door!"

The ancient lady shook her grey head. "To think my step-papa packed me off on that small sloop from the City to go up Hudson's River with no more company than three Indian guides an' his two hired carpenters – imagine, me, a wisp of a girl only eighteen! - sending *me* up here, to the dark wilderness, to claim *his* share of the Wawayanda Patent, giving me all of two barrels o' flour, a couple of axes an' hammers an' a saw, a cow an' a horse an' a cart; an' - *two* pair o' boots!"

"Methinks I'd be 'way too frightened to do such a thing, myself. Were you not afraid, ma'am?" Mehetable asked, looking at the petite, white-haired old lady in awe.

" 'Twould be dishonest o' me to say I wasn't. But I was young, an' I was confident my step-papa wouldn't be putting me in harm's way. I figgered he knew I would be safe. I found out later he had no notion a-tall what he was sending me into, but by then it was done, an' then he come up himself, an' then I met my husband William who come up a couple o' years later, an' he built us this fine stone house here, an' our Indian neighbours were our friends, an' so I say work hard, treat others like you want 'em to treat you, an' put your faith in the Lord. That's my advice to you, young lady."

Sarah Wells Bull shook her head slowly as she drew her needle deftly through the fabric, red and blue thread outlining a bouquet of thistles, roses and lilies. Her wrinkled old eyes were as clear and sharp as her needle.

"Nope, back then...let's see, we first cleared this land after our marriage...started to put up this house in 1722 – right over the spring, it's in our basement – back then there wasn't no talk of boycotts or tar an' feathering the king's officials or sons of liberty or liberty poles. I don't understand what the fuss is all about.

"We *have* liberty. We own our farms. We have our land. We have plenty to eat. We should be giving thanks to our king. If it weren't for him, pretty soon the mobs will be comin' after honest, hard-working people to take away what we worked our whole lives for."

Hannah had returned to the quilting table and resumed her seat. "Mother, I've never heard you talk this way."

"I may be old but I'm not stupid. I can still see better than a lot o' people."

"Maybe," Esther Bull perked up, "things will be better now." While listening to her mother she had been watching the children out of the corners of envious eyes, amused by Chrisse the youngest boy snatching away a finger puppet out of the hands of his young sister Esther, who pulled in protest at the skirts of her cousin Patience.

"My husband Silas says people aren't so angry now that the tax on most things has been repealed. He told me this morning not to fret, the worst is over," Margaret Bull Horton sighed.

Over in the corner Patience made Chrisse return the prize to his sister. The boy glared.

"I hope you are right," Elisabeth Colden remarked. "I sincerely do hope so. But the mob attack on the king's soldiers in the City and their looting of all those poor small shopkeepers was only six months ago; and Isaac Sears is writing a lot of nasty, false things in the *New-York Journal*. Telling folk to tar and feather anyone who doesn't agree with his thinking. They almost tarred my father-in-law five years ago after Parliament passed the Stamp Act. As it was they burned his coach and hung up his effigy. It seems they inspired the Boston rabble to burn and loot Thomas Hutchinson's house."

Mary Carr Bull saw the look in Mehetable's eyes. "There, now! We're distressing our poor Mehetable. Well, sister, did you get the better of that cat-whipper?"

"Shh-h!" Hannah shushed. "Mr. Mills is just outside, on the porch." She looked behind her a moment, then turned back around and laughed. "Well, maybe he did let me take him down a peg or two because times are hard; or maybe because the Assembly just lowered the fee for his peddler's licence; or maybe I'm just getting good at negotiating, like Bess' husband. Mr. Mills agreed to mend our boots and shoes for only six shillings nine pence, if I give him the leather for it. What do you think of that?" She smiled in triumph.

"Hannah, you should be a lawyer." Margaret Horton admired.

"Love to but can't. I'm a helpless woman, remember."

"Hannah, you know I don't like that talk," Sarah Wells Bull admonished. "It's not lady-like. You've been listening too much to John."

"Mother dear," Margaret defended her sister-in-law, "Hannah is only being obedient to her husband."

Hannah gave her a withering look. She glanced over to the corner where Phebe and Patience were entertaining the younger children, and themselves, with a jig-doll, making the wooden figure dance and twirl on their knees rather than on the shingle so as to make less noise.

"Phebe! I told you to have the children recite their letters."

"Yes ma'am."

Phebe reluctantly put down the toy and picked up the book. She opened it up, her cousin looking over her shoulder.

"Hush! Listen to what I say, then repeat," she said to the younger children, a little bit crossly.

Her young charges gathered more closely at the older girls' feet.

"First the letter 'A'."

Phebe cleared her throat, like she had heard the schoolmarm Mrs. Wood, the wife of their Anglican preacher, do at the dame school she held in her kitchen in the wintertime.

"A: In Adam's Fall, We Sinned All."

"A: In Adam's Fall, We Sinned All."

"Not too bad. Chrisse, stop pulling on Esther's hair and sit still. Next. B: Heaven to Find, the Bible Mind."

"B: Heav…Heav…Heavy too Fine, the Bible Mine."

"C: Christ Crucify'd, For Sinners Died."

"Phebe, what does 'crucified' mean?"

"Esther! Don't play dumb. You know what it means."

"I forgot."

"All right," Phebe sighed. "It means they nailed him to a wooden cross to make him die."

"Why did they do that?"

Phebe looked at her cousin for assistance. Patience reached down smiling and pulled up Esther on her knee. She smoothed the girl's disobedient hair back under her little bonnet.

"Because they didn't like what Jesus did."

"What did Jesus do?"

"He told them the truth."

"Oh. What did Jesus tell them?"

"Jesus said, 'Love the Lord your God with all your heart, and with all your soul, and with all your mind; and love your neighbour like yourself. And follow me."

Esther's eyes opened wide.

"Oh." She thought a moment. She nodded her head gravely. "I see."

"D," Phebe continued. "The Deluge Drowned, the Earth Around...."

Hannah put down her new pin-cushion. "Sisters, shall we rest our needles for a well-deserved refreshment?" She turned her head towards the hall. "Rachel!" she called out. In a short moment the Bulls' Negro house slave appeared and waited patiently by her mistress' side.

"Well, ladies. Rachel will serve us. Now, what will it be: coffee, or tea?"

Chapter Three: *Rendering unto Caesar*

"Coffee, strong and black! That's what I want," Elihu Marvin growled. He launched a jet of saliva into the spittoon with an expert eye and bit off another chew from his thread of tobacco. "What about you others?" he asked, glowering around the table.

"Coffee for me."

"Coffee."

"Me too. Coffee."

"St. John? What'll it be?" inquired the tavern-keeper John Brewster, standing attentively by the table, fleshy hands folded calmly above a greasy apron.

St. John hesitated.

"I'll take cider."

The clopping of horses outside was followed by the scraping of boots on the iron by the open front door of Brewster's King George Tavern. Thomas Moffat entered the room escorted by Jesse Woodhull and a few other men. A couple of young boys not yet old enough to shave trailed behind.

"What cheer, gentlemen?" Moffat greeted. "I smell good coffee. But, I was rather hoping for something else."

" 'Tis good to hope. Good for the soul," Brewster replied. "I'll be warming up the punch soon enough." He brought around a tray of pipes and a bowl of tobacco. The fire tong made the rounds and soon the newcomers' puffing added to the already smoky atmosphere of the room, blending with the aroma of nutmeg and cinnamon coming from the loggerhead St. John was holding over the flames. He had selected with care a chair within reach of the hearth but close to the open window.

Mrs. Brewster's plump self bustled over with a large basket dangling from one hand and a tray held by the other. She pushed her way to the table and dumped the basket and tray in the middle without ceremony.

"I suppose you'll be wanting to eat," she sniffed, disdain diluted by thoughts of gain a-coming. In reply came chortling and happy grunting as hands reached forward to take out hot hoe-cakes from the basket and cold pickled tongue from the trencher. Mrs. Brewster went straight away to the bar and carefully recorded in her ledger book the food, drink, pipes, tobacco, and spices for St. John's cider dispensed thus far, sharp grey eyes missing nothing.

"What manner of punch will it be for you today, gents?" Brewster inquired, bringing over coffee and cider. "Sower? I have lime fresh off Ellison's dock on Queen Street, give or take a few days. Or do your souls need some sweetening? I can whip up a good milk punch for you. With fresh strawberries on the side, picked just this morning by twelve vestal virgins. Either way, you'll be getting only the best dark rum from Jamaica our smugglers can smuggle."

The tavern-keeper swept expert eyes over the group. "Lime sower it is. Comin' right up."

Thomas Moffat brought a chair over near St. John. "Michael, I don't believe you've met my brother William. William, Michael St. John."

William shared his older brother's green Irish eyes and thick shock of black hair. He and St. John shook hands.

"Now that you're bosom buddies, here's another to add to your fraternity, Hezekiah Howell. And Nathaniel Strong. Marvin's sons you already know." More handshakes and greetings. "Nat and his family farm a good hunk of the old Daniel Crommelin grant down south towards Oxford. The Marvins are there, too. If I remember right, Michael, your farm is on the western part of the same tract."

St. John gave a nod. "I bought my 120 acres or so from old Ebenezer Seely. I worked for my deed by surveying for him when he divided up the rest of his land." St. John gestured to Strong with his cup. "I know your pa. I surveyed for him, too. I think at one time or another I've surveyed for half the gentlemen in this room! Or at least, for their fathers."

He took a sip of cider. "So, I guess that means I should have a bone to pick with the other half." He feigned a look of reproach towards Thomas Moffat, puffing on his pipe.

"I am being unjustly accused," the miller replied serenely. "I merely received my land from father Samuel, as did my brother William here. 'Twas my father who was the original settler; he came here from Ireland, County Antrim, around...when was that, William?"

"1726."

"Right. Well. Like I was sayin', our father bought from Blagg over there in the clove south of Murderers' Creek, an' then over the years he kept on addin' to his holdings. His surveyor was long before your time, Michael. He hired the Old Colonel, Charles Clinton. My pa figgered if there was ever any argument over his boundary lines, no one would dare go up against the Colonel. He'd chew 'em up and spit 'em out faster than they can wink. They say the Colonel could make milk curdle just by looking at it. Besides," Moffat winked, "an Irish Presbyterian will never cheat another."

"Unless he's lookin' the other way." The tall, lanky figure of Jesse Woodhull ambled over, dragging a stool behind him. "But then, isn't every business all about cheating? Present company excepted, of course."

"Well," Thomas Moffat replied, "an honourable man would never cheat his neighbours. Outsiders, now that's another story. They're fair game. But I don't know if I agree that tryin' to get as much profit as you can is cheating. If a man's willin' to pay your price why shouldn't you charge as much as he'll let you? It's his choice. Now, if you take away his choice, well then, that's different."

"I wouldn't trust any merchant in the City to give me a fair deal of his own accord, that's for certain. 'Specially the iron-mongers. Cheatin' people right 'n left." Elihu Marvin joined in. "I've half a mind to go to Philadelphia. They say Quaker dealers are honest. Why can't I buy good wrought-iron bars in Orange County?"

"Problem is," Moffat pointed out, "Philadelphia is a good five days' journey, twice as long if the mud is deep! Even though the King's Highway goes right by your front door. Twice as long as going to New-York City. So the money you save dealing with honest Quakers you lose by spending more for the privilege of dealing with 'em."

"Peter Townsend's looking to make wrought-iron at his Sterling Forge. That's not too far from here," St. John offered. "And he's a Quaker to-boot. Says he wants to make ships' anchors."

"Make way for punch, lads," John Brewster sang out. He waded his way to the table carrying with both hands a large Delft bowl and placed it ceremoniously in the middle while his wife at the bar behind him eagerly scratched her ledger with her quill.

"Did I hear you talking about forges?" the tavern-keeper asked. "My cousin Samuel is setting one up in New-Windsor down by the river. He'll be making wrought-iron. Steel, too, from what he tells me."

"What! Steel? That means tilt hammers. That means your cousin Samuel will be contravening the sacred laws of Parliament. No tilt hammers allowed. Therefore no steel. As sheriff I will be duty-bound to arrest him next time he steps into Orange County," Woodhull observed with a wink. "But, time enough for that later. First, pass me the punch bowl when you're done will you?" This to Elihu Marvin, who was slurping noisily on the rim of the bowl while tilting it upwards with both hands clutching elaborate handles conveniently cast into the sides for that purpose.

After Woodhull drank his fill the bowl was passed to Moffat, Thomas and then on to Moffat, William and so on down the line until each man had had his turn. The last to drink were the two boys, who came running over from the dart-board to get their portion. Brewster, like a magician, reappeared and replenished the bowl in the twinkling of an eye.

" 'Tis bad luck to leave a punch bowl unfilled," he observed, to the happy scratching of his wife.

"And now," Moffat, Thomas intoned, having risen from his chair, "now that we have dispatched with the first, and foremost, order of business let us proceed to matters of lesser importance." He produced a folded paper tied with a red ribbon, which he undid with fingers surprisingly nimble given their plumpness.

"As duly elected Clerk of the County of Orange of the Colonial Province of New-York, I have the honour, and solemn duty, to publicly read, and post, an Act adopted by our Colonial Assembly, in the name of our Right Sovereign Lord, George the Third, by the Grace of God King and Protector of Great Britain, France and Ireland and Defender of the Faith – " here Moffat winked, there being no Anglicans present "- on the twenty-seventh day of January in the year of our Lord 1770 – "

"But today's June 26th!" Marvin jeered.

"I know," Moffat replied, "but there being a shortage of good paper on which to print the Act, and a shortage of funds with which to pay the official printer, and what with the terrible condition of the roads this past Spring and all; well, here we are, just a few months behind the times.

"Let us continue. It is entitled: 'Chapter 1453. An Act for the Better Regulation of Publick Inns and Taverns in the Counties of Orange and Ulster.'" Moffat paused and looked pointedly at Mr. Brewster leaning back against the bar, listening, and Mrs. Brewster leaning forward from behind the bar, frowning.

" 'Whereas the original design of Inns and Taverns was to accommodate Travellers with necessaries and conveniences, this laudable intent has been perverted to the most mischievous purposes, by furnishing means for the entertainment of Idle and Dissolute Youth to the ruin of families and to the great injury of the publick; let it therefore be enacted by the Honourable Lt.-Governor Cadwallader Colden, the Council and the General Assembly that any person keeping a Publick Inn or Tavern who furnishes Strong Liquors to any child under the age of sixteen years or who suffers such child to play any game, whether dice, darts, cards, bones or other, he, she or they shall pay a penalty of five pounds, to be recovered by the parent or guardian of such child before any Justice of the Peace.

" 'And further, each Inn-holder or Tavern-keeper shall keep at least two good feather-beds, with good and sufficient sheeting and coverings, washed at least once every six weeks, for four persons, no more than two to a bed if strangers to one another, with sufficient hay for their horses in default of which shall be levied a fine of twenty shillings.'

"In the name of the King I hereby post this notice. God save the King etc, etc."

Moffat, calling out to Brewster for a hammer, illegally manufactured, walked over to the posting-wall next to the front door, where several other official Acts of the Colonial Assembly had been posted and ignored. The dart-board was hanging from a nail, illegally manufactured, next to the postings; judging by the torn and defaced papers and the odd dart or two affixed to an Act, the tavern regulars had either poor aim or little respect for the laws of the Colonial Assembly.

"Well, gents, so much for my duties as Clerk. I now switch hats. As Chairman of the Orange County Chapter of the Sons of Liberty, I convene this session to order." Moffat seized the punch bowl. "But first, a toast. To our sovereign king."

"To our king," all present intoned, with varying amounts of vigour. The bowl made its round, around the table and down the line of chairs to the two young boys at the end.

"The subject of today's meeting," Moffat commenced," is to fashion a reply to our brothers in the City, who have asked us to join them in Boston's protest to the king over the shooting in their town last March."

"You mean, massacre!" Marvin rejoined. Ayes in assent could be heard around the room. "Five unarmed men cut down by the king's troops in cold blood, right in front of the Boston Town House."

Hezekiah Howell, a big-boned, thoughtful man, spoke up. "But wasn't there a mob, throwing bricks and rocks at the soldiers?"

"The mob would not have assembled and the people would not have been angered but for troops quartered in the city," Nathaniel Roe pointed out. "As though the people of Boston are foreign enemies or the Irish. It was a provocation."

"An' this is the result! Look here." Marvin retrieved from the news-paper rack an edition of the *New-York Journal,* dated some weeks earlier. He held aloft the front page depicting red-coats firing into civilians. Several were fallen to the ground, blood gushing from their wounds, highlighted in vivid red ink. "I don't see any civilians holding rocks or bricks."

"Maybe they had already launched their missiles," Woodhull jibed. "Here, let me see that." He scanned the article under the picture. "Says it's copied from an engraving by a fellow named Revere. It don't say if he was even there that day."

"As I was about to say, it is unclear what the facts are," Moffat continued, somewhat testily. "The soldiers, however, have been arrested and will be put on trial. This is the way it should be. We are, after all, a country under the rule of law and we should be proud of it. If we, as free Englishmen – I beg the Irish amongst us to indulge me – if *we* have the right to defend ourselves before a jury of our peers, well, then, so too the accused soldiers. It is for the jury to hear the evidence and determine what happened. Until then we do a disservice to ourselves, and to our king, if we jump to conclusions without knowing the facts. After all, there can be no liberty without respect for the law. The defendants have a lawyer appointed, a fellow named Adams."

Elihu Marvin guffawed. "Adams! The 'radical' Sam Adams? That's a riot."

"No, not that Adams. His cousin. John Adams. A young lawyer in the town."

"I know all I need to know," Marvin asserted. "Let's vote!"

"Wait. You don't even know yet what you're voting for." Moffat had unfolded another paper. He read out loud the letter from Isaac Sears on behalf of the New- York City Sons of Liberty. "Not only does Captain Sears want the red-coats out of Boston, he wants them out of New-York City as well; and he wants the merchants of the City to know we think them traitors for backing out of their pledge to stop importing British goods." Moffat's green eyes glittered ambiguously under arched brows. "There you have it, gentlemen. Any discussion?"

A heated debate ensued, the temperature raised a notch by the effects of a third bowl of punch, with mechanics and farmers taking one side and merchants and tradesmen the other. St. John, not a member of the committee though invited to join, looked on in silence. The tavern-keep was watching the proceedings with a hopeful gleam in his watery eyes until slapped in the back of his head by a wet washrag.

"Stop lolly-gagging. I need help with the dishes. An' the fire needs feeding. You never do anything to help me out."

Brewster glared at his wife. "Who milks the cows every morn? Who chopped your firewood today? Who smokes your meat? I do plenty to help out."

Mrs. Brewster would not back down. She returned his stare and held out the washcloth. Mr. Brewster surrendered and glumly took the dreaded instrument, holding the whitish rag at the end of his arm in front of him like a flag of truce as he retreated to the tub in the back room while Mrs. Brewster picked up a large tray loaded with food.

"Dinner, gentlemen!"

In light of the urgent matter of eating, the debate was tabled along with the debaters. Having exhausted her meager supply of Delft dishes Mrs. Brewster fell back on an assortment of redware bowls, pewter plates and the odd wooden trencher or two. Individual forks were out of the question. Foreseeing this, she had graciously sliced the roast pork in finger-sized pieces, the better to disguise its true quantity. As for spoons, there were plenty, made of horn or pewter or wood. Sliced buttered carrots, diced buttered turnips, roasted red potatoes and an intriguing round, flat light green bean completed the vegetable offering.

William Moffat dubiously poked with his spoon at the strange things, as green as his own eyes. "What on earth is that?"

"That, my friend, is what St. John here calls 'Lima beans'," Woodhull explained. "I grew 'em, an' now you have the honour, and pleasure I truly hope, of being the first around these parts to partake of this exotic delicacy."

"Not bad," William conceded, nodding his head as he took another spoonful. "Where d'ye get them from?" he asked St. John.

"My wife's brother, after a voyage he made to the Caribbean. They need rich, loamy soil like we have around the Grey-Court Swamp and the Drowned Lands."

"The Drowned Lands contain good black dirt," Woodhull remarked. "For proof just look at the rushes and cattails that thrive there. If only we could drain 'em and regulate the floods from the Wallkill River. 'Twould make an El Dorado for some farsighted farmer."

"Like you, Jesse, I suppose!" said Thomas Moffat.

"Well, why not me? Don't you like all the hundreds of bushels of grain I grind at your mill every harvest? An' the three or four bushels I let you skim off the side for good measure."

"I am an honest miller," Moffat sniffed. "How would we pay to drain the swamps?"

"Petition the lieutenant-governor and Assembly to levy an assessment on each landowner affected by the swamps to pay for the works. That would be only fair, since the owners are the ones who will benefit."

"The last thing I need is more taxes," Marvin scowled.

"I don't have the money to pay any assessment," said Nathaniel Strong. "Where'd I get the coin?"

"You wouldn't need silver. The Assembly'll do what it always does: permit payment in Colonial bills of exchange."

"Paper money is not worth the paper it's printed on," Marvin snorted.

"That's the beauty of it," Woodhull exclaimed. "It don't matter! Even though it's not legal tender – thank you again, Parliament – and even though the Colonial treasury has precious little silver in its coffers, it don't matter! As long as people *believe* the paper is redeemable, it will have value in their eyes. An' if our Assembly says we can pay our tax in paper, I for one won't be objecting."

"The problem with paper currency is counterfeiting. It's become a plague," Brewster grumbled. "It's bad enough with New-York money. What am I supposed to do when a traveler from Pennsylvania – or worse, Maryland, or Virginia, God forbid – wants to pay for his fare with strange paper? How do I know it's genuine? Who's going to accept the paper from me later? I have to cross the Delaware River to exchange it. And the worst thing is, a Pennsylvania shilling is not the same as a New-York shilling."

"How would you drain the swamps?" Nathaniel Roe asked, turning to a practical question that set all the heads in the room a-nodding.

"I can respond to that," St. John spoke up. "There is a method used in…."

He caught himself. References to New-France might not be welcome here. He looked around the room at the faces of men he called neighbours and friends, the interest flickering in their eyes reassuring. He felt a pang of guilt for doubting them.

"….In French Acadia, called Nova Scotia by the British, the old settlers there built what they called *aboiteaux*. They're like small Dutch dikes but with gates you can open and close to drain the water out of the marshland…." Their method was simple, he explained, planting young tulip trees or willows every so many yards in a double row as anchor posts for the low dike walls made out of cedar logs, filling the space in between the walls with dirt, clay, small rocks. "In late summer when the river is low, we'll open the gates and drain out the swamp behind."

Even Marvin was nodding his head, as if visualizing the thousands of acres they could transform into valuable land almost overnight. Moffat, too, seemed to be silently calculating, stealing a sidelong glance at Woodhull, drawing peacefully on a pipe, while the inn-keeper and his wife kept vigil over them all, like spiders sensitive to the slightest quiver of the web.

Moffat smiled broadly. "A toast! Tavern-keep'! How about two or three bottles of your finest smuggled Portuguese Madeira for our august assembly."

"I think you'll be wantin' four."

"Four it is, then," Moffat acquiesced with a nonchalant wave of the hand. He smiled at St. John and winked. "Did I forget to mention it? As we are engaged in official government business, this splendid collation is courtesy of our generous Colonial treasury. Drink up!"

"How," Hezekiah Howell wondered, "are you going to get the support of the lieutenant-governor for your project?"

"Let us not worry ourselves unduly over that," Moffat replied serenely. "Cadwallader Colden is very responsive to projects benefitting the public. Particularly if he gets a juicy stake in the venture. Well, Jesse, if you and St. John want, I'll be delighted to draft up a petition."

Isaac Sears' appeal carried the day by a whisker, the vote lubricated by ample shots of Madeira. As the men and boys imbibed, the post-rider came through the door with the week's mail. He greeted Brewster and placed his saddle-bag on the bar, gladly accepting a nip of wine.

"Moffat," the post-rider called out. "Woodhull. Roe. Howell....Strong." At the call of his name each man received his letter in exchange for a penny. "St. John. Two pence."

Puzzled, St. John handed over the extra coin and was rewarded with a folded document. With his belt-knife he slit the wax wafer sealing the document. "What is this?" he asked out loud.

Moffat looked over St. John's shoulder. "It's a subpoena, that's what it is. A summons to testify in court. There's a letter with it, as well." As St. John read the letter Moffat perused the summons. Finishing at the same time, they exchanged documents.

"Who is Ethan Allen?" Moffat asked.

"Ethan Allen is an acquaintance of mine in the Green Mountains. I surveyed some land for him he bought around

Bennington, from the New-Hampshire governor Benning Wentworth. I guess he wants me to testify at this trial of his."

"That's what the subpoena says, too." Moffat guffawed, amused. "It's signed by a lawyer, Jared Ingersoll. Says he's Allen's counsel. You're to be their star witness!"

St. John did not share in the humour. "I don't wish to be a witness for anybody. I have my harvest to bring in, cows to milk, and a wife with child."

Jesse Woodhull read the letter for himself. He whistled. "Can't say I blame you for not wantin' to go. This fellow Ethan Allen's suing New-York! Says our officials like Cad Colden and his cronies granted large tracts of his land to themselves, claiming New-York holds title, not New-Hampshire. What's more," Woodhull laughed, "one of those 'cronies' is Robert Livingston, Justice of the New-York Supreme Court. The same judge who is to preside over the trial, or so your friend complains."

Woodhull gleefully returned the papers to St. John. "Well, I wouldn't bet the farm on Ethan Allen's claim."

"What would happen if I didn't show up?" St. John asked.

Woodhull and Moffat glanced at each other. They both shrugged. Woodhull looked again at the summons. "Don't know, exactly. It's only signed by this lawyer here, 'in the name of the court'. I guess nothing would happen unless a judge himself signed it; and then I'd receive it as sheriff and serve it upon you, at your cost. But until then, it looks like you're a free man."

From the kitchen behind the bar came the shrill sounds of scolding and the muffled slapping of wet rags against a soft object, followed by a feeble voice in protest.

"Of course, 'freedom' is subject to different interpretations," Woodhull remarked.

An hour later the last of the Madeira had been uncorked and a final toast declared. Marvin, who had enjoyed more than his fair share and was showing the effects, stumbled back from a visit to the necessary. He plopped himself into his chair and gave St. John a slap on the arm.

"Well," he slurred," what's your decision?"

St. John looked at him glumly and sighed. "I suppose I'll have to go and testify."

"No, I don't mean about that trial! I don't give a hoot about that Allen fellow or Cad Colden's land claims. A curse on that rich friend of yours, Cad Colden. He can go to the devil, along with all his wealthy cronies. The king's fool, that's what he is. He and his toady son the tax collector. Maybe someone should burn down their houses someday. No, I mean, are you with us? Will you join our committee?"

Even as he was mumbling out his question Marvin's eyes had lost their focus and his eyelids were drooping, and soon his head followed suit. He began to snore loudly. Moffat gently lowered the man's head onto the table-board as the assembled in the room prepared to disassemble. Brewster bustled over with a paper on a slate.

"If you would do me the honour of signing at the bottom. The total for today is three pounds, six shillings two pence." Brewster glanced down at the snoring Marvin, snoozing on his table. "There will have to be an extra charge for any overnight accommodations, of course."

"He's on his own penny now," Moffat said, shrugging on his riding coat and reaching for his hat and saddle-bag. "Let 'em sleep it off for an hour or two. But don't let him go longer than that. Otherwise he'll catch hell from his wife."

From behind the bar came loud shrieking sounds.

Brewster sighed.

"Coming, my love."

Chapter Four: *The Philosophy of Milking Cows*

The bed-chamber was pitch black. St. John quietly eased his body out of the warm bed from next to his sleeping wife. He groped for his work-blouse and breeches draped over the back of the commode-chair, carefully rolling the soles of his feet over the floor-boards. He winced with the squeaking of the loose board he had tried to avoid then stifled a grunt of pain as he stubbed his toe against the chamber-pot poking out from under the chair. He limped to the open doorway and closed it softly behind him.

Downstairs he felt his way through the centre hall into the kitchen, first unlatching the inside shutters to let in the faint light of the new-born day. The kitchen – Mehetable called it their "keeping room" - spanned the full north side of the house, windows on the east and west walls taking full advantage of the morning and evening sunlight. He went to the wide hearth, embers still glowing, and sprinkled pine shavings over the hot coals, puffing them into a small flame; then added kindling until the fire blazed a cheerful orange. He swept up ashes into a pail, to be thrown into the lye barrel outside, for making soap later in the fall after the harvest was in. He lugged the empty kettle over to the wash-counter next to the chimney.

The wash-counter like the chimney was of limestone, in the form of a rectangular box, made by Thomas Bull following St. John's design. Two large, open copper basins were set in lime mortar in the counter-top above a small oven, accessed through an opening at the bottom. Between the two basins was a flat area where St. John placed the pot. Just above, a tin spout protruded from the wall, capped by a barrel spigot. The spout came from a rain barrel squatting on a high stand outside next to the protruding beehive oven. The barrel was fed by a long series of wooden pipes elevated on trestles, descending from the small hill directly behind the house, on which there was a spring of fresh water.

The tin spout leaked, and the trestles and pipes got in the way of the chores, to the irritation of the farm-hands; and he and his wife still had to rely on the well for most of their water. But he always felt a thrill of pride and delight every time he turned that spigot and saw the result of his ingenuity come dribbling out of the spout, even if he did not see the slow shaking of his wife's head behind him.

Another wood pipe went from the spring to the necessary, some fifty feet or so behind the kitchen, through which a constant gurgle of water flushed out the basin under the seat of the latrine and into an underground pit away from the backhouse. Thus had done the ancient Romans, St. John imagined. "What will you do when winter comes and the water freezes up?" his wife had asked, her look betraying what she thought of his genius. "I'll think up something," he replied cheerfully.

After placing the kettle over the fire, so that his wife would have one less task to do, he eagerly went outside for the morning chores. He heard his two hired hands stirring in their log cabin, St. John's former dwelling. He walked into the pen next to the barn where the cows were waiting impatiently. They had begun to low as soon as they heard him coming and willingly followed him into the milking stalls on the ground floor of his new barn, leaving their calves in the care of the two indifferent bulls.

The back foundation wall was set into a gentle slope leading up to the squat hill with their spring and a grove of pine trees. The main floor of the barn, used for breaking flax, threshing wheat, shearing sheep or storing things, was accessed from the higher elevation of the terrain behind the barn. From the main floor it was easy to throw hay through chutes in the floor down to the stalls on ground level, or out of the wide doors onto waggons waiting below.

His two farmhands joined him and together they put the six milch cows into their stalls, heads poking through hickory stanchions to prevent their bolting. The cows set to chewing the grass and clover in the feeder in front of their noses while each of the men, seated on stools, took in hand distended teats from swollen udders and began the symbiotic exchange between man and beast where both benefitted and neither suffered and were therefore absolutely equal partners, at least for that moment.

Their fingers pulled at the teats to the sound of milk squirting into the bucket. To pass the time St. John ruminated over the relationship between a man and his cow. "See here," he mused out loud. "The man provides access to feed and shelter, and performs the task of milking necessary to the cow's survival. So, rather than stealing from the cow, in taking its milk the man is actually giving to the cow. The time, energy and effort expended by the man for the cow is in reality expended for himself, and therefore is not a loss to the man but a gain. Both gain and neither loses."

From the stalls to his right and his left came the steady splashing of milk in buckets. The cows flicked their tails in contentment as they chewed on their clover. On his right he heard Cesar clearing his throat.

"I don't know about that, boss. Seems to me there is, in fact, a loss. The cow loses her freedom to go where she pleases. The man, too, loses his freedom to do what he pleases. He's stuck with the chore of milking cows every day."

More sounds of milk hitting milk.

"Unless," came Henry's voice from the left, "unless the man likes milking his cows, and doing all his other chores, so that in everything he must work at he also finds joy."

St. John's cow flicked its tail at a buzzing fly and twitched a hind leg.

"Well," St. John replied, "I guess to that extent there would be true freedom, if duty corresponds exactly with desire."

"Sorry, boss, but I ain't ever goin' to like mucking out the cow stalls. If it was up to me to decide, I'd just as soon let Henry do it all the time."

"I suppose cows don't have the capacity to make decisions," St. John reflected. "Man does."

"*Some* men don't have that right. Are you saying, boss, that freedom means deciding for yourself?"

"Well now, I suppose so, in a certain sense. But being able to decide is only the consequence of being free. It does not define what freedom really is. Free from what?"

"Alls I know is that most of my folk are slaves."

The three fell into a thoughtful silence. From outside birds could be heard singing joyfully.

"I wonder if birds feel happiness," St. John mused. "Hard to believe they're not happy, listening to their singing."

" 'Course they're happy," Cesar replied. "They don't have no bird slave-drivers. No bird king, no bird parliament. No bird government. No bird taxes to pay."

"And no cows to milk or stalls to muck," Henry teased him.

"Birds don't need a government. Only men do." St. John brooded. "Can we ever really hope to find freedom, true liberty, in any government run by men?"

"Why is it, boss, there be two words for the same idea?"

"Well, I don't rightly know why. The French language does not have a pair of synonyms for the concept of freedom. Just one word, *liberté*. The English word 'freedom' comes from the German word *Freiheit.*"

"I didn't know you could speak German."

St. John laughed. "I don't. But I taught myself to stumble through a book by a German fellow named Leibnitz."

"Europeans like big books with big words," Henry declared. "There is only one word we need to be free."

The three lapsed into silence. St. John fell into a long reverie.

"Boss. Boss! We're done with the cows. Your teat's empty!" Cesar laughed, pointing at the cow's hindquarters and tail now twitching with irritation. St. John smiled at himself and rose, giving the cow Rousseau a grateful rub on her back, and picked up his heavy bucket by its hemp strap.

"Thanks for milking Diderot for me," St. John said, referring to the other cow he was supposed to take care of.

Cesar chuckled. "We seen you was lost in one of those day-dreams of yours, boss. What invention you cookin' up now? Not another new-fangled latrine, we hope."

St. John shared in the laugh. He hefted his bucket filled to the brim with rich milk.

"As a matter of fact, I do have another idea. Something to do with a better way of churning butter."

"If it means less work for me, then I'm behind you one hundred and one percent, boss."

"Well maybe not less for you, but certainly less for my wife."

The trio trudged up Pine Hill to the spring-house where they poured the contents of their buckets into tin receptacles sitting on a shelf in the pool of cool water. From another container they scooped out the cream floating on top of the milk placed there the morning before, ladling the heavy yellow liquid into firkins.

They carried the firkins down the hill and onto the covered porch next to the kitchen, placing the containers into a water barrel to keep them cool. Cesar went to feed the pigs while Henry attended to the chickens. St. John brought in a load of firewood.

Mehetable was busy at the fireside preparing breakfast. St. John stole a kiss on the back of her neck and his wife flashed him a smile. He enlaced his arms around her growing belly and nuzzled her cheek, gently kissing each freckle, basking in her soft, warm sweetness.

"Stop," she protested. "Our hands will see you."

"Our hands will see my hands? So be it. We are man and wife, after all."

"There is work to be done."

"There will always be work to be done." He kissed her long and hard and she responded willingly, warmly until breaking off suddenly at the sound of footfalls scraping the steps to the porch. Henry opened the door and brought in a basket of eggs.

"Morning, Mrs. St. John," Henry greeted her, still not used to the presence of a woman on St. John's farm. He put the basket on the side-board and awkwardly took his leave.

Born into a Huron tribe, schooled by Jesuit missionaries, Henry as a youth accompanied French trappers all along the Mohawk until kidnapped by a prowling band of Oneidas - the *Onyota'a'ka* - one of the several tribes of the Iroquois Confederacy, who adopted him into the Wolf clan. Later he met a Protestant missionary and was baptised; and there, at his clan's winter camp, he met St. John, exploring the Mohawk Valley after sojourning in the Green Mountains. St. John was surprised to see this French-speaking young Indian taking Communion and they were both surprised to meet again three years later in Blooming Grove, where St. John was clearing his new farmland and Henry's preacher employer had just died.

Sagacity Brown arrived, opening the kitchen latch and letting herself in. She was the eldest daughter of a neighbour down the road towards New-Windsor whom St. John had hired to help his wife. Although he thought her lacking in common sense and industry he engaged her, however reluctantly, out of need and also out of pity for her father who had recently lost his wife in childbirth and who always seemed to have money problems. Mehetable, too, had not been impressed. "We'll give her a week," she sighed, resigned to the experiment. The week became a month, and then two months.

Despite her hopeful birth-name Sagacity's lack of judgement showed no sign of improvement but she proved to have more energy about her as time went on, as though looking forward to being with the St. Johns rather than in her own home. Mehetable noticed that some days the young lass arrived in the morning, mousy hair disheveled under a threadbare cap, bluish marks around her forearms she was forced to reveal when rolling up her sleeves to wash dishes or knead dough; and oft-times her eyes were red and swollen as though from crying. "Is there anything amiss, my dear?" Mehetable would ask, only to receive a sullen shaking of the head.

After a hearty breakfast of eggs, cheese, bread, beef and beer the men resumed their chores outside. It was almost time for the flax harvest and so St. John set the men to work mending a broken axle on the waggon. He himself spent the morning assembling the three flax brakes he had crafted so that when it came time to crush the reeds each man would have his own machine.

The contraption he built was nothing more than a solid wooden box with three rows of wooden blades, the "knives" running parallel to each other across the top on which the flax reeds were placed. He opened the hinged wooden lid on the top of the box, resembling a huge jaw with its two knives designed to fit in the spaces between the lower knives. He placed a few flax stalks across the bottom knives, then slammed the lid down and pounded it with a mallet so that the knives splintered the tough outer skin of the reed. He opened the lid and took out a few of the mashed stalks.

Cesar had come into the barn and was watching him.

"You done a nice job, boss."

He took a crushed stalk in his hand and looked with interest at the coarse fibres inside. "Hard to believe this soft shirt I'm wearin' is made o' this stuff. But why, if a cotton shirt is made o' cotton, and a silk cravat is made o' silk, and wool socks is made o' wool, why is this thing I'm wearin' not called a flax shirt?"

St. John shrugged. "The English word 'linen' comes from the French word '*lin*'. Meaning flax."

"I wish you would cook up an invention to turn this stuff into thread. Without me havin' to pound it an' soak it an' pound it some more an' running it through the hetchel...."

St. John's brow furrowed. "If only I could learn more about that engine John Ellison was talking about. He said it uses steam pressure as the motive force."

"Henry and me, we're ready to put on the new axle."

St. John followed Cesar to the waggon under a maple tree. Using a pulley and rope slung over a branch, they had raised the rear end of the waggon to take off the wheels and axle. The axle had broken because of the stress placed on it by another of St. John's contraptions, designed by Jesse Woodhull. Drawing inspiration from the workings of a mill, they had fitted out a waggon with gear wheels made of strong hickory wood attached to the rear axle. A long, thin iron blade was affixed below the horizontal gear wheel, rotating as the waggon wheels moved forward, cutting the stalks of wheat, oats or barley like a scythe.

St. John replaced the defective axle with a stronger hickory one reinforced with an iron band fashioned by Elihu Marvin. They hitched up the team of oxen and St John gleefully climbed onto the bench, reins and whip in hand. With a crack and a holler he set the team in motion and the contraption lumbered forward through the tall grass on one side of the house. Looking back over his shoulder he saw with satisfaction the blade turning and the grass flying out behind.

"Well, I guess it works now," he exclaimed, stopping the team and jumping off the bench.

Cesar looked unconvinced. "Maybe. What do we do when the ground isn't level? That blade will get stuck."

"We'll figure something out," St. John said cheerfully.

"I like it," Henry pronounced. He frowned. "Too bad we can't use it for the flax."

"I know. But it won't work for flax since we have to pull up the whole plant, roots and all. But we'll think of something, someday."

They were glad to hear the dinner-bell. The boards were set with pewter chargers full of steaming stew and vegetables from their garden. They sat down on long benches, St. John at one end of the boards above the salt, Mehetable on the other end below the salt, with Henry, Cesar and Sagacity to the sides. Mehetable bid them bow their heads. She said Grace, softly and simply. They then broke bread.

They ate in silence, except for an occasional compliment to Mrs. St. John for the tasty stew or to request the pitcher of cider. They had just passed out slices of peach pie when they heard a rapping on the doorframe.

"Come on in," St. John said to the visitor. A barefoot boy entered, baggy linen pants patched all over, panting from having run. He lifted his straw hat in respect with his left hand. In his right he held a small iron box by its short wooden handle.

" 'Afternoon, sir. Mrs. St. John, ma'am. Ma sent me over to ask for some coals. Our serving girl spilt water all over the fire and put it out. Oh, Ma gives you her regards."

"Sit down a moment, Nathaniel, and have some peach pie and cider," Mehetable had risen and was already preparing a plate.

Young Nathaniel Roe hesitated. "Ma said I was not to tarry or intrude on your dinner." He looked with longing at the slice of pie and cup of cider beckoning from the table.

" 'Tis no intrusion at all. You do us a pleasure. Now come, sit. Here, give me your scoop."

"Yes ma'am! Thank you ma'am."

As the boy regaled himself St. John asked after the boy's ma and pa. Nathaniel swallowed his cider. "They're worried 'cause my sister Faith's not doin' very good. She has the fever."

"Not too bad, I hope." Mehetable's eyes were distressed.

"I don't know how bad it is." Nathaniel looked sad. He had already known the loss of young siblings. The fever was always a thing to be dreaded. "Ma and pa were up all last night next to her, praying."

"Then we too shall say a prayer for Faith," Mehetable said, forcing a smile. "Here, another cup of cider before you go."

St. John went over to the fire-place and, opening the top of the scoop, shoveled in hot coals. He closed the top and brought it over to the boy. "Tell your folks we'll be dropping by later."

Nathaniel thanked his neighbours then bolted out the door with the coal scoop. Henry and Cesar with their own nod of thanks got up and went out to do the afternoon chores. Sagacity quietly cleared the table.

"We'll bring the Roes the *tourtière* this evening, for their supper," St. John said, indicating with his head the meat pie enclosed behind the perforated tin door of the pie-safe. He had made the delicacy with his own hands for his wife yester-eve, stuffing the pastry with chunks of roasted quail, pheasant and venison. Not since his arrival in New-York had he permitted himself to harken back to his life in Quebec.

Mehetable nodded her head. "Yes, I would like that, too."

St. John's face lit up. "In an hour I'll have something interesting to show you," he said, before disappearing through the doorway. True to his word, an hour later he popped back in.

"Come, come!" he exclaimed, pulling her away from her ironing board. She opened her mouth as though to speak, but held her tongue and went out to the porch.

"What is that?" she asked, dubiously.

"That," her husband proclaimed, "is a device that will make your work lighter and more efficient. It is a butter lathe."

Mehetable was puzzled. "You are going to turn butter on a lathe? Like spindles for a chair or spokes for a waggon wheel?"

"No, nothing like that. I suppose the word 'lathe' is not the best choice but it's all I could think of. You see the long leather strap here, running from the bull wheel over to the box above the butter churn? Inside the box is a wheel. When the ox pulls the rope attached to the bull wheel it sets the leather strap in motion, which turns the small wheel, to which is connected this here rod going down into the barrel of the churn. The rod has four flanges, which you can't see because they're inside the barrel. When the wheel turns, it rotates the rod with its flanges, thus churning the butter. You will not have to do any of the churning yourself! It is like the workings of a water mill, only in miniature."

"I see."

"You'll love it, I assure you."

"Yes, I'm sure."

"No, really, just wait and see."

St. John slid the barrel top up the rod to allow his wife to peek inside.

"The flanges," he explained, hopefully.

Mehetable said nothing as she watched her husband take out a firkin from the water barrel and pour the yellow cream into the churn, then replace the lid. He smiled at her reassuringly, then dashed off to the waiting ox harnessed to the bull wheel. He led the beast forward and gave a cheery wave of the hand to his wife.

The large bull wheel turned. The leather strap travelled. The small wheel spun. The rod twirled. The butter churn shook. Mehetable trembled. She took three or four cautious steps back, expecting the staves of the churn to come exploding off any moment.

After a minute of ominous shaking the whirling objects came to a standstill. Mehetable looked over to the bull wheel. Her husband and his ox had come to the end of the line. He ran over excitedly.

He lifted up the lid. A frothy head of whitish foam came spilling up and over the sides of the churn. Little bubbles detached themselves and floated off into the air before popping into oblivion.

"That don't look like butter," Mehetable observed. She peered into the barrel. "I don't see butter. Methinks it looks more like whipped cream."

St. John pursed his lips.

"Well," he said.

He glanced at his wife. "Perhaps it will taste good on the peach pie. If we have any left."

Mehetable looked at her husband. She slowly shook her head and went back into the kitchen.

"Small wheel turns too fast," he muttered. He tasted a lick of the foamy substance from the churn. "Not bad," he mumbled. "Needs some sugar, though."

Glancing up, he saw Henry and Cesar staring at the spectacle from over by the smoke-house.

"Don't you two have work to do?" he groused.

His farmhands skedaddled.

Chapter Five: *The Sassafras Tree*

The next day dawned cooler and less humid. As usual St. John was up and about before daybreak. The moments just before sunrise were his favourite time, no longer night yet not quite day.

He had learned to distinguish the songs of the different birds which made their nests in the bushes and trees around the farm and he amused himself by imaging what they might be singing to one another. The twittering of the robins surely meant they had found a trove of juicy worms in the grass; and the dignified whistling of the brilliantly plumed cardinals was like a call to worship. But St. John treasured most the hummingbirds, with their ruby throats, whose song came from their wings oscillating too fast for the eye to see as they hovered among the orange trumpet vines and wild roses.

After he and his hands finished milking Diderot and Rousseau, and their bovine brethren Voltaire, Montesquieu, Spinoza and Descartes, he went off alone into the woods. Not too far; for he did not want to tire his wife when the time came to show her the prize. He did not have to look long, for the forest was lush and fertile. He marked its location, then went back down for breakfast.

Mealtime over, he gave his wife a kiss and a smile. "Leave the dishes to Sagacity. Put on your boots. I have something to show you."

Seeing the look in Mehetable's eyes he added hastily: "No, don't worry. It's not another invention. It's a creation. By the greatest Creator of all."

Spade over shoulder and piggin in hand, he led his wife up the small hill and into the forest. Within a few minutes he found his *points de repère* and with a flourish showed her the prize: a young sassafras tree, hardly more than a sapling, around whose slender, tender trunk a light-coloured grape vine had taken hold.

Mehetable smiled as her husband dug carefully around the little tree and lifted the precious living ornament out of the soil and into the container. The couple walked back down the hill to the house holding hands, Mehetable holding the piggin by its handle, St. John shouldering the spade.

"It is beautiful. Where shall we put it?" she asked, hugging her husband and giving him a kiss.

"Well. How about by our front door, just off to one side? There our tree and its vine shall receive the goodness of the morning sun and in the late day the shelter of the shade from the oak tree yonder."

And so that is where they planted it, their sassafras tree and grape vine. Carefully he dug the hole and patiently strewed a spadeful of manure at the bottom before gently lowering the sapling with its vine into their new home.

He stooped down, winnowing away the small pebbles so that only the finer soil went around the roots, then gently patted it down. Slowly he poured a small pitcher of water around the trunk, letting the water seep in. Next he took a plumb bob on a string to make sure the sapling was exquisitely vertical, pushing on the trunk a little to the left, then back, then forward until it was perfect. He stepped back.

Mehetable stooped down. She gently adjusted the stalk of the grape vine winding its way upward, hugging its host. She inserted tiny chips of wood between the vine and the bark of the sassafras tree so that the vine would not be squeezing too tightly around the trunk. Next she pulled and tugged softly here and there on the vine, enhancing what nature had started, arranging the large, dark green leaves of the vine to form a pleasing, symmetrical pattern around the young tree, gently fussing until it was perfect. She stepped back.

They clasped hands, hands soiled by the good earth of their land, and contemplated their sassafras tree intertwined with its vine.

"Such a bountiful Eden God has given us," Mehetable murmured. "I wonder sometimes that it is not just a dream. And that I will wake up and find it all gone." She hugged herself closer to her husband, who bent his head down and kissed her forehead. She smiled. "Please be to God to forgive my anxiousness. I know we must trust in Him always, whatever happens. We who can't see beyond the tip of our nose think we know what's best."

"Together our vine and tree will thrive and flourish, you will see. As will our family."

For the final touch he planted cedar stakes in a ring around the tree and vine to protect them from wandering sheep and pigs as well as the occasional deer, attracted to the sweet fruit-like aroma of sassafras.

"We shall put the tree's flowers into our soap," Mehetable said. "Then, when we bathe and wash, we will be always reminded of our tree and vine."

Still hand in hand they strolled along the front of the house, façade facing the King's Highway, the optimistically named narrow dirt road just wide enough for the Conestoga waggons lumbering by from time to time between Philadelphia and Newburgh on Hudson's River, or Hartford or Boston.

"To think we are husband and wife not quite a year," Mehetable mused. They had reached the round stone well in the side yard with its large, old-fashioned sweep. "If I were not a Christian woman I would wager you don't remember the date of our marriage!" she teased him.

"But you *are* a Christian woman, and so you cannot wager, and thus we see the wise benevolence behind God's prohibitions. He has spared you the pain of losing the wager. The date of our marriage is September 20, 1769."

"Aya, God is indeed good." They stopped and kissed again.

"We had best do all our pecking today, for the Sabbath is tomorrow," St. John pointed out gravely, before nuzzling her neck.

"Oh do stop!" his wife admonished. " 'Tis not proper here. We are in plain sight of everybody. An' what is worse, I fear you venture oft-times too close to blasphemy, Michael Hector St. John, what with your light approach to Sabbath-day. God blessed the seventh day and made it holy."

"But it is good, is it not, for a man to kiss his wife, his better half, whom God has given to him to love and protect? And did not Jesus say it is lawful to do good on the Sabbath? And so, our kissing on the Sabbath were pleasing to God; as well as on the day before, I should think."

"Methinks you think much too much!" Mehetable responded, before surrendering softly.

They walked slowly towards the back of the house. "Must you really go to Albany to testify at that trial?" she asked.

"I won't go until after the flax is in and before we have to harvest the corn and wheat. That means the third week of July. Three weeks from now."

"But the summons says you are to appear on July 15."

"I know."

"What will you do?"

St. John shrugged. "I suppose I will write to them and explain," he said simply.

He ducked his head just in time to avoid the water-pipe trestle and they strolled over to their vegetable and herb garden where Henry was pulling out weeds among the cabbage. Although they had a large crop of Indian maize growing on the other side of the road, here in the garden Henry had also planted corn, in several long rows, carefully interspersed with squash plants and bean vines.

"And how are your siblings doing today?" St. John asked.

"Good. The Lord Loya'n'el has blessed my three sisters." Henry pointed to the maize stalks, still not quite knee high, around which the bean vines clung; and below which the broad green leaves of the squash plants spread out like a protective umbrella over the roots.

"The squash leaves shade the roots and keep the soil moist," St. John explained to Mehetable, as if she were hearing of it for the first time. "The bean vine and leaves somehow keep away the insects; and the corn stalks support the beans. Squash, beans and corn. For some reason, as long as an Indian has the three sisters to eat he never seems to get sick, not even the scurvy. But the three must be taken together. I wonder how that should be so."

Henry nodded. "That is true. In each of the three sisters the Lord Loya'nel has given a part of himself, out of love for his children. His children need all three parts. And here," he exclaimed, stooping down then straightening up again, holding a small, perfect freckled red fruit, "here is the Lord's special treat to delight us." He presented it to Mehetable with a smile.

"Why, thank thee, Henry." Mehetable took the strawberry and ate it. Henry was pleased. He gave her a handful more, carefully placing them in her cupped palm.

"Just about ripe," Mehetable approved. "We shall have a gross of good strawberry preserves next week. And pie, if the rhubarb is ready."

"The strawberries should be gathered tomorrow, ma'am. I don't think it will storm tomorrow, lookin' at the sky. But I don't know about the next day."

"Tomorrow is the Sabbath. And we are all a-going to Meeting."

"Not to worry," St. John intervened. "Cesar and I will help you this evening after supper, after letting the fruit have the full benefit of today's sun."

Henry brightened. "Yes. Thank you, brother. Thank you ma'am."

Leaving the farm hand in the garden, the couple went to the shade of the kitchen porch. St. John insisted his wife sit a spell and rest. He brought her a large cup of water and took a cup himself as well.

"You are so much like my own father," Mehetable remarked with a smile. "Can't sit still a moment. Even on the Sabbath."

"If Jesus approved plucking corn to eat or rescuing sheep on Sabbath-day, then I suppose we do not risk fire and brimstone by picking strawberries or milking our cows."

"You have been reading the Gospels." Mehetable was pleased. "I suppose I take after my mother. She came straight out of the Old Testament. 'Abraham's daughter', she called herself. How fitting her name should be Hannah. Although her son, my brother, bears little resemblance to Samuel, even though he carries that name."

"You know, we could ask your father to come here and live with us."

Mehetable squeezed his arm. "Thank'ee. But no, he would never do that. He's too proud. Besides, he has help from Samuel."

"Samuel is at sea most of the time."

Mehetable fell silent a moment.

"I hope our Meeting can find a good preacher," she fretted. "'Tis a long way to the Presbyterian church at Bethlehem or Goshen."

"We could always accept the Bulls' invitation to attend their church, St. David's."

"I don't appreciate your sense of humour today, Mr. St. John. I'd just as soon go to the Catholic mass with all its saints and ungodly relics than go to an Anglican church. It's the same thing, minus the pope."

"But He is the same God, isn't He?"

"Why, Michael! I have not seen you in such a spiritual way before. I confess, I have had some doubts about your true feelings from time to time about it."

St. John looked away a moment. "Perhaps it is necessary for some to experience miracles before they dare to wonder," he murmured. "Perhaps it is seeing the miracle of the morning sun shining on our farm, or the miracle taking place in your womb."

He gently opened his wife's fingers and took out a vivid red strawberry, still attached to its dark green stem, not unlike an umbilical cord. He held it up, at eye level, examining it with interest.

"No mortal philosopher made this."

The remainder of the afternoon seemed to fly by. Every minute was spent on the thousand and one chores needed for survival, and because it was vital the chores be done, there was no choice in the matter but to do them; and as a consequence came the complete, utter peace and serenity – and freedom - of acceptance and surrender.

After finishing her ironing Mehetable turned to baking pies for the Sabbath, while roasting a leg of mutton and stringing up herbs from their garden. Outside St. John and Henry finished picking the last of the strawberries. Henry went to join Cesar milking the cows. The setting sun was obscured by a long band of wispy clouds looking like puffs of uncombed wool dyed pink in its refracted light.

"Looks like rain day after tomorrow," Henry affirmed.

"I hope it don't mess us up too bad with the flax harvest," Cesar worried.

Henry shrugged. "Whatever the Lord Loya'nel wants is good enough for me."

The darkening stalls were quiet except for the soft chewing of cud and the rhythmic squirting of warm milk into wooden buckets.

"You ever think of goin' back home to your people?" Cesar asked the other hand.

Henry shrugged again in the twilight. "Where is home? Who are my people?"

"But don't you miss your father? Your mother, or brothers or sisters?"

"Who is my mother or father? Who are my brothers and sisters?"

Cesar got up and patted Voltaire gently on her side. "Was' the matter, Voltaire? You don't feel like giving much any more, do you? You ain't sick, are you?"

He moved his stool over to the next stall and began milking Spinoza.

Mehetable was not feeling well and the bumpy waggon ride to Meeting made her feel worse. St. John had tried to convince her of the wisdom of spending Sabbath-day at home but she would not hear of it.

The hot, sticky air and heavy grey skies weighed down upon them and the gnats swarming around their heads were diabolic. Even the usually cheerful Cesar, sitting in the back with Henry guarding the heavy iron pot with their picnic dinner, was somber. Their horses, Martin and Luther, so named by St. John over the vociferous objections of his wife ("once a papist, always a papist!") plodded lethargically along the dusty road, a few traces behind the Roes' two carts.

Despite the misery of Mehetable her husband surveyed the land around them with contentment. Once past Daniel Crommelin's old stone house, Grey-Court – built by William Bull – and the smaller Roes' house – also built by Bull - and the Moffat mill on Crommelin Creek, houses were few and far between; but the softly rolling hills of Blooming Grove were a pleasing blend of corn, hops and wheat fields, patches of forest and rocky outcroppings. Looking eastward towards Hudson's River a few miles distant were several parallel mountainous ridges, part of the Hudson Highlands. Not as tall as the Catskills to the northwest, their ridge-tops of exposed granite veined with white quartz seemed to have been carved and scraped out by giant chisels wielded by a mighty hand.

They passed the side road on their right leading southerly to the Woodhulls', the Marvins', the Strongs' and a smattering of Bulls. Another half hour and they passed on their left the road northwards to the Tuthills and Seelys and Goldsmiths along the Otterkill stream. Ahead of them about a quarter mile was Brewster's Tavern and its large sign above the door with the painted, bewigged head in profile of King George, presumably the Third.

The congregation's white clapboard meeting-house sat on a small rise just off the road to their left, gable-end facing the highway at an angle. A small cottage for the minister stood off to one side next to a middling barn. Between the meeting-house and the cottage was a large tent made from old canvas sails.

After stopping a moment at the water trough to let Martin and Luther replenish themselves, the St. Johns drove over to the line of waggons and carts in the meadow where the horses would spend the next six hours grazing and thinking about whatever horses think about.

They went into the shade of the tent followed by Cesar and Henry, who put down their large iron pot on a trestle table with dozens of others, and fell in with the Roes, so prolific they took up almost half the tent. Three generations of Nathaniels were there, plus a Jonas and his Phebe. Mehetable searched for little Faith, found her, and gave her a hug, pushing askew the girl's bonnet and letting loose little sheaves of wheat-blond hair. The Woodhulls and their tribe together with numerous Howells, Seelys and Strongs filled out the rest of the tent. Small families with only three or four children, like the Brewsters and the Marvins and the Moffats, were already inside the meeting-house.

There was no sound of any bell, as there was no bell to ring, there being no bell tower in which to hang a bell. People thereabouts knew what time it was just by looking at the sky, or feeling the way the wind licked at their cheeks, or by the twitching of the cows' tails. The minister's cottage was fitted out with a wag-on-the-wall clock but its wooden gears, said to come all the way from the last century out of Plymouth Plantation, showed their age and the minister's blind guess was usually more accurate than the clock.

Today Reverend Azariah Schoonmaker did not need to guess or look at the clock for the congregants themselves would let him know when they were ready to hear his preaching. It was not called a congregational church for nothing, for unlike the Anglican Church with its bishops and the Presbyterians with their elders these descendants of Calvinist Puritans liked to row their own boat. They would go into the meeting-house and sit down when they were good and ready and not a moment before.

Rev. Schoonmaker peered near-sightedly out the dusty window and saw the Woodhull clan going inside, the sign that his flock was ready for their shepherd He hastily gathered up the squares of birch-bark on which he had written down the outline of the morning's sermon – paper from rags being far too scarce and expensive for his meager allowance - , nervously adjusted his plain linen neckband, slipped on his waistcoat, and prepared to sail out into the maëlstrom of Blooming Grove Meeting. But first he dropped to his knees on the floor and whispered a quick prayer for wisdom, for without God's guidance there was no way in the world he could preach for three hours on his skinny birch-bark outline.

Rev. Schoonmaker was a supply preacher, come down from Kingston in Ulster County with its surfeit of ministers to fill vacancies caused by death, or retirement, or scandal, and with the ardent hope he would hit it off with the congregation and they would call him to stay. He was only thirty years old but his chronically poor eyesight had not been made better by the years of constant reading, mostly at the Divinity School at Yale College; and was getting worse by the week despite his awkward eyeglasses. Most people thought of him as short and stout, due to his rotund body and bespectacled round face but he was actually quite tall.

This was his second Sunday. He thought the first one had gone off pretty well. At least, the people seemed to like it and some even praised it. Only a handful had drifted off to sleep during the morning sermon, and just a few more during the afternoon sermon which, he thought, was understandable given the heat that day, the large picnic dinner, and the drowsy humming of the bees outside.

"Morning, preacher."

"Good morning! Um...Mr. Woodhull?"

"Just plain Jesse. Hope to hear a good 'un today!" Woodhull smiled, not used to talking to anyone at his own eye level. He gave the young preacher an encouraging slap on the back which almost sent his eyewear flying as they shuffled through the doorway.

The inside of the meeting-house was simplicity itself. There were no pews, but benches without backs, some just rough-hewn lumber, others long oak boards, the better to discourage slumber. The benches were not so much arranged as scattered in a casual ellipse of concentric ovals in the middle of which was a chair. In this way, so the thinking went, there would be no pride of place. It did not prevent a subtle contest for the right to occupy the benches closest to the chair, nor did it prevent the several wealthier families with slaves to have them sit in the back rows.

St. John and wife always chose to seat themselves in the middle rows. Cesar and Henry followed their employers to the bench directly behind them, Henry being indifferent to where he sat, Cesar never feeling quite comfortable. The Woodhull, Howell, Marvin and Seely families took up most of the innermost seats. To St. John's left were Isaac and Sarah Bull with restless children wedged between them and to Mehetable's right the family of Mary Bull Horton and her Silas. The Strongs found places behind the Woodhulls, and at either end were Tuthills, and Roes, a few Goldsmiths and some just plain Smiths.

Rev. Schoonmaker bid them rise and open with a prayer.

"Grant us understanding, o Lord, so that we may learn the true meaning of wisdom," he concluded. "Amen."

A Roe couple led the congregation in a hymn. The preacher adjusted his spectacles. He coughed nervously.

"The title of my sermon this morning is: 'Know Thy Enemy.' " He fumbled with the birch-bark. The assembled waited patiently, children excepted. He adjusted his glasses. He coughed again. He gave up on the birch-bark and committed himself to God. He took a deep breath.

The door to the meeting-house opened. A heavy clumping of boots announced a late-comer. It was Jeroboam Brown with family in tow, daughter Sagacity and sister herding their younger siblings as best they could. Brown took his spot just behind the Elihu Marvins.

Rev. Schoonmaker closed his eyes and began to preach. He preached from the Old Testament, he preached from the New, then landed back on Kings. Most of the parishioners seemed to enjoy his preaching, the degree of enjoyment being directly proportional to their capacity of understanding. A few of the men sat with arms folded, eyelids narrowed, but whether from skepticism or somnolence only they knew. All of the children fidgeted, but they knew, and feared, the consequences of venting their feelings. The people in bondage on the back benches watched in silent waiting.

"Now, King David did many sinful things when he was on the throne of a united Israel. But in each instance he realised he had sinned and he repented from his heart. He died faithful to God. Do I suggest, therefore we should all feel free to sin? If King David is here in this Meeting among us, please, stand up now so that we may see you!"

Jeroboam Brown, who had drifted off to sleep, came to with a jerk and rose to his feet thinking it was time for the closing hymn. The women-folk looked at him aghast while their men chuckled. Sagacity, blushing, tugged at his waistcoat. Brown, face darkening, sat back down, slapping away his daughter's hands.

"And what are we to make of King Solomon, David's son, inheriting the throne as he did through the divinely inspired intercession of his mother, Bathsheba the queen? Solomon, who thereupon proceeded to kill off all his rivals. Did he feel remorse? Did he ask for repentance? We do not know. We do know he then prayed to God. Now, what did he pray for? Did he ask God for money, comfort, power? No! He asked God to give him understanding, and discernment. What did God say? He said to Solomon, I will give you wisdom, so that you may discern between good and evil.

"And so Solomon became celebrated for his wisdom. He made wise decisions. He rendered justice with a righteous hand. He ruled his people wisely. He wrote the book of wisdom we call Proverbs.

"But, my friends, what, exactly, *is* wisdom? We look around in our community and we say, 'so-and-so is a wise man' or 'so-and-so says wise things'. But what do we mean by that? Is wisdom what you say, what you do, what you think? Or is wisdom deeper than that? Just *what* is wisdom?

"Something later happened to Solomon the Wise. He turned his back on God. He started to do unwise things. He became a tyrant, and treated his subjects harshly. So God said, 'I will nonetheless let you remain king until you die; and after you, your son Rehoboam shall inherit your kingdom. But, God said, Rehoboam is a foolish man, for he chooses not to discern between good and evil and so is not wise. A king who is foolish deserves to have his kingdom stripped away from him. And so there shall rise up a rebellion against him which will tear his kingdom asunder!' So spake God.

"And so it came to pass, in fulfillment of God's will. There rose up a rebellion against the tyranny of the unwise king, and his kingdom was torn apart."

"Amen!" Elihu Marvin called out. Others around him echoed the sentiment.

The preacher dabbed his sweaty brow with the sweatier kerchief.

"But," he marched onwards, "now then, what of the rebels? Were the rebels any wiser than the unwise king they overthrew? Or did they, too, turn their backs to God? Were those who demanded the overthrowing of the tyrant themselves any less tyrannical?"

The pastor had been preaching for an hour and his kerchief was so wet it only added to the dampness of his forehead. He gratefully drank the cup of water from a proffering hand.

For some of the assembled this was a signal for discussion. Elderly David Smith, the patriarch of the Smith clan, and Justice of the Peace down by Smith's Clove, rose from his bench. "As the apostle Paul teaches us, we are to obey our king anointed by God."

Elihu Marvin, on the opposite side of the ellipse, jumped to his feet. "Did Moses submit meekly to Pharoah? Did he not slay the cruel Egyptian slave driver?"

"Moses Marvin! I think I like the ring of that name."

Marvin folded his arms across a defiant chest and planted his legs. "There came a time when the Hebrews threw off the yoke of slavery and fought for their promised land. What matters if they were sinful people? We are all sinful people. I'd rather be a sinner under a free sun than a sinner under the yoke of slavery! Do you like being a slave, Judge Smith?" Elihu Marvin challenged, jaw thrust forward.

"I am as free a man as you are, Elihu Marvin. Which means I am as free as you to have my opinions."

"Maybe there are some opinions that aren't welcome in these parts."

Richard Bull, sitting next to his brother Isaac, stood up impatiently, a look of exasperation on his weather-beaten face. "If we're all going to talk about freedom, let us all understand what that word means. Free from what? Free from oppression? Who here is truly oppressed? Our king is no more Pharaoh than you, Elihu, are Joseph. God gave us order and rules, and if we go beyond His order and rules that's where we will surely find chaos and ruin. That's a place where no man is free. Freedom exists when we live within God's kingdom. And God has given us a king to live under."

"Richard Bull, you're a long, long way from your Anglican Church. We can show you the road if you've forgotten it." This from Nathaniel Strong.

"And are you, Nathanial Strong, wiser than Solomon?" Judge Smith rejoined. "Are you above God? Didn't the Lord say, 'I hate pride and arrogance, evil behaviour and perverse speech.

Counsel and sound judgement are mine; by me kings reign and rulers make laws that are just, by me princes govern and all nobles who rule on earth.'"

"On condition they rule wisely and in the ways of God," Strong retorted angrily.

Jesse Woodhull, whose immigrant ancestors had long ago jumped from Connecticut to Long Island, along with the Roes and the Strongs and the Smiths and the Brewsters, was enjoying the heated exchange between his distant kin. He saw the look of dismay, however, on the young preacher's face.

He patted the pastor's thigh reassuringly. "Just a regular Sabbath Meeting in Blooming Grove."

Woodhull rose. "God knows I'm no preacher, gents and ladies, but here's my own two bits. Reverend Schoonmaker here will tell me if I get my Scriptures wrong. Wasn't there a time, before King David, when the Hebrews had no king, but instead were led by their judges and priests?

"But then they looked around and saw that all the other nations had kings. So the Hebrews started hankerin' for a king, too. They pestered their wise priest Samuel to ask God for a king to rule over them. An' Samuel says to them, "why do you want a king to rule over you? You already have a King, the greatest King of them all.

"But they weren't satisfied with God and demanded a human king. So God says to Samuel, let them have their human king. But warn them what they're getting themselves into. Tyranny, slavery, arbitrariness, misery.

"I don't know if we can govern ourselves *without* a king, but it seems to me it can't be any worse than being governed *by* a king, as long as we keep our eyes on the one true King."

There was a smattering of *amens*.

"Jesse, I don't know that I disagree with what you just said," Hezekiah Howell weighed in, "but the cause of our troubles is not the king, God watch over him, but Parliament. Arrogant, aloof Parliament and arrogant, aloof ministers. That's the heart of the problem."

Rev. Schoonmaker struggled to his feet, sweating more profusely than ever.

"Yes, the heart! That is where the problem is, and that is where the remedy will be found. The human heart."

He dabbed his brow. "Friends, let us recall where he was, the Apostle Paul, when he wrote, 'love God and one another with all your heart'. He was in a Roman dungeon. Thrown in prison for having simply said, God loves you and asks for you to love Him back, through his Son the anointed one. What kind of man is he who talks of love and compassion from inside a prison?

"That man, friends and neighbours, is a man who understands where true freedom is found. And where it is not found. It is not to be found in human institutions and governments which rise and fall. It is not to be found in the emotions and passions of the moment, which come and go like the wind and clouds. It is found only in the one who allowed Himself to be tortured and killed in the most excruciating agony for our sakes, all while saying: Father, forgive them, for they know not what they do.

"Forgiveness! Search your hearts, brothers and sisters. Ask yourselves, is not the spirit of forgiveness the path to true freedom?

"Of all God's commandments which is supreme? Jesus said it is this: thou shalt love the Lord thy God with all thy heart, all thy soul and all thy strength; and thou shalt love thy neighbour.' When the clever lawyer then challenged Jesus to define 'neighbour' what did Jesus do? He told a story. And *whom* did Jesus choose as the hero of His story? Not only was His choice an outcaste, a Samaritan despised by the Jews, but it was this same Samaritan who rescued an injured Jew left to die on the roadside by his fellow believers. If the outcaste has more love in his heart than God's own chosen people, what does that say about us, followers of God?

"Jesus said, before you criticize your brother for the speck of sawdust in his eye, first pull out the log in your own eye. Paul said, 'You have no excuse, you who pass judgement on someone else, for at whatever point you judge the others, you are condemning yourself, because you who pass judgement do the same things'. Christians! Be devoted to one another in brotherly love. Cast aside your selfish pride and forgive your brothers, as Joseph forgave his."

The morning sermon came to an end and the worshippers, led by the children, went out to the tent for the mid-day dinner. It was the Tuthill clan's day to take care of the water, and their children were dispatched to the preacher's well with buckets. The women-folk busied themselves with spreading the food out on the tables while the men-folk clustered around to exchange news.

By tacit understanding an unspoken truce was declared and politics was avoided. By unspoken custom sitting apart were families, dressed in black, who had lost a child or mother or an elderly ancestor within the past few weeks. No one invoked the departed; everyone knew their time would come soon enough to don mourning clothes.

A group of older children came up to their parents with a petition for permission to play. Permission was granted on condition the game was scholarly. The children agreed to the condition. They removed to the preacher's open barn door and in the shade of the eaves organized a spelling bee. The dozen or so oldest boys elected John Marvin captain of the bee by open ballot.

The captain ordered everyone to sit down on the ground and began to announce the rules of the game. Tall and skinny, his white linen shirt hanging loosely on his frame like the sail of a skiff in irons, the captain towered over his disciples sitting cross-legged below him, a pubescent Moses laying down the law.

Seeing this, the younger children, boys and girls, white children, slave children, wriggled their way from the cloister of the tent and ran over to the barn, like a swarm of bees to the hive. There being no more room in the shade, the newcomers chaffed in the hot sun. A few tried to crowd into the cool space already occupied by the older children and were rudely shoved away.

"We were here first!"

"You don't own the barn. It doesn't belong to you!" the rebels retorted.

The boldest among the younger boys pushed back, provoking a tussle while the majority of the children, whether through meekness or indifference, looked on without committing themselves one way or the other.

The captain was impatient.

"Stop it! Sit down. Find another spot!" he commanded the newcomers.

"Who anointed you king?" replied the bold boy. "I'll sit wherever I want to."

"Like hell you will. Go on. Scram! If you don't like it here go find someplace else."

The bold young boy dug in his heels and refused to budge. The captain, his authority threatened, flushed in anger and gave the younger child a brutal shove. The lad fell back but regained his footing and held his ground. His face, too, was infused with wounded pride and he raised his balled fists in front of him.

A look of confusion crossed John's face. He was perplexed. This was not the reaction he expected from his inferiors. Reason dictated there must be only one leader. Younger children were to wait patiently for their turn just as their older siblings had had to do. Why could young Absalom Smith not see this?

In a flash John's anger at Absalom's stupidity overcame his reason and he sprang forward, knocking the young boy down on top of other children trying to stay out of the fight. The noises of juvenile warfare and the cries of the non-combatants reached the ears of the adults under the tent. With an inaudible curse Elihu Marvin got up from his bench and hurried over to the battleground with several Smiths and Roes and Strongs on his heels.

The two boys were locked together and so consumed with the desire to annihilate the other they were oblivious to everything else. Strong hands clamped their necks and pulled them abruptly apart, then dragged them away, the brawlers squirming in furious protest.

The older boys immediately organized another caucus. Vacuums are impossible in any society. Voids will always be filled, for better or for worse.

Young Nathaniel Roe emerged as the new leader. He repeated the rules for the bee lain down by his predecessor for the benefit of the newcomers, divided the group into two even teams, and let the game begin.

In an instant the fight was forgotten, as quickly as a birch-bark sermon.

Chapter Seven: *Justice Shall Be Done*

Cadwallader Colden smiled sardonically as he read once again the letter and summons St. John had handed over. He chuckled.

"He's a fighter, this Ethan Allen! Head-strong and hot-headed, is he." Colden, despite his sixty years in his adopted land, still spoke with the Scots burr of his childhood. "But, I'm afraid, what the man shows in boldness he lacks in intelligence. The fight was over before it began, and he is the only one who dinna ken that fact."

The old Scotsman was looking shrewdly with sharp hazel eyes at the younger man, who had come to him for advice and who clearly did not want to testify.

"We'll let Mr. Allen and Jared Ingersoll have their day in court and present their case. But it will be dismissed on the motion of Mr. Duane and the other lawyers for New-York, without needing to call to the bar secondary witnesses such as yourself. Your testimony would be immaterial."

"It's just that I've got to get the flax in and I only have two hands to help. "

"Say no more, young lad," Colden replied breezily, as though speaking to a somewhat dense adolescent, dismissing the comment with the wave of an elegant hand accustomed to being obeyed. "Allen's claim will be dismissed because he has no proof Governor Wentworth had any royal authority to issue his grants. The Colony of New-York, on the other hand, has the original letters patent granted by Prince Edward, the Duke of York and Albany, declaring that the Colony of New-York encompasses all the land east to the Connecticut River north of Massachusetts. The duke's patent was confirmed under the seal of King George III six years ago. And so, you see, Ethan Allen's case is hopeless."

The lieutenant-governor absently stuck a finger up under his white powdered wig and scratched his scalp, then picked up an elaborate round container made of cherry wood inlaid with light maple veneer in the form of the cross of St. Andrew. He proffered the box to St. John.

"Snuff?" he offered.

"Ah, no, thank you just the same."

Colden shrugged and took a large pinch for himself between thumb and forefinger. He opened his mouth and inserted the tobacco between his lower lip and gums, rubbing it in thoroughly with a quick brushing motion. He smacked his lips and inhaled with satisfaction, then coughed.

"Your Excellency, you must not move your noggin' so," a woman's voice scolded. "Sit still! Or else it won't do."

The plump woman sitting just to the side and behind St. John was looking crossly at the lieutenant-governor, then relaxed back into a contented smile as she saw him obey her orders meekly. Her lap was tucked underneath a small folding camp table on which sat a large, amber-coloured lump of wax in the shape of a human head on which her agile fingers were busy at work. She sighed happily.

"Yes, I declare, this will be the finest bust I shall have ever sculpted. Your friend Dr. Franklin will be pleased, I'm sure. But you must promise me you will not move your head or else I shall pack up and leave! You don't want that now, do you?" the woman admonished, as if speaking to a disobedient child.

"No, Miss Wright, I don't want that. I promise I shall not budge. But you must finish soon for I have business in the City to attend to. And a meeting with General Gage. We must prepare for the arrival of the new royal governor."

"I would be pleased if you could introduce me to the good general. Perhaps he would like me to do his bust, too."

"I would be delighted, my lady." Colden spoke stiffly, trying to keep his head rigidly still. In so doing he resembled a waxen figure himself.

"He's no stranger to the court-room, Jared Ingersoll," Colden said, trying to please his taskmaster by keeping his lips frozen like a ventriloquist. "Yale graduate. Used to be the King's Attorney for Connecticut. The mobs threatened to tar and feather him at the time of the Stamp Act troubles. Coerced him to resign."

The elderly man snorted loudly, whether from disdain or from the snuff was hard to tell. Miss Wright shot him a stern warning look across the bow. "Like they did with Andrew Oliver, the stamp agent in Massachusetts. Intolerant rabble! Sailors, vagrants, Negroes! A band of shiftless banditti.

"And even here, in New-York! The mob attacked Fort George, whipped up to a frenzy by the pirates McDougall and Sears, aided and abetted by none other than the Livingstons! They burned my coach and sleigh, burned down Major James' house, looted dozens of shops, threatened to kill everyone who disagreed with their radical republican views. Turbulent Bedlamites! And they call themselves 'sons of liberty'. They're free to swing, if I had my way.

"Sears finally realised he was being manipulated by the Livingstons. What does he go and do? He and McDougall and their 'Liberty Boys' dump the Livingstons – turncoat Presbyterians! - and join with James DeLancey, of all people. The richest man in New-York! My daughter Betsy is married to DeLancey's brother Peter, you know. But Peter is a gentleman.

"Thanks to Sears' mob, DeLancey's men swept the elections last year and ran the Livingstons out of office."

Colden chuckled grimly, in his throat so as to not provoke the ire of Miss Wright. "I was only too happy to oblige DeLancey's request to revoke the appointments of all the Livingston sheriffs and clerks and justices of the peace. Except for the Judge, of course. He's appointed for life, much is a pity. A haughty, conniving, vindictive family, those Livingstons! I was glad to be able to teach them a lesson.

"But, lo! What's the first thing DeLancey does after crushing the Livingstons? He tears up the non-importation pledge! And thumbs his nose at King Sears! Which is why the rabble is back to supporting the Livingstons.

"So the Livingstons with their million acres and the DeLanceys with their million pounds hate each other. If it weren't for me our Colony would fall apart. The king is relying on me to hold the fort until the new royal governor arrives. Thank God my daughter is safe in London, safe from the likes of Sears and his outlaws.

"An iron hand, that's what's needed, or else the lower sort will only be emboldened to stir up more trouble. You see, all this talk about 'equality' and 'justice' is so much clap-trap. It's resentment and envy what drives them."

St. John was only half-listening. He, too, was conscious of envy, envy for all the wonderful volumes of books gracing the walls of the wood-paneled room. Books were a luxurious rarity on the frontier. Lining the shelves were volumes in Greek, Latin, French and English; Plato, Aristotle, Cato, Aquinas, Newton, Descartes, Buffon.

Closer to hand was a thick volume written by Colden himself, the *History of the Five Iroquois Nations*, the first book Colden loaned him when they had met. Next to it was his deceased daughter Jane's book on the flora of New-York, the second book St. John had borrowed, although he had to struggle through it, having forgotten long ago most of his Latin. Colden's other famous book, *Plantae Coldenghamiae*, had earned him international fame among botanists and a warm endorsement from Carl Linnaeus, whose treatise *Systema Naturae* had been carefully placed next to it on the book-shelf.

Sitting on the grand table was another heavy tome. *Blackstone's Law Commentaries* was the title, embossed in large gold letters. The elderly man saw the look of curiosity in St. John's eyes.

"Are you interested in reading law? Well, you will enjoy Professor Blackstone. This, my young friend, is a real treasure. Published in London a fortnight ago, figuratively speaking! I bought it for my son. It will help bring order out of the chaos of our muddled judiciary. You know, most of our judges have never read a law book in their life. The only legal work they know is the *Constable's Pocket Book*. Moore and Coke are strangers to their intellects. Legal precedent is a meaningless concept.

"Pray excuse me for not being able to loan to you our Blackstone. However, you might be interested to know that Robert Bell, the Philadelphia auctioneer, has advertised another large estate sale. He has a Blackstone, I believe."

"I would gladly give an acre of good land to be able to go. But I haven't the time."

"Yes, yes, your flax harvest, your cows, your honey-bees, pregnant wife and all that. I know. I too, was once young like you. I am fortunate to have had both the blessings of a farmer and those of a philosopher, a cultivator of the soil as well as of the mind. I see that in you as well."

"His Excellency may not have told you, but I am from Philadelphia and I know Mr. Bell quite well. I did his bust last year," Miss Wright purred. "I shall be glad to inquire of him should he come across a volume of...whatever it was you gentlemen was talking about."

There was a light rapping at the door, then a black serving girl entered with a silver tray and silver tea-pot; and porcelain tea-cups with silver spoons.

"Set it down anywhere, Rebecca, but mind the Blackstone! You may pour out. Sugar, young man? Cream?"

"Black is fine."

"So be it. Miss Wright?"

"No, thank you all the same. I am nearly finished with my work. Perhaps you gentlemen will excuse me while I stretch my legs."

"Very well....Thank you, Rebecca."

The men sipped their tea.

"The Chinese philosophers claim their tea has great medicinal value," Colden mused. "Some of my fellow physicians are of the same opinion. It is obvious tea stimulates the heart muscle as well as the mind. Not to mention the bladder."

"I wonder though if it has any preventive power."

"Aye, that's the important question, hain't it? The power to stymie the malady before it takes hold, rather than merely lighten the symptoms. Since all diseases result from an imbalance of the humours in the body, made worse by their distribution throughout the blood, it is obvious that any substance which tends to keep the humours in their proper balance and correct proportions to one another ought to prevent the disease."

"In that case, we know that tea is not such a substance, since many are the tea drinkers who succumb to the yellow-fever, the small-pox, and other distempers."

"Well," Colden pointed out, "our casual observations are not dispositive. We do not know, for example, that tea, taken alone, is not effective. Perhaps it is the addition of other food that reduces the salutary benefits of the tea. Come to think of it, I have never myself had the fever since childhood, and this despite numerous outbreaks of the small-pox and cholera in the communities in which I was living."

"I suppose then what we are lacking is knowledge of the facts."

Colden poured out another cup for his guest and himself. "The problem is our lack of experience. We need subjects on whom to test our theories; but in so doing we might only be securing their deaths. That is why I am dead-set against this mania come out of Boston which pretends that in order to cure the small-pox, all one needs do is to infect the patient before-hand. If ever such an illogical, immorally reckless notion ever was spawned, it would pale before this idea. Imagine, deliberately infecting a person with the very evil sought to be avoided! Absurd. Besides, I understand it was the Mohammedans who invented this foolish theory.

"And yet, none other than Cotton Mather has espoused this. And I have to admit his data from the great small-pox epidemic of 1723 are intriguing. Physicians all know that at least one-third of all healthy adults will die of the disease within ten days of being infected; fifty percent of all older children; and eighty percent of all younger children. Mather claims that only 2 to 5 percent of those inoculated died."

"It's no wonder we all live in fear of the sickness," St. John felt obliged to contribute, glad his wife was not present.

"Nonetheless," Colden lectured onwards, "Mather's experience must have been a fluke, an aberration. I for one am not ready to abandon the only true effective remedy, which is the immediate and thorough purging of the blood. Bleeding the patient, you see, is the only possible way to remove the bad humours. But inoculation, never!"

"To be completely frank, Dr. Colden, I've been thinking of getting myself inoculated, and my children and wife."

"Do not venture there, young man, at the peril of your life. I was, as a matter of fact, in the middle of composing a letter to Franklin and our mutual acquaintance Dr. Priestley. Priestly shares my skepticism over inoculation. Franklin, on the other hand, is misguided. He believes in it. His own young boy died of the small-pox, you know. Not only does he recommend inoculation for adults, but he also insists on it for children, even if against their parents' wishes. But I have given up trying to convince him of his error.

"No, I am writing to him about the transit of Venus last year. Not that Franklin disputes my calculations; he is hopelessly lost in higher mathematics, as you may know. I am merely indulging his request for clarification on the subject of the errors I have discovered in Newton's own conclusions from long ago. Franklin, I am afraid, seems to be the only natural philosopher in the world who understands the point I have made."

Colden shook his head sadly at the thought. "But you know, getting back to your wish to expose yourself and your loved ones needlessly to the perils of the small-pox, you will no longer have to travel up to Boston, or down to Philadelphia to visit Dr. Rush. Our Colonial Assembly will be granting a license to a physician in Goshen village, not far from your farm, to inoculate. His name is Tusten, Benjamin Tusten. The compromise in the law will be, that no inoculations shall be allowed within a quarter-mile of any other dwelling or place of business. If some people wish to deliberately infect themselves, so be it; but it must not be allowed to spread. Oh, and make sure you are well prepared for it: you will be mighty ill for two to three weeks. If you survive that long."

St. John finished his cup of tea. "Regarding my idea about windmills...."

"Yes. Your windmills! It slipped my mind. I tried it once, myself, years ago around the time I had my canal dug. You know, I was the first one in all the Colonies to build a working canal."

Colden frowned. "Unfortunately, it's all clogged up now. Tenants, you know. Can't rely on them to do any more than what's in their own self-interest. They don't use the canal, so they let it go. Now, the problem with the windmill was, well, the lack of wind. Constant, strong wind, I mean."

"You are right that the winds here are not as steady as on the coast. But the problem to be solved, I think, is not so much the lack of force, but rather the resistance of the object we want to turn. In other words, if we could find a way to make our vanes lighter, and capture the wind more effectively, we would overcome the problem of light winds."

"If you can come up with an intelligent design, I will nominate you for the American Philosophical Society," Colden said, smiling broadly. "After all, it was at my urging that Ben Franklin founded it." Colden rose from his chair, signaling the visit was at an end. The old man reached for a large volume behind him on a shelf and handed the book to St. John.

"Have you ever read Thomas Hobbes' masterpiece *Leviathan*? No? Well, then you will enjoy this. The rule of law or the tyranny of the mob, that's the choice."

He walked his guest to the stoop outside the front door. "And about that summons to testify, do not have any concerns. If it should ever be brought to Judge Livingston's attention, you may rest assured, justice will be done."

He gave St. John a wink and closed the door.

Chapter Eight: *A Troublesome Cook-Book*

"Let us see here," St. John muttered to himself. "Take the whites of six eggs…whip them with a whisk until frothy…where is our whisk?" he asked Judas.

Judas stared at St. John, green eyes glittering with the reflection of the fire.

"It must be here somewhere…." Annoyed, St. John walked from the trestle-table over to the earthenware pot on the cupboard shelf from which all sorts of cooking spoons, ladles and gadgets protruded. Judas followed the man with his eyes.

"It would be helpful if I could see what I am looking for," he remarked. The light from the hearth did not reach beyond the table, leaving the back of the kitchen in shadows. Although not yet dusk, only a greyish glow filtered in through the west window due to the overcast sky of early autumn. From outside came the raucous calling of crows.

He thought of lighting the betty lamp. "Too smelly," he decided. He felt something soft brushing against his calf. Judas purred, then jumped up onto the apron of the cup-board and looked at St. John.

"If you value your life you'll be wanting to jump back down before my wife sees you."

The cat regarded St. John, thinking it over. Not wishing to lose face, the creature first took a moment to lick his paws nonchalantly with an insolent tongue before hopping down to the floor and following the man back to the table.

The door from outside opened and Mehetable came in armed with a basket of apples.

"You are working in the dark."

"I didn't want to use the tallow-lamp. I don't feel like putting up with the smoke and smell this evening."

"We have the whale oil lamp in the parlour."

"Whale oil is too precious to waste on my cooking. And we have no more bayberry candles left. That will have to wait 'til candle-making next week."

Mehetable put her basket down on the cup-board apron. Judas retreated silently to a corner and resumed grooming himself.

"With our apples I shall bake us a good pie tomorrow."

St. John came up to her and gave her a kiss. "And I shall bake us a tasty treat for tonight. A *soufflé*, in celebration of our anniversary."

"Michael St. John! I wish 'twere our anniversary every day, that I might be relieved of the chore of cooking! But what, pray thee, is a *'soufflé'*?"

"It's a baked delicacy, light and puffy, made with egg whites. There is a tavern-keep in the City, fellow named Fraunces, who prepares the latest French pastries and desserts. I dined there with Pastor Tétard last Spring. Fraunces claimed he's the only one outside Versailles who knows how to cook this dish. But now he's gone and published it in his little three-penny recipe book here. Tétard sent it to me by the post." St. John gestured at the pamphlet.

"It has been a long time since I have tasted good French pastry," his wife remarked. "Not since I was a little girl in New Rochelle. Madame Sorrel, it was, who made it for us. She owned a bakery. She was the mid-wife for my mother when I was born. My father said, 'who better than a baker to pull out sweet warm things from the oven?'"

She peered into the large earthenware bowl on the table next to the open pamphlet and the small basket of eggs. "Why, you have not even yet begun," she exclaimed.

"I was trying to find the egg whisk. I have looked high and low for it."

Mehetable looked at her husband and sighed, shaking her head softly. "Here it is. On the side of the table. Isn't this what you were looking for?" She held up the small fan-shaped tool, fashioned from a dozen thin twigs from an apple tree. "It was right under your nose all the time and you never saw it."

She glanced at the pamphlet on the table. "Are you sure you know what you are about?"

"It can't be witchcraft! It's just a cake. I thought, what a fitting dish for our first anniversary in our new house. As we have had our barn-raising, we shall have our cake-raising."

"I have seen you make your *tourtières* but I did not know you knew how to bake anything else."

"I have not baked anything other than meat pies since I was a child in my mother's kitchen."

"And so we shall relive your childhood tonight."

"Anything but that," he replied. He held up the cook-book to the light of the fire and studied the recipe. He laughed softly under his breath. "He is quite amusing, this fellow. 'Take heed to part the yolk from the white with care, lest your soufflé not rise in the air, and whip the white to a peak just right, that you may offer a heavenly delight.' Well, it seems simple enough."

Mehetable was doubtful. "I don't know about that. I would be afraid to attempt it, methinks."

"Afraid of a soufflé? It is nothing but cream, eggs, flour, some butter; and a bit of sugar and ginger I'll add, with some strawberry preserves. It will be a 'heavenly delight', you'll see."

Judas in his dark corner licked his paw silently, watching them out of the corner of his eyes.

As her husband laboured over his creation Mehetable hung the tea-kettle on the crane over the fire. "Thank'ee to save a bit of the ginger for my tea."

"Do you have the nausea again? Ginger, honey and cider work wonders I find."

"I prefer chamomile and bee-balm from our garden, thank'ee just the same."

St. John lined the iron baking-pot with lard and sugar, poured in the base of egg yolks and flour followed by the folding-in of the whites, then placed the lid on the pot and slipped the vessel into their bake-oven built into the side of the chimney, still hot from the day's baking and to which he added a scoop of coals. He turned over the sand-glass and helped his wife into the old, rickety rocker. He fixed her chamomile and ginger tea and hot cider with a splash of rum for himself and joined her by the flickering fire.

Judas padded over and regarded St. John a moment, then helped himself to the man's lap. The cat purred. The couple sipped their drinks, looking silently into the capricious flames.

"I don't think I feel comfortable around Sagacity's father, Mr. Brown," Mehetable remarked. "Forgive me if I am not charitable towards him, but I can't help it. Methinks he is a cruel man. An' it seems he does not say nice things about you behind your back. Mary Bull Horton has told me. After all the help you gave him, too. Loaning him Henry and Cesar for his corn harvest, giving him money to meet his taxes, hiring his daughter."

"Well, he did give us something nice in return." St. John caressed Judas' neck. The cat stretched out languidly.

"A cat, yes! The creature does not like me."

"He's good at catching mice, though."

"I feel ill at ease, the way he watches me with those strange eyes. I will be sure to put a sachet of angelica in each of our rooms to ward off his evil."

"Angelica... *Angélique*...." St. John murmured absently, looking into the fire.

"Not a former belle of yours, I hope."

"No.... There once was a wise good man I knew. In Quebec. Jacques Lamoureux. He loved his daughter so. Angélique was her name. She was to marry a friend of mine. I wonder if they ever did. Or if they survived...."

"There is a new family come to Blagg's Clove. I believe their name is Lamoureux. Mary Horton keeps me informed of all the gossip in town." Mehetable laughed. "Thanks to her I know what every family has had for breakfast, dinner and supper and who is secretly courting whom. I believe Mary said this new family come up from the City. They are Huguenots. I imagine they worshipped at the French Church. If so, they would know Pastor Tétard."

"Well," St. John replied," if they are Calvinists they would not be related to my Lamoureux family. Strange coincidence though. That is not a very common name in France."

"But then, neither is yours."

"It's your name, too, now!"

"Yes, and what a name, if I can truly believe your translation, Michael Hector St. John de Crèvecoeur. Broken heart! It lends an air of romance and tragedy to you."

Her chair creaked as she rocked gently back and forth. "Psalm 51 was my mother's favourite," she murmured. "A broken spirit...a broken and contrite heart will find welcome with God."

Mehetable paused to sip from her cup. "I oft-times have wished my father had taught me French."

"I would teach you but you resist."

"Surrender is never easy."

They sat a moment in silence.

"I think I have almost forgotten how to speak my own native language," St. John mused. "The Old World seems so far away, so...alien. The old ways are no longer my ways. And yet, although attracted to the New World, I feel myself as though I am an alien to it. Just as the old ways are alien to me, I am alien to the new. And yet, here I am."

"I, too, sometimes feel I do not belong to this world of mortals."

St. John dumped Judas to the floor, to the cat's displeasure, and hugged his wife tenderly. "Don't pack your bags anytime soon. That is a command. As Paul says, 'wives, obey your husbands.'"

"An' he says, 'husbands, love your wives. An' I know you do."

"Twenty minutes! It's time."

He rose and padded eagerly over to the bake-oven, picking up along the way heavy cooking leathers. He reached into the oven, dragged out the heavy pot, and lovingly placed it on the table.

He retreated a step and took a deep breath. Mehetable stood next to him. They regarded the pot. The embers hissed. Judas licked his paws. St. John looked at his wife and smiled. With a gloved hand he reached for the handle on the lid and, like a magician unveiling his marvel, whisked off the lid with a grand "*Voilà!*"

They saw inside the pot a flat, yellow-brown substance resembling a thick porridge. A large bubble rose up to the surface and burst with a popping noise.

"I thought it is supposed to be puffy."

"There must be something wrong with that recipe," St. John muttered. Face darkening, he grabbed the recipe-book and flung it onto the hearth, narrowly missing the flames. "Or something wrong with the author!" he exclaimed in anger. "A charlatan, a fraud, that's what he is. His book's no good."

Mehetable, at first shocked by the sudden outburst, softened. She looked with pity at the vexed face of her husband.

"We should not blame our shortcomings on the author of the book if we don't understand what he says."

She placed her hands on his red cheeks and gave him a kiss. "'Tis the heart that counts," she said. "It was a lovely thought. But from now on I will do the baking." She kissed him again.

Mehetable donned the leathers and brought the pot onto the hearth. With the long fire-poke she pushed a trivet over some embers, then placed a fry-pan on it. She greased the pan, then added a cup of corn meal to the pot and whipped the contents before ladling it out in large round spoonfuls onto the sizzling pan. In the wink of an eye she was dishing out golden strawberry-ginger corn-cakes for the both of them. They sat down at their table, content with the light from their fire-place and the glow from their corn-cakes as the only illumination they required.

Mehetable bowed her head. "Thank Thee Lord for the food you give us. Thank Thee for your love and wisdom. Pray forgive me for the bad feelings I have harboured towards our neighbour; and pray give us strength and wisdom to forgive those who do not understand. An' may you bless their hearts as well as ours. Amen."

Sitting in a dark corner, looking at them silently, Judas slowly licked his paws.

Chapter Nine: *Stirrin' the Wrong Way*

St. John looked up at the heavy grey clouds pushing down upon them, like a press about to squeeze apples waiting in the tray. A stiff wind was blowing from the southwest. "A perfect day for threshing wheat," St. John remarked. "As well as for making cider afterwards."

"I volunteer to go up the hay loft," Cesar grinned.

"I'm sure you are only too happy to do so. Leaving Henry and me with the flailing!"

In a flash Cesar was up the ladder and soon forkfuls of long wheat stalks fell to the floor below where Henry and St. John were waiting, flails in hand, on either end of an imaginary circle twenty feet across. Once the pile was knee-high they began to beat it with their heavy clubs swiveling whip-like on a leather strap connected to the handle of the flail, separating the heads from the stalks.

"Back go the flail and down she come! Up go the flail an' give me rum!" Henry chanted.

The men were stripped down to their naked torso and soon bathed in sweat. An hour passed, then they turned over the pile with forks and began the beating anew. It was simple work; it was hard work; but the steady rhythmic continuity of it all was mesmerizing, and the miracle repeating itself once a week in their own bake-oven rendered the task sublime.

After dinner they returned to the barn just in time to greet the storm. They opened wide the barn doors to let the breeze come through, then forked up the broken straw and threw it down the hatch to the stalls below. They swept up the chaff and heads of grain onto a large tarpaulin, raising it up to the hay loft with a rope and pulley. Henry pulled the short straw and so climbed up to the loft from where he shoveled out, little by little, the contents of the tarp, which drifted down to an identical tarp waiting below. As the objects wafted downwards the wind below across them, winnowing out the chaff from the good kernels of grain hitting the tarp like pellets of rain.

The chaff swirled all around the barn, flying into their hair, clinging to their backs, coating their arms and sticking to their skin, their sweat acting like glue.

"Boss, you look like you been tarr'd 'n feathered."

St. John laughed. "You rather resemble a chicken yourself."

They gathered the corners of the tarp and filled up a barrel with the grain. Within the hour four more hogsheads were added to their autumn collection of barrels lining the walls of the barn.

"Our fall harvest will be almost as plentiful as the summer," St. John observed. "The first dry day next week we'll go to Moffat's mill."

"Tomorrow we'll squeeze apples?" Cesar asked.

"Tomorrow we'll squeeze apples," St. John agreed. He looked out the open door at the heavy rain flattening the grass and turning the dirt paths into mud. "Who's ready for a bath?"

"It ain't Saturday."

"You're not fixin' on sleeping in your straw suit, are you? Straw belongs in your bedding."

"Mistress will see us."

"Mistress is 'way yonder in the lean-to making soap. Speaking of which, there is a slab of soap in the bucket by the door."

With that St. John slipped off his wooden shoes and work trousers and, stark naked, grabbed the soap and stepped outside onto a large flat boulder. In an instant he was soaking wet from the rain. He sang as he scrubbed himself with the soap, raising first one arm, then the other high in the air.

"...hold up the sceptre and the crown...never let them down...." The lyrics escaped from his lips unbidden. Eyes clamped shut, he saw the smoky maple fire, the burly man in the red knit cap. But then the smell of the camp-fire was replaced by the sweet scent of sassafras.

He relaxed and enjoyed the freedom of being without clothes, without shame or guilt even if for only a moment, there under the pure water falling from the sky. He felt a sudden warmth on his forehead. Opening his eyes he saw that the sun had pierced a breach through the clouds on the horizon to the west.

"Looks like the storm is about over. At least, this storm. If you want to clean up, now's the time."

They had nothing with which to dry off and so shook themselves like dogs, then waited a few minutes before putting their clothes back on. St. John assigned his hands a few chores to do before the evening milking, and walked down the muddy path behind the house towards the open lean-to next to the smoke-house.

He could smell the stench even from fifty yards away. My poor wife, he thought. He had firewood to chop, but perhaps there was still enough time before the milking to relieve her at the soap-kettle.

The lean-to was smoky, the wind having died completely. Mehetable and Sagacity looked miserable. The smell of the bubbling brew was awful. Stray wisps of hair escaped from under his wife's cap and bothered her eyes as she stirred the hot liquid in the cauldron while Sagacity shoved another piece of firewood into the flames underneath.

"I'll have to think of a better way to ventilate this place," St. John offered.

"Aya, and none too soon." Mehetable was cross. "Sagacity! I told you, not so much lye. It won't thicken. And not so much salt, it is way too dear!" she scolded the girl, who resentfully put down her ladle. "Put in three more scoops of fat now to coarsen it."

"Here," St. John offered, "let me stir for a while." He took the heavy stick out of his wife's hands and began to move it. He had to use both hands, the liquid was so dense.

"You're stirrin' the wrong way!" Mehetable almost screamed. "You have to stir to the right! We have enough evil around us as it is. Here, give it back to me. You can put in more sassafras flowers."

Taken aback by his wife's outburst, St. John clamped his lips tight and did what he was told. He then went over to the far side of the lean-to, wrestled a squat length of log upright, grabbed the axe, and split the wood with one furious blow. One after another, log after log was torn asunder, split apart until a huge pile had built up.

St. John hardly paused, resting only a moment to remove a piece of bark from an eye before resuming his onslaught. After stacking half the split wood against the wall of the smoke-house he brought the rest in a hand-cart over to the wood-box on the kitchen porch. He went inside to feed the fire, came out, and stalked over to the cattle-pen to milk the philosophers, who were snorting in impatient indignation for being treated with so little respect.

The brilliant red, orange and yellow of the turning maples were luminous in the morning sun the next day and the air was crisp and cool. St. John, Henry and Cesar devoted their time to pressing apples behind the kitchen. They took turns cranking the heavy iron screw pressing down upon the fruit, a barrel underneath receiving the juice. They were assisted by Henry Wisner's son Gabriel and his friend from the village who, not having much in the way of farm chores, were glad to earn a few kegs of cider and a bushel or two of wheat to take back home to their families.

"Come November we'll be clearing another acre for more apple trees," St. John remarked. "I'll be calling on you lads to help me. Also with cutting up firewood."

"Pa says if you want him to draft you a will, what with your new wife and baby and all, this would be a good time to do it. Says he'll be glad to accept a bushel or two of flour for it. Oh, an' Ma says she could be your Missus' mid-wife if you want."

"You tell your folks thank you for us. That will be fine."

Over on the kitchen porch Mehetable and Sagacity were churning butter, with Margaret Bull Horton lending them a hand. They had already filled two firkins full.

"Sagacity, take them up to the spring-house. Bring back two of cream. Remember this evening to take back to your father a firkin of butter."

After the girl, sulking at the chore, had left Margaret shook her head. "You are indeed an angel, Mehetable. Giving away your good butter to that ungracious man."

"I am not an angel, an' at the moment we have more than we can use ourselves. So you will also take away a firkin. Come the cold of the winter my husband is a-going to lay up as many barrels of butter he can to sell down in the City. He thinks with his six cows we can make eight hundred pounds of butter a year, which means we ought to be able to sell half if we're fortunate."

"How is he going to get the butter to the City?"

"He has a deal with John Ellison down by New-Windsor village on the river. We're going to ship our extra flour with him, too, on his sloop. He has his own ice house for to keep the butter cold on the boat."

Mehetable suddenly stopped churning and put her hand to her stomach.

"There dear, set a spell. Give me the stick." Margaret helped her friend to a chair and began churning.

"Have you thought of a name yet for your child?"

"I dare not think on it."

"Are you going to call upon Dr. Tusten?"

"I don't like physicians. I don't trust them. They seem to only make things worse, my mother used to say. All they are good for is making you drink vile things to induce you to vomit; and then they bleed you to death. I'd rather pray and place my fate in the hands of God."

"I can be your mid-wife, if you like. I do it for most of my sisters and brothers' wives."

"Thank'ee, Margaret. That will be fine."

Sagacity returned to have the churning stick thrust into her reluctant hands.

"I don't mean to pry," Margaret said to Mehetable, "so do let me know if I were indiscreet, but – I notice your husband does not talk much about himself. Most of the folk around here think he come down from Canada and so assume he was born there; but others say he was born in France."

"You are right he don't like talking about it much. He did come down from Canada, true enough, but he was born in France. As was my own father."

"Are his father and mother still alive?"

"This is what I know: his mother died when he was a young boy. His father is still alive, but has always been in poor health. They used to write to each other long ago, from time to time. I think they had a bad quarrel when Michael was a boy. I believe Michael has a brother who takes care of their father and I have the impression Michael and his brother are not terribly fond of each other."

Margaret hesitated, biting her lower lip. "Some say your husband…fought in the French wars. They say he was in the Battle of Quebec. On the French side."

Mehetable sighed. "Yes, I know there are people hereabouts that don't like that notion. But the past is the past. He had a duty to do. He did his duty."

The glopping sounds produced by Sagacity's churning were becoming deeper in tone and the task became more arduous. The young girl's forehead was covered in perspiration. Margaret had her sit down and took over the stick.

"It's not always easy knowing what your duty is," she reflected. "I see how it affects my brother Thomas. Him and my other brother John don't see eye to eye on anything having to do with the mother country. I am glad things have settled down now." Margaret continued churning slowly. "Thomas' wife Mary – my sister-in-law – is with child. Again."

She sighed. "The Lord has seen fit to put them through many trials. But, He has also blessed them with almost as many children who have survived. They lost their first baby, David, almost twenty years ago, then later Thomas, and then another baby Thomas…then there was Abner, five years ago; and then little Isaac just before you came here, Mehetable. But now Mary's pregnant again, and hope begins anew, like the spring.

"Oh dear, I have distressed you. I am sorry for speaking so foolishly."

Margaret gave the stick back to an unhappy Sagacity and comforted her friend. "There dear, everything will be all right. Just trust in the Lord."

Margaret put her arm on St. John's as he passed by with a load of firewood for the kitchen. "Your wife is not feeling well," she whispered.

He looked at Mehetable, hunched miserably in the rocker in the corner of the porch, eyes closed. "Fever?"

"I think she is just tired. She has a bit of the nausea."

St. John nodded. He went inside and stoked the fire, then reemerged and went over to his wife. He put his hand on her forehead, then stroked her shoulder. "Come, let's put you into bed. You need rest. Margaret and I will take care of dinner."

Mehetable opened her eyes and shook her head. "I will be fine. Just let me bide a spell." She closed her eyes again and rocked slowly in the chair.

While Mehetable napped the two other women and St. John fixed dinner and set the boards. The food had been simmering all morning over the fire, a venison stew with root vegetables Mehetable had started early in the day, and loaves of pumpkin cornbread and roasted corn in the husk.

St. John went to fetch his hands and the boys rather than ring the bell, out of deference to the sleeping Mehetable, who woke up anyway when they all clumped past her to go into the house, halting first to wash their hands in the tub by the door.

At board Mehetable said Grace in a subdued voice and then they dug in. The cat slunk among their feet under the benches, restless.

"You boys going to go to school this winter?" St. John asked.

"Yes sir," Gabriel spoke up. "Me and Davie Carpenter here, we're going to the new academy in the village. Dr. Tusten is to be the master."

"Tell your father I'll be coming by next week with his flour if he can set aside an hour for us to make up our testament."

St. John smiled at his wife, sitting opposite from him at the other table end.

"Judge Wisner has offered to draw up our will. It would be the wise thing to do, don't you think? And Sarah Wisner will be your mid-wife."

Mehetable put down her spoon with an abrupt thump on the table. The eating stopped. The dinner companions looked at her, spoons suspended aloft.

Mehetable, eyes squeezed shut, was weeping, bitterly. St. John arose and hastened over to her. She shook off his hands angrily.

"Go away!" she sobbed. Perplexed, her husband backed off.

"There now, dear, don't be distressed," Margaret soothed her, stroking her trembling hands. She looked up at St. John's worried face. "She's just tired. It's to be expected. Don't you start fretting, too. I can't have the both of you distressed, now, can I?"

"I guess I ought not to be talking about wills and testaments and such things. I'm sorry. Gabriel, no need to mention it to your pa right now." He smiled reassuringly at his wife.

"But do you still want me to tell ma she's to be the mid-wife?" the boy asked.

"Of course. Why not?"

Mehetable stopped sobbing and glared at her husband. Taken aback, he held up his hands in supplication.

"What is it? I thought you liked Sarah."

"I want Margaret," she said, coldly.

St John glanced at the two women. "Margaret? Why, of course it shall be Margaret!" He beamed at Mehetable, who did not return his smile.

"I believe I do want to take to bed after all," Mehetable said to Margaret.

"Of course, dear." She helped her friend rise and walked with her out of the kitchen and into the hall, then up the stairs.

St. John sat back down in his chair at the head of the table.

"Umph," was all he could say.

Judas jumped up into his lap and made himself comfortable.

Chapter Ten: *Settling for Mr. Punch*

Slaughtering pigs was the one farm chore St. John dreaded. Taking down and dressing a buck, or butchering a steer was one thing; sticking pigs and hearing their agonized screaming in your ears was another experience altogether. St. John had Cesar and Henry along with young George Bull, loaned by Thomas, take care of it while he prepared the huge iron kettle, also loaned by Thomas, for boiling water.

After executing Xerxes and Haman, saving as much of the swines' blood as they could, they trundled the porcine corpses to the oak tree where St. John was waiting. They hooked each carcass, one after the other, on the rope and tackle slung from a stout branch, plunged it into the boiling water of the crucible to scald it; then removed it from the water and placed it on a rectangle of wide planks resting on the grass. They scraped off the bristles from the pig's skin for to make brushes later, lopped off its head and feet with an axe and then slit open its belly to let its intestines and organs spill out onto the boards, steaming in the cool air.

The stench was sickening. Henry gathered up the intestines for making sausages and the other organs for stew along with the head and feet to be pickled in brine; and the blood would be used for a pudding. Cesar guided St. John and young George Bull in butchering the carcass into portions for curing in the smoke-house as hams, shoulders, and bacon before eventually finding their way to a fine pewter platter on their elegant dinner table.

With relief St. John hitched up Martin and Luther and clambered into the waggon loaded with stuff to take into Goshen village. He made the five-mile trip in a couple of hours, the road twisting and turning along the contours of the hills. After a stop at the tannery to exchange his load of bark and raw hides for fresh-tanned skins he turned his horses towards the cooper's.

William Allison's place was a bee-hive of noisy activity. St. John found him wielding a windlass next to the barrel-to-be, for the moment a collection of curved staves standing upright in a circle, held at the bottom by a hoop and blossoming upwards like a bouquet of flowers.

The rope around the tops of the staves tightened with each crank of Allison's windless, pulling them together until their perfectly beveled sides joined up to form the perfectly curved sides of a barrel. A helper fastened hickory hoops around the sides while the cooper with his hand tool deftly carved a groove around the inside perimeter of the barrel staves parallel to the top and about an inch below, his only measure his eyes and experience. With a mallet he pounded into place the barrel top, fitting neatly into the beveled groove he had just cut.

"One more done, just a hundred more to go," he smiled wearily. "If I can get me more staves, that is." He looked hopefully at St. John. "You don't, by any chance, have any more today for me?"

"Afraid not. I'll be clearing more land soon and then I'll have plenty for you. I was counting on riving them in the winter. I was thinking you might have half a dozen barrels to sell me right now."

Allison shook his head, gesturing at his busy shop. "It's all bespoke work. I can take your order but it won't be ready for a month. And only then if I can get more staves. What kind do you need? Slack, or wet?"

"Wet barrels. For brine. Got hams to cure. Tongues to pickle."

"The best I can do is give you those three old barrels over there I was going to use for scrap. Can't guarantee they're leak-proof."

Allison wrote down St. John's order in his ledger-book, taking advantage of the moment to do some proselytizing. "Have you decided yet which militia you want to join up with? Goshen's the best one around these parts, you know. The fact I'm now the captain has nothing to do with my opinion, of course," Allison grinned.

"Well," St. John fumbled, "you see, I guess I'm sort of...bespoken for the Chester milita which is Elihu Marvin and Nathanial Roe; unless it's the new Blooming Grove unit they're thinking of forming, which is Nathaniel Strong and Jesse Woodhull. But then, Capt. Bull asked me to join his unit, although he's in Ulster County. Where my farm is, I'm right in the middle of you all."

"Judge Wisner speaks highly of you. Says you have professional military experience. An officer. You know Indian ways. That's what's needed here in Goshen since we're on the frontier. Well, you chew it over and let me know when you've made the right decision."

St. John called on the Wisners, only to be told the judge was not at home. "Today is court-day," Sarah reminded him, nodding her head at the wooden frame building across the main street. St. John gave Mrs. Wisner a jug of honey, a keg of cider and a skein of wool in part payment for her son's help with a promise of a bushel of flour later. He was glad she did not broach the topic of mid-wiving. At Josiah Carpenter's general store he stocked up on staples for Mehetable, and a box of tea for a neighbour. "Don't worry," Carpenter grinned. "It's good smuggled Dutch tea." As for the dozen perfect English sewing needles he also bought, Carpenter shrugged. "It's what our ladies want," he defended himself.

St. John chose to return home by a different route, along the King's Highway through tiny Chester settlement. Behind Yelverton's Inn men and boys shouldering muskets were drilling, led by Nathaniel Roe. In front of the inn was a Conestoga waggon, canvas cover proclaiming "Peter Gardiner's Amazing Traveling Puppets".

Inside the great room the fire was blazing briskly. At the small corner table a portly man with white powdered hair pulled back into a short queue was polishing off his dinner with enjoyment, chatting cheerfully between spoonfuls with his skinny companion sipping from his cup, a look of melancholy in his eyes. A subdued young Negro man sat next to him, evidently a slave, looking even more melancholy. A few steps away a very tall, gangly man was standing in front of the fire, gazing into the flickering light as though searching for something important and not finding it.

"They'll be hungry and thirsty when they're done," Abijah Yelverton said with a satisfied smile, referring to the militiamen as he served St. John at the bar with a noggin of cider to go with the plate of sausage and cabbage. "You thinkin' of joining a militia?"

"I'm sort of bespoken to Captain Allison over in Goshen. Unless it's Captain Bull. Or Jesse Woodhull."

"I know it's not mandatory no more. Used to be all able-bodied men under sixty. But still. Well, you'll make up your mind, one way or the other." He plopped down a news-paper he had been reading. "See here. Seems that red-coat Captain Preston has been acquitted of murder at his trial up in Boston. That don't sit right with me. That ain't justice!"

"But it was a jury that decided he didn't order his men to fire."
The tall stranger had come over from the hearth, holding a
black-jack of beer he had been nursing. He had a large nose and
piercing black eyes under a shock of unruly black hair. "A jury
comprised of Boston men. Sitting in judgement of an English
officer. Accused of murdering Boston civilians." The stranger's
eyes supplied the logical conclusion to his syllogism without
the need to vocalize it with his lips.

"Well," Yelverton mumbled, mindful of the man's pocketbook
and the joys it might contain for the innkeeper if it could be
coaxed to open wider, "I suppose you might have a point.
Where ye bound for? We have a bed to spare. You can have it
all to yourself. Unless another guest drops by later. Which
seems unlikely."

"I'm headed for Boston. I was planning on spending the night
in Newburgh before crossing the river on the ferry tomorrow."

"Newburgh's a good twenty mile from here. You'll not reach
it before nightfall."

"Look, friend, my farm is a couple of miles up the road to
Newburgh. You can tag along with me and stay if you like; or
push on if you feel like it," St. John offered.

The stranger smiled at the gesture. "Much obliged." He
extended his lanky arm and almost crushed St. John's hand with
a hickory grip. "Name's Abner Lancaster. Out of Bucks County,
Pennsylvania."

He paid for his drinks and food with a Spanish dollar that
instantly raised the man's esteem in the eyes of the innkeeper.
"Hope to see you on your way back," Yelverton said with utter
sincerity, handing the small change reluctantly back to the tall
traveler.

"I plan on staying a long time in Boston, but I'll be sure to keep
your place in mind."

"If you slept here tonight, you could see the puppet show
tomorrow," Yelverton pointed out doggedly. "That gent over
there says he puts on quite a performance. He's heading back
down to Virginia for the winter after doing a circuit in New
England. Here, take a look at his broad-side. I recruited our
neighbour boys to run 'em over to the towns around."

The innkeeper pushed over a stack of parchment-like
handbills. Across the top, bold black lettering arranged in a
half-circle proclaimed "Mr. Punch and the King of Prussia".
Underneath was a wood-cut print depicting a grinning Mr.

Punch landing a blow to the crowned head of the unfortunate monarch with a slap-stick.

The stranger politely declined the invitation. St. John paid for his dinner and the two men left the inn together. They tethered the man's horse, saddle-bags bulging, to the waggon and, seating themselves on the bench side by side, struck up a conversation as St. John whistled Martin and Luther forward.

They passed the drilling militia on their left and Peter Townsend's house on their right as they drove on up the winding narrow road heading eastwards. By and by they came upon the disheveled clapboard house owned by the elderly Joseph Drake and his wife overlooking the Grey-Court Swamp. St. John halted the horses and jumped down. "I'll just be a minute." He disappeared into the small house carrying the box of tea. He was back in an instant. "They have a hard time getting by," he explained.

They clopped their way up a steep rise leveling out on top of the ridge. Coming towards them along the highway was a small, beat-up cart pulled by a mangy beat-up horse. St John nudged Martin and Luther over to the right to let the cart pass.

He recognised the large, plump driver and gave him a cheery wave of the arm. Rev. Schoonmaker acknowledged the salutation with a half-hearted flick of a hand, his bespectacled face looking sad. A round-topped traveling trunk and worn brown bag filled the back of the small cart plodding past them. St. John doffed his hat and gave a final nod to the departing preacher before resuming their pace.

Mehetable's welcome warmed when she learned the traveler was bound for Boston. "Perhaps you would be so kind as to deliver a package to my father and brother for me." Their guest inclined his head in acquiescence, despite the lack of any room in his already bursting saddle-bags. St. John was delighted to show his guest around the out-houses of his farm and his myriad inventions and other contraptions. Lancaster insisted on helping milk their cows, to Cesar's joy, then split log after log, each one with a single mighty blow of the axe.

In honour of their guest Mehetable laid out her best – and only - pewter dishes, and St. John broke out a bottle of blackberry wine. In the middle of the table stood a silver candle-holder, a marriage gift from her father, and the pleasing fragrance of their bayberry candle complemented the simple elegance of their meal.

Their cat was not pleased with the stranger. Judas looked at the tall man nervously, then paced to and fro by the door until Mehetable let him out, fleeing through the legs of the hired hands coming in. Sagacity served them silently before taking her place at the table, glancing at the stranger out of the corner of her eyes. Mehetable had them bow their heads and recited a prayer.

"Mr. Lancaster's on his way to Boston to practise law," St. John informed his wife.

Their visitor offered an apologetic smile. "If I may amend your statement slightly, I am going to Massachusetts to claim an inheritance. My mother's father has died; and as my parents are gone I am the next of kin and the only heir. I may wind up doing some law if I can't make a go of my grandfather's farm. At least," Lancaster smiled, "he died owing no one. In fact, it was I who owed him. But his death forgives my debt."

"So you will not be living in Boston-town?" Mehetable asked. "I am sorry to have imposed upon thee with my packet."

"I am pleased to deliver it to your father since I will assuredly be visiting Boston. My grandfather's farm is not too far away. It is in Middlesex County. A borough called Lincoln. Perhaps you are more familiar with Concord, of which Lincoln was formerly a part."

Their guest had been raised in Coryell's Ferry on the Delaware, near the York Road. "Thanks to an introduction from our pastor I was able to read law in Philadelphia in exchange for my services as a clerk. But then my grandfather died, and so I thought, why not try New England and farming?" He smiled. "The only profession held in lower esteem than lawyering is medicine."

"But it should pay better, methinks."

"He studied under John Dickinson," St. John supplied.

Their guest, seeing Mehetable's blank look, explained. "You may recall his *Letters from a Farmer in Pennsylvania*. Caused quite a sensation. He laid out clearly and logically why Parliament must respect our rights as a free people."

"I am sorry but I don't have much of a head for politics."

"It's not a fault, I assure you. Politics, like acid, eventually corrupts everything it touches. But I admire Dickinson for his call for peaceful change. He is against the use of violence. Using violence to achieve your ends is foolish, for it will only engender more violence and in the process poison your own soul."

Their visitor departed early the next morning with a parting gift of bread and sausage. Mehetable's mood had brightened considerably. Even Sagacity was almost pleasant. What the cat felt no one could tell, as Judas had vanished into the night and had not returned.

It was Mehetable who insisted they go see the puppet show that afternoon. "I have never in my life set foot in a tavern. So now I will see with my own eyes the wicked devil's den where our men-folk idle away so much of their time."

St. John forked over their coin to a beaming Yelverton pouring drinks at the bar, then looked around for a chair for Mehetable, nodding his head in greeting at the many familiar faces. The noisy great room was crowded with folk from all around, men and women, all standing except for the lucky few in the dozen or so chairs directly in front of the puppet theatre set up in a corner. Women sat in all the chairs but one, where a man was slouched.

As St. John approached he recognised Jeroboam Brown. St. John doffed his hat, smiling. "Pleased to see you again, Mr. Brown. Your daughter has been a God-send to us. If you don't mind my asking, my wife Mehetable is here."

Brown, still slouched in his seat, looked up. His bloodshot eyes appeared yellowish.

"So?"

"It's just that there are no empty seats."

Brown closed his eyes and settled further down in the chair.

"As I said, my wife would be grateful for the courtesy of a chair."

Brown did not reply. The people around them had stopped their chatter and were regarding the two men.

If Brown's eyes had been open he would have seen St. John's own blue eyes smoldering. As it was the man was surprised to find himself suddenly lifted up and flying through the air into the wall between the puppet theatre and the open back door of the tavern. Before he could recover St. John grabbed him and punched his face hard for good measure then dragged him out the open doorway. Once outside he kicked the man in the ribs, raised him up, and sent him stumbling to the barn with a final kick to the man's backside.

Seething, St. John came back in. Mehetable was looking at him, aghast. He escorted her to the chair. She sat down, numb. He made his way back to the bar where Yelverton was staring at him.

"I turn myself in. You're the constable. Arrest me."

Yelverton looked at his uncle Elihu Marvin and Nathaniel Roe standing nearby and raised his eyebrows. The other men shrugged. Yelverton turned back to St. John.

"I didn't see nothin'. Don't know what you're talkin' about. How about a drink? Cider for you, isn't it?"

St. John exhaled. He looked down abashedly at his still-balled fists resting on the bar.

Finally he looked up at the innkeeper and gave him a weak smile.

"Cider's too good for a fool. I guess you'd better make it punch this time."

Chapter Eleven: *A Child Is Born*

The tiny light of the two Advent candles flickered in the reflection of the dark looking-glass suspended on the whitewashed walls of their bed-chamber. Mehetable's protest over the popish practice melted away as quick as snow in spring as she watched her husband carefully arrange a bouquet of mountain laurel and ivy laced with cheerful, bright red cranberries between the candle of Hope on the right and the candle of Bethlehem on the left of their commode. He saw her weak smile in the looking-glass, turned and their eyes met.

Hester Woodhull brought a cup to Mehetable's lips and helped her drink. She passed a soothing hand over her friend's forehead. Through the small window the last rays of the December sun filtered through to alight on the colourful squares of the quilted bedcover blanketing the legs of St. John's wife. Margaret Bull Horton put another small log on the fire which crackled in appreciation. She then put a few embers in the bed-pan and passed it carefully between the quilt and blanket underneath, moving it around slowly, taking care to not burn the cloth or Mehetable's legs.

St. John stole a kiss on his wife's forehead before Margaret shooed him away. "Go see to it there be plenty o' hot water. Hester and I will tell you when the time is right."

Jesse Woodhull was standing by the fire in the kitchen smoking a pipe. St. John poured out a generous cup of rum for his friend and one for himself. "Make it grog?" he asked. Woodhull nodded. St. John took the kettle from over the fire and splashed in a dash of hot water with a scoop of honey for good measure and handed the cup to Woodhull.

"Pull up a log and make yourself comfortable," St. John said, amused at the quizzical look on his guest's face. They each brought over a chair and sat down.

"Nervous?" Woodhull guessed. St. John, sipping his grog, nodded.

"Well, that's to be expected. I was too with my first-born. Nervous, too, with my next born! An' the next! It don't change. 'Course, we deal with our nerves; but our women suffer the pain."

He sipped his grog reflectively, staring into the fire. "If you were born in '35 as I believe you told me, then you and me are the same age, but I married Hester when I was only eighteen."

"And that's when you settled in Orange County?"

"That's when we settled here, yep. An' I'll admit it was thanks to the generosity of Hester's pa. With her dowry, and a loan from my father, I bought us our first two hunnerd acres. 'Course, land here was cheaper back then. When I seen my Smith cousins startin' to look this way, an' then the Howells an' the Strongs an' the Brewsters, I figured it would be a smart idea to buy up more land. I was right, it seems. 'Course, I got the idea myself to move here from my other cousins, the Roes. They and the Seelys were the first ones to come here from our town on Long Island.

"Orange County! Now that's a name bound to attract all good Protestants. King William and Queen Mary and their House of Orange. I always thought it ironic that England should invite a Dutch king to their throne, and this, barely a generation after we English took away New Amsterdam from Holland. But, on the other hand, it shows shrewd common sense, don't it?

"Now, my wife Hester's family, they come down from New Paltz in Ulster County. You know Zack DuBois, the tavern-keep up on Murderers' Creek by Bethlehem Church? Well, Zach's my wife's brother. Their grandfather Louis DuBois founded New Paltz. So my wife is descended from the French Huguenots."

"Now that's an interesting bit of news," St. John said, pouring more rum into his friend's cup. "My wife Mehetable's father is a French Huguenot as well."

"Howells also count as my relatives, at least through marriage if not blood. Hezekiah married my niece Juliana, my brother Nathaniel's daughter. Howell fought under brother Nathaniel, with General Amherst in Quebec.

"But," Woodhull smiled, "that war is long past. A toast to England, and a toast to France."

The door from the porch swung open and a young woman came in carrying a pail of milk. Seeing Woodhull she stopped to give a half-curtsy and a shy smile. Woodhull smiled back. "Hello, Charity."

"Evening, Mr. Woodhull."

"Henry still milking the philosophers?" St. John asked. The girl nodded. Turning to his guest, he said: "We'll have supper soon as he's done."

"I suppose you had to let the other girl go," Woodhull remarked. "What with the schooling you gave her pa. I'm surprised you kept her as long as you did. Well, Charity's a good lass. She's a Goldsmith, after all. What happened to your other hand?"

"Cesar? I'm afraid he has left me for a woman. To think he would put his own happiness ahead of mine. He is now in the throes of marital bliss, as am I."

"Well, you're going to need help. You can't run this farm with just you and Henry. Not if you enjoy eating and drinking, that is. I have two young Negro slaves I could spare, if you'd like. Brothers. I'll part with them for next to nothing. Or take just one now, the other later if you feel the need."

St. John stood up abruptly. He turned his back to his neighbour, pretended to fuss with the fire. After a moment of thought he turned around, smiling.

"I'll take both." He and Jesse shook hands.

They took their supper, cold pork pie and beer, seated by the fire. Henry had come in and sat at the table. John had Charity run up a pie to the women upstairs.

"Moffat has sent in our petition to Colden to drain the swamps," Woodhull informed his host. "The inspectors'll be me and Nat Roe, you'll be a trustee along with Elihu and Joseph Drake, and we'll make sure you get the surveying contract when the time comes. Yessir, it's all about land. That's where the wealth is. Whoever controls the land, controls the wealth. 'Liberty and Land!' as they say."

St. John stole a glance at Henry peacefully smoking his calumet. There was an amused look in his warm brown eyes. Can you be truly free as long as you are clinging to a piece of earth to the exclusion of everyone else? Are you truly free if you live in fear of losing it? his eyes seemed to inquire.

Charity returned to the kitchen. "Baby will be coming soon. But Mrs. Horton says, don't come up yet."

St. John wordlessly put down his trencher and bolted upstairs.

He sat on a stool for the next few hours holding his wife's hand. The candles had burned low but he did not move. His wife's discomfort was intense but she said nothing, until her hand jerked in his own and squeezed it tight.

"It's time. I feel it nigh."

Margaret gently but firmly pushed St. John away from the bed and the two women busied themselves around Mehetable.

"Here, take the quilt," Margaret commanded St. John. He obeyed, looking around in a mild panic for a place to put the object, eyes passing right over the blanket chest against a wall. He dumped it on the commode chair.

"The water! I'll go fetch the water!"

"Hester has already gone to get it. And the knife. And the cloth. You can best help by letting us do our work. And by praying."

At the end of half an hour of pacing he was called over to the bedside.

"Hold your wife's hand now. Push, Mehetable. Push! Baby wants to come out now. Push! You are doing fine, dear. Push more. You can let go. You can scream. Holler if you will! Almost over, dear. One more time, push!"

Mehetable sobbed and cried and gave a last low sigh which flowed into the new high-pitched cry of a new-born baby. She squeezed her husband's hand and sobbed again, pain replaced by relief and joy. In the semi-darkness Margaret and Hester busied themselves with cleaning baby and mother, cooing softly to this outraged newcomer to a cold, dark world.

"Give her some water to drink, Mr. St. John," Margaret said. "Make yourself useful now!"

Obediently he poured a cup from the pitcher on the commode with a shaky hand and let his wife drink the pure water from their well. With a sigh of happiness she let her head float back onto the pillows and smiled.

"I want to see my baby."

St. John stood back to let more light pass as Margaret gently lowered the fussy baby swaddled in a cotton cloth to Mehetable's bosom. Mehetable held the bundle with joy and cradled the gift in her arms, kissing the baby's warm head, smiling in peaceful bliss.

"'Tis a little girl, methinks."

Margaret smiled. "You are right. Mothers always know, don't we? A beautiful, blessed little girl."

St. John's heart leapt. A girl. He was stunned. Somehow, he realised in surprise, he had always imagined to himself a little boy. A girl! The idea was startling. And then a slow smile crept across his face. A little baby girl. He hovered near his wife, impatiently waiting his turn to hold their new-born child. A girl.

But baby had other ideas. She had found her mother's breast and was greedily partaking of her mother's nourishment. St. John struggled to contain his impatience, gave it up, and resumed his pacing at the far end of the room. A girl. What colour will her hair be? What joyful songs will she sing? What name shall she carry?

"Mr. St. John! Come and hold your new baby girl."

He walked in a daze through the fog to the bed and received from out of the shadows the soft wiggly bundle floating towards him. As he felt for the first time in his arms the warm living miracle, felt for the first time the soft gentle heartbeat and smelled the sweet soft scent of her being he was aware of a sudden, surging wave of warmth washing all over him, inundating him, submerging him in a sublime, indescribable plasma of peaceful, uplifting awe. He was ascending, a child holding a child in his arms. He sensed with unmistakable certainty the miracle occurring in his own heart.

Baby cried. It was the most beautiful sound he had ever heard. He hugged her to his heart as she cried again, then reluctantly yielded her back to his wife.

He pulled a startled Margaret Horton into his arms and gave her a big kiss before she could escape; then captured Hester Woodhull, who, forewarned, yielded peacefully. St. John then bounded down the stairs. He danced into the kitchen.

"It's a girl! It's a baby girl!"

Sharing his joy, Woodhull clasped his neighbour's shoulders and shook his hand, followed by Henry. St. John attacked Charity shying away in a corner with a big kiss and a hug, then gladly accepted the cup proffered by Woodhull. The three men all took a chair by the fire, St. John first insisting that Charity join them in a toast.

"What will you name her?" Woodhull asked.

St. John was nonplussed. "I don't rightly know. Mehetable did not wish to discuss it beforehand, and to tell the truth I was thinking we were to have a boy. I don't know. Something different. Something...meaningful, symbolic."

"Well, there's Esther, for courage; or Hannah for faithfulness. Or Mary for holiness."

"Biblical names are so commonplace."

"Old New England names are nice. Quaint. Names like 'Hope' or 'Constance' or 'Faith'. Then there's always Charity," Woodhull nodded, smiling, at the girl next to him. "Or Sagacity, or Felicity. Or even, I suppose, Fecundity. But I guess that might raise a few eyebrows."

On Christmas Eve St. John was pleased to welcome a steady stream of well-wishers from all around. Faithful Margaret Horton served as hostess in Mehetable's bedchamber. In the kitchen Martha Drake, their elderly neighbour from Chester, had helped Charity all day with the cooking and the day before with the baking so that every available table-top and counter was piled high with a feast for their guests.

As Mehetable was in bed – and would remain there for another week, if Margaret had her way – St. John had free reign to decorate their home in the festive style of Normand Catholics and Sussex Anglicans. Green boughs and red cranberries were everywhere and multiple sets of the four candles of Advent were in each room as well as the kitchen.

All the chairs in the formal parlour had been shoved against the walls. In the middle he had set up a small table on which he had placed a large Wassail bowl. Come mid-afternoon Thomas Bull and wife Mary passed through and Bull led the assembled in *Wassail, Wassail All Over the Town,* followed by a toast to Mehetable; then another carol, followed by a toast to St. John, and then another in honour of baby.

Even the most severe among the Puritans present gave in to the Christmas cheer of their Anglican neighbours and joined in the singing.

"And now," Thomas intoned, "a *Hymn for Christmas Day*." He led them with his fine tenor voice:

Hark! How all the Welkin rings
Glory to the King of Kings,
Peace on Earth, and Mercy mild,
God and sinners reconciled.

Joyful all the nations rise,
Join the Triumph of the Skies,
Universal Nature say,
Christ the Lord is born to-day.

The octave of Christmas passed by quickly: Christ's Day, St. Stephen's Day, Holy Innocents; and finally, on Epiphany, the sixth day of the new year, Mehetable left her bed, and, cradling baby in her arms, was escorted downstairs and to the kitchen by her husband. He led her to a grand, polished walnut and cherry Windsor rocking chair.

"*Joyeux Noël*," he smiled, presenting to her his gift, newly delivered via an Ellison sloop from the City. He helped Mehetable settle down on the soft cushioned seat, baby still in her arms. She rocked blissfully in her new chair, gratefully accepted a cup of hot tea.

"Charity!" he called out. The young woman put down her hot iron and approached as St. John handed her a small packet wrapped in fine silk cloth, burgundy bow glowing on a green ribbon.

"Henry!" The hired hand walked over from the table where he had been sipping his coffee. The man took his gift with a smile and a shake of the hand.

"Peter. Andrew." St. John's voice was stern.

The two black youth, seated with Henry at the table, looked at each other in surprise. The older boy questioned Henry with quizzical eyes. Henry grinned and gestured with a nod of his head. They rose and warily came forward by the fire. St. John was regarding them severely. They returned his look nervously.

St. John's face broke out in a smile. "Please step forward, Peter Toussaint."

St. John brought forth from behind his back a parchment document in a gilt frame. A small red bow was affixed to the top.

He presented it to the young man, who took it with confused hands before looking up at his master with a puzzled expression.

"That is for you. It is your Articles of Manumission." Peter stared blankly at the man, not comprehending.

"You are released from bondage. You are a free man."

Peter was stunned. He stared at St. John. He began to cry. St. John gravely shook his hand and shoo'd him back to his chair. Peter's younger brother didn't have to be summoned twice. Andrew Toussaint's eyes sparkled as he rushed forward, almost stepping on St. John's toes, and eagerly reached out his hands to claim his prize.

"I would be pleased if you were to decide to remain here with us on our farm, at the usual wages. But that is for you to decide. And now for breakfast."

Their table was graced with the centre-piece silver candle-stick in a small green ring of pine boughs. Bowls of bright oranges and red apples were on either side of the candle. After Mehetable said a prayer they enjoyed a leisurely meal.

As they sipped their tea St. John produced a small box wrapped in satin cloth, with a tiny red ribbon and bow, and presented it to their little girl nestled in her mother's arms.

"For our little child. May she cherish it in joy and peace."

"Please to open it, I'm sure," Mehetable murmured, kissing their baby's head.

St. John obliged and, slowly, solemnly, he opened the top of the small wooden box. He held up his gift to baby.

It was a pewter ring. He displayed it for his wife to admire. It had an oval centre-piece fashioned of hardened wax. Engraved across the wax were the words "*Agneau de Dieu.*"

St. John playfully pretended to slide the ring onto baby's tiny finger. She chortled and grasped the gift in chubby, clumsy little hands.

"When Pastor Tétard arrives we'll have everything ready for your baptism, won't we," St. John cooed to the baby. He looked up at his wife. "Tell me again you like the name. I want to be sure."

Mehetable smiled. "I am sure." She looked down gently at her little girl. "It is a beautiful name. Such a lovely sound to it. America-Frances. I do love it so."

St. John lifted his cup of cider.

"A toast! A toast to our little baby girl.

"To America-Frances."

Chapter Twelve: *The Poison of Pride*

The cold April wind whipped up white caps on the blue-grey water of Hudson's River. Captain Nicoll was at the helm of the lateen-rigged sloop sailing away from Ellison's jetty into the bay and into the flow of the southerly tide, leaving behind them the small village of New-Windsor and the mouth of Murderers' Creek at the foot of Sloop Hill. He sent the vessel flying into a broad reach, the almost sheer sides of Butter Mountain looming ahead on the west bank and Breakneck Ridge on the east. The ship's master tacked twice and they were in the narrow channel between the mountains, pushed along by the favourable winds and outgoing tidal current whose rhythms and whims dictated all human endeavour along the river.

Even the three tough crewmembers and their captain joined with their passengers to look up in awe at the steep granite cliffs towering above them, only a stone's throw away as they glided by. John Ellison, the owner of the *Harmony*, gave an excited poke to the arm of his guest. "Look up there. Closely, now. Do you see her?" He was pointing to a crevice mid-way up the cliff.

A large dirty-white bird with dark blotches had come soaring out from its craggy aerie. The fish-hawk circled lazily around in ever smaller concentric rings; then in a flash the avian hunter dove into the water and emerged with a flapping sea-bass in its claws. It struggled upwards towards its nest, rising and falling on the currents of air, encumbered by its heavy, wriggling prey, and did not perceive, shooting from behind straight as an arrow, the enormous bald eagle come to assert the right of the strongest. But, sensing the approaching attack, the fish-hawk let loose its claim which dropped towards the water only to be snatched away by the eagle in mid-air. The aggressor flew off with its prize in one direction while the victim carved a circle in the other and, within moments, found itself another fish.

The mountains hugged the meandering river so closely it appeared, when looking back northwards over the stern, that the gateway through which they had so recently sailed had been swallowed shut; and looking forward over the bow, towards the invisible City fifty miles to the south, the channel seemed to reach a dead-end. Yet still they were being pushed and pulled along, a captive to wind and current.

By the time they reached Haverstraw on the west bank the tidal flow had reversed itself and so they hove to in the lee of a cove near the tiny village, passing the night under the protection of a pair of nesting bald eagles high above in the tree tops. They set sail before dawn on the tide and crossed the Tappan Zee long before the zenith of the noon-time sun. On the east bank the mountains surrendered to the rolling green hills of Westchester and the vast estates of Pierre Van Cortlandt and Frederick Philipse competing with their mills for every advantageous stream and landing-place, around which small villages had sprouted up along the shore.

They passed Spuyten Duyvil, the Devil's Gate opening into the Harlem River on their larboard beam; and to starboard on the west rose up the regal cliffs of the Palisades, granite sentinels guarding New-Jersey, facing their rocky complements across the river on the heights of *Manahatta*, York Island, all green forest and rugged ravine. The City itself was still out of view, but the bay could be seen in the distance stretching out to the Narrows off Staten Island. Ships at anchor and ships under sail were everywhere.

"I've never seen it so busy," St. John remarked. "Especially at this time of the year. I would have expected to see less sail."

Ellison grimaced. "It's fear, I'm afraid. No one knows what's going to happen next. The merchants in the City have been importing as much as they can since the news of that genteel little tea party in Boston last December and what with King Sears renewing his agitation for another non-importation pledge. The retailers are scared and so they've been hoarding, as though afraid the spigot's going to be turned off.

"At least the market for country fare will always be good. Like what we have in our holds. Food. Beef, pork. Flour, butter, apples. People still must eat, you know, and His Majesty's officers pay in good pound sterling.

"But o Lord! You should hear them grumbling about the shortage now of tea! You would think they were being deprived of air. No tea ship has come here since the *Lord Dunmore* last October and that cargo is long since drunk. Since Parliament passed the Tea Act last year few captains, whether American or British, dare bring the stuff here."

"But I should think we would welcome the new law. Since it drops the tax on tea to almost nothing, only three pence."

"But it gives the East India Company a monopoly on the tea trade. And the right to appoint its own agents. If we swallow that, then nothing will stop Parliament from monopolising every other trade we do. And taxing everything they force us to buy from them."

"What do you think will happen?"

"Don't know rightly. They say Governor Tryon refused to turn away the next tea ship, whenever it comes, but at least he agreed to have the cargo kept locked up. But that doesn't suit the Liberty Boys. They've threatened to throw their own tea party. Seems they're a wee bit jealous of Boston for stealing their bragging rights."

The afternoon wind was now barreling down from the westward quarter and the sloop flew along the shore of Manahatta. The granite heights abruptly gave way to low hills pocked with scattered farms and orchards, ponds and swampy meadows. The small hamlet called Greenwich Village rolled past, surrounding by forests of tall trees just starting to unfurl their foliage. The outskirts of the City hove into sight, the steeple of Trinity Church towering over rooftops and chimneys puffing out plumes of dark grey smoke. Through the trees appeared King's College, elegant stone towers flanking an imposing edifice also of stone, as though a piece of Anglican Cambridge had transplanted itself to the New World. The ruins of an old Dutch windmill and then the dilapidated, crenellated walls of Fort George came into view, resting on a low rise of ground like a tarnished crown sitting askew on the head of its monarch, badly in need of refurbishing. The British colours streamed in the wind atop the flagpole.

Nicoll had his crew come about, to head up the East River separating the City's wharves from the heights of Brooklyn and its farms and orchards beyond. Behind the Great Dock rose the grand buildings of the imperial government: the fort, the customs house, the Royal Exchange with its cupola, and the mansions of the wealthiest merchants at the foot of the Broad-Way. On Bowling Green a more recent newcomer glittered in the afternoon sun: King George the Third, mounted on his steed, grandly surveying his restless domain from atop a marbled pedestal.

They passed the old fish market at Coenties' Slip, then Cruger's Wharf and Crommelin's and beyond that the slave market. Sailing by they could see all the way up Broad Street, past the ancient Dutch houses with their stepped gables to the grand painted brick façade of City Hall and the gothic spire of Trinity Church to the west on the Broad-Way. Just beyond City Hall rose another steeple, not as tall and not as grand as Trinity's, proclaiming the site of the French Church on King Street.

The wharves bristled with the masts of countless ships. Nicoll at the helm maneuvered the small sloop with a deft hand, his crew reefing and trimming the sails of their own accord while the master directed *Harmony* towards Ellison's wharf near the foot of Crown Street. His bo'sun blew three times on the brass horn to alert the dock-workers, always lounging about waiting for their next job, to make themselves ready to receive the heaving lines.

Coming in off the slack tide, their vessel moved slowly, but steadily, towards Ellison's flag fluttering on the wharf. There was no one about. Irritated, Ellison turned toward his bo'sun. "Sound it again." The sailor obliged, but with no greater effect. Even the depot door at the head of the wharf remained shut, as though his clerk had decided to take the day off. Ellison, cursing, and Nicholl, stoic, scanned the docks along with their crew and St. John. In an instant they all understood.

Thirty or so rods away off their starboard bow they saw a large British merchant-man, *London* embossed in large gilt letters across its stern, tied up along the lee side of Murray's Wharf. An agitated cluster of men was milling about on the quay. In a moment dozens more joined them, running down from Queen Street, dressed up as Mohawk Indians, yelling war-whoops and brandishing clubs and hatchets. The invaders swarmed up ladders and ropes over the sides onto the deck of the ship. There was the sound of wood splintering; then out of the melee on the ship's poop large rectangular objects were flung over the gunwales into the water, to the cheers of the people on the wharf.

"Looks like the tea ship has finally arrived," Nicholl remarked wryly. "Eight bells. Just in time for the afternoon pouring out." With the captain at the helm and the bo'sun working the jib back and forth they coaxed the sloop up against the wharf. The two crewmembers leapt the few feet onto the planks as the sloop's low beam came alongside, the bo'sun throwing them first the bowline, then the stern and finally the spring which they made fast to the bits.

"Mr. Nicholl, I'm going to find out what's going on. Mind the ship."

"Aye, Mr. Ellison. I'll have my pistol loaded."

"No. No weapons. If the mob assails you use your tongue."

Ellison led St. John to his warehouse between the quay and Queen Street. The door to his office was unlocked, to Ellison's disgust. But the heavy interior door to the storerooms was padlocked, to his relief.

From off in the distance floated the brassy notes of an off-key cornet playing a mock funeral dirge. Through the narrow office window they could see clusters of men coming towards them from Murray's Wharf. But they were strolling, laughing and bantering as they went, looking like an amused crowd leaving a Chinese fireworks show and feeling satisfied they had had their money's worth. Most of the men were jack-tars and dock-workers of all stripes and colours but here and there appeared apprentices from the chandlers' or sail-makers' and even the well-dressed toff or merchant. Many of them were singing as they went by.

Through the door entered Ellison's young clerk Richard who, because he was the man's nephew, greeted them casually, spirits uplifted by the spectacle at Murray's Wharf. He took his uncle's reprimand in stride, gladly paying the price of the merchant's ire in return for the thrill of excitement he had just shared.

Ellison saw the sparkle in his nephew's eyes and growled. "Don't you start getting any ideas, now."

"But Uncle Jack, it's just the Liberty Boys having some fun," Richard laughed. "It's a regular jubilee."

"Destroying people's property is not amusing."

"But, it's not the people who own that tea. It's the East India Company. Whose shareholders are all in England."

"Not all of them," his uncle replied, smiling in spite of himself. "I suspect our own lieutenant-governor has an interest; and James DeLancey and his brother Oliver and a few others of the 'better sort'. What did your republican friends do with the ship's captain?"

"He wasn't on board. The captain's James Chambers. The same bloke the Liberty Boys honoured in October for *refusing* to carry last year's tea! I guess he's not so popular anymore."

Ellison acted as his own factor through a network of relatives among the City merchants and retailers. St. John's barrels of flour and ham and casks of butter were for the most part already bespoken through prearranged contracts; and the rest Ellison would sell at auction in the market. St. John was free to attend to other business.

He took his leave and stepped out, his travel chest staying behind on the boat to be sent for later. He walked the short distance up to Queen Street. Here the crowd fresh from the festivities over the *London* was swarming in front of the Merchants Coffee House on the corner, like bees trying to enter a hive with no place for any more bodies. Many of them gave up the effort and started off along Queen Street towards Whitehall.

St. John found himself following them. In no hurry, he strolled down the cobbled avenue lined with the fine brick buildings of the City's merchants. Their window-panes glimmered with the fading orange-pink glow in the western sky as the lamp-lighter went about his chores, putting his candle to the brass whale-oil lamp affixed to every seventh house. A cart-man was hawking the last of his load door-to-door, large kegs of water from the City's only drinkable source, the Tea Water Spring up Chatham Street towards the DeLancey farm. The vendor had to struggle against the current of people flowing west towards Whitehall and Fort George.

As Queen Street turned into Dock Street near Hanover Square the current became a flood, as though the City's entire male population and not a few female members had decided to meet at the foot of Broad Street, pitch-pine torches swirling grandly in the twilight air. They were milling around the stoop of a grand red brick building whose sign depicted a crown resting above a coiffed feminine face in profile, over which appeared the legend "The Queen Charlotte's Head".

On the far corner a knot of boisterous young dandies had burst into song.

> *"Farewell, master, farewell! No more dams I'll make for fish...*
> *nor scrape trenchers, nor wash dish!*
> *Freedom! Hey-day, hey-day, freedom!*
> *Freedom, hey-day, freedom!"*

"What is going on?" St. John accosted a well-dressed young man in a burgundy suit with ruffled shirt and silken neckband.

The young macaroni was amused. "What? You haven't heard? Have you just fallen off a ship?"

"As a matter of fact, I have. Figuratively speaking."

"Well, stranger, inside Mr. Fraunces' tavern here we have the Governor's Council. Complemented by the leaders of the Assembly. And our Committee of Correspondence. It would seem they are negotiating the fate of Captain Chambers of the *London* and Captain Lockyer of the *Nancy,* who, I am told, are at the present moment being royally entertained at the Merchants Coffee House by a few of the Liberty Boys."

"I was rather hoping to have a good supper and a sound sleep."

"You will get neither at Black Sam's tonight. Mr. Fraunces no doubt is preoccupied with more weighty matters. Try Hull's Tavern up the Broad-Way. But make sure you come back for the bonfire tonight. Captain Chambers' teak furniture ought to burn right nicely."

St. John wended his way to Whitehall. In front of him loomed in the darkness Fort George where he could sense if not see nervous royal grenadiers watching anxiously, or bitterly, on the ramparts as dozens of flickering torches paraded on the grounds below the walls to the accompaniment of jeering voices. He turned northward and walked past Bowling Green, where the equestrian king glowered in the dark.

He veered onto the Broad-Way. Here were the magnificent mansions of the wealthiest merchants and officials, Judge Robert Livingston at No. 3, the Van Cortlandt house two doors down. Further up the street was the King's Arms Tavern, looking run-down and sad, whose sign of the lion and unicorn was hanging awry on only one hook.

At No. 18 he turned into the inn kept by Robert Hull. The proprietor was not in, being himself down by the excitement at Fraunces' Queen's Head tavern and so St. John registered with the man's clerk, gladly paying extra for the luxury of a bed all to himself in a garret room. He arranged to have his trunk picked up, and took his supper in the crowded great-room where he had to wedge himself onto a bench between a tipsy mariner reeking sweetly of rum and an itinerant vendor reeking not so sweetly of a week on the road. St. John did not linger over his meal.

He went for a stroll, *au petit bonheur la chance*. The upper Broad-Way was quiet, and the graveyard next to Trinity Church quieter still. St. John drifted among the silent tombstones, looming almost mockingly out of the soft dark ground.

Brooding, he continued his stroll up the Broad-Way, then turned right onto King Street. At a white picket fence he paused. The old French Church with its stone walls and steeple would have been at home in any small village in Moselle. It sat there cold and forlorn, as though abandoned to an uncertain fate on the shores of an uncertain new world. Candlelight flickered through the small window of the presbytery.

St. John tapped on the door with the knocker. After a moment the door creaked open and a grey, wizened face peered out, frowning.

"Your business, sir?" the old man inquired, brow furrowed with suspicion. He was clutching the edge of the door as though ready to slam it shut in an instant.

"Might Pastor Tétard be at home? Jean-Pierre Tétard." St. John politely raised his hat.

The old man's face took on an even more unfriendly demeanor. "And who might be asking?" The gatekeeper's words bore a faint French accent.

"De la part de son ami, Michel-Guillaume Jean de Crèvecoeur. Ci-présent."

"Speak English!" the man growled. "The old ways are gone. Dead and buried. Along with most of the old guard."

"Pastor Tétard is not among them, I trust."

Seeing the alarm, and affection, in the stranger's face, the old man softened. "No, Tétard is still among the living, as far as I know. Although I don't know very much nowadays! He's still alive. But lucky to have survived."

He swung the door open and with a nod of the head invited the visitor to come inside. He gestured toward a lame chair with a broken back while he seated himself on a stool by the fire. "I'm afraid to not be able to offer you a refreshment," he said gruffly.

"And Pastor Tétard?"

"Tétard. Yes. Well, he's no longer pastor here. We don't have any pastor. Hardly any members left. It's like preaching to the stone walls. That's why Rev. Kettlelas has gone back to Geneva. Or was it Amsterdam? No matter."

"Pastor Tétard baptised my daughter Fanny and my son Guillaume-Alexandre. My wife is again with child and so I was hoping...."

"You will find him back at his farm outside King's Bridge. On the Boston Post Road. Near the Morris estate. I hear he preaches from time to time at the Dutch church up there. Runs a French academy."

Disappointed, St. John watched the play of the fire.

"Why did he leave?" he finally asked.

"Why do they all leave?" the old man asked sourly. Answering his own question, he resumed, "they leave because of the poisonous atmosphere. The poison of pride. Churches aren't immune, you know. Pride poisons every human heart. And more than anything Satan delights in inflaming the pride in Christian hearts. When he can drive a wedge between Christian brothers and sisters he thinks he is driving a stake in God's heart. He is wrong, of course. But then, that is why he is truly the prince of fools."

"You said before that he is lucky to be alive."

"I did. And so he is. Lucky to have been able to escape from the back window of this house."

"Whom was he escaping from?" St. John was thoroughly puzzled. "Pastor Tétard is the kindliest man I have ever known."

"Kindly, yes. But too stubborn for his own good. It was young Bonnet who set the Liberty Boys upon him. To get revenge."

"Revenge? For what?"

"When the elders called Tétard to preach a few years ago he saw that most of our young families no longer spoke French and were leaving us to join Trinity Church. So Tétard shrugs and says, might as well preach in English. But Bonnet's father, our richest member, got angry and had the Company in Geneva send over this pastor named Daller who shows up one Sunday when Tétard's at the pulpit and announces he's the new pastor and tries to show Tétard the door. Bonnet and the other elders got into a fist-fight right in front of the altar. The next day he and Daller show up with two arrogant lawyers, William Smith and John Morin Scott, and threaten to sue. Bonnet had plenty of money to pay lawyers and the elders didn't so they gave in to the bullying.

"But after all that, this fellow Daller ups and leaves. So the elders bring Tétard back. Then Parliament goes and passes the

225

Tea Act last year and Bonnet's family joined the Sons of Liberty. Now they told their pastor he had better start preaching what the Sons wanted to hear or else. Tétard refused. The next thing we know, they start sending letters to Tétard threatening him with death for preaching a gospel of peace instead of resistance to the Tea Act. Tétard, being stubborn, ignored the warnings."

Here the elderly man finally allowed himself a smile. "*Tétard le Tétu, comme on disait.*" He shifted his skinny bones on the stool.

"And so, late December last year, who rides into town but Paul Revere, and gets the Liberty Boys all excited with news of the tea party up in Boston. The next night a few o' them had a bit too much liquid cheer and decided to pay a friendly visit here. Tétard left through the rear window while his well-wishers were banging on the front door."

The old man's smile turned bitter. "I knew Revere's father. Apollos Rivoire. A fellow Huguenot from France. Who, like all of our forefathers and mothers, fled the tyranny and persecution of King Louis and the Catholics, hoping to find peace and freedom of worship here in America."

St. John thanked his informant and took his leave. Hands thrust into his deep coat pockets he walked slowly down the lane, brooding. At William Street knots of people, mostly men and most well-dressed, were making their way uptown towards John Street, passing other knots of men not well-dressed making their way downtown towards Fraunces' tavern and Whitehall, all of them bypassing the occasional lone female figure seen lurking here and there in shadowy doorways. Shopkeepers weren't the only entrepreneurs whose business suffered when the Liberty Boys threw a party, St. John thought.

Up the road a-ways a short line had formed outside the John Street Theatre, the only such establishment in the Colony. St. John strolled over. The building was a large wooden barn-like structure, set back from the street by a courtyard, painted bright red and illuminated by dozens of torches. Plastered on a bill-board outside was a large parchment broad-side, trumpeting the show inside, the American Company of Actors proudly presenting William Shakespeare's *The Tempest*.

St. John was tempted. So that explained the gleeful song he had heard down by the tavern, he thought. Without realising it he found himself at the door where a man stood collecting money. His face and naked torso were smeared with brown and red colours and he wore an elaborate costume evoking the scales and slime of a large fish. He leered at St. John and held out his open hand, palm up.

"Come on inside, hey-day hey-day, come on inside, Caliban say! Voyage to a mysterious isle and see the magic of Prospero beguile! Plots against kings, treacherous conspiracies, and best of all, the ravishing beauty of Miranda! All this enchantment for only three shillings. You'll be wanting the gentlemen's box seats, of course."

"I'll take the gallery."

He handed over his three pence and went inside.

Chapter Thirteen: *The Glass that Runs for Thee*

St. John chose to not take his breakfast at Hull's and went for an early morning stroll along Broad Street down to the Queen Street docks. He was glad for the cold dawn air, for it made wearing his heavy wool great-coat a comfort rather than a burden, and he could carry all his documents in the coat's endless deep pockets.

At the corner of Queen and Broad he stopped to linger at the window of Rivington's *New-York Gazetteer.* The publisher must have had a box seat view of the goings-on of the day before, St. John thought, without even having to leave his shop. A face appeared from behind the window and then a pair of hands, slipping a freshly-printed ha-penny sheet into a display case. He went inside and bought a copy.

Up Queen Street dock-workers competed for space with farmers debarking off the ferry from Brooklyn and others driving teams down from Harlem. Up ahead sat the Merchants Coffee House and he was not surprised to see a crowd of people, crowds of people apparently having become the norm in the City. A brass band was with them. An energetic man climbed onto a chest and raised a stick like a conductor's baton, then gestured for his musicians to bring horns to lips.

A mock cheer went up from the spectators to the brassy strains of *God Save the King* warbling from the French horns and cornet. On cue, the door of the coffee house swung open and a small procession stepped out, heralding not the king but the chastened captain of the *Nancy*, escorted by a proud guard of Liberty Boys to the raucous acclamation of the assembled. The onlookers followed the cortege as it lead Captain Lockyer, not to a kettle of tar, but to a small sloop waiting at the wharf, the brass band bringing up the rear, now playing a funeral march. The gulls swirling overhead squawked in protest.

St. John continued his way up Queen Street to Beekman's Slip. Just past the quay he entered an ancient, rambling wood-clapboard house whose sign announced Jasper Drake's Tavern.

The great-room was dark and smoky notwithstanding the fire and because of it. The proprietor was bustling about among his patrons seated at a couple of long tables, some eating their breakfast, others digesting theirs and all drawing heavily on clay pipes. St. John's eyes watered.

Drake gave the newcomer a friendly hail and pulled out a greasy pipe from his apron. St. John declined. The tavern-keep was stout and cheerful, so much in contrast to his emaciated, subdued cousin, St. John's neighbour down by the Grey-Court meadows.

"Good to see you again! How fare my cousin and his wife?"

"They are well. They have entrusted me with a few things for you."

"All in good time. First have some breakfast."

Drake sat his guest down at a table in the corner and brought out pitchers of coffee and cream, butter and bread; then a bowl of porridge and a plate of ham. As St. John ate he read his *Gazetteer*. He skipped the usual mundane notices offering rewards for runaway slaves or announcing estate auctions and absorbed Rivington's account of the prior day's Tea Party. By and by Drake came over and helped himself to a chair.

"Exciting times, what?" he beamed, sparse wisps of thin grey hair floating about his balding pate. "The Sons of Liberty are good for my business. And they are true to their word. They are liberating me from my debts. But, I suppose things are quiet up there in the wilderness of Orange County."

St. John pulled out some papers from a pocket of his coat draped over the chair. "Here, a copy of your cousin's will. He wants you to be his executor. The original is with Judge Wisner in Goshen village. There's also a letter describing his property."

The door to the tavern opened and a couple of jovial men entered, one short, one tall. They spotted Drake and came over to the table, plopping themselves down without ceremony on the two remaining chairs.

"We already ate," said the shorter of the two, a barrel-chested man with curly iron-grey hair, declining Drake's invitation for breakfast. "And a fine meal it was, courtesy of the coffee house and Widow DeBrinni. But we'll take some more of your own good strong java."

St. John recognised the man as the leader of the brass band outside the Merchant's Coffee House. Drake had more mugs brought over and made the introductions. "This here is Michael St. John, my cousin Joseph's neighbour up in Orange County. Michael, meet my son-in-law Captain Isaac Sears. And his partner, Captain McDougall. What's the latest, gents?"

Sears took a swig of coffee, then regarded St. John closely. "Is your friend a believer in the Cause?" he asked his father-in-law.

"Don't worry. I vouch for him."

Satisfied, Sears nodded his head. He broke into a wide grin, showing teeth more black than white. "The curtain's come down on Act I. Now for Act II of our little play. North and Dartmouth are already pissing mad over Boston. I'd give half my fortune to see the scurvy scums' faces when they hear from Lockyer about our own tea party! Now we have to keep up the pressure.

"We've got the wind in our poop and a full head o' sail. See, Their Lordships can't take this sitting down. They cherish their pride too much to not react. So, they're bound to do something drastic.

"According to the London press, it looks like they're going to have Parliament – the king's puppets all of them! 'cept Burke, of course – punish Boston. Who knows? Maybe the king will send more troops. Or try to force a landing of another shipment of tea. No matter what, the fools can't see beyond the tip of their pointy noses and they'll stumble right into our hands. They're playing *our* game now. And they don't even know it." As Sears chatted cheerily his partner listened, sharp hazel eyes under a freckled brow and receding red hair studying St. John closely, whose own russet-red hair was pulled back in a tight queue.

"So we just sit and wait?" Drake asked. "Waiting don't suit you."

"Hell no. Our next move is non-importation. DeLancey and the merchants don't want none of that again, but they'll have to change their tune as soon as the newest outrage from London comes ashore. Which will happen any day I'm sure. Then all hell will break loose."

McDougall, who had been stirring his coffee thoughtfully, spoke up. His voice had a rich, deep Scots brogue. He spoke slowly, struggling against a stutter.

"Anyone... with half a brain can see that North and, and Parliament are going to do something punitive. Foolish people don't become wise... overnight. They'll walk right into our trap and then we'll send off our letter to Sam Adams and John Hancock calling for an...an inter-colonial conference. A provincial congress, as it were. We'll show Parliament they, they can't divide and conquer the Colonies like they think they can. But, all the Colonies will have to accept, finally, that we are all in the same boat. And that we must row together or sink.

"New-York, our own Colony, is key. At least, we know that if Parliament tries to force any more tea on us there won't be... any one here willing to risk their neck to act as the company's agents."

"You can't be sure about that, Mac," Sears grumbled. "I don't trust those three blokes to keep their word."

"What three blokes?" Drake asked.

"White, Lott and Booth," McDougall explained. "The three fellows DeLancey recommended to the East India Company to be, to be their tea agents. Isaac and I had a friendly little chat with them. We persuaded them to turn down the commissions. White and Lott don't have much...much backbone, but Benjamin Booth's a tougher nut. 'Tis pity he's a Tory."

"He's conniving and clever. Like a Livingston," Sears muttered, suddenly rankled at his off-again, on-again allies.

"Booth has a country estate in Orange County, doesn't he?" McDougall was looking at St. John.

"Well, he's next door in Ulster County. Between my farm and Thomas Bull's farm. Married a Bull woman."

"Don't know the name."

Drake spoke up. "Booth's not far from the Clintons."

"George Clinton?" McDougall asked. "He's a good Whig and a good, a good friend of the Cause."

"But Booth isn't," Sears interjected, dark eyes flashing. "That's all I need to know. If you're not with us then you're against us. And thus my enemy."

McDougall again looked at St. John. "What's the mood in Orange County?"

St. John put down his mug, contemplating his coffee as though reflecting.

"Mixed. The Church of England people and the German Lutherans are more conservative than the Presbyterians and the Calvinists."

"And where do you stand?"

St. John poured himself another cup of coffee. He looked at McDougall, a half-smile on his lips.

"On the side of freedom."

He raised up his coffee mug. "A toast to liberty."

"Here here!" Sears clinked his cup against St. John's and Drake's. McDougall sat still, watching St. John intently.

"Then come to our next meeting here, on Thursday."

"Unfortunately, I must return home before then."

"Then I must impose upon you with a request for a favour. You are acquainted with Tom Moffat and…and Henry Wisner?"

"Very well acquainted. I consider them to be among my closest friends."

"Then if I may I will entrust you with a letter to them from our committee Where are you… staying here in the City?"

"At Hull's."

"Very well. I'll send the letter over… over by messenger."

They shook hands on it. "We're off to meet with the Committee of Correspondence," Sears told Drake. "John Jay, William Smith, James Duane… they're the windlass we need to trim our sails for where we want the ship to go."

St. John turned to other business with his host. "Your butter, pork and flour should be ready to be picked up today. At Ellison's." He signed over the bill of lading to his friend. They parted company, St. John pocketing the tavern-keeper's order for a July shipment and an eclectic assortment of Spanish dollars, Dutch guilders, pound sterling and Colonial bills of exchange in his purse.

Like all travelers from remote parts his pockets were crammed with letters from folk back home for delivery to correspondents in the City. Fulfilling most of his neighbourly mission by noon, he stopped in at the old Royal Exchange where he knew the Chamber of Commerce would be meeting for the weekly dinner.

The merchants were milling about the bar in the long room upstairs. He found his friend William Seton, talking to a thoughtful-looking young man who was shaking his head slowly. As St. John approached, Seton gave a smile of welcome and extended his hand.

"Pleasant trip, I hope? Michael, let me introduce you to my good friend and stubborn, pig-headed, opinionated lawyer John Jay. Mr. Jay, Michael St. John. A gentleman farmer from Orange County."

Jay seemed flattered by Seton's description. "It is indeed a remarkable coincidence I have myself noticed: how often it is that people who disagree with us tend to be stubborn and opinionated! Not to mention, pig-headed. If only they could be rational and reasonable like me and we'd all get along so much better."

"I have been attempting, in vain it would seem, to explain to John here the error in his thinking. That non-importation is an effective means to achieve a purely political end. It is not and can never be, since all it does is ruin the very people we would all like to see flourish, namely, our own citizens. And therefore it is divisive, at a time when we must be united. "

"But my dear friend, your own reaction as a merchant proves the very point I make. If you, a merchant, are distressed by the pernicious effects of non-importation from England, you can well imagine the distress on the part of the merchants in England and especially, in London, who no longer have a market to export to. We need only recall how our non-importation pledge five years ago forced Parliament to repeal the Revenue Act."

"Well, at least we do agree on one thing: no more violence. You and James Duane and William Smith have got to impress that upon Captain Sears."

"More to the point, upon McDougall," Jay replied. "He supplies the brains to Sears' brawn. The City's boldest smuggler, and wealthiest as well," he explained for St. John's benefit. "Hard not to admire a man with his principals and courage. He's become quite an expert on Montesquieu and Locke."

"If so he will agree with them that violence is not the answer to tyranny because it will only engender, in the long run, more tyranny. It is logic and reason that must win the day."

"Unless the party who opposes you is himself illogical and unreasonable. In that case, then what?"

"Then we eat. They are calling us to table." Seton slipped his arm under Jay's and the two strolled over to dine as though they had merely been debating the weather. St. John trailed in their wake.

The meal, catered by Samuel Fraunces, was excellent. Dinner was topped off by generous bowls of syllabub, ladled out by Black Sam himself.

"Some years ago I bought your recipe-book," St. John informed him. "I am pleased to report that I have now mastered all your recipes. Except for one."

Hours later St. John awoke to a pounding headache. He squinted out the small window of his garret room and saw the setting sun hanging over the New-Jersey shore. He forced himself to his feet, shrugged on his coat, and winced his way down the stairs to the great-room.

"Water," he croaked to Hull, putting up glassware in his cabinet upon the bar.

The tavern owner looked with pity at his guest. "I don't think you'll be wanting to drink our City water," he said. "It's only fit for washing dishes. I don't have any more Tea-Water at the moment, but the cart-man should be coming by any moment now. How about some coffee while you wait?"

After three cups St. John felt much better. By then the Tea-Water man had made his round and St. John drank a quart without pausing. After a visit to the well-named necessary out back he stepped out onto the Broad-Way. He headed north along the cobbled street.

From somewhere church bells were tolling mournfully. Up ahead from around the corner of Crown Street a grim figure emerged dressed in black. From behind his black hat fluttered black crêpe, falling over the black cape on his shoulders. Here most of the old houses were of the Dutch vernacular, with stepped gables and low stoops. The funereal figure stopped at each door and, as it opened, doffed his black hat and with a black-gloved hand passed a packet to an extended palm before going on to the next house.

It was the *Aanspreecker*. St. John had witnessed it before in Albany and Kingston. The funeral-bidder went from house to house among the neighbours, inviting them to the defunct burgher's going-away celebration. The tolling bells he heard, St. John realised, were coming from the old Dutch Church a couple of blocks away. After the funeral would be a sumptuous feast at the house of the deceased, and the mourners' grief washed away by toast after toast in memory of the departed.

He found himself following the Tea-Water cart, aiming for the spring up ahead, just beyond the colossal iron-clad liberty pole towering sixty feet up into the sky like the main-mast of a land-locked ship. Across the top, gigantic golden letters screamed the single word "LIBERTY!" glittering in the light of the dying sun.

He returned to the Broad-Way via Murray Street, wondering what had become of the British general. He thought of the Dauphine Redoubt, the general twirling the globe with his fingers, inviting him to become a British army officer. The young French lieutenant placing his right hand on a Bible, repeating the solemn oath to never again take up arms against the British Crown.

Back on the Broad-Way he passed by the Georgian brownstone of St. Paul's. Flanked by a graveyard and with the river in its rear, the church looked upon the road, as though turning its face away from the brothels crouched yonder by Chambers Street, known by the locals as the Holy Ground.

St. John walked the two blocks south to Trinity Church. He paused. The narrow portal door on the side was open as well as the wider main door through which most of the people were passing. He went into neither. He went instead into the graveyard.

He walked among the tombstones, searching for the oldest. Perhaps he found it, on a small plot not far from the nave. Richard Churcher, a long-forgotten hand had chiseled into the cold stone. Died in 1681, at the age of five years. Richard's brother Charles rested next to him. He enjoyed a longer life, dying at the age of seven in 1691.

A large, reddish brownstone tombstone whispered the final resting place of a more recent but equally transient traveler:

> *Here lyes the Body of Abraham Williams,*
> *Who Departed this Life*
> *November 30, 1760 aged 29 years.*
> *Stay, Reader, stand and shed a Tear;*
> *Fear and think on Me, Who now lyes Here.*
> *And as You read the State of Me,*
> *Think of the Glass which runs for Thee.*
> *In Christ alone I put my Trust,*
> *To rise in Judgement with the Just.*

The bells of the Dutch Church nearby stopped tolling. Swallows twittered hungrily as they swooped among the small trees gracing the gravestones, finding all the nourishment they needed in the air around them.

St. John left the cemetery and strolled down towards Fraunces' tavern.

Chapter Fourteen: *A Worthy Temple*

Saturday, April 15, 1775 was a cool but sunny day. Patches of snow and ice still clung stubbornly to the earth but the promise of springtime had not been forgotten. St. John whistled cheerfully as he placed the tin box holding their supper of cheese, ham and *tourtière* in the cart; and for six-month old Louis-Philippe, porridge and apple-sauce. He was careful to not overlook the keg filled not with cider, but with the good, pure water from their spring on Pine Hill.

He fussed with the old quilt he had spread out for the children to sit on, then went to fetch Martin and Luther. As he hitched them up he heard impatient little voices from the kitchen and Mehetable's softer tones. In a moment Fanny with her little brother Ally in tow burst out of the house like excited bubbles from a bottle and flung themselves into their father's arms.

"Windmill, papà, windmill! Be a windmill!"

St. John lifted up his giggling daughter high into the air over his head then moved her around in a giant circle while she screamed in delight as Guillaume-Alexandre tugged at his father's leggings. St. John deposited Fanny onto the quilt and swooped up Ally in his arms. He waltzed his son around the horses and cart, moving the boy up and down like the piston of a steam engine.

There was just room for the cradle in the back of the cart. St. John lent a hand to his wife with a warm kiss on her cheek. He held their baby swaddled in blue while Mehetable climbed onto the leather seat and adjusted her skirts to let the small bronze box filled with hot embers warm her legs. She took baby back into her arms and kissed his head.

With a cheery wave to Henry and the brothers Toussaint St. John put the horses into motion. They followed the cart-path through the hills behind their farm and onto the trail just south of Purgatory Swamp. They passed by the Horton farm, then a few minutes later the trail to the old Bull homestead off on the right. After another three-quarters of an hour they reached the Goshen Road and headed west.

"Papà, when will we get there?" Fanny complained. "Will it be soon? Will it?"

St. John turned his head, speaking over his shoulder. "We're almost to the Tustens' house. It won't be long now 'til we reach the village."

Satisfied for the moment, Fanny sat back down. A few minutes later she sprang back up.

"Papà, when will we get there?"

"Soon, America-Frances. Soon." He pointed with the stock of his whip at a stone stele set to the side of the road indicating to travelers the direction to Goshen.

"Just as soon as we go by that, that whatchamacallit up ahead on the road."

"Papà, what's a whatchamacallit?"

"A whatchamacallit? A whatchamacallit is a – a thingamajig."

"Oh."

St. John reigned in at the physician's modest clapboard farmhouse hugging the road. In the yard was the young doctor himself helping wife and infant son into their buggy. He came over to greet them.

"Grand day for a fair, wouldn't you say?" He sported a fine new brown suit. A red cockade graced his black felt hat.

"Couldn't ask for better," St. John agreed.

"Howdee, Mrs. St. John. And who do we have here? A new addition to the family?"

"Louis-Philippe. Born October 22, 1774."

Dr. Tusten did not take offense that his services had not been requested for the delivery. He was used to the suspicion his profession engendered. He could shrug it off all the easier to the degree his reputation had grown from his successful small-pox inoculation practice.

"And who do we have hiding in ambush in the back here? Don't tell me... let me guess. Of course, it must be Fanny! But who is that little Indian hiding behind you? Guillaume-Alexandre, I see you. Surrender!"

The giggling children ducked down behind the side-boards.

"Fanny looks good. No ill effects from the inoculation?"

"Nothing long-lasting. We are all fine. Although it is not the happiest memory of my life."

"You should do Ally soon. Young children are the most vulnerable to the small-pox, you know." He smiled reassuringly at Mehetable. "I've now inoculated over eight hundred people. Haven't lost a single child yet. Only a few elderly folk."

They clopped along the low ridge leading down to the village. On their right hand, to the north, they could see Thomas Bull's large farm and his elegant five-bay Georgian stone house, visible through the still-naked trees. To Fanny's delight and her father's relief they soon came upon the Albany Post Road and on into the village.

The township of Goshen sat on the western frontier. To the south lay the Town of Minisink then New-Jersey where the last portion of the new boundary line survey had finally been completed, by their Goshen neighbour Samuel Gale. The men milling around the spanking new court-house, grand double-doors gaily decked out with the white, blue and red bunting of the British flag beneath an elegant Greek pediment, were unanimous. The Colony of New-York and, more importantly, the County of Orange, had been cheated.

"It's highway robbery, nothing less," William Allison declared. Like all the other men he was arrayed in his finest Sunday attire for the inauguration of the new court-house. "We ought to invite those boundary commissioners here and give'em a taste of our new gaol, from the inside out. What do you think, Judge Wisner?"

The judge shrugged. "I'm not exactly impartial either, you know. It's not possible to be indifferent when your own self-interest is involved. But after seven years as a judge I've learned that in most disputes both sides have valid points. The royal commission made a reasonable compromise between New-York and New-Jersey. The only alternative to compromise is war."

"Well," Jesse Woodhull laughed, "we ought to send those commissioners up to the Hampshire Grants. Cad Colden's still doling out land up there to his cronies despite the king's order to stop. Which only makes St. John here's friend Ethan Allen and his boys fight harder. They kidnapped the judges and even the sheriff Colden appointed and held them for ransom! It's a regular war up there in the Grants."

"As I was saying," Wisner continued, "war is the consequence of not being able to reason together."

"And if the other side don't want to be reasonable?"

Wisner shrugged. "That's the problem, isn't it? Last October in Congress John Adams read Franklin's letters from England about his humiliating cross-examination in front of Parliament. As he puts it, those vain, foolish squires and lords are hopelessly corrupt and dead-set on crushing our spirit. Franklin though still believes war is not inevitable. Jay, Duane, the Virginians, they're all hoping the boycott will work again like before."

"No boycott's going to push the red-coats out of Boston," Woodhull retorted.

"I doubt it, myself. Well, Franklin is supposed to be back from England in a few weeks, in time for the next Congress. Maybe he'll have something new to report."

"If it's war they want, it's war they'll get!" Elihu Marvin joined in. He was holding his hat in his hand and his straw-blond hair glinted a fierce red in the sun. "They've closed off Boston port. They've sent over two thousand more grenadiers. They gave all our territory in the Ohio to Quebec – French papists, to-boot! An' now Parliament says we don't have the right any more to pick a jury to hear our trials! I'd rather die than let 'em treat us like a bunch of Irishmen. Sorry, Tom, no offense intended."

"No offense taken," Moffat replied. "I am not an Irishman. I am an American."

"Judge Wisner!" Josiah Carpenter, now Goshen Town Supervisor, approached. "Captain Woodhull, Captain Marvin, Captain Allison... time to go and meet our guests of honour coming in from Yelverton's on the Chester Road."

Away he led them, taking by the elbow Wisner, Orange County's delegate to the Continental Congress. The county's other leading citizens were already seated in a long waggon decorated in the same manner as the court-house, bedecked with garlands of flowers and vines woven by the maidens of the village. They were driven away by a pair of white Arabians with plumed headdresses, flanked on the right by Woodhull on his horse, as county sheriff and militia commander of Blooming Grove, and on the left by Marvin, newly appointed justice of the peace and militia commander of Oxford. Allison brought up the rear at the head of his village militia company.

They returned a half hour later, proudly escorting their guests, Judge Robert Livingston, the lawyer James Duane, and George Clinton representing the Colony's official Assembly as well as its illegal Provincial Congress and now Ulster County's delegate to the Continental Congress as well.

The supervisor and Rev. Kerr from the Presbyterian church were waiting patiently for them on the reviewing stand erected on the road in front of the court-house. Before the steps stood a dozen men and older boys at attention, holding at the ready bugles or cornets, fifes and the odd French horn, flanked on either side by a drummer. As the cortege drew near the supervisor turned his head to the brightly uniformed leader of the militia band and nodded.

On the downswing of the baton the drums tapped out a tattoo, drawing the bugles into a fanfare noteworthy for their high degree of originality, before cornets and horns joined in the fray, all with their own unique understanding of melody and tonality. The fife players could not be heard at all but, undeterred, could be seen vigorously puffing away.

The guests of honour stepped onto the platform where a colour guard stood at attention on the right, holding the Union Jack with its crosses of St. George and St. Andrew; and on the left, a militia guard holding up slightly higher a homespun flag with the words "UNION AND LIBERTY" writ in red above the image of a snake which, unlike Franklin's segmented serpent, was wholly intact, coiled, and dangerously ready to strike.

The reviewing stand faced the new court-house, in front of which the people had gathered, squeezing in as best they could. The fine stone building, which had taken Thomas Bull almost two years to complete at the cost of 1,800 pounds voted by the Assembly, was two stories tall, centre gable facing the street. Granite steps led up to the double entrance doors over which was a glass transom with a three-leaf clover design. Above the transom was the Greek pediment all in white, in the centre of which reigned a crown atop the royal coat-of-arms.

For its finale the band did not play *God Save the King*. Instead the inauguration committee had decided upon a psalm by William Billings, which most everyone had already heard many times in church and meeting. They sang:

> *"When Jesus wept, the falling tear*
> *in mercy flowed, beyond all bound.*
> *When Jesus groaned, a trembling fear*
> *seized all the guilty world around."*

A quiet settled over the people. Rev. Kerr rose, in the centre of the stand, and led the crowd in a prayer. "Almighty God, may your blessings be upon our leaders You have chosen to go to Congress. May they walk in the ways of Your Wisdom and may the fruits of their endeavours be pleasing to You.

"We have gathered here to inaugurate a court-house. But we dedicate it to You, the source of all truth. For without Your true law there can be no true liberty. May our new court-house be forever a temple worthy of Your justice."

The ceremony was the most important celebration in Orange County's brief history. Present were not just one but three delegates to the Continental Congress and a supreme court judge as well, and the people were expecting an oratorical performance worthy of the occasion. Judge Livingston, being a Livingston, spoke first, cloaked in the ponderous mantel of severe dignity adopted by all judges since time immemorial. He concluded his eighty-minute peroration with a stern admonition to respect the law. "If you value your own legal rights, then you must respect the rights of your neighbours as much as your own."

There was a polite but wan smattering of applause, the Livingston clan not being particularly admired in the backwoods wilds of Orange County. The next orator, lawyer James Duane, spoke with a manner of squinting his eyes as though the light were bothering him. When he praised the generosity of Orange County for sending waggon-loads of food to besieged Boston, the crowd began to warm to him. But then he stepped into a puddle.

"Let us avoid violence at all costs, for the wages of war are misery and despair. Let wise words be our weapons." A smattering of boos and jeers rippled among most of the younger men and boys in the crowd. Undeterred, Duane ended his talk with a plea for reconciliation with the Mother Country. "Let us petition the king. To let us form an American Union. With an American Parliament. Beholden not to the British Parliament but only to the king."

George Clinton personally knew a third of the men standing before him and could recite by heart the names of their wives and children. He was tall and stout, like the other visiting dignitaries coiffed with a white bob-wig under his three-cornered black hat. As Moffat presented him to the crowd they cheered wildly. Clinton doffed his hat and bowed, beaming. He did not bother with a written speech, or for that matter, any speech at all. Instead, he chatted with the people, although it was a one-sided talk, given in a booming voice for all to hear. His tone only grew serious when he announced the new law, just passed by the Colonial Assembly, that all able-bodied men aged 16 to 60 were required to be active in a militia unit under penalty of fine or prison.

"But," he continued, "I know here in Orange County I am preaching to the converted. I have no doubt all the brave men before me here today will answer the call of duty with honour." He pulled out a white silk kerchief and dabbed his brow, then, returning the cloth to its pocket, he threw back his shoulders and adopted his most dignified pose, prominent chin tilted slightly upward. He paused a moment for dramatic effect, observant eyes scrutinising his audience shrewdly.

"I am honoured to represent the County of Ulster in the Continental Congress," he declared. "But I also represent in spirit all my brothers here in Orange County. Brothers, let us all stand united in our convictions. Let us not dwell in a house divided for, as Lord Jesus himself tells us, such a house cannot subsist. But let there be no misunderstanding: whoever is not with us, is against us. And we will not let dissenters from our noble cause divide us. I pledge to you I will do my duty to *our* country in the Continental Congress. We will *not* back down, we will *not* give way to tyranny, even if we must die to stand up for our rights."

A masculine wave of cheering and applause swelled up from among the assembled. Clinton shone. He thrust out his right arm dramatically, pointing to the new building. "We here dedicate this court-house to the ideal of freedom from tyranny, freedom from oppression. We will settle for nothing less than liberty under God!"

The band struck up a vigorous martial tune to the clapping of the crowd whipped up to a jubilant pitch, their enthusiasm honed all the more by the prospect of food now that the four hours of speeches were over. As the dignitaries disappeared inside the court-house for their guided tour, the Goshen militia assembled, chanting and hollering, soon joined by their brethren from Chester, Oxford and Blooming Grove.

In their midst was Judge Wisner's son, Gabriel, grown into a tall strapping young man. His comrades lifted him onto their shoulders and, surrounded by the rhythmic chanting of their peers, they wended their way up the granite steps to the front doors of the court-house. They stopped directly in front of the noble Greek pediment above the doorway, displaying the embossed crown and royal coat-of- arms. With the band playing on, and the assembled shouting with hoarse voices, Gabriel brought up a chisel in his left hand and a hammer in his right. He paused, then raised his right hand clutching the hammer. With two or three mighty well-aimed blows he struck away the royal crown, then obliterated the royal arms. His companions whooped with joy.

Watching at a distance, in stunned silence with his friend St. John, Thomas Bull wept.

Chapter Fifteen: *A Pledge upon a Bloody Deed*

"Papà is it done yet? Is it ready yet? Is it? Is it?" Ally was jumping up and down on his short little legs in eager anticipation

"Whoa, there. Hold your horses. It's almost ready for you." St. John said, making a final adjustment to his invention. "There! Perfect. It fits just right. "

He bent over, hands on knees, looking at his boy with a huge smile. "How about if we wait until after dinner? That way it'll be more fun," he teased.

"No, papà, no! Now. Now papà!"

"Well, all right, if you insist." With that St. John swung his little boy squealing with delight up into the air and set him down into the little wooden seat he had affixed to the beam of the plough. With the help of Peter Toussaint and Henry he hitched up their oxen Abel and Cain. With Peter leading the team and Henry guiding the plough St. John walked alongside his son on the uneven ground. They had not gone far when a clattering of hooves on the road made them pause.

Four horsemen were galloping up the rise from the east in a swirl of dust. The leader was Isaac Nicholl, the sloop master's brother. With him was young Jonathan Tuthill, William Moffat and neighbour Bird's-eye Young. They saw St. John and reigned in their mounts. St. John lifted up Ally in his arms and walked with a quickened step to the riders, their horses steaming in the late April sun.

"It's war! News just come in from Connecticut," Nicholl exclaimed, breathing hard.

"There's war in Connecticut?" St. John asked, puzzled.

"No, not there! The battle was in Massachusetts, in Middlesex County. Five days ago. Town called Concord. Gage sent a regiment of red-coats to seize powder and guns. Massacred a unit of militia when their backs were turned. We showed 'em! Drove 'em all the way back to Boston! Kilt a hundred lobster-backs! Maybe more!"

There was another clattering sound from around the corner of the house, made not by shod hooves but by dainty feet shod in wooden clogs. Fanny had run over at the sound of visitors and now clung to her father's legs, looking up in scared awe at the mounted men, her reddish-auburn hair protected by a cream-coloured bonnet.

"We're passing the word. Jon here's goin' to Allison in Goshen. Nat Roe and Jess' Woodhull are already headed for Sugar Loaf and Warwick. Me an' Moffat an' Bird's-Eye are a-goin' to Yelverton's to round up Elihu Marvin's boys. All militia companies are to be at the ready to march to Boston at any time an' their captains are to meet tonight at Yelverton's."

"Here now, your horses need water."

Reluctantly Nicholl and his companions dismounted and led their animals over to the trough by the well.

"Bide here a spell and have a bite to eat and a bowl of coffee."

Nicholl looked at St. John incredulously.

"We're at war, man! Eat? You'd best get down your musket and pack your bag and find your company. Blooming Grove or Chester?"

"I'm with Bull."

"Captain John? If you mean John Bull, he's a good man. Looks like there's to be a combined Ulster-Orange Brigade under George Clinton and Colonel Hasbrouck. So all our companies will be together in one way or another." With that the three men mounted their horses and rode off down the King's Highway, Tuthill splitting off to his right onto the path towards Goshen.

St. John, Ally in his arms and Fanny and Henry by his side, watched the retreating messengers in silence.

"So it's war then," he finally murmured.

Ally, content to be resting in his father's arms, looked up questioningly.

"Papà, what's 'war'?"

St. John looked at his young boy tenderly. He bit his lip, furrowed his brow.

Fanny, jumping up and down in excitement, exclaimed: "War is when men can't agree and so they hate and kill each other. Papà, are you going to join the militia?"

Ally trembled. He burst into tears and buried his head in his father's chest.

St. John glanced at Henry. "You and the Toussaint boys had best get on with the ploughing."

St. John stood still beside the well-sweep, gentling rocking the sobbing Ally in his arms. The sassafras tree by the front door had just woken up from winter's sleep, its fragile buds pinkish-white against the dark green nascent leaves of the grape vine gracing its trunk. Slowly St. John strolled around to the back of the house, to the kitchen porch, while Fanny pranced ahead, yelling excitedly.

Mehetable was in the rocking chair by the fire nursing Louis-Philippe. "Fanny, go help Charity outside in the vegetable patch."

St. John pulled up a log and sat down next to her. He stared into the fickle flames of the fire.

"What are you going to do?" Mehetable asked softly.

St. John, still holding Ally now asleep in his arms, looked at her, tried to smile.

"I don't know."

They both stared into the fire.

* * * * *

Four weeks later St. John and his hands loaded up the waggon with their woolen cloth from the spring shearing for cleaning down at Satterly's fulling mill in Blagg's Clove. On the way he would stop in at the town meeting, to be held at the Congregational church rather than Brewster's tavern, the turn-out expected to be overflowing.

The meeting-house was packed to bursting. The benches had been shoved against the walls and everyone was standing, looking at plump Thomas Moffat standing on a long make-shift platform along with Hezekiah Howell, Elihu Marvin, Nathaniel Strong, and Zach DuBois. Moffat, holding a parchment document, was motioning to several other men to join them.

Nathaniel Satterly, the mill owner, stepped up followed by two others St. John did not recognise.

"This meeting is now in session!" Moffat had to shout out in order to be heard above the noise of the crowd. The gathering fell into a grudging silence.

"Good. Thank you. Before turning to the business of this document I am holding in my hand, I am pleased to report to you that Ethan Allen and Benedict Arnold have captured Fort Ticonderoga, taken the red-coats prisoner and seized all the guns and powder. They are advancing into Canada as we speak!"

The meeting-house erupted in a volcano of cheering and shouting. A dozen or so elderly men in the back, along with another dozen not so old, watched in a pocket of silence.

Moffat gestured for quiet. "You all know the gentlemen standing next to me. No need for me to repeat their names. They have each of them volunteered, along with me, to act as your Committee of Safety and Observation. As you have no doubt already heard, our Congress in Philadelphia have asked patriots all over America to form local committees to assist the heroic resistance to tyranny by our Massachusetts brethren and to carry out the orders of the Congress.

"Do I hear a motion to accept the gentlemen before you as your Committee?"

"No need for any motion!" Elihu Marvin shouted out from somewhere in the crowd. "We accept them by acclamation!" The men crowding around the platform yelled out their agreement with cheers and whistling. The men towards the back watched in silence.

"Motion made, seconded and passed unanimously," Moffat duly noted in a ledger-book he had placed on the podium next to his ink and quill. He lifted up the parchment paper. "Now if you'd all be quiet you will be able to hear what I'll be reading."

He had to hold the paper at arms-length to make out the words. "It's from our brethren in the New-York Provincial Convention. Every town has been asked to accept the same pledge. It's dated Saturday, April 29, 1775. The 'Pledge of Association'. Listen up:

> 'Persuaded, *that the salvation of the rights and liberties of America depends,* under God, *on the firm union of its inhabitants, taking all measures necessary for its safety*

and to prevent anarchy and disorder; we, the Freemen and Inhabitants of the County of Orange! *being alarmed by the bloody scene now acting in the Massachusetts-Bay, do, in the most solemn manner,*

'Resolve, *never to become slaves; and to associate under all the ties of religion, honour, and love to* our Country, *to adopt and carry into execution whatever measures may be recommended by the Continental Congress and by our Provincial Convention, for the purpose of preserving our Constitution, and opposing the execution of the several arbitrary and oppressive Acts of the British Parliament, until a reconciliation between Great Britain and America, on constitutional principles (which we most ardently desire) can be obtained;*

Therefore, *we will in all things follow the advice of our General Committee, for the preservation of peace and good order, and the safety of individuals and private property.' "*

To make sure everyone understood what they were being asked to pledge to, Moffat read the document out loud once again.

"An' I'll throw in my own two bits just to raise the ante a little," he added. "There can be no liberty without respect for the law. An' our present royal government has no respect for the ancient hallowed laws of all Englishmen.

"And now we will open up the floor for discussion but *one man at a time* in order to assure 'the preservation of peace and good order'!"

The floor erupted at once in a cacophony of clamouring voices, all talking at once.

"Silence!" Moffat yelled. "One at a time, I said. There can be no discussion unless we all respect the rules. Raise your hands." Arms shot up into the air, resembling so many masts in a crowded harbor.

The group in the back, mostly men of Judge Smith's clan out of Smith's Clove, began a low, heated exchange among themselves. Several others gravitated towards them, Isaac Bull and brother Richard, elderly Ebenezer Seely and sons, school-master James Peters and friend Fletcher Matthews from down the road at Matthews' Mill. The circle orbited around the judge's son, Claudius Smith, with his own son Richard and friend James Flewelling.

Their angry buzzing reached the ears of an irritated Thomas Moffat. "Quiet back there!" he thundered. "One speaker at a time, gentlemen!"

With a loud banging sound Claudius Smith threw together a couple of benches and jumped up onto his own platform in the back of the meeting-house. Although not tall he was a muscular man with a strong jaw and vigorous face under a shock of insubordinate nut-brown hair with streaks of grey. He had a robust voice to match his physique.

" *'O heavy deed! It had been so with us, had we been there,'* " he boomed out the quotation from Shakespeare's *Hamlet*, in a mocking theatrical tone. He pointed an accusing finger at Moffat standing with the others on the platform. " *'His liberty is full of threats to all – to you yourself, to us, to everyone. Alas, how shall this bloody deed be answered?'*" His voice was heavy with sarcasm, eyes roving over the stunned meeting-house.

"Their 'pledge' is pure madness an' they will lead you all, like the docile herd of swine you are, right over the cliffs of Gadarenes into the sea to drown. How are *we*, loyal subjects of the crown, to answer the bloody, *mad*, deed of Massachusetts? Not by following these mad-men into the ocean! Nor by logic. The sword of reason is but a blunt instrument when thrust into the belly of fools."

An outraged Elihu Marvin recovered his tongue. He would have rushed the rump speaker were he not hemmed in by the packed bodies surrounding him. "Let me at 'im! I'll kill 'im, by God!" he spluttered. "Pigs? Fools? Mad-men?"

Moffat had regained his composure. He cupped his hands in front of his face. It was his turn to be mocking.

"Hail! Hail, King Claudius! Wise, good King Claudius! Remind us all how your namesake became king of Denmark! You're the proverbial pot calling the kettle black." The crowd broke out in laughter. "King Claudius galloping to the rescue of King Lear!"

Unfazed, Smith responded in an even louder voice.

"Fish don't know they're wet. Mad-men don't know they're mad. A pox on your committee! A pox on your pledge!"

He leapt down to the floor. "*My* revenge knows no bounds. Come on, boys. Let's find us a place where we can breathe the pure air of freedom." He shoved his way out the door, followed by his sons and their friends. A furious Jeroboam Brown, flanking Marvin's right, pulled out an object from his pocket and hurled it at the departing dissenters. The apple splattered against the wall next to the doorframe. A bit of apple landed on the shoulder of elderly Judge Smith. He brushed it off with a flick of his hand. He remained standing where he was.

Marvin's sons Seth and Elihu Jr. made to go towards the door, fists balled in anger. Nathaniel Roe held them back. "Let it go. Let 'em hang themselves."

Moffat on the platform in front resumed answering questions from the floor. St. John found himself next to Isaac Bull and sons, and brother Richard. Isaac Bull raised a hand and shouted out his question.

"If we promise to obey our Congress, and if our king orders us to obey his Parliament, what then?"

"Then you must follow your oath."

"But some of us – a lot of us here – took an oath before God to obey the king, when we served during the French Wars, or as justices of the peace or judges. Even *you,* Thomas, as county clerk. Are we to break our oath to God? Is Congress above God?"

"Did not God bless Saul as king, only to curse him after he turned his back on the Lord? It seems to me if our sovereign acts in ungodly ways we are released from our oath to the sovereign, although never to God."

Richard Bull spoke up. "In what way has King George turned his back to God?"

"Well, for one thing, by giving away our lands in the Ohio to the ungodly French Canadians led by their papist bishops."

"You can't trust the French," Brown yelled out angrily. "A curse on all of them."

St. John, standing next to the Bulls, encountered Brown's staring eyes.

Moffat moved on to another questioner. Richard was whispering heatedly in his brother's ear.

St. John gave a perfunctory nod to the Bulls and made for the doorway.

He heard behind him the angry splattering sound of an apple smashing against the doorframe as he slipped out the door.

Chapter Sixteen: *Miracle Shoes and the Doll without a Face*

It was unusually pleasant weather for an August day. St. John and the Toussaint brothers had just walked onto the kitchen porch from threshing wheat in the barn while Mehetable came down from the attic room where the weaver was still busy at their loom. They all plopped down onto whatever available seat they could find, glad to be able to relax if only for a spell. Mehetable put the sleeping baby Louis-Philippe in the cradle and sat on a low stool, rocking him gently with one foot on the runner. The kitchen windows were open to let the breeze flow through and they could hear Charity finishing up her chores inside.

Henry ambled over from the vegetable patch with a large basket of greens and an armful of Ally, squirming and wriggling to escape once he espied his mother on the porch. Fanny was prancing and skipping barefoot behind them in her thin white homespun blouse, long red hair flowing behind her. Henry went into the kitchen to give Charity the basket then came back out, holding a smaller basket. He made himself comfortable on a stump next to the porch and beckoned to Fanny.

"How you would like a little doll?" His face the colour of soft red clay broke into a smile.

Fanny clapped her hands and nodded eagerly. Henry pulled out from the basket a half dozen dry corn-husks and a cob and proceeded to fashion her an elegant doll, magically transforming the corn leaves into a fine satin skirt and dainty blouse with puffed sleeves. The corn silk became luxurious hair and a strip of husk a fashionable bonnet.

"The doll's face," Henry explained, "will be left to whatever you imagine it to be."

He presented the gift to a happy Fanny who hugged the doll to her cheek and kissed it.

"That way she is no one, and everyone. And therefore at one with the one and only."

"Thank you Mr. Henry! Ma, look! Look! Isn't she beautiful?"

From down the King's Highway they heard a clopping sound accompanied by the creaking of a cart. On the cart sat a spare, skinny man in black vest and black cocked hat. The cobbler from Newburgh, seeing Henry and Fanny, decided to turn into their path-way and see what might be acting. St. John got up and strolled off the porch to greet the visitor.

"G'day, folks."

"G'day, Mr. Mills. Business good?"

"That remains to be seen, Mr. St. John. My fate is entirely in your good hands." He flashed a toothy grin and his thin long nose quivered as though sniffing the air.

"Lord I hope not," St. John replied. "I don't know that I want that responsibility."

"We can use your good skills today, methinks, Mr. Mills," Mehetable spoke up. "Our daughter has grown since you last came by, as you can see. Ally needs Sabbath shoes. And Mr. St. John could use a new pair o' boots."

"By the strangest coincidence, ma'am, I happen to have a few tools of the cordwainer's art with me and so I would be happy to oblige. Would you like for me to use your own leather?"

With that the deal was struck and Jacob Mills set up shop next to the porch under the shade of a large parasol he affixed to his cart after unhitching his mule and tethering it in the shadow of a maple, bribing the beast with an ample feed bag.

"Miss Fanny first," he said, offering her a seat on a stool while seating himself on his own stool with a small ramp on which his customer placed her bare right foot. With a practised eye he selected a wooden shoe and had her slip her foot inside. Nodding his head as if to say 'I thought so' he then examined her toes, instep and arch while she giggled.

All of a sudden Mills straightened his back and looked at the little girl, blue eyes aghast under raised bushy black eyebrows.

"Oh my Lord. Oh my Lord. What do I see here? I can hardly believe my eyes!" he exclaimed.

Fanny, falling silent, looked at him with her own rounded eyes green as Indian peas.

"It's your...your toes. You...you have five of them!"

Fanny giggled. She wriggled her toes, all five of them.

"I've never seen such a strange thing before."

Mills' face abruptly took on a serious look. He slowly shook his head at the girl with a grave air.

"Tell me the truth now. Have you always had five toes? Or did one of them suddenly grow on your foot when you weren't paying attention?"

Fanny giggled again. "My other foot has five toes, too!"

Mills looked at her in astonishment. His jaw dropped. "No! Let me see. I think you'll be pulling the wool over my eyes…. Well, I'll be! You *were* telling me the truth."

Mills looked at her shrewdly, eyes narrowing in his raw-boned face. "I bet you always tell the truth, don't you Fanny?"

"I hope so Mr. Mills. I try to. Mamà says telling the truth makes God happy."

"Quite so. Quite so. Well, truth is I'm going to whip you up the finest Sabbath shoes in all the Colony. Here, you can have your feet back."

From his cart the cobbler produced a work-bench with all sorts of vises and clamps. Awls, pliers, punches, hammers and other tools of his trade protruded from slots along one side. He placed the wooden model matching Fanny's wooden shoe into a jig, then took the tanned leather Mrs. St John had given him and, with an expert eye, cut out the pieces he would need with a pair of sharp sheers, humming a hymn to himself all the while. St. John was watching him work with interest.

"Yessir, these are interesting times," the cat-whipper said, manipulating his awl and threaded needle and thus whipping the cat. He held up a rectangle of heavy leather supplied from his own bag. "I'm down to my last stock of English leather soles. Don't know what I'm going to do when that runs out. I guess I'll have to use smuggled Spanish soles.

"Don't understand why it should be you can't get good leather soles made here at home, but that's the way it's always been. But then, maybe things'll be changing soon. Looks like we'll be making a lot more things we hardly used to make a-tall. Cannon. Muskets. Bayonets. Saddles. Even war-ships!

"Yessir, what with Congress offering rewards for folks who build powder-mills and steel foundries and cast cannon, looks like business everywhere ought to be booming. Even for cobblers like me!

"Seems to me like this ain't no ordinary family quarrel. If killing hundreds of regulars by Bunker's Hill and invading Canada ain't war, then I guess I don't know how to define it anymore. An' if it's war, why then, our soldiers will need good leather boots. Lots of them."

Mills glanced up from his work at St. John.

"I suppose you'll be needin' your new boots for the militia service. Or are you planning on enlisting in the new Continental Army? Let's see, if I recall right there's four regiments to be raised in New-York. It's only a six-month enlistment so I guess that means the fighting has to be over soon! I suppose you'll be in joining up with James Clinton's Third Regiment, seein' how's he's your neighbour?"

The cobbler saw St. John shaking his head.

"Then I guessed wrong! Not surprised, I usually get things all backwards. So you're in the militia after all. Well, word just come in from our Provincial Convention we're to have each militia company pick every fourth member to serve as a Minute-Man. That's an apt name, Minute-Man. Within minutes o' hearing o' that Thomas Moffat got himself elected their captain! But I guess you already know that."

The cobbler, threading a needle, darted a quick glance at St. John out of the corners of his eyes.

"Actually, that's news to me."

"I suppose that means you're with Captain Allison's militia in Goshen."

"The truth is…"

St. John paused. His gaze settled on his daughter yonder by the porch, fussing happily over her doll.

"Truth is, I'm not enlisted with any militia. I paid the fine instead," he said softly.

Mills held up the finished shoe, admiringly. "Nice piece of work, if I do say so. We'll put on the buckle later."

He looked again at St. John.

"The true test is coming up. If the shoe fits, wear it!" Mills laughed. "Or so they say."

He started in on Fanny's other shoe. "Or, here's another saying us cordwainers like: make sure you pick the right shoe, 'cause you'll have to live with it a long, long time."

He chuckled. "Yessir, when Daniel Morgan's riflemen marched by here last month for to take the ferry at Newburgh, I made a pretty penny. You see, as soon as I learnt Congress was raising an army I figgered they would be needing a lot o' footwear. So I made up as large a batch o' boots as I could with my own hands. Problem is, I only have two of them! Hands, I mean. All my 'prentices have run off to join the army. But I can't blame them for breaking their pledge to work for me. 'Prenticeship papers notwithstanding. There are some things more important than whipping shoes, don't you agree, Mr. St John?"

The cobbler turned over the shoe and fixed it to a horn. With his small hammer he proceeded to tap in the pegs through the heel on the sole.

"Yessir, no judge or justice of the peace hereabouts would fine an apprentice for breaking his bond if he went off to fight the red-coats. Half our judges have enlisted, themselves! Yep, there are pledges; and then there are pledges. Some pledges, folks don't mind if they're broken. 'Course, before you can break a pledge you have to swear on it first! Or sign the paper, as the case may be."

Mills took out a small case and opened it up, displaying an assortment of buckles.

"The fine silver buckles in the back row are English, if you prefer."

"Pewter will be fine," said St. John.

"Pewter it shall be for the little lass." Mills began sewing on the leather loop into which he had placed the oval buckle.

"Yessir, seems like most of the men in New-Windsor have signed the Pledge of Association, and just about everyone in Blooming Grove and Oxford. I hear there have been a few hold-outs, though. 'Course, over down in Smith's Clove a lot have refused outright and aren't ashamed to tell everyone out loud! Imagine. I guess for some folks shame knows no bounds. I hear tell your neighbour across the road, Josiah Gilbert, also refused to sign. So did old Ebenezer Seely. And Richard Bull. Thomas Bull, too, but no surprise there."

The cobbler shook his head sadly. "May God have pity on their souls. I don't know who can vouch for their safety anymore. Not our local judges! The few judges and justices of the peace who refused to sign, why, guess what? They've all been turned out of office. Ain't judges no more. By order of the Committee of Safety."

Mills whistled casually through his teeth.

"You see, anyone who refuses to sign the Pledge is, by definition, a traitor. What's that special language the Committee uses? Oh, I recall now. 'Persons inimical to the Cause'.

"I suppose we can make allowances for the Quakers, perhaps. Although, you understand, there are plenty o' people here-abouts who aren't quite as tolerant as m'self."

The cobbler looked up from his sewing at St. John. He flashed a grin.

"I have principles, after all. I believe it's only right to give someone fair warning before you shoot."

He held up both shoes, pewter buckles and all, and displayed them to his host.

"I've learnt in my trade that you have to be very careful. Mistakes can be fatal. The same holds true for the customer. Once your shoes are made to your order there can be no changing your mind. You'll have to accept the consequences of your choice.

"Well! Let's see how our little Miss Fanny likes these."

Fanny came dancing over, still hugging her little doll, as soon as she caught wind of her name.

"Can I try them on? Can I?"

"I do hope the shoes fit you right," Mills said, adopting a worried expression. "After all, you're the little girl with the five toes. I don't know if we can squeeze them all in."

"They fit! They fit!" she squealed.

"Well I'll be. So they do. Fancy that. I guess miracles do happen. From time to time. We'll have to take them off, though, Miss Fanny. Don't want to wear 'em out too soon."

"Can I still wear them a little bit more if I promise to just sit here and not touch the ground?" she pleaded. "Please? Please? I don't want to take off my meerkle shoes."

Mills looked up at her father. St. John shrugged his acquiescence.

"If it's good with your pa, then it's good with me," Mills said. "As for *your* boots, Mr. St. John, I don't need to see your toes. I've got me a good idea already of the shoes you wear. Besides, I still have the model noted down from the last time."

"How about a bite to eat?"

"I'll be happy to take you up on your offer after I finish your boots. In the meantime, though, I wouldn't be adverse to a little liquid refreshment. I suppose you're a tea-drinker?"

"I'm sorry but we don't have any tea. Can't offer you coffee, either. Beer, cider or water?"

Mills straightened his back, stretching his arms. "Not good for one's bones, hunching all day over a cobbler's bench." He winked at Fanny. "Why, I used to be five inches taller. I'll have beer, thank'ee."

St. John went inside the kitchen, leaving the cobbler alone with Fanny.

"Yep, little miss, your pa's a fine man. You should be proud to have a father like him."

Mills rummaged in his cart, pulled out a large wooden model, set it in the jig, and began cutting out the leather for it. St. John came back with a mug of beer for the cobbler.

"I'll be up in the barn for a little bit if you need me."

The cobbler, nose deep in the mug, nodded his head and gave a cheery wave of the hand. He finished half the portion in a large gulp and wiped his mouth with the back of his sleeve.

"Yessirree, he's held in high esteem by a lot o' folks around here, that pa of yours. Thomas Moffat admires him greatly. Jesse Woodhull thinks the world of 'im.

"'Course, over Newburgh way where I come from folks don't know your pa very well. They know he's good friends with the Coldens. An' the Coldens are good friends with Thomas Bull. An' Bull's good friends with Benjamin Booth. Isn't Mr. Bull's sister married to Mr. Booth? I believe I got that right."

Mills looked up from his stitching at the girl. He smiled.

"Do you think good friends ought to tell each other the truth?"

Fanny, seated on the stool, had her legs extended, making her shod feet twirl around in small circles, admiring her new shoes.

"Why, yes sir, I do. I do think friends must tell each other the truth."

"Well, am I your friend, little miss?"

"I am sure you are, Mr. Mills. You made for me these wonderful meerkle shoes."

"Yes, and they are *your* miracle shoes. Just for you, and no one else. Tell me now, has your pa seen much of Thomas Bull lately?"

"No. I mean, yes! He went to Mr. Bull's house when his nephew Ebenezer got married to… to Elizabeth Lama…Lama–"

"Lamoureux," Mills supplied. "Go on. I'm listening."

"Then pa helped them measure some of Mr. Bull's land for a gift for Mr. Ebenezer and his new missus."

"Go on."

"I think my papà and mamà went with Mr. and Mrs. Bull to a church. In New-York City. Trinity Church. For to baptise Mr. and Mrs. Bull's little boy… Cad… Cad…

"Cadwallader. Cadwallader Bull."

"They were gone a long time. They took baby Louie but Ally and I had to stay with Mr. and Mrs. Drake. I was scared. Mrs. Drake is a nice lady though."

"Does your pa talk much about Mr. Bull?"

"Oh! Papà doesn't talk much about anyone. He likes to mind his own onions, is the way he puts it."

"Do you know Benjamin Booth?"

"Sure. He's a nice man. He gave me a bon-bon to eat."

"When did he do that?"

"When he came here last week. With Mr. Bull. And Mr. Bull's son Ab... Ab..."

"Absalom. Was anyone else here? Besides your own family, I mean."

"I don't think so... oh! Mr. Booth came with his nephew."

"William Booth?"

"I think so."

"What did they talk about?"

"I don't know. Mr. Booth didn't look very happy. 'Cept when he gave me the bon-bon and I gave him a smile."

"Was anyone named Smith here?"

"No. I don't think so. I don't remember anyone named Smith coming to our house. 'Cept for Charity. Charity Goldsmith. She's our helping girl."

"What about your ma? Now, she's a fair lady, your ma. I bet she has a lot o' nice lady friends."

"Mrs. Horton used to visit us. But she doesn't anymore. Mrs. Drake's here a lot. Sometimes we see Mrs. Roe. But not very often like before."

Fanny looked wistful. "Mamà's still sad. My Grandpapà died last year. He lived in Boston. My Uncle Samuel was there, too. Mamà says she's worried about him. She wants Uncle to come live with us. But no one knows where he is right now."

"I'm sorry to hear about your ma's father. Your other grandfather, now, I bet he must be a nice man."

"I guess so. I don't know. I have never seen him. He lives far away. Some place called France. I'm named after it!" Fanny giggled. " 'Little Fanny went to France to see horses prance and ladies dance; and there she met the jolly king, who smiled at her, all in a trance'! "

"What a clever little rhyme, my girl! I bet your pa made that one up, didn't he? I suppose he likes kings, would you say?"

"I guess so. Papà says, he tries to like everybody. 'God makes it sunny and rainy on good men and on bad men', he says."

"I wonder how he must feel about the fighting going on up in Boston."

"Oh! He doesn't like it. He doesn't like war. Mamà told me he was a sojer once. In a war. In Canada. He got hurt. He got captured. They made him promise he would not fight any more. Then he came here. An' he met mamà. An' then he got me! I'm his reward to make up for all the bad things that happened to him! Me!" Fanny twirled her feet in delight.

Mills proudly held up a new boot. "Here now, what do think of this master-piece, little miss? Think your pa will like it?"

"It's beautiful, I'm sure. Is it a meerkle boot, like my shoes?"

"Well, now, we'll just have to wait 'n see. Only time will tell. Now, you take your shoes off now and give 'em to me to shine and wrap up nice and pretty, and then go fetch your pa to try his boot on for size. And remember to tell him after I'm gone how much I look up to him, will you remember that?"

Fanny nodded, taking off her miracle footwear, and then bolted away barefoot, up the path to the barn.

St. John came down by and by. Bits of wheat stalk garnished his hat and the back of his blouse. The sight made Mills grin.

"You fixin' to be your own scare-crow? Here, try this one on to see how it fits."

St. John obliged. "Seems to be just right. It's so comfortable I could dance. If only I knew how to dance. But say! Fanny tells me they're meerkle boots. So I guess I'll be able to do anything I want with them on."

"Miracles do happen, I suppose. But as for me, well, I'm no magician. I'm just a poor humble cat-whipper with very limited powers. But, who knows? Maybe those boots will work magic for you someday."

The cobbler helped St. John pull off the boot with a backward heave and a tug. He started in on the other boot.

"Yessir, magic, witchcraft, sorcery, miracles! And the devil. There are good angels and there are bad angels. How to know which one it is what's calling you? Now, take that young George Bull. You know, Thomas Bull's son. Can't figure what has gotten into his fool head. You know he was a student down at King's College? Just about ready to graduate, he was, when he gets it into his mind to go and join the British Army! Now where could he have gotten such a foolhardy idea? I wonder.

"An' to think he was in the thick o' the fighting in Charlestown, on them twin hills Breed's and Bunker's... on the side of evil! I pity his poor parents. What must they be thinking. But then, I suppose the parents are to answer as to how their children turn out. Don't you think, Mr. St. John?"

"Thomas Bull's nephew, Ebenezer, is in the Continental Army. His son Daniel's in the Ulster militia."

The cobbler smiled and his eyes crinkled. "Quite so. Quite so. Well, if there's anything you'd like me to convey to Mr. Bull, I'd be glad to oblige, seein' that I'm headed up their way after I'm through here."

Charity Goldsmith emerged from the kitchen. "The table is all set for dinner, if you please." She went to the bell hanging on the porch and gave it a vigorous clanging. St. John with a courtly bow and sweep of the arm let Mr. Mills precede him onto the porch and at the wash-tub while Henry and the Toussaint brothers came down from the barn.

They arranged themselves around the boards, even baby Louis-Philippe in his cradle nearby, while Mrs. Drake and Charity brought over pitchers of water and cider before joining them.

"Mr. Mills, Mr. Belknap, I believe you know each other." St. John gestured with his hand.

"Hiya, Jacob."

"Howdee, Josiah. How goes the weaving?"

Josiah Belknap was a short, plump man with a large bald spot in the middle of his head. He nodded it energetically.

"Tolerable well. More than tolerable! Mrs. St. John has a good, solid, straight loom. What a delight to work on, a perfectly square loom! A crooked loom makes crooked cloth, you know."

Mehetable was counting the *convives* around the table. She frowned. Including the baby there were only eleven. "Where is America-Frances?"

Charity arose. "I'll go look for her, ma'am."

"Try up in the barn," St. John suggested. "Well, Mr. Belknap. How go the blankets?"

"I have finished the one and will soon be starting the other. I should be done just before the next Sabbath. Thank you again for putting me up - and for putting up with me! Where will you have the cloth cleaned when I'm done?'

"I'll go to Satterly's mill in Blagg's Clove. He owes me for some surveying work."

Mehetable bowed her head. "Let us give thanks. Fanny and Charity we will include in our thoughts." Grace invoked, the bread was broken and the meal begun.

"Business good, Mr. Belknap?" Mrs. Drake asked. "I am sure you will forgive me, but I am handy on a loom and for that reason I do not call upon your good services."

"No need to apologise, Mrs. Drake. Yes, business is tolerable good. More than tolerable! An' it looks to get even better. Since we are not allowed to export our wool anymore, an' since our army needs thousands of blankets and uniforms, why, I am sure to be busy night and day, all week long, week after week! Excepting the Lord's day, of course. Although, exactly how anyone's going to be paid, no one's figured that question out yet. I don't know if a trust this new Continental paper money yet."

"Everyone's got work to do, that's for sure," Mills added. "Colonel Hasbrouck in Newburgh's converting one of his mills from flour to gunpowder. So's Thomas Moffat up here. He an' Henry Wisner on Crommelin Creek. Wisner's also building a musket factory over in Goshen. Seems like everybody's got a finger in the munitions pie."

"Where are we to grind our grain, then?" Mrs. Drake worried.

"You'll have to take it to Matthew's on Murderer's Creek; or Ellison's near the river now that Moffat's switched from grain to gunpowder. 'Course, Satterly's keeping his grist-mill. Either way it's a long haul for you." Mills flashed a grin. "Seems like guns are cherished more than grain."

"Where is Charity? Where is Fanny?" Mehetable asked to no one in particular and to everyone.

At that moment the door opened and Charity entered. She looked apologetic. "I couldn't find her."

"Excuse me." St. John got up and went out the door.

He walked up the path to the lower stalls under the threshing floor. Empty. He went around in the back up the short hill and into the barn. He called out her name. The only response was a flapping of wings and the rustling sound of cooing doves under the eaves. He climbed up the ladder to the hay-loft. Empty.

She was not up at the spring. She was not in the corral with the philosophers. A sudden dread seized him. He ran across the yard to the other side of the barn past the vegetable patch with the second planting of corn just knee high, past the smoke-house and the corn crib on its stilts until he reached the pig-shed and pen in a remote corner of the yard, placed as far away from the house as possible.

In the pen a long, fat sow grunted a greeting, lying on her side, while her little ones fought greedily over their mother's teats. In the shed other sows and the two boars were in a corner, snoozing. St. John sighed in relief.

St. John walked slowly back towards the house. Perhaps she was at the latrine. Or, the well. He quickened his step.

As he came up to the vegetable patch he stopped. "Fanny!" he called out. He went into the garden, wading through the corn-stalks to the far side where the corn gave way to other plants. He halted abruptly at mid-step.

A broad smile crept over his face.

Fanny was curled up on a tuft of grass, face shaded by the soothing leaves of the three sisters. Her eyelids were closed and she was breathing gently. Her little hands were clasped together, close by her chest, softly rising and lowering with each breath. In her hands she was holding her corn-husk doll, timeless face upturned towards the timeless sky. She was fast asleep, far away in another world.

St. John stooped down and carefully cradled his daughter in his arms. He rose up, gave her forehead a kiss, and walked back towards the kitchen, lost in thought.

Chapter Seventeen: *The Purifying Flames of Equality*

The village of Newburgh huddled on a couple of narrow, winding dirt lanes hugging the bluffs along the river. St. John decided to spend the night at Weigand's Tavern up by the cemetery, where he was received correctly but suspiciously by the proprietor.

"Heading for Boston?" Weigand asked, sandy eyebrows arched, looking over St. John's shoulder out the open door where his waggon-cart and horses stood, cargo covered by a tarp.

"No. King's Bridge. To see a friend."

"A friend of the Cause, I'm sure."

"I have no doubt of that. The flour and beef in the cart won't be making the trip with me. *That* I'm delivering to your quartermaster here. Isaac Belknap's his name, if I have been correctly informed."

The tavern owner grunted. "That's his name, all right. You can find him at Mrs. Hasbrouck's farm down the road a-piece. "

Trintje Hasbrouck's rambling farmhouse looked as though its stone walls could have been hewn by William Bull. The house reigned on a bluff with a commanding view of Hudson's River and the Taconic Mountains stretching all the way back to Connecticut. Most of the autumn leaves were down, but a few red, orange and yellow stragglers still clung stubbornly to the trees they considered their own, refusing to abandon their homes.

A militiaman directed St. John to a barn where farmers were unloading barrels from their carts. St. John queued up and waited his turn. A short, plumpish man in a brown felt hat was standing in an open doorway of the house, one of several doors made in the heavy Dutch style under the sloping Dutch roof. From his resemblance to the weaver St John guessed he was the man's brother, Isaac the Quartermaster. The man bustled over to the head of the queue and spoke to an officer recording in a ledger-book the wares unloaded from the waggons. A skinny man with a pock-marked face followed, frowning up at St. John seated in his cart.

"Howdee, Zack."

"Mr. St. John." Zack DuBois' reply was stiff, eyes searching first his interlocutor, then the back of the cart covered by the tarp. Reaching the head of the line, St. John alighted and recognised Isaac Nicholl, doing duty as clerk.

"Howdee, Isaac."

Nicholl, seated at the table, nodded his head slowly in reply, a scowl on his face. What do you have?" he asked coldly.

"Twenty bushel of fine-ground flour and eight hogshead of smoked beef."

Nicholl motioned to one of the men to untie a sack. He looked inside the open bag and grunted. He picked at random a barrel and had the fellow knock off the lid. He peered inside, poking at the meat. Nicholl started to barter over the price. St. John cut him off. "I want you to pay me what you paid the others. Less ten percent."

Nicholl's eyes narrowed. "What's your game?" he asked slowly.

"No game. You asked me my price. I gave it to you."

Nicholl sat back down and made his entries in the book. He wrote out a receipt and signed it. Wordlessly he handed it to St. John. He glanced back at Belknap, arms crossed over his chest, standing quietly with DuBois, still frowning. Belknap shrugged. DuBois turned his head and spat on the ground behind him.

"Take it to the paymaster. Sam Brewster, over there in the house," Nicholl said, already looking past St. John's shoulder to the next waggon waiting in line. St. John tipped the brim of his hat, climbed into the seat of his cart and nudged his horses.

The November evening turned cold and windy. Inside Weigand's Tavern the great-room was dark and smoky. A boisterous crowd of wayfarers, toasting to liberty and George Washington, besieged the long supper table, faces made ruddy by rum and the light of the fire on the crackling hearth. St. John took his supper in the shadows, standing alone at the bar along the wall opposite the revelers around the fire-place. Weigand, cup in his own hand, joined in the bantering of his guests while his serving girl replenished their drinks.

By and by the proprietor came back behind the bar to have his own supper. He glanced at St. John.

"You said you have family in King's Bridge." Weigand's German accent was enhanced by the beer he was drinking.

"No family. Just the old acquaintance I mentioned. A preacher I know."

"You're taking your cart?"

"I figured I'd sleep in it along the way."

Weigand shook his head. "I'd advise against that notion. Westchester's become a dangerous place. Highwaymen, bandits, thugs." Weigand, sipping from his cup, looked closely at his guest over the rim. "Cow-boys. Tories, that is."

St. John shrugged. "I'll take my chances. Can't be that bad."

"The Tory ringleader in Westchester doesn't stop at robbery. Murder suits him better. Used to be the county sheriff over there. Fellow named Peter Colden. I don't suppose you know his grandfather, the lieutenant-governor?"

"I know the man. As I do a fair number of people."

Weigand polished off his beer. "Well, stranger, if you survive the Tory cut-throats and make it to King's Bridge you'll be seeing a lot of our boys. One of my own sons included. They've set up camp somewhere around there. Under George Clinton. Looks like they'll all be home right after Christmas, seein' as their enlistments expire by the end of the year. 'Course, who knows what will happen up in Boston? Maybe Billie Howe tries to break the siege. Maybe Washington decides to attack Howe.

Or maybe General Howe leaves Boston and sails down to New-York with his admiral brother."

The front door opened to admit a group of men led by a tall figure. "Evening, Colonel Hasbrouck. The back room's ready for you. Go on in."

"Much obliged," the man said over his shoulder, walking towards the back, followed by a half dozen others. St. John recognised John and Isaac Nicholl and the stout figure of Isaac Belknap bringing up the rear.

"The Newburgh Committee of Safety and Observation," Weigand informed his guest. "The agenda for tonight is how to deal with spies." He regarded his guest narrowly. "They're all around us, you know."

"What time is the first ferry tomorrow morning?"

"Probably around 8 o'clock."

"I'm turning in. Thanks for supper."

St. John slept passably well thanks to the earplugs he fashioned out of a wad of tobacco and despite the two other men in his bed. He was glad now to be on the ferry, breathing in the cold autumn air. Martin and Luther, blinders on, munched contentedly in their feed bags, unmindful of the tossing of the boat. An hour later he was on the river road heading south.

He spent a peaceful night at Peekskill in the lee of the village church and by noon the next day reached King's Bridge, guarding the crossing over the Harlem River from York Island. Patriot militia were encamped in the fields with a contingent of soldiers in homespun shades of blue, red and brown. No one challenged St. John as he went into town.

He halted at a tavern, devoid of patrons other than a man with a heavily lined face seated on a bench, cup in hand, staring numbly into the fire, a news-paper laying on his lap. The proprietress, an ample woman north of fifty whose rouged cheeks only made her look older, recited her culinary offerings for the day. St. John chose a bowl of soup and half a loaf of bread.

"You don't eat much for such a robust man," she observed, the sod of Ireland in her voice.

"Truth is, I'm anxious to look up a friend of mine. Perhaps you know him. Jean-Pierre Tétard."

"I do indeed."

"Where can I find him?"

"Not here." She was watching her guest with suspicion.

"Where, then?" Seeing her expression, he added: "He baptised my first two children. We'd like him to baptise our third baby. I was also hoping he might know something about the whereabouts of my wife's brother. He had a warehouse in New Rochelle."

The woman softened. "Pastor Tétard, good patriot he, volunteered for the army. Colonel Morris sent him up to Albany to serve with General Schuyler. He's the regimental chaplain and the general's interpreter, seein' how's they're trying to convince the French in Canada to join with us. Schuyler had him go with our neighbour General Montgomery and his men into Quebec. A man came through this morn' sayin' they've taken Montreal, but we'll just have to wait 'n see. I don't trust rumours."

"His wife, then? If you could tell me where their house is."

"She's gone to live with a sister in New Rochelle. She went there after they burned the house down. And Pastor Tétard's school as well."

"Who burned their house down?"

"Tories."

The morose man near the fire stirred. "Damn them all. May their souls rot in hell."

His voice was slurred. He looked with bloodshot eyes at St. John. "But revenge shall be not long in coming."

The man grabbed his news-paper and held it up in the air, shaking it furiously.

"See what they write! Lies. False, despicable lies. Trying to deceive people by their clever arguments and fancy words. An' this Anglican preacher fellow is the worst of the bunch!" Approaching St. John menacingly, he suddenly thrust the offending paper into the traveler's face. "See for yourself!" he nearly screamed.

St. John took the paper. It was an old edition of Rivington's *Gazetteer* featuring an article by a certain "A. W. Farmer" of Westchester, opining that peace brought prosperity and war devastation, and economic ruin for small farmers.

"Sorry but I'm afraid I don't have a head for numbers."

"Numbers? Numbers?" The man was beside himself. "It ain't about numbers. His real name is Seabury an' he's an Anglican preacher up here tryin' to turn ordinary folk against the Cause by talkin' in that secret code of his. It's written between the lines! You have to know how to read between the lines!" he shrieked.

He snatched the news-paper and hobbled angrily over to the fire-place. He balled up the paper and flung it into the fire. "May they all burn in hell," he nearly sobbed.

He pointed to another news-paper hanging on the rack, a copy of the *Journal*. "The real truth is there. That one we keep."

The proprietress, who seemed used to the man's ways although unhappy at the waste of good paper, turned to St. John. "You may as well spend the night here before pushing on to New Rochelle," she said, guessing at his intentions.

St. John set out just after dawn and a breakfast of hoe-cakes and bacon. Outside the village he passed a cross-roads and an elegant mansion set back from the highway. A small group of militia were camped in the yard. "The Morris house," a passer-by informed him. "Colonel Morris is at the Congress in Philadelphia. But his brother Gouverneur is here now, holding the fort. Tories are on the prowl everywhere, you know."

The cold northeasterly wind whipped off the Long Island Sound and raked the fishing village of New Rochelle with its bone-chilling tines. The sky had turned dark grey. He saw the Anglican church, formerly the French Huguenot chapel, doors locked and windows shuttered. He skipped the tavern despite the inviting thread of smoke wafting from the chimney. From nearby reverberated the rhythmic clanging of a blacksmith, sounding brittle in the chill air. In the middle of the village huddled the houses and shops of the artisans and mechanics, with the merchants and chandlers, rope-makers and sail-makers lining the streets leading down to the waterfront. In the village common local militia were gathered around a large camp-fire, cups in hand.

St. John stopped his team in front of a house displaying a wooden sign depicting a loaf of golden-crusted bread. He tied the horses to the rail and went inside. The smell of fresh-baked dough leavened the air and the cheerful room had a feminine touch to it. Behind the counter was a smiling elderly woman with spectacles and behind her, shelves offering large round rolls and loaves of bread.

"Vous désirez, monsieur? How may I serve you today?"

"Je vous serais très reconnaissant si vous pouviez me mettre en contact avec une ancienne amie de la famille de ma femme. Il s'agit de Madame Sorrel."

265

"Mais c'est elle-même avec qui vous parlez."

Madame Sorrel's face lit up when she learned the reason for his visit; and darkened just as quickly.

"Do tell Mehetable how happy I am to hear she is well, and with three healthy children of her own! But I am sad to say I do not know where Samuel is. The last we saw him – meaning my husband the baker and I – was the time he brought us the sad news of their father's death. He sold the warehouse and went back to Boston.

"He did say he was going to have a bigger, faster schooner made. My husband believes he turned to smuggling. But since then, with all the ports in Massachusetts closed, I don't know where he would sail out of, if not here. But he hasn't been back. I do hope he is alive and well."

St. John made the rounds of the waterfront mechanics and merchants. With the approaching winter the smaller vessels and fishing sloops were laid up on the shore and the larger ships tied up at the docks. What little activity there was, was found indoors. No one he approached knew where to find Samuel although several knew who he was.

It started to snow. He drove back up to the tavern on the Boston Post Road and ducked inside. A lively group of sailors and fishermen were pulling on pipes by the fire and gossiping while in a corner an intense game of dames was underway with onlookers giving unsolicited advice to both players, who ignored their pearls of wisdom.

St. John arranged with the owner for his horses to take hay and shelter. He took for himself a noggin of flip and stood by the hearth, listening to the gossipers, waiting for an opening. The men were chatting merrily in the lilting vernacular of the Atlantic seaport towns of the French coast. An older, bearded man was observing St. John, attired as he was in the plain dress of a prosperous farmer.

"Prenez une chaise et mettez-vous à l'aise," he invited, gesturing with his pipe at a well-worn chair in the corner.

"Je vous remercie." St. John drew the chair nearer the hearth and sat down.

"What's your business here, my man?"

"I am looking for my wife's brother. Samuel Tippet."

The old fisherman reflected a moment. "I know the fellow. Saw him six months ago, in New-London. Right after the frolicking started up Lexington way." He puffed on his pipe. "He was running the blockade with a couple of daredevils out of Setauket. They were taking rum down to French Hispañola and bringing back powder and muskets. But then he hooked up with a fellow named Townsend. Solomon Townsend, out of Oyster Bay."

"Do you know how I might get word to him? My wife's brother, I mean. He has not written us since their father died."

The man pulled on his pipe. "You'd be better served looking for him up in Connecticut. Try the Blue Whale Inn, at New-London. Or maybe Long Island."

"I have a neighbour where I live, a Townsend who came from Oyster Bay. Perhaps I'll follow your advice."

As with Madame Sorrel, St. John had to struggle at first to find his French but after a while it came back to him and he relaxed, like a canoe-bound explorer resting in a calm eddy after overcoming the rapids. The tavern had news-papers, not only from the City but also from London and Paris. He devoured the French papers first.

The bearded man observed the stranger discreetly. Seeing him staring off into the fire, he ventured a question.

"You've been living in America a long time, isn't that so?"

St. John returned to the present. He nodded. "Fifteen years. I've almost forgotten our native language."

"You are from the north of France, judging by your way of speaking," the man observed. "Calvados?" As the stranger did not reply, he asked: "Family still over there?"

After a moment of silence St. John stirred. "My father, Augustin. Guillaume-Augustin. His estate's outside of Caen. A retired magistrate of the county court. He's always been in poor health. My brother takes care of him. And is to be my father's heir."

"Older brother, I take it."

"No, I'm the oldest. But the traditional law of primogeniture is not strictly followed in our part of Normandy. It seems by quarrelling with my father I lost my birthright."

"And so, prodigal son that you are, you have wandered the world in search of your fortune."

"In search of something, you are correct."

"A noble name, Augustin! Our new commander of our new Continental Army has a father with the same name. Augustine Washington. His son General George seems an honourable sort." The man took on a somber look. "My two boys are up there now. With the army around Boston. The fishing season not even done, they walked over to New-Haven and volunteered with Israel Putnam's Connecticut boys. May God walk with them."

The fire crackled in the hearth. The man brightened. "I'm sure it won't last long. Like a nasty summer squall. It'll all blow over and they'll be back home before we know it. Besides, it's only a six-month enlistment."

The tavern served ordinary fare for dinner, setting up the dishes on a long table along the far wall. The diners helped themselves to what they wanted and sat, or stood, wherever they found a place. A lick of chill air from the front door being opened and a half-dozen men came in from outside, brushing off the snow from their hats and over-coats and stomping their booted feet.

The tavern-owner bustled over, scenting something in the air. He addressed one of the plain-garbed militiamen, then with a beaming smile shook the hands of two of the newcomers, evidently strangers. They conferred in low tones with the owner, looking carefully at the diners in the room, who stared back at them, food forgotten for the moment.

The bearded man stood up from his chair by the fire. "Tell 'em, Jake, they're with friends here," he exclaimed, in English. He addressed the two strangers. "We all have boys up there with you," he said, hazarding a guess. "New Rochelle is patriot ground."

Jake, who wore a blue ribbon pinned to the collar of his shirt indicating his militia rank, proudly introduced the two travelers.

"This here is Mister Henry Knox, an advisor to Gen'r'l Washington; an' his brother William of the Worcester militia." Knox, a tall, plump young man, squinted near-sightedly at the diners then attacked the dinner table with relish. A couple of sailors yielded up their chairs to the two strangers.

"Excellent fare. Excellent!" Knox exclaimed between mouthfuls. "I'm famished. We saw the snow coming when we set off this morning from New-Haven. I'm hoping it'll blow over soon. How far are we from King's Bridge?"

" 'Bout eight miles," Jake replied.

"I thought so," Knox nodded. "An' from there I calculate ten miles down York Island to the City."

"General Clinton's at King's Bridge."

Knox' jaw dropped. "General Clinton? At King's Bridge? But how can that be? Henry Clinton's holed up in Boston, with General Howe."

"George Clinton. From Ulster County, New-York."

Knox broke out in a relieved laugh, enjoying the joke on himself.

"See what happens, when kin is fighting kin."

"How is the situation up there outside Boston? Army faring well?" The tavern-keeper was anxious. "We heard there might be trouble a'brewin' in the ranks. What with enlistments expiring... no gunpowder...."

Knox lost his smile and gave the owner a sharp look. "Nothing of the sort," he retorted. "The army is in fine shape. True, enlistments are coming due, but the General is confident all true patriots will stay the course. Besides," he dropped his voice almost to a whisper, "we have a plan. Just give us a couple of months."

"What is it, this plan?" Jake asked.

Knox shook his head. "It is enough for you to know that we are thinking. Not what we are thinking." He winked. "The good Lord's Providence will care for us."

St. John spent the night in the tavern's drafty attic on a pile of straw on the floor. He woke up to a flaming red sky in the east. The snow squall had left them the evening before, headed for New England while Knox and company headed for King's Bridge.

The road west towards Hudson's River took St. John through meandering hills white under a thin blanket of new snow until he reached the rolling farmlands near a small village. The spire of a church poked above the trees and thin grey threads of chimney smoke twisted upwards. Closer to him rose a thick column of heavy, black smoke. Drawing closer he saw a dwelling on fire. Figures stumbled back and forth carrying leather buckets between the house and a well. Tongues of bright orange-red flared out the doors, licking around the eaves of the smoldering roof. A chapel nearby was also afire, engulfed in an inferno of red.

The road took him alongside the conflagration. The several desperate men and women working the bucket brigade looked exhausted. Their puny pails of water could not appease the greed of the fire. Even along the road the heat was intense. At a distance a crowd stood by, offering no help to the beleaguered.

Some were jeering while their companions laughed. Others simply watched in somber silence.

"It's the Reverend Seabury's house," an elderly man informed St. John in response to his question. "And our church," he added bitterly. "Isaac Sears paid us a visit this morning. With a band of Liberty Boys and local skinners. Took away Seabury with him. Said his next stop was Rivington's printing press in the City."

With a moaning sound the roof of the house caved in and crashed into the roaring unforgiving inferno below. The roof of the chapel next door followed suit. The spire with its cross on top was the last to hold out until it, too, collapsed into the flames, crumpling and burning as quickly as a despised ha-penny news-paper.

Chapter Eighteen: *Jubilee*

"Hallelujah! Brother, hallelujah!"

Cesar was jubilant. He was near dancing with joy. He hugged first his wife, then St. John.

"Hush, you be quiet now lest you wake up our baby," his wife scolded. She was smiling nonetheless.

"Let 'im wake up. Let the whole country wake up. Let 'im wake up to being a free man in a free country. Wake up to freedom!" Cesar jumped up and began dancing again, forgetting for the moment the slow dripping of water falling on his bare head from the leak in the roof, creating a muddy mess of the dirt floor of their cabin. A sudden bang of thunder like a huge bass drum, then the steady staccato drumming of a mid-summer downpour.

Cesar remembered the leaky roof. He stepped out of the water, looking up.

"Got to get me new shingles," he said ruefully. He left unspoken the fact money was scarce.

Rebecca tried to comfort their baby, now crying in her arms. "Don't you get all excited and carried away now," she said, whether to her baby or her husband was not clear. She looked up at their visitor. "Is it true, New York has joined?"

"It's a fact," St. John replied. "Henry Wisner said he and our other delegates to Congress didn't feel they had the authority when it came to a vote on July 2. But the Convention in White

Plains has ratified it. We now live in the free and independent State of New York."

"New York had to join. They had to, you see. It is written." Cesar rejoiced. He pulled out a grimy bottle and three wooden cups and poured out a drink for all of them. "I been saving this for a long time. A toast! A toast to freedom. A toast to no more slavery, no more slave-markets, no more slave-ships, no more slave-drivers."

Rebecca took a sip, sighed and shook her head. "Don't count your chickens too soon. *My* folk are still in bondage."

"You'd be wrong, love. Jubilee is here! Preacher read it out loud, at church. I heard him with my own two ears. Mr. St. John has it right there, in his hands! Read it again, Mr. St. John. She don't believe yet."

St. John obliged. He pulled out the rumpled ha-penny sheet being hawked by the hundreds by entrepreneurs in the City.

" '...We hold these truths to be self-evident, that all men are created equal, that they are endowed by their Creator with certain unalienable Rights, that among these are Life, Liberty and the pursuit of Happiness – that to secure these Rights, Governments are instituted among men, deriving their just powers from the consent of the governed – ' "

"There!" Cesar interrupted. "You heard it again, Becky. There's no turning back. Not now. An' may the good Lord forgive me for feelin' proud, but I am, I *am* proud o' being part o' this wonderful thing here. I'm so proud I want to join up with the army down in New York City to fight the enemy."

"Hush! I don't like that talk. You ain't joinin' no army. You don't have to! You're already free. Me and baby need you at home. What I am supposed to do if you're off fightin' the British? What's a-going to happen to us if you git yerself kilt?"

Cesar was shaking his head. "True, I am not a slave. But why can't I sleep or sup in a tavern or inn, only the barn? Why does my labor count for less than white folk? But all that, that has to change now. It has to. It is written."

"You're staying put, right here," his wife declared, giving her head a peremptory nod. She rocked her baby in her arms. "Your duty is to your family first."

"But don't you see, love, that by fightin' for our country's freedom I'm fightin' for our baby's freedom?"

"Isaiah won't be enjoying any freedom if he starves to death. Besides, workin' as you are at Mister Brewster's forge, you *are* fighting for freedom. Our army needs guns an' ammunition, cannon and chains. Where'll we git 'em if there ain't any workers to make 'em?"

St. John sighed. "I can't pay you, Cesar, as much as Brewster can, so I won't even mention how much I could use your help on my farm," he mentioned anyway. "Bumper crop this year! And no hands to help me, except for Henry.

"The Toussaint brothers enlisted last week, joined Isaac Nicholl's regiment under George Clinton's Brigade in Harlem-Town. Jesse Woodhull's son Ebenezer went with them. Most of the Roe boys have left for the army or the militia, and Nat Strong and his sons, too. No one has any hands to spare."

The party fell silent a moment. The only sounds were the patter of rain on the roof and the dripping of water on the floor; and baby Isaiah's contented cooing as he nursed.

Cesar was stubborn. "If I don't go an' fight now, it'll be too late. It'll be over before I git my chance. Gener'l Washington's goin' lick them red-coats, camped high 'n mighty like they think they are on Staten Island. The war'll be over by September an' I won't have seen none of it."

"There are over four hundred British ships in New York Harbor," St John murmured. "Seventy ships of the line, or so they say. Each one with fifty cannon or more. And thirty thousand troops."

"How many soldiers did Pharaoh have? How many chariots? How many horses? An' what did Moses have?" Cesar nodded his head, content to leave his question suspended in the air.

"Don't you start comparing George Washington to Moses," Rebecca rejoined. "Don't be adding blasphemy to your long list of sins, Cesar Jones."

Cesar was undeterred. "If he's the one who leads our people to freedom I'll be pleased to call him the Lord himself, blasphemy be damned. Look, love, Massachusetts has just declared that all Negro slaves who want to enlist are to be allowed to do just that; an' after the war is over they'll be free men. I bet New York'll do the same. An' if the Congress adopts that resolution about givin' each soldier who hangs in for the duration a reward of a hunnerd acres of land out West, why, we'll have our own farm, our own house. Ours, Becky. An' no one else's. Our own farm!"

Rebecca looked imploringly at their guest. "Mr. St. John, do please talk some sense into my mule-headed husband."

St. John cleared his throat.
"Anything left in that bottle of yours, Cesar?"

* * * * *

St. John held the reins loosely in his hand. Martin and Luther knew the route they had to take. Down the road smoke was drifting up into the hot August sky from Brewster's tavern chimney, undoubtedly tended by Mrs. Brewster if husband John was with his militia company somewhere down in the City. The tavern sported the same old wooden sign, only that now above the bewigged profile of the patrician head was the legend "The Gen'l George Inn".

The horses pulled to the right onto Round Hill Road. By and by they reached the bridge over Satterly's Creek. They veered onto the road following the creek south to its source. Here Nathaniel Strong's farmhouse was nestled snugly in a narrow little valley, among a few other scattered dwellings. Strong, too, was not at home, he and his sons being with Jesse Woodhull's militia around Westchester.

He passed by the Howell family farms. Two husky Howell boys were hitching up a team to a wagon, like St. John's loaded with barrels. A mile further along and Woodhull's own large farmhouse and barns came into view, at the foot of Musket Hill, where his younger sons and their slaves were busy with cattle in one field while others were harvesting the last of their crop of rye with the cutting contraption Woodhull and St. John had designed.

At Blagg's Clove he bore right, in the direction of Smith's Clove and a few minutes later reached the mill. Here Satterly had dammed the stream to form a large mill-pond, taking advantage of the hilly, rocky terrain to place the stone foundation of the mill-house at an elevation well below the pond. As a result they were able to install a large overshot wheel, generating ample power to turn a multitude of different gears at once, lathes and machines to grind grain, saw timber or wash cloth, depending on the season.

There was an empty wagon next to the mill-house, coupled to a mangy horse, glaring at the intruders The mill-race was open and the rush of water and loud clattering racket from the slowly turning wheel gave a pleasing sense of logic and purpose to life.

Nathaniel Satterly was Woodhull's quartermaster and had left his middle son Obadiah in charge. He was directing several older boys in the operation of the machinery. St. John barely recognized William Moffat's son, also William, who had shot up a foot since he had last seen him; and Nathaniel Strong's young nephew was sprouting facial hair of which he seemed inordinately proud.

Two Negro men ambled outside beside St. John to unload his wagon. A skinny freckled young man carefully counted the barrels before they piled them into hand-carts, trundling them over to the hoist running along the outside wall.

The freckled youth extended his hand to St. John. "George Seeds, pleased to meet you. I counted twelve barrels. Twenty-four bushels o' wheat, am I right?"

"That's right."

Seeds laughed. "Last week Joshua Seely comes in here with a wagon-load, an' I counted wrong. Mr. Seely got all upset. Accused us of tryin' to cheat 'im. Mr. Satterly was getting ready to go off with his militia, an' he turns to Mr. Seely and says, 'if we wanted to cheat you you'd never know it.' But then afterwards he warned me to be more careful. An' so I checked with you. But I don't care much anyhow seein' how's I'm off to join the army soon as my wife an' me have our baby born."

Seeds hollered up to the loft. Someone hollered back. The vertical ropes attached to the hoist started to move, taking the barrels up with them, pulled from above over a set of pulleys and a windlass powered by the mill-wheel. Seeds disappeared inside the mill-house. As St. John watched the last of his barrels rising up to the top floor of the building, the Howell boys pulled in with their wagon to wait their turn at the grinding-stones. St. John gave them a nod, then stepped inside.

Jeroboam Brown was standing on the open top floor. His eyes were fixed on the miller's apprentice pouring Brown's grain into the hopper out of the last of his barrels. The running mill-stone could be heard inside the wooden vat rotating over the stationary bed-stone as it ground the grain being fed from the hopper, while the vertical shaft of the spindle coming up from below and to which the running stone was affixed creaked and groaned with each revolution.

The ground grain hissed its invisible way down the enclosed chute from the mill-stones above to the receiving box below. Brown bolted downstairs to the main floor, almost bowling over St. John. His son Absalom was standing watch over another worker who was transferring the flour and bran from the bin into large burlap sacks to be hoisted back up to the drying floor before being sifted.

"Don't you worry none, Mr. Brown. Your grain will be all accounted for," Obadiah said dryly, clearly not fazed by their difference in age. He had a good three inches and thirty pounds' advantage on his customer.

Brown, arms folded, flushed red at the miller's son. His face darkened as he noticed St. John looking on. He glared silently at the new arrival with yellow eyes. His son Absalom, standing a few feet away, imitated his father. From behind St. John the two Howell youths came in.

"Make sure you don't mix up my good wheat with that Frenchman's," Brown growled at Obadiah. He turned his head as though to spit; remembering where he was, he caught himself just in time. He swallowed, reluctantly.

Obadiah laughed. "Why Mr. Brown. Don't you know that it's a French stone that just ground your good American wheat? If you want good flour you use a French burr. Every miller worth his salt imports his runner-stone from France."

"An' don't you know my boy that while your pa is about to risk his neck defending our country against the enemy, you, his son, is about to grind the grain of a friend of the enemy? That man's a traitor."

The apprentice stopped his sifting and looked up. The freckled young man coming down the stairs froze. Obadiah lost his smile Uncertainty replaced youthful cockiness. He looked at St. John.

"Go on, tell 'em," Brown jeered. "Tell 'em the truth. Tell 'em why you won't sign the Pledge. Tell 'em why you refuse to join a militia. Tell 'em why you like nothin' better than to sup with Tories like Thomas Bull and Cad Colden, sipping tea with your wealthy bastard Loyalist friends.

"Either he's a coward or he's a Tory. Take your pick. An' you, Obadiah, you are willing to grind this man's grain?"

Brown stepped closer. Absalom followed suit. From behind St. John the Howell boys closed in. Seeds came down a step on the stairs from the top floor. William Moffat pushed down on the long bar closing the gate of the race outside. The mill-wheel shuddered to a stop. The spindle and mill-stones ceased turning and the air fell still.

"He ain't one of *us*," Brown went on. "He don't belong *here*. He used to be an officer in the French Army, fightin' against us in the French Wars. He's got American blood on his hands. An' you, Obadiah, you shook his hand," Brown mocked.

Seeds standing on the stairs looked down at his right hand.

Brown took a step closer.

"Go ask your pa about your Uncle Jedidiah," Brown hissed, addressing Obadiah but staring at St. John. "Jedidiah. Taken prisoner by the French and their Indians at Fort William Henry. Along with my own father. And then...then they were butchered. Murdered, in cold blood. Scalped. An' this Frenchman was there, tellin' his Indian friends what to do, I'm sure. Watchin' it all from beginning to end. I bet he was smiling the whole time."

Brown came nearer.

"Ever wonder why he loves that Indian hand of his? He even brings that savage to Meeting. Yessir, a regular Indian-lover, is our Frenchy. Catholic, too, I'm sure. He may go to Meeting, but he's still a pope-lover at heart."

Brown moved forward.

"The Tories are stirrin' up all the Indians all along the frontier, even as I speak, watchin' us, waitin', getting' ready to strike. An' to do that they need their spies, don't they Mr. Frenchman? Spies to tell 'im what towns are vulnerable, which of our farms have all their men-folk away in the army so they can do their bloody work against our women and children, alone at home. Spies like that friend of Frenchy here, Thomas Bull. Tories, spies, traitors. An' you're willin' to grind this man's grain? He's a traitor to the Cause."

From behind St. John the Howell lads grabbed his arms, twisting them up behind his spine. One of them knocked off his hat and grabbed his pony-tail, pulling his head back.

Obadiah, standing between St. John and his accuser, regarded the accused. "So, you're a traitor, is that it?"

St. John, head pulled back, returned his stare.

"You say so."

"You have nothing to say about their accusations against you? Defend yourself if what they say is false."

St. John was regarding Obadiah. He said nothing.

Obadiah tried again. "Speak up! Say something to defend yourself, will you? Is it true or is it false?"

St. John maintained a steadfast silence.

"Then I wash my hands of the whole thing," Obadiah said bitterly, walking away. "Do what you want with him."

The two black slaves outside were surprised to see Seeds' head sticking out from under the hoist pulley in the loft door above them. They were more surprised by his yelled instructions. They looked at each other, shrugged, then went to work.

They had just finished reloading St. John's wagon with his unopened barrels of grain when the owner of the barrels himself came flying out the open door of the mill-house and landed on the ground at their feet. He lay on his side, coiled up, gasping for breath through clenched teeth, blood flowing from his nose and a wound in his head. Suddenly he started to retch, turned his head, and vomited.

One of the slaves, heedless of the hostile curses from inside the door, ran with a bucket to the mill-race. He came back and took off his shirt. He dipped the shirt in the cool water and sponged St. John's face, wiping away the blood oozing on the outcaste's cheeks and temple. He looked closely at the wound, cleaned it with water, then helped St. John sit up. "Drink," he said.

St. John cupped his hands and drank. The slaves, ignoring the yelling from behind them and the whipping reserved for them later, helped St. John to his feet and into his wagon. They unhitched his horses and handed him the reins. One of them slapped Luther and the team started ambling home.

St. John slumped on the bench, barely holding the reins. The blood oozed anew from his temple. When he opened his eyes again, he saw his horses had chosen to follow the Oxford road skirting Smith's Clove.

The terrain was rugged. The wagon lurched and jerked. The path twisted and turned among huge outcroppings of rock. Deformed trees had somehow taken root in the inhospitable soil, gnarled branches tangling overhead. Dark caverns could be seen here and there among the slabs of ancient stone, half-hidden by wild rose bushes growing in profusion along the side of the road.

They followed the tracks down into a narrow hollow. Rounding a bend in the path, Martin and Luther came to a sudden halt, jerking St. John back to consciousness.

The road was blocked by a quartet of horsemen. They sat immobile in their saddles, eyes silently appraising the wayfarer, his horses, his wagon, his cargo. Pistols appeared in the hands of two of the men. Their leader, stocky and muscular with unruly nut-brown hair streaked with grey, finally broke the silence with a loud laugh.

"Well, well, look what fate hath caste our way!" Claudius Smith rejoiced. His cohorts snickered behind him.

Smith grandly nudged his mount around St. John's wagon, inspecting more closely the load of barrels. He leaned over and pushed against a barrel. "Why, it's full!" he declared. "A dry barrel, it is. An' so, I deduce it must be grain. Well, well, well."

Smith peeked inside a barrel then finished his tour of the wagon and coaxed his horse so that the beast's nose was nearly in St. John's blood-caked face. His left eye was swollen black. Smith whistled. "My, don't you look lovely. Had a spat with your wife? She must be real handy with her fists."

Smith frowned as though puzzled. "Except you're headin' *for* your farm, not comin' away from it, aren't you, Mr. St. John? So, I guess I'll have to rethink my hypothetical.

"I know! You're a-comin' from a visit to your good pal Jesse Woodhull over in Blagg's Clove. Except Colonel Woodhull's away with his hodge-podge rebels on the other side o' the river, isn't he, Mr. St. John.

"So tell me. What on earth are you doin', wanderin' about like you are, with a bloody head and a black eye and a wagon full o' grain but headin' *away* from Satterly's mill? Don't tell me you and your traitor friends have had a fallin' out? A little misunderstanding perhaps among the misguided miscreants who call themselves 'patriots'?

"You're one of them at heart, now, aren't you, Mr. St. John. Or could it be that your heart's still in France? I wonder, just wonder, if perhaps you might not just be pretending to be an American. After all, a skunk don't ever lose its stink. You were in the French Army, weren't you? Fightin' on the side of the papist enemy, isn't that right?

"I believe you have British blood on your hands, don't you, Mr. Papist Frenchman? I believe you just might be a spy, just pretending to be neither fish nor fowl, the better to betray our one, true king and sovereign lord. Isn't that the truth, Mr. St. John? Isn't it? I believe you're nothing other than a papist, a spy, a traitor."

Smith spat on St. John's face.

"What? Has the pope-loving spy nothing to say? Has the traitor lost his tongue? Out with it, Mr. Frenchman. Are you a traitor to the king our lord, or aren't you? Is it true or is it false?"

St. John said nothing. Furious, Smith slipped off his saddle onto the running-board of the wagon, seized St. John by the shoulders and threw him bodily onto the side of the road into a tangle of thorny rose bushes.

"Thus do I treat with traitors!" Smith yelled. "I hereby confiscate this grain in the name of our lord, King George. And I declare this wagon and these horses to be contraband."

He grabbed the reins and settled himself on the wagon bench.

"Mr. Flewelling. Please be so kind as to secure my horse to the back of the wagon. Mr. Matthews, kindly lead the way."

With a gentle flick of the wrist Claudius Smith set Martin and Luther into motion. As the wagon and riders moseyed away Smith turned around on his seat and flashed a departing smile in salute.

"God save the king!"

Slowly, painfully, St. John disentangled himself from the rose bush. He got slowly to his feet. He put one foot behind the other and began the long walk home, a small thorny branch still clinging to the crown of his bloody head.

Chapter Nineteen: *Waiting for a Miracle*

The room was dark. All the rooms were dark in the Lamoureux' small farmhouse. The shutters were closed, allowing only a dim, grey light to filter through a few narrow slits. All was quiet, except for the muffled sounds of someone weeping gently as though her heart were being squeezed with a pain too unbearable to utter.

A hazy hint of daylight crept in from the central hall through the doorway of the parlor, as the front door of the house was opened. Footfalls could be heard on the doorsill. A murmur of voices from the hall. The hall floor-boards creaked under the weight of new visitors, their shadows cast onto the trapezoid grey of the floor. Shod feet shuffled slowly into the room.

A white hand motioned softly towards a pair of chairs against a wall, barely discernable in the dark. Voices whispered, black satin rustled like a soft breeze wafting through a field of wheat. The minutes passed by, measured by heartbeats, not the tall clock in the corner whose hands had been stopped at twelve. A chair creaked, a child fidgeted. By and by the sobbing softened, the suffering heart soothed by the balm of sleep.

Figures arose in the dark, silhouettes bowing before floating towards the open doorway. As mourners left, others arrived, like water from a mill-pond flowing slowly over the mill-wheel, turning lazily.

Mehetable accepted her husband's extended hand and arose from her seat. They left the parlor and emerged from the back door of the house into the late November afternoon.

A repast had been laid out on a buff linen cloth spread over a table. A knot of younger men in militia dress was standing nearby within easy reach of the food, laughing between mouthfuls. St. John tried to ignore their hostile stares as he and Mehetable walked by. Further away, all dressed in black, were three generations of Lamoureux women-folk and beyond them the men and boys. Mehatable moved towards the women while St. John went to the men to offer condolences. He fell in with Joseph Drake, who had just left the house with his wife. Drake's lined face was grim, long white hair escaping from under his hat. Silently they walked to the men, searched out the elder Lamoureux, then paid their respects to his son John, the father of the deceased lad.

Near at hand was the small family graveyard. Freshly turned dirt and a humble brownstone marked the spot of the young man's final resting place. A musket had been placed against the grave-stone, barrel up and on the end of the barrel rested his cocked hat.

St. John looked down at the grave, deep in thought. *Tabaldak wants it that way*, flashed through his mind. He absently prodded the edge of the grave with the toe of a boot, then rejoined Drake, talking with John Bull and Thomas Moffat.

"This is the fourth one I've been to this week," Bull was saying. "Three were in Ulster. Sad times indeed."

"He was in Isaac Nicholl's regiment wasn't he?" Drake asked.

Bull nodded. "Nicholl was here when I arrived at noon. Said Robert was the only one killed in his company. A few others wounded, though. Took a ball through the kidneys. Must have been a horrible death. I pity his poor brother Joseph, who was with him. He had to break the sad news to their parents. An' then wait for Howe to leave before fetching the body to bring back home for a proper burial."

"Chatterton's Hill?"

Bull nodded again. "On the north flank, along with the Ulster militia, close to White Plains. Howe attacked from Scarsdale and Clinton – Henry, of course – came up from King's Bridge. General McDougall was dug in on the summit with his New York City boys and militia from down south. At least our boys gave 'em a beating before retreating."

Bull gave a snort of anger. "Washington losing first Long Island then the City is hard to swallow. Thank God my son Ebenezer is all right. His wife has grief enough with the death of her brother." Bull gestured towards Elizabeth Lamoureux Bull in mourning dress with her sisters.

"Jesse Woodhull lost a brother, too, General Nathaniel," Drake reminded them. "Murdered by a British officer after surrendering at Jamaica Pass." Drake shook his head sadly. "Nathaniel was also Mrs. Howell's father, and Nat Strong's father-in-law, and Isaac Nicholl's, too. One man dies, and thirty families in Blooming Grove and Long Island are in mourning."

"The past is past. We bury our dead and move on," Moffat replied tersely. "We have a war to fight. Washington's in New Jersey now on his way to defend Philadelphia. That means the only thing between us and Howe is General Heath's brigade and Nicoll's militia in Peekskill. If the red-coats had wanted to, they could have rolled right over Heath to seize our Assembly up at Poughkeepsie. As it is, Howe could always cross the river and attack us. Or have Cornwallis do it, seein' that he's already on our side of the river in Jersey. They know how important Orange and Ulster are.

"We guard the river route to Canada. We feed half the Continental Army. Orange County's vulnerable. The British could whip through us like a scythe through a wheat-field."

"Unless the French king decides to help our cause," Drake offered half-heartedly. "Franklin's in Paris. So is Adams. Maybe they can persuade him."

Moffat snorted. "By the time that fat monarch makes up his mind it'll be too late for us. We have to help ourselves. Can't count on a Catholic despot to come to the rescue of Protestant republicans."

"We need guns. Muskets. Powder. Money," Bull muttered.

"We need soldiers," Drake replied. "Young men willing to enlist for the duration, not just six months. What's Washington going to do next month when all the enlistments run out? He's already lost half his army what with dead and wounded, prisoners, deserters. Canada won't join us, not since Montgomery was killed and Ethan Allen captured. Nova Scotia wants to be the fourteenth state but that won't happen, not with the British Navy based in Halifax. We have no allies."

The men fell silent. Droplets of rain fell on the brims of their hats.

"We need a miracle," Drake mourned.

"God helps those who help themselves," Moffat replied.

Bull and Drake went to give their condolences to the women-folk. Moffat took St. John by the elbow and they strolled a-ways under the mist.

"My nephew ought not to have insulted you so," Moffat said. "But William is head-strong." He stopped and regarded St. John.

"My friend, there are a lot more like William in these parts. The young lads like him an' Seth Marvin an' the Strong boys an' the Howells don't know what you an' I an' the Thomas Bulls of the world have lived through. The patriots in Newburgh an' New Windsor know even less. The boundary line between Ulster County and Orange is only an invisible, political one. An' it's a very thin line.

"The New Windsor Committee of Safety has arrested Cadwallader Colden the younger for harboring opinions 'inimical to the Cause'. Even though he signed the Pledge. He must have said something to someone that was indiscreet. Or maybe because of his father, who knows? Now, Colden lives in Hanover Township. The Hanover Committee refused to arrest him. An' so the New Windsor patriots took it upon themselves. See what I mean?

"General Clinton's after sendin' half our militia down to Jersey to support Washington. That leaves only a handful left to guard the river and even less to protect our western frontier. Winter is knockin' on our families' doors and the larders are nearly empty. There are a lot o' scared, hungry, desperate people hereabouts. It might be tempting for unscrupulous persons to accuse someone of being a Tory as an excuse to steal his property or get revenge for some past insult.

"I have only one of five votes on the Committee of Safety. And I, too, must be careful."

Moffat cleared his throat. "The Committee summoned Ebenezer Seely to prove his loyalty. He refused to appear. So we condemned his farm. Fletcher Matthews', too."

Moffat glanced side-long at his neighbor. "The Patriots in Goshen are pushing to have all 'foreigners' arrested. Judge Wisner, for one. A visit to your father in the old country might be worth considering. At least for the time being. I will do my best to protect your farm."

St. John looked off into the distance. A flock of wild geese was flying overhead in a V-formation, honking loudly, driving all the smaller, less vociferous birds out of the sky.

"I'd best get back home," he said.

The long, dreary ride back in their cart stretched into a long, dreary winter. The snow lay thick on the ground and drifts from the early April blizzard surrounded their home, holding them hostage when St. John finished the long letter to his father he had started on Epiphany.

"....and so the joy of Washington's victories at Trenton and Princeton have faded into the grey dullness of the winter like a fire reduced to embers, having no more fuel to sustain itself. And now all eyes are turned on Franklin and France in the hope that the flames will be rekindled anew.

"There is great fear among our neighbors. The summer campaign is about to begin and no one knows what Howe in New York intends to do. Will he attack Philadelphia? Will he sail up the Hudson and attack Kingston? Ethan Allen was paroled by the British but now he and the Green Mountain Boys have declared Vermont to be an independent republic. They have gone back to raiding New York settlers and burning their farms. Will they join with England? But our greatest fear is our naked frontier, exposed as it is to Butler's Tories and Brandt's Mohawks. Orange County is like a fruit being squeezed in a press.

"America-Frances is blossoming into a beautiful young girl. She has her mother's green eyes and your auburn hair turning strawberry red in the summer sun; and my freckles. Guillaume-Alexandre is a spirited boy, a feisty little colt. He wants to join the army and pouts when I tell him 'next year'. Louis-Philippe is talking now but he is meek and does not say much. Or perhaps he is merely wiser than us.

"Mehetable says a prayer for her brother every day. He responded to the letter we wrote, entrusted to our friend Peter Townsend who, as a Quaker, was allowed to pass through the lines and visit his family in Long Island with whom brother Samuel was sailing. But the British have probably learned by now from their Tory spies that Peter is forging cannon for Washington, and so he will not risk any more trips to Oyster Bay. We will need another way to communicate with Samuel.

"I shall entrust this letter into the care of a merchant friend in Philadelphia with instructions he include it with his own correspondence on his next ship to France. I think nonetheless that if this letter should ever be read by you, it will be something of a miracle. But perhaps that is what we are all waiting for, a miracle."

Sitting by the fire after supper St. John read the letter out loud to his wife, at her spinning wheel in a corner. Fanny sat next to her, working on her sampler. Near the hearth Henry was teaching Ally how to carve a birch broom. Philly was asleep in the cradle, rocked by the foot of Rebecca, rocking her own baby in her arms.

"If you please, Mr. St. John," Rebecca said, "read for us from the book of Isaiah." She looked down at her sleeping enfant. "Chapter 53. Perhaps Cesar will hear, wherever he is right now."

St. John obliged.

Chapter Twenty: *The Time Is Nigh*

"I won't hear of it." Thomas Bull was adamant. "You don't have the luxury to refuse." He turned to his son Daniel. "Go on. Git with it."

Daniel gave a salute, then limped over to their team of slaves standing mutely with sickles in hand. His cousin Thomas and friend Alexander Millikin joined them. With a spirited "Huzzah!" the young men grabbed a sickle each and they all began the arduous chore of reaping wheat under the stubborn September sun.

"It's bad enough you had to plant your crop late for want of help. Let's not make it worse by letting it rot in the field."

Bull and St. John went over to the oak tree by the corral where John Bull, Joseph Drake and Henry were rigging up rope and pulley. Henry went to fetch the young steer. The animal balked, sensing danger while its father glowered from the corral and the cows in the stalls moaned. The men pulled the beast to the tree, tied him up, and dispatched him with several well-aimed thrusts of the knife.

The butchering took the better part of the morning. Mehetable put aside her churning to lay out dinner on a make-shift table in the shade of the maple tree, helped by Mrs. Drake. She rang the triangle.

Thomas Bull was bid to lead them in prayer. He was silent a long moment, then spoke softly. "Lord Almighty. In you alone do we find true freedom. Through your Son we have freedom from the slavery of sin. Let us not either be slaves to fear. But O have we need for your strength now... we are a family divided.

"We have sons in arms against each other, nephews in arms against our sons, and I know not what to think. Neighbors pitted against neighbors, the seeds of enmity sown all around. Please, Lord, bring a speedy end to this quarrel. May men's hearts be filled with your love and not the devil's hate. Comfort those who are afflicted, soothe those who suffer, that is, all of us. Help all of us friend and foe find the freedom that only your love can give. May your peace reign on earth. Amen."

The neighbors ate in silence. Not even Fanny, wedged in next to Bull's slaves with her brother Ally, dared speak. Suddenly Captain John banged his fist on the table.

"I am not at a funeral! 'Tis no time to mourn, but to celebrate. We are witnesses to a new beginning. A toast to the birth of the free State of New York. Let us embrace the fate God has for us with joy and cheer. Let those who believe, have faith."

"Our fate is truly not our own," Drake agreed, a little ambiguously. "But within a few weeks we will know what it is."

"There now, Joseph! You sound like my brother Thomas. 'Doubting Thomas'. "

Drake lifted his hat to brush off the sweat on his forehead with a sleeve. "If not being able to see into the future is doubting, then I guess I deserve the nickname. But I don't know that Washington will prevent Howe from seizing Philadelphia. I don't know that Gates and Arnold will stop Burgoyne from taking Albany and Kingston. I don't know that Henry Clinton won't come up from New-York City to attack us."

"Let 'em attack. We'll whip 'em," young Alexander Millikin exclaimed, freckled face excited. "We're ready for the red-coats."

"When is your leave over?" Mrs. Drake asked.

"We have to go back in three days. Me an' my brother James and my brother Nathaniel. And Daniel here. James is captain of our company and Nathaniel is lieutenant. Plus it'll take us a good whole day to walk back to the fort from home. It's only about twenty mile, but we have to climb over Black Rock to get there."

"Which of the forts are you at?" Thomas Bull asked.

"Fort Clinton. On the south side of Popolopen Creek, right where it runs into the river. Right across from Anthony's Nose. Zach DuBois' in charge of our regiment. His brother Lewis is holding Fort Montgomery on the north side o' of the creek."

"Is General Clinton there? George, I mean."

"I don't know. He wasn't when I took my leave. He was goin' up to Kingston for to vote on the new state constitution, bein' our governor as well as our general. His brother's there, though. Colonel James."

"Our brother William's boys are with Gates in Saratoga," John Bull remarked. "Along with my son Ebenezer." His face darkened. "But my other son has run off to join a Loyalist regiment. Let us hope he is far, far away. South Carolina would suit me."

Thomas Bull raised his cup solemnly. "A toast. An' a prayer. May all our boys come home safe and sound. An' may this war end soon."

As they arose from the boards a whinnying of horses came from the highway. They heard Fanny's dog barking. A half-dozen mounted men with shotguns and pistols drawn were coming towards them up the path. "Easy there," Drake murmured. "It's only Isaac Nicholl. He's just been appointed acting sheriff, you know, 'til Woodhull's back."

Drake raised a hand in greeting. "Howdee Isaac. Seth Marvin, is that you? And Bird's-Eye? Nat Roe, too. If you're looking for cattle thieves, you've come to the wrong place."

Seeing Drake and John Bull, Nicoll motioned for his men to put down their weapons. He kept his own pistol exposed. He looked with cold dark eyes at St. John, standing next to Thomas Bull.

"Had any visitors lately? Present company excepted." Nicoll searched the man's face closely.

"May I ask the purpose of your visit?" St. John inquired.

"Two prisoners escaped from the Goshen jail last night. Claudius Smith and his son Richard."

"We haven't seen them. And they would not be welcome. They're not here."

"If you don't mind we'll see for ourselves." Nicoll dismounted and gestured for his posse to do the same.

"I do mind. This is my home."

Wordlessly Nicoll led his men, pistols drawn, through the kitchen doorway and into the house. They emerged ten minutes later and marched up to the barn. Nat Roe glanced at his neighbors, an apology written in his eyes. From the barn they went to the smoke-house; then the henhouse and pig shed and finally Henry's cabin before coming back to their horses.

St. John offered them a drink. Nicoll brushed aside the offer without a word, turning his back to the outstretched hand.

As he put his foot in the stirrup his shoulders were grabbed from behind and he was spun around. St. John landed a blow to his jaw, sending him reeling backwards into his horse. Seth Marvin, already on his mount, pulled out his pistol. John Bull and Joseph Drake grabbed St. John and pulled him away. Nicoll rose to his feet. He stood stock-still, eyes locked on St. John's.

"As acting Sheriff of Orange County, State of New York, I place you under arrest for assaulting an officer of the law. You will report tomorrow morning to the jail at Goshen." He turned, swung himself into his saddle, and led his posse down the road.

* * * * *

Only a narrow beam of light squeezed through the narrow square of the barred window, just enough to make the gloom of the tiny room gloomier. From somewhere in the basement jail there was a banging of tin cups and voices raised in profane singing.

"O Lord, save me," intoned a voice nearby. "Rescue me from the exquisite torture of their tuneless music. Or, if you would, perform a miracle and change the vinegar of their voices into fine wine." St. John's cellmate was stretched out on his pile of straw on the dirt floor serving as his bed. "On second thought," he continued," if you don't mind, my Lord, I think I'd prefer being pardoned."

St. John tired of holding up the stone wall against which he was leaning and flopped back down on his own bedding of straw. His companion propped himself up on an elbow and picked at his teeth with a blade of hay as though he had just polished off a sumptuous meal. "Funny thing about prison," he mused. "You lose all sense of time. Night, day, everything's grey. I've almost forgotten how long I've been here, or why I'm here."

"Why *are* you here?"

"You've asked me that before."

"Yes, and you have not answered."

"Perhaps I have and you failed to understand."

St. John got up and went over to the bars that formed the door. From the end of the corridor came a rattling sound as of keys in a lock, then the creaking of hinges. The militiaman, serving as jail guard, came into view, trailed by Joseph Drake.

"Visitor, Mr. St. John."

"Thank you, Davie. Give my regards to your pa."

"Will do, Mr. St. John." David Carpenter retreated back upstairs.

"Here's some dinner for you. I'll slide it under the door," Drake said. "Enough for your supper and breakfast, too." His face was leaner and sadder than ever and his long white hair disheveled.

"How fare my wife and children?"

"Don't you worry. Mrs. Drake has them under her wing. An' the Bull brothers took in your apple crop. Your wheat's in the barn, ready to be threshed. Only you'll have to take it to Ellison's to mill."

"I can't thank you enough."

"You've done as much for us. Go on. Eat."

"Food can wait. What's the news?"

Drake's tired eyes grew dark.

"Not good. Fort Clinton and Fort Montgomery are lost. Henry Clinton took them two days ago. We lost a lot of good men as well. And boys." Drake turned his head away and brushed his eyes. "We lost half our militia. Dead, wounded, captured," he said softly. "Three hundred casualties out of six hundred men...Thank God Jesse got away.

"Our militia never had a chance. The enemy was five times our number. Putnam never sent us reinforcements like the governor asked. They held their ground as long as they could, then those who survived escaped by diving into the river. The Clintons and some of the other officers made it back to Newburgh, but Zach DuBois was taken prisoner. Colonel Allison, too. Our neighbor, Jonathan Tuthill. Captain Archibald Little, out of Oxford.

"Ulster got hit hard. I pity the Millikin family....They lost three boys killed. Alexander and his brothers."

St. John was stunned. Drake wept a moment in silence before composing himself with an effort.

"Sir Henry has two thousand red-coats and Beverly Robinson's Loyalists not twenty miles away from us right now. Our only hope is Saratoga. Gates and Arnold gave Burgoyne a bad whipping at Freeman's Farm and had him almost surrounded last we heard. But Howe has taken Philadelphia. Drove Washington into the hinterlands."

St. John's cellmate stirred in his corner. "And so the pudding begins to thicken. The time is nigh, gentlemen. The time is nigh."

Boots sounded in the corridor and David Carpenter reappeared, keys in hand. He selected one and put it into the lock, turning it. He swung open the door.

"Twelve o'clock noon. October 8, 1777. Your ninety days are up. You're free to go, Mr. Barrabas."

St. John's cellmate stood up, calmly brushing away bits of straw from his pants and shirt. He stepped carefully over the trencher of food on the floor and into the corridor.

"Peace be with you, gents."

* * * * *

St. John awoke with a start. He heard it again, the sharp crack of gunfire. He sprang up and tried in vain to see out the small window but the dawn had only just been born. He heard the other prisoners exclaiming fearfully.

From outside all around he heard excited voices and the pounding of boots. More guns went off. Then a metallic clanging as though pots and pans were being struck. A church bell began to toll.

As the sun rose St. John, peering on tip-toe out the window, could see part of the road through the village thronged with people turned out in a spontaneous celebration of joy despite the black bunting shrouding doorways. People were hugging each other, exalting, weeping, laughing. Young Carpenter came down. He stopped at St. John's cell, inserted the key into the lock and opened the door. He was smiling, eyes shining.

"Burgoyne surrendered! He and his whole army, surrendered to Gates!"

Carpenter took St. John's right hand and pumped it excitedly. "New York is saved. We licked 'em. It's all but over now." The prisoners down the corridor heard and began yelling out in derision. "God save the king!" one of them screamed. Others simply cursed.

"Why am I released? My thirty days are not yet up."

Carpenter shrugged. "Do you need to know the reason? Judge Marvin told me to let you go. And so here I am. And here you are. Free to go." He turned to the other prisoners. "Shut up down there or you won't get anything to eat until tomorrow."

St. John followed his jailor up the stairs to the main floor. He went out the front door and into the street, squinting against the morning sun.

He set off on the long road home.

Chapter Twenty-One: *An Honorable Man*

The February storm had dumped another half-foot of white powder onto an already laden landscape. With a flick of the wrist St. John set Diana into motion, pulling the sleigh behind her. He let Ally sit in his lap and hold the end of the reins, content to let the boy believe he was in control of their fate.

As they slid along St. John recalled with painful longing the festive times before the War, parades of cheboggins with families riding on top, laughing and waving to friends and neighbors, trailing behind them their heavy logs compacting the snow in the road. They would stop at every other farmhouse along their route where hot mulled rum and cider awaited them with a slice of pie or *koeckjes* next to a welcoming bonfire....

There were no bonfires in sight today. Diana labored through the snow, pulling the pung along the neglected road to Brewster's where a dozen sleighs and their horses lined the fence. Inside the tavern the punch bowl had already made its first round and the discussion was heating up, rum, at least, not being in short supply. St. John took a turn at the bowl and settled onto a spot on a bench, listening to Moffat explaining the purpose of the meeting, Woodhull sitting next to him. He hoped his son didn't realize the stony stares from some of the men were directed at them. Woodhull's smile and handshake with St. John kept their mouths shut.

Washington and the army were spending the winter in Pennsylvania within a two days' march to British-occupied Philadelphia, at a place called Valley Forge, Moffat was saying, along with the Hudson Valley's 4th New York Regiment. He read aloud a letter from Capt. Strong, Nathaniel's brother, encamped with his two sons and three score other boys from Blooming Grove and Cornwall and hundreds more from neighboring towns. Strong pleaded for food, for blankets, and especially boots and socks, for most of his men had none.

Moffat asked the assembled to pass the word to bring all contributions to Jesse Woodhull's place within the week. Woodhull, his sons, and any other volunteers would take down to Valley Forge as many sleigh-loads as they could muster. One of his own sons, Ebenezer, was down there, Woodhull reminded them.

"Now," Moffat said, "we turn to other business. You all know by now our new neighbor William Denning here, the army's deputy quartermaster for New York." Denning, newly installed at Tory Peters' former house by Matthew's Mill, produced a letter from his pouch whose seal had already been broken.

"This is from Gen'l Washington's aide-de-camp, Alexander Hamilton. He asks your Committee of Safety to prepare for the arrival of the General's adjutant, the Markee de La Fayette, Major-General of the Continental Army... a French nobleman... served in the French Army....Headin' to Albany to meet with General Schuyler. Should be reaching Orange County in two day's time. I think we ought to have a company of mounted militia meet him at Warwick, at the Jersey line."

At Woodhull's insistence they agreed to offer St. John's home to the marquis. "Make 'im feel at home if he don't speak English much."

The morning of the day after saw Blooming Grove and Warwick militia encamped around Baird's Tavern. A sentinel announced the arrival of New Jersey militia approaching from the south. As the company plodded nearer a tallish, thin officer in a long elegant greatcoat nudged his mount into the lead.

Woodhull's eyebrows shot up. He glanced at his companions, just as surprised.

The slender officer sported in his hat the black cockade reserved for the rank of general, pinned to the white cockade of the French Army. Yet the face under the hat was too young. It was as though a precocious boy were playing officer for the day. But the bold brown eyes returning the New Yorkers' stare were anything but playful.

Major-General the Marquis de La Fayette stopped his horse, doffed his hat and bowed his head. The New York party did likewise. The general turned to the New Jersey men and thanked them warmly in a proper British English heavy with the accent of his native country. He and his fellow officers then stepped forward into the embracing welcome of New York, the Jersey men invited to join them.

John Baird's stone building was not large. There was barely room for a score of men and boy general. With his hat off, standing in front of the fire, he looked even younger despite the white wig.

"I thank you gentlemen for your gracious hospitality," he began. He was reciting from memory, stumbling over his pronunciation every now and then.

"And for your ardent support of the most glorious cause in the name of humanity that has ever been witnessed....Brothers, we are fighting to liberate the human spirit. To liberate human beings from tyranny, from oppression, from bondage. We are fighting for the right of *all* people to breathe freely, to live freely, and if necessary, to die freely."

He raised his cup. "A toast! I offer a toast to universal liberty; to universal fraternity; to universal equality."

La Fayette's young age was forgotten. There were cheers and warm handshakes all around. The general introduced his fellow officers and aide-de-camp and William Denning reciprocated, before beckoning St. John.

St. John inclined his head. "*Monsieur le Marquis, j'ai l'honneur de vous offrir l'hospitalité de ma femme et moi ce soir. Michel-Guillaume Jean de Crèvecoeur, à votre service.*"

The young general's eyes showed a flicker of surprise. He bowed in return. "*J'accepte votre aimable invitation.*"

Mehetable had been told to be ready for overnight guests and she had laid out the long table in the formal dining room with fine china - hastily borrowed the day before from Mary and Thomas Bull. Rebecca was busy upstairs making the master bedroom comfortable for the marquis. Henry had the fire going with Ally's help and Mrs. Drake was tending the soup and stew in the kitchen with Fanny when the party of men arrived. Fanny's pet spaniel barked a greeting from outside.

Mehetable had rouged her cheeks and lips and blushed at her husband's amused look as he introduced her to the marquis, who bent to kiss her extended hand. She was arrayed in her finest Sunday dress, with a white silk shawl - a gift from Elizabeth Colden - carefully draped over her shoulders to hide several threadbare spots.

Her shy smile glowed with a soft radiance, and the panache of freckles across her cheeks were as tempting as ripe strawberries. Her green eyes sparkled. She had never looked so beautiful to St. John. He felt himself wishing his guest of honor could lodge elsewhere for the night.

The marquis was given the place of honor at the head of the table, Mehetable on his right, St. John to his left. Marie-Joseph Gilbert du Motier was his birth name, the marquis explained to Mehetable. Before his second birthday his father, a colonel of grenadiers, was killed fighting the English at the Battle of Minden. His mother died when he was twelve, and right after that, her father.

"And so, fate would have it, I, an orphan, inherited a vast estate. But there is no glory in wealth. Glory and honor are found only on the field of battle. And so when I completed my college I enrolled in the Royal Army. Thank you." This is to Rebecca who along with Henry were serving the diners. If the marquis noticed the simplicity of the meal it was not evident.

"When I was sixteen I married Marie-Adrienne Françoise de Noailles. Her father the Duke d'Ayens is close to the king. She, too, is heiress to a fortune. But money means nothing to me. My treasure is my two daughters, Henriette and Anastasie."

He turned to St. John. "It is for them that I fight for you. You *are* an American now, are you not? After all, you speak your French with an American accent."

St. John was silent for a long moment.

"How strange life is. My mother, too, died when I was twelve. I too have a daughter, my first-born, America-Frances; and two sons."

La Fayette smiled in delight. "What an apt name you chose for your daughter. You must be very prescient. Perhaps some mysterious spirit was guiding you. I understand from Mr. Woodhull your father is a baron?"

"That is true. His estate is at Pierrepont, near Caen."

"He also mentioned you served during the fall of Québec. How comes it you found yourself in New York?"

"Divine Providence. And a fortuitous hurricane."

"Permit me to observe you have uttered an oxymoron. It is not by accident you are here. You and your brother patriots in this room are part of the great family of new men who are willing to sacrifice everything they hold dear so that all men may live free. Anything less than that is dishonorable; and a life lived in dishonor is not worth living at all."

"How did you meet General Washington?"

"Letter of introduction and a recommendation from your ministers Silas Deane and Benjamin Franklin in Paris. Even though," La Fayette added with a smile," the king and my father-in-law made sure the English minister, the Duke of Gloucester, knew of their 'outrage' at my disobedience of the king's order of neutrality."

"But will the king remain neutral?"

"Your Benjamin Franklin is a very persuasive man. There are many at Court who advocate war with England and sending a French force and the French Navy to assist America. The king and his ministers have been watching and waiting. Perhaps our remarkable victory at Saratoga will tip the scale."

"Let us hope the Iroquois feel the same way. The Oneida excepted, all the other Iroquois tribes pledged their loyalty to the king of England. The Iroquois would rather die at the stake than go back on their sacred promise. The Oneida, too, live by their word of honor."

The marquis looked with curiosity at his *compatriote*. "I would have expected you to be familiar with the Huron and Abenaki, the traditional allies of France. But you seem also to know about the Oneida, if I am not mistaken."

"I spent a winter living with their Wolf clan, before settling here."

"I see." La Fayette regarded St. John closely. "I am not at liberty to divulge the purpose of my mission, but I will say that the temperament and ways of thinking of the Oneida are of interest to me."

"If your Excellency will indulge me. The Oneida proved their valor at Fort Stanwix. Thanks to them General St. Leger's grenadiers and Iroquois allies were forced to retreat. The Oneida are just as courageous and honorable as the other Iroquois tribes. But they are also shrewd. They will not be persuaded that an attack on Canada would be in their best interests. Or serve any useful strategic purpose," St. John concluded gently, guessing at the reason for the visit to Albany.

La Fayette's eyes flickered. "To have on our mission an experienced officer familiar with the Oneida would be of great assistance."

St. John's eyes met Mehetable's.

"I am the sole support of my wife and children. But I am flattered and honored," St. John demurred.

The marquis nodded his head slowly.

"So be it." He brushed away his disappointment with a smile. "Your wife tells me you go by the name of Hector. Hector, the reluctant warrior, the tragic doomed hero of Troy." He turned his head, smiled at Mehetable.

"To part from one so lovely for even one day would be more than unbearable."

Supper was followed by toasts all around, cider having to do for the lack of wine. Jesse Woodhull raised his cup. "Long live the king!" he intoned. "Of France."

Each diner in turn offered a toast, Mehetable included. Her eyes gazed into St. John's for a long, long time. She smiled and raised her glass.

"*À mon cher mari.*" She took a sip, eyes not leaving her husband's, enjoying the look of surprise on his face blooming into desire.

"And now," La Fayette said, "I would be delighted to meet your daughter with the marvelous name."

St. John obliged. He disappeared into the kitchen and re-emerged with Fanny, forced to wear her Sunday shoes for the occasion, bringing brother Ally in tow, boots too large for his feet.

"Major-General. Sir. May I present to you a fervent advocate of freedom," St. John said, in English. "Freedom from chores, freedom from shoes, freedom from peeling potatoes. My daughter, America-Frances. America-Frances, I present to you Major-General Marquis de La Fayette, adjutant to General George Washington."

Fanny's eyes grew round. "A markee! A markee! Papà, what's a 'markee'?"

La Fayette had risen from his chair. He bent down to the young girl and took her hands in his.

"Young miss," he said gravely, "a marquis is nothing more than an anachronism."

"Oh. I see." Fanny wriggled in excitement. "You know General Washington! You're friends with General Washington! And now I know you! I'm friends with a friend of General Washington!"

"Yes you are. And, young miss, he is a great man. An honorable man. And so you are friends with a great and honorable man."

The marquis stooped further down and whispered in Fanny's ear. She giggled.

He straightened up, half a head taller than St. John and towering over his children. "It is with great regret, dear miss, that I must take my leave on the morrow. But I will tell my own daughters someday that I once met a young lady who was friends with General Washington and whose name was America-Frances."

The next morning after a casual breakfast, outside ready to depart, La Fayette took St. John by the shoulders, embracing him in the style of the French.

"*Mon ami, deux pays, une seule fraternité. Il n'existe qu'une seule vérité. On se doit de la reconnaitre. Au revoir.*"

St. John holding hands with Mehetable, Fanny and Ally on either side, watched the general and his party disappear down the highway to New Windsor. Philly peeked through a window from inside the house.

"Papà, what was he saying? What did he tell you?" Ally asked.

"Two countries, one brotherhood...." St. John murmured. "There is only one truth. We owe it to ourselves to see it."

"Where is it, papà? Can I see it too? Please. I want to see it, too. Show me, papà, show me."

Wordlessly, St. John lifted up his son and placed him on his shoulders. He took Fanny by the hand and she her mother's and they walked towards the front door of their house, Fanny's spaniel wagging his tail behind them. St. John halted.

The slender sassafras tree stood straight despite the crown of snow on its dormant branches. The grape vine, too, was sleeping, its tendrils spiraling up the trunk of the young tree in a gentle embrace.

St. John gave his wife and children a hug and a kiss.

Chapter Twenty-Two: *A Helping Hand*

St. John knelt in the semi-darkness of dawn before the fire-place and blew the embers into a flame. Mehetable, still not quite awake, lugged the pail full of heavy ashes towards the kitchen door. She pushed back the bolts on top and bottom and fumbled with the latch. She swung the door open and stepped out onto the porch.

Her cry of anguish ripped through St. John's heart. She screamed again, and again....

"What is it? What is it? Mehetable...." Frantically he searched for the butcher knife on the counter, grabbed it, and rushed to the open doorway.

He collided with his wife stumbling back into the kitchen, sobbing hysterically. "It's horrible," she gasped. She clung to her husband, burying her head in his chest. "Why are they doing this to us? Why? Why?" she cried.

Confused, arms around his wife, St. John tried but failed to see past the half-opened door. He gently set Mehetable, weeping bitterly, down in the rocking chair and, half-crouching, knife at the ready, cautiously slipped outside onto the porch.

The sight was sickening. Fanny's dog's head had been cut off and placed on top of the butter churn facing the door. Its teeth were bared and its tongue, swollen and blackening, protruded onto the wooden top, steeped in its own blood which ran down the sides of the churn into a dark pool on the porch deck.

"What in the world...." Dazed, St. John turned his head to his right and saw the dog's headless body swinging gently three feet away, suspended from the hook from which their dinner bell usually hung. The dog had been disemboweled and its guts spilled to the deck. The stench made him want to retch. Already flies were gathering....

His breath shortening, stomach tightening, he glanced all around, weapon at the ready, in the corners, out towards the vegetable garden, the smokehouse. Henry came running, down from the spring on the hill, water splashing out of his pail.

"Brother, is the missus all right? What has happened?" he exclaimed. As he reached the steps to the porch he stopped short, grimacing with revulsion.

"Oh Lord no. Lord no. Not the little misses' pet dog."

Henry took a step backwards, dropping his bucket. He looked at St. John, his coppery face full of sorrow. About to speak, his glance shifted beyond St. John, to the half-closed door behind him, and his eyes grew wide. His arm thrust forward, finger pointing to the door, trembling.

St. John whirled around and he caught his breath.

Across the door words were written, painted in large red letters: *Papist! Out of Orange County. Or Your Head is Next.* The message had been written in dog's blood.

* * * * *

"Thank you both for helping my wife bring in the harvest. And threshing it. And for shucking the corn."

Thomas Bull's drawn face was barely visible in the gloom. The fingers clutching the black iron bars were livid. "A day later and the storm would have ruined us."

"We're still waiting for a response from Governor Clinton." George Booth, Bull's brother-in-law and nephew, tried to sound encouraging. "Maybe he'll grant your petition. At least give you a trial."

Bull's hacking cough was painful to hear. "Seein' that the governor was the one who ordered me put in jail in the first place," Bull wheezed, "I wouldn't bet the farm on it. But thank'ee just the same."

Their eyes now accustomed to the dark, his visitors could see the half-dozen shroud-like figures sprawled on the straw-strewn dirt floor of the cell behind Bull.

He slapped a hand against the clammy stone wall. "Perhaps it serves me right. To be imprisoned in the very building I built with my own hands."

"We tried to get more signatures on the petition," Booth apologized. "But most folk, especially Newburgh way, are too scared to put their names to it. They're all afraid of the Committee."

"Ah yes. The Committee. The 'Committee to Prevent Conspiracies'. A fine-sounding title. In the service of a noble cause. Locking up innocent people without a trial."

"The war could well be over soon," Booth tried to be comforting. "Henry Clinton almost lost his army in Jersey and barely got back to New York and now Philadelphia is ours again. The French king has declared war on England and has sent us silver and arms. The French Navy is trying to blockade the red-coats holed up in Newport. Nathaniel Greene and John Sullivan have besieged them."

"Newport! Newport's not going to win the war. It's a stalemate. Just like the battle in Jersey last June. My son George fightin' for the British and my brother Isaac for the Americans. In the same battle, God save us."

A bored guard escorted Booth and St. John back to the street. The rain had been coming down hard and the road was a morass of mud. They tarried under the court-house portico, above which the word "Liberty" had been chiseled in place of the demolished royal coat of arms. A farmer in his cart was struggling up the road, huddled under a tarp while his oxen plodded forward as best they could in the muck.

"It's a hell of a mess, ain't it?" Booth remarked. "My brother Benjamin has fled to the City and now they're accusing my son William of being a spy, just because he wants to visit his beloved uncle. They don't dare touch me, of course, knowin' as they do I'm a patriot through-and-through. My militia service speaks for itself."

Booth looked at his friend. "You're fortunate, with your farm bein' in Orange and not Ulster. Governor Clinton and his attorney-general John Morin Scott will throw in prison without question anyone accused by a local committee for havin' the wrong opinions. There's a fellow out Newburgh way, Silas Gardner, who's condemned to hang for the heinous crime of sheltering a British officer's wife who got separated from her husband at Saratoga."

"Prisons don't always require bars," St. John remarked, face tense.

Booth glanced sidelong at St. John.

"Have you made up your mind?"

St. John did not answer.

"I suppose you'd sail out of Philadelphia."

"It's closer than Boston, true. But the risk of being captured by a British ship and treated as a prisoner of war is greater since they are patrolling all around the Chesapeake. I guess I'd have to leave from New York on an English ship. And from there cross over to France. But I don't know that Gov. Clinton would give me a pass to leave."

"Must you go?"

"Must we do anything except 'fear God and die'?"

They had stopped to let the wagon waddle past. St. John tried to not sound bitter; and failed.

"The only one willing to grind my grain is Ellison way over in New Windsor. But when I try to drive down there masked men jump out of the bushes and turn me back....No one will supply me with barrels, or tan my leather, or help me with the harvest.

"But worst of all," he said softly, "this from people I used to think were my friends...."

St. John was staring at the muddy ground, struggling to confess his fear as though it were a shameful flaw. He looked again at Booth.

"We've been getting death threats."

Booth nodded his head slowly. "I've seen that kind of thing before. My brother Benjamin...."

St. John suddenly grabbed his friend's shirt. Booth was staring into frantic blue eyes.

"Now they're threatening my wife and children! It's not enough for the cowards to threaten me but they have to go after my family?" St. John cried out. "I can't take this any longer. Why don't they show themselves? How can I defend them? I don't know who these monsters are! The children are afraid to sleep at night, we jump up at the wind blowing in the trees, afraid what we'll find when we open our door...and every other day a new message, a new threat, this one pinned to a tree, next time painted on a rock, sayin' if I don't flee, they'll kill my family...."

St. John let go of his friend's shirt, trembling hands balled into fists. "My head feels like it's clamped in an infernal vise, squeezing tighter and tighter and tighter while they whip-saw my body back and forth, back and forth from Tory to Patriot, Loyalist to Rebel then back again and again and again. I try to keep peace with each only to earn the hatred of both...."

St. John exhaled abruptly, tried to collect himself.

"My father has asked me to come home. He has been calling me for a long time but I resisted. I can't ignore his voice anymore. He has promised me forgiveness and a reconciliation with my brother, who is very ill. I must answer. Before it is too late. But I can't leave my wife and children alone to fend for themselves, and I can't take them all with me. I can't leave and I can't stay. I think I'm going mad."

Booth saw his friend look at him again. His eyes were beseeching.

"I don't know what to do."

The rain had stopped and the sun was beginning to reassert itself through the stubborn clouds. "O Lord," St. John murmured. "What has happened to our Eden?"

The two men parted ways, Booth heading north to his farm near the Bulls', St. John turning right onto the road to Blooming Grove. Arriving home, he found the kitchen door barred shut. Surprised to be knocking on his own door, he waited, then knocked again. He went to the window and called.

Mehetable's scared face peered through the panes. She vanished. He heard the latch rattle, the creaking of the bar and the groaning of hinges.

Mehetable's eyes were red from crying. Rebecca was at the cutting board, eyes cast down, making a stew. Fanny was in the far corner, spinning thread from the distaff held in her hand. Henry sat next to her, sewing a patch onto a pair of britches. Rebecca's son Isaiah was curled in a ball in another corner, fast asleep. They were quiet, Fanny and the two boys shucking corn no exception.

"Major Strong has been murdered," Mehetable wept softly. "He was killed this morning at his house. Seth Marvin and his brother came by and told us. They almost accused us of hiding the killer. They went through the whole house. They finally left an' told us to bar all the doors."

"Did they say who the killer is?"

"Claudius Smith and his sons. Before they killed Major Strong they robbed Jesse Woodhull's family and stole their silver."

St. John took his wife in his arms for a long moment. Still embracing her, he murmured: "I must go see them. The Strongs, the Woodhulls."

"You can't leave us. Not now."

"You will be all right. Smith won't be coming out this way. For sure he's holed up in his lair in the Ramapo Mountains or on his way to Westchester."

The afternoon shadows were longer by the time he reached the Strong homestead, in the dark vale near Satterly's Creek. Folk from all around were gathering as the news spread, some coming from as far away as Newburgh; or Haverstraw on the river where Woodhull was posted. Strong's sons, on leave as had been their murdered father, were gone with Sheriff Nicoll's posse on the manhunt but, Woodhull remarked, it was searching for the needle in the haystack. As Mrs. Strong was his niece, he took the grim duty upon himself to sit with her throughout the evening.

St. John rode back home in the dark, brooding. *Lord, why have you abandoned us?* In a spasm of despair he hit the horn of his saddle with a frustrated fist, provoking a confused snort from Irene. Terrified wife, children tormented by nightmares he was powerless to soothe, invisible enemies all around, nowhere to take them, nowhere to go. Nowhere....

In pitch blackness he clambered wearily onto his kitchen porch. He heard a strange rustling sound. A sudden chill of dread went down his spine. He felt a crushing pain to the side of his head then to his gut and then the hard ground. Voices, coarse and loud out of the dark, cursing, his head spinning, throbbing, the searing pain in his brain burning as though from the blade of an axe, someone pulling him upright by the arms ready to sever them from their sockets, shaking his body, punching without mercy his face, his nose, his mouth, his wife and children screaming from far away, far away...so very far away....

* * * * *

Lions surrounding their prey, circling ever tighter, feline bulls of Bashan. Blood blooming out of Private Stéphane's face like a red rose, soft brown eyes serene, mouth opening like a cave, echoing, *It's not blasphemy to tell the truth, tell the truth, tell the truth....* The lions, snarling, pouncing, ripping apart his body. *Traitor!* they scream. *Traitor! What more proof do we need?* A young French lieutenant shaking his fist, *You're just a coward, hiding behind this pretense of virtue! Aren't you? Aren't you?* Scalped corpses asleep in the smoldering ruins, René's blue eyes shining. *"Please accept this in remembrance of the truth...."* and Anne-Marie sobbing, crying her heart out, mother and child at rest on his dead friend's chest. *"Tabaldak wants it that way,"* Megeso smiles, pewter cross and scalping knife dangling, and a little boy sobbing, his sister in her miracle shoes, nodding her head in understanding. *"War? War? War is when men can't agree so they hate and kill each other"....* Rev. Schoonmaker tied to a stake engulfed in smoke, flames licking at his writhing body, sweat flooding his beatific face. *"Forgiveness! Brothers! Forgive each other, as Joseph forgave his brothers...."* And a tortured figure nailed to a tree, lips mouthing the words: *"Forgive them Father, for they know not what they do...."*

St. John woke up from his delirium and looked into Mehetable's eyes, and through her eyes into her soul. Her tears were gentle and her smile was sweet as she leaned forward to kiss his forehead. She collapsed onto him, sobbing softly.

The days stretched into weeks and the weeks into months. St. John could sit up in bed enough to sip his wife's carrot soup and stare out the window. He asked for his journal and quill; Henry made up a batch of ink from the fireplace soot. St. John wrote. He wrote to forget, he wrote to remember what it was like to hope, to dream. He wrote about the America he once knew.

New Year's day, Epiphany, was greeted by a snowstorm and the rest of the winter of 1779 followed suit. With the exception of the capture and hanging of Claudius Smith it was as though the world stood still. When, abruptly, the sun re-emerged on an early March day it was as though a miracle had occurred, so sharp was the contrast with the darkness they had endured. And then Samuel appeared.

Mehetable was overwhelmed with joy. She fell into her brother's arms, sobbing. They hugged each other for a long time, quietly. Fanny, squirming with suppressed excitement, could hold back no longer. She erupted in a squeal of delight and threw herself onto her mother and uncle. The bubble of silence burst and let forth years of compressed feelings, fears and hope in a cloud of bliss that let them dismiss their worries and troubles, if only for a day.

Samuel like his sister had jet-black hair, pulled back into a queue, already heavily streaked with grey and starting to thin. His face was sallow as though stamped by repeated fevers and deeply lined from the tropical sun and salt air. His shoulders though were brawny and his grip strong despite the absence of his little finger.

"Taken as a souvenir by a pirate off the coast of St. Lucia," he explained, letting Fanny, Ally and little Philly marvel at the stump. He entertained them for an hour with stories of his adventures.

"Is a privateer like a pirate?" Fanny asked.

"Well...think of it like this. A privateer is to a pirate what a committee of safety is to a robber. They both take things away from people; but the one does it for a noble cause and the other for selfish reasons."

"Oh." Fanny looked disappointed. "I guess that means you don't get to keep what you rob. You have to give it to the gummermint."

"Well, we get to keep half of what we...find; an' the other half goes to the government. But we only ask for donations from enemy ships."

"Can I be a privateer, too?" Ally asked. "I would like to go with you. Are you going to go away in a ship again? Can I go with you? Please?"

Samuel laughed. "I think I've had enough of the sea for a while. A long while."

St. John, still limping, escorted Samuel around the farm with the help of Henry. He showed Samuel the two new hired hands mending a fence in the distance.

"It's been hard for me to find good help," he said. "They are not interested in hard work; and they demand exorbitant wages knowing there's a shortage of labor. None of the reliable ones around here will work for me."

Samuel shrugged. "It's the same with a ship's crew. Only with the ocean all around they can't bail out so easily. But there's a trick to making 'em work. I'll find a way to persuade them."

"There's more money to be made in the powder mills and gun foundries. Even my wife's helper Rebecca has gone to work at Brewster's. I thank you again for coming here. You could have followed your friend Solomon to his uncle's iron works at Sterling Forge. It was Peter who made the chain across the river for Washington, you know. I'm sure he's happy to have the extra hands."

"I'm staying here."

They halted by the well near the road. Samuel's lean face flushed red with anger as he looked at the most recent outrage from the day before. An unseen hand had written in red paint across the stones: *Death to the Traitor.*

* * * * *

Mehetable did not want their children to see her sobbing. She cried throughout the night, nestled in her husband's arms.

"Michael, I don't want you to go. Oh, it breaks my heart....But if you don't go they will kill you. Sure an' they will come back one night and kill you...or all of us. Our children...." Mehetable moaned softly, heart squeezed in a painful spasm of despair. "Our children...you have no choice. We have no choice. Samuel can take care of us, they will know he was with Solomon Townsend on the privateer ship, he's joining the militia...You must go...I don't want you to go!" she cried in his chest. "But you must...for our sake...."

He caressed her long, soft hair, nuzzled her cheek, tried to comfort her even as he fought back his own tears, not knowing if they were the tears of a lover, the tears of a coward, or both.

At a family council the next morning they decided that after the flax was harvested St. John would try to leave, taking Ally with him. "Thomas Moffat and Judge Marvin promised they'd vouch for me with Gov. Clinton to get me a pass to leave Orange County," St. John told Samuel. "I'll ask my friend William Seton in the City to arrange for a safe-conduct through the British lines from Sir Henry."

"How do you manage to communicate with Seton?"

"John Ellison down by New Windsor. Ellison has the trust of both sides. He's allowed to go back and forth to the City. At least, until someone accuses *him* of being a spy for one or the other."

But at the beginning of June the news that Sir Henry Clinton had captured Stony Point on the river sent a ripple of panic throughout the county. The regiment of Continental regulars under Lord Stirling posted in the foothills west of Goshen were rushed to reinforce the small fort at West Point leaving the Orange County frontier exposed to raids from Tories and Indians. Calls went out to the isolated farmers out west along the Basherkill to pull back to the safety of the center but were ignored as crops and cattle had to be tended. Rumors of massacres from the western valleys were rampant. Moffat counseled St. John to wait.

"This is not the moment to be asking for passes."

In July came the exuberant news of Mad Anthony Wayne's defeat of the British garrison at Stony Point. A week later Moffat came to Pine Hill.

"Governor Clinton's with Washington in New Windsor, at Tom Ellison's house. Gen. McDougall was there, too, come up from West Point. George – the Governor, that is – he says, well, he got me an' Elihu's letters all right but that Judge Wisner also wrote to him, sayin' he learned about your plans and objected, sayin' you were a Tory spy and would betray our fortifications. I told 'em Henry was plain wrong, you're no spy, you need to go to France to see your father.

"George then turns to Mac and asks him for his opinion, and McDougall says, he knows you and has no objection as long as you don't try to come back before the War is over. So, Mac will sign a pass for you but first he wants to question you. He's stayin' tonight with Ellison's son John but leavin' tomorrow so you best git up there this evening.

"Good luck and may God be with you."

St. John rode with Ally behind him in the saddle, alert for bushwhackers. At Matthew's Mill they took the fork northeast to New Windsor rather than southeast to West Point and by late afternoon crossed over the Silver Stream on the narrow bridge spanning the rocky gorge where John Ellison had his mill, wheel clanking over the rush of water. Ahead were his fields and elegant Georgian stone mansion, built by the ubiquitous William Bull, with barns and out-houses around which dozens of workers and a handful of slaves were employed.

Ellison's farm lay on the ridge running parallel to the river. On both sides of the road to Newburgh squatted hundreds of patchwork tents. The road was busy with men in carts, men on horseback, men on foot. St. John found Ellison in his barn, serving as store-house for the troops. He told his friend of his plans. Ellison was not enthusiastic.

"Passing through the lines with your safe-conduct is one thing. Surviving the anarchy of Westchester is another thing all together. Between us at Peekskill and the red-coats at King's Bridge is a devil's den of thieves, murderers, cow-boys and cutthroats."

"New Jersey is the same."

"Aye, that is true. But I have another suggestion, provided you can wait another week. I have a pass myself, for my sloop, to bring down food to our prisoners on the ships. No doubt half of it vanishes on the docks as soon as we unload it. Perhaps the other half never makes it to the ships, either, for all I know. Poor bastards. But you and your son will be secure with me, regardless what happens to the food."

Ellison invited St. John and Ally to stay for the night in the bunkhouse. "I can't offer you a room in my house," he apologized. "General McDougall and General Knox outrank you, I'm afraid. They're still with Washington at my father's house up the road. The General thinks my father's chimney's too smoky – he's right, it never has drawn well – but he can keep a better eye on the river up there."

Alexander McDougall and Henry Knox rode in just before sunset, one tall and lean, the other tall and rotund. McDougall remembered St. John and greeted him cordially. Nonetheless he questioned him closely over supper, Moffat's recommendation notwithstanding. Satisfied, he procured a quill and bottle of ink from his aide and put his signature to the document.

"But," he added, "you will still need a pass from the British."

"That I'm hoping to get from William Seton."

"I suppose you'll be staying at his home."

"He would have offered, but English officers have taken over the whole house. Seton and his family sleep in the attic. I'll be staying at Drake's."

"Give him my regards."

General Knox was content to let the others converse while he finished his meal. He put down his knife and rose from the table.

"Think I'll go and visit Brewster at his forge. It's just down the hill a-piece."

"General Knox. If you don't mind my asking. By what miracle were you able to take all those cannon Arnold and Allen captured at Fort Ticonderoga in '75 and bring them in the dead of frozen winter over the Green Mountains two hundred miles to Boston?"

Knox adjusted his spectacles and shrugged, smiling.

"It *was* a miracle, wasn't it? I guess we must've had a helping hand."

Chapter Twenty-Three: *Choosing to Flee*

"...Carpenter...Coleman...Decker...Dunning, Benjamin and Jacob; Howell..." The names of the forty-three dead were pronounced like the tolling of a church bell. With each name a cry of anguish arose from a wife or mother or father or child. "...Little, James and John and Samuel...Lt. Col. Benjamin Tusten. Gabriel Wisner...."

Mehetable had not wanted to go. Supported by her husband and brother, she supported Mrs. Tusten and her three-year old boy; and they supported Sarah Wisner and the Judge and all the other grief-stricken families of Goshen town. The names of the fallen were still reverberating between the walls of the church long after the reverend reached the end of the long list and the apogee of his final prayer, until succumbing gently to the cries of the suffering black-shrouded figures huddling in the pews. A long quiet ensued.

Judge Wisner stood up, shoulders back. Eyes red and swollen, he began singing slowly in a low, mellow voice. Soon other men joined him, also standing, and women and children as well, hands holding hands, eyes lifted upwards, and the words of "Christ Has Risen" now rang out in defiance of the darkness surrounding them. Into each succeeding song they poured the sorrows of the heart until there was nothing left to pour.

From the church they went with Mrs. Tusten, her son, and her deceased husband's parents and sat in their mourning parlor. It was too difficult to comprehend, the elderly Tusten murmured, himself a former militia colonel. Too hard to grasp. Col. Hathorne's report of the ambush by Brandt's Indians and Tories and ensuing massacre on the cliffs overlooking the Delaware River forty miles away to the west was simple and plain. Too difficult to comprehend, Col. Tusten repeated.

In response Washington dispatched a company to guard the towns and assured the bereaved that General Sullivan's regiment would hound Colonel Brandt to the gates of hell. The suffering of the Iroquois women and children would prove to be equal to the rest. Infinite, indiscriminate suffering knows no inequality. All must suffer alike.

Mehetable and St. John spent a last night together in their dark chamber. She did not come downstairs at dawn, did not want to see them leave. She did not want her children to see her crying.

Samuel drove St. John and Ally with their sea chest of clothes to Ellison's wharf on the river. Ally was thrilled to take the tiller of the small sloop. Once in the narrows Ellison's mate took over, and they were careful to stand on deck in plain view with a salute to the soldiers on guard on the cliffs of West Point, their flag signifying they were bound with food to the prison ships. They repeated the display as they sailed down the river until arriving the next day at the docks near Whitehall.

A British officer approached, two soldiers behind him attired in the uniforms of an American Loyalist regiment.

The bored British captain greeted Ellison laconically. He frowned at St. John's pass from McDougall and looked at him with suspicion. "What's your purpose here?"

"My son and I, we hope to find passage to England."

"Oh you do, do you?" The officer seemed to find the answer amusing. He gestured to the town sprawling behind him. "There are thousands of other refugees, just like you. All chomping at the bit to kiss the soil of the Mother Country. And where is your safe-conduct to pass through our lines? How do I know you are not a rebel spy?" He smiled cynically.

"William Seton can vouch for me. I was hoping he could arrange for a pass."

"Indeed! It would seem he has not been successful in that endeavour." The captain's smile turned into a brittle glare. "Is that not a French accent I detect? You *are* French, aren't you? How strange, that you should pop up here right at the moment your Most Christian Majesty's navy has been espied just beyond Staten Island, lurking off the Jersey coast. My, my. Just a coincidence, I suppose?"

One of the Loyalist privates spoke up.

"Beggin' your pardon, sir, but I know that man. He calls himself 'St. John' but he really is a Frenchman. Used to be in the French army. My father knows all about him and his rebel friends. Gen'l La Fayette was a guest at his house."

"And just who might your father be?"

"Fletcher Matthews."

"Ah. I see. Your Refugee leader here in town. Well now, Mr. St. John, if that's your real name, what do you have to say for yourself? Is it true, La Fayette stayed at your house?"

"Well, yes, but –"

Furious, the officer slapped St. John's face with the side of his sword, sending him reeling backwards to the ground, taking Ally with him.

"Tie his hands. The boy's, too," the captain seethed. Rough hands carried out the command, then sharp kicks prodded the captives to their feet.

They were marched up the Broad-Way under the curious stares of vagrants and street peddlers, past the charred ruins of Trinity Church still not rebuilt from the fire three years earlier that destroyed most of the West Side. Make-shift huts had sprouted up everywhere. Even the stray dogs looked less famished than the people.

The business of the Holy Ground seemed to be as prosperous as ever, although crude tents fashioned from torn sails had replaced the burned down bawdy-houses. The women of virtue now roaming the streets in broad daylight seemed no less and no more virtuous than before the signing of the Declaration of Independence. Here and there curtains parted in windows, grasped by bony fingers.

The captives were prodded past King Street, the French Church now a horse stable for British officers. On Crown Street they were pushed along until abruptly reigned in before the looming brick mass of the Livingston Sugar House. Above the main door was a crude hand-painted sign bearing the hallmark of a bored soldierly wit:

Welcome All Ye, Who Have Chosen to Flee
Through these Doors into Liberty

"Keep the boy with us. We'll ask the colonel what's to become of him." The captain smirked. "A wee too wet yet to send to sea, methinks. Perhaps the General could use another stable-boy."

With a push and a shove in his back St. John exchanged the light of the day for the gloom of the prison.

Chapter Twenty-Four: *Chosen to Be Free*

The pain in St. John's side would not go away. It was alleviated in no respect by the damp, rotting plank flooring or vermin-infested straw on which he lay. He was too weak from hunger to stand up, and too sickened to stay down. He rolled onto his back, eyes opened upwards looking for light in the darkness. He commanded his lifeless right palm to open and his arm to rise in the air. They did not obey his command, yet they rose anyway. They fell back to the floor, rose again, fell again. The exercise was repeated with his left arm, then his legs.

The body next to him stirred. The voice of a man moaned, fell silent. From somewhere in a corner floated the sounds of a parched throat rattling. From another corner came a feverish trembling followed by a harsh hacking. In another cell someone was retching. The smell of putrefaction lay heavy in the still air as another corpse began to decay, too impatient to wait for the morning death-cart to make its rounds.

The rotten straw was not the sole home of the vermin. Insects had taken over the mold-covered sea biscuits occupying the wooden trencher a guard had shoved under the cell door. It helped pass the time weeding out the bugs before dipping the biscuit into the pitcher of brackish water to moisten it before being swallowed.

By and by a feeble hint of daylight began filtering through the narrow slits along the tops of the cells. The arched brick vault-ways vaguely emerged out of the gloom. The iron bars being black took longer to appear. The listless bodies stretched out on the floor were the last to materialize.

Voices murmured. Some spoke of delirium, others were rational, owned by newcomers to the fold who had not yet lost all health and strength. A few throats whispered prayers, others muttered frail curses. No matter what the form of the utterance all were of the same substance. Pleas for mercy.

Minute banal events took on great significance. The occasional odd biscuit without any worms, the paroled prisoner come back to empty the chamber pots of their filth, the arrival of the death-cart and removal of the latest dead bodies. The advent of a new inmate having chosen the door to freedom.

Days, weeks, perhaps even months passed. Or perhaps not. Eternity knows no time. Into the absence of the world had flowed another reality and the truth of its beckoning shimmered through the darkness and its thundering call whispered in the silence. St. John watched and listened.

It was almost casual, as though a non-event, the morning of his visit. The young boy's face was hardly discernible but his voice was cheerful, like the first robin calls of spring. How or why he had been let in no one knew. The knowledge was not relevant to the fact that he had come.

He brought with him shallow baskets of fresh baked bread and pitchers of fresh water. Patiently he made the rounds, disappearing a few moments when exhausting his supply before reappearing with new baskets and pitchers. The sustenance he brought went beyond the nourishment of the food and glowed long after he left.

Only in suffering is surrender easy. St. John gratefully ate of the bread and drank of the water. He rose to his feet, shakily but surely, for the first time in a long time, as though without any conscious effort on his own part. He took a few halting steps. It was as though he were floating, rather than walking.

The day of his release came not long after. The guard said nothing, motioning silently, grudgingly with his hand for St. John to follow him down the long brick corridor then up the stairs.

There was no ceremony, no paperwork, no words exchanged. His departure from prison was as inevitable and effortless as breathing and thus transpired the most monumental occurrence in the most everyday way.

The guard with a jerk of his head directed St. John to the doorway. Like its counterpart outside, above the doorframe was a sign, writ in the same hand but with different words. It read:

Fare Thee Well, All Ye
Whom I Have Chosen to Set Free

PART THREE: BROKEN HEART

Chapter One: *A Stranger in his Own Country*

"Describe for me again your farm. I would like to hear more about your strange native fruit and vegetables. And your American potatoes. I have cultivated what you sent to me but you will have to be the judge."

St. John obliged. He spoke slowly, fumbling for the correct words. He shifted uncomfortably on the dainty salon chair, his brother's clothes chafing him.

St. John's father listened, eyes closed. His long sparse white hair came trickling over his shoulders onto the upturned face of his grandson, tickling him. Ally giggled. His grandfather smiled, eyes still closed, and absently rocked the boy resting on his lap.

"And now, again, tell me about your wife. And my two other grandchildren." St. John obeyed.

His father opened his eyes. The soft blue orbs were partly obscured by a whitish haze along the circumference, like the evening sky veiled by so many *moutons*, wisps of floating clouds fluffy like sheep. He regarded his son strangely, as though not able to believe they were sitting together in the same room.

"It must have been terrifying, your shipwreck on the Irish coast," the elderly man mused, for the fourth time. "It was a miracle you and Guillaume-Alexandre survived."

The boy perked up on hearing his name. He looked up in wonder at the white haired man, watching his lips move as though understanding the strange sounds they were producing.

"It was, indeed, a miracle."

"It was Providence that brought you safely to shore."

"And into the kind arms of the O'Leary family."

"It was no less miraculous how you survived that winter in New York City. With no food, no hearth." Baron de Crèvecoeur fumbled with the blanket around his legs. St. John stood up and stirred the embers then put another small log on the fire. The flames took hold, crackling and dancing. His father scowled.

"That is for Robert to do. You can't go around spoiling the servants. God knows they're becoming more and more insolent with each passing day. Just like the peasants." He shifted painfully in his armchair, eyes closed again. "The newspapers say New York is a ruin. People in rags. Crime, prostitution, vice. Nowhere to live but tents and hovels." He shook his head.

"There is suffering, that is true. But hardship is like rain. It brings forth beautiful flowers as well as ugly weeds. It was thanks to my friend William Seton I was released from prison, and through him I met a kind Quaker couple who took me in, destitute though they were. My bed of straw in their barn was more luxurious than their thin bed in their flimsy shack. Ally, at least, had a decent bed at the home of Seton's friend in Flatbush."

"How did you manage to pay for your voyage?"

"Seton again. The elders of Trinity Church paid me eleven pounds to survey their grounds and some other land they bought nearby from departing Loyalists."

"And Dublin? How long were you in Dublin?"

"Only long enough to find a ship's master willing to take us to Liverpool on my word of honor to repay him in the future. He took pity on Guillaume-Alexandre, shivering in his borrowed suit of clothes. He was interested, too, in hearing what I had to tell him about the war."

"Ah yes. The war. The great American Rebellion. That remarkable, admirable, awful, interminable conflict. Will I live long enough to ever see it come to an end?"

"Maybe it's already over and we'll learn about it when the next ship comes in."

The elderly man broke out in a fit of a harsh coughing, causing Ally to bounce up and down on his lap like the ship caught in the storm waves they had just been discussing. St. John took his distressed son onto his own knees.

A middle-aged woman hurried into the salon. She fussed about the old man, who brushed her away feebly with a gnarled hand.

"Your cousin Marie-Céleste is a sweet angel," he wheezed, regaining his breath, "but she would not make a successful seer. She will tell you I have not long to live. But she is wrong."

"Shush, uncle," Marie-Céleste admonished. "You must not say such foolish things. I will bring you some tea."

"You know, since your brother died I have had to depend on your cousin. She has been a Godsend. But she is too pessimistic. Just like all the charlatan physicians in the county. They have all been predicting my eminent demise for decades. And yet my heart is still beating, even if my brain is not functioning as well as I would like. Or other parts of my body. My son, would you like to hear a valuable bit of fatherly advice?"

"Yes, father, I would."

"Here it is: do not grow old."

"I will try my best to follow your wise counsel."

"And here is a second piece of even more valuable advice: avoid doctors like the plague."

Marie-Céleste returned with a silver tray and tea-set, and a cup of apple cider for the boy. She sat down with them. Even though it was August the chill from the sea air made the blazing fire welcome.

"I look forward," the old man rasped,"to reading your book. Once you translate it into French. I don't believe there has ever been an author in our family. A writer of books, I mean. Plenty of scriveners, myself included, who have bored the good citizens of Caen with endless reams of pompous legal drivel.

"Which reminds me of my third bit of precious advice: avoid lawyers. They are even more deadly than doctors. Physicians will bleed you but lawyers will suck your blood straight from your veins. Like leeches."

He took a sip of tea. "When will it be published?"

"That, I don't know for sure."

The old baron grunted in derision.

"Strange, isn't it?" his son mused. "Here I am, my adopted country at war with England; sitting with my father in France, at war with England; waiting to hear from my English publisher, about to print and sell a book about America."

"And who has paid you an advance of...how much did you say it was?"

"Only thirty guineas. But it was enough to pay our way over to Amsterdam. And to repay the kind Irish captain. My publisher has promised more if the book sells well."

"Thirty guineas! You're not much of a negotiator, are you?"

"I would like to read your book," Marie-Céleste announced. "But first you will have to translate it into French."

"I wonder if I can do that," St. John replied. "I have almost lost my ability to write in my own maternal language. Or even to speak it the way I want. It's a struggle. I get bogged down like a wagon in the mud."

"You have a unique, exotic way of speaking French, that is true," his cousin replied. "And, you have an American accent. But I find it charming."

The elderly Crèvecoeur snorted. "Charming? There's nothing seductive in broken grammar and mangled words. My son speaks fractured French like a peasant from Brittany. I know Englishmen who speak our language better."

He made a temple of his hands and brought them to his chin. He regarded his son with veiled eyes.

"You're going to have to devise a means of support for yourself. If all you get from your English scribbling is thirty pounds a year you won't have even enough to keep a clean suit of clothes on you. God knows I can't support you. My tenant barely pays enough to keep up the château.

"You will have to do something about your French. Your way of speaking declares you to be a stranger to your own country. And your manners. You are too free and easy. You lack the refinement of a nobleman. Too rustic. You are like a farmer's pine stool sitting in a salon of polished walnut and satin sofas. One Benjamin Franklin in high society is more than enough."

The elderly baron gestured with a flick of the wrist at the wall behind him adorned by the copied portrait of the very same American philosopher hanging above the mantel-piece, fur cap and spectacles adorning the second most famous face in France.

"I have invited a special friend to come and meet with you," he said. "The Marquis Turgot. I would not expect you to remember him. He is the brother of the king's minister of finance. Or should I say, was, being that the minister just died recently. The marquis's aunt was a cousin of your mother and her brother, Michel-Jacques Blouet.

"Turgot, like you, is interested in natural philosophy and passionate about agriculture. I have shared with him your correspondence from the New World, however few and far between your letters to me may have been. He is keen on renewing your acquaintance. He will be dining with us this evening. Four o'clock sharp. Turgot is never early and never late. The sun, the moon and all the stars in the heavens regulate their movements by looking at him. If only he could regulate my own internal movements."

The old man succumbed to another fit of coughing. Marie-Céleste administered a large glass of water.

"Should drink more of that," he muttered. "Does miracles for the insides of a man."

"I wonder if maybe it would be better to have the marquis come next week. My grammar...."

"Posh. Don't concern yourself with that. It's educated conversation you need. Turgot won't care how you speak."

"I feel like I ought to first go back to our Jesuit college."

"You can't. My God, how ignorant you have become, lost in the wilds of America. The Jesuits were expelled from France almost twenty years ago. Marie-Céleste, my dear, kindly go fetch that book with the gold binding in the shelf above my desk. That's the one. Thank you."

The elderly baron opened the leather cover and lovingly perused the pages before handing the tome to his son.

"Since you are so self-conscious, study this. It's the *Discourse on Style*, by Count Buffon. Whatever you need to know to write well, it will be in there. Buffon is also big on potatoes. And rubber, what your Indians call *caout-shak*. And the animal kingdom, at least the furry specimens. He can't stand insects and so he discounts entirely their importance in the order of the natural world. I imagine Turgot will want to introduce you to him. Buffon is without doubt the most respected natural philosopher in all the world. Franklin notwithstanding. He's been in charge of the Royal Gardens for years."

True to the baron's word Turgot's coach clattered up the drive on the stroke of four. He was met at the door by the baron's manservant Robert who, taking the marquis' cloak and hat over a crooked arm, showed him into the library where his host was waiting with his son. After much bowing and embracing the baron presented his son to the marquis.

"You would not recall the last time we met," Turgot said, "but I do." He was a handsome man with large, inquisitive dark eyes and a prominent cleft chin. His elegant white bob-wig coiffed his head as naturally as St. John's seemed out of place.

"You were a very young student back home on leave from the Jesuit college in town. You showed me your bird collection. I was impressed."

"I remember, your Excellency. Please allow me." St. John escorted the marquis to a display case in a corner of the library. Behind the glass were numerous birds in a state of mild decay, their bodies dubiously preserved by the young scholar. Robert poured out generous goblets of brandy and with a low bow presented a glass to each man.

Sitting by the fire the marquis peppered St. John with questions about Canada and America.

"You may know," Turgot recounted, "that I was briefly – very briefly! – governor of Guyana, our South American colony. Must have been around the same time you were living amongst your Oneida friends in New York.

"The jungles of South America are full of fascinating creatures. Monkeys, orangutans, snakes, even carnivorous fish! Birds small and large, with beautiful colored plumage, enormous beaks. The untold diversity and infinite variety of the animals forced me to ponder about the origin of it all.

"And how strange the flora. I have always been intrigued by the plant they call potato. They eat only the portion growing in the soil with the roots, in the form of a roundish tube. They thrive on it and never take ill. The potato is not mentioned in the Bible, of course, and so here in France and Spain the people refuse to eat it. They fear it is the devil's poison."

Robert's hand emerged into his field of vision long enough to replenish his glass. "Parmentier put on quite a dinner a while ago featuring nothing but dishes made of potatoes to prove they are edible and nourishing. The king's foreign minister Vergennes was there, as were Benjamin Franklin, Buffon, my brother, myself. I am sure your father has a copy of his treatise. You would do well to read it."

"As a matter of fact, I have."

Turgot's eyebrows shot up. "But I understand you have only just arrived."

"That is true. I did not read the book here, but rather in America."

"Please excuse my astonishment. I do not associate learned books with the wilds of the American frontier."

"I was acquainted with the deceased lieutenant-governor of New York, Cadwallader Colden. He had an extensive library."

"Colden. Of course. Well. I have a copy of his book *Plantae Coldenghamiae* in my own collection. We corresponded from time to time. He, too, admired the potato."

"Michel-Guillaume," the baron interjected, "also fancies himself an author. Although I shall wait to see the empirical evidence of that assertion before passing on its veracity."

"So you have written a book! What is the name, and the subject you treat?"

"At the suggestion of my London publisher it will be called *'Letters from an American Farmer'.*"

"And the central theme is....?"

"The endless bounty of that land. And its invigorating effect on the common man. Free to let bloom his natural instincts for innovation. Free to work the rich soil of his own land. Free to chart his own life. They work hard because they believe that through their own diligent efforts they too someday can become that rich landowner or merchant."

"And their spiritual life?"

"They are, overall, a devout people."

Turgot grunted. "They remind me of the Dutch. Devout in everything having to do with making money."

"Well, it is true Americans always have one eye if not both on commerce."

"At least they do not appear to be a lazy people."

"In America nothing stands still. There is a latent energy in the very air."

"Would that our peasants here in France partake of that air."

"Well, so it is too with the slaves in America. But free blacks work just as hard as whites. See, it's like a kettle of cold water. Take away the wood for the fire and the water lies dormant. But give the kettle the means to heat itself, and the water will take that energy and transform itself into a frenzy of steam. That power can produce a lot of useful things."

"Unless the steam does not have an efficient outlet. Then the kettle will explode," the Baron rasped. "If there is pressure, there must be a release or else you will have destruction."

"But can ordinary men be counted on to put the steam to good use?" Turgot asked. "That requires wisdom. Do the *peuple*, the lower classes, have such wisdom?"

Turgot's arched eyebrows supplied the answer to his own question. He pulled from a pocket a small silver box and pinched a bit of snuff, sniffed then sneezed. "There! I feel much relieved." He held up the silver box, admiring it. "It is clear that tobacco is good for the bodily humors," he declared.

"As I was saying, I fear the lower sort are incapable of governing themselves. They lack the judgment, the enlightenment, the intelligence of their betters. Your experience in America notwithstanding. I suppose we shall have to let their little experiment play itself out. We will then have the empirical evidence as proof they lack the wisdom and discernment necessary to rule which only the noble classes possess.

"To counter your example of steam, I would invoke the image of a natural lake fed by a pure mountain spring. As long as it is tended by a wise overseer the pond will remain pure. But inevitably word of the pond will reach the ears of other men, most of whom are not enlightened or wise. They will all rush to exploit that pond and in so doing pollute the pond. They wind up destroying the very thing which attracted them in the first place.

"That is why the Supreme Creator has ordained a specific order for man to follow, to protect man from his own foolishness. When that order is upset chaos and ruin will follow. No, it is evident that the well-being of all requires the educated, sober mind of the wise overseer."

The marquis gladly let the baron refill his glass with another generous dash of brandy. As the marquis drained half of it in one gulp the baron's manservant announced the arrival of dinner-time. Their guest was escorted to the seat of honor in the drafty dining hall, clutching his goblet now drained of its content and wobbling on somewhat unsteady legs.

Turgot smiled at the sight of the table ornamentation: three vases in the middle, each with the preserved flowers of the potato plant, white petals in the middle vase, lavender in the others. He smiled even more as the first of the entrées was brought to table: a steaming tureen of potato and onion soup. It was followed by a dish of finely diced roasted potatoes and carrots in maple syrup, then a dish of braised beef and whipped potatoes. The pièce de résistance: potato crêpes, stuffed with finely minced potatoes, chives and Indian maize.

When informed he was eating maize, the marquis took on a troubled look. "Maize? Indian corn? You should have warned me. I know that Franklin and Parmentier have praised it, but maize unlike the potato is fit only for pigs and peasants. And Indians."

"There now, my dear Turgot. It is simply a matter of growing accustomed to it," the baron remarked gleefully. "Here, have another serving." The baron himself shoveled another corn and potato crêpe onto the marquis' plate.

"You can thank my son for the inspiration behind this splendid repast I had Cook prepare. He is quite an expert on Indian corn and New England potatoes, or so he says. Perhaps he should write a book about them. Only this time," the baron added, glancing at his son," try to negotiate a better price than thirty guineas."

Turgot elicited from St. John a description of the varieties of potato in North America and urged him to write a treatise on the topic. "I have Bartram's study on the potatoes from the southern Colonies, so if you do me this pleasure we can complete the American picture. I will have it published in Paris for you. It will secure your election to the Agricultural Society, and, who can tell, possibly the royal Academy of Science as well.

"In the meantime, come to Paris with me. You will be my guest, quai du Dauphin. I am sure you and Buffon will hit it off in grand style as well. I suggest you read his articles in Diderot's *Encyclopédie* to prepare yourself. I, too, contributed an article, on cotton. There! It's settled. I will send my carriage for you…shall we say two weeks from today?"

"If you please, four weeks. I will need to have a new suit or two of clothes made."

"Four weeks it is then."

With that the three men retired to the library for a glass of porto. The marquis gestured at the portrait of Franklin.

"The sage who tamed lightning! Lightning rods have become all the rage. '*Eripuit caelo fulmen sceptrumque tyrannis*'. 'He snatched the lightning from the sky and the scepter from the tyrant.' Or so my brother wrote.

"The last time I visited Franklin he explained to me his design for improving upon his stove. Ingenious. I had one made and installed in my apartments. I'll show you when you come to stay with me. Using just atmospheric pressure the stove recirculates all the smoke from the fire and burns it off while at the same time doubling the efficiency of the coals."

He produced a pipe, a long wooden instrument with carved figurines along the thick stem, decorated in the same fashion as the whale-bone powder-horns of the mariners. He showed it lovingly to St. John.

"Speaking of smoke, this pipe was a gift from the local chieftain in Cayenne. I had one sent to Buffon as well. He is a great believer in the medicinal value of tobacco, as am I.

"The carvings on the pipe are interesting, don't you find? Superstitious nonsense, of course. The primitive mind is too quick to leap to conclusions without understanding the facts. Intellectual rigor is what they lack. What, you do not smoke tobacco?"

"No, thank you just the same."

"Trust me, you don't appreciate what you are missing. Future generations will praise the healthy benefits of tobacco, as they will the potato."

The manservant poured more porto into the marquis' glass.

"But first," Turgot took a sip, smaking his lips in satisfaction, "we must strip away the shrouds of superstition and the tyranny of religious dogma and let the light of human reason be our guide. Governed, of course, by the refined, sober mind of the enlightened philosopher. There we will find, in the boundless power of the human intellect, true freedom."

Turgot raised his glass of alcohol high in the air.

"A salute to the age of reason."

St. John raised his glass.

"To true freedom."

The baron twirled his goblet in his wizened hand.

"A toast to whomever can cure my gout."

Chapter Two: *A Short Walk to Eternity*

The news reached the tailor shop in the village just as the fussy master tailor was finishing up the fitting for St. John's new suit.

"Sire, I beg of you, do not budge so. The pins will fall out."

Impatiently St. John restrained himself. Father François, a plumper, greyer incarnation of the priest of St. John's youth, was standing a few feet away, hands clasped calmly together over his berobed *embonpoint*.

"All in good time, my son. All in good time. The American sailors will not be leaving us any time soon. I've hidden them at the rectory. They're taking supper. And by the looks of them, they have not eaten for quite a long time."

"Where did you find them?"

"They found us. Or rather, André the fishmonger's son. André was bringing his boat into port. They came up to him out of the fog in a rowboat. André was afraid they'd get thrown into

321

prison so he brought them to me. And I know you speak their language. And so here we are."

Fitting finished, Father François escorted St. John to the rectory next to the church. To reach it they had to traverse the village square with its ancient, tired fountain having ceased long ago to produce any water, to the apparent indifference of the inhabitants. They passed the hatter's and the wine merchant's and the baker's, the tinsmith's and the fishmonger's. Although hardly afternoon none of the shops appeared busy. The air was heavy with a morose lethargy.

As though reading his thoughts Father François offered an explanation.

"Taxes," he said. "Taxes, taxes, more taxes. And now they have dredged up anew long-forgotten feudal dues and fees and other *droits de seigneur* owed to the lords, on top of the traditional *taille*. The shopkeepers and artisans are not happy. They blame the insurgents in America for draining the royal treasury and the church for collecting her tithes.

"The peasants especially are suffering, for they know not how to cope with the added burden. They are suffocating under the load," the priest sighed. "And in suffering have forgotten to whom to surrender their burden."

They reached the church, an ancient stone relic from the twelfth century erected in the age when the Viking dukes of Normandy ruled England with an iron fist along with Brittany, the Loire and Aquitaine. The rectory was on the far side of the graveyard.

"Would you like to pay your respects to your mother?"

The two men made the pilgrimage together. It was but a short walk to reach eternity. Marie-Françoise Blouet was resting near the shade of an oak tree, planted at the same time as the mortal remains had been returned to the earth. A grape vine grew alongside the grave, embracing the crown of the granite memorial. Thirty-five years had done nothing to alter the simple tombstone with its simple inscription of the name of the departed and the simple depiction of the dove in timeless flight carved in the stone above her name from before the beginning of time.

Sunlight played over the grave and the breeze from the sea murmured in the leaves of the tree. A leaf was dispatched from the guardian and floated down, the message and the messenger one and the same. It caressed the broad green crown with its budding young fruit, as it came to rest in the generous leaves of the grapevine. I am the vine, you are the branches. I am the true vine, the Father the vintner. Abide in me. Abide in my love.

Father François crossed himself and St. John rose to his feet. It was but a short few paces to the rectory and through the doorway into the illusory life of the world. The five sailors, clothed in the short blue vests and once-white pants of low-ranking naval officers, were at the small trestle table in the kitchen finishing the last of the priest's cheese and polishing off a bottle of wine. They looked up at the sound of footfalls.

"Howdee, gents," St. John greeted them in American English. "Looks like you're a long way from home."

The Americans stopped their chewing and looked in surprise at this French nobleman chatting with them in their own vernacular.

"St. John's my name. Michael St. John. Where are you folks from? And why on earth were you rowing around in a longboat in the fog?"

A young officer, sandy-haired, short and wiry, stood up and leaned over the table to shake St. John's proffered hand. "Pleased to meet you," he said, grinning widely. "George Little speaking. Lieutenant in the United States Navy." His voice revealed a heavy New England accent. "And this here's me mates. Samuel Wales, Alexander Story, John Collier. An' Clement Lemon. His parents came from France but he don't speak the language."

"And the rowboat? In the fog?"

"Well, as for the rowboat, we figgered it was too far to swim across the English Channel not to mention the water's a wee too cold for my taste. As for the fog, we have to thank God for that. It allowed us to make our get-away without being seen."

"Get-away from what?"

"The English jail we were in. A rotten barge, actually. In Portsmouth harbor. Almost six months we were there. Since March 1781, after our ship *Protector* was captured."

The sailor named Samuel Wales spoke up. "What's the news from America? Has your General Rochambeau finally made a move to help Washington? Where's Admiral DeGrasse? Is the war over?"

St. John could only shrug. "I don't have the answers to that. The last news we have is that Rochambeau was still in Newport with his army and DeGrasse with his navy somewhere in the

Caribbean. Washington was in Newburgh. The war shifted to the Carolinas – "

"We knew that much," Wales cut in bitterly. "We lost Charleston over a year ago. Your Admiral D'Estaing scampered like a scared bunny out of Savannah. Tarleton and Cornwallis walked all over Gates. Benedict Arnold raided Richmond, almost captured Governor Jefferson. It was one disaster after another down South."

"As I was about to say," St. John continued, "Nathaniel Greene has turned the tables on them. He crushed the Loyalists at King's Mountain and thrashed Tarleton at Cowpens. La Fayette was pushing Cornwallis into the Virginia swamps."

The sailors fell silent as they digested the news.

"*Que les messieurs m'excusent,*" Father François murmured an apology, forgetting their guests did not speak French. "I must prepare for the evening mass. You are all most welcome to attend," he finished, hopefully, then turned to St. John for help, realizing his invitation was not understood.

"Perhaps," St. John suggested, "you can light a candle and say a prayer for these sailors and our men in America. I will bring them up to the château."

"Take care the mayor doesn't see you. He doesn't know the difference between Americans and Englishmen. He'll have them arrested as British spies. You'll have to take our new friends as soon as you can over to Caen and have the Admiralty Court certify them as American officers."

St. John hired the candle-maker's son to drive the sailors while he led them in his father's cabriolet to the château. The ancient road spoke of the Roman engineers who had laid out the highway in the time of Augustus, with as much mathematical precision and uniformity as the undulating terrain would allow. Their arched viaducts still spanned the occasional narrow ravine, their engineered stone and cement evidence of the ability of human reason to re-fashion the objects of the world but proof of nothing more than that. Unbidden, he saw for an instant the serene blue eyes of Father René. "The baker who believes the bread he makes proves he can create the wheat is foolish indeed," the priest smiled.

Baron de Crèvecoeur made little attempt to hide his irritation at the unexpected guests in their tattered, dirty uniforms. "Overnight guests are expensive. Money's tight," he grumbled.

"My father says 'Welcome. Make yourselves at home'," St. John translated cheerfully for the sailors.

"Tell our visitors," Marie-Céleste suggested, "they can stay in the two good bedchambers. They won't mind wearing your brother's clothes while I have their uniforms mended. And I'm sure they will want to bathe." With a slight curtsy she left to have the servants carry out her will.

"Please don't think we're ungrateful for your hospitality," Lt. Little replied to St. John's translation, "but we don't want to tarry long. We want to get back to the fight. How far away are we from Lorient?"

"Lorient? The naval port? That's a good three days' ride. There is a stage-coach from Caen that passes by twice a week."

Little paused. "We have no money to pay the fare. Let us work here to earn it. Clement's a smithy, Samuel's a carpenter. The rest of us will help with the harvest."

"You are in the Old World. Things work differently here....Please don't concern yourselves with work or money. The first thing we must do, I'm told, is to have you pass muster as bona fide American sailors with our officials in Caen."

The Americans ignored the injunction for the next morning at dawn they were up and about, chopping firewood, weeding the gardens, mending fences. Samuel Wales and Clement Lemon got it into their minds to fix several decrepit window frames in the château which took them all of the afternoon, Ally lending them a hand.

The baron was amazed. "They accomplished in one day what my smith and carpenter take a month to think about." Now that the sailors had proven their worth, and had bathed regularly, the old man was ready to accept them albeit at a cautious distance. He went so far as to invite them into his library for an evening drink. Not understanding the conversation, by-and-by he drifted off to sleep, his grandson curled up beside him, wide-awake, listening with wide eyes to the stories of the sailors' skirmishes with the British Navy.

St. John told the Americans about his family and farm west of Hudson's River.

"I have had no word of them for two years. I wrote to them from London but didn't receive a reply. I wrote them another letter and posted it just before you washed up on the beach yonder, but it'll take two months to reach them, assuming it's not lost at sea or waylaid due to the war."

"Give your letters to me," Lt. Little said. "From Lorient we're heading for Boston, by hook or by crook. I have an uncle there, a sea captain. Gustaves Fellowes is his name. He made a fortune as a privateer. He's a warm-hearted, generous fellow, he is. If anyone can make sure your letters get to your family, it will be my uncle. If it wasn't for the war I'd go myself. I have cousins in Orange County."

"I knew an Archibald Little," St. John recalled. "A militia captain. He was captured at the Battle of Fort Montgomery. I trust he is still alive, but I don't know for a fact. Three of his relatives were killed on the Delaware River in a Tory-Mohawk ambush two years ago."

Lt. Little's expression did not change, except for a hardening of the eyes. "Small world, ain't it?"

"Perhaps you know my wife's brother, Samuel Tippet. He was a sailor, too, although now he's with my family tending the farm."

"World's not that small, I guess."

The baron made the arrangements with the Admiralty Court to receive their American guests. "And you will be staying in town with Countess d'Houdetot. Sophie doesn't spend much time in Calvados anymore so we're fortunate she's here. I'm sure you will remember her, and her husband the count, my second cousin. If you see him, that is. He spends all his time now at Versailles fox hunting or playing cards at his club in Paris. Sophie is a great lover of your American rebels. She worships Franklin. No doubt she will trip all over herself to have you meet the philosopher king."

The American sailors were wide-eyed at the medieval city, its castles, its cathedral and twin abbeys. Mme. la Comtesse, Sophie d'Houdetot was gracious in her unbridled effusion over her guests. She fussed over them as though their mother. Through her connections the hearing at the Admiralty's was a perfunctory pro forma affair and their passports had already been signed and stamped.

After dinner she had them write to Benjamin Franklin, residing in the Paris suburb of Passy. "I'm sure he will help you find an American vessel, and clear it through our minister of the Navy, the Marquis de Castries."

She advised St. John to write to Franklin as well. "He might be able to open some doors for you, you know. But we have to be careful. The dear man is inundated with all sorts of office seekers and sycophants. I'll write to him myself to introduce you."

The countess that evening entertained her guests with her poem in praise of Franklin she had recited at her *fête champêtre,* staged in his honor at her château in Soissons the year before. Strumming a harp, she declaimed:

> "*Our Nestor of America,*
> *Greatest friend of Humanity*
> *Who with wisdom and wit guides us*
> *To Knowledge and thus to Liberty*
>
> *His sublime Philosophy*
> *This Buffon of* Philadelphie
> *Whose glorious name shall shine,*
> *throughout all Eternity*
>
> *All Hail the new Solomon, on Earth as in Heaven*
> *Wise tamer of lightning, savior of his brethren!*
> *His spirit shall light the way to Happiness*
> *for us and all Posterity.*"

St. John dutifully translated the panegyric into English for the benefit of the Americans. They applauded politely, balancing uncomfortably on the dainty salon chairs of the countess.

A fortnight later Franklin's replies to their letters arrived at Baron de Crèvecoeur's château. After supper St. John excused himself and went to the library where he spent half the night writing. The next morning he carefully folded and sealed his letters to entrust to Little, one to his wife, one to William Seton, others to Jesse Woodhull, Thomas Moffat, and Joseph Drake; and a letter to Capt. Gustaves Fellowes.

Their guests each received from Marie-Céleste a simple *besace de pèlerin* they could carry easily slung over a shoulder into which she placed their uniforms, darned and laundered along with two new pairs of stockings. When St. John, having driven the Americans himself along with Ally to the village to board the stage-coach, informed them they were equipped with pilgrims' shoulder-bags, Little gave a grin.

"My ancestors in Massachusetts were pilgrims from the Old Country, landing in a new world. Maybe we'll find out we're pilgrims to a new nation. He and his mates shook their host's hand. "If we don't meet again in paradise, then maybe we'll have to settle for America instead."

St. John and Ally, holding hands, stood still for a long, long time, watching the departing coach carrying away the American pilgrims with the precious epistles in Lt. Little's shoulder-bag, watching the coach becoming smaller and smaller until fading away all together as though nothing more than a dream.

Chapter Three: *At the Altar of Reason*

Only once before in his life had St. John been to Paris, and the memory was but a dim haze. As the coach rounded a bend in the road remnants of the ancient stone walls of the city came into view. They were waved through the St.-Honoré Gate by the guard and the customs collector, there being no merchandise to declare and thus no tax to pay.

Inside the wall the boulevard ran straight and wide, flanked with the grand houses and estates of the nobility, unlike the warren of whitewashed hovels and narrow streets in the poor neighborhoods. They trotted by churches and convents, the Jacobins on the left, the Capucins on the right. The Palais des Tuileries loomed ahead, the opulent Palais-Royal, home of the Orléans branch of the royal family, on the left. Further along and the side streets took on a more popular air, crowded with tradesmen and artisans of the finer sort, shops displaying glittering arrays of clocks and jewelry, exquisite furniture and haute couture mingling with the occasional bookstore. Beyond, over to the north, crouched the dome of the large grain market, the Halle aux Blés and to the south towards the river, the Palais du Louvre and rising beyond that the towers of the Palais de la Cité and the cathedral of Notre-Dame.

The coach had to slow to a crawl, its pace dictated by the whims of the people populating the crowded streets, paying no heed to the impatient coachman and his sheltered passenger. It bore right, towards the Seine onto the Place de Grève and the imposing Hôtel de Ville, the city hall, before turning onto the quai du Notre-Dame, then onto the bridge crossing over the Seine onto the Île St.-Louis. The flying buttresses of Notre-Dame rose up above the houses to their right and the twin towers of the Bastille castle far away to the left, above the tops of the elegant townhouses lining the quai du Dauphin onto which their coach was now alighting. It stopped at number 30 and the coachman jumped down to open the door for St. John.

Turgot's uniformed manservant showed St. John to his rooms upstairs while the coachman brought up the baggage. The marquis, St. John was told, was out dining with Messieurs Buffon and Lavoisier and was expected back before nightfall. The marquis' honored guest was to make himself at home while awaiting his host's return. In the meantime the honored guest would be pleased to take a hot bath and dine at the marquis' table.

St. John ate quickly and set off to explore the city while there was still light. He returned just as the lamplighters were making their rounds and his host's carriage was pulling up inside the courtyard serving the townhouse. With a drink in one hand and a pipe in the other Turgot gave his guest a tour of the marquis' cabinet of curiosities occupying the second floor of the townhouse. Stuffed birds and preserved mammals and reptiles competed for space with specimens of plants and flowers living and dead along with unusual rocks and minerals.

Turgot described each specimen in loving detail and explained his friend Buffon's system of classifying them as well as his distaste for Linnaeus' competing method, which included insects and was therefore defective *a priori*, for elevating pests to a level of study to which they were not entitled.

"Tomorrow," the marquis informed his guest over supper, "I shall bring you over to Sophie's salon. You will meet Count Buffon; and Lavoisier if he can tear himself away from his chemical experiments. Condorcet the mathematician. Sophie's cousin will be there, Louise d'Epinay and her lover Baron von Grimm. Duke de la Rochefoucauld, perhaps. The duke's another one enamored of the American cause. Unless he's with Count d'Houdetot at the card tables run by the Duke de Chartres, the king's cousin."

St. John pleaded for more time.

"As you wish," Turgot grunted "But do not wait too long. I have already informed the countess about your arrival and she is anxious to see you again. She is very influential in court and can be the key to open many doors for you. In the meantime you can take advantage of my library and complete your treatise on potatoes or whatever else takes your fancy."

St. John spent the next three weeks writing feverishly, venturing out only in the evening. His fashionable suit of purple velvet and lace no longer seemed stiff and uncomfortable. But there was no getting used to the hostile glares of the people in the streets, the peddlers, the poultry-sellers, the *sans-culottes* whose long baggy pants were stained indelibly with the ink, grease, paint or lead of their trades. Even the prostitutes lurking in every other shop-door bore a sardonic look as they lured him with cynical eyes.

He adjusted his attire, opting for the plainer clothes of a country Norman squire which were, even so, in marked contrast to the dirty chemises and ragged dresses of the beggars, wandering laborers, runaway farm boys, pickpockets, police spies. Fist fights erupted on every other corner, attracting throngs of jeering onlookers eager to place bets on the contestants producing out of nowhere an assortment of homemade clubs and small knives.

Side-stepping one such brawl of an evening, he passed by an old church on the fringes of the quarter, built over the former swamp land known as the Marais, gothic tympanum above the portal depicting the suffering of humanity before the Judgment as well as after, a mirror carved of stone reflecting the brutality of the fighting on the street nearby. The church doors were shut tight, bolted and padlocked.

The inflamed eyes of the spectators were focused solely on the combatants, blind to the crucified figure in the tympanum praying for their forgiveness a scant few feet away. A gilded coach rolled by. Its occupant, adorned in the pure white gilded lace of a bishop, fixed his glaring eyes on the ragged crowd in preference to the host of love in the portal above. Apples splattered against the sides of the coach.

St. John skirted the crowd, narrowly avoiding a citizen reasoning with another with the aid of a hammer clenched in an erudite fist, the better to enlighten his fellow. The first knot of street philosophers had by now been reinforced by scores of others eager to expand the debate. They grabbed a passing handcart out of the reluctant hands of its selfish owner and set it on fire, then looked around for other combustible objects to consecrate in the purifying flames of equality. A tall man clothed in the garb of a glazier hoisted himself up onto a barrel and, laughing, shouted out encouragement, pointing out other prizes for the taking to his companions, men and women along with a few boys all rushing to join in the spoils.

The way home being blocked by the swelling crowd of frolickers, St. John elected to detour north, away from the river. He walked up rue du Temple, turning into rue des Francs-Bourgeois. Most of the magnificent *hôtels particuliers* had long ago lost their original lustre, transformed into rooming houses, shops, tenements. He passed by the ancient almshouse which had lent the street its name, then felt his way through a series of alleyways back towards the river, emerging onto rue des Rosiers. In an instant he regretted his decision.

The revelers had overflowed down the street, leaving in their wake more flotsam and jetsam in the form of burning furniture, barrels, hemp sacks, anything they could ignite with their torches. As the flood advanced doors and windows in the buildings just ahead of the deluge could be heard snapping shut, one by one, like rows of dominoes falling in sequence. Peddlers fled by, as fast as their hand-carts would let them run. Stray dogs barked and ran about excitedly.

A celebrant grabbed one and, laughing with his companions, threw the terrified mutt through the window of a *charcuterie*, splintering the panes and shattering the glass all over the display of hanging sausages and hams. Undeterred by the sharp shards eager hands reached in to grab everything edible in site. The bakery next door, the wine shop, and the cheese store were treated to the same respect. The proprietor of the cheese store, tugging on one end of an enormous wheel of goat cheese tucked under the arm of a citizen, was soon chastised for his bourgeois selfishness with a club on the head. The club was then turned against the head of the cheese aficionado to remind him of the importance of sharing with one's brothers. As the two philosophized, the one with the club and the other with the knife, a third philosopher graciously relieved of their burden the debaters who, the cheese forgotten entirely, were totally absorbed in demonstrating to the other their respective Natural Rights.

The human wave washed over a pushcart peddler under a yellow hat. A scream squeezed out of his throat. He was lifted off the ground and held aloft by gleeful hands before tossed around like a sack of potatoes until falling through careless fingers back down to the unforgiving cobblestones almost at St. John's feet. As the peddler's head was pulled back and mouth forced open by one reveler another forced a morsel of ham down the man's throat almost choking him while another urinated over his body to the sound of jeering laughter.

"...and so with this Holy Water we baptize thee in the name of the Father, the Son and the Holy Ghost," the mock priest mocked. Re-buttoning his *braguette,* patting his fly fondly, he bent over his neighbor writhing on the pavement and solemnly drew the sign of the Cross in the air with his short club over the peddler's sodden head, yellow hat stilled firmly pinned to the man's long dark hair; then, with face suddenly contorted, in a snarl of rage gave the man a hard kick to the ribs.

"Get out of our neighborhood, dirty *youpin*. Go back to Saint-Martin where you belong!" he screamed.

As the tormentor raised his club he did a *girouette* like a weather vane then went flying backwards into the arms of his surprised *confrères* before being grabbed again and thrown to the ground, now receiving as he had given at the hands of the Norman country squire who had thrown himself into the mêlée. St. John in turn was grabbed but twisted away and flung himself towards the peddler trying to raise himself off the ground. The snarling crowd surged towards them but suddenly shrank back as a flaming torch was thrust in their faces before arcing back and forth menacingly, forcing the rioters away from their prey. The torch was held by the tall glazier who, laughing as carefree as before, ordered the mob away by the gleam in his eyes and the boldness of his stare, like a lion tamer in a circus.

Walking backwards, not taking his eyes off the confused mob, the glazier gestured with a nod of his head towards an alleyway. "Get yourselves into there. Fast. Move!" he ordered the peddler and St. John.

They walked as quickly as the peddler's bruised ribs would allow and soon emerged on rue Saint-Antoine. Their savior led them past the Church of Saint-Louis then turned down rue Saint-Paul. He stopped in front of a shop with a small but exquisitely ornate storefront of glass framed by a façade made of oak and stained dark walnut, embellished with carvings of the sun, the moon, calipers, chisels, a mallet and a compass. Behind the window were shelves displaying small bottles and glassware of all shapes and colors. The sign hanging overhead announced *Jacques Bongaillard et Compagnie, Verrerie.*

"This is my glass shop. Come in." He led them in the darkness through the display store and into his workshop. He fumbled with his hands on a table, found what he was looking for, and lit it.

In the light of the lamp the peddler looked ghastly.

"I must offer you my deepest gratitude," he murmured in pain through clenched teeth, looking forlornly at Bongaillard.

"My *compagnons* and other brothers sometimes get carried away," the glazier replied breezily. "First thing, let's get rid of that silly hat." He found the pins and removed them, then the offending object.

"I'll need to have it back, you know," the peddler pointed out sadly. "It's the law."

"All in good time, my man. Right now what you need is a bath. My house is across the courtyard. I'll tell my wife to bring out hot water."

He returned and led his guests into the open ground between the shops on one side and the squat houses of their owners on the other, holding the lamp and dragging behind him a foot-tub. He placed it under the mouth of the well pump and bid the peddler to strip off his clothes. "I'll work the pump. You're in no condition."

A plump woman appeared into the light of the lamp lugging a bucket whose contents she dumped wordlessly into the tub, glancing only briefly at the men as though used to seeing disheveled and naked strangers in her courtyard at all hours of the evening.

"My wife and partner," Bongaillard explained "Marie-Élisabeth. She runs the glassware business and I take care of the workshop." He slapped his wife affectionately on her rump. "Bring us a bite of supper. And with it the old pants and blouse Jeannot left behind." She merged back into the darkness without a word.

"Ah yes. A faithful partner. That's what every man needs in life." The glazier chuckled. He handed the peddler squatting in the tub a square of greasy soap. "Best decision I ever made, marrying Marie. Second best decision, leaving my father to set up my own shop. With a little help from Marie's dowry, of course."

A hand emerged from the circle of dark clutching some clothing. Bongaillard took it. The hand disappeared.

"I don't need any father to tell me how to live my life. Or anyone else. I'll do as I please."

He handed the clothes to the shivering peddler. "Here. Come meet us in the shop when you're dressed."

Over the cold supper he shared with St. John in the lamplight – the peddler steadfastly refusing to take anything except a glass of hot water - Bongaillard gleefully recounted for them every detail of his seven years on the road as a *compagnon*, a journeyman glazier, then his return to Paris and brief stint under his father.

"And now I'm my own boss. I make the rules and do as I wish. Of course, the guild has rules, but they're reasonable and for our members' own good, and so I adopt them as my own, as if I made them. What do you do in life, my friend?" This to St. John.

Learning his guest had a farm in America, and had just had a book published, he poured out another drink, and the two glasses of wine and one of hot water clinked together in a solemn toast to liberty.

"Freedom. Freedom from laws imposed by the wealthy onto the poor. Freedom from the tyranny and rules of religion. Freedom to use reason as our guiding light."

The peddler sipped his water, regarding Bongaillard in a quiet contemplation.

"And, not least of all, freedom to have a fun life," Bongaillard exclaimed with a laugh. "And what fun it's been! All at the altar of Cupid, if not Bacchus.

"You know," he confided with a wink and a nod," I lost count how many young farm girls I deflowered. Right behind the backs of their naïve fathers, too! Serving girls, shop girls. A few pretended to resist, but they were only trying to increase my ardor. Why, in a village just outside of Toulouse where my *compagnons* and I worked a while, I succeeded in knocking up four girls. I won the contest, hands down. Of course, when the ungrateful maidens starting crying and implying that marriage would be in order, we knew it was time to take our leave.

"But best of all was the convent we worked on in Lyon. A lot of broken stained glass to repair. We busted a fair number of nuns, as well. You'd be surprised what lies beneath that pious look."

Bongaillard snorted. "Hypocrites, all of them! Priests, monks, nuns, bishops. Going around with their saintly airs, lecturing people on what's allowed, what's not allowed, while they themselves lord it over the rest of us. We're just as good as them! We're better than them, since we don't pretend we're superior to anybody."

Marie-Élisabeth came quietly into the shop to remove the tray of plates.

"More wine!" Bongaillard ordered. He was in a jovial mood. He pinched then slapped the backside of his wife, who departed in silence.

"Of course," he continued, "the fun doesn't have to stop just because you're married. I suppose you know that very well, my brother."

The peddler gazed at the glazier in thoughtful silence.

"You know, when the 'better sort' look upon me in the street, or at work on some church or rich man's estate, they're thinking to themselves, 'ah, poor ignorant fellow, has to work with his hands to scrape up enough to eat each day.' Little do they know! I can read, I can write, I can cipher just as well as they. "

He leaned back, still smiling. "Such blind, proud people. Blind to their own pride and conceit. Not only are all people born equal, women as well as men, with the same natural rights to flourish, to prosper, to enjoy life; but we are all born naturally good as well. Rousseau has proven this. It is the church and the nobility that destroy the natural goodness in people. It is the institutions of the wealthy nobles, the bankers, the church that poison people's spirits. Get rid of them, and the natural goodness of the human heart will flourish. We don't need any Bible or God to tell us what to do. We can figure it all out for ourselves."

The peddler pushed back his chair and arose, with a little difficulty. He found the yellow hat and the pins. He secured the headware to his hair, calmly, almost meticulously.

"I must go now. It is long past the curfew for Jews and I have a long way back to Saint-Martin. I cannot thank you enough. I will return your kind lending of your clothes when I can."

"Keep them, brother. They're no use to me. My apprentice, Jeannot, left them behind when he ran away. Ungrateful scoundrel. Breaking his pledge, and along with it the rules of his apprenticeship. Some people know no shame. I'll whip him to the bone if I ever catch him. The law allows it, you know."

"I, too, must take my leave," St. John said. "Perhaps someday we will meet again."

335

"You know where to find me. If you ever need new windows or fine bottleware." Bongaillard grinned.

"Or an introduction to other free-thinkers who worship at the altar of truth."

Chapter Four: *Rose Water, Garlic and a Scent of Lebanon*

The Marquis Turgot held up his right arm, commanding his party to stop.

"Not yet. I will tell you when the exact moment has arrived."

In his left hand he was holding his Swiss pocket-clock. He was scrutinizing the time-piece as though mesmerized.

"Three minutes still to go."

An audible sigh escaped from the heavily rouged lips of his sister. She shifted uncomfortably on her beslipper'd feet, hidden underneath her enormous red and white striped hooped skirts, the *pannier* sculpted in the form of a bell whose narrow neck was pulled impossibly tight around the duchess' waist, making the act of breathing a challenge.

"Really, dear brother, at the very least we can sit down in the coach and wait."

She took a deep breath. As she inhaled, the movement of her diaphragm caused a sparkling band of diamond-encrusted stars, thirteen in all, to emerge in a field of blue silk from the taffeta folds below her waist and rest atop the red and white stripes of her skirts. As she exhaled the stars disappeared, whisked back into the recesses of her pannier by a hidden mechanical device. With each breath, the three-masted warship sailing atop the crest of her curled and scaffolded coiffure gently tossed and swayed as though riding the waves. Above the main mast fluttered a miniature red, white and blue flag, and on the sides of the bow was inscribed *U.S. Liberty*.

"Two minutes left." Turgot was without pity. The only extra accouterment he had adorned for the occasion was a small flag with red and white stripes behind a circle of blue with white stars in the middle, pinned onto his tri-corn hat, its twin affixed to his coat lapel.

"In everything, precision must rule. The slightest variation can distort the data and thus the result."

"My dear Turgot, there is nothing more imprecise than Paris traffic and therefore all your attention to exactitude will be of no avail should we encounter a street blocked by a dead mule or rioting apprentices." Despite his comment Count Buffon was also studying his own time-piece.

"Nonetheless," replied Turgot, "there must be a rational basis for all our actions, and the law of averages will, in the long run, always prevail. Since we cannot measure in advance the effect on our timing of a random event, the logical mind will rely on the average as proven by empirical observation and experience. And my own observations show that on average it takes my coach forty-three minutes to reach the d'Houdetot *hôtel,* at this time of the day. One minute left."

"Our clocks are not in agreement. Mine shows...ah, there it is. Now there is one minute left. So we see that, if our instruments are not accurate, the results are not reliable."

"Time's up! Sister dear, you shall enter first. I have allowed an extra three minutes for you to install yourself in your seat. Coachman, the doors."

Despite the six-foot height of the entrance the Duchess de Beauvilliers had to carefully bend at the waist to an almost forty-degree angle to make sure her liberty boat would not shipwreck itself against the top of the doorframe. Fortunately the duchess' seat was directly beneath the open square of the trap door in the roof, whose cover had been slid forward. The liberty ship popped up above the roof of the coach, bowsprit proudly pointing the way forward.

Despite Buffon's fears they did not encounter any dead animals or tumultuous *sans culottes*. They arrived at the d'Houdetot townhouse just as the December sun was setting. They had to wait on the street as an enormous coach lumbered its careful way out of the courtyard through the arched passageway. The royal coat of arms of the Orléans branch of the Bourbons was emblazoned on its doors.

"This is not good. Not good at all." Turgot was shaking his head. "Thirty-nine minutes! How do we explain this aberration? Now we must wait four minutes."

"Upon my soul, Turgot, let's just go in now!" Buffon exclaimed. The duchess nodded her head, too vigorously, causing the liberty ship to almost capsize.

"It would not do to walk in right on the heels of the Duke de Chartres," Turgot replied. "He has fooled us all, coming so early. No doubt he has a night at the theatre or another amorous escapade lined up."

"He wouldn't care. Not him. He prides himself on breaking rules."

"Nonetheless." Turgot was firm. "I told la Comtesse the precise time of our arrival to provide her a fixed point of reference to rely on. It is hard enough to plan for protocol when guests just pop up whenever they please."

St. John took advantage of the lull to pull out the letter he had received from Sophie and post-script by her husband the count. He read it again to refresh his recollection of the personalities he would be encountering, carefully enumerated and described for him by his hostess in her flowery, perfect handwriting. Her husband's blunt words were to the point, his careless masculine hand evoking fox hunts and games of whist over whiskey and pipes.

"I don't care for these *réceptions* and *salons à potins* and *soirées mondaines* where one hears nothing but fancy talk and gossip and witty platitudes and philosophical theories," he complained. "I'd rather spend my time more profitably with my old comrades in arms at the club rue de l'Université discussing military strategy over an honest game of cards. I am eternally in your debt, my dear, for having accepted our modest invitation, for your attendance exonerates my own, thus liberating me to follow nobler pursuits. I beg of you, my dear, under no circumstances are you to stand me up for if you were to fail to appear I would die of boredom. So you see, my life is in your hands. But a word of kind advice: take care you do not yourself become a *savant* like them. We already have far too many intellectuals for the good of the world...."

The sounds of animated voices greeted them as the footman led them to the open doors of the salon. Françoise-Hélène Étienne Turgot, la Duchesse de Beauvilliers was the first of the Turgot party to enter, pushed from behind by the hands of her brother. Because of her hoops she had to go through the doorway sideways, taking tiny mincing steps on the balls of her feet like a ballerina while at the same time bending her knees, ducking beneath the United States flag spanning the width of the doorframe in order to bring her ship safely into port. Having navigated her way past the hazard of the doorway, she popped into the room, stars and stripes flashing and *U.S. Liberty* bobbing triumphantly at anchor on her head.

"*Ah...ma foi...mais c'est formidable!*" More exclamations of admiration and delight.

The duchess beamed beneath the rouge and wax caking her face, taking care to not smile too much lest the paint crack. The small silver and gold stars glued across her right check glittered. From amidst the feminine firmament in the middle of the room, from which arose a forest of towering headdresses sprouting three to four feet high from the heads beneath them, Sophie emerged. Draped in a pink and yellow chiffon dress with a simple cameo on her bosom, she glided over to the duchess, long wavy dark hair streaked with grey, allowed free reign to fall down her back below her waist.

"My sweet Tini. The Muses have surely made you their captive. Such inspiration! And so you make us your captive with your stunning presence." Countess d'Houdetot's smile was radiant. With effort she managed to reach out and hold her guest's hands in her own, the ducal hoops preventing any closer contact or embrace. Benjamin Franklin smiled serenely at the duchess from the cameo nestled happily in the ample bosom of the countess.

"Mimi...how gracious you are. So...natural."

The hostess led the duchess by the hand clockwise around the salon to present her first to the duke then the other guests already present while her lover Saint-Lambert launched into orbit Turgot, Buffon and St. John counterclockwise. More guests arrived. Sophie effortlessly appeared at the doorway to greet each while at the same time carefully herding them around the clock-face to assure that all introductions and salutations were properly performed *de rigueur.*

If the entrance to the gilded room was twelve noon then le Duc de Chartres was two o'clock. Having just been introduced to the Marquis de Condorcet at five o'clock explaining why differential calculus proves the stability of the solar system, St. John was rescued by his hostess in violation of her own planetary laws and whisked away to meet the duke.

The king's cousin, tall and fleshy, wore a dark-blue military uniform with burgundy sash around the waist, royal blue sash at a slant across the chest, and burgundy boots up to the knees. He was chatting with a shorter man in a white bob-wig while puffing on a cigar between sentences, casually flicking off the ashes onto the floor with a ringed finger. With perfect timing the countess slipped into their conversation.

"Your Royal Highness. Monsieur Necker. I am so pleased to present a dear friend and cousin of my husband's family,"

Sophie d'Houdetot began, her right arm draped casually around St. John's shoulders and her left hand holding his. "Sieur Saint-Jean, Michel-Guillaume. And, he is an American, no less! Whose father is the Baron de Crèvecoeur, the retired magistrate near Caen.

"Our dear cousin Michael has just published a book in London, about America. Michael, please behold our sweet friend Louis-Philippe-Joseph d'Orléans, Duc de Chartres, an ardent crusader for liberty and equality and reason."

La Comtesse tapped St. John lightly on his shoulder, her prearranged signal for him to bow. Before he could the duke had transferred his cigar to his left hand and reached out enthusiastically with his right. He shook St. John's hand, English style.

"A book about America!" the duke exclaimed in English. Sophie smiled with pleasure at the duke's reaction. "Your timing could not have been better. I should be delighted to read it. As will, I am sure, our friend Mr. Necker," the duke's words taking on briefly a sardonic overtone, "taking into consideration the Royal Treasury's considerable investment in the American cause."

Necker, unperturbed, inclined his head slightly towards St. John.

"You can't read the book quite yet," Turgot informed the duke. "The royal censors must first approve it."

"Pinheads, all of them," the duke was dismissive. "They even insist on censoring cook-books. No need for *me* to wait. I'll get my copy from my English friends.

"But this is indeed a happy occasion, for France and for America," the duke continued, lapsing into French. "No sooner do we learn that Admiral DeGrasse, thanks to Count Bougainville's heroic tactics, has driven away the English fleet from the Chesapeake, we find out last week that the result is nothing less than the surrender of General Cornwallis and his entire British Army to Rochambeau and Washington! And best of all," the duke paused to take a happy puff from his cigar, "I win my wager with the Prince of Wales."

"I would advise against selling the lion's pelt before having killed it," Necker put in a little lugubriously. "The lion still has its teeth even if a paw is gone. The bankers in London and Amsterdam and Zurich are hedging their bets. I see little chance of France being paid back her loans to America unless a treaty is signed and America proves she can govern herself."

"Which is," Turgot smiled sardonically," precisely why the king and Count Vergennes were delighted to accept your resignation. The king's ministers do not want to hear the truth. Especially from a foreigner, and a Protestant to-boot. As finance minister, you were a thorn in Vergennes' side. As was my brother before you."

Necker shrugged. "Your brother and I agreed at least that unless the government reduces spending and cuts the huge royal debt, and taxes the nobility and clergy, we will never have a balanced budget. Or enough food for the people."

"Then the government must also stop controlling the price of bread. It discourages production and thus results in shortages," Turgot rejoined.

"Sometimes economic truth must yield to political reality. If the price of grain and bread should be allowed to fluctuate, in times of famine the people will starve and they will imagine all kinds of conspiracies. And the scapegoats will be the bankers and the royal councilors. And so we go full circle. For the government to be able to afford to subsidize bread the Royal Treasury must cut spending and broaden the tax base. And bring down the royal debt. "

"Nonetheless," cut in the duke, whose own gambling debts were astronomical, "the war in America is drawing to a close. All my English friends, even the Prince of Wales himself, are telling me the same thing. England has lost. The tide has finally turned in Parliament. And the king's ship has to go where the tide goes. What I want to know is, once Parliament lets Lord North begin treaty negotiations, what effect will that have on our own war with England? And not least of all, where do I invest to profit the most from American independence?"

"Vergennes doesn't want the Americans to negotiate a separate peace with England," Turgot reminded them. "He wants France to come away with a few choice prizes for our trouble."

Necker casually blew out a ring of smoke. "If Vergennes thinks he can outsmart Franklin, he is jousting with windmills."

"I offered Franklin my coach so he could come here this evening," the duke sniffed. "But he declined. We rarely see him anymore at the Lodge, even though he's been elected our Grand

Master. He is happiest spending his time with his grandson Temple or Madame Helvétius."

"And what, may I ask, of your projects for the Palais-Royal?" Sophie asked. "You plan on building a new theatre, I hear. And shops. Cafés. A public garden. A casino."

A fleeting look of disdain roiled across the ducal brow before subsiding into a smile. "It took longer than I would have wished to obtain the king's permission. Not to mention my father's. But now the plans are being drawn up. There will also be a marketplace, and a distillery. The park and everything else will be open to everyone, including the common people.

"The park though, will not compare to your Royal Gardens, my friend." This to Buffon. "By the way, congratulations on your son's engagement. I am sure they will make a good match. How old is the *demoiselle*?" The duke's eyes gleamed.

"Young enough. Marguerite-Françoise is her name. Her father is the Marquis de Cepoy."

"Yes. I know."

"My son is away on duty at Martinique and so it will be a rather long engagement."

"You must be sure to introduce me to the lucky young lady."

At that moment new gasps of admiration announced the arrival of another guest. She was attired in a lacy white dress reminiscent of a spring snow shower, her brassy curly hair falling freely upon bare shoulders. She was wearing a straw hat with rakish curl to the brim, complementing perfectly the perfect oval of her face and her large hazel eyes. Even before la Comtesse could announce her name, the duke had beaten her to the doorway.

"Certainly has an eye for the ladies," Turgot remarked gleefully. Buffon looked uncomfortable.

"Who is she?" St. John asked.

"Madame Vigée-LeBrun," Turgot furnished the answer. "Louise-Élisabeth Vigée-LeBrun. If you attend the next salon you will no doubt see a few of her remarkable portraits. Such colors! Such bold uninhibited brushwork! There is a refreshing freedom about her art. She has become the favorite of the queen. Not to mention the duke. Her father's house was on rue Saint-Honoré, a stone's throw away from the duke's apartments in the Palais-Royal. She and her husband now reside rue de Cléry."

"But," Buffon added, "since it is the duke's own wife Louise-Marie who is the patron and champion of Mme. Vigée-LeBrun, and given that the queen can't stand the duke, our young artist knows very well exactly where to draw the lines. And the right perspective to take. All to the duke's chagrin."

Turgot was looking with amusement at his protégé's face. "How long has it been, your living with us in Paris? Three months? You remind me of your compatriot John Adams, now in Holland, when he was introduced to the rarefied air of our Paris society. Franklin, on the other hand, fits right in, being himself something of a libertine. His grandson Temple is the living proof. As is Madame Helvétius. To the dismay of his fellow ambassador Adams," Turgot chuckled.

"Indeed," he continued, "I would say that in order for one to be accepted in society it is desirable, nay, absolutely mandatory that one have at least one lover if not several. Exceptions can be permitted for mathematical geniuses or scientific prodigies. Their eccentricities only add to their charm, and therefore they can be excused from the rules. But if you wish to succeed as an author, playwright, artist or philosopher you would be well advised to take a lover, preferably a well-connected one in whatever circle you wish to orbit around."

"There there Turgot, you have missed your mark. You are giving our friend the wrong impression. Unless you have been leading a secret double existence, you yourself have not any lover, nor do I."

"I note your use of the present tense. In the present you and I are simply too old. Anyway, you, Buffon, can have no moral inhibitions whatsoever on the subject, your wife having died twelve years ago. You are perfectly free to do as you please."

"And I am pleased to indulge my interests in natural history and the calculus. And, like our dear departed Voltaire, in debunking superstition and false thinking wherever I find it."

Louise d'Épinay, Sophie d'Houdetot's cousin and seasoned *salonnière* herself, had joined the circle and was listening with amused interest.

"As long as you are not too indiscrete in expressing your views," Turgot observed, giving a smile to d'Épinay. "You can't risk, my dear Buffon, a second condemnation by the Sorbonne. Not if you value your pension."

"My friend, I am too old to worry about the theologians any more. They can have my body, but Reason has my soul. How can any intelligent person believe it all started with Adam and Eve? Talking serpents? The dead rising from the tomb? We should only believe what we can see."

"Suppose a man is blind?" Louise d'Épinay smiled.

"I meant figuratively, not literally. What we can perceive, measure, and test."

"Therefore what we cannot perceive, measure and test does not exist?"

"I mean to say that a rational mind cannot accept a supernatural object as a truth."

"Does an object's existence depend on its acceptance by rational minds? What do we do if some but not all rational minds accept it? If I, for example, accept it but you do not, which of us is the irrational one? And who decides? Another mind which may, or may not be, rational?" D'Épinay's eyes were shining.

"What then are we to do about love?" she asked. "Or anger? Kindness or cruelty? Goodness or evil? If there exists no independent basis for these phenomena, then it must mean they exist only in the individual's mind and nowhere else except perhaps in the minds of others who think the same way. And therefore we are free to be as cruel as we want and no one has any moral right to tell us otherwise, since objective morality cannot exist, there being no God of Goodness.

"And yet it seems to me," she smiled, that every human being longs to do 'good' even if many do the opposite."

It was Turgot's turn to smile, not without a hint of sarcasm. "And so we see that people do indeed rise from the grave. Is it not Rousseau himself that I just heard from your lips?"

"Poor Jean-Jacques!" Sophie, having rejoined them, exclaimed. "Such a lonely, tormented soul was he. He never understood why I could never accept him as a lover despite all my efforts to illuminate his thinking. His exalting womanhood to the point of placing us all on a pedestal as though we are unthinking objects of beauty and virtue and nothing more can never be my definition of equality with men. It is not women's task to raise men to a higher level of virtue and I am sure I do not wish to take on this added burden."

"And so," Turgot smiled mischievously, "like water, women should be free to take the easiest route: lower themselves to the level of men. If men are free to smoke, drink, swindle and swear so too are women."

"But do you not see the injustice in holding women to a different standard than men?" Louise d'Epinay rejoined. "If men are base and mean, then so too are women. If men are capable of intellectual brilliance and genius, then so too are women.

"Here is where our poor Rousseau hit the mark. The answer to inequality and oppression is education. Education for all children, from the earliest age possible. Education gives birth to reading and reflection, which in turn refines human intelligence and thinking, leading ultimately to enlightenment. In the light of intelligent thought the natural good in people will grow. Education is the path to liberation."

"Provided," Buffon cautioned, "that people are educated correctly. Based purely on reason and logic. Free from sentimentality and emotion and dogma. And above all else, religious superstition."

Baron von Grimm, d'Épinay's lover, had joined the group. "Liberation is all well and good; but then what? At liberty to do...what, exactly?"

"To think. Rational thinking is everything," Buffon sniffed, reaching for his snuff box.

"But then," Louise d'Épinay rejoined, "applying your formula there would be no place for poetry, or theatre, or music, or literature, or virtue or even love. All the things that make life worth living. The things of the heart."

"Well," Buffon conceded, grumbling, "I suppose you do have to have those subjects. As long as there is no mention of God or the Bible. After all, we don't want to indoctrinate young, malleable minds with foolish ideas. The goal of education is to be completely free from indoctrination in order to grow up with an open mind. Only with an open mind are we able to perceive truth, protected from the fog of superstition and ignorance and conceit.

"Do you know that in America there are no schools? Excepting a few colleges for older children, educated abroad as youngsters, of course. And so we see the unfortunate result: unbridled religious belief. It dictates everything they do. Such a cruel, unforgiving tyrant is their religion! It deceives them into false thinking. Americans even believe that God has blessed them in their struggle for independence. We need only recall their ambassador Mr. Adams just before he was sent to Holland. Such a narrow-minded Puritan!"

"I recall Mr. Adams as an intelligent, happy man." Baron von Grimm smiled.

"Intelligent, yes. Happy, true enough. I find that kind of child-like happiness most irritating. But his religious belief only proves his ignorance.

"The proof of their ignorance abounds. At the Royal Gardens I am bombarded by the bombastic letters of their pseudo-philosophers claiming the most absurd things. All sorts of fantastic animals somehow unknown to enlightened minds in Europe. Deer-like animals six feet tall at the shoulder! Bears standing nine feet tall! Every intelligent man knows that large mammals do not exist in North America and South America and never have.

"This is a fact which I have proven in my Law of Degeneration. Since it is a fact that all animal life originated in Africa, and that all the large mammals are found only there (surely the elephants of India were later introductions by men) and that the farther away from Africa one goes the smaller become the mammals, why then, it is obvious that only the smallest of mammals can exist in the Americas.

"My Law of Degeneration applies with equal force to the native Indian peoples in America. As they are far removed from the place of the origin of mankind they are a degenerate race. It is a fact that Indian men have small sexual organs and little appetite for sexual relations. That is why their women have had to concoct all sorts of bizarre superstitious rituals to entice their men to mate, in order to allow their race to survive. It is for that reason their birth-rate is so low and their numbers are dwindling."

"Well," Necker said gloomily," the same cannot be said about our Parisian natives. Do you realize that last year there were 6,000 illegitimate births within the old city alone; and I am counting only the ones that were found abandoned on the church steps and registered so the true number is surely higher. One-half of all births every year, out of wedlock. Our orphanage houses are bursting. So is our budget to feed them. From a balance sheet point of view those who create these future thinkers should be obliged to pay for them. But short of force, and the means to know who they are, this is impossible."

"If you don't mind my asking, Count Buffon," Louise d'Épinay asked, "why do you get so perturbed at seeing Christians like Adams so happy?"

"Because, my dear lady, they're fools. And I can't abide fools."

"Why are they fools?"

"Because they waste their time in superstitious nonsense. Religious ecstasy and the like kind of emotions distort the logic process. They hinder intellectual progress."

D'Épinay's eyes twinkled. "Thomas Aquinas? René Descartes? Mr. Adams helped draft the Declaration of Independence and is an expert on Cato and Montesquieu and Locke and the English Magna Carta. Is Mr. Adams intellectually hindered?"

"They are exceptions to the rule. "

"How so?"

"Well, take for example our Catholic Church and the extreme fringes it leads to: the Jesuits. I should know, since I myself was educated at a Jesuit college. How I hated that Jesuit father who taught us Greek. He reeked of garlic and rose water. Why were they expelled from France? Not because of garlic and rose water, but because they were narrow-minded, preaching that all intellectual inquiry had to be done through the lens of the Bible which dictates the conclusions we must reach."

"Where in the Bible does it say that?"

"It doesn't but that's what they preached."

"Do you disagree with Linnaeus' system of classifying animals?"

"You know I do. His grouping of animals into 'families' and 'orders' is absurd. It is arbitrary and therefore false."

"Therefore different kinds of animals cannot be related to each other?"

"Not that, but there is an underlying truth which Linnaeus misinterprets."

"Therefore a person's erroneous understanding of a fact does not prove that the fact itself is erroneous?"

"That is correct."

"Therefore a person's erroneous understanding of the Bible does not prove that the Bible is false?"

Buffon frowned. "In and of itself, no; but one needs only to read it for one's self to prove it is false."

"How so?"

"God created the world in seven days? A sample of all the animals in the world could fit in Noah's ark? Jonas could survive three days in the belly of a big fish?"

"Where in the Bible does it say we must interpret those words literally as opposed to metaphorically?"

"It doesn't."

"So why do you?"

"Because that is the accepted interpretation."

"What is more important, the words themselves or the message behind the words?"

"The message, of course."

"Can messages be conveyed through metaphor and allegory?"

"Of course, and very powerfully as well."

"Why do you choose to base your opinion of the Old Testament upon a literal rather than metaphorical interpretation?"

"Because that is what they all preach."

"And what they preach is false?"

"Yes."

D'Épinay's eyes crinkled. "Therefore you accept a false interpretation of the Bible as the true interpretation of the Bible?"

"Madame, I choose to not accept the Bible at all. It is a fairy-tale. I pay it no mind whatsoever. To me it is as inconsequential as a flea." Buffon took another pinch of snuff, sniffed, and sneezed into his sleeve.

"Then why does it make you upset at seeing Christians like Adams so happy?"

"I am not upset!"

"Pardon but you look angry."

"I am not angry! You misinterpret my expression. It is due to the tobacco. No, I am merely...dismayed, disgusted at seeing such people so... so foolishly happy all the time. As if they know the truth, and I don't! The only true path to happiness is through intellectual progress. Scientific progress. If only you and I, Madame, could live long enough to see the wonderful new world of happiness and peace that science will bring future generations to come."

"Mr. St. John. I would like to introduce you to someone." La Comtesse had slipped her arm under her guest's and now waltzed him away to the other side of the salon.

"Liza dearest. I am so delighted to have you meet our genial American friend. He owns a plantation in New York. He has just written a book about America. Michael St. John, Louise-Élizabeth Vigée-LeBrun."

St. John inclined his head and accepted the artist's soft, slender hand emerging from soft white lace, kissing it. A subtle musky perfume like the scent of Lebanon suggesting wildflowers but promising something deeper, mysterious. As he held her hand in his he looked into the doves of her eyes. Her irises were not so much hazel as green, sparkling with shades of light amber. The smooth light oval of her face bore only a suggestion of artistic embellishment, there being no need for it. The few discreet freckles on her cheeks floated on her delicate skin as naturally as creamy orange poppies in a field of lilies. Only her strawberry lips wore rouge.

The smile on her lips was mirrored in her eyes. "*Enchantée de vous faire la connaissance*," she murmured, still smiling. "*Racontez-moi un peu de l'Amérique. J'aimerais en savoir plus.*"

St. John, still holding her soft, warm hand, obliged. "America is a beautiful country..." he began, then stopped. He saw reflected in the green of the artist's eyes the verdant fields of young barley rippling in the spring breeze, offset by a dash of amber brown from his grove of chestnut trees. There was a little girl with auburn hair romping through the meadow close by, and as she approached him she was a little girl no more, her buttery yellow bonnet now a smart straw hat....

"Are you feeling all right?" Liza squeezed his hand gently.

St. John blinked and his eyes refocused. "Tomorrow is December 14, isn't it?" he asked as if seeking the answer in her eyes. "She will be eleven years old..." he murmured. "S*es chaussures miraculeuses*...."

Madame Vigée-LeBrun's eyelashes fluttered and she smiled, quizzically.

"You know," he continued, "she once met the Marquis de la Fayette. He whispered something in her ear. She laughed, her little girl's laugh tinkling like a lamb's bell. I wonder what he said to her."

They were walking slowly now, as though strolling along the manicured gardens of the Tuileries. "You asked me about America....It is impossible to capture with words her indescribable beauty. Majestic mountains, lush green valleys, rolling hills, fertile farmland; and then the streams, the rivers, the wild ocean. There are only four or five small cities of any consequence; otherwise the traveler will see only scattered villages and snug, tidy farmhouses with grist mills here and there along the numerous streams that come cascading down from the heights covered in pine trees, hemlock, birch, oak and maple.

"I wish I were an artist like you. Perhaps then could I paint for you the incomparable splendor of a landscape shining in all the vivid red, orange and yellow hues of a New England autumn, contrasted by the steel grey-blue of the ocean pounding passionately against the rocky shores. It can carry your heart away."

"It would seem that she has." The artist's amber-green eyes glowed beneath the delicately curved brim of her *chapeau de paille*. A subtle flourish of pink miniature roses caressed the right side of the crown of her hat, complimented by the restrained exuberance of a single white ostrich plume brushing softly erect against the left side.

"Tell me more." She squeezed his hand in hers. "Tell me more about your life in America."

Observing the artist and the farmer from her command post in the center of the room, Comtesse d'Houdetot was smiling in delight.

"Étienne, *mon cher ami*," she said to Turgot by her side, "I think the seed we have planted might bear fruit. With just the right amount of watering and nurturing. Let us now put our thoughts together and proceed to the next phase of our plan. How do we best arouse the interest of the foreign minister in our American cousin?"

"Let us enlist the aid of Buffon. Trees, I should think, will supply the answer."

"Trees? Do you mean, the things with leaves? As in forests?"

"Trees," Turgot nodded. "To build ships. Naval stores. Vergennes is desperate for a good, steady source of tall, mature hardwoods such as they have in America as well as resinous trees like pine and fir. Our Navy needs them badly. With the English gone from America and the Americans in our debt, why, their market is ours for the asking I would think."

La Comtesse was watching her protégé, still holding hands in a corner of the salon with the artist, while absorbing Turgot's suggestions. She nodded her head.

"Let's do that. You and Buffon work on Vergennes. I and my husband and M. Necker will concentrate on Vergennes' naval minister the Marquis de Castries. He owes my husband the count a favor or two."

Turgot rubbed his hands together. "It is like the snare France set for Cornwallis in Virginia: Rochambeau and Washington approaching from the land, Admiral DeGrasse from the water.

Toc! They converge in perfect harmony at the end-point of the snare. Like trapping eels in a river."

Sophie d'Houdetot watched as Vigée-LeBrun leaned towards St. John, whispering something in his ear.

"Perhaps our garden will not need much tending, after all," the countess remarked. "She looks more radiant than ever. And if you've held her baby – it's hard to believe she's already two years old! – you would see the wonderful effects on both mother and child of breast-feeding. Once again, Rousseau was right."

Sitting warm and snug in her generous bosom, Benjamin Franklin smiled.

Chapter Five: *Baffled by the Truth*

Count d'Houdetot was not a man to waste time. Promptly at two o'clock he returned from the king's fox hunt to find St. John dressed, bewigged, powdered and perfumed, sitting at the count's elegant mahogany writing desk in the middle of the count's elegant gilded library, one of four elegant chambers comprising his apartments in the king's palace at Versailles.

"Capital! The marquis respects punctuality." The count didn't bother to change out of his riding outfit. They walked down endless glittering hallways, the count's booted stride beating the cadence like a metronome, until reaching the far wing of the palace where the naval minister, the Marquis de Castries, had his offices.   D'Houdetot opened the grand door without ceremony and they stepped into a small antechamber where from behind a desk an aide arose.

"Stay put, my son. I know how to navigate the channels here." St. John followed his mentor, sailing into the minister's salon, which the practical and studious Castries used for working rather than socializing. Scribes were scribbling away in a corner while officers came and went through doors leading to other rooms of the minister's complex, the count's own son among them.

The naval minister was poring over a yellowed map spread out over a table near the enormous fireplace where enormous logs were burning briskly despite the blossoming of spring. He looked up; smiled at the count. His glance alighted on St. John, bowing awkwardly in his new suit, a present from the countess, the clothes not fitting quite right. Castries' small, alert eyes and square face gave him an air of no-nonsense efficiency.

"And so, César, you permit me at last to meet the author of that new book on America you've been touting, as well as the cartographer of that old map of New England and Canada I pulled from the king's archives. The map I can read but the book I cannot, my proficiency in English not being at the level I would wish."

"Well, my dear Gabriel," the count remarked, "I, too, must confess I have not, myself, read the book. But I have it on good authority – namely, Sophie – that it is a masterpiece and a treasure of practical information on our infant ally. As for the map –" he gestured toward the table " - that I cannot vouch for. I was not aware of it."

"It was Count Bougainville who brought it to my attention. He mentioned it in correspondence regarding the natural resources of America compared to the South Pacific, after his voyage around the world. He had presented the map to Louis le Bien-Aimé just before the disaster at Québec."

St. John, aware he was undergoing an examination of sorts, tried to stifle his surprise. He had forgotten all about the map.

Castries was regarding him closely. "I would like for you to translate your book into French. But in the meantime why don't you summarize for me what the book says about America. By that I mean her resources, her industries, her markets, the temperament of her people. Here, let us sit down."

He motioned towards a round table and its quartet of elaborate *rococo* chairs looking too dainty to support any true weight. He pushed a lever on his table and as if by magic a servant appeared. "Cognac, *messieurs*? Good. Feel free to indulge your tobacco, César." The count had already pulled out his gold cigar case and presented it first to the marquis, then to St. John before concluding the ritual with a casual snip of his cigar scissors. The servant brought over the small fire-box and opened the lid to allow the men to light their cigars with a pair of elegant silver tongs.

The count and the marquis puffed happily away, as St. John, glad for the excuse to put his cigar down, launched into a description of America's resources, Castries interrupting him frequently with questions.

"And now, what think you about the potential market for our French exports? After all, we would want to sell more than we buy."

"America needs precision tools. Measuring equipment, scientific instruments, machinery. Good writing paper. Fine porcelains. Americans don't yet have the means to make those things. Although they will learn quickly. What's missing is a reliable mail service between our two countries," St. John allowed ruefully. "Merchants need to communicate with each other. France needs a dependable fleet of packet boats to carry correspondence back and forth with America."

"Yes, I know," Castries grimaced. "The peace treaty hasn't even been negotiated yet but already the English merchants are back to plying the waters of their erstwhile enemies."

Count d'Houdetot's elegant, refined face took on an even ruddier glow thanks to the fine cognac. He took a puff on his cigar, eyes gleaming as though contemplating his next move in a game of cards.

"Lord North has resigned and Shelburne is the new secretary of state," he mused. "Rockingham is back as prime minister. And the king won't have anything to do with Fox or the anti-war whigs. To me that means one thing: the war is not over yet. King George is too proud to admit defeat and so he'll have Shelburne, in charge of colonial affairs, push the Americans to agree to their own separate parliament independent from London but owing allegiance still to the king."

"Like Scotland," Castries reflected.

"But," the count continued, "Franklin will never accept that. Not since the time the king and Dartmouth publicly humiliated him in front of Parliament over the Hutchinson letters. Franklin would sooner die than swear allegiance to the king he used to love. He will not agree to anything less than total independence."

"And fishing rights," Castries added. "Or else New England won't go along. But there he had better tread carefully for we want those same fishing grounds. And then there's New York and Virginia's claim to all land west to the Mississippi. Which our Spanish ally wants. And finally, compensation for all the towns the British burned to the ground. Without offset for all the Loyalist property the insurgents condemned."

"And there's the rub," the count exclaimed almost gleefully, putting down his cigar and rubbing his own hands as though cleansing them of the scourge of peace. "The Tories in Parliament have staked their lot with their destitute brethren from the Colonies. They can't back down now. And if the king refuses to sign a peace treaty, I win my wager with the Duc de Chartres."

The count chuckled. "The duke is always careful to hedge his bets. Even if he loses his wager with me, both he and I stand to win a lot more if the war continues. We've been reaping a good return with every shipload of guns and powder Beaumarchais manages to slip into America. The playwright makes more money selling arms than he does from tickets to his theatre-pieces. Which is considerable. The duke has dragged me three times to see *The Barber of Séville*. One more time and I'll turn into an Italian republican."

"Right now King George's council are holding their collective breaths over Gibraltar." Castries pulled thoughtfully on his cigar. "The British attack is imminent. If we and our Spanish partner can hold the island the English will give it up. And then we will be in a position to dictate terms. As long as Franklin doesn't ruin it all by deciding to break his treaty with us and negotiate a separate peace. With the threat of American hostilities gone we lose valuable leverage. As long as the threat is there we have more to gain."

"How can you know what Franklin is proposing to the English?"

"We have our sources" Castries said smugly. "The British aren't the only ones with spies, you know. The American delegation's former secretary was a British agent, unbeknownst to them. But the British didn't realize we were spying on their spy.

"The only ones who aren't spying on the others are the Americans. But Franklin doesn't need to spy. He just speaks the truth of what he is thinking. Hearing the truth is such a novelty to politicians and diplomats that it utterly confounds them. And thus the secret to Franklin's cunning."

The cigars and the cognac came to an end at the same time and with them the discussion. The naval minister went back to his maps and his worries over Gibraltar, while the count and St. John returned to the apartment, there to bathe as for the count before going back to Paris and his club, and there to wait as to St. John for the coach from the Duchess de Beauvau.

It was an hour's ride through the royal forest to the village of Saint-Germain-en-Laye and the duchess' Château du Val. As he had done every Sunday for the past four weeks St. John reviewed the chapter of his book he had translated into French and would read before the duchess' guests. He finished and closed the book.

Moodily he watched the countryside roll by. His pulse quickened as he saw, on a rise in the distance, the Château de Marly surveying the valley below.

The coach passed through the village of Marly-le-Roi disturbing the dominical peace of the chickens and geese and leaving a royal cloud of dust in its wake. The villagers were at mass. The stone chapel with the Sun King's pew was quiet. There were no accusing fingers to point with blame and no accusing eyes to see the fleeting look of shame. The coach rolled on.

The cabriolet with its single white horse was waiting patiently on the road from Paris. The leather hood was lowered. Slender hands graced with soft lace were folded on a lap.

The coach coasted to a stop. The two chestnut horses inched a few more feet forward. One of them extended his neck to nuzzle the muzzle of the white horse. His companion, jealous, nicked his neck. The coachman descended.

The driver of the cabriolet stepped down from his perch in the rear. He drew back the hood and extended a gloved hand. The figure in the flowing snow-white chiffon dress and soft straw hat with rakish brim alighted. Her scarlet lips curved up in a smile and the pearls of her white teeth sparkled. She stepped up into the coach.

With a flick of the wrist the coachman set the chestnut horses in motion. The coach continued on its journey. But not in the direction of the Château du Val. Not quite yet.

Chapter Six: *The Art of Jumping to Conclusions*

"We can only pray." Turgot moped.

"Now, now Étienne. Let us be optimistic. Of course he'll receive us." Countess d'Houtedot was relaxed in her cushions, oblivious to the jostling of their coach. "I know our dear friend is very busy, what with the peace negotiations and his experiments; but he will not refuse old friends."

"But he did not respond to your invitation."

"Well, I am sure there is a good reason for that. He may have misplaced his mail. Or some English spy may have waylaid it, or his grandson overlooked it."

"We can't be sure he'll be at home. He might be over at Lavoisier's laboratory today," Turgot worried. He relaxed into a smile at the thought of the scientist.

"I admit being impressed with Lavoisier's experiment. The evidence is clear as glass. Combustion of an object does not result in the loss of matter. Priestly's phlogiston theory is false."

"Phlogiston, dephlogiscated air, invisible acids flying all around us, inside of us! I have a hard time grasping these notions," Sylvie laughed. "All those new substances they have discovered. The one Lavoisier calls 'hydrogen', and his 'azotes'. And that other one. I forgot his name for it."

"Oxygen," Turgot supplied, taking in a deep breath of the stuff as he spoke. "The mysterious ingredient in the combustion process. When objects burn they do not release phlogiston as Priestly claims, for the simple reason it does not exist. Priestly still won't let go of his pet theory, though. Friend of Franklin or not, he's wrong but cannot accept it, despite the evidence before his eyes. Ergo Lavoisier's repeat of his experiment at the Academy last week, to nail the coffin lid shut."

"But I still don't understand how it should be that his sulfur weighed more after he burned it than before. And why does wood weigh less?"

"Oxygen," Turgot shrugged. "We can't see it but the proof was there before our eyes. Oxygen must be always in the air and the fire makes it attach itself to the sulfur. That is why the sulfur after combustion weighs more than before, not less. When wood burns it gives up what Lavoisier calls 'carbonic acid' causing smoke and making its 'hydrogen' attach itself to the 'oxygen' to form water vapor. The ashes weigh less than the original wood, but the overall weight of all the elements in the experiment remain constant. Or, as he puts it, '*Rien ne se perd, rien ne se crée, mais tout se transforme.*'

"Lavoisier has proven it, thanks to that wonderful measuring machine he has. Without the precise calibration of his special scales no one would have noticed. And so we see the strange twists and turns of serendipity Whoever would have imagined that science could owe such an extraordinary discovery to the collection of government taxes. It was only because the tax collectors didn't want to be cheated that this machine was made, to which we add the fortuitous event of Lavoisier himself being a tax collector, a *fermier général.*"

"As was my own father," the countess remarked. "But the only thing *he* discovered in collecting taxes was universal hatred."

Their coach had followed the cobblestoned Passy Road near to the top of the rise with its view of the River Seine below and Paris beyond and now rambled through the gates of the Hôtel Valentinois. The mansion sat before them, the two wings separated by a courtyard and connected by an atrium of columned archways through which a glimpse of the park and pool beyond could be seen through vines of ivy and grape twisting around the columns.

Slender pointed iron rods punctuated each gable end of the mansion wings. Through the open doors of the carriage house a cabriolet was visible and horses whinnied in the stable.

"Good. He's here," Sophie smiled.

"Unless he's at his neighbors taking a bath."

"Well, no, his cab is in the carriage house."

"Le Veillard would have sent his coach for him. Come to think of it, I wouldn't mind taking a cure in his mineral springs myself."

"Then again," the countess worried, "he could very well be across the road, at the Château de Passy. Count Bougainvilliers and his children are favorites of his. He is trying to set up his grandson with their daughter, after failing with Mme. Brillon's daughter last year. But he and Mme. Brillon still adore each other. Just look at the humorous stories he writes for her! And her love poems to him."

"I would think Mme. Helvétius would be jealous."

"She is too enlightened to be jealous. She accepts that he loves all women and that all women love him."

"He seems to love everybody. You will never hear him say anything unkind about anyone. I daresay he even loves the king of England even while abhorring the monarch's foolish behavior. If George were to drop by and play a game of chess with him, all would be forgiven in an instant."

The coach had come to a stop at the top of the carriage circle next to the main archway in the middle of the atrium. The coachman waited patiently on his bench. Birds chirped cheerily in the linden trees.

"He could be in Paris after all," Sophie began to fret. "The Masonic Lodge is meeting tonight. The Marquis de la Fayette is speaking about the American Declaration of Independence and the Duke de la Rochefoucauld will explain the constitutions of New York and the other states. Since our dear friend helped write the Declaration and asked Rochefoucauld to translate the state constitutions into French, it would not be surprising if he were attending the Lodge tonight. Particularly since he is the Grand Master."

"It's only an honorific title. His stature is magnified that much more by his absence. Between the gout and the peace treaty there's little room left for freemasonry."

"Would that I could have seen him enter the Lodge that day with Voltaire on his arm! What rhapsodic encomium of wisdom and wit I would have heard. Two great lights, only one still with us."

"I heard the two great philosophers were rather embarrassed and at a loss for words. They kissed each other awkwardly and then mumbled some platitude or other. Something about universal brotherhood etc etc. More impressive was the ceremony *after* Voltaire died. They crowned our friend with a halo of laurel in front of Gaudet's painting of Voltaire rising from the tomb to be greeted by Truth and introduced to the souls of Corneille, Racine and Molière."

The countess was looking out the window. "The truth is, nobody seems to be home. And yet his cabriolet is here."

"The truth is evident. He's not at home. No one is here. Not even his servants."

"It *is* strange that his *maître d'hotel*, M. Jacques, hasn't come out," Sophie agreed. "M. Jacques always knows when guests arrive and he always comes out to greet them."

"There, you see. That's our proof. He's not at home."

"I would think," the marquis continued, "we would at least see some signs of life in the Chaumont wing. Chaumont would not have gone back to his château in the Loire at this critical stage of the treaty negotiations. He has too much money of his own at stake. Indeed, if it weren't for Jacques-Donétien Le Ray de Chaumont the Americans would never have procured enough arms to defeat the British.

"He outfitted with his own fortune John Paul Jones' *Bonhomme Richard*," Turgot explained to St. John. "Which he named to honor the author of *Poor Richard's Almanac*."

"I suppose," the countess said, "he might have gone into the city to greet his fellow ambassador and wife. They have just arrived from Spain. Mr. Jay's wife Sarah is with child so it is natural they would not venture out here."

"Unlikely. Even though he is casual with protocol it would not be *de rigueur*."

"I would like to meet Sarah. Her father is governor of New Jersey and her Livingston uncles in New York are judges. Her cousin Robert helped draft the Declaration of Independence. It is said the Livingstons own half of New York."

Turgot, tapping his fingers on the window pane, was only half-listening. "This is throwing our schedule all off! How can I order my day in the midst of this uncertainty of waiting? You know, he might be home after all. Playing with his neighbors' kids."

"Well, he does love young people."

"This might turn out to be the first peace treaty in the history of the world written with the assistance of school children."

Turgot rapped his cane against the frame of the carriage.

"Driver!"

The coachman sprang down from his seat to open the door for his mistress and her party. Turgot marched them into the atrium, turning left towards the south wing. Swallows darted through the air among the ivy and grape leaves on the trellis above, transforming the atrium into an aviary.

They were startled to hear a muffled explosive sound, as though a cannon had gone off, but far away in the distance.

"Perhaps the peace treaty negotiations have blown up," Turgot smirked. "Or else the English have decided to renew their claim to the French throne."

Reaching the grand doorway Turgot pulled down on an ornate lever. From inside could be heard the chiming of bells. In a moment the door swung open and the excited face of a young man beamed at them. Wigless, his sandy brown hair was standing on end, each strand extending upwards as though being pulled by invisible threads, before softly settling back down.

"*Ah, mais c'est vous, Madame la Comtesse. Et Monsieur le Marquis. Et votre ami. Soyez le bienvenu.* "

With that, Temple Franklin invited the party inside.

"We're all in the laboratory. We've been having a splendid time," he chatted cheerily in French as they walked down the hall. "Playing with the electric fire."

They stepped into a dark room, closed blinds allowing only slivers of sunlight to filter through. Long tables supported instruments of all sorts, measuring scales, a Leeuwanhoek magnifying machine, glass vials, organized in a neat and tidy fashion. There was a whiff of smoke in the air and the scent of sulfur as though something had burned.

A group of figures clustered around a table. On the table sat six large glass jars with metallic-looking rods and wires protruding between them, culminating in a sort of wand held by a young pretty lady. Her hand, holding the base of the rod encased in a sleeve of caout-shak, trembled.

"Don't be afraid, Geneviève. Go on," a young companion encouraged her. "It won't hurt you. As long as you don't let it get too close."

Behind her a stout elderly man with long greying brown hair flowing back over the shoulders of his plain brown coat smiled encouragingly. With a steady hand guiding the young lady's he helped her bring the rod to within a few inches of another, larger rod with a pointed tip, rising from a wax-like square on the table. All of a sudden there was flash of intense light followed by a loud clap as though a pistol had been fired at close range.

The young lady sprang back. The elderly man beamed. The spectators applauded.

"Bravo! Well done, my dear Mademoiselle Geneviève, well done. You are an excellent student." The man retook possession of the rod from her trembling hand.

"The electric fluid!" Turgot exclaimed. They moved closer to the table where the faces of the young observers were illuminated by delight and amazement.

"But how, Dr. Franklin, does it work?" This from a tall young man standing next to Temple.

"There is nothing in the world better than electricity to turn a vain man into a humble man," their mentor replied. His French was halting but correct. "I can tell you the *how* of it, but I cannot tell you the *why* of it.

"How it works: we saw that rubbing our glass rod with wool then touching it to the metal ball on top of the jar excites the water inside. Because the iron bodkin is connected by wires to the jars, it too becomes excited and, when brought close to the larger rod, provokes the electric fire.

"I can show you how we can induce it to do this, but I can't explain to you *why* it does it. But, I suppose a man can enjoy eating his roast quail even though he does not know quite why the wood in his oven burns."

"*We* will surely enjoy eating our roast chicken for dinner this afternoon," Temple said, lifting up a large wire cage from which an angry clucking came. He put the cage back down on the table. "Who would like to have the honor of dispatching Jeanne d'Arc to avian heaven? Guillaume?"

Guillaume Le Veillard made a face, shaking his head.

"I'll do it," the tall young companion said.

"Then it's all yours, James. I'll give Joan of Arc her last rites."

Temple handed the caged bird, their expiatory offering and dinner-to-be, to M. Jacques then busied himself with rubbing the woolen cloth on the glass rod before applying it to the jars forming Franklin's *batterie*. Finished, he turned his attention back to the imprisoned martyr to their hunger.

"Chicken. Do you accept God as your one and true Father, and his Son as your one and only Redeemer? Do you repent and ask Him to forgive you for your wicked ways?"

Temple looked gravely into the bird's eyes. The chicken squawked.

"Good," the young dandy said, nodding his head. He raised his right arm over the cage. "By the authority of the Holy See given to me, I pardon you from all your sins and suffering forevermore in the name of the Father, the Son and the Holy Spirit. May you have lasting happiness and peace; and find it in your heart to forgive those who are about to cook and eat you for their dinner."

His young male companions tittered as he made the sign of the Cross, then took the cage from M. Jacques and placed it back on the table, onto a hard wax platform. He nodded at his friend James Le Ray de Chaumont.

James grasped the bodkin by its rubber handle and brought it to the cage. There was a loud popping sound and the halo of electric fire flowed into the metal. The chicken inside stiffened as though being pulled in all directions, the pungent smell of sulfur mingling with the odor of burnt feathers. Temple removed the bodkin from his friend's hand and put it back in its stand.

He, Guillaume and James peered into the cage.

"Yes, I would say Joan is now one with eternity," Temple affirmed with satisfaction.

Geneviève, standing next to her brother Guillaume, was weeping softly. He put an arm around her shoulder.

"There now. It's only a chicken."

M. Jacques, wearing his gloves, took the cage and disappeared into the hall. Franklin came back from the windows where he was opening the blinds. Countess d'Houdetot, smiling, extended her neck. Franklin, smiling, leaned forward and kissed her neck, first on the right, then on the left, and then again on the right.

"Sophie. Happy you have come by. Étienne." Smiling warmly, he nodded his head at Turgot, Franklin's version of bowing. His eyes fell on St. John.

"Dr. Franklin. I am so pleased to introduce you, finally, to our dear cousin from Normandy, now an American although always French in heart. The author of the book we have sent you. Mr. Michael St. John de Crèvecoeur. Michael, Dr. Benjamin Franklin, the Archimedes of the New Age and Minister Plenipotentiary of the new United States of America."

Franklin, again, nodded. He was looking at St. John quizzically. "Have we not exchanged correspondence?" the older man asked, continuing in French.

"Yes, your Excellency. " St. John replied in English. "You were so kind as to assist some American sailors I was sheltering in securing a berth to return to the United States."

"Yes, I recall that. I receive so much correspondence that I find it helpful to have my memory jogged a little." Turning to Sophie and the marquis: "Come. Let us sit on the terrace and enjoy a bit of tea. It is too beautiful a day to dally inside."

He slipped his right arm under the left of the countess who placed her right hand over the philosopher's own. They strolled leisurely down the hallway, Franklin's cane in his left hand, chatting while the others walked ahead and, led by Temple, outside onto the shaded terrace overlooking the park and pool.

They sat down on wrought-iron chairs adorned with a frenzy of elaborate motifs depicting vines and flowers running wild in an orgy of unrestrained exuberance. M. Jacques served them their tea.

"You will be staying for dinner with us, of course," Dr. Franklin stated. "You will meet our new American colleague come to assist in our negotiations with the British. He has been serving as our minister to the Spanish king. The Marquis de la Fayette will be showing him the way to our humble cottage."

"But is he not engaged this evening at the Lodge?" Turgot asked.

"I believe so. But that is not until 8 o'clock. Time a-plenty to return to the city."

M. Jacques, listening tactfully, digested the information, then went over to a long bench with a tall back on which were hung a variety of instruments. He had produced a notebook and pencil.

"Our readings," their host explained to St. John. He spoke in his careful French out of deference to the others. "As I am not certain to be home every day at the same hours he records our data in my place. We also have a sun-dial you might want to take a look at, over yonder." He gestured towards the object near the pool, where his grandson and friends were playing with a large toy sailboat rigged with a set of long wires they were manipulating, like a kite on a string.

"Compiling the raw numbers is the easy part. What to make of them is the challenge. But I wonder, just wonder, if with enough patience and time – would that I had more of that! – we should not eventually be able to see clear patterns in their relationships to one another so that we could predict accurately changes in the weather. What a boon that would be to farmers, mariners, not to mention old philosophers suffering from the rheumatism."

"Speaking of time, we must not overlook the importance of recording precisely the hour and minute of each phenomenon," Turgot declared. "Is that Swiss clock I gave you proving to be accurate?"

"It is, reasonably so. If only you could present to me a clock which can make time stand still, and I would be eternally in your debt."

Franklin paused an instant to measure the impact of his pun before continuing.

"The rapidity with which new discoveries in science pop up every day makes me regret having been born too soon. I should have delayed my entry into this world a wee bit longer. Imagine the new world a thousand years hence which science will have created.

"You observed the killing of the chicken with the electric fire. And so you may also easily imagine the cooking of the chicken with the electric fire, or the heating of the house with electricity, and even artificial light. Although it strikes me that the light produced by electricity is not the exact same phenomenon as the light produced by the sun. Then again, what, exactly, is light?"

"Perhaps," Turgot said, "we should adopt the Hindu religion. That way, we can look forward to being reincarnated at a future date when science will answer these questions for us."

"I think," la Comtesse laughed, "I should prefer *not* knowing. Is not ignorance bliss? The mystery, the wonder, the excitement of not knowing and even the fear of something unfathomable can be so romantic."

"Or tragic," Franklin observed. "As we see with our American Indians. They simply accept strange phenomena, like gunpowder and fire-water, without questioning it, and are thus vulnerable to exploitation.

"But to their credit they do not jump to conclusions. If they speculate at all it is speculation done with an honest acknowledgement of it. I too must remind myself to not mistake speculation or opinion for truth. Science to be true must always, I think, proceed upon actual observations, with the facts carefully collected, and the natural philosopher permitting himself to make no conclusion that goes farther than what those facts will warrant."

"The same then should hold true for human relationships," Sophie observed. "We fashion opinions about people without knowing who they truly are, what they have experienced, or what is in their hearts."

Franklin smiled. "Would that moral science keep pace with natural science, that men would cease to be wolves with one another and that humanity someday live up to its name."

"Benjamin. If men are wolves, then a philosopher or a scientist is simply an intelligent one, a *lupus eruditus*. And far more dangerous, don't you think?"

Sophie had moved from her chair and claimed a spot on Franklin's lap. She stroked his long hair languidly. "And yet, you do not strike me as being wolfish in any way," she continued, laughing. "Nor can I conceive that you have ever been wolf-like."

"Well. Perhaps I am merely a wolf in sheep's clothing."

He put his hand on the chiffoned thigh of the countess. "A wolf sheds his coat once a year; but his disposition, never. I ask myself, are human beings born to be like wolves, violent and selfish, or is wolfishness an acquired trait? Since I cannot see what the facts of the matter are, I will pass on speculating. I would venture, though, the question: in Christian countries, how many people observe Christ's birthday, and how few observe his precepts?"

"It is an inverse proportion," Turgot declared. "Proof enough, therefore, that the holy premise is false."

"Or, on the contrary, evidence of its truth, if we mortals are disposed towards *un*-holiness." Sophie was delighted. "May our dear departed Rousseau forgive me. So we are back to our point of departure: are humans born good, or are they born bad?"

"Here we best let the facts tell us," Franklin said. "Although, we cannot recognize bad without first perceiving the good. Otherwise we have nothing against which to compare it."

"Yet even an infant will spit out vinegar having never tasted sugar," Turgot remarked.

"But," Sophie rejoined, "is sugar good for the infant? Or is it a sweet deceiver?"

M. Jacques had set the table with cloth, silverware and small china along with crystal wine glasses. He uncorked a bottle and held it under Franklin's nose. A nod of the head and a smile signaled the pouring of the wine into the glasses. A young serving girl brought out a dish of dainty pastries and a plate of cheeses.

"Let us now deceive ourselves with something sweet," their host invited. "And take comfort from our ignorance in a fine glass of Bordeaux. Which is, I venture, neither too bitter nor too sweet."

Perceiving the sweets and the wine with innate senses the young men, leading Geneviève by the hand, came running up.

"I say, Granpapà, how about lending me your cane?" Temple helped himself to a tart and a glass of wine and his friends followed suit. "The wind is picking up, and kicking up nice waves on the pond."

Franklin handed the cane to his grandson. "*Amusez-vous bien.*"

Gulping down his pastry and downing his wine, Temple took the cane and hastened back down to the pool, trailed by the others. Franklin, delighted, watched. His grandson, disciples on either flank, stood at the lip of the pool. He straightened up tall, like an orchestra conductor and waved the cane like a large baton over the wind-whipped water, chanting solemnly in the process. He unscrewed the crook of the cane and removed something from within. He again waved the cane majestically over the pond, then flung his other arm outwards, releasing a liquid over and onto the water. In an instant the surface of the pond went from waves to a flat calm despite the wind.

His friends broke into applause and cheers, even though they had witnessed the trick before.

"Now let's see you walk on it," James' voice could be heard.

"Remarkable, that discovery of yours," Turgot exclaimed. "Who would think that such a small quantity of oil could tame such a large surface, and so quickly. How do we explain this?"

"I cannot explain it for a certainty, this smoothing of the water, although I have my ideas. Here again, we can appreciate the consequences even without understanding the *why*. I still don't have any practical uses for it, and so it remains for the time being simply an amusing divertissement. Which is why I enjoy carrying a bit of the oil in my cane.

"When I first sailed to London in 1757 I noticed one of the ships in our convoy left behind a wake that was perfectly smooth, whereas the other ships' wakes were as rough as my ship's own. The next day I observed the same phenomenon, only involving a different ship; and this, immediately after a sailor had dumped a bucket of waste off the ship's stern. I recalled Pliny's story from eons ago, Greek sailors smoothing the angry seas with oil to appease the gods. In England I found myself by a pond on a windy day. I procured a vial of oil, and poured it onto the water. Immediately the surface became smooth as glass. I concluded that the oil, being slick, prevented the wind from grabbing hold of the water and lifting it up, thus letting it lie flat. How the oil could spread itself so thinly and so quickly, I do not know.

"It occurred to me this might be a useful device for sailors or fishermen struggling to come into port in heavy seas. But, the winds and currents are simply too strong. The ocean currents follow their own laws. As every mariner knows."

"Those currents," Turgot remarked, "are of considerable interest to the Marquis de Castries. As well as to our friend here, Mr. St. John, who is charged by our naval minister to establish a packet-boat service with America. I would venture you are the ideal teacher on this subject, from your experience as Deputy Post-Master General for the American Colonies."

"Your project is a welcome one, Mr. St. John. It will kill two birds with one stone: the merchants will profit immediately, and the post office eventually from the revenue. Commerce increases correspondence, and correspondence increases commerce. And so they go on, mutually augmenting the other.

"We found out that four packet-boats a month were not adequate. Accidents and delays due to weather are frequent. I would advise you to suggest five ships to Castries. That is what the English do. As they leave on the first Wednesday of the month, the French ships should leave on the third Wednesday. Such a schedule would benefit both France and England, as well as America, for it will cut in half the waiting time between sailings.

"I have another suggestion to offer you. The packet-boats are not advised to carry cargo but they are suitable for passengers. If you divide their holds into separate apartments after the Chinese manner, and caulk them tight so as to keep out the water, you will see that if a leak should happen in one apartment the others won't be affected, and so the ship will be less subject to sinking. This, if you make it known, will encourage more passengers and thus increase your revenue. It will also encourage travel and thus broaden our knowledge and understanding of other peoples.

"Are you aware of the phenomenon of the current circulating clock-wise around the Atlantic? I call it the Gulf Stream, because it seems to emanate from the Gulf of Mexico. I deduced it from data I collected during my voyages between England and America. This knowledge will be of help to your navigators. I told Captain Jones about it; and the English Captain James Cook when we met before his tragic voyage to the Hawai'i Islands. I will give you a copy of my chart to present to Castries."

"I can't thank you enough, Dr. Franklin," St. John replied. He would have bowed were he standing up. "I will be sure to acknowledge your gracious and wise contribution."

Franklin brushed away the compliment with a wave of the hand. "It is reward enough for me to be able to increase the knowledge and comfort of mankind. Accolades aren't necessary."

"About the book I have written...."

"Book? Book. Oh, yes, of course. Your book. Rest assured I will be delighted to read it."

M. Jacques approached. He was carrying a silver tray over which an elegant silk cloth was draped. On the cloth were two small *cartes de visite* laying side by side. M. Jacques presented the tray to his master, who picked up the two calling cards and glanced at the writing on their face.

M. Jacques cleared his throat. "The Marquis de la Fayette and Mr. John Jay present their compliments."

Chapter Eight: *In Pursuit of Happiness*

The dinner table was laid out in opulent elegance, made more ornate by the contrast with the plain garb of the host. La Fayette was at the seat of honor, Franklin anchoring the other end. The American ambassador from Spain and St. John looked at each other from their middle seats. Hugging Franklin's right arm was Comtesse d'Houdetot; on his left his grandson Temple then Turgot; and filling the chairs in between were his young friends from the neighborhood, augmented by spa-owner Louis-Guillaume Le Veillard and Louis-Donétien Le Ray de Chaumont, Franklin's landlord.

The diners were festive as they finished their roast sacrificial chicken and lamb followed by plates of fine cheese and grapes. The table was not so long as to prevent La Fayette from talking to Franklin and vice-versa.

La Comtesse was playful. "It is rare indeed I can have your lap all to myself. Is not Mme. Helvétius coming?"

"She has, I am afraid, a slight case of the grippe. If she would only sleep with her window open her health would be the better for it."

"Had she only accepted your proposal of marriage her health would have been better, as your open window would then also be hers."

"If only," Turgot intervened, "she had accepted *my* proposal for marriage *my* health would have been the better for it. I am pining away from a broken heart."

"Is it not intriguing how half the population yearns to become married and the other half regrets it!" Sophie laughed.

"That should not surprise us. The recipe to a happy marriage," Franklin said, "is best illustrated by a simple experiment. Take two rough objects, bring them together, and then rub them against each other. What do we observe?"

"Heat?" Temple offered.

"Yes. Caused by?"

"Friction," Geneviève supplied.

"Correct again. What do we do to eliminate the heat?"

"Eliminate the friction."

"How do we eliminate the friction?"

"Move the two objects away from each other."

"By the same token, if standing next to a fire is too hot, what is the remedy?"

"Move farther away," James joined in.

"Lambert has shown that the intensity of light – and by that I infer also heat – diminishes proportional to distance. And so the remedy to friction and hot temperature is to move farther away. If happiness in marriage is inversely proportional to the degree of friction and heat, then we can conclude that distance does, indeed, make for a happy marriage."

"Distance makes the heart grow fonder?" Sophie raised her eyebrows. "If that is so, why does my heart yearn to be closer to you the closer I am to you?" She moved her chair right next to Franklin's and draped an arm around his shoulders.

"Because you have removed one of the premises to our syllogism. We are not married."

The Marquis de la Fayette was observing with amusement the stunned look on the face of the newly arrived American ambassador.

"Perhaps," the marquis said, "we can propose an inverse corollary to Dr. Franklin's law of marriage. If distance makes the married heart grow fonder, then does not time do the opposite? Time makes the married heart grow colder? What do you think, Dr. Franklin?"

"I think," he replied, "that a wise man will stand neither too close nor too far from the fire; but will see that since the flames and hence the heat are never constant but always changing, he too will have to be always changing."

"And so," Sophie concluded, "it is change which brings happiness."

"I would think, my dear," Turgot said, "that it is not so much the change, but the changing. The act in and of itself."

"But does that bring true satisfaction? True happiness?" Jay had regained his composure and decided to join in the fun, his French almost as fluid as Franklin's thanks to his Huguenot descent. "Your supposition is that happiness is not a stable state, but is rather an instable, volatile chimera. A constant searching. A grasping after smoke which dissipates as soon as you close your hand around it. That strikes me as dissatisfaction; and a dissatisfied man cannot be happy."

" 'We hold these truths to be self-evident: that all men are created equal; that they are endowed by their Creator with certain unalienable rights, that among these are life, liberty and the *pursuit of happiness.*' " La Fayette recited in English.

"We take due note," said Turgot, "that the American Declaration does not say that 'happiness' is guaranteed. It is the right to search for it and try to obtain it, if you can."

"And that," Jay observed," is the role of good government. To guarantee the opportunity. Nothing less, and nothing more. It is up to the individual to succeed or fail based on his merit and hard work, without any influence or interference, taking away or giving to, by the government, I would think. It is not good government which deprives people of their opportunity; and it is not good government which lavishes gifts on people, as that renders them lazy and dependent."

"As one of the drafters of the Declaration, Dr. Franklin, how do you define 'happiness'?" This from La Fayette.

Franklin took another sip of his tea. "I would say, a man who has had a good meal does not think about hunger. He might, however, still have a few thoughts for food. Please pass me the dish of candied ginger."

"Happiness," Franklin's neighbor and friend Le Veillard offered, "is found in the joy and comfort of one's family. In a loving home. In the love of God. "

"God does not change," Jay remarked. "If you measure your happiness against your love for God, whose love for you is constant, your happiness will be constant. If you measure your happiness against material success and comfort which are unstable, your happiness will be fleeting. Your happiness depends on what you decide to value."

"But," the countess remarked, "what of the hungry? The poor without homes? The orphans of Paris? The sick and the lame who cannot work and thus cannot feed themselves? Are they happy? *Can* they be happy in such a condition?"

"I can't think of anyone happier than the Apostle Paul," Jay remarked, "and he was in a Roman prison. He defined his happiness based on his relationship with God."

"It seems to me," Turgot interjected, "that the Declaration is a political statement, not a philosophical dissertation. And if God created all men equal, how is it that you Americans permit slavery?"

"For the same reasons the English, French and Spanish permit it in their Caribbean colonies," Jay replied, with a sigh. "And it is abominable....but we excuse it. If it were not profitable we would not see the vast energy expended to try to justify it based on every pretense other than the true reason, which is money."

"Inequality is a fact of life. There will always be those more intelligent than others. Healthier than others. Stronger than others," Turgot rejoined.

"And wiser than others, my dear Étienne," Sophie remarked, "who are not necessarily among the most intelligent, healthiest and strongest. A man can be very intelligent but not wise."

"If you give the *peuple* the power they will abuse it. They will destroy rather than construct. You will be left with chaos."

"Unless," La Fayette said, "you have wise leaders. Honorable leaders. George Washington, for example. And a system of government flexible enough to accommodate dissent without shattering."

"Washington has slaves. Jefferson owns slaves." Turgot was sardonic. "There are plenty of Christians who are slave owners."

"That is true," Jay admitted. "I confess, I am among them. And we are torn by it. As we are all torn by our weaknesses and shortcomings. But that does not mean we do not wish to be rid of the curse. Like a man too taken to drink. He truly wishes to be sober but the temptation overwhelms his will."

"It can't be abolished overnight," La Fayette declared. "That is why we are working, here in France, to create a gradual emancipation of slaves in the colonies so that future generations, not seeing themselves as being deprived of property, can accept a slave-free society."

"You are right, your Excellency," Jay agreed. "It must be gradual, and it must be prospective in order to be accepted. Even so, it is like pushing boulders uphill. I tried to include the abolition of slavery in the New York State constitution but was defeated. We will try again when the moment is ripe, only the next time we will be wiser in our approach."

"A written constitution," Turgot observed, "is not a guarantee of success. Look at your Articles of Confederation. Despite this document the states refuse to cooperate with each other. Your army is near starving because of it. Virginia and New York are fighting over the Ohio territory and New York and New England are fighting over Vermont. I wish your new republic well, but I have my doubts."

"Reasonable men will find a way to solve their problems," Jay shrugged.

La Fayette turned to St. John. "And how goes your little America-Frances? She is well and flourishing, I hope?"

St. John slowly stirred his spoon in the cup of tea M. Jacques poured out before adding a dollop of cream.

"I only wish I knew. I have not had word from my wife or friends despite my letters to them. My son Guillaume-Alexandre at least is here, at school in Caen. And, if I may inquire, how are your own children?"

La Fayette's eyes flickered a moment. "I am sorry to say my first-born daughter Henriette died shortly after I met you in New York, although I only learned much later. But, Anastasie is doing well; and she has a young brother now. He is named George Washington du Motier de la Fayette.

"You are right, Monsieur Le Veillard. There is nothing more delightful than family. Nothing more precious than our children. Don't you agree, Mr. St. John?"

"Yes. Yes, of course." The tea in his cup swirled slowly around. In its eddy *des moutons* had formed, little swirls of cream looking like so many embryonic lambs before vanishing. A figure emerged in their place, looking like a doll without a face.

"To that, your Excellency," Le Veillard said, "I would add one's wife. Have we not taken a solemn oath before God to love for all time this woman who trusts us, depends on us, bears our children whom we love? What do you think, Dr. Franklin?"

"It is the wise man who goes into marriage with his eyes wide open. And who during the marriage keeps them half-shut."

Jay laughed. "I for one am quite *happy* my dear Sarah has come with me. I could not imagine being separated from her. Especially across the huge ocean. Even one week would be too much. I pity our poor friend John Adams, all alone in Holland without his beloved Abigail. I take it, Mr. St. John, your wife is back home in New York?"

"Yes."

"Then you must miss her dearly. It must be difficult for you, not knowing how she is faring."

"I try not to think on it."

"Where is her family? In New York as well?"

"Her brother Samuel is with her, on our farm in Orange County. Might you perhaps know Pastor Tétard? Jean-Pierre Tétard. He performed our marriage."

"I do, although by name only. He is in Philadelphia, working for Robert Livingston, our foreign minister. Do you know Gouverneur Morris or his brother William?"

"I have met Gouverneur, at the Chamber of Commerce. Where, on another occasion, you and I were introduced by William Seton. Around the time of the tea party. I seem to recall, *unhappily*, having enjoyed Samuel Frauncis' syllabub without enough moderation. It seems so long ago."

"A lot has happened," Jay agreed. "For a long time I had hope for a reconciliation with the Mother Country. But there comes a time in every man's life when reconciliation between two opposing principles is no longer possible."

"And so you have war," Turgot remarked.

"Or," Sophie observed, "it is war which made the reconciliation impossible."

"Reconciliation is always possible," Le Veillard said, smiling. "At least, in that realm where the King loves his subjects. It is never too late. Even at death's door."

St. John watched Franklin's neighbor fingering a small oval cameo, suspended on a delicate gold necklace, resting on his left breast. It had been a long time since St. John had seen a *scapulaire*. The crown of thorns had a glow to it, and the eyes an open invitation.

"If *political* reconciliation is not possible," Jay said, "diplomatic reconciliation can be had with England. But only on a footing of equality. The independence of the United States does not depend on recognition of this fact by England. And America – or at least this American – cannot accept independence as though it were a negotiation point. Why should we negotiate over something we already possess?"

"Perhaps," Franklin said to Le Ray de Chaumont, "you would be so kind as to convey for us our note introducing Mr. Jay to Count Vergennes and the king. He will need to come to Versailles to present his credentials."

"Certainly. And Mr. Adams…?"

"Mr. Adams is detained in Holland for the time being. He is intent on obtaining a loan from the Dutch banks. And, lawyer that he is, Mr. Adams would prefer to talk with Mr. Oswald only after the gentleman has been given full powers to treat by his masters in London."

"A view shared as well by *this* lawyer," Jay remarked. "There is no negotiation with a servant of the master. Negotiation presupposes equal status. That is the essence of independence. There is only one master I am dependent upon, and it is not King George."

La Fayette and Jay took their leave, Jay thanking Franklin for his offer to share his lodgings. The countess and Turgot prepared to follow suit, Sophie craning her neck to allow Franklin to kiss it. St. John, dependent upon them, bid *adieu* as well to their host.

"I cannot thank you enough for your kind advice. And thank you as well for sending my letters to my family."

Franklin nodded. His blue eyes were bright behind his glasses.

"I am *happy* to help. You know, there was once a man who loved children. 'Be like they,' he advised, 'for heaven is reserved for them.'"

"Adieu."

Chapter Nine: *The Image in the Mirror*

Turgot's manservant brought it up to his rooms at no. 30 quai du Dauphin, the dainty soft snow-white envelope lounging on the luxurious burgundy satin cloth draped negligently over the silver tray. Closing the door, St. John tore open the envelope and was enveloped in turn by a whispering of Lebanon. He devoured the letter hastily. He put it down on the elegant red damask cloth of the commode. He looked into the mirror.

His cloak was lying on the bed. He grabbed it and put it on, fumbling for the tie-strings. He reached for the bottle of perfume, splashed a few quick drops onto his fingers, rubbed it into his neck. He adjusted his wig, fussed with the powder. He looked again into the mirror.

He barely glanced at the manservant opening the door to the street, ignored the man's parting salutation. The sun, veiled by a delicate curtain of wispy clouds, was sinking behind the church spires to the west. Behind him peeked the moon, eager to reclaim its due.

He did not hail a cab and he did not call a coach. He walked on foot as he preferred to do. As he had done a dozen times over the past dozen weeks. He did not stop to admire the play of the fading light on the river and he did not linger over the beauty of the flowers in the park. Crossing the bridge onto quai Notre-Dame he did not notice the cathedral reigning above the rooftops.

He passed the charcoal-grey conical towers of the Palais de la Cité and the Conciergérie while the Palais du Louvre loomed up ahead. He ignored the beggars stretching out their arms and stepped over the vagabonds sprawled along the way. He turned right onto rue Saint-Denis.

He did not smell the faded stench of blood from the slaughterhouses nearby nor the putrid scent of decay from the prison and morgue in the Grand Châtelet. Gypsies eyed him narrowly. He followed rue Saint-Denis under the gothic archways of the Grand Châtelet and crossed over rue Saint-Honoré. He turned left into rue Mont de Marthe, his feet his guide. They knew le Marché des Halles would soon come into view and, not far from there, on rue de Cléry, her townhouse.

The clopping of horses and rattling of wheels on the cobblestoned street. Elegant white-stocking'd calves passing by and satin-hooped skirts lifted high, thwarting the puddles, staying prim and dry. The lady's shoes were exposed with her platform heels and ballerina toes, refusing to get wet despite the water all about from the early evening shower, her miracle shoes impervious to the perils around her. And on her finger, *l'Agneau de Dieu*.

His own shoes were splattered with mud and the cobblestones were slick and wet. They glistened in the glowing street lamps claiming man-made authority against the fading sun's faltering light. More passers-by, a coach, a cabriolet, Gentlemen and Ladies hurrying to the theatre, to the cafés, to a *rendez-vous gallant,* avoiding the shadowy figures lurking in the doorways or huddled in an alley or jumping forward to clutch at an unwilling arm.

Through the columns and archways of a garden park illuminated by torches he saw people strolling, chatting, stopping a moment to reminisce, to embrace. A man and his wife in plain dress were laughing, talking to their children. A beggar approached and the man put a protective arm around the shoulders of his daughter and they moved away. The girl glanced behind her at the outcaste, his face caste down, while her own face was in shadows under her bonnet, butter-brown. Her father hugged her closer to him and took her hand in his, and the leaves in the trees whispered in the breeze: It's a girl, Mr. St. John. A baby girl. Come hold your new baby girl.

The cobblestones fell silent under the gathering moonlight. Fewer feet hurried by and the carriages were quiet. If vagrants were still lounging in doorways or brigands lurking in alleys St. John did not see them. His sullied feet knew the way they had to go.

They led him along the quai du Louvre. The Palais de la Cité and the Conciergérie rose up to his right. The towers of Notre-Dame soon appeared and he walked over the River Seine across Notre-Dame bridge.

The door to no. 30, quai du Dauphin opened. Turgot's manservant looked at St. John in surprise. Wordlessly he stepped to the side to let his master's guest climb up to his rooms. He followed in a moment, carrying an oil lamp, its flame glowing softly.

St. John opened the door to his suite. He took the lamp and with a nod of the head to the servant closed the door behind him. He went to the dressing-commode, placed the lamp down. He looked at the dainty damask cloth and the dainty perfumed letter sitting on its dainty soft envelope. He picked up the letter and the envelope, then the lamp. He went over to the fire-place and stooped down.

He removed the glass from the lamp, exposing the fire. He took the letter; then the envelope and held them over the lamp. The paper burst into flame. St. John cast it into the fire-place.

He stood up and went to the commode. He placed the lamp down. He looked into the mirror.

Below, in his butler's pantry, Turgot's manservant was startled to hear a loud noise. It was the brittle crashing sound of glass, shattering into a million shards.

Chapter Ten: *Time Will Tell*

It seemed as though all of Paris were crowded into the fields known as the *Champs-de-Mars* between the River Seine and the military school. Boys had climbed up into trees thinking to get a better view. Spectators stood on the tops of carriages and sat on makeshift risers placed in wagons rimming the fields. The more daring of the curious could be seen on rooftops and the less daring on balconies on the buildings across the river.

The choicest places were reserved for the nobility, foreign dignitaries and the philosophical elite. For them chairs had been set up in a ring in the middle of the field. All their wealth and privilege did not prevent the light drizzle from falling on them. They did however allow for the procurement of umbrellas, which glistened under the occasional bashful peek of the late afternoon sun from behind the shifting grey screen of clouds.

Even those with seats were impatient, not the least of whom was Ally. He squirmed and fidgeted under his umbrella, uncomfortable in his new suit of clothes, stockings and shoes wet and not a little muddy.

"When, Papà, when? When will it happen? Why is it taking so long?"

His father pulled out a pocket-clock.

"Here. You can see for yourself. It's only 4:45. Fifteen minutes left to wait."

Turgot produced his own time-piece. He frowned.

"Your clock is not right. It is 4:52. Only eight minutes to go."

"But I bought it only recently. From Lépine's shop near the Louvre. They assured me it keeps accurate time."

"It is evident they were wrong."

"But Lépine is the clockmaker for the king."

"Even more proof that it is wrong."

Impatience is contagious and Sophie's grandson Frédéric had caught the bug. He looked up at his grandmother.

"When will we see it? Is it going to start soon? When?"

Turgot leaned forward in his chair and looked to his left across St. John and his son.

"What time do you have, Dr. Franklin?"

"As much and as little as our good God desires."

"No, I meant, what does your time-piece say?"

"I prefer to not look at it. Waiting is easiest when you're oblivious to time. Looking at the clock will not make the wait shorter. On the contrary, it makes the wait seem longer. And yet we torment ourselves by looking.

"Have you ever noticed how, when walking at night in the dark, you don't seem to mind the steep hills? Yet those same hills seem so tiring and painful in daylight. Oft-times we're happiest not knowing. That is to say, when our knowing cannot possibly affect the outcome. As is the case here. Five o'clock will come, of that we can be certain. And it will be five o'clock according to the Robert brothers' time-piece. Or that of Professor Charles, since he is the one who designed the experiment."

Frédéric, regarding the old man smiling at him, nodded his head.

"Dr. Franklin, is it five o'clock yet? When will it be five o'clock?"

"Sophie. With your kind permission." Franklin handed to her his large umbrella and then, twisting to his left, gently lifted young Frédéric with surprisingly strong arms and placed him on his lap, heedless of the rain now falling on his hat and dripping down the brim onto his nose. Sophie handed back the umbrella.

"I think you can see the machine better from here. There! What do you think of it?"

"It looks like a big strange ball."

"Or a Chinese lantern," Sarah Jay offered, sitting between Ally and her husband John.

"Dr. Franklin, what is that long thing for?" Frédéric was curious now, forgetting all about time.

"I know," Ally put in excitedly. "I read about it in the bulletin. And saw the drawings."

"Well then," Franklin said, "perhaps you would be so kind as to explain it."

"They are...they are making the air hot in that oven. And then the pipe brings the hot air into the big ball."

"And why do you suppose they want to do that?"

"So the ball can fly in the sky."

"And why do you think heated gasses will make it fly?"

Ally fell silent, frowning. "I don't know why."

"Well. Have you ever sat down next to a fire-place on a cold winter night?"

Ally and Frédéric nodded.

"Did you ever feel the cold air come sneaking in from behind you and steal into the fire-place, and then see the embers and sparks go flying up into the chimney? Well, that is because when the air passes over the fire it gets hot. And hot air gets excited. When it gets excited it spreads itself out. That means it gets thinner, compared to the common air around it, which stays the same thickness. That's what is called density. The common air is denser and the hot air is less dense, and so it's as if it is lighter than the common, colder air. And so it goes up. It rises."

Seeing Frédéric's puzzled look, Franklin tried another tack.

"Have you ever taken a straw, stuck it into a glass of water, and blown your breath through the straw? Good. You saw bubbles come up to the top of the water. That was air. Air is less dense, and so lighter, than water. And so it rises up. Hot air does the same thing through colder air."

"But," Turgot interjected, "this machine here is not relying on simple heated air. That would be the Montgolfier brothers' globe."

"That is true," Franklin said. "Which would seem to have the disadvantage of requiring a constant fire of burning straw underneath the globe even while in the air. Professor Charles' invention is to use the inflammable air, what Lavoisier calls 'hydrogen'. That is produced by the pouring of oil of vitriol onto the iron shavings in the kiln they have set up over there. It is fed into the *globe aérostatique* via the pipe. It seems the inflammable air has the advantage over simple heated air because it maintains its thinner density even after it cools down."

"Out of what material do they make the globe?" the Duke de la Rochefoucauld asked, adjusting the monocle on his prominent Roman nose. "It looks like varnish."

"It is, in a manner of speaking," Turgot answered. "I was happy to learn we can finally put to good use the sap from that South American gum tree, the Indians' *caout-shak*. Professor

Charles had the Robert brothers mix up a vat of it with linseed oil to produce the varnish. They then painted it over the taffeta silk stretched out over a rounded wooden frame to make the globe. After it hardened they removed the frame to create a hollow space."

The globe in question, looking to be the size of a large coach, seemed to want to rise up from the platform on which it was tethered, restrained only by its cords. Workers were busy around the pipe while three men having the air of being in charge directed others at the kiln. One of them, dressed in the robes and colors of the Sorbonne, climbed the short ladder onto the platform and gestured with a hand towards a brass band between the platform and the Military Hospital. As the band finished its fanfare the professor gestured again.

From the military school's *parvis* came a loud boom as a cannon was fired. The crowd fell silent. The workers on the platform prepared to release the globe from its bondage. The people in the chairs leaned forward on their seats, holding their breaths.

"This is bad. Very bad," Turgot muttered unhappily, looking at his pocket-clock. "Seven minutes past five."

Another detonation and the workers let go the ropes. Cheering and applause rippled through the crowd and the brass band starting playing again as the bright orange ball floated up and away high above the field underneath the grey ceiling formed by the clouds. It seemed to stand still for a long moment, hovering, then was whisked by the wind away into the clouds until it was nothing more than a tiny bright dot before vanishing altogether.

The curious object having disappeared, some in the crowd sought to fill the void by turning to the other curiosity nearby, which happened to be the famous American sage.

"Monsieur le Docteur Franklin," a well-dressed man approached. "What do you think of this invention? Seems rather like a new expensive toy. What use can it possibly have?"

Franklin shrugged. "Of what use is a new-born baby?"

Turgot was impressed. "If a small globe can fly like that, then why not a larger one? And why couldn't it be equipped with a cabin? Large enough for several men. Think of it. Imagine how fast one could travel from city to city, country to country."

"Or how quickly our mail could be exchanged. No more waiting in the dark for months on end," Jay observed.

"It would be a useful device for cartographers and explorers," St. John agreed.

"I can foresee," Franklin observed, "a magnificent way to expand our knowledge of the weather. Air currents, temperatures, moisture. It could be another step towards predicting accurately the weather, to the benefit of everyone. That is why, like the new-born baby, this aerostatic globe should be nurtured. It could bring untold gifts to humanity."

The Duke de la Rochefoucauld was enthusiastic. "Not to mention the military. I can see right now a thousand and one uses for this thing in our army. From such a high vantage point we could easily spy on everything our enemies are doing. Their maneuvering, their numbers, their weaponry, their supply lines. We could even destroy them by dropping missiles on them by the air before they even reached our borders. Truly, a marvelous thing, this flying globe. How fitting to be launched from the Field of Mars."

"Well," Franklin replied, "it is a fact that Caligula, just as George Washington, was once a new-born baby."

"The ancient Greeks," Mrs. Jay remarked, "knew it well, that law that says that every thing created by human beings has not only the propensity for evil as well as for good, but the certainty."

"All I know," the duke remarked, "is that if we don't seize the opportunity the enemy will. Let he who wishes to be a slave be the first to cast down his weapon."

"Safeguards," Turgot said. "New inventions need not be violent to protect us from the enemy."

"But," Sophie replied, "we are already presupposing that having an enemy is inevitable. Why must that be so? Surely all human beings, being endowed with intelligence and reason, are capable of overcoming their own selfish desires for the good of their brothers and sisters."

"Madame," the duke rejoined, "have you never observed a will contest? Nothing illustrates the state of familial affections more than a dear departed with a lot of wealth. Or, for that matter, a deceased with very little wealth."

"There will always be an enemy," Turgot stated flatly. "We had best accept this fact if we and are children are to survive and flourish. The question is therefore: how do we best manage the enemy?"

"The first thing, I suppose," Jay said, "is to recognize who the real enemy is."

The countess, outnumbered, fell silent a moment, then said: "Perhaps the true slave is he who insists on holding on to his weapon."

Jay looked at her with interest. "I wonder. It is a question a lot of people lately in America have wrestled with. But what then do we make of the Book of Exodus? Did not Moses himself direct Joshua to go and fight to the death the evil Amelakites? As long as man is walking the earth the enemy is stalking him. It is the wise man who recognizes who the enemy is. And who is willing to fight the good fight."

"As you Americans have done," the duke replied. "Congratulations are in order, Dr. Franklin, Mr. Jay. When, if I may ask, do you expect the treaty to be formally signed? It has been a long pregnancy."

"And not a painless birth," Franklin replied. "The treaty – our birth certificate? – will likely be signed next week. Both treaties: America's with Britain, and France and Spain's with Britain. But it is, essentially, the same document we worked out almost a year ago, and which Congress approved this past April.

"Mr. Adams wrote me this morning suggesting next Wednesday. We will see what Mr. Hartley says."

"I, for one, am rather sad in the midst of this joyful event," la Comtesse remarked. "I dare not think, Dr. Franklin, that this will mean your stay with us will soon be at an end. I could not bear the thought of your leaving. You could, you know, simply stay with us. Why risk another hazardous ocean voyage?"

"I am indeed tempted, my dear Sophie. Tempted indeed. But, happily, as long as the object of one's duty is the same as the object of one's temptation, there is no conflict and thus, only peace. I am duty-bound as well as delighted to stay here until I receive from Congress permission to leave this post. Which ought to take a fair amount of time, as the treaty will first have to be sent to Philadelphia to be ratified; then re-shipped to London to be ratified by Parliament; and then finally back to Paris for the royal ratification of your king.

"And thus we see, in all things there are good, and bad. Because Professor Charles' flying globe has not yet achieved adulthood, we are deprived of quick mail service. Yet, a lengthy and cumbersome process of ratification will produce a corresponding benefit: a prolonging of my current gratification in your society."

"We will treasure every minute of it. And at the same time dread the passing of each minute."

"There my dear. You do yourself a disservice. You are under no duty to think about the passage of time. On the contrary. You owe it to yourself to reflect on other things. Always. To the exclusion of the ticking of the clock or the running of the sand.

"I have often wondered about this thing we call 'time'. I remember, when I was just a wee lad in Boston too young to be apprenticed yet, I would sometimes wander down to the marshes. One day I found myself in a delightful world where time did not exist. I know that because I recall marveling at the pure beauty of every moment that day. I was supremely conscious of being suspended as it were in a realm where I was in a state of pure, delightful being, with neither a beginning nor an end.

"That day of pure delight seemed to me at the time, and to me even now, as being infinite in duration, as having unfurled itself immeasurably, imperceptibly slowly. Now, when I was middle-aged I often remarked how the days seemed to pass by much more quickly; and now that I am an old man they positively fly by.

"I ask myself, why should that be so? I think, although some might have a different experience, that the answer is found in a ratio. You see, when I was a six-year old lad each day was only one two-thousandths or so of my experience on earth. As a forty-year old each day was equal to one over 14,600. As a seventy-seven year old man it is one over 28,100. And so that might be why time now seems to shoot by. Each day appears to my senses as a much smaller portion of the whole."

"And so," Jay remarked, "that would explain why a man in prison suffers so, having nothing to distract his thoughts. He is aware – horribly aware – of each upcoming future minute of boredom, of nothingness, that awaits him. And is in a state of tedium, if not agony, because of this awareness. I imagine that is what hell must be like. It follows, then, that if awareness of the passage of time is unpleasant or worse, then the unawareness of it is happiness."

"Or bliss. However we choose to call it. But I would propose a slightly different conception. If one is in a blissful state then by definition one is not aware of the passage of time at all. Just like one who is in the light cannot be in the dark. In such a blissful state it follows that time simply does not exist as an independent thing. If infinity is indivisible, then eternity is immeasurable as well. Eternity is of the same nature as infinity."

"Are you saying, Dr. Franklin, that there is no such thing as time?" Sarah Jay asked.

"I am supposing that as long as there is more than one object in existence then perforce each object exists in a relation to the others. Therefore for those objects time exists, as it describes a relationship. But if ultimately only one object exists, then, no, time cannot exist as there is nothing else against which to measure it."

"But can that be? That only one object exists?"

"Not in this world. And there, my dear, we have come to the limits of my poor mortal intellect."

The drizzle had stopped and the sun finally emerged through the clouds. The party rose and made their muddy way over to their coaches. As Franklin prepared to embark St. John approached him.

"Dr. Franklin. I must take my leave of you now, perhaps for a long while. I will always treasure our acquaintance."

"When do you leave?"

"My departure will be entirely dependent on *your* schedule, Dr. Franklin, since it is conditioned upon the signing of the peace treaty. And so, I imagine as soon as it is signed and sealed."

"Mr. Adams has asked that his secretary be chosen to carry the originals to Congress. I imagine you two ought to sail together if your ship can go on to Philadelphia after New York."

"And thank you again for your kind suggestions regarding the mail service and the Gulf Stream. By the way, I have had lightning rods installed on all the ships."

"Then you are guaranteed to arrive safely in port."

St. John offered his *adieux* to the Jays and Rochefoucauld as well.

"Of course," he said to Jay, "Governor Clinton shall be the first to whom I will present my credentials. But as to the United States? It would be so simple if you were still the president of the Congress."

"A mere figurehead if ever there was one," Jay replied. "I much preferred my brief tenure as Chief Justice of New York. But you are right, it would be the current president, General Mifflin. Thomas Mifflin."

"How should I address him? Your Highness? Your Excellency? General?"

"All three would not be objected to by him."

"I am not aware," Turgot remarked, "of any animal known to man which can survive very long without a head. The United States do not have a king; they do not have a prime minister; they have no executive chief of any kind. How long can the several states live in harmony with each other?"

"Being that they have never lived in harmony with one another, the question presupposes a fact which has yet to be proven," Jay smiled. "But you are right in asking it. The Articles of Confederation do not work. They have never worked. That 'rope of sand', Washington calls it.

"State assemblies are no different than the men who comprise them. That is to say, selfish. That is why we need a strong national government. Otherwise our ship will founder. America cannot survive as a nation of disparate, jealous little sovereigns held together only by the moral inspiration of one man, no matter how virtuous he may be."

"Well," Turgot observed, "only time will tell."

The sun once again had chosen to disappear. The rain was coming down now in buckets.

"Only time will tell," Jay agreed.

The Duke de la Rochefoucauld gave a parting wet wave of the hand as he mounted into his carriage.

"*Adieu, mes amis.* I foresee a time, not far in the future, where France will learn from your example and she too will glow in the light of reason and liberty. How I look forward to that day! *Salut.*"

Chapter Eleven: *Von Steuben Answers Washington*

It was a desolate tableau. Greyness reigned, a vague, ill-defined, ambiguous grey. Grey sky, grey water, grey buildings. What was not grey, was black. Blackened shells of burned-out houses, crumbling shops, decaying wharves. The Union Jack hung limply on its flagpole sticking up over Fort George like a weary exclamation point. Up beyond Bowling Green west of the ruins of Trinity Church stretched the village of shacks, walls of rotting driftwood and roofs of discarded sailcloth.

British Navy vessels rocked listlessly at anchor or slouched along the docks. Here and there from tired chimneys charcoal-hued smoke meandered upwards, twisting around in slow spirals to form giant question marks in the bleak sky. In the streets red-coated figures ambled aimlessly about. On every third or fourth house a small red cloth hung on the front door like a sad flag.

The English pilot motioned with his hands. The French First Officer relayed the motion with his own hands. The helmsman turned the wheel and the ship began to come about as the bo'sun barked the command to trim back the remaining sails even further. Sailors aloft carried out the order while others on deck handled the lines. The ship shuddered to a stop. From the wheelhouse six bells tolled.

Anchors splashed into the cold waters of the bay, chains groaning. The French consul worried the papers in his deep breast pockets lining the inside of his coat. His fingers trembled. A sharp shudder seized him. Feverish, he grasped the railing with livid hands.

"Here. Let us go into the cabin. You must sit down."

The consul shook his head, clinging more tightly to the railing. His eyes were locked in a blank stare. Suddenly he began to jerk, first his arms, then his torso, then his head. His young secretary planted his legs and put his hands on either shoulder of the sick man, now convulsing violently. There was nothing to do but wait out the storm.

By and by the attack passed. The young man felt his companion's arms slacken although his hands still gripped the railing.

"Stay here," James said, needlessly. "I'll go fetch you some water."

James returned in a moment. He was accompanied by a somewhat older young man, his simple attire proclaiming him to be an American. James held the cup to the consul's lips and helped him sip.

Captain du Moulin approached. "We'll be going ashore now. I've ordered your trunks be put in the boat. We'll have the ship moved dockside and then unloaded, probably tomorrow." The captain was looking at the French nobleman's pale face. "Are you sure you can climb down the ladder?"

Accepting the silent nod of the head in response the officer moved on to other business, leaving the three men waiting at the rail, staring into the grey unknown.

* * * * *

An untidy assortment of bric-a-brac adorned the shabby docks of Whitehall. Sloppy coils of old rope competed for space with piles of torn sails and broken rigging. Women dressed in rags rummaged through the piles watched by bored men. Two stray dogs were fighting over the carcass of a gull. On the lee side of the wharf a ship was tied up. Civilians were trundling trunks on board or the odd piece of furniture.

The sailors in the longboat shipped their oars and made fast to the floating dock lashed to the pier. They stepped out to assist the alighting passengers. The English pilot led the French captain of the *Courrier de l'Europe* and the others onto dry land before departing for the nearest rum mill. But first he hailed a grenadier in tattered red coat and breeches more brown than white.

"Where's your commanding officer?"

The redcoat looked disdainfully at the pilot. He jerked his head toward an open doorway in a house at the foot of Dock Street. "Where he always is, mate. At his favourite grog shop."

"Bring him here."

A sullen glare then a sardonic smile and mock salute and the soldier ambled over to the shop. He swaggered through a sparse cluster of civilians pushing hand-carts piled with baggage and burlap bags, heading toward the ship on the wharf. With them was a man in the uniform of a British lieutenant. Mechanically he saluted Captain du Moulin and the pilot, then gave a curious glance at the Frenchman in aristocratic garb and his younger companions.

The British lieutenant stopped with a jerk. He stared a long moment at the man attired in the vestments of a French court officer, reddish hair only lightly powdered and pulled back into an ornate clasp.

"Mr. St. John? Can it be you sir?"

"I beg your pardon?" The French consul spoke with difficulty.

"It has been a long while, hasn't it. I'm George. George Bull."

The consul stared blankly into the young man's ruddy face with the prominent nose.

"George? Yes...yes, of course it is. George. George Bull!" He extended a weak hand to shake the young man's. "Tell me. How is your father, your mother?"

"My mother has died, I regret to tell you. My father took it hard. But he is better now. He has remarried. He was very ill, you know, being in gaol two years then under house arrest. At least the rebels didn't steal his farm like they did with so many others. My brothers have something to inherit. As for me, I'm about to leave, as you can see."

He jerked his head towards the ship nearby. "We're going to Nova Scotia. Most of the others in town have already left. Any day now and the rest of the British Army will be gone, too. Washington's chomping at the bit, no doubt, to make his grand entrance. He's waiting up in Westchester with his rebel army."

"So we have heard." The French consul's young American companion spoke up cheerfully. "John Thaxter's my name. We met a fleet of British ships crammed to the gunwales with your fellow redcoats off the coast." He stared boldly at the other American dressed as a British lieutenant. "I happen to have the Treaty itself in my pocket."

George Bull ignored him. He was looking at his former neighbor with a look of sympathy.

"But say. Here I am rambling along about myself. Please excuse me. And please allow me to express my condolences. I would have made them sooner, of course, but what with the war and all – "

"Condolences?"

"Yes, I'm so sorry. I know it must have been painful for you. As it was for my own father. Losing a mother one loves is hard, naturally, but I imagine it must be even more wrenching to lose the wife you love. Again, I'm sorry about Mehetable. She was such a sweet – "

"Mehetable? Mehetable?" The French consul grabbed Lt. Bull's shoulders violently. "Mehetable?"

Bull, taken aback, looked into the man's feverish eyes.

"I'm...I'm sorry sir...I thought you knew. Sir, she died, three years ago..."

"No! No! No! No! No!" The man screamed in Bull's face, clutching his arms. He collapsed at his feet. His hands, laced around the major's boots, grew rigid. His legs, sprawling on the cobblestones, began to jerk spasmodically.

James crouched down next to him, gripping the man's violently twitching shoulders and cradling his head to prevent its banging on the ground.

"Ça va, doucement, cela passera..." James tried to sooth him, struggling to keep the man's shoulders and head from beating the cobblestones, helped by young Thaxter kneeling on one knee while the captain looked with uncertainty at the convulsing figure on the ground.

"Mr. St. John, sir. Are you all right? Can you hear me?" Bull was anguished.

"It will pass soon," James told them. "He was very ill on the voyage. He has had several of these convulsions. He can't hear you right now. He has already lost consciousness." James had shifted to a sitting position so that the man's head could rest on his thigh.

"It has been a terrible thing, this war." Bull was bitter. "Thank God it is finally over."

"This is such a sudden blow for him. Monsieur de Crèvecoeur talked of nothing during the voyage except his longing to finally see his wife and children again."

"Then at least you may tell him that his daughter Fanny and her brother Philly were spared. I am not sure where they are, however."

A colonel approached. Lt. Bull saluted him, informing him the French gentleman was very ill.

"Please excuse me for not rising," James said, looking up from his crouch. "This is Mr. St. Jean de Crèvecoeur. He has been commissioned by our Most Holy Majesty, King Louis of France, as consul for New York. I am his secretary. James Le Ray de Chaumont. With Mr. John Thaxter, secretary to his Excellency John Adams."

"Colonel Hughes here." His voice was slurred and he smelled of whiskey. "Do you think he can stand up?" The British officer's own equilibrium seemed questionable.

"Not yet. He will come out of it in a few moments. He spoke of a friend he thought might still be living here. Mr. William Seton."

"Aye, Mr. Seton. Know him well," Col. Hughes said. "He is the magistrate here. Up the street, at the City Hall." The officer ordered his sergeant to fetch Seton. He commanded a corporal to commandeer a chair.

William Seton and the chair arrived at the same time. Hughes filled him in. Seton crouched down and placed a hand on his old friend's shoulder. He looked intently into his face. Their eyes met.

"I am so sorry you have had to hear the bad news in this way. Come with me. You will be my guest."

Crèvecoeur rose to his feet slowly, supported by Bull and Seton. Seton addressed James.

"Have his baggage brought to my house. At no. 5, Wall Street."

* * * * *

The storm had come crashing in shortly before midnight and showed no sign of leaving any time soon. The howling wind lashed remorselessly the panes of the windows with heavy tongues of rain mixed with sleet. In the greyish light of the room the bed was hardly visible even though it was late morning. The feeble fire sputtering beyond the hearth served only to make the room feel even colder.

Seton, seated by the bed, rose to give the fire a poke and put on another small log, one of the rare survivors from the household's dwindling stock of wood. He resumed his place by his friend's bedside. He picked up the book again and continued reading out loud.

" 'When the righteous cry for help, the Lord hears; and delivers them out of their troubles. The Lord is near to the broken-hearted, and saves the crushed in spirit.' "

Seton looked at his friend, half reclining on thick pillows, eyes closed, then read another favorite passage in his well-marked Bible. "A voice says, 'Cry!' And I said, 'What shall I cry?' All flesh is grass, and all its beauty is like the flower of the field. The grass withers, the flower fades, when the breath of the Lord blows upon it. Surely the people are grass. The grass withers, the flower fades; but the word of our God will stand forever.' "

His friend opened his eyes, focused on Seton.

"Thank you." He looked at the pale grey square of the window, looked at the nebulous orange of the fire. He struggled to sit upright.

"Here. Have some tea. And broth."

Crèvecoeur declined and leaned his head back weakly.

"What day is today?"

"Friday. November 21. You arrived two days ago. I am glad you slept through. You had a very hot fever." Seton placed a hand on his friend's forehead. "Not so bad now."

"Tell me what you know about my family. My children. My farm."

Seton hesitated, looking with compassionate eyes closely at his friend. "What I know comes second-hand. By way of the Booth family. The sad event occurred in late 1780. Not long after you and Ally had sailed for England. If I may, your son Ally...?"

"He is in good hands. He is at school in Caen."

Seton nodded his head, relieved. "You may have heard of the law passed by the New York Assembly, declaring the right to seize and sell outright all Loyalist property. They had already confiscated most of it and were renting it out, but then they took that final step. Well, your friends Moffat and Woodhull were able to protect your farm from being seized. But it would appear there were Patriots in the area who were unhappy about that. Some of them – just who, exactly, we'll probably never know – put the torch to your house and barn one night.

"Your children were saved by your brother-in-law. But he went back in to rescue your wife and neither came out. This, according to the farm-hands. They also reported they heard Indian war-whoops and saw a few 'Mohawks' dancing around the flames. Strangely, no other farms were molested by these so-called Indians.

"The acting sheriff at the time – I think his name was Howell - accused your Oneida foreman – Henry I think his name was – of being in cahoots with the 'Mohawks' and threw him in jail. A few days later he was found dead in his cell."

Crèvecoeur closed his eyes. "Where are my children now?"

"I do not know."

Crèvecoeur appeared to slumber. Seton stood, picked up the tray with the tea set and empty bowl.

His eyes opened again. "I think it's time for me to rise." Ignoring his friend's protests he struggled weakly to his feet.

"You will find your clothing hanging in the *Kast*." Seton gestured at the massive Dutch walnut armory opposite the bed and retreated to a rocking chair by the fire. He sipped his tea while his guest dressed. "Anna Maria will not be pleased if you have a relapse."

"She is faring well, I trust." Crèvecoeur's voice was low.

"As well as any woman given the circumstances. It is her faith that sustains her. As did her sister Elizabeth's – my first wife, you recall – up to the moment she died."

"And your son – "

"William Magee is returning from school in England. I will put him to work as clerk in the counting-house on Water Street."

There was rapping on the door. James entered. "Good morning, sir. I am happy to see you are feeling better. Good morning, Mr. Seton."

"*Bonjour à vous, M. le Ray. Je vois que vous nous avez apporté des journaux.* "

"*Oui, vous avez raison, Monsieur. Mais comment se fait-il que vous parlez francais? Et si bien en plus.*" James was astonished to be addressed by their host in French. He was carrying the three newspapers to which Seton had referred under his arm.

Seton smiled at the compliment. "I had a good teacher. Pastor Tétard."

"Where is Tétard now?" Crèvecoeur asked.

"Philadelphia. With Robert Livingston, Foreign Affairs Minister. He wrote to me he was planning on moving back to New York. After Washington has taken possession of the City. Which is supposed to occur tomorrow. November 22."

"That's what the papers here say," James agreed. He gave the *Gazette* to Seton and the *Packet* to Crèvecoeur.

Seton read the article out loud. " 'Under order of General Washington: The definitive Treaty being concluded and the City of New York to be evacuated on the 22nd instant, His Excellency the Commander-in-Chief proposes to celebrate the Peace, at that Place, on Monday, the First Day of December next, by a Display of the Fire-Works, and Illuminations....' "

Seton looked up from his *Gazette*. "Well, I'm not certain the British Army can complete their evacuation on time. Not with the storm. Here, this will interest you. 'The Pacquet *Le Courrier de l'Europe*, after a stormy passage, arrived from Port Lorient, having as passenger John Thaxter, Esq., Secretary to John Adams, Esq., Ambassador from the United States of America to the States General of Holland, charged, by the American Commissioners with the Definitive Treaty, signed by them on the 3rd of September and on the part of Great Britain, by Mr. Hartley, which Mr. Thaxter, on Thursday morning November 20th set off to deliver to the Honourable General Mifflin, President of Congress.

" 'On this ship came also Hector St. John, Esq., appointed by the Court of France to be Consul, and Superintendent of Pacquets, now established between this City and Port Lorient. The Design of the Pacquet Service being to facilitate communication between France and America, and the concerns of commerce between both countries.' "

Crèvecoeur smiled wanly at his young secretary. "Well done."

"I had help from Mr. Seton. " James nodded at their host. "Thank you again for letting me use your shop. And bringing me around to Mr. Rivington and Mr. Holt."

"My pleasure. I would be honored if you and Mr. St. John were to agree to establish your consulate in my building on Water Street. I have plenty of room and a good suite giving onto the street. And for your packet service office as well, it being so handy to the docks."

"Thank you, my friend. I accept." Crèvecoeur had arisen and gone over to the window, staring out at the bleak greyness of the day. He had to lean against the *Kast* to support himself.

"I wonder where she is buried...or if she was interred at all." He turned his head towards his friend. "I wish to go to there."

Seton put an arm around his shoulders. They both looked down at the muddy street below.

"You can't travel now. The roads are impossible and you're still very ill. Washington will be arriving any day, so will Governor Clinton to set up the new government. Your presence will be needed here, as the French representative. I am sure the first thing they'll do is to establish a postal service. You will be able write to your friends in Orange County about your children. Come. Take a seat by the fire."

Like a child Crèvecoeur allowed himself to be escorted to a chair. They all sat down, James absorbed in the papers.

"Here's another notice. 'The Chevalier Anne-Robert de la Luzerne will be departing next week from Philadelphia to present his wishes to the Commander-in-Chief. The French Ambassador is a beloved friend to America.' " James put down his paper. "We'll need to find lodgings for him."

"I'll take you around to Black Sam this afternoon. " Seton offered. "His rooms are still the most elegant in town, or what's left of it. Over a thousand houses have burned down since the war began, you know. No doubt General Washington will also be staying at Fraunces', unless he goes to Cape's Tavern on Broadway. John Cape just bought it from old Roubolet a couple of weeks ago for a song. The Loyalists have had to sell for bottom dollar. "

"What are all those red flags I see by the doorways?"

"Auction flags. Departing Loyalists selling their belongings. Or the house itself. I bought an estate myself last month at an auction, up the Bowery. I'm renting out the house and farm to a returning Exile, as they call themselves. They've been trickling back into the City, reclaiming their property, buying up Loyalist houses, speculating."

"I am grateful you have not left. Are you not fearful of retribution?"

Seton smiled. "I am confident I will not be molested. Everything has been arranged with Major Tallmadge. For the moment it is best to leave it at that." He shifted in his chair, looked again at his friend.

"It seems a miracle, your return to New York, and as the French consul, no less. The Lord works in mysterious ways. I am happy for you."

"Many kind people helped me. Countess d'Houdetot. Her husband. Duke de la Rochefoucauld. The duke has taken Ally under his wing."

A sudden shudder shook his body and he closed his eyes, determined to fight it off. By and by it passed.

"I published a notice in the *Mercure* in Paris with our sailing schedules and rates. I will need to do the same thing here in New York, and work with the port captain, the merchants. Would you be willing to assist us?" he asked, voice weak.

Seton smiled his acceptance. They shook hands on it.

"I also have been asked to represent the Academy of Science and the Agricultural Society, and the Royal Gardens. I brought copies of their periodicals I want to translate and publish. We have medical devices and laboratory equipment for Dr. Stiles at Yale. And for Governor Livingston, King Louis' offer to the citizens of New Jersey to establish a botanical garden...."

As he spoke Crèvecoeur's eyes drifted over to the small blaze in the fireplace. He stared into the fire. He saw a dark shadow flicker across the light, then a terrified woman screaming in the flames....He shut his eyes, fighting back the tears. *Requiescat in pace.*

Seton was watching him closely. He put a hand on his shoulder. "Are you all right?"

Crèvecoeur looked up and nodded, convincing neither his friend nor himself.

"Mr. Seton," James spoke up, "you will have to educate us on your money ways. How are we to effectuate payment for the mails? For the exchange of merchandise?"

"The same way as before. Inefficiently." Seton remarked. "The Colonies could never cooperate before the war, or during the war, and now that they call themselves 'States' it seems to make no difference.

"We need a national bank. Chartered by the Congress. Empowered to issue money and to back it up. And the government needs the power to lay taxes to pay off our enormous debts, and establish sound credit. The merchants have always known this. But the large estate owners and farmers oppose it. And so we muddle through.

"But change is in the air. We won our freedom so now we will have to pay our way. The young lawyer, Alexander Hamilton, has drafted a plan for a national bank. It has merit. However, he is married to General Schuyler's daughter and so without any effort on his part he has thereby incurred the enmity of Governor Clinton, Clinton and Schuyler being arch rivals.

"Clinton is furious at Congress as well. He believes New York has been saddled with an unfair share of the national debt to pay off. On top of the State's own debt. And Congress waffling over New York's claim to Vermont and entertaining Massachusetts' and Virginia's claims to western New York is the icing on the cake. The battle lines for a new war are being drawn even before the governor and the Commander-in-Chief have made their grand entrance.

"But, let us render unto men what belongs to men and unto God what is God's. This afternoon there will be a special service of thanksgiving at St. Paul's. I would be honored if you were to attend with me."

* * * * *

November 25, 1783, the day so long awaited in some parts and so heavily dreaded in others finally dawned. Whether winter Patriot or summer Tory, all but the dying, and even a few of them, watched the last of the departing redcoats march down the Bowery from their camps around Murray Hill and the DeLancey farm, onto Chatham Street and then Broadway to join up with the grenadiers evacuating Fort George, heading to the docks to board their ships. Their slumped shoulders and downcast faces were at odds with the brash piping of the fifes and bravado of the drums.

Like water swirling in to fill a void civilians, gaunt and hungry and shivering in the tattered rags they called clothes, poured onto the streets. James Le Ray wanted to go up to the Bull's-Head Tavern on the Bowery to see Washington come down from Harlem Heights but deferred to his master's still-wobbly legs.

They went instead to Cape's Tavern on Broadway, where a squad of men in buff-and-blue uniforms and black-and-blue Union Cockades on their lapels had assembled on horseback, their leader with gold épaulettes and colonel's sash waiting in his saddle with a dignified air. Soldiers and civilians alike sported a green sprig of laurel pinned to their hats. Everybody today was a Patriot. Thanks to James' foresight he, the French consul, and William Seton were suitably adorned as well. Seton pointed out Samuel Broome talking with James Duane and other civilian leaders.

"And yourself?" Crèvecoeur asked.

"I'm *persona non grata*. Not allowed to join their club of returning Exiles. No hard feelings. I prefer to work behind closed doors."

Seton introduced Crèvecoeur to the Tavern owner watching from his open doorway.

"Gen'r'l Knox will be coming in first to secure the City, ahead of Washington," John Cape informed them. "Around twelve noon. Which means right about now."

James came back from reconnoitering the street, excited.

"Knox is coming."

Around the corner from Chatham Street they came, Major-General Knox in the lead followed by his officer corps at the head of a company of dragoons and light infantry, then a corps of artillery and foot soldiers. Children, women and not a few men dashed in and among them, marched along, then dropped back out to be replaced by other civilians. With a call to attention and the raising of a sabre the Patriot Exiles saluted the procession. Knox sent the brigade with its field guns on down Broadway to Fort George before leading the company of Exiles back to meet up with Washington at the Bull's-Head.

"Washington and Clinton an' all the rest will be parading down Queen to Wall Street," Cape told them. "An' then the raising of the United States flag. Now, if you gentlemen will excuse me, I have two dozen punch bowls to attend to...."

They walked down to the remains of Trinity Church. An hour later the tall figure of the Commander-in-Chief emerged, sitting straight in his saddle astride a fine grey horse, leading the procession up Wall Street towards them, passing by City Hall with its huge American flag draped from the balcony. On his left rode the governor, Gen. Clinton on his bay mount, bracketed on either side by waving and cheering civilians. Behind them came their general officers, then Gen. Pierre van Cortlandt's Westchester Light Calvary. The Commander-in-Chief swept his eyes right, left and back again, doffing his tri-corn hat with the brush of green laurel.

The generals veered to their right onto Broadway. As they rode by, Washington's eyes rested a moment on Seton's and he gave a slight nod, as though in appreciation. Although smiling his eyes looked distant, and very, very tired.

They halted at Thames Street where, in front of Cape's Tavern, Knox and Exiles were waiting at attention. There was a moment of silence. Then a wide grin flashed across Knox' round face. He took off his tri-corn and waived it around over his head and led his men in a round of cheers for the Commander-in-Chief. Hats, gloves and hand-bills went flying skyward. On Knox' command a squad of riflemen raised their guns in the air and let off a stupendous *feu-de-joie*.

Seton led his party over to Bowling Green, to wait for the salute and the raising of the United States flag over Fort George. Standing by the remains of the equestrian pedestal, the mounted king having been pulled down in July 1776, they heard angry muttering rippling through the crowd. The huge British flag was still fluttering regally in the air atop the tall pole rising above the ramparts of the fort, as though mocking the people below.

"The Brits cut the halyards on the pole," someone remarked. "Greased it, too, by the looks of it."

"Cut it down! Burn it!" voices cried out.

Knox' artillery corps stood in formation along the east wall bordering the street, waiting for the generals to come down from Cape's for the ceremony. Their commander was striding back and forth in front of them, fuming, conferring with a junior officer. Through the gates could be seen a company of infantry on the parade grounds.

From the direction of Cape's came the clattering of horses and the shouting of commands to make way. As the people parted, Washington and Clinton with their entourage emerged on horseback. Coming up from behind Washington was Gen. Knox.

"Well I'll be the son of a Hessian general's whore!" Knox swore. He was glaring in anger through his eyeglasses at the Union Jack taunting them from on high. He jerked his mount out of formation, motioning his aides to follow him. Knox led his officers straight for the open gates of Fort George and the offensive object protruding high in the air from within like an obscene gesture.

After a moment several soldiers came running out of the fort and disappeared into the crowd clustered around Pearl Street only to re-emerge a few minutes later and plunge back into the bowels of the fort. By and by loud cracking sounds emanated from within, as though from a hammer. The pounding continued, then paused, only to resume again until, poking up from above the farthest redoubt guarding the southwest angle of the fort, a human head in a sailor's tarp cap appeared.

Slowly he inched his way up the flagstaff, greased pole glistening in the sunlight, then, his torso secured by a loop of rope twisted around a cleat, raised an arm and nailed in another wooden cleat, then another a foot higher, and so on, until he had climbed up to a point above the grease, the spare halyards he had brought up with him trailing down to the ground below. Here he let his hammer fall and, clasping his legs around the pole sailor-fashion and grasping the pole above his head with his hands, began to haul himself up. The crowd yelled up words of encouragement.

His head and shoulders disappeared into the folds of the Union Jack. In a flash the flag came hurtling down. The soldiers below were chanting now as the man ran the new halyards around the pulley, then slowly descended back down. As soon as his head disappeared below the ramparts the halyards were in motion, and then the Stars and Stripes emerged, grandly filling the sky, accompanied by thirteen volleys booming from the Battery.

* * * * *

Samuel Fraunces greeted each guest personally coming into his establishment, then with a bow and extended arm directed the dignitary to either the great room to his left on the main floor, or behind him to the narrow stairway leading to the firmament of the upper floor, depending on rank as to officers and status if civilian, as determined by the restaurateur's practiced eye.

That sharp eye, appearing even greener in the ruddy swarthiness of his face, dilated in recognition as the French consul, unaccompanied, handed him his *carte de visite.*

"Enchanté de vous revoir, Monsieur l'émissaire," Fraunces murmured, inclining his head again. "Was your *soufflé* a success?"

Crèvecoeur forced a smile.

"It is a story best left untold."

"Governor Clinton's reception is on the next floor. In the ballroom." Another bow, and Black Sam turned to greet a party of other civilians.

Crèvecoeur was welcomed by the Exile leader Samuel Broome, posted at the first of two doors servicing the ballroom. Broome presented him to Gov. Clinton, who, like van Cortlandt, Col. Weissenfels and the several civilians already present, was standing by the long rectangle made up of three banquet tables on which all the fine china surviving the British occupation had been laid along with spoons and knives, of which only the *couverts* at the ends were of silver. Clinton, in turn, introduced to the others the French consul who found himself greeted warmly as though he were the king of France himself.

Clinton did not notice the ironic look in the eyes of the man whose fate he had once held in his hands.

"The Commander-in-Chief is in his rooms," Clinton informed him. "Major Tallmadge has gone to bring him." As he spoke the hallway outside reverberated with the sounds of boots and in a moment the General himself came striding into the room, followed by Knox, Nathaniel Greene, Tallmadge and Baron von Steuben with their aides. Salutations and cheers rose up in greeting from all around.

The governor escorted the Commander-in-Chief to the head of the table and then took his place at the opposite end, standing as were the others behind their chairs. Fraunces himself appeared and, uncorking the first of many bottles of madeira, reverently poured out, the first glass presented to the General. On command from Clinton all glasses were raised.

"A toast to the United States of America."

"To His Most Christian Majesty Louis the Sixteenth."

"Let us drink to the United Netherlands.... the American Army."

"To the Fleet and Armies of France."

"I propose a toast to our fallen heroes...and their widows and orphans."

"May America forever be the sanctuary of the persecuted and the oppressed, the vindicators of the Rights of Mankind....and may the States in close union guard forever the temple they have created in the name of Liberty, and with Justice support what courage has gained."

"May the remembrance of this day be a lesson to princes and tyrants."

Washington asked them to bow their heads.

"I would like to offer up a prayer of thanks. To our Supreme Commander, without Whom all life is without meaning; and with Whom our lives can have hope. May that Almighty Being's Wisdom and Mercy infect us all, and may his Peace descend on your city. May we welcome with loving arms the valiant soldier and returning exiles, and treat with grace the repentant ones who ask for our forgiveness. Amen."

The sun had set by the time the diners took their leave, not a few on unsteady legs. The streets were lit up by bonfires at every corner attended by civilians and ex-soldiers throwing their own impromptu party.

Major-General Baron Friedrich von Steuben had a difficult time negotiating the steps, even with the help of his aide Capt. Walker.

"*Putain d'enfer! Verdammten Scheisstreppen,*" he swore in two languages under his breath.

"*Ne vous inquiétez pas, mon général,*" Walker comforted his commander, supporting the vast uniformed bulk with difficulty. "*Vous voilà les pieds sur terre. Nous y serons bientôt de retour à nos chambres.*"

"If you are staying at Cape's we can walk together," Crèvecoeur offered. "I'm at a house in Wall Street."

"I'm sure that will be fine, sir," Walker replied, with a noticeable Cockney accent. "But you'll have to speak in French if you don't know German, otherwise the general won't understand you."

Crèvecoeur and the army's Inspector General accordingly conversed in French as they made their slow way up Broad

Street. Crèvecoeur learned the baron planned on becoming a United States citizen and living in the City.

"But first I shall be paid all the damn wages the damn pigs in Congress owe me!" he exclaimed in French to a startled passerby. "Almost six years with nothing but Continental dollars to show for it. Damn."

"There, general, it will be all right," his aide soothed him. "We will all be offered land grants for our service."

"Land? Where? In Indian territory? I'm too damn old to learn how to farm and too damn old to wait for the land to have value enough to sell. Damn. Let New York give us some of that good Loyalist property Clinton has seized in payment of our wages. Damn."

As they neared the bonfire at the top of Broad Street they heard a group of skinners singing in loud boisterous voices.

"King George, he sent his Hessians, his Tories and his whores
To steal from our possessions, our lorries and our stores
But then they met us Yankees, who showed them how to fight
And away they ran like frightened sheep full of fear and fright.

"We hung up André by his neck, we'd do the same for Benedict
Be careful now, you refugees and Loyalists, be careful, watch
your backs!
For when you're caught you'll soon be taught
The fate in store for turncoat dirty rats.

"To all you Tories, royal dung, you tool of the Tyrant Fool,
We, the Sons of Liberty, will show you how we deal with you!
When you come a-crawling, asking for repentance
When you come a-begging, asking for forgiveness
Instead you'll reap your just reward: the bitter taste of
vengeance!"

"What are they saying?" Von Steuben demanded to know. "Damn English language!"

"They are saying," Capt. Walker informed him, with a wink to the French consul, "that to forgive is divine."

"Then," von Steuben roared, "tell them they are damn fools. The only way to deal with the enemy is to annihilate him. To forgive is to die."

"Gentlemen. The general would like for you to sing your song again."

The skinners obliged.

Chapter Twelve: *News of a Miracle*

"Here is my letter to Governor Clinton about the packet service. You can hand deliver that one," he said to James. "But," turning to Seton, "how do we send mail to New Jersey or New Haven?"

"I can answer that," James said. "It's in the *Gazette*." He read out loud. " 'The Deputy-Postmaster William Bedlow, at the former house of Judge Horsemanden, no. 38 Smith Street, wishes the public to know the post will arrive every Wednesday afternoon and be set out the next morning at 10 o'clock.... Rates to be published tomorrow.' "

"Let's talk with Mr. Bedlow. Smith Street is only a block away."

"It's Sunday morning."

Crèvecoeur walked over to a window and peered out. He turned around, with a shrug.

"This is New York."

They stepped out onto the muddy street. In a week the City had changed from ghost-town to boom-town judging from the febrile activity all around. They had to step past a crew of carpenters installing a large new sign above the door of their neighbor Mrs. Verplank's house at no. 3 Wall Street. "Aaron Burr, Attorney and Counselor-at-Law" read the sign, an image of a gavel and balance signifying the right of the proprietor to argue in court.

"You know prosperity must be lurking just beyond the corner when the lawyers start coming into town," Seton remarked. "Edward Livingston, Alexander Hamilton. Like vultures circling overhead, they seem to sense a killing. Now it appears we have Colonel Burr. He must be renting from Mrs. Verplanck. Her husband Samuel spent the war up at his estate in Fishkill, you know, as host to Gen. von Steuben. He didn't share his wife's love of the British. Judith's love, it seems, extended to General Howe himself, judging from the paintings of Eros he gave her.

"And now, of all things, there is a shortage of licensed lawyers since all Loyalist barristers were stripped of their right to practice. I've been asked to stay on as a magistrate until new judges are appointed for the City. Right now my sessions are full of only petty crimes but the new judges will have to deal with a quagmire of civil claims by returning Exiles."

The ground floor of no. 38 Smith Street was organized chaos. A small queue had formed in front of a newly-built counter behind which a young clerk in glasses was struggling with his tables of conversion to the irritation of a customer holding the foreign coin before the clerk's nose. In a back room behind him were stacks of loose papers piled high on tables where a harried-looking man was working.

"He's in there," the clerk jerked his head in response to their question.

The short plump man, like his clerk, wore eyeglasses. His thinning hair, pulled back into a tie, was coming undone.

"What you see before you, gentlemen, is seven years' worth of mail the British have left behind. I found it in their post-office and had it brought here. I've been working at it all week-end and I'm still only half-way done. I will post a notice in the newspapers for people to inquire at the shop if they think it worth their while. Your business, sirs?"

Crèvecoeur and Seton presented their cards.

"Pleasure to meet you gents," the man extended his dusty hand. "William Bedlow. Lately of Philadelphia. I was working under Mr. Hazard, the Postmaster himself, until requested to come here. But say, I recognize your name, Mister St. John de...de...ah, excuse me I can't pronounce the rest of it. Not from the newspapers, but – yes, I remember now."

Excitedly he walked over to a huge set of shelves he had built along a wall in the form of dozens of small boxes where he had been placing old mail. "Let's see...did I put it under 'S' or under...yes, here they are. Under both the letter 'C' and the letter 'S'.

"I found letters you wrote; and letters people wrote to you. How they all wound up in the British post office, I can't tell you. But here they are."

Bedlow handed over two bundles tied in ribbon. Crèvecoeur took them, numb. His eyes fell on the date written in a strong masculine hand on the top of the first letter: Boston, December 17, 1781....

"Are you all right, sir? Here. Sit down, make yourself comfortable over at this desk. I suppose you'd be attending the dinner at Cape's tonight with the French Ambassador? They say he's due in from Philadelphia...."

Crèvecoeur was not listening. The wax seal had already been broken long ago. With shaking fingers he spread open the papers. Silently he started reading to himself.

> "Honorable Sir: I received your letter of September 29, 1781 by the hands of the five officers of the naval vessel 'Protector'. I read it attentively. Your readiness to assist them in misfortune, and the important service you did them made on my mind an impression so strong that I at once took all the steps I thought needful to gain information by letter of the state of your family in Orange County. My effort was in vain; the war interrupted all communication. I then made up my mind to go there myself, and told my wife, who approved the plan.

> "A week after I left Boston I was lucky enough to meet the Sheriff of Orange County, Jesse Woodhull, Esq., who as Colonel of the militia was with his regiment at the post at Fishkill. Your letter, which I handed him, was the first he had got from you since you left the British prison at New York, he told me. He asked 100 questions about you, and Ally, your misfortunes, etc. I learned from him the sad death of your wife and the deplorable condition of the children, taken in by a destitute couple named Drake near your farm. Horror-struck at the news, I at once made up my mind to bring them away from that unlucky place and take them with me to Boston, and raise them up with my own children. The Sheriff approved my plan. He said, 'You cannot do a greater service to my old friend and good neighbor, Mr. St. John.'

> "Fortunately the snow was deep, and the roads well-trodden. I at once busied myself with arrangements for getting the children to Boston as comfortably as possible; and especially to clothe them warmly. My wife had provided for that, and luckily, for everything was so out of order that I could not have found in the whole County of Orange either woolens or suitable flannels.

Before leaving I inquired with Sheriff Woodhull what had been the expenses of the children since the death of their mother, and offered to put 40 guineas in his hands. He would not take it, saying that the sale of some horses and cattle, which had escaped the plunderers, had brought money enough to pay for their support, which could not indeed have cost much, judging by the condition I found them in. As to your farm and outlands, I advised him never to allow their sale without your consent.

"We treat your dear children as our own. As the Lord would have it we have a boy and girl of their ages, with whom they live on the best of terms. My wife and I love them as if they were children we had lost and recovered; were we so unfortunate as never to see or hear of you again, we shall educate them as our own. Not knowing what religious principles you had given them, I take them to church with my household, and they offer to God the same worship that we do. If you receive this, please tell us your wishes on this point; we shall be glad to conform to them.

"I am, sir, your humble servant,

Gustaves Fellowes."

Crèvecoeur looked up at his friend. "My little lambs are in good hands," he murmured. He read the letter again, out loud for the benefit of the others. When he finished he carefully folded the papers and tucked them away in his breast pocket.

"If you'll excuse me. I have some letter-writing of my own to take care of. And something else of no less importance."

Bedlow was weeping. Seton, who had gently taken hold of his friend's arms, was looking intently into his eyes. He smiled.

"Let us first go together to St. George's Chapel. Beekman Street is a fair hike but the walk will do us good. My friend Dr. Rogers has come back to town and has been invited to give this morning's sermon."

* * * * *

"We have come together to give thanks. Thanksgiving to God for giving to us a new life. May we use His gift wisely."

Dr. Rogers bowed his head.

" 'Out of my distress I called on the Lord; the Lord has answered me and set me free....Thou art my God, and I will give thanks to Thee; Thou art my God, I will extol Thee. O give thanks to the Lord, for He is good; for his steadfast Love endures forever....' "

It had been a long, long time since St. John had taken communion. He heard the tinkling of the bell, saw Father René standing before him, a halo of sunlight around his bald pate. Do this, in remembrance of Me....

"Go now in peace. And come back, if not next Sabbath for Episcopalian service, then Thursday, December 11 for Congress has declared that day a day of fasting, thanksgiving and prayer."

Seton stayed to visit with the Rev. Dr. Rogers. James took his leave and disappeared. Crèvecoeur walked slowly back to Wall Street by himself, although he was not alone.

* * * * *

The fever made its return. Mrs. Seton did her best to make her guest comfortable. At last he could sit up, back against the pillows, and read his correspondence. To James and Seton he entrusted the packet service. But affairs were sluggish.

"It's to be expected," Seton remarked. "It will take a few months for people to learn what they can import from France, and export back. Money is scarce, and credit scarcer. But that might change soon. John Church and his brother-in-law Col. Hamilton, and their father-in-law Gen. Schuyler, have formed their new bank. They've asked Alex McDougall to be its president, a shrewd choice to increase support from the Whigs. I have been asked to serve as First Cashier. It will be called 'The Bank of New York'."

James entered with the mail. "Here is a letter from the Marquis de Condorcet. Congratulations! You have been confirmed as a corresponding member of the Academy of Science. You are requested to report to the Academy on everything and anything of interest."

"That's a tall order." Crèvecoeur slumped back down on his pillows, exhausted. He closed his eyes.

"Here's a response from Dr. Bard to our subscription notice for the Journal of Medicine...a letter from Dr. Ezra Stiles of Yale College...Colonel Wadsworth in Hartford....This one is from Pierpont Edwards, in the Connecticut Assembly, about your proposal to have the Royal Gardens sponsor a museum in New Haven....

"But I think you'll want to read this one here first. It is from your daughter, Fanny."

Crèvecoeur, head slumped in the pillows, opened his eyes with a start. He stared at the young man.

"Please read it for me."

James obliged.

> " 'Dearest Father, it was with so much joy I opened your letter and learned from your own hand you have returned to New York, and as French Consul no less. Our dearest savior Capt. Fellowes showed me as well your letter to him and your request for more particulars on how he came to find us. I implored my adoptive father to permit me to respond.
>
> " 'It was time, dear father, for Providence to take pity on little brother Philly and me. For when Capt. Fellowes got to Chester we had neither stockings nor shoes, and were almost naked, and it was very cold. Little brother, being younger, did not feel the misery of our lot so much as I, but he cried a good deal. And I who remembered so well your tender care and that of poor Mother – how I did grieve when I thought of all that! And 'twas very often.
>
> " 'Mr. Drake and his wife, not knowing who this stranger might be that came to claim us, did all they could to persuade us to stay with them. They alarmed little brother, and he began to cry, saying, 'I don't want to go with that stranger.' I said to them, 'We cannot be more wretched than we are now; why should you want to keep us? You can hardly feed yourselves. This man must wish us well, else he would not have come such a long way. Perhaps God has sent him to us.'
>
> " 'I remember this too: I got into the strange man's

sleigh with the greatest eagerness, for I thought it would take me away from the place where I had lost my mother, and had suffered so much. Capt. Fellowes had to pull Philly away from the arms of Mrs. Drake, he crying, she crying. O Father! How good and warm were the clothes this good man had brought with him! How I trembled with joy when I put them on! You could not yourself have been kinder than this blessed man was to us.

" 'When we had a big river to cross on the ice, which he knew would give me a great fright, he always told us a pretty story to distract us. When we got to Hartford, some of his friends asked him, "What have you got in your sleigh?" "Two lost children," he said. "They were lost; and now they're found. I am taking them to Boston, where my wife will soon make them forget all they have had to bear. We have seven children, now the two little lost lambs will make nine." That was just what he said.

" 'In Boston how I liked being pitied, being put into warm clothes, having enough to eat when I was hungry, and especially to fear no longer being attacked by Indians. Philly began to laugh as soon as we got there. They let me sleep the first night with Abigail, the oldest daughter, who is near my age. I love her as if she were my own sister; she is kindness and sweetness through and through. Philly was put to bed with little Gustaves, who is only five months older.

" 'The next morning Mrs. Fellowes combed our hair, and gave us clothes like the others, and sent us all off to school together. Not only did she wash and dress us herself every morning, but she had us sit by her at the table, and gave us the best there was on it, for she said, 'These poor children have had a hard time, they must now have more care than our own.'

" 'I have been very useful to Mother, too. I help her every morning with the younger children. She has a baby eight months old, a little girl, and they gave her

my name, for I am her godmother. They named a
whaleship 'Fanny', too – she sailed three months ago
for Brazil. Do not worry over us, dearest Father, for
Philly and I are in loving hands. I say a prayer for
Mother every night and I am sure she is watching over
us, too.

Your devoted daughter,

Fanny.' "

As James finished reading he carefully folded the letter. He
looked at the consul. Crèvecoeur's eyes were closed and he
appeared to be asleep. But the glowing light radiating from the
fireplace was reflected in the glistening wetness of his cheeks.

Chapter Thirteen: *Beneath Thin Ice*

No. 3 was the longest edifice on Wall Street, having more
frontage than even the City Hall down the street. Its elegant
Georgian façade exuded an aura of imposing dignity and wealth
in every bay window draped with the finest dark burgundy
damask curtains. The butler, Jamaican by the lilt of his accent,
led them to double French doors ornate with gilded rococo
vines and flowers. He knocked, discretely.
"Come in." The voice was pleasing, melodic.
They found the owner of the voice seated in a grand walnut
and cherry armchair with plush burgundy upholstery behind a
luxurious polished mahogany table. His office was also his
library, and the carved walnut bookcases lining both sides of
the fireplace were not wanting for tenants. A cheerful fire
blazed.
"Pray be seated," the lawyer murmured, rising from his chair
and gesturing to its identical siblings. "A bit of brandy?" He
poured out two small snifters' worth from the fine French
decanter whose amber contents reflected the rich red of the
room. He took none for himself. He resumed his seat and
regarded them with soft hazel eyes.
"Mr. St. John. Mr. Seton. I am honored to make your
acquaintances."
There was no escaping the penetrating, domineering eyes.
They seemed to know the answers before the questions were

even formed. Although still a young man his lustrous brown hair was starting to thin in front, making him appear that much more intelligent. His blue jacket with dark blue satin lapels was cut from the latest French design.

"And now, how may I be of service to you?" His cool reserve was suddenly broken by a quick smile in the handsome face. It bespoke of warmth, an invitation to come and relax by the fire and chat a spell.

"I am sure you have read in the papers about the loss of our packet-ship," Crèvecoeur said. "The *Courrier de Saint-Louis*. Shipwrecked off Long Island last month."

"I recall the incident. We have had a brutal winter. One tempest after another. But surely the vessel was insured?"

"It was, through the Royal Assurance Society in Paris. But bogus claims are being filed in court here in New York against the policy and we will need to engage legal counsel to assist us."

The lawyer let his eyebrows rise in mock astonishment. "Citizens filing false claims? Committing perjury? Lying to our honorable judges? That's a serious charge." He flashed again his charismatic smile. "But not as uncommon as people think." He read the papers handed to him. He looked into the fire, lost in thought. He turned his bright eyes back to them.

"Their lawyer is a very good attorney. Hamilton and I are working on two or three large matters together right now, as co-counsel. We are all very busy thanks to the Trespass Act. His case under the Act might be the first of ours to go to trial."

"I've been threatened with a lawsuit under the Trespass Act myself," Seton remarked ruefully. "I saved an Exile's house from ruin by having British officers live there and keep the place in good repair, and now this new law says I am supposed to pay the returning owner rent for six years. I never got a penny for my efforts. And, should not returning Loyalists have the same right to damages?"

"Ah, but you see, Mr. Seton, you have overlooked the noble purpose of the new law: to reward the winners at the expense of the losers. And the fact that returning Exiles have the right to vote, and Loyalists don't."

There was the sound of steps outside the hallway door. The flowery knob was turned and the door swung open. An older boy with a scholarly air walked in. He saw the visitors seated in front of the table and hesitated.

"I'm sorry to have barged in," he said. "Please excuse me. Sir, I have brought the local mail." He laid a bundle on the corner of the table.

"That's all right, my boy. Have you finished the calculus problems I gave you?"

"Yes sir."

"Good. Now you will have time to read Socrates. I expect a report this evening after supper. You may go now."

The boy bowed and left, closing the door softly behind him.

"Bartow is a promising lad. My wife Theodosia's youngest son. I told him if he truly wants to attend Columbia College when it opens later this year he had better impress Governor Clinton and the new regents. His French grammar needs work, as well. My wife is literate in French but her health is not always the best."

"I would be delighted to assist you there, Mr. Burr, but I will be leaving next week for Boston," Crèvecoeur replied. "To see my own children. It has been a very long time....I can put you in touch, though, with an old friend and teacher. Reverend Tétard. Once the Assembly approves the act to transform King's into Columbia College, he is to be appointed professor of French."

"The name sounds familiar...my wife may be acquainted with him. I believe she had her daughters study the classics and French under him, before the War."

Crèvecoeur looked out through the window onto the snowy street outside. The sun was fighting to regain supremacy through the dark clouds.

"For some Americans it seems the War is not over...."

Aaron Burr smiled. "Indeed, warfare rages all around us. It lies in wait, simmering just below the surface of our civility, but always ready to erupt at the drop of a glove or a careless comment. It has no beginning, and it has no end. War is an eternal state. And so we have our judges. And I a source of income. Speaking of which we should address the question of my fees."

Contract concluded the lawyer accompanied them to the street door. He did not offer his hand, bowing instead, while his Jamaican servant stood ready to open the door.

"When you pass through New Haven give my regards to my cousin Pierpont Edwards. He wrote to me about your plan to establish a museum with the help of the French Royal

Gardens....When do you suppose you will be visiting your estate in Orange County? I believe you said it was near Chester."

"On my return from Boston. I am thinking about crossing the river at Newburgh."

"Mr. Hamilton and I have been asked to handle a case up there. It involves a long-simmering dispute over land."

Again the engaging glimpse of a smile. "Wasn't it Horace who said, 'Through every generation of man there is constant war?' Man hasn't changed much in two thousand years. Ergo, laws. The flurry of new laws the Assembly is passing in New York will be of great benefit. To us the lawyers."

" 'The more laws you have, the less justice.' Cicero, I think." Seton frowned. "But don't ask me which one."

"It was Marcus. I would add: it is foolish to think you can legislate people into acting justly. Laws do just the opposite: they teach the dishonest how far they can go; and remind the virtuous how impotent they are."

Another flash of the charming smile. "A virtuous people need no laws. Show me a society with an abundance of laws and I'll show you a depraved people. Who think that by adding patch upon patch to the hull of the ship they can cure the rot. Sooner or later that ship will sink. From the weight of the patches if not the rot."

"But, Mr. Burr, I hear you have been nominated for the State Assembly. To serve as lawmaker!"

Burr laughed. "And I pledge to do my very best to repeal unjust laws like the Trespass Act. But in the meantime life goes on. Like a stream flowing beneath a surface of ice. When you're driving your sleigh to Boston be mindful of it. The ice, I mean. Theodosia's uncle the old general reports that it is starting to thin in Connecticut."

* * * * *

The road glistening in the wan daylight of late March twisted and turned through small hills and vales until opening up onto a tableland of snow-covered fields. The irregular rows of stone fences shrouded in white uniforms guarded the sides of the road like minute-men asleep at their posts. Curls of smoke rose from scattered chimneys and bonfires in the woods where maple-sugaring was underway, and here and there could be heard the cheerful jingling of sleigh-bells competing with his own and the shouting of excited young voices absorbed in a blissful moment of timelessness.

Ahead on a rise lay a village visible through the naked limbs of the trees and on a higher eminence a large mansion, presenting a fable-like display of fanciful turrets and gables. As he passed through the village people were about attending to chores. The houses looked sad in the grey of the afternoon and even the mansion needed repair. The sign in the avenue said "Winthrop Street" and the traveler bid his horse to bring the sleigh to the tavern set back from the road. He went inside.

"Captain Fellowes?" the tavern-keep repeated. "He lives in his house in Town. Up the road just a-piece. Right after you cross the Neck. On Orange Street. 'Course, his wife owns that grand mansion on the hill you just passed. 'Pierpont Castle', everyone calls it. Grandest place in Roxbury. But it's her uncle and cousins what live there."

The traveler sipped his cider. "Strange coincidence," he murmured. "Pierpont...."

Seeing his hands trembling the tavern owner asked, "Stranger, you feelin' all right?"

The man nodded. "Just a wee bit o' the nerves."

He attempted a smile. "I don't know which is harder to bear. The fulfillment of the hope so long in coming seems to agitate my nerves almost as much as the fear I used to have that it was lost forever."

The tavern-keeper eyed the stranger warily.

"Are you sure you're feeling good? What's your business, may I ask?"

Drink finished the traveler put down his cup.

"To witness the unfolding of a miracle. Much obliged."

As his sleigh glided down the sloping road he saw the Town of Boston unfurling itself before his burning eyes, stinging from the cold wind. Church spires punctured the low-hanging clouds, tall masts of ships imitating them along the wharves and piers lining the irregular shoreline of the semi-island on which hundreds of houses huddled between the water and the hills for mutual protection against a harsh world. The Long Wharf extended far out into the bay ahead to his right, on which dozens of houses crouched, looking like old London Bridge.

He passed over the narrow Neck reeking from the low tide and the rotting remains of the British gates, the stench reinforced visibly by the sight of a decomposing body hanging from a garret, crows and gulls fighting over the spoils. To his left a few horses were standing, stoic, in a snowy yard and to his right was a shipyard and rope-walk building. The shipyard gave way to chandlers' shops and forges where smithies, at least, had work to do, glad to be near the warmth of their fires.

A large sleigh passed by loaded with firewood while another had assorted barrels of nondescript goods. A cross-street appeared, then another with the inevitable taverns. Between them were houses and a few shops, not a few with mullioned lead-pane windows under a brooding Elizabethan overhang. People were out and about, breaking up icy paths, tending to their chickens and cows in their barns behind their houses, the waters of the grey-green bay, glinting in the dim veiled light of the setting sun, never a long walk away.

The traveler stopped a passer-by and asked a question.

"Up ahead. By Harvard Street. The big house with the fancy gables and cod-fish weather-vane."

The house, cod-fish weather-vane pointing the true way the wind was blowing for those who cared to notice, sat on a very large lot reaching all the way down to the bay and a cluster of piers and a wharf where several sea-going ships were tied up. There was a carriage-way, freshly shoveled of snow, leading from the street down the side of the house to outbuildings in back. A steady yellow light glowed through a window. The traveler eased his horse into the carriage-way and stopped.

He sat for a long, long moment in his sleigh, looking at the grand portico sheltering the ornate double-doors. A ship's bell was suspended on one side. A brass whale-oil lamp was on the other. Each door boasted a large silver knocker in its middle. The stranger stared at them.

The knockers were weighty and made a dark ponderous sound. The doors opened.

"Sir?" the black butler inquired.

"To see Miss Fanny. And Mr. Louis-Philippe. Tell them …tell them their father is here." He handed the calling card to the stunned servant. He stepped inside the house.

The grand, wide hallway was dark. A soft yellow light bloomed through a doorway to the right, its essence captured and reflected in a rainbow prism of reds and blues by the cut-glass of the chandelier overhead, like the promise writ in the post-diluvian sky. Floating towards him on the light came the soft harmonic chords of a spinet and the higher tones of a harp and then a low voice, the soft, sweet singing of a girl, her words, like the light, captured for all time in the glass of the chandelier....

"Sir? Sir?" The butler's voice murmured from nearby, yet so far away. "I say, please follow me. Sir, can you hear me?"

The voice was singing words he could not understand and the melody was unfamiliar. But the message was clear. He walked into the salon.

The music stopped abruptly. The fingers of the woman at the harp froze in mid-pluck. The hands of the girl at the piano rested suspended over the keys.

Fanny stared at the stranger. Then her eyes closed and her face looked pale in the glow of the oil lamps. When they opened they were looking into the eyes of her father, kneeling before her chair.

Her green eyes asked a question to which no answer was possible. Her hair, darker now, a lustrous auburn, was curled in front and glinted red in the gleam of the light and the freckles on her cheeks glistened wetly as tears slowly meandered down her cheeks. She turned her face away, looked down at her hands still resting on the keyboard, her ring, *Agneau de Dieu*, embracing a finger. She closed her eyes again. She was crying, softly.

"Fanny...my dear daughter. Don't you know who I am?" His hands sought hers but she pulled her own away.

"Father! Father!" an excited boy came squealing into the room and threw himself onto the kneeling man's back, encircling his arms around his father's neck.

"Louis-Philippe, dear boy, is it really you?" Crèvecoeur gently disengaged the boy's arms and hugged him in turn. "Philly..." he almost whispered. "My son. My dear boy...." He squeezed him tight against his breast then held him at arms'-length, the boy's radiant face mirroring his father's.

He felt a hand on his shoulder. He turned around. Fanny was standing there. Crèvecoeur let go of Philly and let his daughter, in her turn, collapse into his arms, sobbing and laughing at the same time. They cried together, the three of them, crying and laughing in the elegant parlor of a Boston sea captain's home, three hundred miles and a lifetime away from the place that had been their home but was no more.

Chapter Fourteen: *Squaring the Human Heart*

All that remained were the foundation and the chimneys. Five years of rain, snow, wind and sun had swept away the memory of what had once been. Weeds and ivy were growing in paradise and their tendrils snaked among charred timbers. A fragment of copper, an iron hook, a twisted hinge from a door long since gone.

He went to where the barn used to stand. Here too only stones were visible. The smoke-house was no more and the pigsty had vanished, like the chicken coop, corn crib and granary, all evaporated into the air like a mirage in the desert. A rustling sound, the scurrying of feet and a chipmunk squeaked in protest at having been disturbed. The creature ran out from a clump of weeds underneath which, somewhere, the three sisters were weeping.

He slowly walked back to where the kitchen had once been. Nary a stone was left from the chimney but the lime-coated bee-hive oven was intact, waiting patiently for the bake-shovel and *tourtière* which were no more.

The round stone well was there even if the wooden well-sweep and bucket were not. September 20, 1769 the stones seemed to sigh. He peered down the well, let drop a pebble but he heard no sound. He turned around, looked towards the rubble where the front door of the house once stood. He approached.

The sassafras tree was taller now, branches unfolded a few feet above his head. Miraculously its bark revealed no trace of the conflagration as though it were impervious to fire. In the dappling shade cast by its young green leaves re-born only a few days before, the grape vine flourished around the trunk, standing straight in the midst of the ruins.

He fell down to his knees and cried.

* * * * *

" 'This Indenture made this second day of May in the Year of our Lord one thousand seven hundred and eighty–five by and between Hector St. John, Esquire, Consul of his Most Christian Majesty Louis XVI for the States of New York, Connecticut and New Jersey party of the first part, and Thomas Moffat Esquire of the County of Orange, party of the other part....by these presents doth sell, grant and convey to said Thomas Moffat all that tract of land lying and being in the patent of Wawayanda, County of Orange, once forming a part of a certain tract of land belonging to Daniel Crommelin known as Grey-Court, being bounded and described as follows....' "

Aaron Burr finished reading the deed out loud and looked at both men sitting on the bench before the table, behind which Burr was standing, document in hand.

"There it is, gentlemen. I have checked it carefully against the deed into Mr. St. John, but you are, of course, free to verify for yourselves. Otherwise kindly sign where indicated. Thank you. Mr. Moffat, I hereby deliver the deed to you. It is now your property."

Moffat folded the document and put it into his vest pocket. He put a hand on Crèvecoeur's shoulder.

"I promise to search again. But don't hold out much hope. The fire was very hot. Nothing remained, except for stone."

Abijah Yelverton came over. "Will you be staying another night, Michael?"

"If you have the bed, yes, I would like that. I plan on going up to Bull's this afternoon, then I'll look up Jesse Woodhull tomorrow. Then it's back to the City before I return to France."

"If you stayed another week you could see the trial. I'm letting Mr. Burr here and Mr. Hamilton hold the court in my barn. Looks like it'll be quite a show. That land is worth a hell of a lot o' money. Truth is, though, no one knows really exactly where the boundary lines are."

"Well, gentlemen," Burr purred, "where the boundaries are in anything depends on who is drawing the lines." He shook Crèvecoeur's hand.

"*Bon voyage.*"

* * * * *

"Dear Hector. With pleasure I learned you and your children were granted honorary citizenship by New Haven, and by Hartford at the same time as the Marquis de la Fayette. Their example inspires me to seek on your behalf a similar honor from the Republic of Vermont in recognition of your efforts on the part of your generous King to endow a college here with gifts of his munificence viz. a library of learned treatises and scientific treasures so that we may educate our children in the ways of the New Reason. I have asked the governor and council to name our new town in your honor 'St. Johnsbury' and its sister town 'Vergennes' for your Foreign Minister. I trust they will adopt my request.

"I was flattered to receive your book on America. Permit me to return the favor to you, in the form of a copy of my own book I have had printed in Bennington by a brave friend of Reason and which I present to you, enclosed. *Reason, the Only True Oracle* is the title of my modest work which I humbly place in your hands. Good sense, logic and reason should be the only oracles we teach our children to consult and only in reason can we find the Truth, freed from the stifling boundaries of Christianity and the worship of their false idol. I know you correspond with Mr. Jefferson, now in Paris, and I would be grateful were you to share my book with him as well, for I sense in him a kindred spirit.

"There can be no false prophets for those who worship the Truth of Reason. And, as every person 'has been endowed by our creator with reason', it stands to reason that every person, once freed from religious fervor, will develop a thirst for virtue, love and tolerance; and will conduct themselves accordingly. I look forward to that day, for America and for France.

With kindest regards, your friend,

Ethan Allen."

Crèvecoeur handed the slim volume to James. "Pack it with the other books in the trunk I'm bringing to Mr. Jefferson."

"It's almost noon. You'll need to get ready soon for the ground-breaking ceremony."

"I'm stepping out for a moment. I need a breath of fresh air."

He walked over to Nassau Street, ambled towards the City Hall on Wall. The air felt more tepid than fresh. The American flag hung limply over the cupola, below which the Congress was still not quite settled in. In this neighborhood, at least, there was a little more activity thanks to the handful of men serving as the federal government but even so every other building was still vacant. The only businesses seeming to thrive were the grog shops at every corner and the purveyors of the two oldest professions at work between the corners, the only distinction being that the lawyers put out signs openly proclaiming their trade. Wandering hogs grunted among the garbage and stray dogs were everywhere leaving their calling cards at random on the once clean cobblestones now caked over with a decade of decay.

"Oysters, my man. Get yer oysters for the day. Five pence the dozen. Yer wife will love you for it."

"*Koeckjes*? *Kruller*?" An old Dutch lady in rags accosted him. He had no appetite but bought a half-dozen anyway. An androgynous beggar stumbled towards him from the mouth of Broad Street and was surprised to find thrust into an outstretched paw sweet biscuits instead of coin.

Trinity Church was still biding its resurrection. Small yellow daisies bloomed among the stones, heedless of what had once been, patiently awaiting the vision to come. From across the river the Palisades sat unperturbed, as patient as the daisies, the jagged cleft in the middle of the cliffs up which Howe's grenadiers had climbed to assault Fort Lee splitting the curtain of rock like the veil torn asunder.

The old brownstone tombstone of the twenty-nine year old Abraham Williams had not changed either. "In Christ alone I put my trust...."

Crèvecoeur trudged back up Broadway to *Maagde Paatje*, Maiden Lane, the once pristine country creek long since filled in. He entered his house with the storefront serving as the consulate office. He found the chargé d'affaires waiting for him, recently arrived with the signed orders permitting him to return to France. Together they walked back to Broadway and then on to the new roads laid out west of the fields where the Liberty Pole had once reigned and the Tea Water Pump still presided.

"How long will you stay in France?" Count Barbé-Marbois asked.

"That," Crèvecoeur replied, "will depend on the state of my health. And on the grace of the king. Or at least Marquis de Castries."

"You do not believe you can find a cure in America?"

"I am not sure what to believe."

They reached the corner joining the new streets christened Barclay and Church where the land had been rid of the nuisance of nature and the terrain leveled. Other dignitaries were arriving, most on foot, a few in carriages, carriages in the city being few and far between. A small group was forming on the staked-out lot, mingling around the mayor and the Spanish consul Don Diego María de Gardoqui.

The Spaniard and the two Frenchmen embraced. They were joined by Gardoqui's chaplain Rev. José Phelan and the tiny congregation's unofficial pastor Rev. Charles Whelan. Encouraged by the example of their shepherds ordinary folk began to materialize, as though emerging from the secret basement rooms and garret lofts serving them for so many years as clandestine chapels and still not convinced they were free to worship as they believed.

"It is a glorious day. Catholic Christians need fear no more," Rev. Whalen greeted them. A carriage arrived, and three of the four trustees of the newly-chartered church emerged to the smiles of their comrades in faith. They were led, along with the fourth trustee, to a short platform in the middle of the small lot by Mayor Duane acting as host and were joined by Barbé-Marbois, Gardoqui and the two pastors.

Duane welcomed the foreign officials and introduced the trustees of the church: citizens James Stewart and Henry Duffin, Portuguese merchant José Roiz Silva, and Michael St. John de Crèvecoeur, French consul. The mayor's remarks were brief and he relinquished the podium to Rev. Whelan who led the assembled in a benediction and prayer.

"For Catholics in New York two dates will be cherished: November 26, 1784 when by Act of our Assembly religious toleration became the law of this State; and June 10, 1785 when the Assembly approved the charter for the Catholic Church of New York." After a ripple of polite applause the pastor resumed.

"May the Lord bless Charles the Third, by whose generosity one thousand silver Spanish dollars are now on deposit in the Bank of New York for the construction of our new chapel, and his Ambassador Don Diego who worked and prayed so hard on our behalf; and His Most Christian Majesty Louis the Sixteenth, from whom we hope for a similar blessing through the good offices of his consular representative, Sir St. John de Crèvecoeur, who was so instrumental in bringing about the Act of the Assembly and underwriting our new charter. And may God watch over our Prefect Apostolic Msg. Rev. John Carroll in Baltimore who sends his prayers and greetings to you the faithful. He will be here in October for the laying of the cornerstone, God willing.

"And now I ask our honored guests and benefactors to say a few words. May St. Peter's Chapel stand forever on this hallowed ground."

* * * * *

The voyage on the *Courrier de New York* following Franklin's Gulf Stream took only twenty-five days. Mercifully, for the fever had returned. The stage coach ride to Caen was a calvary of rough roads fallen into disrepair through terrain causing the coachman and his armed guard to maintain a constant vigil against highway bandits. There were signs of drought as they crossed dry streambeds and stunted crops in parched fields.

Crèvecoeur did not want to leave his sons, spending summer with Countess d'Houdetot at her estate at Soissons northeast of Paris. "Then stay," Sophie smiled. They went for long walks in the countryside and read books together long into the evening. One week they went to see the Duke de la Rochfoucauld at his château at Roche-Guyon; another week they visited the Duchess Beauvau and her husband at Marly-le-Roi. In October they went to Paris.

"I shall enroll the boys in Maître Lemoyne's school, with my own grandson Frédéric," Sophie announced. "Your general Nathaniel Greene's young son is there already, as well as other Americans. With two sons enrolled Maître Lemoyne gives a discount on tuition: only 2,400 pounds for both. Full pension, and his food is actually nutritious."

Crèvecoeur forced a smile and gave Sophie a kiss on the neck. His yearly honorarium of 3,000 pounds from the Naval Ministry was not enough to cover his expenses and the money from the sale of his book had long since been spent. It being useless as well as distasteful to ask his father for help Crèvecoeur set about writing an expanded third edition. That winter he became a virtual recluse, writing feverishly all day in his rooms at the d'Houdetot *hôtel* and only stepping out on occasion to visit his sons; or to see Jefferson and La Fayette on Monday afternoons or to be led by Count d'Houdetot, Sophie and her lover Saint-Lambert to see an opera or concert, or Beaumarchais' *Le Mariage de Figaro*. Every other Sunday morning he went to mass.

They watched Beaumarchais' play at the Comédie-Française from the private box of the Duc de Chartres now d'Orléans thanks to his father's death. The floor was given over to *le peuple* who booed and hissed the grandly lecherous Don Almavira and cheered Suzanne and Figaro at orchestrated moments led by a tall man Crèvecoeur recognized as the glazier from the Marais. When Figaro, decrying the abuses of the nobility, declaimed *"Noblesse, fortune, un rang, des places: tout cela rend si fier! Qu'avez-vous fait pour tant de biens? Vous vous êtes donné la peine de naître, et rien de plus..."* the crowd chanted the words along with the actor, led by the Duc d'Orléans himself, the king's cousin leaning out from his box above the floor, pumping his right fist in the air to the cheers of the people below, his left hand securely snuggled in the warm bosom of his lover, Marguérite-Françoise de Buffon, her husband having been sent to quell a slave insurrection in the French Antilles. Thus had King David dealt with General Uriah.

Thomas Jefferson, too, had seen the play and was enthusiastic.

"I wish I could understand spoken French better. But, no matter. I studied beforehand the written text Monsieur Beaumarchais was kind enough to give me."

His voice was soft, his drawl unhurried. The greyish-blue eyes in the handsome face shined with delight, sorrow for the moment forgotten.

"A sober lesson to the privileged who would abuse the power of their position to satiate their selfish desires. Which, indeed, can never be satisfied, as Monsieur Beaumarchais observes," La Fayette remarked. The red and blue cockade he had designed highlighted his velvet lapel.

" *"En ce fait, même trop c'est jamais assez.'* Did I get that right?" Jefferson smiled deferentially.

"*C'est parfait*," Countess d'Houdetot assured him.

Her lover Saint-Lambert nodded in agreement. "*Parfait.*"

"We will speak in English now!" An intense young man with a long, serious face interjected, looking around the salon as though he were the host.

"Well of course we shall," the even younger young lady seated on the canapé next to him agreed. "English is the new language of political thought, no? And all peoples here speak it, no?" she looked around the salon at the other guests not expecting disagreement.

The much older husband of the young lady, standing by a window in the splendid uniform and sash of the Swedish Ambassador to France, continued smoking his pipe as though lost in thought or otherwise. Baron Erik Magnus Staël von Holstein had no comment, perhaps because he did not, or could not, or did not want to, understand his wife of six months.

The proprietor of the *hôtel particulier* and therefore the salon in which they were all sitting at 183 rue de Bourbon smiled broadly at the young Madame de Staël.

"My dear Anne-Louise, English, as it is practiced in America has become the language of change. Beaumarchais notwithstanding. And we are honored to have the oracle of the revolution in Mr. Jefferson. But in political thinking, our Montesquieu still reigns supreme. Would you not concur, Mr. Jefferson?"

Jefferson, his lanky body almost too much for the dainty Louis XV salon chair on which he found himself sprawling, allowed for a shy smile.

"I do, Monsieur le Marquis. But I would also add to your pantheon J. J. Rousseau. On political philosophy as well as on education. "

"See how we are all of one mind!" The serious young man exclaimed. "Government must be made to answer only to the people. If it does not, then it is in breach of contract and must be overthrown. Along with all of its repressive laws. There must be a new beginning. As Rousseau said, crime does not make people criminals. It is law that turns good people into criminals. Why should a man be thrown in jail for speaking his opinion? Why should it be a crime for a poor starving man to steal food for his hungry family?"

"Or for a banker to steal money from his clients?" Anne-Louise, Madame de Staël laughed.

"Or from the government's pacquet boat service," Crèvecoeur muttered, receiving a sympathetic glance from the American ambassador.

"If dishonest bankers are the rule then your father Jacques Necker," Sophie said to Anne-Louise, "is the exception that proves rules are not absolute."

"Which is why he was shunned by the king's government!" the young man exclaimed. Jacques-Pierre Brissot ran his fingers through the mass of his thick brown hair as though expunging for all time the unwanted lice within. "Corruption cannot tolerate virtue."

"My father," Madame de Staël rejoined, "would be mortified to hear such flattery, sincere Calvinist that he is. He would say, 'He who thinks himself without sin condemns himself.' "

"Remove the Laws of Moses and you remove the notion of sin," Brissot replied. "Then Man, freed from guilt, can flourish, free to think and speak as *his* spirit moves him."

"Until he bumps heads with another free-thinker with opposite views. Then what?" Baron von Holstein was ironic.

"Then they talk. Debate."

"And if one of them pulls out a knife?"

"In a civilized society, with the proper education of our children, such things will no longer happen."

"And thus we can look forward to the abolition of all laws," the Baron smiled.

"Exactly!" Brissot nodded his head enthusiastically. "Exactly. That day will come, and not a moment too soon. I do not want to spend another four months in the Bastille. Although I would gladly do it again to defend my right to say and write whatever I wish, even if it does offend the queen. Mark my words, someday in our lifetime the Bastille will be pulled down. That will signal the dawn of the new age of tolerance and mutual respect between men."

"Men?" Madame de Staël arched her brows. "I am grieved that we women must be doomed to continue in our intolerant and disrespectful ways. But, I suppose, such is the inevitable result of cultivating the heart more than the brain. Don't you think so, Madame la Comtesse?"

"Oh, I do. I do indeed," Sophie replied. "Ovid, our *Präceptor Amoris*, tells us so. 'Whether you call my heart affectionate, or you call it womanish, I confess, that to my misfortune it is soft.' To the men, the steely lamp of reason. To the women, the dark weakness of the heart. We are quite doomed."

"Doomed, yes, that is the word," Madame de Staël laughed. "But I prefer our modern philosophers like Jean-Jacques to ancient Romans. 'Nothing is less in our power than the heart, and far from commanding we are forced to obey it.' "

"Better yet, our dear Benjamin," Sophie raised the ante. "The heart of the fool is in his mouth, but the mouth of the wise man is in his heart.' "

"But best of all," rejoined Marie-Adrienne Françoise de Noailles, the Marquise de la Fayette, "is He who said, 'blessed are the pure of heart, for they shall see God'."

She turned to Jefferson. "I am so sorry, Mr. Jefferson, for the loss of your young Lucy. I have asked for a special mass for her."

Jefferson gave a polite nod of the head. Casting his eyes to the side to hide the pain only served to reveal it.

"But now, tell me. How is your lovely daughter Patsy adjusting to school? She resembles you so much. L'Abbaye de Pentemont suits her well, I hope. The good sisters are quite used to exempting the daughters of Protestant foreigners from the Holy Mass."

Jefferson shifted uncomfortably on his dainty seat. "I cannot thank you enough for your introduction to the Abbey. Patsy is very…fond of the nuns….I visit her every Sunday."

"When can we expect your younger daughter Polly to join you? Will you also place her in the Abbey?"

Jefferson hesitated. "She is very attached to her aunt and uncle and cousins in Virginia. Since the death of her mother she has known no other family. I have not been successful yet in my endeavors to have her make the voyage to France."

"I imagine though you will have her enrolled in the Abbey with her sister once she arrives," Mme. la Marquise persisted.

"I suppose you are right….I wonder, though, why it should be that in such an enlightened society there is no other option for giving one's daughters a good education, unless they are tutored at home. The same needless distinction between the sexes is practiced in America, of course, after the child attains a certain age."

"How progressive you are, if I may say so, Mr. Jefferson. There is no reason not to educate girls and boys together, and every reason why it should be good for them all." Madame de Staël's smile had an edge to it. "In that way girls will benefit from the uplifting, enlightened wisdom of the boys."

"Have you received word lately from dear Franklin?" Sophie hastened to intervene. "I am beside myself for fear he has not received my correspondence."

Jefferson gave a short nod of the head. "Mr. Franklin and Gen. Washington are distressed, as am I and Mr. Madison, over the inability of the States to cooperate with each other. The General has called for a conference to revise our Articles of Confederation. As usual, the driving force behind the call is money. Or the lack of it. We do, after all, owe a deep, deep debt to France. Of gratitude as well as money."

"How is it possible to sail a ship without a captain?" Baron von Holstein asked. "A country without a king, or a prime minister, or a governor. Your ship, if I may be permitted, is *sans gouvernail*. It is rudderless."

"That is indeed a problem," Jefferson admitted. "Although the Swiss Republics seem to manage. However, we are thirteen fiercely independent bodies strung out over a thousand miles. Plus the new Northwest Territories in the Ohio Valley."

"For which, Mr. Jefferson, you are to be congratulated, for advocating a total ban on slavery in the new lands." Brissot leaned forward eagerly. "All friends of mankind - " he glanced at Madame de Staël next to him " - that is, humanity, are watching your great experiment in building a new society, one which will reject, not for base money reasons, but for virtue alone, the enslavement of people. People in their natural state would never enslave another, since no one wants to do something to another which he himself would not like."

Baron von Holstein gave an audible sigh. He packed his pipe, which he had laid down to cool off, into his ornate gold case.

"I must take my leave, my good general and my dear marquise. For this evening I am a slave to my duties as ambassador. Another reception at Versailles in the guise of a tea party with the queen. If only, Mr. Jefferson, I could become a naturalized American, even just for the evening, and thus enjoy the immunity conferred by Her Highness' low regard for your new country and everyone associated with it. Good day to you all. Anne-Louise, my dear, I will send the coach back for you."

A sharp click of the heels and he was gone. Brissot reached into his pocket and pulled out a pamphlet. He handed it to the American.

"I would be honored for your thoughts and comments. It is my essay on reforming our criminal laws in France."

"I can't thank you enough," Jefferson murmured.

Nicholas, the Marquis de Condorcet was escorted into the salon by the *maître d'hôtel*. Jefferson brightened. All stood to greet him. He bowed deeply before kissing the extended hand of the Marquise de la Fayette. For la Comtesse he reserved a special kiss. Nor was young Madame de Staël spared the lips of the beaming mathematician, who held both of her hands in his a moment.

"I singled out Anne-Louise for greatness, you should know, from the moment I heard her recite a poem she had written at her mother's salon, what, eight years ago? - when she was still a mere little girl. She will no doubt carry on the great tradition of our Paris salons when we of her parents' generation are no more.

"I hope your talks are going well with Vergennes and Calonne, Thomas. Being stuck at the Mint as I am, I am far out of the loop of things."

"As I am learning, Nicholas, treaties are never easy things. Commercial treaties in particular."

"It is indeed a pity I am not controller-general. You would find negotiating with me as easy as talking to yourself in the mirror. We think alike. Free ports. No restrictive duties. No government meddling. No government controlling every little detail. The people know what they need and what they want. Let them decide But, I'm afraid, there is great fear of change in our ministers. And so many fingers in the pie.

"The royal government over the years has delegated the entire machinery to outside investors to administer everything: tax collecting, finance, manufacturing, food distribution. Trade guilds and their monopolies. No one wants to give up their slice of the pie. Not least of whom the ministers' bureaucrats. For them it is power. Your difficulty, my friend, is that you must ask those who enjoy the power to give up the very thing they strive to keep."

"I'll settle for the moment for duty-free ports. Or at least no duties on our rice and whale oil. Or tobacco."

"But will your individual States give up their insistence on the same right to impose? Americans have only one France to deal with. French merchants have thirteen Americas to understand, each with its own set of taxes and imposts. And we understand so poorly."

"If you would permit me." Brissot had come over, unfazed by his lowly birth for which he had compensated by adding an honorific "de Warville" to his name. "Your treatise on free trade resonates well. I submit that France and America are not rivals for prosperity but partners. We are of one mind, Mr. Jefferson! Both our countries are societies based on agriculture and the fruit of the land. The agricultural production of France and America do not compete but rather complement the other. All the focus on manufacturing is like two men arguing over who owns a tiny pond when they both share an enormous lake."

"The two activities require a different analysis," Condorcet replied. "But I see no reason they cannot live in harmony with one another. Economic activity like everything else in human society can ultimately be reduced to mathematical proofs. From there it is simple. Just solve the equations."

"Human beings cannot be reduced to mathematical calculations," Brissot retorted. "The human heart cannot be squared. We are a people of the good earth. Happiness can only come through growing your own food, your own crops, on your own farm. Like in America. With no feudal lords or peasantry. Or royal taxes. Each family owning its land, responsible for its own success or failure.

"Manufacturing, by contrast, is demeaning and dehumanizing. Enslaving people to work for a tiny wage like in our textile industries in Rouen, or Reveillon's wallpaper factories, given a pittance compared to the profits reaped by the owners, living in unhealthy cities and slums full of pestilence and vice."

"I couldn't agree with you more." Jefferson replied in his soft unhurried voice. "City life demeans the worker and perverts the wealthy with its lure of luxury and comfort."

Brissot nodded his head enthusiastically. "The right to own and work your own farms and mills is the only source of virtue and happiness! Just as our friend Crèvecoeur describes in his inspiring book about your bountiful land, its benign forests, its fertile valleys! You have read it, have you not?

"America, the new paradise! I am organizing investors to form a company to settle in your lush Ohio valley. Like in the Garden of Eden, the fruits of the land just waiting to be plucked and eaten."

Jefferson found himself inhaling the aromatic, fruity fumes emanating from the breath of the ecstatic young man who, in his eagerness, had brought his face only inches from the

American's. Jefferson retreated a step, then turned to Condorcet.

"About your book on the abolition of slavery. I would like to have it translated into English and published in America. I fear, though, that in our southern states there is an ocean of resistance. If the Negroes are liberated they will become the new masters, or so the thinking goes. Our black servants outnumber the masters ten to one in Virginia, for example. Or on some plantations, two hundred to one," he said ruefully, reddening slightly.

"Then," Brissot cut in, "there must be a revolution by the slaves. Like what's going on presently in our Haïti colony. If it is good for the oppressed white people of America, so too must it be for the oppressed black people. Don't you agree, Mr. Jefferson?"

Young Madame de Staël glided in deftly. "I've been meaning to ask you, Monsieur le Marquis," she addressed Condorcet, "about your paper on voting and elections, and majority rule. I confess I did not understand completely your mathematical proofs. But your conclusion seems clear enough, that you will have a greater probability of achieving the 'correct' outcome when you have a greater number of voters. I ask myself, though, how your theory evaluates whether an outcome is the correct one or not."

"That outcome is correct, which pleases the greatest number of people," Condorcet replied.

"Suppose fifty-one percent of the voters approve killing the other forty-nine percent. Is that a just result?"

"My dear, do not confound mathematics with morals. I am simply saying that in any election it is not advisable to have more than two candidates. There is a good chance that none of the three will receive a majority of the votes. The same holds true when voting on issues or propositions. Otherwise, no one is happy and no one can agree. And so you have a mess."

"That does sound like our Congress," Jefferson agreed.

Brissot resumed his pursuit of the American. "Mr. Jefferson. As the Marquis points out, there is an ocean of misunderstanding between our two cultures. I think – and I flatter myself that General La Fayette and Monsieur Crèvecoeur agree – that the key to nurturing trade between our countries is to first educate each about the other. '*Le Bureau des Luminaires*' Monsieur Crèvecoeur calls it. I prefer a simpler name. *'La Société Gallo-Americaine.'* More down-to-earth. The French-American Society. Its members will consist of the leading lights of France and America. Philosophers, scientists, writers, lawyers, merchants. Ambassadors...."

"An interesting idea. Let me give it some thought."

"But wait." Brissot gestured excitedly with his hands. Jefferson shrunk back imperceptibly, as though fearful the young man was about to grasp his lapels. "It will be more than just a vehicle to promote culture and trade. I envisage a forum for the exchange of ideas, social philosophy. We will have speakers. Topics like education. The right of women to vote. The abolition of slavery. I have a few comments on your interesting ideas about black people. "

"My ideas on black people?"

"Yes, in your stimulating treatise, *Notes on the State of Virginia*. My wife Félicité and I read it in London. We find the original language much better than the French translation."

"It really was intended for only private publication. And to answer a few questions from Count Barbé-Marbois."

"You are so modest. Everyone admires your elegant pen and brilliant mind. I agree completely with your condemnation of city life as corrupting and evil. Also your abhorrence of debt and your praise of frugality and thriftiness. And especially your hatred of slavery and the tyranny of the clergy.

"Anyway, I myself can have no opinion on your observation that black people in America are intellectually inferior or physically less attractive, having never been to your country, at least, not yet! Although I am eager to go. But I can appreciate your suggestion that once freed from bondage they should be encouraged to remove to Africa. But I have different reasons for that, having nothing to do with miscegenation or racial wars.

"If your plan is adopted, it should be for the purpose of colonizing Africa with black farmers, who will export their exotic crops to France and America and import our produce. On French and American ships. Our seaport towns like Nantes and Bordeaux will flourish. They will drop their opposition to banning the slave trade and abolishing slavery in the French colonies since they will have crops to transport in the place of humans."

"And the sugar cane planters?" Condorcet asked. "They are wealthy and therefore control the opinions of the ministers and merchants. But there could be a better argument. Why should it not be true that they can stand to gain more money if they paid their laborers? Paid workers will have to buy food, clothes, lodging. All of which could be supplied for a fee by the plantation owners. Paid workers will work much harder than slaves. And therefore bring in more profit.

"I think I will look into what mathematics has to say about this."

The *maître d'hôtel* whispered in Madame de la Fayette's ear.

"*Le dîner est servi*," she smiled to her guests.

"Come. Let us proceed to the table." La Fayette linked his arm to Jefferson's. To Condorcet he remarked, "And perhaps you can devise a mathematical explanation for the enjoyment we feel when seated before an appetizing repast with fine wine and even finer company."

"I accept the challenge." Condorcet bowed. "Ultimately, in the final analysis all human life can be explained by numbers. Mathematics, you see, is the ultimate truth. And therein lies the final solution."

Chapter Fifteen: *The Irony of it All*

"The numbers just didn't add up. The votes weren't there. And so there was a complete acquittal for my client."

The quartet was strolling among the gardens of Les Tuileries, enjoying the late spring air, the twin conical towers of the Palais de la Cité rising in the nearby distance, the needles on top pointing to the sky like accusing fingers.

Jean-Baptiste Target stopped and pointed his own finger at the top floor of the former palace of the Valois kings.

"The irony of it all," Target said. The lawyer sniffed. For the benefit of the American ambassador he explained.

"One of the first things Louis the Sixteenth did when he came to the throne in 1774 was to restore the royal tribunal, the Parlement de Paris. Which had always sat since the days of Saint-Louis over there, in the Palais. Above the Conciergérie, the prison. That is where the trial of my client took place last year.

"The king had offered my client a choice: he could defend himself in the king's own council, or before the Parlement de Paris. I was astounded at this gift from Providence. Of course I advised the cardinal to elect to appear before the Parlement.

The Pope was outraged, but the trial proved his fears unfounded.

"Sixty-four magistrates, of whom most are trained lawyers and the rest men of the clergy, heard the evidence. But even had they been wooden statues the outcome would have been the same. The evidence left no doubt. Cardinal de Rohan was innocent of the charges. To the mortification and chagrin of the queen.

"You see, he had been completely duped by that conniving woman. Not the queen, but by the real crook Jeanne de St.-Rémy. 'Comtesse de la Motte' she called herself. She and her unscrupulous husband and her lover. It was her lover who forged the letters they palmed off to the cardinal as coming from the queen. And so, thinking he was pleasing the queen, he gave his promissory note to the jewelers who released the diamond necklace to the crooks."

"I had a difficult time understanding the accounts in the newspapers," Jefferson admitted. "It seemed to me that if anyone had been swindled, it was the defendant cardinal. After all, he paid for the necklace. Not the Royal Treasury."

"Oh, do not feel inferior. It was a magnificent scheme. Wonderfully complicated. So complicated, in fact, that the magistrates saw right away that our poor naïve cardinal was hopelessly incapable of masterminding such a fraud as the queen charged. If he was guilty, it was not for being venal. It was for being gullible."

"It *was* fascinating," Sophie agreed. "Poor Cardinal de Rohan. To be deceived and manipulated by his own lover. The very woman he shared his bed with. She not only procured an accomplished forger – her real lover! – but managed to find a prostitute who is the queen's look-alike, who completely took in the cardinal. But who can fault him? He was infatuated with the queen. And desperate to find a way to curry her favor."

"And that way," the lawyer continued, "was nothing less than a stroke of utter genius by our dear Jeanne. Employing the charlatan mystic Count Castiglione to convince the cardinal of what his Eminence wanted to believe: that the false letters asking him to buy the diamond necklace were truly from the queen.

"And so, once again we see, it is not very hard to persuade people to believe what they want to believe regardless of the truth."

"Well," Jefferson said ruefully, "I can attest it's not pleasant to be falsely accused. I was so myself, by my detractors in Virginia claiming I fled from my duties as governor when Cornwallis invaded. But why is it the people believe the queen herself was the inventor of the scheme? That makes no sense to me."

"Well, as I said, people will make up their minds not based on the facts, but on their prejudices. The fact is, the people hate the queen."

They had taken a path that led down to the river. Scores of girls and women, heads wrapped in shawls to protect them from the sun, skirts tied above their knees, were standing ankle deep in the water washing laundry. Several glared at the well-dressed party passing by high and dry. One of them raised her voice.

"Rich people, with their airs. That's the American ambassador, isn't it? Red hair and all."

"There are two red-heads."

"I mean the tall, skinny one. Trying to cheat the treasury of our tax money...." Her companions took up the call to arms, jeering words the unflattering meaning of which the ambassador sensed rather than understood. Target hastily led the party back up to the more rarefied air of the royal gardens. A splattering sound as of mud hitting dry ground pursued their heels.

"I apologize on behalf of our disgruntled citizens. Next to the queen, America has become the new scapegoat. Not surprisingly, it is about money."

"I know the problem only too well," Jefferson said, glumly. "I have been pleading with Congress for the last three years to at least make a partial repayment. Not only does America owe France almost six million pounds, but thanks to Franklin's charm it is without interest! I cannot blame your people for throwing mud at my back. Particularly in light of your finance minister's horrifying report on the French debt. To which America's contribution is not insignificant."

Jefferson sighed.

"Debt is truly an evil to be avoided at all costs."

"America's debt to France is not overwhelming, compared to the whole," Target pointed out. "But you are right, the figures are shocking. The French current deficit, according to Calonne, has reached the astronomical sum of one hundred million pounds. Forty percent of our national revenue. The total royal debt is a thousand million pounds! Half the tax receipts each year go to pay the interest on the debt. Which makes the people hate the bankers and the government even more."

"At any rate, the people have gotten their wish. Calonne resigned." Jefferson observed.

"But does hatred for the messenger change the underlying truth of the message?" Sophie asked.

"It's not just hatred of the one man that has all of Paris – indeed, all of France now – heating up," Target replied. "The royal government is bankrupt. Yet the king asks for even more new loans. He needs the loans to pay the interest on the loans he already has. Lenders are scared they won't be paid back. Plus, Calonne let the price of grain and bread fluctuate freely which has the common people terrified.

"The king's attempt to create a puppet court of hand-picked nobles to rubber-stamp his requests for more money and castrate the Parlement de Paris was the last straw. For me as well, I must admit. So now the lower clergy, the merchants, the mechanics, the lawyers, even some of the nobles are clamoring to bring back the *États-généraux*. I am with them."

"The three General Estates – clergy, nobility and commoners – haven't been convened since 1614," Sophie pointed out. "No one alive even knows how to do it or how to elect the members."

"Well, the devil, as they say, is in the details."

"There have been riots in the provinces," Sophie fretted. "Noblemen and priests have been murdered. The pamphleteers are enflaming the people."

"The royal government wants time to figure out what to do. And without giving up power. The irony is, by playing for time the king betrays his lack of the very power he still pretends to have. His government is beginning to realize how illusory true power is. Power derives from the people's perception of it. The people are beginning to perceive that beneath his ermine robes the king is nothing but a man. A scared, frail, bankrupt man."

"What does this mean for French-American relations?" Crèvecoeur wondered.

"America just as well might not exist for the king. He has other things to worry about. The lawyers, the magistrates, we won't let the king manipulate us anymore."

"But we can't have the government default on its loans," the Comtesse worried.

"Oh, to be sure we in the Parlement de Paris will agree to give him another loan because we won't let the government collapse. But it will be on our terms, not his. He will have to cut the royal budget and tax the clergy and the nobility. And he will have to rescind Vergennes' trade treaty with England. The French merchants are upset because he reduced the duties on English textiles, which means they are forced to lower their prices to compete or close shop and fire their workers."

"But free trade and lower duties are exactly what is needed in France, and what the Americans like the English also want," Crèvecoeur pointed out. "How else are we to stimulate trade between our countries?"

"Buy more books," Jefferson said. They had reached the rue de Rivoli and the first of several elegant bookstores mesmerizing the American ambassador with an enticing array of seductive selections. He stared with longing at several new titles.

"Let's go in," Sophie urged.

Jefferson hesitated.

"I can't go into this one, I'm afraid. Not until I pay off the debt I owe the proprietor."

He smiled sheepishly. "It's just that I love books so much. I spent two thousand francs last year on books, I'm afraid. I still owe him six hundred. It is such a delightful shop."

They passed a vintner's, whose carved oak-paneled storefront was stained a rich, comforting dark reddish-brown, redolent with the look and smell of a fine country wine cellar and its inviting bacchanal delights. Here, too, Jefferson lingered.

He smiled ruefully. "I owe two hundred francs here. Three francs a bottle for a good Bordeaux, you know. It *is* shameful, isn't it? A laborer in Paris earns only two francs a day."

They crossed rue de Richelieu. The street was busy with the life of the city. In this quarter even the beggars were courteous and the prostitutes well-dressed. Elegant carriages shared the way with smart cabriolets and the restaurants and cafés were *égayés*, overflowing with witty conversation and laughter. They stopped to watch a pair of jugglers and a *saltimbanque* performing stunts on the sidewalk while a musician nearby entertained with his violin, in competition with an organ grinder not far away. Jefferson was delighted, handsome face lit up.

They walked up rue de Richelieu, past the jewelers, the milliners, the dressmakers. At a tailor shop they paused while Jefferson went inside a moment. He came back out in less than a minute.

"Well, they won't have my new suit until next week. It's the new season, you know, and so it must be silk. Tomorrow being Tuesday, and I won't have the proper attire for the king's levee or Vergennes' dinner for the diplomatic corps. I wonder if I should stay home."

"The only one I know who is Monsieur Jefferson's height and build is your husband," Target said, looking at the Comtesse d'Houdetot.

"I will arrange it," Sophie replied.

There was a clockmaker's next door. The display window was a cornucopia of wonderful mechanical gadgets of all kinds: table clocks, pendulum clocks, Bavarian cuckoo clocks and Viennese dancing clocks, windup dolls and walking toy soldiers.

"Look. What are those large globes?" the Comtesse asked.

"That machine, my dear," Jefferson replied, "is an orrery. It shows all the planets in orbit around our sun; and all the moons around the planets, those that have them. You put them in motion by means of the silver crank on the side. We have in Philadelphia an inventor, David Rittenhouse, who has made one or two. This one here is even more elaborate. Just look at the beautiful cabinet...satinwood and mahogany I think. I've always wanted to own one," Jefferson confessed.

"The silver and gold inlay is exquisite," the Comtesse agreed. "I am sure it must cost a small fortune."

"It does," Jefferson said, sadly. "Fifteen thousand francs. I have already inquired. The other day, it was," he said almost apologetically. "Just as much as the new coach I have on order. The phaeton I shipped over from Monticello is too plain."

Their stroll took them to the Palais-Royal. The linden trees along the sides of the vast interior court were just starting to blossom as well as several smaller, newly planted trees with exotic bright yellow flowers peeking timidly through the thorny branches protecting them.

"Your acacia trees seem to have survived their first Paris winter," Jefferson remarked to Crèvecoeur. "As did the ones you gave me. I enjoyed your lecture about them at the Academy.

I wonder though if our American transplants are meant for Europe."

They found themselves entering the grounds of the Palais-Royal.

"Isn't the architecture of Paris magnificent? How grand the Palais is." Jefferson gestured towards the elegant Roman arches of the Duke d'Orléans' arcade. He enticed them around the gardens and fountains of the immense courtyard, entranced by the rich shops and boutiques, clockworks and cafés under the arched passageways, pointing out in minute detail each exquisite architectural feature thrilling his eyes.

They chose a charming café close by rue de Rivoli and sat at a table outside. An intricate wrought iron fence tipped with gilded fleurs-de-lys enclosed the terrace. Their coffee was served to them in fine porcelain and the sugar dispensed with small silver spoons. Target ordered a liqueur. Jefferson was delighted by the small sweet pastries served on a silver dish.

"When you come to dine at the villa on Sunday," Jefferson said, "I hope to be able to replicate this. Or rather, I hope James will."

"Has he finished his training?" Target asked. "It is easier to qualify as a lawyer than to become a certified pastry chef. But then, you sent him to the finest school, did you not?"

"We will see if he passes the test next Sunday at my house, with my guests as the jury. And judges."

They all felt the sting of a pair of hungry eyes staring at their plate of pastries. The eyes belonged to a disheveled man whose unshaven face was thrust half way through the iron bars forming the enclosure, livid hands gripping the metal as though it were a cage, or a prison. A bright yellow acacia flower was pinned to his lapel, a splash of brilliance on his otherwise drab apparel. He turned his eyes towards theirs.

"Here now. Go away. Leave us in peace, my man." Target was cross.

The countess rose and went to the fence. She handed the beggar a franc.

"Sophie. You should not be encouraging them. He will only spend it on drink," Target said, sipping his own.

The man accepted the coin with a slow nod of the head, bright eyes shining at his benefactor.

"I suppose," Sophie said, resuming her chair, "it was more for myself than for him."

The beggar was looking intently at Crèvecoeur. Their eyes locked onto each other's for a long instant. Then the man with the yellow acacia flower vanished as silently as he had appeared.

The void was quickly filled. They seemed to appear out of nowhere, from all directions, like ants at a picnic. Some were men, a small few were women, some old, some young The head-waiter bustled over, shooing them away crossly with a swishing motion of his towel, as if swatting at so many flies. He offered the party his excuses.

"It is getting worse every day. They come from the country; they come from the *banlieues*, the surrounding towns. These *banlieuesards* aren't even real beggars. They have jobs. What they don't have is a sense of shame. More pastries, *messieurs-dame*?" he asked perfunctorily before departing.

"I suppose," Target mused, "if a man has to feed his family he will swallow his shame even if he has a job. The taxes are too high for them. It can't go on like this. But even in America, we have read, the farmers and mechanics are rioting over taxes."

Jefferson was nodding his head. "Daniel Shay and his band. They have my sympathy, I confess."

"I can appreciate the irony of it all." Target was amused. "Here's this patriot Shay whose farm fell into ruins because he was off fighting the British, who's not paid a cent what's owed him for his service, then is told he must pay taxes with money he doesn't have because the government won't pay him what he's owed."

"And so," Sophie completed the picture, "that ardent crusader for liberty and leader of the Revolution, Massachusetts, crushes the farmers' revolt so that the county courts can foreclose on their farms."

"The law can often be cruel," Target agreed.

"And when it is," Jefferson replied, eyes suddenly flashing, "the people have the absolute right to rebel."

"But even if it means violence? Shedding blood?" Sophie protested.

"Especially if it means shedding blood!" Jefferson exclaimed. "A little blood-letting now and then is good for the body, and good for the soul. It takes precious blood to secure precious freedom."

"It seems Shay has fled to Vermont," Target remarked. "So at least his own blood won't be shed. Unless Vermont turns him over to Massachusetts. Will Vermont do that?"

Jefferson shrugged. "Vermonters have a rebellious streak themselves." He turned to Crèvecoeur.

"I enjoyed Mr. Allen's book. If you see him upon your return to America give him my thanks. And please don't forget that Ally and Philly are to dine at my house every Sunday evening."

"I will be sure to bring them," Sophie assured him.

"I ardently wish your new United States success," Target said, "but the case of Vermont seems to be evidence of the contrary. If New York and Vermont can't stop their fighting each other, what hope is there that thirteen states will ever cooperate?"

"Well," Jefferson choose his words carefully, "it was New York's Governor Clinton, after all, who personally led New York militia to help General Lincoln and Massachusetts crush the farmers' rebellion. Much to my own dismay, I will say."

"Maybe," Sophie observed, "your constitutional convention will produce a new contract all the States can live with."

"We will see. They convened in Philadelphia last month, in May. Mr. Madison is hopeful he can reign in the monarchists like Hamilton. They both seem to agree that a bicameral legislature is necessary. I have my doubts. This 'Senate' as Hamilton calls it smacks of Roman aristocracy. We don't want another House of Lords stifling the will of the 'commoners'. Nor do I want to see another tyrant king, by whatever name you choose to call the head of state. The weaker the government, the better. The only thing more evil than debt is power. It will corrupt whomever it touches."

"Like politics?" Target smiled.

"Like politics," Jefferson agreed, nodding. "Another evil one should avoid if one can."

"Politics is to government what manure is to the cow," Target remarked. "An unavoidable by-product. Which despite its smelly side has utility. Our King Louis may be on paper the absolute monarch but in reality the true power is in the people. How to direct that power to good ends is the dilemma. Beneath the surface of the cool, majestic mountain-top reigns a boiling cauldron waiting to erupt. And there are an infinite number of would-be cooks scheming and conniving to stir up the pot, for their own ends. The Parlement de Paris doesn't have the monopoly on budding politicians; clubs are springing up all over the city."

"The pamphlets they publish say the most cruel and false things," Sophie fretted.

"Well, let's not be surprised," Target rejoined. "*'La politique, l'art de tromper les hommes.'* "

"Politics is the art of fooling the people?" Jefferson muttered in English to himself.

"D'Alembert said it first, not me. "

Target insisted on paying the bill and the party strolled over to the Rue Saint-Honoré. Jefferson consulted his new silver time-piece.

"James and his sister should be done with their errands by now," he remarked. "I had the coachman take them to the markets near the Halle des Blés. No sense making them walk all the way back to the villa."

"It's not every master who lets his servants ride his coach to do their shopping," Sophie remarked.

"You are spoiling them," Target agreed.

"Mr. Jefferson," the countess replied, "is simply being kind. Kindness is in his nature. Just look at the fine clothing he insists on having made for James and his sister. He dresses them as regally as though they were royalty."

Jefferson's phaeton, recently refurbished and re-gilded, came rolling up, pulled by two chestnut geldings. The coachman dressed in fine gold livery leaped down and opened the door. Sitting demurely inside was Jefferson's young slave James Hemings, facing his younger sister Sally. The coachman bowed deeply.

Jefferson, reddening slightly, kissed the countess' hand then shook the hands of Target and Crèvecoeur.

"Until next Sunday." He climbed into his coach and the coachman closed the door before hoisting himself back onto his driver's bench. From on high he cracked his whip to drive away the several beggars who had approached the coach windows.

The phaeton rattled off, leaving the beggars behind for the beggars still to come.

Chapter Sixteen: *Stronger than the Tomb*

The short, plump Vice-President of the United States of America had arrived in town only two days earlier and had been hastily sworn in by the Congress. Nervously, he smoothed back the long, curly grey of the hair sprouting on his temples, causing it to fluff up rather than lie down. The round, bald top of his head resembled an ostrich egg sitting uncomfortably in its nest.

He paced a moment, then sat back down on the chair from which he had just sprung, upholstered in a rich, dark red damask like the two others on the short dais, like all the others in the grand Senate Chamber. Above him, the arched vault of the ceiling was painted sky-blue with a golden sun reigning in the center surrounded by a halo of thirteen stars. In a second John Adams popped back up and resumed his pacing, hands clasped behind his back.

Behind him Senators mingled with Representatives and members of the foreign diplomatic corps. In front of him the three magnificent French window-doors, flanked by red damask curtains, were wide open, revealing the balcony beyond guarded by granite columns and a flowery iron grillwork, bathed in the cheerful noontime April sun. A table had been placed to one side of the balcony, draped in a red damask cloth on which a large red damask cushion sat and in which a brown-bound Bible lay.

A loud cheering and singing arose from the multitudes crowded outside, overflowing Wall Street and down Broad. Church bells, which had chimed throughout the City in unison precisely at 9 o'clock that morning, began ringing anew, the carillons in the tower of the newly resurrected Trinity Church nearby pealing the loudest. The brass and fife band lining the steps of the new Federal Hall down which a deep burgundy carpet descended to the street struck up Yankee Doodle, then the crowd and the band embarked on the melody if not the exact lyrics of God Save the King:

> *"...Joy to our native land, Let every heart expand,*
> *For Washington's at hand, With Glory crowned."*

From directly below came another chorus, heavy with the nasal pronunciation of Boston, intoning:

> *"Fill the bowl, fill it high, Firstborn Son of the sky,*
> *May He never, never die; Heaven shout 'Amen' ".*

There was a stomping of boots on the stairs and an excited Sergeant-at-Arms burst into the Senate Chamber. He hastily composed himself and stood at attention, shoulders perpendicular to the open doorway.

"The – the President...His Majesty...the President-Elect – the...the General...his Highness...the - His Excellency, George Washington!"

In the doorway appeared not George Washington but Baron von Steuben.

"Damn!" he growled at the Sergeant-at-Arms and brushed past, shaking his head.

From the end of the line still standing on the stairs came a booming command.

"Make way! Make way for the President."

Like the waters of the Red Sea the men just inside the doorway dutifully obeyed and miraculously parted to form an open corridor.

Into the breach marched state senator Aaron Burr, smiling.

"Thank you, gentlemen."

"His Excellency General George Washington!" the Sergeant-at-Arms exclaimed, clicking his heels together.

The tall figure of Washington appeared, dressed in a simple suit of brown Connecticut cloth with silver buttons embossed with an eagle, dress sword at his side. The men in the room let loose a spontaneous cheer and applauded. Even the foreign diplomatic corps could not help joining in the celebration. Washington allowed himself a sober smile and a brief bow of the head. On his left was Governor Clinton and on his right General Knox, who took it upon himself to clear a path to the open French doors where Adams was waiting, on the dais with the three chairs under a red damask canopy.

Adams cleared his throat. "Sir – the Senate and the House of Representatives of the United States are ready to attend you to take the oath recognized by the Constitution...which will be administered by the Chancellor of the State of New York."

"I am ready to proceed."

Adams bowed. He led Washington out onto the balcony then stepped aside.

The cheering did not abate for twenty minutes. In the distance, from the Battery, cannon boomed out. From the Senate Chamber men squeezed out onto the balcony behind

Adams and Washington. Adams glanced nervously behind him, as though praying the architect Pierre L'Enfant's porch would not collapse from the weight.

By and by Chancellor Livingston took his place to the right of Washington. From between them a hand lifted up the damask cushion with the open Bible. The crowd fell silent. The Chancellor nodded his head and Washington placed his right hand on the divine *Logos*.

"Do you solemnly swear that you will faithfully execute the office of President of the United States, and will, to the best of your ability, preserve, protect and defend the Constitution of the United States?"

"I solemnly swear...so help me God." He bent his head and kissed the Bible.

Livingston, beaming, turned towards the crowds below and shouted, "Long live George Washington, President of the United States!"

The vocal hurricane of ten thousand people roared from the packed streets. Washington bowed deeply. The cheering rushed on in endless waves. Washington bowed again. From the Senate Chamber came cheering and applause as well. Washington bowed once more. After a few minutes and countless more bows Washington gave up and retreated into the Chamber. From the harbor a warship boomed a 13-gun salutation.

"That would be our Spanish frigate *Galveston*," Don Gardoqui remarked proudly to the French ambassador Count de Moustier sitting to his left.

The count, who did not have a warship to play with, replied with an arch of the eyebrows, "Let us hope it is not firing real shells. I believe in any event protocol requires only eleven guns. Rhode Island and North Carolina refuse to accept the new Constitution and are thus not part of the so-called Union."

"You are too pessimistic, my friend," Gardoqui smiled. "They will come around...see how all Americans adore him. They worship the ground he walks on."

"Exactly," De Moustier responded. "And like a pendulum, the higher it is lifted into the air, the greater the fall. How long will Americans heed his message of virtue and honor?"

From the look in Washington's eyes as he faced the Congress from aside the vice-presidential chair he seemed to be troubled by the same thoughts. He stood there stiffly, waiting for the chattering to cease. He pulled out a manuscript from his pocket with one hand and fumbled for his reading glasses in another pocket. The assembly fell silent and watched, fascinated, as the General now President tried to remove his spectacles from their case while clutching his speech, almost dropping the case; gave it up, turned to the fireplace mantel, rested the case on top, and, after prying open the lid with clumsy fingers, managed to extract the glasses and place them on his commanding nose. If the French ambassador barely contained a smirk most of the assembled were close to tears at the sight.

Crèvecoeur, seated between de Moustier and the French chargé d'affaires Louis-Guillaume Otto, fumbled in his turn for his writing paper and pencil. He need not have hurried, for the President was slow to begin his discourse, as though collecting himself. When he began to speak it was in a deep but low voice, so that even those in the closest chairs had to lean forward to hear.

"...in response to the public summons...it would be...improper to omit in this first official act my fervent supplications to the Almighty Being who rules the universe...that His Benediction may consecrate to the liberties and happiness of the people of the United States a government instituted by themselves for these essential purposes....No people can be bound to acknowledge, and adore, the Invisible Hand which conducts the affairs of men more than those of the United States....."

The Spanish ambassador was frowning, lips moving silently, struggling to understand the President's flowery oratory. De Moustier did not understand all the words but let his face show he did not care to. Crèvecoeur was grateful the President was speaking slowly, almost ponderously.

"....I behold the sweetest pledges... no local prejudices or attachments, no separate views or party animosities...since we ought to be persuaded that the propitious smiles of Heaven can never be expected on a nation that disregards the eternal rules of order and right which Heaven itself has ordained...on the experiment entrusted to the American people...."

The Dutch ambassador nodded his head vigorously in approval. De Moustier stifled a yawn. Washington, who was holding his paper in his left hand with his right hand in his coat pocket, paused long enough to transfer the paper to his right hand and place his left in the other pocket before soldiering on.

"....Having thus imparted to you my sentiment...I shall take my present leave; but not without resorting once more to the benign Parent of the Human Race in humble supplication that, since He has been pleased to favor the American people with opportunities for deliberating in perfect tranquility...for deciding, with unparalleled unanimity, on a form of government for the security of the Union and the advancement of their Happiness, so His Divine Blessing may be equally conspicuous in the wise measures on which the success of this Government must depend."

His inaugural address finished, Washington waited out the standing ovation with patient resignation, then took his leave accompanied by Knox and Chancellor Livingston to attend a service at St. Paul's. The national Senators stayed behind to take up the first order of business, formulating an official response to the President's address.

"I will be proposing," a senatorial voice intoned, "that in response to his 'most gracious speech' –"

He was cut off by a howl of outrage from the Senator from western Pennsylvania.

" '*Gracious*'?" he shouted. " '*Gracious*'? Only God is 'gracious'. How dare you suggest good republicans adopt the very formula used by the House of Lords to flatter the tyrant king, who thinks himself God? Yes, I am well aware," William Maclay allowed sarcastically, "that our new Caesar dreams of nothing less than the monarchial glory and power of his British namesake. And that there are legions, some in this very room, who are dying to prostrate themselves – prostitute themselves! - at his regal feet."

The Chamber erupted in a volcano of angry shouting and yelling. A gavel was heard pounding weakly, and ineffectively, for silence and decorum. As the French legation descended the stairs de Moustier smirked.

"Ah, yes. Perfect tranquility. Unparalleled unanimity. With such words of wisdom so did the Roman experiment play itself out."

That night the entire City was lit up with illuminations and transparencies. Crèvecoeur escorted his daughter from their house now on Queen Street over to the John Street Theatre where strollers had stopped to admire dozens of large transparencies back-lit by lanterns, depicting angels descending from heaven to bestow on the President the crown of immortality. The governor's mansion on Pearl Street had candles in all the windows behind which shadows could be seen, perhaps the President at dinner with Clinton.

Rounding the corner onto Broadway Fanny gasped in surprise. They both stopped and stared. Across the street there arose from Bowling Green the gigantic person of the President in his buff and blue military uniform, looking upwards where the allegorical figure of Fortitude was poised, a shield in her one hand and a sword in the other. The enormous transparency, illuminated from behind by dozens of large lamps suspended from a platform, was flanked by the figures of Justice on the right and Wisdom on the left.

The mansions on Broadway had the grandest illuminations and the French and Spanish ambassadors' homes competed to be the grandest of the grand. From the windows of Don Gardoqui's house lanterns radiated through transparencies showing the graces, the muses, figures of antiquity and a fairy-tale world of castles and chivalry, like so many Flemish tapestries. Not to be outdone, de Moustier's windows and doors were ablaze with scores of lamps and candles illuminating fanciful allegorical images of America's past, present and future.

Because of the decorations they were obliged to go into the house via the servants' door in the back garden. The doorman led them to the main salon. Here too candles and whale oil lamps were everywhere, of which two dozen burned in an enormous crystal candelabra suspended from the high ceiling. At the piano sat a rather frumpy lady playing a minuet, her enormous hoops hiding the chair in which she was presumably seated. Her hair was done up in the latest French fashion and powdered white, looking as though a giant sugar loaf was resting on her head. Circumnavigating the loaf were thirteen large gold stars glittering in the light.

Crèvecoeur bowed deeply to Count de Moustier who, brandy glass in one hand, returned the gesture, looking not at Crèvecoeur but at Fanny. She curtsied.

"Vous êtes sans doute la plus charmante jeune fille de la ville de New York," the count proclaimed, kissing her hand. "And it is my good fortune to be able to see such a charming young lady for a third time since your arrival...in December, wasn't it?"

"Yes, Monsieur le Comte. I was visiting with Colonel Wadsworth and his family in Connecticut last fall. General and

Mrs. Knox were kind enough to bring me to New York in their coach on their way down from Boston."

"And what might your plans for the future be?" The count was still holding the young lady's hand in his paw.

The music stopped and the guests without drinks in hand applauded politely. Rescued by etiquette, Fanny invoked the duty to applaud as an excuse to extract her hand from the count's. The lady at the piano smiled a curtsy then resumed playing, singing along this time in a wavering, watery voice in reasonably close approximation of the melody.

"Your sister Madame de Bréhan is remarkably talented," Sarah Livingston Jay complimented de Moustier, whose eyes flickered with amusement at Mrs. Jay's naïveté. Her husband John coughed into his sleeve. "Not only does she play music beautifully but I understand she painted all the transparencies around your lovely house with her own artistic hand."

"You are too kind, my dear lady," de Moustier murmured. "The talents of my *sister-in-law* are more varied than you can imagine. However, inspired though she is, her talent is nothing compared to that of her sister Antoinette, my dear departed wife."

"Will we be meeting the Count de Bréhan?" Mrs. Jay inquired. Again her husband coughed, louder this time. Mrs. Jay looked at him, puzzled.

Crèvecoeur intervened. "Madame de Bréhan drew the portrait of General Washington for the third edition of my book on America. The General was pleased."

Louis-Guillaume Otto, chargé d'affaires for the French Legation, joined their circle. He gave a short bow to no one and thus to everyone but his gaze was directed to Mrs. Jay. She gave him her hand, which he held in both of his.

" *'L'amour est un tyran qui n'epargne personne,"* Otto quoted with a sad smile. *"La moitié de ma vie a mis l'autre au tombeau.'"*

"Corneille?" Mrs. Jay guessed.

Otto nodded. "Our French Shakespeare. It is hard to believe it has been over a year since she died, isn't it? If I were a poet like Corneille perhaps I would write, 'The death of one's beloved entombs the heart as well.' "

"Then allow me to reply through Alexander Pope. 'Hope springs eternal in the human breast.' "

"*Ma chère amie*, If anything can rob sorrow of its sting, it is your gracious smile," Otto said. "Although our Elizabeth is gone, and my baby boy as well, I am blessed to have you forever as my sister-in-law."

"By your marriage to my dear sister you are a Livingston for all time."

Otto, turning to Fanny, inclined his head, kissing the back of her hand. "*Enchanté de vous revoir, Mademoiselle America-Frances.* For the second time in as many days!

"You can see," he said to the Jays, "how she is taking good care of my dear friend." He relinquished her hand and clasped her father's.

"The three widowers," Otto managed a smile, including de Moustier in their circle, who, with a short bow of the head, went to greet new arrivals. "December 17, 1787 it was," he continued, softly. "Fifteen months ago, but it seems like a mere fifteen days."

"Only three days after my birthday...." Fanny murmured.

Crèvecoeur, who had been one of the pallbearers, nodded slowly. "The heart, my friend, is stronger than the tomb."

The French vice-consul LaForest entered the salon with his new bride on his arm. Other guests followed them in, while others left.

"This year 1789 seems to be the year for marriages as well as the birth of new governments," Mrs. Jay remarked. "Not least of which in the Livingston families. My cousin Alida has married Mr. Armstrong, and at least one if not two nieces are to be wed as well. Soon, my dear," Sarah said, turning to Fanny, "you will be fighting off the young men, as pretty as you are. Unless you have plans already...."

"I'm sure I don't, Mrs. Jay," Fanny demurred. "I don't see the hurry," she said with a smile. "I told my father I will not get engaged until after I have sailed around the world. As the master on one of Captain Fellowes' ships."

"The ocean is no place for a lady. Are you sure you wish to hold your father to such a condition? You might wind up never getting married."

"There's not a chance of that happening," a confident young voice emerged from the throat of a confident young man who had joined them, with a hint of a Dutch accent. His thick blond hair was swept back from his forehead and his cool blue eyes smiled. He bowed to Mrs. Jay, then to America-Frances.

"I am pleased to meet you. Frank van Berckel," he announced, making his own introduction, there being no one else to do it. Mrs. Jay did not look pleased.

"At your service," the brash young man continued. "My father is the Netherlands minister here."

"Miss Fanny St. John's father is the French consul in New York," Mrs. Jay supplied.

"Yes. I know."

Madame de Bréhan had launched herself into a cotillion and the guests were lining up for a dance.

"May I?" Without waiting for an answer van Berckel took Fanny away by the arm, beating Bartow, Aaron Burr's stepson, by a step and a half, mouth half open with his invitation. William Magee Seton tapped Bartow on the shoulder. "Let's flip a coin for the right to be next," he suggested.

"I think," Mrs. Jay remarked to Crèvecoeur, "your daughter's ship may wind up sailing without her."

"Will Monsieur Washington be passing by?" Mme. LaForest asked de Moustier, who had rejoined them. "I do wish to meet him."

"He has already paid his respects. He has gone on to Chancellor Livingston's to watch the fireworks scheduled for later tonight. But come to the reception I am giving in his honor next week. Plan on arriving exactly ten minutes after the appointed hour. They say he is punctual and not likely to linger very long." De Moustier smiled. "Just as I imagine will be the fate of the United States. But say. I see in our doorway the next best thing to the President. His Vice-President."

De Moustier was all smiles and charm as he bowed to John Adams. Adams bowed awkwardly in return, then kissed the back of Mme. LaForest's hand, Mrs. Jay's, then Fanny's.

"Will we have the pleasure of meeting Mrs. Adams tonight?" de Moustier asked.

"I am afraid not. Abigail won't be coming down from Braintree until I have secured a house. But it so happens I am about to sign a lease. A beautiful place, really. Richmond Hill, it is called. Up about a mile out of town, near Greenwich Village. It reminds me of my own house and farm. Surrounded by lovely orchards, meadows. There is a splendid view of both rivers. You will do us the honor of visiting us there."

"I and Madame de Bréhan will be delighted. If you will pardon me, I must go and greet other guests."

Several Livingstons had entered the salon followed by Senator Izard and his wife Alice, not a Livingston but from the rival DeLancey clan, now all but decimated. Izard spotted Adams talking to the French representatives and came over, Alice beside him.

Izard, arriving at a spot a few paces in front of Adams, suddenly stopped, bowed his head, and dropped to one knee.

"Your eminent Highness. Or rather, your high Eminence. I mean, your gracious Majesty...majestic Graciousness? O dear, I used that obscene word again, didn't I? Please, please o Lord, spare my head. I have constituents who need me."

Adams' expression changed from annoyance to mirth in an instant. He chuckled, then laughed along with Izard who had risen to his full height. His wife shared with the French delegates a look of astonishment.

"It *was* too funny, wasn't it," Adams finally managed, looking like anything but vice-presidential.

"You didn't seem to think so at first," Izard said irreverently. "In fact, I thought you were about to bite that fellow from Pennsylvania's head right off his neck."

"I confess I wanted to but at six feet three Senator Mcclay would be more than I could chew. Or even reach. But did you have to egg him on by referring to me as 'His Rotundity?' "

"It was only to show him how fair-minded I am, after my calling him 'His Asperity'."

"You see," Izard explained to the others, "we in the United States Senate have not let the grass grow under our feet. Within just seconds of President Washington's noble inaugural speech we wasted no time in getting down to the truly important matters facing our country. That is to say, how we are to officially address the President. And treat each other. Mr. Adams' pleas for a rational debate of ideas, rather than name-calling and personal attacks, were proof of his anti-republican, royalist leanings. And when the Vice-President had the temerity – "

" – the royal nerve," Adams corrected him.

" – the royal nerve to suggest we address the President as 'Your Excellency', a few of our fellow sages felt it was imperative to smother this newborn changeling before he grows into another monstrous monarch. And the best way to do it, they felt, was by demeaning those they disagree with and yelling louder than everyone else. And thus spent the wise Senate its afternoon."

"And how it will undoubtedly spend tomorrow as well," Adams said with a sigh. "As I must preside over this august body in my role as Vice-President I do not have the luxury of absenting myself, as several of our less dedicated members have. But say, Monsieur Otto - *mes amis* - you must not allow yourselves to get the wrong impression. Teething pains are inevitable in a growing infant."

"The American experiment is a valuable teacher for France," Otto assured him. "Your teething pains might help my country steer a course of moderation and avoid biting off more than we can chew."

"It seems to me," Sir John Temple had joined them, "France will inevitably adopt a constitutional monarchy as we have in England. But not until your countrymen rid themselves of the notion of the 'three estates'. It's too cumbersome a machine to produce anything except endless debate."

"I sincerely hope," Adams weighed in, "you are right, and that Louis' agreement to convene the Estates-General will result in a wise, reasonable new form of government for France that will conduct itself with dignity. Like our American Senate. But permit me to have a few reservations. From what I read in the newspapers there seems to be lacking a unity of belief and purpose. There is even, if I may, an absence of belief. How can a farmer expect his beans to grow and thrive if he refuses the pole needed to support the vine?"

"Oh, *Monsieur le Vice-Président*," de Moustier, back in port, demurred. "Things are not so dramatic as all that. Our 'beans' are only one small crop among many. France is a wealthy country. Our culture is the envy of the world. The sky is not going to come crashing down, I assure you. Ah, I see the lieutenant-governor has arrived. Please excuse me once again."

"It is not that France lacks wealth," Jay remarked, "but it is concentrated in too few hands."

"How to pry open the hands is the real question," Adams agreed. "It will be done, though. If not voluntarily, then by force. And then you will have a devastating civil war.

"I am sorry," he said to the French diplomats, "that your grain crop failed last year. If I and Mr. Hamilton had our way we would have sent an armada of flour in partial repayment of the debt we owe you. With the new Congress we may have better luck."

"Perhaps with Necker back at the Finance Ministry things will turn around," Jay offered.

"The problem in France," Otto replied, "is political as much as a question of finance. And politics, I have found, at its most fundamental level, is a question of heart."

" *'Ceux qui voudront traiter séparément la politique et la morale n'entendront jamais rien à aucune d'eux,'* " Mrs. Jay quoted.

Sir John Temple, seeing Adams' frustrated expression, gracefully offered a translation for the benefit of the Vice-President.

"Rousseau, is it not, Mrs. Jay? 'Those who would separate politics from morals will never understand either.' Did I get that right, Monsieur Otto?"

Otto nodded. "Quite right....If there is a common desire to do good born of love for others then miracles can happen. If on the other hand the preponderant motivation is selfishness, then any ultimate success you obtain is due to the lucky fluke of coincidence, and is not likely to be long-lasting. Your American Revolution would not have succeeded were it not for the virtue and sacrifice of the many."

"And its legacy," Adams nodded in agreement, "cannot continue but for virtue and sacrifice in the generations to follow. How do we keep these truths alive?"

"It may be," Otto shrugged, "that every generation will need to be tested anew. Faced not with petty inconveniences but with a fight for survival itself. Otherwise, the valor and virtue only sacrifice can bring will turn to complacency and ingratitude. And such a society will inevitably collapse, either from its enemies without, or the enemies within."

"I think," said Jay, "to truly understand 'sacrifice' requires in each person a revolution. A revolution of the heart."

"Well, my dear," his wife murmured, "I would say your heart is about to be tested. Here comes my brother."

Jay sighed deeply. "O Lord give me strength."

Henry Brockhulst Livingston did not so much walk as swagger. After paying his respects to Mme. de Bréhan and her lover the ambassador he stalked his way over to his sister and his brother-in-law and their cabal of monarchists.

"Sarah. So good to see you." He bowed stiffly to his sister. "John." Another bow, to his brother-in-law. "Monsieur Crèvecoeur, Monsieur Otto." Bow. "Monsieur et Madame....?"

"LaForest. Our vice-consul and his lovely wife," Crèvecoeur supplied.

"Delighted." Another bow. Then, as if noticing Adams for the first time, he smiled.

"Mr. Vice-President." Here he bowed very, very deeply. Adams grew red.

"Dear brother," Sarah forced a smile. "Where is Catherine, your lovely bride?"

"Indisposed, I'm afraid. Something the doctors call 'monarchial distemper' also known by its other name, 'federalitis'. But don't worry, it's rarely fatal, merely annoying."

"I have never heard of such a malady," LaForest remarked. "What are its symptoms?"

"An irritation of the nerves caused by verbal flatulence, accompanied by bouts of nausea provoked by prolonged exposure to pretensions of grandeur. The doctor prescribed bed rest at our cottage in the country up by Harlem, far removed from the gassy airs swirling around Federal Hall."

"I see." The French vice-consul's eyes were, however, puzzled.

Jay cut in to cut off the incipient Adamsonian eruption. "My dear Henry. How is your law practice going?" he asked his brother-in-law and former law partner.

"Couldn't be better. Business is booming now that we in New York have our own paper money and that means plenty of contracts just waiting to be drawn up. And then broken. And then it's off to court we go. How nice to be needed."

"If not loved," Adams remarked dryly, having recovered his composure. "I've always found it remarkable how people hate lawyers until they need one."

"Like some people's attitude towards God," Mrs. Jay agreed.

"Oh, please, dear sister. Don't let's start comparing us lawyers to divine beings."

"Far be it from me, dear brother, to do so. The only ones I know of who think that way are lawyers. Present company excepted, of course."

"It is amazing, isn't it Mr. Vice-President, how many men of such high intellectual pretensions flock so eagerly to such a maligned profession," Livingston smiled sardonically, immune to his sister's sarcasm "Are the lawyers the cause of the malignancy, or is it the people they represent?

"The law," Adams replied archly, "is a noble profession. It is thanks to the unscrupulous few that the public have such a disdain for the rest of us. Much like the New York State Senate, I hear. As a state senator perhaps you can enlighten us as to why your august body could not even agree on electors to vote for the Presidency?"

"For the simple reason, your Excellency, that the choice for President was a foregone conclusion and the selection of Vice-President too inconsequential to concern ourselves with. We in the New York Senate have more pressing matters to attend to."

Seeing the steam starting to escape from the Vice-President's ears Crèvecoeur thought it a good time to continue their social rounds.

"Louis," Crèvecoeur smiled at Otto, "would you care to accompany America-Frances and me in paying our respects to Don Gardoqui?"

"Will you be able to pull your daughter away from all her admiring suitors?"

A very fatigued-looking Fanny was being twirled by a very tall young man while Seton, van Berckel and Bartow Prevost Burr looked on impatiently, the indefatigable Mme. de Bréhan still pounding away on her piano. As she was whooshed by, her father caught her eye and she nodded. At the first available pause she did a quick breathless curtsy to the disappointed beaux and made her escape with her father and the count.

"America produces fine-looking young men," Otto said, smiling.

"Well," Fanny replied, laughing, her left arm looped around her father's right as they strolled onto Broadway, "one of them is Dutch, the ambassador's son; and the tall one is Dutch and French.

"Say," she said, stopping suddenly, looking at her father. "He told me his name...it is Daniel, Daniel Crommelin Verplanck. He just came here from Holland. He lost his wife recently. But he said his mother and father lived here, and that his father's father had owned a lot of land in the Hudson Valley. I seem to remember that name, Crommelin.

Crèvecoeur gave his daughter a hug. He held on to her tightly a long moment.

"That would be Daniel's grandfather who was the original owner of the land where our farm used to be."

They walked a few more steps in silence, Fanny between her father and the count. The count offered to her his left arm, which she accepted, still lost in thought.

"I have often wondered why it should be," she finally said, "that I had to lose my mother that way. Or why things happen the way they do. If she had not died the way she did Philly and I would not have suffered so; but then I would not have prayed to God as I did and I would not have been blessed with the kind Fellowes family. I often have thought that were God to take me away now I would have no right to complain because of the lifetime of love I experienced with those wonderful people."

They were walking slowly along the fringes of the cemetery bordering Trinity Church. Its graceful newly reborn tower and spire were outlined against the starry sky. Fanny pulled the men's arms more closely to her.

"I used to wish mother were buried somewhere we could visit, but now I think, it is better the way it is. She is with God; and God is everywhere. And so is she."

The narrow gate to the cemetery was open, as though beckoning them to enter. They went in, silently, as though of one mind and one heart.

"Long time ago, in Chester that winter with Mr. and Mrs. Drake, I would think, how futile and pointless life is. But then in Boston my new mother and father showed me that life, our lives, do have a purpose. We usually can't see it; or understand it; but it is there. And it exists independent of ourselves even though we are a part of it, and it is a part of us. We are part of a purpose which is greater than our own selves, and it will go on fulfilling itself long after we are all departed from this life."

Gravestones rose up in the reflected light from the moon, tall ones, short ones, grand ones, humble ones, as varied as their departed owners and just as similar. All had died as they had been born and all now knew the truth, for better or for worse. There was a tombstone off by itself at the end of the row, neither large nor small and close by was a very small marker. Otto led them there.

He dropped down to one knee before the plot. The words etched into the cold stone were not visible but they did not need to be read. The unfathomable purpose and meaning of it all were inexpressible.

Unbidden, the words from the young soul resting just behind them came to Crèvecoeur's lips.

"In Christ alone I put my trust...."

Chapter Seventeen: *Of Vows Broken and Vows Spoken*

"It's revolution in France! The people have defied the king!"

James le Ray de Chaumont had burst through the Queen Street door into the consulate office, panting and breathless. He clutched a bundle of newspapers under an arm and a packet of mail in his hands. Crèvecoeur and Fanny were taking their tea at the small table in the bay window alcove while Otto was finishing a report in the office.

"I went out in the tender to the *Courrier de l'Empire* and the first thing Captain du Moulin yelled out was that Paris is in the hands of the people. They have forced the king and the National Assembly to abolish the Old Order. La Fayette is drafting a declaration of rights. The entire country is enflamed. Here, which do you want to see first? Newspapers, or letters from the Duke de la Rochefoucauld? Or your official correspondence from Court?"

Hearing the news Otto hurried into the room. William Seton and his son emerged from their counting house next door. They all wore the same incredulous expression on their faces, messenger and recipients alike. Otto broke their stunned silence.

"Revolution? Impossible. Can it be true?" He extended a hand for a newspaper, unfolded it frantically and began reading. James plopped down in a chair and spread out another newspaper on the table. Fanny and Crèvecoeur hunched over it. For William Magee's benefit Crèvecoeur read out loud, translating into English.

> " 'Paris, 6 August 1789....The glorious light of the dawn of the New Age is shining on France. The long chain of events turning France upside down since Mirabeau's bold defiance of the King, and the Third Estate pledging June 20 to not disband until a Constitution is adopted, and the new National Assembly's proclamation of allegiance not to the King but to the Nation; to the taking of the hated Bastille Castle on July 14; to the

King's withdrawal of his troops and his submission to the will of the people before the National Assembly on July 15, saying 'I entrust myself to you, help me save the State'....

" 'And now, not two days ago, our glorious National Assembly abolishing for all time the unjust feudal laws, *les droits de seigneur*, the tithe and the *taille* and the taxes and the privileges of the nobles and the clergy. The Old Order is no more!

" 'And the King himself bowing to the will of the deputies, they applauding the King and shouting *Louis XVI, Restaurateur de la liberté française.'*

" 'But, would the King have deigned to drink the precious water of liberty had he not been forced to the well by the people of Paris? Would he have brought back Necker on July 15 but for the people's demand? Would he have tolerated the appointment of La Fayette as Commander of the National Guard had the people not insisted? And would the bourgeois deputies of the Third Estate have stood up to the King were it not for the clamoring of the citizens of the capital, clamoring for justice and equality, led by the King's own cousin the Duc d'Orléans, 'Philippe Égalité' who magnanimously threw open his Palais-Royal to the leaders of the people and the cry of Camille Desmoulins: 'To arms! To arms!'

" 'The ship of revolution that has been launched must now be guided by sure hands safely into port. The Assembly has work to do, it must fulfill its pledges of August 4. There is a Constitution to be drafted, and La Fayette's Declaration of the Rights of Man and the Citizen to be refined, debated, and adopted so that our glorious vessel can sail safely and serenely into the haven that awaits her. All Hail, the New Humanity!' "

Crèvecoeur leaned back in his chair, pensive. He got up and went to the far side of the table, picked up the bundle of mail and began sorting it hastily. He pulled out two letters, one from

the Duke de la Rochefoucauld and one from Thomas Jefferson.
He opened the American's first.

> " 'What a glorious thing, the storming of the Bastille,
> that symbol of royal oppression and tyranny! The
> people have spoken and their music has played, a
> resoundingly beautiful symphony. Theirs is the power
> of the ocean against which no king can withstand, no
> matter how regal or how grand. What matters if blood
> has been shed and a few heads cut off? The mighty have
> stumbled, and the proud king is humbled. Arbitrary,
> brutal despotism shall reign no more in France.
>
> " 'Be not concerned for your sons, they are well and
> under the protection of Duc de la Rochefoucauld. Most
> of the rioting and looting seems to have abated and the
> peasants' burning of the châteaux and desecration of
> churches in the countryside have calmed down. Here in
> Paris there is still constant agitation and nobody is
> working, all thronging to the hundreds of political clubs
> that are springing up overnight. But, 'tis all for the good
> and noble cause of revolution.
>
> " 'We will see soon enough, I'm sure, that the
> enlightened ends will justify the sometimes harsh
> actions of the masses. In the end, Reason will triumph. I
> am sailing soon for Virginia although I regret not being
> able to stay and witness the dénouement of this
> exciting passion play. I admit it has made my blood run
> fast, for the first time in many years.
>
> Yours,
>
> Thomas Jefferson.' "

Fanny's eyes mirrored her father's. "Open the duke's, father.
Read it to us please."

Crèvecoeur broke the seal and, unfolding the paper, scanned
the writing with his eyes. He sighed in relief. Rochefoucauld
sounded confident, and there was a short postscript from Ally
and Philly.

"Your brothers are well."

"May I read the letter?"

"I would prefer you did not."

"Father. I would think I am able to bear whatever the duke may have to say."

Crèvecoeur relented reluctantly, handing the letter over to his daughter.

Her frown deepened as she read. Her eyes reflected horror and disbelief. She finished the letter and passed it to along to the count, who had been watching her with sympathy.

"How is it possible that people can do such things?" she asked quietly. "Are these human beings, that massacre crippled invalid soldiers and parade around with severed heads on poles?"

Otto, holding Fanny's hands to comfort her, tried to be optimistic. "Rochefoucauld is a shrewd judge of men and, more important, a good man. He and the other wise men of our caste – Mirabeau, Talleyrand, La Fayette – will help turn France into a constitutional monarchy. Perhaps your brothers will someday be elected to the Assembly."

News of the revolution was on everybody's lips, that day and the next, and the next. It competed for people's attention with the Bill of Rights, adopted just the day before the news from France hit the New York presses. Hundreds of toasts were drunk to France each night in the City's taverns. Vice-President Adams, at the weekly reception he hosted with wife Abigail at Richmond Hill, was glum.

"I foresee nothing but chaos and horror ahead for the French people," he repeated, shaking his head sadly. "They know not what they do."

He was no more optimistic six months later. Otto had bedecked his new house on Cherry Street inside and out with bright red, white and blue flags and banners of all sizes in commemoration of the Franco-American Treaty of Alliance of February 1778 and the American and French revolutions. And, in celebration of his own future marriage. A string quartet was playing discreetly in an alcove.

"It is not," Adams insisted to the Dutch ambassador van Berckel and Sir John Temple next to him, "that I oppose the overthrow of idle aristocrats and overbearing bishops and cardinals and the establishment of a National Assembly. Did I not sign with my own hand our Declaration of Independence? And thereby risk my neck, my farm, my family? How can I not applaud the Declaration of the Rights of Man and the Citizen, which sounds so much like our own Declaration and Bill of Rights."

"So then why, Mr. Adams, such concern?" Sir John Temple smiled amiably. "Our French brethren will continue to do what they excel in doing: engage in endless harmless debate." He dropped a wink at the French diplomats to rob his remarks of offense. "As long as they are talking there is little chance of the anarchy you fear."

"My fear is based on the utter lack of balance in the system they have constructed, a legislature composed of a single enormous assembly with no counterbalance and which doesn't even speak for the capital city, itself at war with the assembly and the king. And secondly, their idolatry of Reason as their new religion. I know not what to make of a republic of thirty million atheists."

"My dearest friend," Abigail Adams remonstrated gently, slipping her arm around her husband's, "it is true the French tend to excess in their enthusiasm; but let us not exaggerate. At least they profess a belief in a Supreme Being. Does our own Declaration go any farther than that?"

"My concern is that once you remove God's command to love Him and your fellows above yourself as the object of your desire to please, you are left with seeking to love and please yourself above all else. Imagine thirty millions of individual little gods, each striving to put himself ahead of everyone else. If the loving God of Moses and Abraham and Jesus does not in their minds exist then why should they have any higher scruples than Genghis Khan?

"From among the deputies in the National Assembly and the Parisian political clubs - where I suspect the true power now resides – there will emerge as leaders those most adept in the fine arts of cynicism and rhetoric, paying only lip service to the 'will of the people' and the 'rights of man' in pursuit of their own ambition."

"Now hush, John. I see Mr. Maclay yonder. No more talk of the French revolution."

"He will want to talk of nothing else. He is, after all, Jefferson's surrogate in the Senate. His mouthpiece.

"Mr. Maclay is holding the fort for him until our new Secretary of State arrives in New York," Adams explained to Temple. "Perhaps, Sir John, you might be able to deflect his attention away from France. For example, by provoking him to talk about renewing hostilities between your country and ours?"

"I would be more inclined, not to say delighted," Sir John replied, "to talk to Mr. Jefferson. About war, about peace, indeed, about any topic, merely for the pure joy of talking with him. But I am afraid he will not condescend to converse with me, as I am only chargé d'affaires for His Majesty's government and not a plenipotentiary. Until the king appoints an ambassador to your government Mr. Jefferson refuses to do more than acknowledge my existence as a human being. And a lowly one, at that."

"We were," Abigail Adams reminded her husband, "so very close friends with Thomas while we were staying in Paris. Let us not let philosophical differences stand in the way of friendship."

"See how Senator Maclay's disciples orbit around him," Adams sniffed. "What Washington feared is coming to pass, I am afraid. Political partisanship. Manipulation, scheming, ambition. Deceit. What Mr. Jefferson does not understand is that our nation needs a strong executive to counter the cupidity of the Congress. Which is rapidly establishing its credentials as the new club of republican aristocrats. Mr. Jefferson fears the 'one'; I fear the 'few' who would poison the baby before he has a chance to mature."

The Jays had arrived accompanied by the Hamiltons and Aaron Burr, followed by Rufus King and his wife. Otto, assisted by Fanny as hostess, welcomed them. After a moment of chatting Otto navigated them past the shoals of the republican radicals and around to the foreign diplomatic corps and the Adamses.

To Abigail's dismay Senator King launched with enthusiasm into the French revolution.

"Isn't it exhilarating," he exclaimed. "To see the French people following in our footsteps. Freeing all those political prisoners from the Bastille in the name of equality! Standing up to the tyrant king! I feel like we're kindred spirits." He smiled delightedly at the French consul. Crèvecoeur replied with a polite nod.

Alexander Hamilton regarded the younger man with cool blue eyes blazing with a cool blue flame.

"Rufus. You know not whereof you speak. You have been reading too many propaganda pamphlets. There is nothing admirable about the behavior of the Paris mobs. When they stormed the Bastille it was not to free political prisoners of an arbitrary king. There were, to be precise, exactly seven prisoners: four of them were convicted forgers, two of them were violent lunatics and the last one a rapist, locked up at the request of their families.

"The mob assaulted the Bastille to seize gunpowder for their canon and muskets. And in so doing they massacred the eighty or so crippled soldiers garrisoned there along with a few dozen Swiss Guards. And to top off their honorable, egalitarian gesture they tortured the commander of the prison and the mayor before cutting off their heads and parading them on pikes through the streets of Paris. To the joy and admiration of the people. And Mr. Thomas Paine."

Senator Maclay, hovering nearby, could not resist the call to arms. The fact that he was a head taller than Colonel Hamilton was not apparent in the eyes of the new U.S. Secretary of the Treasury or to anyone else who was watching.

"The Bastille was the legitimate reaction of the people to whom the king had lied. Like all monarchs he lies, and like all monarchs, and those who kneel before him, there is no punishment too extreme."

"Even by mob rule? Without a fair trial?"

"Good ends justify distasteful means."

"What then of this noble document, this Declaration of the Rights of Man and the Citizen? 'All people have the right to be free from oppression, from arbitrary punishment?' That no one shall be harassed for his opinions, his political beliefs, his religion and all have the right to think and believe what they will, free to express those thoughts and beliefs?"

"The Declaration had not yet been drafted on July 14."

"And so, had it been adopted, the mobs storming the Bastille would have waved copies in their hands instead of guns and swords and pikes?"

"Ah but you see, my dear colonel, the document *has* since been drafted, and therefore we see the salutary result of the irrepressible wisdom of the people."

"La Fayette proposed the Declaration *before* the mob took the Bastille. Let's not pretend the Parisians were motivated by a desire to guarantee freedom of opinion. The Declaration was not the consequence of the mob riots."

"No; but they both were the result of intolerable oppression."

"And so," Abigail Adams intervened with a smile, "we see that France, like the United States, is at a crucial fork in the road: either she elects to obey the rule of law; or she chooses to follow the tyranny of the lawless."

"Quite right, Mrs. Adams, quite right," Maclay replied. "And there you put your finger square on the critical question: how is the rule of law to be exercised? Not by an exalted king, but by the people's representatives. Your husband's insistence on denying the Senate the right to remove the President's appointees is no different than Louis' insistence on having veto power over the Assembly's laws. In both cases the executive cannot be allowed to overturn the will of the people."

The Vice-President could contain himself no longer.

"But the will of the people, in America at least, has been entrusted to the President to the same degree as to the Congress. It is nonsense to say that the President in exercising his judgment thereby violates the prerogatives of the people. The fact that he is chosen by electors rather than directly is beside the point, since the electors themselves are chosen by the people's state representatives."

"None of whom, by the way, are chosen by the majority of Americans since men without property are excluded from the franchise as well as women altogether," Sir John could not help pointing out.

"And with good reason," Adams retorted. Seeing the look in his wife's eyes he added hastily, "at least with respect to the property qualification. The French Assembly has adopted a similar law. Otherwise, vagabonds and vagrants, the illiterate and unschooled, would prevent the legislature from accomplishing anything of value. Worse, it would only encourage lawlessness.

"Just look at that Paris journalist Jean-Paul Marat and his *L'Ami du peuple*. Exhorting the mobs to lynch on a lamp-post everyone who disagrees with his opinions. La Fayette running around Paris with his militia putting down one riot after another like volunteer firemen dousing never-ending flames. That, my friends, is what America can expect if there is only a weak executive and mob rule."

Before Maclay could reload Abigail decided it was time for a change.

"Mr. Burr. You are so quiet! Perhaps you are, after all, the wisest one in our group."

"Far from it. But I do see merit on both sides of the fence. And so don't mind me if I sit on it for a while."

"Congratulations, Mr. Burr, on your appointment as State Attorney-General." This from Sarah Jay. "Theodosia must be pleased."

"So she is! Even more so than her mother," Burr teased Mrs. Jay gently. "I bring Theo - my daughter - to my office whenever possible. I have no doubt she will make a fine lawyer someday. Or attorney-general. Her career may have to take place, however, in a country with a more forward-looking social outlook – for example, perhaps, France if one can judge by recent events."

Burr gave a short bow of the head to Crèvecoeur. "It was the women of Paris, after all," he continued, "who forced La Fayette to march with them, seven thousand strong, to Versailles last October and it was the women who forced the king and queen to go back to Paris with them. And to publicly reaffirm the authority of the National Assembly."

"Perhaps you are prescient, Mr. Burr," Mrs. Adams rejoined. "I admit I was at first taken aback at the...boldness of the women in Paris society; but I could not help admire their intelligence and influence on political thinking and current affairs. Why should not women in America have a similar role? Or better still, the right to vote and be elected to office?"

"One revolution at a time, my dear, one at a time," Adams murmured. Maclay was regarding Mrs. Adams with a horrified look on his face. John Jay was amused.

"Senator," he needled, "our Ten Amendments to the Constitution are too conservative, don't you think? Why don't you sponsor an Eleventh Amendment: the right of women to vote and hold office? Now that I am Chief Justice I will be happy to fend off any lawsuit to strike it down."

"Judge Jay," Abigail laughed, "it is not just the right to be a politician that we women are wanting. Why can't my daughter Nabby – or at least, her baby girls – become financiers like Mr. Morris, or physicians like Dr. Bard?

"Hello, Doctor. Would it be too early to reserve a place at the Medical School for our granddaughter?"

Dr. Bard smiled. "For you, Mrs. Vice-President, no request can be refused. How old is your granddaughter?"

"She will turn five next month. It is not that she is particularly precocious; rather, we anticipate it will take our society perhaps a dozen years or so to recognize equal rights for women. Our dear, enlightened Senator Mcclay here will be leading the charge to amend the Constitution to that effect."

For once Maclay and Adams were united in interest, judging from the glance they exchanged.

"How noble of you, Senator," Dr. Bard praised him. Maclay could only stare.

"How is President Washington's health?" Abigail inquired. "He is recovering well, I hope. He did not attend Martha's Friday reception as usual."

"Just a very bad cold and sore throat. I have him resting in bed. Nothing like the scare he gave us all last summer."

"I shudder to think that Mr. Adams is just a heartbeat away from the Presidency," Abigail said, passing from word to act.

"I, too, Madame," Senator Mcclay intoned.

"And how is *your* health lately, Judge Jay?" Dr. Bard inquired, looking with a puckered professional eye at Jay's left temple. "It seems to have healed all right That was a nasty blow you took. Damn rioters. Unprincipled, gullible fools."

"France," Jay explained to the Adamses, "is not the only place you have mobs and riots. As you well know, coming from Boston.

"This scar," he pointed to his temple, "is proof that a rock is a rock regardless if you're in Paris or Boston or New York."

"Some angry republican, perhaps, upset at one of your papers in support of a strong Federal government?" Adams asked.

"Well no, not quite," Jay laughed, "although it is true I had to dodge not a few republican missiles now and then. Hamilton had it worse, seeing he wrote most of the articles. No, this souvenir was courtesy of the riot two years ago over medical cadavers. Here, Doctor, you explain. It was your hospital, after all."

"Two boys on a lark climbed up a ladder to peek inside a hospital window. Some foolish medical student thought it would be amusing to scare them by waving the severed arm from a cadaver. The boys almost fell off the ladder with fright. They told their father, a bricklayer, and the next thing we knew all the workingmen in the City stormed the hospital and took two medical students captive, for desecrating the dead. Paris has its Bastille; New York has its City Hospital.

"Well, at least these two medical students weren't decapitated. But they were held hostage in my own house. After the mob broke in and took it over. I tried to reason with them, but it was like talking to the cadavers. More and more rioters converged around the house, threatening to kill the students – and me, as well – for by now we had become necrophiliacs as well as grave-robbers.

"Fortunately Governor Clinton and Mr. Jay along with Baron von Steuben were able to round up a few dozen former soldiers and they came to our rescue. Mr. Jay discovered that it is not easy to reason with people throwing rocks at your head."

"Or for that matter, with people who have rocks *in* their head," Jay added.

"I can attest to that," Sir John Temple said. "As the crowd dispersed a few took it into their heads that it would be a pity to waste the rocks some were still holding; and because of the close similarity between medical cadavers and Englishmen they decided that my house, too, should be looted."

Otto approached Crèvecoeur and whispered in his ear. Crèvecoeur gave a nod of assent and excused himself from the group.

Governor Clinton and Chancellor Livingston had arrived a few minutes before. Otto, placing himself in the middle of the large ballroom, waited for the string quartet to finish its piece then raised his arms in the air for attention. As the room fell silent he smiled.

"Friends of America, Friends of France. Honored guests. Thank you for blessing us with your presence tonight.

"I have had the honor of living in your beautiful country for over ten years. I have seen with my own eyes your valiant struggles, your courage and strength and perseverance in the face of doubt, in the face of uncertainty, starvation, treason, and a seemingly invincible enemy surrounding you. But you never lost your faith, and you never gave up. You sacrificed your homes, your treasure, your health; many their lives, their families, their happiness – but you never sacrificed your virtue, or your sacred honor.

"We have many heroes in this room with us tonight; many more who cannot be here. We take pleasure in those honored guests among us now, and with joyful sorrow we take remembrance of those who are with us no more. Please join me in a moment of silence to honor those Americans, and those Frenchmen, who gave their lives so that we may celebrate the spiritual birth, and union, of our two nations in joy and freedom here tonight."

After rendering homage to the absent President, Otto introduced the governor; the chancellor; the Vice-President, judges and secretaries and senators and representatives and so on until virtually every male in the room had been acknowledged.

"A toast to the United States of America, its Congress, its courts, its President; to its new Constitution and Bill of Rights...and a toast to France, her king, her Assembly and to her new Constitution and Declaration of Rights, may they be swiftly approved and adopted.... And to that fateful day exactly twelve years ago, February 6, 1778, when our two glorious nations sealed their destinies together with an oath bound in heaven to stand by the other, so help us God.

"And now, a last and final toast."

Otto set down his glass, smiled and held out his hands. The young lady with the auburn hair and the miracle shoes came out to the center of the floor in her simple white chiffon dress, smiling radiantly. She took his hands in hers, turned, and smiled at her father.

Crèvecoeur, too, was smiling as he walked out to meet them. He kissed his daughter on her checks, and then for good measure her forehead; and then he embraced Otto, his friend and son-in-law to be. He went to Fanny's right side and held her right hand while she, his daughter and Otto's bride-to-be, held her future husband's right hand in her left, feeling the coolness of her special ring warm against her fingers.

"America-Frances St. Jean de Crèvecoeur has graciously accepted to become my wife; and she has graciously allowed me, Louis-Guillaume Otto, to become her husband. Our vows will be exchanged on April 13, 1790. At the altar of St. Peter's Chapel, on Barclay and Church Streets in the City of New York."

To the sound of applause and words of good tidings Otto reached behind him to the table and brought forth a glass of wine for the three of them. In unison they raised their glasses, inviting their guests to do the same.

"To America. To France."

Chapter Eighteen: *The New Humanity*

The ancient stone wall loomed ahead out of the rising fog. The stagecoach rolled up to the arched gateway. The horses slowed then stopped of their own accord. The raucous voice of the driver outside on his bench came through the window, exchanging guffaws with the guard. Inside the coach the passengers waited in silence.

The door abruptly swung open.

"Get out. Have your passports ready."

The passengers obeyed in silence. From the door alighted first the elderly man in the frayed grey robes of a village priest, then an unshaven man in the garb of a mechanic with a red knit liberty cap pulled down around his dirty brow. The gate-keeper, himself unshaven and whose National Guard uniform was as tattered as the mechanic's clothes, leered at the priest holding out his passport.

"Who do you swear obedience to, old man?" he challenged.

"To the Nation. To the Convention. To all true Patriots."

"I think you are not telling me the truth, Citizen. Prove to me you don't worship in secret your obscene false vicar." The National Guardsman smiled mockingly. "Tell me you duly subordinate your precious King of the Jews and his precious Mother to the glorious State. Go on. I want to see proof."

Calmly, not taking his eyes off the sardonic guard, the priest extended his other hand and opened it, palm up. The guard's eyes gleamed.

"I accept your proof," he said, watching the coins clank into his own open palm. "Now for you," he resumed, turning his eyes on the mechanic. "Give me your passport."

He examined it with a critical eye.

"This looks to me like a forgery. What's your business here, Citizen? What need does a mechanic from Caen have to come to Paris?"

The mechanic lurched forward on wobbly legs. He gave the guard a drunken smile, exchanging leer for leer. He opened his mouth and exhaled a pungent puff of his aromatic breath in the guard's face. The man recoiled in disgust.

"I have," the mechanic rasped, "an invention to sell. A great new kind of machine. It's a work of genius, it is!" he boasted before letting out an inebriated belch in the guard's direction.

"So you claim, Citizen." The guard was already rummaging through the travelers' trunks stowed on the back of the coach, which the driver had opened. "Show me this invention of yours. Where is it?"

The mechanic grinned and tapped his temple under the *bonnet rouge* with a dirty finger. "It's all up here...Citizen."

"Prove to me your passport's genuine."

Stilling grinning, the mechanic dropped a few coins into the guard's palm.

"That's not sufficient proof."

"I have no more coin. Only *assignats*. Here. Take it, my good man and share in the wealth and prosperity of our glorious nation. Now let your fellow revolutionary and ardent republican go about his business."

With a shrug and a jerk of the head the Guardian of the Revolution gestured to their coach. He handed back the passports then stepped back, already looking with longing eyes at the wagon waiting a few paces behind.

Once through the city gate the fog began to dissipate as the stagecoach emerged onto rue St.-Honoré. On their left beneath the early spring sun the gardens, shops and cafés of the Palais-Royal were thronged with people. Snatches of music from a brass band came from behind the trees and a crowd of laughing men and women were watching a puppet show set up on the walkway closest the avenue. On their right, closer to the river, a tall, slender wooden structure marked the Place de la Révolution, sunlight glittering off the edge of the metal blade raised high in the air.

The coach turned its back on the Place de la Révolution, heading north onto rue de Valois. The two days' journey ended at the Place des Victoires, the bronze statue of King Louis XIV long since melted down into cannon balls and bullets. The driver made no offer to help his passengers with their trunks, disappearing into the stage coach office. Next to the office building was a hack stand and next to that, a hack with horses munching in their feed bags.

"Where to?"

"Rue des Vieux Augustins, number 19," the priest told the hack driver, helping the man with the luggage. "The Hôtel de la Providence – "

"As if I don't know!" the driver replied sarcastically. "All you country people want to go by there. As if you're on some sort of pilgrimage."

"It's just a coincidence."

The cabbie smirked and bid them to climb aboard.

It was not a long ride to the Rue des Vieux Augustins. The cabbie halted outside no. 19. A porter emerged from the entrance to the hotel and trundled the trunks inside. The mechanic paid for their ride, handing the coin to the grinning hack driver.

"Ask for the assassin's room. Number seven, second floor." He snickered. "Enjoy your stay. You'll be well provided for, I'm sure."

Mme. Grollier eyed the two visitors warily as they filled out the police forms and slipped them across the counter. She read each over carefully several times. Frowning, she handed back to the mechanic his form.

"You wrote '1 April, 1794' for the date. If the police see that – and believe me they will - you'll lose your head. Me too, maybe. Fill out another sheet." With that she slipped away the offending form and slid over a clean one.

"13 *Germinal*," the priest murmured to his companion. "Year Two of the New Humanity. I mean to say, the Republic."

The hotel owner read over the new version, nodding her head. Satisfied, she demanded two nights' lodging in advance.

"Can't be too careful," she defended herself. "You never know. You two might be next. After all, Danton himself was arrested only yesterday. If he can be accused, so can you."

She turned to her porter. "Gilles. Take these citizens upstairs to their room. Number nine."

The porter, carrying one of the trunks, led them up the steps then down the gloomy hall. He paused beside the door marked No. 7, set down the trunk and put his hand on the knob. He turned to them, hopefully.

"For just an additional small token I'd be happy to show you her room."

"No, thank you anyway, Citizen."

The disappointed entrepreneur accepted his tip at number nine and left the guests to themselves. They went in, closing the door behind them.

Father François, looking at Crèvecoeur, put a finger to his lips, then padded about the sitting room, rapping on the wall adjoining the neighboring suite, listening, then repeated the same exercise in the bedroom, finally dropping to his knees to peer under the bed and then up the flue of the chimney. Only after scanning carefully the decrepit molding across the tops of the walls and the faded reddish tiles on the floors did he nod his head. Even so, he whispered.

"It would have been wiser if I had kept my mouth shut downstairs," he said. "So, the great republican revolutionary leader Danton is under arrest. I'm not surprised. You could see it coming. Ever since last July when Marat was assassinated. That leaves France now with only one dictator. Robespierre."

The priest frowned in thought. "Danton's arrest complicates our plan. I was hoping to approach his man on the Committee of Public Safety through a mutual friend. Now I don't know who we are to bribe."

"Perhaps the prison guards."

François shook his head. "You have to bribe them to visit a prisoner, true enough; but they won't risk their heads letting a prisoner go without a release from the Committee."

"But my son-in-law wasn't arrested by the Committee, or the Commune. They probably don't even know he exists. It was someone high up in the Foreign Ministry who accused him to the police. To get rid of him so a relative could take his place."

"We can't even be certain he's still in the Luxembourg prison."

"My daughter believes so. My only comfort is that he's not in the Conciergérie."

The priest was lost in thought. His eyes wandered into the bedroom and beyond that, the wall shared with number seven.

"Charlotte Corday came from Caen, you know," he mused, voice still low. "Father was a lesser noble. Descended from our great poet Corneille. I saw her once or twice, when I was visiting the Abbaye-aux-Dames. Remarkably beautiful, she was Calm, serene. Like a heroine from a Corneille drama. Well, in killing that monster Marat she did what no man in France had the courage to do. She paid for her courage with her head, that is true; but she willingly paid the price."

François looked down at his hands, examining them, as though seeing them for the first time.

"I confess, I do not have such courage."

He looked up at his companion. "I did not have the courage three years ago to stay true to my vows and I am not a braver man today. May God forgive me for my cowardice."

"Peter himself denied the Lord three times."

François had begun to weep softly, bitterly.

"It is so easy to fool ourselves. All those years, I was only play acting, playing at being a village priest, a shepherd to my flock. How easy it is, to delude one's self, when times are good. But there comes a time when every man and every woman will be put to the test.

"That moment for priests came in November 1791. And I failed the test. I pledged obedience to the State as my new lord to save my worthless skin. And thereby pledged my soul to the devil.

"And Satan did indeed arise, incarnating himself in the person of Jean-Paul Marat. One thousand two hundred priests he ordered murdered, butchered with knives and axes and pikes. How, how oh Lord was that possible? Here, in France, in Paris, at St.-Germain Abbey not thirty minutes away from this very spot. Five days and five nights the agonized screams, the diabolic laughter around those bonfires from hell, the executioners from down South – and our own Faubourg St.-Antoine! - singing gaily the *Marseillaise* as they chopped off their hands and feet and then their heads and tore out their palpitating hearts, the gutters running red with their blood...and where was I? Cowering under my bed."

François wiped his eyes with a sleeve of his robe.

"I am not worthy to untie the straps on their sandals."

There came a knocking on the door to their rooms.

"It's just me, your porter Gilles."

Crèvecoeur got up and undid the latch. As he did so the door burst open, hurling him backwards onto the floor. He looked up to see two rough-looking men glaring at him coldly. One had on a black hat and black jacket, the other wore a red liberty cap and printer's apron. Both sported the blue, white and red cockade of the Revolution. They stalked into the room and motioned several men outside to follow them in.

"François Debonnaire? Hector-Jean Michel?" Not waiting for an answer the man in black gave a signal to his devotees who proceeded to throw the priest and mechanic to the floor, face down, in order to tie their wrists together with a short length of rope.

"I am Commissaire Bourrot. In the name of the Revolution you are under arrest, pursuant to the authority given me by the Law Against Suspicious Persons. By reason of counter-revolutionary behavior." He gave a nod of the head and the two Enemies of the State were pushed out into the dark hall, while Bourrot and his fellow commissary searched the traitors' belongings for evidence. A minute later they emerged, Bourrot tucking the proof safely away in his pocket, the woolen lining not quite muffling the tinkling of the money and jewelry no longer needed by the counter-revolutionaries.

They wended their way south on rue de la Monnaie and then onto the Pont Neuf, the bridge anything but new. To their left, above the Palais de Justice, rose the spire and twin rectangular towers of Notre-Dame, cathedral no more but now re-christened the Temple of Reason. On the left bank of the river the ancient streets were even more narrow. The captives were pushed along the Rue Dauphine then through the Cour du Commerce whose medieval houses looked down on them with resignation, frightened eyes mindful of their neighbor Danton's arrest peering out from behind curtains grasped by tentative hands. Crossing over rue St.-André, not yet re-baptized, the condemned and their captors turned onto rue des Cordeliers. Commissaire Bourrot bid the guards to halt in front of number 30, before the entranceway to a courtyard.

Faded garlands of flowers were hanging reverently around the archway from which dangled small ornaments in the shape of pyramids, mountains, trees, the sun and the moon. On the ground an urn held burning incense, tended by a woman of indeterminate age crouched nearby. Her straggly dark hair unrestrained by any bonnet tumbled confusedly over her broad shoulders covered by a tattered linen *fichu*. Her eyes glittered as she watched the *commissaire* strike the two prisoners with his cudgel, forcing them down to their knees in front of the urn.

"Bow down! Bow down, I say. Give a prayer to our martyred mentor. I want to hear you ask for his forgiveness. Louder! I can't hear you. *Bah, foutre!*" Cursing, he kicked François in the rump, hurtling his head face down on the cobblestones. The woman jumped up and, screaming and cursing as well, produced her own baton and began putting it to good use on the backs of the two prostrate men while dozens of other women materialized out of nowhere to add their epithets to the chorus of cussing.

"All right, that's enough, *sale salope*. Herodias the whore, that's who you are!" Bourrot laughed, shoving the crone aside.

"Ah, but you worshipped our dear departed M. Marat, didn't you, you old slut. Well, you'll soon be seeing him again, no doubt." He motioned to his cohorts to pull up the prisoners back onto their feet and push them onto the street.

They reached rue du Théâtre Français. They marched up the sloping street towards the granite and marble building with its row of coldly classical Greek columns and broad steps. Across the wide double doors a sign had been plastered, proclaiming the theatre closed by reason of counter-revolutionary conduct.

Up ahead, on the other side of rue Vaugirard, loomed the mathematically correct, imposing façade of Roman Republican architecture, the Luxembourg Palace of Marie de Médicis, now the imposing face of a republican prison.

Chapter Nineteen: *The Debt Is Forgiven*

The hard, cold stone floor had not become any softer or warmer over time and the bread had not become any less moldy nor the water less putrid. But the air seemed changed, the atmosphere imperceptibly different. Sniffing the air, their comrade in misery sensed it as well.

"Ah, the sweet scent of springtime. Honey and lemon. The linden trees outside in the gardens must be starting to bud," he mused. His companions stirred listlessly on the clammy floor.

"How I miss Danton," Duflot continued. Crèvecoeur's friend from worn-torn Québec had lost most of his hair but wore the same sardonic look.

"I had gotten rather used to his voice, loud as he was even though all the way over on the other side. The room reserved for dangerous, Very Important Enemies of the State. Like the *femmes* Noailles. The old demented Duchess of Noailles, her daughter the Duchess of Ayens, and her granddaughter who were brought in last month. They don't come more dangerous than that."

He grinned in the semi-darkness. "I guess you recognize we don't count. No, we're just small fry, unimportant little fish caught up in the net of republican virtue.

"Forgive me father for being perverse, but I think I should have liked to have seen Danton on the guillotine. I imagine he must have made a final, brilliant speech before losing his head. After all, great men die a great death. That's what they all crave, isn't it? Glory in life, and glory in death."

The Debt Is Forgiven

"They say," Father François remarked from somewhere nearby in the gloom, "that Charlotte Corday taught them all how to die. With dignity and grace."

They fell silent. From far away, outside the prison it seemed, gay voices were raised in singing to the sound of a drum and flutes, the by-now omnipresent *Marseillaise.*

"The perverse justice of it all," Duflot remarked, absently plucking a straw lying at his feet on the floor. "Danton condemned by the very Revolutionary Tribunal he created. But that was not to be his cardinal sin. His crime was to let himself be outmaneuvered by Robespierre."

Duflot picked up the straw, held it up admiringly. He began to tear off thin strands of fibre.

"Let's see....How to kill thee, let me count the ways...So many to count, so many to lose their heads. First the king, poor bewildered soul was he. He refused to shed the blood of his people and for that he lost his head instead. Then let's see...the king's sister Madame Élizabeth. Charlotte Corday. Princess Lambelle. Actually, no, I made a mistake there. Please excuse me, gentlemen. She didn't make it to the guillotine. They disemboweled her in the Conciergérie and sliced off her head right there after one of the mob cut out her heart and ate it. Impatient people. I can't stand impatience."

He peeled off another strand of straw. "Where was I? Oh, yes. We can't forget Brissot's Girondin party, now can we? His chum Roland may have once been Minister of the Interior but that didn't save his head. Or his wife's, the real genius behind his ambition, you know. Then the others: Vergniaud, Barbaroux. Then Brissot himself; and Condorcet. Actually, he was poisoned, or so they say. Pity he couldn't think up a mathematical theory to make himself immortal.

"Thousands more, too many to remember...the Duc de la Rochefoucauld, and his wife. No, wait, there I go again. The duke was stoned to death long before he could reach the guillotine. Ah, the choicest prize, the queen herself! The vendors made a fortune that day selling their lemonade and *petits pains* to the festive spectators.

"Then there's the king's cousin the Duc d'Orléans. Ah yes, Philippe Égalité. He lived up to his nickname, didn't he, showing *le peuple* everyone's equal under the blade. And let's not overlook old Le Veillard, Franklin's friend. And his other friend, the great genius Lavoisier. It would have been more appropriate to execute Lavoisier by a firing squad, don't you think?

"Camille Desmoulins –serves him right, for writing the false lies Marat used to convict Brissot and his Girondins. And Danton along with him. Like Saturn, the beast of revolution devouring its own children.

"But I do feel sorry for Camille's wife. Poor Lucille. Condemned to lose her head for the treasonable crime of being Camille's spouse. Poor, poor Lucille."

There was the loud clanking sound of an iron gate being opened, then the thudding of boots on the floor.

"Yea, as I walk through the Shadow of the Valley of Death I shall fear no evil," the guard recited gleefully. His companions laughed behind him as they strolled among the clusters of prisoners huddled about on the floor of the large room, careful to avoid stepping in the overflowing chamber pots but indifferent to the occasional hand or wrist crushed beneath their boots.

"Bichette? Oh where are you, my little Bichette?" the guard sang out, glancing again at the document in his hand. "Come now to papà! Mademoiselle Bichette? We know you are here."

The young maiden was betrayed by her sobbing. Like an owl the guard pounced on her, pulling her up roughly by her hair.

"Such fine, lovely locks you have, my dear. Well, by this afternoon they'll be all shorn off, just like a sheep. The blade likes a clean, unobstructed pretty little neck, you know."

"Wait a second, stupid," one of the other jailers intervened. "There are two women named Bichette here. Which one is it?"

The first guard looked dubiously at his paper. "I don't know, it just says 'Bichette, the serving girl'."

"You, over there," the second jailer yelled out to another young woman coiled into a terrified bundle on the floor. "I see you. That's the other one," the man exclaimed triumphantly.

"That's all right. We'll take both. With the two of them we make our quota for this morning. There now, my two young ungrateful whores. Stop whining. You'll enjoy the rarified air of the Conciergérie. For all of one night."

Father François rose to his feet. He approached the two girls and their tormentors.

"I will hear your confessions," he offered in a strong voice. "May God our father have mercy on you. And on your captors."

476

With a snarl of rage the chief turnkey lunged at the priest and struck him to the ground with the back of his cudgel.

"You! You'll be the next to go. Start saying your own prayers now."

They left, pushing the two crying girls ahead of them and out the gate.

Even the cynical Duflot lapsed into silence.

Father François knelt down on his knees and said a quiet prayer for the two girls and their tormentors.

"That was a brave thing you just did, priest," Duflot said "If not foolish."

François gestured angrily with his hand.

"I am the biggest coward in France. I pledged. I am also therefore the biggest fool as well."

"If the archbishop of Paris can pledge obedience to a dictator then I suppose a simple priest can be excused for not being a saint."

Duflot shifted from one buttock to the other as though in so doing he could make the stone floor softer.

"Your cowardice pales before my own," he said softly. "I am the champion of cowards. A medical marvel seeing how's I can walk upright even though I don't have a backbone. You see, I was in the Assembly, when it was called the Legislative Assembly; then I was re-elected for my district when it was renamed the National Convention.

"What high hopes we had! What high-minded theories and flowery speeches! At the Jacobin Club, on the floor of the Assembly, you never heard such clever arguments, such elegant political philosophy, such convincing sophistry. But they were like so many rotten trees in the forest, grand on the outside, hollow on the inside. And one by one they fell.

"I thought I was clever, shrewdly watching which way the wind was blowing before voting, before taking a stand, not because it was the right stand to take but because it seemed the safest. Most of us were like that. Silently we sat there, the quiescent majority, in the middle between the monarchists to the right of the president's chair and the Girondins – Brissot's party – to the left while above us all, up on the 'Mountain' to the far left sat the members from the Paris Commune.

"At first it was almost imperceptible, like your bath when the maid gradually adds warmer and warmer water until you realize too late you're about to be scalded. One by one the king's supporters left, as one by one the Montagnards increased, fed by Marat's mobs and Hébert's thugs from St.-Antoine.

"When the Girondins used Marat and bribed Hébert to invade the Assembly with their mobs and terrorize the king they thought they were being smart, intimidating us all to support them. But they didn't understand they had made a pact with the devil, and the devil always gets his due. Out of the slums of the city arose Danton, and in the wink of an eye the Commune was his and with it the mobs of Marat and Hébert. And, just like that! he overthrew the king and tore up the Constitution. And we – I – sat there in the Assembly and let him do it. Because we – I – had only quivering sacks of jelly where our testicles should have been.

"But Danton's deal with the devil was no better than Brissot's. For no sooner does Danton overthrow the Constitution than Marat orders the massacres of September '92. And now Danton learns along with the Girondins that once you let the genie out of the bottle he doesn't want to go back in.

"Look at my face, my friends. Look closely, now. You are looking at the face of an imposter. I am only pretending to be a man. Just like our Assembly, pretending to be the lawgiver, like our king pretending to be a ruler, or our courts pretending to dispense justice. The truth is, I am false. I am counterfeit, through and through.

"Are you therefore surprised that I voted in favor of the motion to condemn the king to death? Accused of treason, for the high crime of breathing through royal nostrils. His pleas to the royal heads of Europe to *not* invade France and to *not* restore his monarchy could not be stronger proof of his conspiracy to crush the Revolution. How fitting it is that I, a phony man, should vote in favor of a phony motion. No man in the Convention pronounced the verdict '*La Mort*' as solemnly as I did that day.

"At least I wasn't asked to vote for the Jacobin massacre of the five hundred children in the Loire. Or the drowning of the citizens of Nantes by the boatload. Or the butchery in Lyons and Bordeaux and the Vendée. I was spared the discomfort of eating my dinner with a guilty conscious.

"I suppose, after the Girondins were arrested by Robespierre and Marat, I should have realized it was time I retired to my farm. But then Marat was murdered. Robespierre's Law Against Suspicious Persons was approved. And quitting the

Convention was viewed as a Suspicious Activity. And so, like the Dutch boy holding his finger in the hole in the dike, I dared not leave while dreading to stay."

"How then did you get here?" Crèvecoeur asked.

"Through the same door you did," Duflot replied sourly. "*Why* I am here, you mean? Well, why not? What did I do to merit being spared? Why should I be superior to all the thousands of other deserving Citizens who have enjoyed the hospitality of the State? And quite a few non-citizens as well. Mainly English. Poor tourists, didn't understand that once Great Britain declared war on Republican France last year all English people on French soil were automatically Persons of Suspicion. There's even an American here! Thomas Paine. Or is he British? No matter. His head's probably safe either way.

"In answer to your question, I'm here not because I voted against Robespierre. I'm a guest of the Nation because my neighborhood Committee of Surveillance had me arrested. They arrested me because I did not have a Certificate of Good Citizenship. I did not have a Certificate of Good Citizenship because the Committee refused to accept my application. The Committee did not accept my application because the Chairman wanted to sleep with my wife. My wife did not want him to sleep with her nor did I. And so here I am. As to my wife...." Duflot could only shrug.

"Now it's my turn to ask. Why are you two here?"

"My crime," Crèvecoeur supplied, "was to write the date on my police form in the Christian fashion."

"And I compounded his felony," François added. "By telling him to write 'Year Two of the New Humanity' 'rather than 'Year Two of the Republic'."

"Revolution is too serious a matter for humor. We in the Convention solemnly adopted the Girondins' new calendar to erase every vestige of the old pagan gods and Christian dogma. This was of paramount importance. You see, if you don't like the taste of the wine, why, just put it in a different bottle. Stick on a new label, invent a new name! And voilà, just like that, it's wine no more. And if it offends you to see your neighbor still drinking from his old bottle and still calling it wine, then the solution is obvious. Eliminate the offending object. Throw him in prison, crush his spirit, cut off his head!

"What more glorious way to celebrate the New Age of Humanity than by renaming the months of the year. And so we have the new months of Spring: the windy Ventôse, the fertile Germinal, the flowering Floréal. Or, as one of the English inmates here called them, 'Wheezy, Breezy and Sneezy'. And even better, every day of the year now has its own special name, thanks to Fabre d'Églantine, the Girondins' poet-artist. The late poet-artist, I should say. He lost his head with all the rest despite his panegyric eulogy to nature. I hope you've memorized them all – it's a capital offense to forget even one, you know."

"I've lost all track of time," Crèvecoeur murmured. Today must be...?"

"I've invented my own new starting point to measure time. I call it the New Age of Duflot. It's based on the date the Noailles ladies came here. The crazy old duchess – she's the one you can hear singing late at night – is the grandmamà of Marie-Adrienne. You know, your friend La Fayette's wife. Adrienne's in some other prison. I wonder if she still has her head on her shoulders. And now I put you to the test. On what date did they arrive?"

"Let me see," Crèvecoeur played along. "That would be...12 April?"

"*La mort*," Duflot pronounced gravely. "Death to you! It's no longer April but Germinal and '12 April' is Horse Chestnut – *Marronier*. The day before was Romaine Lettuce and the day after was Arugula. Christmas Eve is Sulfur and Christmas Day is Dog. Newton – not Christ – was born on Dog and the holiest day of the year is now *la Fête de la Révolution*, 1 Vendémiare, or as you heretics prefer, 22 September. Got it?"

The iron gate could be heard opening again. Like a breeze rippling through a field of wheat voices were murmuring back to them and soon bodies surged towards the figure of a woman in a long dark shawl carrying a huge basket from which she was tossing chunks of bread into eager hands. The peasant woman passed by Crèvecoeur and threw out the manna before disappearing into the further reaches of the room. Another woman followed her with another basket and behind her a boy lugged jars of water which he left here and there among the prisoners.

Crèvecoeur shared the food with his companions.

"Are you certain Otto was released?" he asked, not for the first time.

Duflot gestured impatiently with his free hand, the other clutching his piece of bread.

"As much as we can be certain of anything today," he grumbled. "Just before you were thrown in. And no, he wasn't sent to the Conciergérie. He was set free. Why that was, my dear departed informant Marie couldn't say. May she rest in peace. I hope you enjoy the irony of your situation. As for me, I have a friend on the Commune who owes me a favor….

"If I ever get out of here, I think I'd like to immigrate to America. Tell me, why didn't you go back when you had the chance?"

"Because of my two sons. I was in Caen when Danton's coup d'état and then the September massacres took everyone by surprise. I was frantic for news of my boys. La Fayette fled and General Dumuriez defected to the Austrians after losing Belgium; and then I heard the Duc de la Rochefoucauld was in hiding. But afterwards the Comtesse d'Houdetot got word to Father François she had Ally and Philly with her in Switzerland. But then my son-in-law Otto was thrown in prison. François and I came to Paris hoping to bribe his way out."

"And where is your daughter?"

"I don't know."

The by-now all too familiar sound of the iron gate swinging open doused the desire for further conversation. The jailor, wading through the masses among the Very Important Enemies of the State, cheerfully sang out the names of the morning's two dozen chosen to be trundled in the tumbrels over to the Conciergérie, the last stop before the Place de la Révolution and eternity.

The turnkey watched in satisfaction as eight Carmelite nuns were herded over towards the gate. Mission almost accomplished and quota almost filled, the demi-urge was in a jovial mood as he strolled over to the area housing the Not So Important Enemies of the State.

"One more sheep! Just one more *mouton,* and my quota is done. Now let's see, who do we have here on the list…Duflot. Duflot, where are you? Present yourself." Crèvecoeur seized Duflot by the arm and held him down.

"You're staying put. I've owed you a debt these past thirty-five years and I'm paying it now."

Duflot struggled to pull his arm free as Crèvecoeur tried to stand up.

"The debt's forgiven. Let me go," Duflot whispered angrily, as Crèvecoeur, shaking his creditor to the floor, started towards the jailor. But Father François blocked his path.

The priest pushed Crèvecoeur away and turned towards the approaching guard, who was looking at the trio with an expression of sardonic amusement.

"How gratifying to meet people who appreciate the benefits to society the Revolution has brought."

"The Lord is my Shepard. As I walk through the Shadow of the Valley of Death I shall fear no evil," the priest replied to the jailor. "My son, I am ready to hear your confession."

"So it's you again, my fine fat friar." The jailor was grinning in delight. "You didn't think I had forgotten you, now did you?" He lunged forward and slapped the priest hard with a swipe of his stick across the face. With his other hand he grabbed his victim by the folds of his robe and twisted it tightly such that the priest's face was almost touching the jailor's.

"Go on! Pray!" the guard screamed. "Pray to your precious Savior, your Almighty God! See if He hears you! See if He cares! Well, go on. I'm waiting. Let's see a miracle. Let's see Him save you!"

François regarded his tormentor calmly.

"He already has."

A puzzled looked flickered across the jailor's eyes, replaced by a gleam of fury. He struck the troubling martyr to the ground with his cudgel and called out to his cohorts. François regained his feet and gently brushed off the dirt from his sleeves and the dust from his sandals. He stepped forward and walked away, trailed by his guards in silence.

* * * * *

The iron gate swung open and the dark shrouded figures bustled through carrying their baskets of bread. They meandered their way through the sagging shapes sitting and lying on the floor until reaching Crèvecoeur. The figure in the lead, wisps of grey hair escaping from beneath her hood, moved on without stopping. Her companion, hood drawn tightly over her head, came to a soft halt in front of him.

She reached into her basket and withdrew a quarter-loaf of bread. With a slender hand she held it out to her father.

Crèvecoeur searched his daughter's eyes.

"How did you know I was here?" he whispered. He longed to hug her but dared not.

Fanny made a show of handing out pieces of bread to outstretched arms around her.

"Your friend Duflot. After he was released he found us. Louis-Guillaume and me. We've been in hiding at a friend's house, a member of the Convention. Our friend is close to one of the leaders on the Committee. That's how Louis was able to get out. But our friend has to be careful. You must be patient."

She pretended to look around for the water jug, found it and set it down at her father's feet.

"You must drink," she said.

His daughter lifted the jug and with a twist of the wrist undid the cork in the spout. Slowly she raised the earthen vessel and, carefully holding the tin cup tied with a long string to the neck, slowly began to pour.

The water trickled out of the jug and into the cup, making the gurgling sound of a spring whose water, soothing and cool, swirled in leisurely lazy circles around the gently bubbling source rising to the surface from deep below. The pure water flowed among the firkins resting on shelves in the pool, filled with the good sweet butter of their cows fed on the rich green clover from the fertile fields of their farm, the little girl with the reddish auburn hair and cream-colored bonnet offering a sip to her father, reaching out with his own hand to partake of the source of their lives.

He drank. The smile offered by the father to his child was radiant, and eternal, and in its infinite light flowed the promise of pure, infinite and unfathomable love.

Into her father's outstretched hand his daughter gently placed a small smooth object.

"You must be patient. You must persevere. You must hope."

She pulled her hood securely over her head and rose back on her sandaled feet, lifted up the large basket, and silently stole away.

Crèvecoeur watched her go. She receded into the masses of groaning humanity before disappearing from his sight.

He looked down at his fingers, curled over the palm of his left hand, holding her parting gift. Unbidden, like the day lilies bordering the golden fields of his farm unfurling their bright orange-red petals in reply to the sun, his fingers opened.

Slowly, with the fingers of his right hand, he gently took the ring, pewter sparkling like silver and the wax like fine gold. He let the ring, *Agneau de Dieu*, glide effortlessly onto his *annulaire*, the third finger of his left hand as though it were an *alliance*, a wedding band born anew.

It fit as though the ring had been born with him, and he with the ring. He closed his eyes and smiled, heart broken no longer.

Afterword

The real-life Michel-Guillaume Jean de Crèvecoeur was born in Normandy in 1735 into the landed gentry. His life was adventurous, exciting, romantic, tragic – and in many ways, miraculous.

Little is known of his early years. Banished to a Jesuit boarding school in Caen, he was packed off to relatives in England after a quarrel with his father and became engaged to an English girl who died soon after. In 1765 he pops up in the Colony of New York after serving as a soldier in the French Army defending Quebec from the British assault in 1759. Now a citizen of New York, calling himself Hector St. John, he marries an American and settles down to the life of a gentleman farmer in the wildnerness of Orange County in New York's Hudson Valley.

When war breaks out in 1775 his desire for peace and reluctance to choose sides, coupled with his French heritage, stoke the suspicions of his Patriot neighbors, leading to persecution and imprisonment by Patriots and Tories alike, until he finally escapes to France. Within two years he undergoes a miraculous metamorphosis from unknown broken man into famous author and royal diplomat. He returns to New York as first French Consul in 1783 in the company of John Adams' secretary carrying the Treaty of Paris, just in time for Washington's triumphant entry into the City – only to find tragic news awaiting him.

His book *Letters from an American Farmer* is on the shelves of most libraries even if the author himself has melted away into obscurity. Few people today know that he was one of the founders of the first legal catholic church in New York, St. Peter's, and the town of St. Johnsbury is named after him, at the behest of his friend Ethan Allen. He corresponded with Benjamin Franklin and socialized with the leading philosophers and politicians of the day both in the United States and France. His daughter with the poetic, symbolic name America-Frances was to be married at St. Peter's to a French diplomat soon after Washington's oath of office and the electrifying news of revolution in France. Fanny and her husband survived the Reign of Terror, as did her father, and her husband Louis-Guillaume Otto was appointed by Napoléon to the court of Vienna as French Ambassador.

The historical events depicted in my novel – from the siege and battle of Quebec to the unfolding of the American War for Independence to the federalist post-war New York and then the Reign of Terror, are accurate and based on historical record. Crèvecoeur's personal life in its main points is factual as well, based on a biography by his grandson Robert published in Paris in 1883, a short biography of his daughter Fanny written by a friend around the same time, and a biography by Julia Post Mitchell appearing in 1916. The real Crèvecoeur's life in Canada and New York before 1783, however, is almost a blank page. He participated in momentous history and knew many of the leading actors of the day, yet his own life was amorphous. Even his name was poetic – and prophetic. For Crèvecoeur, in French, means "heart-breaker". He is the perfect vehicle for the theme and message, secular and spiritual, I want to convey.

I also refer the reader to my article on the man and his life in Orange County, New York published in the *Hudson River Valley Review* in the Spring 2018 edition, under the auspices of Marist College in Poughkeepsie, New York and its Hudson River Valley Institute. The footnotes contain a trove of information and sources.

Map of French Canada, New York and New England 1759

Map of Ulster and Orange Counties, State of New York

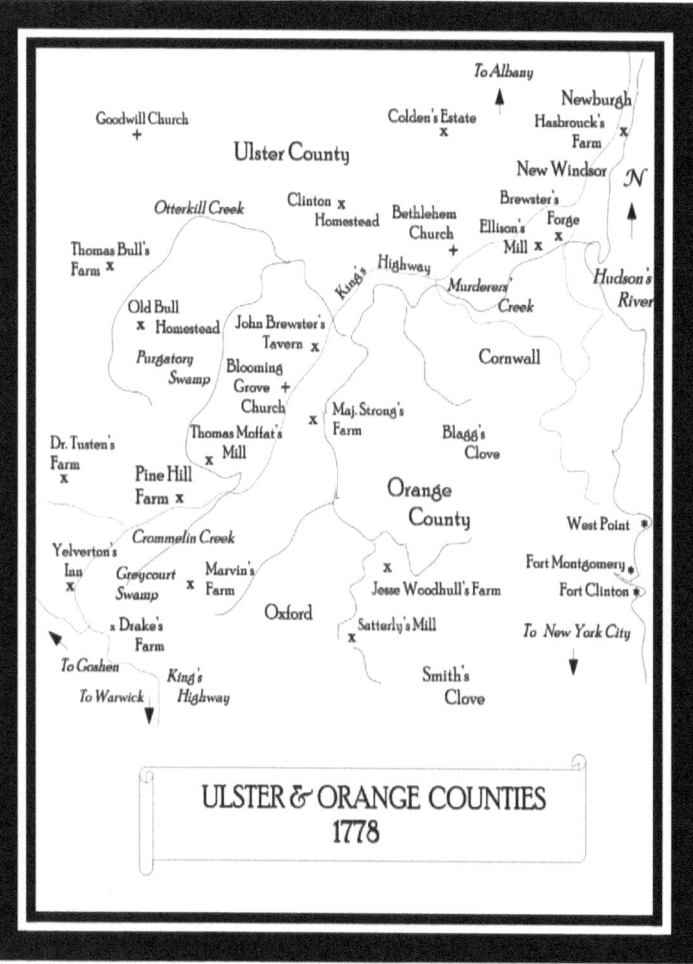

Ulster County

To Albany

Goodwill Church
+

Colden's Estate
x

Newburgh
Hasbrouck's
Farm
x

New Windsor

𝒩

Otterkill Creek

Clinton x
Homestead

Bethlehem
Church
+

Brewster's
Forge
x

Ellison's
Mill x

Thomas Bull's
Farm x

King's Highway

Murderers
Creek

Hudson's
River

Old Bull
x Homestead

John Brewster's
Tavern x

Purgatory
Swamp

Blooming
Grove +
Church

Cornwall

x

Maj. Strong's
Farm

Dr. Tusten's
Farm
x

Thomas Moffat's
x Mill

Blagg's
Clove

Pine Hill
Farm x

Orange
County

Crommelin Creek

West Point ✴

Yelverton's
Inn
x

Greycourt
Swamp

Marvin's
x Farm

x

Fort Montgomery ✴

Fort Clinton ✴

Oxford

Jesse Woodhull's Farm

x Drake's
Farm

Satterly's Mill
x

To New York City

To Goshen

King's
Highway

Smith's
Clove

To Warwick

ULSTER & ORANGE COUNTIES
1778

489